TALES
FROM THE
RADIATION AGE

BY JASON SHEEHAN

Novels
Tales from the Radiation Age
A Private Little War

Memoir
Cooking Dirty: A Story of Life, Sex,
Love and Death in the Kitchen

TALES
FROM THE
RADIATION AGE

Jason Sheehan

PUBLISHED BY

47NORTH

Text copyright © 2013 Jason Sheehan
Originally released as a Kindle Serial, July 2013

Published by 47North, Seattle

www.apub.com

ISBN-13: 9781477848913
ISBN-10: 1477848916
Library of Congress Control Number: 2013943420

Cover design by Cyanotype Book Architects
Author photo by Laura Sheehan

For Laura, who once again had my back and gave me the time I needed to play with my dinosaurs.

"*The technology underlying cell repair systems will allow people to change their bodies in ways that range from the trivial to the amazing to the bizarre. Such changes have few obvious limits. Some people may shed human form as a caterpillar transforms itself to take to the air; others may bring plain humanity to a new perfection. Some people will simply cure their warts, ignore the new butterflies, and go fishing.*"

—K. Eric Drexler, *Engines Of Creation: The Coming Era of Nanotechnology*, 1986

E P I S O D E

1

In Which I Am Almost Immediately Killed Right Dead

SO WHAT STORIES SHALL WE TELL TODAY?

Smart man said once, "If history were taught in the form of stories, it would never be forgotten."

Wasn't me that said it. Other times, other places, I've *claimed* it was me, but no. It wasn't. Don't make it any less true that it wasn't me. Don't make it more true neither. The words are true because they are true. That's what matters.

I know 899 stories about the Captain and every one of them is true. I could tell you about the time we stole a candle ship and flew her to the burning husk of Chaozhou for noodles. How we all ate by the wreck of the Jinshan Bridge and watched sea monsters fuck in the poison water and how he called it a field trip. An educational outing.

I could tell you about the week we spent Scooby Doo'ing after ghosts in Judiciary Square with Maxim Vitsin or about the Battle of Jackstraw or how himself looked standing on the shoulder of a war robot advancing on Kansas City or how he sounded, weeping, with his best friend dying in his arms and the color of the flower he wore in his buttonhole when we threw the funeral—full dress, 21 guns, the nines.

He damn near executed me once, so I know precisely what his pistol tasted like. He preferred beer to whiskey, but I never once held that against him. Several of his teeth were false. He wore a partial and was vain about it. Sometimes he snored and sometimes he didn't.

But to look at you, I know that's not what you're here for. Not the man, but the *stories* of the man, right? Because if history got taught as stories, no one would ever, ever forget.

Smart man said that once. Maybe it was me. Maybe not. So give us a lash of that oh-be-joyful and perhaps we can just start from the beginning.

Once upon a time there was a man named James Barrow. Everyone called him the Captain. He was the bravest, the strangest, the best and worst man I have ever known. And I first met him while I was working for the King of Denver.

Pretending to work might be the better description. I spent my days drinking canteen chicory, riding a gimp-legged metal desk that rattled and slewed every time I touched it, and fussing about with papers, rulers, and thick, bound land assessments in a way calculated to make me seem busy enough to be left more or less alone without ever really accomplishing anything. I was, at the time, a consultant in the laying of roads—fortuitously placed in one of the less-ruined wings of the Gray Castle with a typer before me, a pen in hand, an automatic under my arm, and a cheery view through one cracked blast-glass window over the decapitated head-piece of one of Mad Lord Phillip's Type IXs.

I knew nothing about roads, save that they were supposed to go straight and flat, most-ways. It's important you know that. I was (and remain) a cheat and a swindler, a fast-talker, a crook, a liar both by trade and vocation. I was (and remain) a man you should never loan five dollars to, never trust with a secret, your daughter, or anything even passing precious to you. Not a *bad* man, mind, but not your godly paragon of human decency neither. Should I find you alone on the street one day and in need of aid or service, I might be the luckiest thing that could happen to you. Cannot resist a chance at chivalrous action or the opportunity to prove my better nature, me. But when we've done with our dance—once we've fixed your tire, driven off the hooligans, or found what has been lost— you should certainly check your wallet and watch. I've never stolen the nickels from a beggarman's cup, but I have taken dead men's shoes. And hats, coats, shirts, ties, and, occasionally, identities. There's a difference there. Slight but vital.

Anyway, my liar's heart and the head over which I looked every working day from my wobbly desk were the reason I was where I was—part and parcel of how I'd come to find such gainful employment among the coterie of competent men pledged to serve his Stevenness, the King of Denver.

See, it was large, that head. And it had fallen close enough to King Steve's own chambers that it'd nearly put an end to the reign of one of the West's least dreary temporary monarchs. But in the moments prior to its being decapitated from its proper neck-wise place, that head had sat atop the shoulders of a 100-foot-tall war robot under the command of mad, bad Lord Phillip Sumner and his Kansas reavers. During his final brash, foolish (and very nearly successful) assault on the Gray Castle, said kill-o-bot, along with five others of its kind, had risen up from the siege lines surrounding

Denver and had stomped all over various houses, shops, fortifications, and roadways in their hurry toward glory. So, too, had thousands of Lord Phil's soldiers, muties, steam tanks, metal men, cowboys, conscripts, centaurs, militia, assassins, eye-shooters, face-biters, gun hands, and assorted flatland rabble, all of them scrambling along in the shadows of monstrosity, shooting up the place but good.

Oh, it'd been a hooly, that battle—all thundering guns and glory, waving flags, valiant deeds and blood up to the knees. Or at least that's what I'd heard. Personally, I'd spent the entirety of it far and away. Up north in the Free Republic, well clear of any yucky blood or accidental glory, laboring away at the card tables and whiskey stills and saving my vital energies for such a time as a man of my particular talents might make himself useful. Dying at noble causes never made any man rich. That's just wisdom. But hold 'em, 7-card, and Chinese 3-tier, on the other hand, occasionally did. And far fewer men have met the reaper while sitting at the card table than do amid such eruptions of martial splendor.

So at the tables was where I'd stayed. There, and propping up the long oak at a variety of low-end boozers where a man with smart ears might hear a dozen fascinating things before breakfast. For days and nights and days I bided until the un-wiser had settled their tiffs on the streets of the Queen City and word had come north that Denver, lovely Denver, had weathered her troubles. Needless to say, all that stomping, shooting, scrambling and assaulting had chawed things up catawampusly, breaking much of the city beyond all simple repair. And while this made times rough on the citizenry (those who'd survived the troubles, anyway), it also made lots of paying work for them that knew how such things might could get unbroke—and a nearly equal amount for them what could *pretend* at knowing, too.

Which, of course, had been my cue to saddle up and scuff off, post haste.

Fleeing Denver, I'd had to pass through closing siege lines three miles deep (another rousing tale for another rainy day, I promise).

But coming home again was a husking frolic by comparison. I made the trip in two days on promises and bootleather; found my way to the Castle, to the offices of the King's civil councilors, and then, ultimately, to my desk with its unsteady constitution, macabre view and regular pay.

At least I didn't have to spend my days looking into the dead head's eyes—just the cool, smoke-blacked curve of its brainpan. And this I did happily, day upon day, as myself and twenty or more of my contemporaries typed, measured, fussed, smoked loose silks, ate our Royalty rations, collected our four dollars daily of Royalty pay, pored over water-stained paper maps of Denver-that-was, and feigned work at the reconstruction of the Queen City, always with this inspiring view: constant memento of how close Denver had come to falling, and a reminder of how profitable wars can be for them that aren't directly involved in their execution.

So this was where the Captain found me, once upon a Tuesday morning.

He himself came strolling in pretty as you please and I recall that I didn't make much of him in the moment—likely didn't even look up from my busy fussing at nothing for more than a blink, give or take. Just another freebooter, him, in his ragged field jacket and dolly tankers, stepping through a hole in the south wall that'd once been a proper door and standing there atop a bit of convenient rubble with hands on hips like he owned the place complete.

Trust me, friends: I'd seen the lot. All manner of folk came passing through the Castle in those days. Lords and Ladies of the Quality. Princes and princesses who traveled inside protective nanite screens and always smelled of cheap cologne. Kinglets of all variety. Charlatans, hucksters, con men. Pushers of snake oil, nanoquackery, and patent medications. Scientists. Half-scientists. Common weirdoes. Carpetbagging generals with bottlecap medals rattling on their topcoats. The wounded, halt and lame come grubbing for commissions or handouts. Press-gang lieutenants with their cold and appraising eyes, and new-minted officers with their polished pauldrons, gleaming pistolry, and ceremonial pig-stickers rattling against their rubber boots. Painted ladies swept through the halls and the arms of fancies and swells. Ambassadors from the East and enigmatic characters from the Further West treated the Castle like a common fleabag, always popping in and out on mysterious business, but the whores, at least, had the decency to linger. All of this I'd seen and more.

And yet the Captain's timing was, as they say, fortuitous. As I've already truthfully stated—for the record and all, hand on noble heart—I knew precisely what a cat does about the laying of roadworks. I'd talked my way artfully into my position, had arrived in the offices of the civil council in socks that were little more than ankle warmers, but in a pressed shirt, braces, nipped vest and polished shoes, and carrying a briefcase of once-fine leather. None needed know that I'd recently won the drag playing at dice in a top-hatters bar just down the road, or that the case contained nothing more than half a sandwich. Like likes like, as they say, and when the King's boys had caught sight of me in the hallways, sitting among such a collection of trash and demolished men that one might've thought we was all waiting for the relief or directions to a tubercular ward, they'd immediately scooped me up from my place in the line of likely far more qualified applicants, hustled me through a door, into a chair, and pressed a cup of chicory into my hands while they tut-tutted over me like a long-lost brother come from a terrible direction. Had I arrived with an Oxford jacket and a fine hat as well, I might've gotten myself appointed straight to the council itself. In the moment, though, the roads had suited me just fine.

And yet I'd know from the jump that it could not possibly last. Eventually, some sharp mind was going to get trig to the fact that I hadn't the foggiest notion of axle weights, aggregates or binder materials. And of late, that sharp mind seemed to be contained within one up-jumped fella with tape-fixed spectacles and a limp who'd been coming 'round my desk more and more regular, breathing sour, rotten-tooth breath on me and asking questions about my progress. It was always *How are we feeling about the I-25 bridge buttressing, Mr. Archer?* and *When do you think you will be submitting your first report to the Infrastructure Working Group?* or somesuch.

So he had me worried, that one. About my future employment, sure, but also about what might happen once it was determined that I'd been defrauding the crown out of four dollars a day plus lunch. Kings, as a rule, do not like being fooled. Makes them seem just as dim as most of them truly are. And they tended to grossly overreact to such cleverness among their subjects with things like public lashings and trips to the gallows tree.

Which is all to say that I was in a traveling kind of humor on that particular Tuesday. A state of flux, you might say, wherein I found myself weighing my want of comfort and folding money against the need to keep my neck un-popped.

So when the Captain stepped to the square and center of the room and announced loudly that if there was any man present who spoke a piece of Techny and wanted for some fresh air and exercise he ought to pipe up clear and present himself fastly for work, I found myself, quite without thinking, clearing my throat, easing up to my feet, and saying that I did, in fact, speak Techny like I'd been born to it, thanks, and could certainly go for a romp.

Now there was three problems with this right off.

Firstly, I liked neither fresh air nor exercise. What I liked was regular pay, a safe bed, and chewing something other than my own teeth. I liked sitting 'round on my bonafides and turning invisible under the faceless gaze of a complex bureaucracy. Becoming part of the landscape, that is. Like a desk, me. Or a particularly handsome chair. Then collecting a handful of dollars and alleying out ahead of suspicions. To me, a day out-of-doors was a waste of a day. And if there was running involved, it was an abject failure.

Secondly, I had no idea who this grinning banco was in his skrogged-up battle dress and shaggy hi-top, and had no reason to believe he hadn't meant to lure a fella out, shank him, gut him, stack his bones, and wear him like a skin suit.

Thirdly, at the time I spoke about as much Techny as I did Shelta, Banjacki, Pachee or Spotter—which is to say a dozen-dozen words of each, maybe, and most of thems the dirty ones or dealing with asking where the shitter was. Not exactly fluent, in other words. I had a fair handle on Spanglish and the smuggler's tongue of the Frontera. I knew some Viet, bit of cant, spoke Leet like a pro; had some Frog, German like an ace, a smattering of Swede, Cantonese with a terrible accent, a piece of the modern Polari used among the working boys and girls; had a handle on Padonkaffsky from some previous adventures among the Ruska, and had picked up a piece of Romani camp-slang while about it. But Techny was different. Wasn't a language so much as a *code*: a highly specialized bit of engineering ridiculosity spoken by them as spent most of their time talking to machines.

Still, I'd always had the ear, as they say. Aunt Nells like my Aunt Nell, me. Languages had always come simple—so much so that I often had four or five of them in my head at any one time, each arguing with the other. And since, out the corner of one eye, I could see that limping Civil Council smarty advancing on my position with a black-hand kind of look about him, I decided in the moment that it was probably best if I were for out, and right quick, too.

So up I come then, on the bounce, and say, "Yeah, over here, boss! I talk Techny and could absolutely do with a ramble, sir."

The Captain, looking me up and down quickish, replied, "Say something smart then."

So I asked him where the shitter was.

He looked around at the two partners he had with him—one of the female persuasion, the other male the way a two-legged and tattooed ox might be—and they both shrugged like to say, *I Dunno... Sounds Techny to me.*

So then the Captain smiled and pointed—fingers shaped like a gun and aimed straight at my heart. "You're our man," says he. "We leave directly."

Which they did, turning tails and making for the same hole they'd come in through like the house was on fire and there was no sense looking back.

I had to up-pegs and scramble to catch up with my new friends, but on my way out in their wake I couldn't help but walk by Mr. Bad-Breath-and-Glasses. And walking by him, I couldn't help but say, "That report to the Infrastructure Whatsis is on my desk, chum. It's not *quite* done yet, but be a dear and deliver it for us, will you? Looks like I've some pressing business outside the walls and I can't say as I know when I'll be returning."

Then I smiled my dodger's best, patted the man on one cheek and, that being that, went on my way, case in hand and with a bounce in my step. Anything was better than getting caught, thought me. An out was an out was an out.

And that was how I met the Captain.

The three of them, the Captain and his crew, set a brisk pace as they turned and twisted through the barmy and occasionally falling-down corridors of the Gray Castle, which had once been the Capitol Building of the great state of Colorado and now was merely the center of the Western universe.

They wound, the Captain in the lead, as though trying to shake loose tails, going up stairs here and down them there, detouring through the canteen kitchen (where the Captain tore loose a leg from a roasted six-footed chicken in passing and I pilfered a last cup of chicory in a cracked mug) and more than one private office where various Lords and councilors stopped flapping their gums long enough to stare in affronted outrage at the vagabonds traipsing through their solemnated territory.

To none of these men did the Captain give the slightest sideways attention, only pressing on at a hard canter and charting a course of his own devising while, behind him, his companions took their pick of anything not nailed down—stealing, by my count, four pens, two neckties, one hat, someone's breakfast, a switchblade knife obviously repurposed as a letter-opener, a sheaf of very official-looking papers that disappeared inside the woman's jacket as neat as can be, a screwdriver, a fistful of wrapped candies from a bowl, two phones, and a lamp with a shade done in a pattern of airships under sail which the Captain made the big fella put back.

"Really?" he asked. "Another one?"

"Like it," the big man rumbled. "Gots boats on it."

"Put it back. We're working."

Roundaboutishly, we came to the north wing, the Colfax Avenue side of the Castle, which was less used for being the more damaged in the recent unpleasantness. Twice here, the three of them—the Captain and his two lieutenants—stopped short as though of a single mind and vanished into nooks and doorways. Waited for the space of five breaths. Came out again nodding to continue on.

The first time it happened, I found myself suddenly alone in a hallway lit only by the light spilling in through bullet and blast holes, beams cutting crazy angles through the plaster dust raised by our passage, and I dropped to one knee, elbows to my ears, arms wrapped around my head in anticipation of the blow from behind I'm always half-ways expecting.

But the hallway behind was empty. There was no sound. And when I made my feet again, the three of them was standing, staring at me, trace of a smirk upon the Captain's smooth and otherwise unlined face.

"Not the most effective job of hiding I've ever seen," said him. "Do you think you turn invisible when you cover your eyes?"

"Tell me what we're hiding from and perhaps I could do better," I replied, brushing the dust from my pants.

The Captain looked at me, tilted his head like a dog's, leaned a fraction of an inch closer and said simply, "Enemies."

The second time it happened, I was faster. Went to cover in a doorway and counted five. Saw nothing but dust. Heard nothing but my own ticker and the blood rushing in my ears. Wondered (not for the last time) what enemies might be pursuing this man and whether they were only in his head, and when I peeked out again, the three of them were already out and moving, coat tails flapping, turning a corner down the way.

Once again, I had to dash to catch up—coming tight around the bend only to find myself seized bodily, spun around, then stopped short with a big hand on my chest and the Captain's face hanging before mine, one finger to his lips.

"Shh . . ." he said.

Near up on him (and fearing, at least dimly, for my beloved life and tender limbs), I clocked the man close, smelling old sweat in the weave of his clothes, the chicken grease on his fingers, and the faint odor of diesel fuel like a faded cologne. He wore a gray-green Vandegrift jacket, open at the waist and maligned all about with various patches and insignia of no discernible order. On his hip there was a lashed Colby over-under: a two-shot barking iron, heavy as a bastard and made for putting down mean dogs, metal men, garbage trucks, medium-sized dinosaurs and that sort of thing. Beyond that, there was a blade on his belt and a knife in his boot (neither appearing in the least bit ceremonial). I could see the cross-bits of a shoulder rig beneath his jacket, creasing the heavy cotton shirt he wore, and, in the cuff of his right sleeve, a Jesus gun that peeked out whenever he gestured large—which he did near on every other second.

His blue eyes shone even in the dark, like with a fever heat. His brown hair badly wanted a washing and a tight cut to match the bits and pieces of doughboy uniform he wore, plus the arsenal hung about his person. And his voice, when he spoke, was warm. Excited. *Alight*. His words—even the mean ones—somehow came out dragging smiles.

"Door," he said, gesturing to the one, crookedly hung in its frame, just over his shoulder. "When we go through it, you are part of the team. Understood? Just nod."

I nodded. He took my chin gently in one hand, turned my head to face the girl traveling with him. "Jemma Watts," he said. Tall, blonde-headed, thin as a whippet, and dressed like a frau in homespuns over breeches and clunky boots, all with a brown leather jacket thrown over the top. She was watching the door like she expected it to try something sneaky any moment.

The Captain tilted my chin up, meaning to show me the man who was holding me tight from behind, arms pinned to my sides. And the fact that I could see the crown of his head behind me and the sweep of his shoulders stretching out beyond mine like wings spoke to the plain blasphemous size of him.

"Logue Ranstead," said the Captain. "Say hi, Logue."

"No," said Logue. And now that we were friendly, his grip slackened not a bit.

The Captain brought my chin back down again, his face close enough to mine that I could feel his breath on my lips. "He's grumpy, Logue. Doesn't like new people. Or government people. Or being inside. Or outside. Or that fact that we had to get up before breakfast today. And he's mad that I made him leave behind that lamp." His eyes cut away from mine. "You mad at me, Logue?"

"Yup."

"You see?" the Captain said, turning back to me. "But we have work to do. Important business. More important than breakfast, which is really saying something. Have to talk to some people, you understand? Nod."

I nodded.

"Techny people. Smart, smart Techny people who have something that I want. And are we going to steal it?"

I nodded again because it seemed like the right answer, but I was mistaken. He removed his hand, smacked me on the forehead lightly with the heel of one palm, then took my chin again and waggled it one way and then the other, shaking my head for me.

"No," the Captain sing-songed. "We are not going to steal it, Captain. Because we are not thieves."

Jemma snorted without looking away from the door and the Captain shot her a look, but quickly corrected himself. "At least we are not thieves *at this moment*. We're going to buy it, this gadget that the smart people have. Cash on the barrelhead, or the likeliest facsimile thereof. Fair and square like gentlemen, which is what we are. Okay?"

"Okay," said me.

"Good. Because most of these smart people? They were war engineers under Dr. Martian. That's a flashback, right? Or they were part of the Mountain Resistance. Few of them worked for Bunny Legree and his Redlegs. One or two for the Western Anarchist Front. There are some Kansans in there. Jayhawkers even. Small group from the Gunbarrel Pioneers who used to work for Squirrel Lasseter and the High Country Rangers. This making any sense to you?"

Baffled, I shook my head. I tried to keep up on my politics as much as the next crooked bastard, but honest, there had been a hundred wars. So many that no one even bothered to keep track any more. So many that a quick man might walk through three in a day if he rises early and doesn't take too long at lunch. A hundred kings or queens or lords or governors or presidents of this block or that one, all scrabbling over something. A hundred armies. A hundred damn fools with volcano fortresses and their underwear on outside their pants. A hundred lads and gangs and battles over this or that. A hundred churches in Denver alone. A hundred cathouses, a hundred offices of civil betterment, a hundred amusements for any man with a ready smile and two dollars in his hand. A hundred tiny, fleeting nations where, once, there had been just the one.

"Doesn't matter," said the Captain. "They have a thing and we want it. Simple as that. Only trouble is, so do a lot of other people. Mad scientists mostly. Rogue generals. Warlords. The King." With his free hand—the one that wasn't holding my face—he began ticking off possibilities on his fingers, shaking his hand, showing me the snout of his hold-out gun again and again. "Crazed billionaires. Doomy Prophets. Local militia. The law. Fools. Idiots. The usual. And some of them are old friends of the smart Techny people we're going to visit, and some of them are old friends of ours. But the fact is, we need the gadget worse than any and all, so we're going to go there and we're going to get it. Roger that?"

"Roger that," said me.

"Like gentlemen."

"Like gentlemen," said me.

"And you're going to translate for us. Clear?"

"Crystal," said me. "Just one question?"

"Shoot, cowboy."

"Who are you?"

And the Captain laughed—one short, sharp bark, enough to shake the gloom out of the shadows in the quiet and the dust—and then, before I could react, his hand went tight as a vise on my chin and he leaned forward and kissed me, hard and wetly, right on the forehead. He pulled back. I could feel the stir of drafts cooling his spit on my skin. He tilted me one way, then the other, staring at me like a prize he wasn't sure he wanted. And then he smiled, brilliant like a clean dawn, and patted me gently on one burning cheek. "We're the fucking OSS, Duncan. And this is gonna be fun. You'll see."

At which point I felt myself released from behind and saw Jemma Watts rise up and boot the hanging door off its hinges. My world suddenly suffused with light and sound, I stepped uncertainly out into the ruin of the world, following close after the shadow of the Captain and his crew.

In the streets outside the Gray Castle was the usual press of all humanity's sad remnants. Soldiers and pieces of soldiers walked their watches in the livery of King Steven the Uneven's bonded militia, most carrying bats and batons with plexi tower shields on their backs and lysing pistols on their belts. Beggars begged and shopmen sold. Petitioners to the throne passed by on their busy errands and, everywhere else, the world just went on pretty much like it always had with horse cabs and carriages, hansoms and pedal-bikes jamming the tangled streets, shuggoths slorking through the smoky sky with tentacles nearly brushing the ground, tophatters and cowboys passing the time with the working girls who traded close up on the kingdom center, and ten-foot-tall exos with battered armor and battle ribbons on their polished gatling barrels sharing street corner real estate with shouty preachers carrying on about Jesus and Shiva and The Good Man who comes from the West.

Above all the tumult, on the high wallwalks or balconies of the Castle proper, stood the King's housecarls—true soldaten, them, with their long rifles and chubbed-up nanocystine body armor. They wore image amplification headgear that made them look like bugs. Like *tres moderne* gargoyles come to life in defense of the realm.

It took fifty steps to cross the current extent of the royalty holdings, coming up against the close-set palisade wall that'd been thrown up, post-yesterday's-war, to separate the King and Quality from the flotsam churned up by decades of weird—all of it washing up against the bastions of power but kept at bay by barricades made of I-beams and Quikcrete, street signs, hurricane fence, a moat, punji stakes, shattered hunks of masonry and hand-lettered signs warning of death by electricity, leopards or lead.

I followed the Captain, Logue and Jemma 'round the quiet side of the wall from the inside, walking past the laid-over statue of King Steven (complete with mincey spectacles and one arm pinned up in an empty sleeve), the erection of which had been suspended after the likeness of his Stevenness kept showing up mornings with pencil mustaches scratched under its hawkish nose or giant, veiny pink dongs superglued to its trousers. Rumor had it that it was the King himself who'd been doing that—sneaking out nights, shaking his guards, and having a bit of fun at his own expense—and true or no, that rumor had always made me like the man a bit more.

We ducked out a side gate watched by a fat militiaman with a face full of boils. The man did not salute the Captain, but rather looked away, seeming to find something terribly interesting inside his nose at the moment we went through the gate.

And then we were out into the market, which grew like a scab trying to cover the wound of grass that'd once been the Capitol's ornamental lawn. Dozens of scavengers had laid out their blankets or tarps and set upon them a wild happenstance of goods—nuts and bolts and license plates and organic processors and hammers and cans of peaches and bullets and servomotors and scrawny, plucked chickens and window glass and blue jeans and children's toys and guns and buttons and loose cigarettes and monitor screens missing their cases and datasticks packed with who-knew-what. Here and there was carts a-jangle with bells, offering burritos, falafel cooked in oil as old as Ol' Nick, or lattes for the dullards who didn't appreciate the charms of a right splash of chicory. Under heavy guard of bats and stunners, there were men selling plastic liter bottles of gas and kerosene and, in one case, a working Bang and Olufsen turntable record player playing a fuzzed-out version of *Sympathy for the Devil* by the Rolling Stones through a blown speaker box. Out along the margins were the bookmen and pettifoggers, the parts merchants, the makers and repairers. A brace of robots done up like tarts shook their coin slots on either side of a greasy ground sheet covered in boxes of eyes, slick lozenges of vat-grown skin, and the discombobulated pieces of other robots. There was a sign—a tent of paper, written in a childish hand and set on a corner of the sheet, weighted with a disembodied hand. It said simply EVERYONE NEEDS A FRIEND SOMETIMES.

Oh, Denver my Denver...Queen City of the Plains, jewel of the Western Confederacy. You have never seen a place more beautiful and more vital than Denver after the war. Never a place more fun. Can I tell you how excited I was? I had something to do and somewhere to go, which—for all my prattle of comfy desks and warm meals—has always been the true weakness of me and all my kind. I had a gun and good shoes. I knew nine kinds of powerful kung fu (most of them verbal) and had boon companions with whom to travel. A nice girl, a big fella, and the Captain, who'd scooped me up and kissed me on my head for no good reason.

The OSS? Didn't believe it for a minute. I'd had some small experience with the Office of Special Services in the past, and these folk, I thought, were not them. *Could* not be them, no matter their jive.

The OSS were gray-suit men. Old bulbs and dimwits. Either cankered geezers all liver-spotted and wheezing with love for a country and a time that was gone and never coming back, or bloody-handed and hard young wreakers of unknowable havocs with dead, flat doll eyes and mercurial hearts, equally as responsible for the ills and sufferings of the world as they were for occasionally preventing worse.

Hated a government man, me. Could smell them at a hundred yards off and knew enough to change direction. At that moment, the OSS was the last functioning agency of what had once been the United States of Whatever. Final survivor of a system whose ninth-term president currently lived in a rat-holed manse in hillbilly country, giving speeches to the woodpeckers and penning screeds against secessionists, anarcho-syndicalist elements and litterbugs.

The world had moved on. No one cared. Now that sea monsters rolled in the cold deeps and whole buildings grew from seeds. Now that generipped dragons nested in the bellies of old Oklahoma missile silos and men grew wings to fly through the wrecked playgrounds and scorched steel canyons of dead cities, who had time for paying taxes or the rule of law? After wars and depressions and terrors and worse, after Florida had sailed and Texas had declared itself a sovereign nation and Buffalo had been lost to French-Canadian agitators and Manhattan had taken the bomb in its teeth and New Hampshire had melted and California had stopped returning all calls and Seattle had been leveled by the quake-nami and places like Bowie and White Deer and Limerick and Toad Lick and Mobeetie and Barstow had just dried up, blown away, turned to goo or been forgotten all complete, all that had survived of apple pie, America, and democracy was its blackest impulses. Free will. Self-determination. Greed. Malice. Lust. Secrets upon secrets. And the OSS was the embodiment of it all—dark, powerful, and crooked as a bent nail.

No, I thought, watching the three of them stride out powerful into the scrum and eddy of the day. The Captain and his crew were proper villains, thank god. And I told myself that I could tell. That I *sensed* in them some parity, some sameness of spirit. Kindred spirits, I thought. Like likes like.

"Gentlemen," said the Captain, even as he was beset by the least timid of the begging children and squalling monstrosities made by war and science. "Let's prop up the local economy."

His voice boomed—a man accustomed to shouting orders in the strangest of dins—and his crew responded. With a small handful of coin and the wrapped candies she'd lifted from the desk of the Chief Secretary to the Secretary of Secretaries, Jemma scraped off two-thirds of the children and Pied-Pipered them off somewhere away. And Logue, making like a house or a hill that has suddenly lifted its skirts and begun to walk, crashed mountainously into the throngs mobbing the fuel sellers and began hooking greasy gallon jugs that'd once held milk with one hand while sprinkling silver eagles like rain from the other.

"You," said the Captain, wheeling suddenly upon me. "Find coffee. Three of them. Hot and white and sweet. And pay in coin."

And when I told him that all I had in my pockets was Royalty scrip (which wasn't *entirely* a lie, mind, since I kept my hard money in places other than my pockets), he snorted through his nose. "No, I prefer mine un-spit-in, thanks. Make do, Duncan."

At which point he turned back away and was gone, plunging into the crowd with a flipper-baby lifted onto one shoulder and a gang of urchins grabbing after the flapping wings of his jacket. For a moment, I could track him by the sound of him singing along with the music—*pleased to meet you, hope you guess my name . . .*—and for a moment more by the squealing of the children that surrounded him. But then he was gone and the day was only a day and I was alone. Free. Or so I thought.

What never occurred to me in the moment was that that'd been the second time he'd called me by my name. Called me *Duncan*. Not my only name (and certainly not my true name, as you well know), but just the one I'd been tarnishing most recently. Duncan Archer, layer of roads, teller of lies.

It took me quite some time to recollect the oddity of that. And by the time I did, I wasn't even sure it'd happened the way I recalled. So when, on a day much later, I would approach his Captainness in a quiet moment and ask him about it—ask him how he had known me and, for that matter, how he'd called me by my name—he would look at me like I had lobsters crawling out of my ears.

"You're tired, Mr. Duncan Archer," he would say with a sigh. "It's been a long day with a longer night on its back. Go get some sleep."

Which, you'll notice, did not answer my question at all.

I did my duty and, in the end, traded bullets for coffee from a pretty girl completely unimpressed with my first tactic, which was to demand three coffees (and one chicory for myself) for free, in the name of King Steven the Generous.

"Fuck you and your king," she said, without even looking up from the ragged, hardbound textbook on TAL effectors and viral phage insertion protocols she had open on the counter in front of her. But when I reached—even ever so slowly and with the greatest of care—for the automatic pistol slung up under my left arm, she looked up at me with sweetly purple eyes, big as manga, batted her artificial lashes, split the tiny bow of her mouth just enough to show me the double row of chromium shark's teeth she had inside, and smilingly promised that she would chew the eyeballs right out of my head before I ever touched leather.

"Such language!" said me. "And from such a pretty fish. I'm only meaning to trade, lovely. Two bullets for three coffees and one chicory, sugar and milk all—9mm, castle-made, guaranteed to go bang or call me liar to my face."

She asked four. We settled on three. She told me that she carried no chicory, and I told her it was a poor world we were living in that didn't cater to the tastes of the refined imbiber of root juice.

"You talk funny," she said.

"No, I speak like a man who knows just what he wants to say," I replied, then thumbed three bullets from the clip onto her plank and asked her where she'd gotten her teeth done. She told me to lean real close so I could read the maker's mark off 'em.

I laughed. I liked her. Man I was then, I would've thoroughly enjoyed whiling away a morning watching the cagey dart of her pretty bought eyes and listening to her threaten my life. Sooner or later, I would've fallen in love with her. Married her. Raised up a passel of shark-babies. History would've been a very different thing. But then Jemma was there, suddenly beside me, hand on my shoulder like a mate, calling the girl Katarina and asking, please, for hers black and another sweet, no milk, and Katarina was calling me terrible names and asking why in the fuckity-fuck-fuck hadn't I just *said* I'd come from the Captain, and I was saying well how was I supposed to know that Himself—who I'd only just met, mind—would swing such a heavy weight with pretty little shark-mouth coffee-sellers, and all was a mess and tumult of loud voices and rude words when I stopped and stepped back.

"The man asked me for three, white and sweet," said me to the ladies, worried—actually *worried!*—that I'd perform less than satisfactorily on this first, vital mission with which I'd been tasked by the Captain.

And Katarina laughed and Jemma shook her head like to make her wheatstraw hair sway. "No," she said. "He told you that because that's how he takes *his* coffee and he just assumes that everyone must like theirs the same."

She lifted her cup then, full and hot and black as sin, and drank from it with a perfect joy. She touched her tongue to her lips when she had done. Rolled her head loosely on her shoulders. "One thing about the Captain," she said. "He's never been wrong about a goddamn thing in his life."

Jemma said goodbye to Shark Face, hugging her and kissing her on both cheeks and reminding her to study hard because good boys didn't like dumb girls, then turned back to me.

"Come on, then. Let's go. Grab the other cups. Our ride is waiting."

Our ride, such as it was, was a pale green technical that looked like an end-of-year welding project at a school for drunken malcontents and multiple amputees.

Parked half up the curb along the pitted ribbon that'd once been Colfax Avenue, it was green in precisely the way that nothing in nature ever had been. The green of hospital tile. Of insane asylum men's rooms and the shirts of colorblind Eastern European gangsters.

It was green and assembled variously from one light pickup truck lashed up with three-quarters of a ton of old radiators, hubcaps, corrugated sheet steel, bits of iron gate, dented trash can lids and a thousand wire hangers. There were running boards made from what looked like old battleship parts, and angry eyes painted on where the headlights ought to have been, an open bed mounted with what appeared to be a grenade launcher pilfered from some alien species that believed in neither aesthetics or barrel length, and a tailgate made of stove iron and set with eight-inch gleaming steel spikes.

"Marlene," said Jemma as we approached—me warily and juggling three coffee cups, she with satisfaction, like a woman returning home after too long away. "Marlene, Marlene, Marlene..."

The vehicle, such as it was, was surrounded by a mob of children—filthy things with hatchet faces, ragged stumps of wings poking through torn plasmid shirts and the odd horn or scabrous bit of brass fitting, all sprouting tufts of gray-white fungus where graftoid infections had set in. There were a dozen of them, carrying Little League baseball bats studded with screws, or antique revolvers scurled with rust. One had an ice axe, its head spray-painted Day-Glo pink except along the teeth of the blade where it'd been scraped lovingly clean with a razor.

Flint-eyed moppets, the lot. Little monsters who'd never known a world less strange than this one they'd been given unto and who likely slept nights in a feral knot, like moles, weeping together over parental units who'd abandoned them or been lost to war or chance or madness.

Jemma marched straight into them. I bumbled along behind. The day was blue and clear and smelled of coffee and kerosene. Someone had thrown a new record on the player, and over the din of voices the Sex Pistols skronked along, whining for Anarchy in the UK, which was funny because, after so many years, they'd finally gotten their wish. London had been burning for two years, radiation and viral transcriptase levels so high that even the rats had fled. Compared to that, the kingdoms of the Western Confederacy were wild paradises that, if they didn't kill you, could make you live forever in the plasticky embrace of the weird.

If they didn't kill you.

If.

Dying made everything sad, so if you didn't just die of something silly or ridiculous—if you weren't stomped flat by a giant robot or eaten by a sea monster (rare in Colorado, but not unheard of) or shot on the street for a nickel; if you weren't press-ganged onto the crew of an airship and died screaming in the dank of the boiler room as it fell from the sky like a poisoned bird; if you didn't get cholera, hepatitis, super-AIDS, Panamanian brain spiders, or one of those diseases where your skin crawls right off your body; if you didn't catch nine kinds of cancer from eating radioactive dog food and expire messily with your insides leaking down your legs; if you didn't join some army or other and die from landmine or laser fire or discombobulator ray or a knife in the face; if you didn't starve; if you didn't blow up for no reason; if you didn't ever grow old or slow or boring—well then, son, you were living in Funville, USA.

Happy, was I. Off on a lark and agog at the beauty of the world. And for a blink, perhaps, I was paying less than complete attention to my surroundings, so when Jemma Watts slipped through the outer ring of defenders (little boys parting smirkingly, averting their gaze from her bright eyes and proud breasts), I wasn't quite quick enough on the jump and found that they had closed up tight against me.

"Pitch off, topper," said the one nearest me, mumbling around a wiggly horrorshow of monster teeth and distended, crude stitching along both of his cheeks. "We don't know you, so fugoff."

And I says, "Carrying joe for the team, kid," and shows them all the cups in my hands. "So if you young gentlemen could kindly step aside..."

"Bring some for us?" said a different small beast. "How sweet."

"Take that iron off'n ya, too," said another.

"Oh, Jemma!" I called, but she was gone 'round the other side of the monstrosity, to parlay with the chief of the eastern defenses or somesuch, and the small beast with the ice axe—a girl beast beneath all the grime and poverty leathers, unless I was terribly mistaken—twirled her prize expertly in one hand and said, "No help for you there, papi. Howza give usn's two dollars and we only snap you sticks?"

"How about I throw you in that puddle and give you a bath?" I countered, advancing a half-step.

"Howza take one more step an' Tuesday chuff your lights?" said the first beast again, at which point the girl-creature stopped making fancy with her axe and raised it like she meant to rumble.

And just when it appeared as though I was going to end my morning in an axe-fight with a ten-year-old girl, I heard the engine roar to life, saw Logue (who'd somehow snuck massively through the defenses) heave his two milk jugs into the pickup's bed, and felt the Captain step up beside me.

"Army?" said him. "Report."

All the children drew upright and to attention with a snap, clubs and cudgels shoulder-arms, eyes fixed and glassy. It was the first boy who spoke, his tone as pinched and professional as any proper soldier's.

"Sir, Marlene secure, sir. No trouble, no noseys."

"And what's this then? Repelling boarders?"

"Sir, yes sir. Orders were to stop anyone we don't know from approaching the vehicle, sir. An' ain't none of us knows this topper."

"So you planned on killing him?"

The boy appeared to think seriously about this for a second. "Sir. We was going to rob him first, sir. Orders is orders."

The Captain smiled. "Good man." He reached over my shoulder and took a coffee, white and sweet. "At ease, troop. This topper is one of ours now, understand? Get a good look."

The children stood down. All except the girl. "This one?" she asked. "Him's on your rolls, an' I'm still guarding the truck?"

"Every tool has its use, Tuesday," said the Captain. "Every man has his value."

She kicked at the dirt with the toe of a boot held together with silver duct tape gone black with grime, eyes downcast. "Not fair . . ." she said, voice suddenly that of a child denied candy. Or, you know, blood.

The Captain crouched down and looked at her until the color bloomed in her cheeks. He took her gently by the back of the neck and leaned close, whispering something into her ear. When he was done, he clapped her on the shoulder and handed her his coffee, stood up and saluted her. She stood straight, fixed a serious look on her face, bit her bottom lip, and saluted him back, touching the tip of her axe to her forehead.

"Army dismissed," said the Captain, then turned to me and took another coffee to replace the one he'd given to Tuesday and which she was now loudly defending from a tangle of grabby boys by biting any hand that came close. "I'll take that. Now get in the truck."

"What'd you say to her?" I asked him.

"That she could have your shoes and shooter when you died, but until then she was to watch out for you extra-special."

"And will she?" I asked, looking for a place to ride and realizing that the bed of the truck was the only seat for me.

"Orders is orders," he shouted from the passenger side, climbing into the hump seat between Jemma and Logue. "But I wouldn't turn my back on her if I were you."

On first glance, Marlene's open bed looked to be a fairly uncomfortable place to ride. In actuality it was worse.

On the flats-and-straights she curried out nice so that it was only my back and heels and tail-place that suffered. But throw a capful of gravel under her tires and I was choking the horn just to stay mounted. Eventually, I found that if I planted my spine against the back of the cab, my boots against the gunpost, and held on for dear life to the side rail and the lip of the bed, it was merely like taking a ride in a clothes dryer, minus the warmth.

But my comfort notwithstanding, we rattled along, down the wrecked and stomp-holed streets which had until so recently been in my care, passing out of downtown headed easterly on the remains of Colfax Avenue, through the siege zone (still being recovered by Royalty work crews and pioneering survivors), and out into the neighborhoods beyond, which had either been spared or savaged, depending entirely on the inequity of moments spent at war.

We crossed the newly cut trench lines at Colfax and Downing Street, rolling up and over a punched steel causey that'd been thrown across the gap and that I wouldn't have been able to draw on my best day as a road engineer, let alone oversee the construction of. I had to hold fast to keep from being thrown when we came crashing down the other side, digging nails into body panels as Jemma jinked Marlene around the crumbling lips of chuckholes and moonscape craters carved by high explosives, then closed my eyes and wished for strength when she hooked a screeching right turn onto Humboldt Street and plunged us into the deeps of the pillaged lands—them that the invading hordes had lived off of during the siege.

Here, things were even stranger. There were whole sections of homes and shops that'd been completely untouched—which sat wearing lace curtains behind unbroken window glass and sprays of yellow and red and blue g-mod flowers. Cheesman Park was half a summer fair and half a refugee camp, with OD tents still clustered on the flat places, aid societies doling out blocks of soy protein, freshly extruded children's toys, and seeds for simple home appliances, and a dozen-dozen chickenwire dishes sprouting from the tops of the barb-wired concertainer walls. But the grass was coming back, too, and fast-grow trees sprouted achingly green shoots that you could hear growing if you stood close.

In the least lathered neighborhoods children played beeps-and-muties in the greenways and men grilled pink lozenges of cloned buffalo protein over backyard fires or roasted chiles in drums made from spent artillery shells. The world, such as it was, hardly looked ruined at all but for the beep checkpoints where the battle police lounged with lazy malice, experimenting with various forms of harassment and waiting to ventilate any looters, anarchists, late-arriving Kansans, or other unsavory elements that might stand still long enough for them to unlimber their iron and get to shooting.

But in the worst-wrecked neighborhoods the work gangs wore biohazard suits and pig-snout rebreathers to cut the smell of dying. The bulldozers rolled night and day, scraping clean lots which would then be churned and seeded with stands of banana trees, television plants, ugly, glittering solar bushes tied into the still-gimped city grid, or fast-forward bamboo. Bodies were burned in pits, then sodded over and coaxed into becoming fertilizer for tufts of carbon-fiber nanotubes that grew like alien grasses (tough to see, even in clumps of a million).

The smoke from the fires turned the air murky. We passed POW's in bumblebee-stripe canvas jumpers working in chain-gang formation, shoveling stone and digging holes with no overseers at all save a cloud of humming video drones as small and quick as gnats and one bored shotgun bull on a barded automatic horse with one knee fitfully sparking. The prisoners' good behavior was vouchsafed by the shaved patches on the backs of each of their necks and the fresh catgut stitching. That was where the little bombs had gone in. Press a button and boom. One more body for the buckytube farms.

This got me thinking how, on the one hand, here was another plain argument against warring for a cause (it's no fun for anyone but the winners, and even then only rarely) and, on the other, how I could maybe turn a nice buck selling tinfoil hats to escaped convicts.

Like to block the signals from the remote detonators, right? For them that were quick enough to escape but didn't have the pesos to get their little head-poppers dug out. It would be a scam with zero worries about dissatisfied customers, for certain.

While I was pleasantly cogitating over my newest business notions, Jemma cut sharpish around a one-seater blistercar tootling down the road, hopped up a curb, and suddenly jumped right on the brakes, jamming me against the back wall of the cab in a way that was likely comical to anyone who was not me.

I shouted for mercy that was not forthcoming and banged the flat of one hand on the cab while she was backing traction. I was busy getting my legs untangled from my shoulders in the truck's bed when she shifted again into drive.

And then she was rolling slow through the side-yard of a shot-holed and gaping white-picket Tudor open to the elements like a face with its teeth punched out. And that was where I saw the child she'd nearly run down.

The child—the boy-child—with his matted hair, bloated belly, sagging diaper gone gray with age and pyoderma sores running down his legs. The child who sat in the dirt poking at a ripe, dead centaur with a stick. The child who did not move, did not scream or cry, who did nothing but watch us pass by with wide, dry and staring blue eyes and a look of absolute, blank disinterest. Inside the cab, the heads of the Captain and his crew rotated in unison, eyes tracking, saying nothing, just watching until this boy with nothing, with no one to love him or save him or see to the care of him, receded into the clouds of our trail dust. There was nothing to be done. Nothing them like us might do save take on the weight of a child dying.

As for me, I just turned my face to the heavens, looked into the blue and perfect infinity of the sky, and let the sun cure me of all my mortal ills. *Ain't nothing there worth seeing*, I told myself. *Ain't nothing you haven't seen before.*

Later, when this story comes all a cropper, when it is chockablock with dinosaurs and distressed damsels and blimp fights, and you ask yourself, how ever could this silly little man—this lying swindler, this inveterate avoider, this cheating, uppish yack—ever do such a damn fool thing as sign on and stay a'friended with a man like the Captain, you remember that boy. Him's the reason. The answer to whatever why's might plague you.

Him and a thousand other things like him, all turned to memories now in the great wide weird of the world. One wall-eyed and dying boy in a dirt lot in Denver, lost to all goodness, all niceness, all help.

See, there are them that make their choices and them that suffer for the choices others make, you understand? For the first sort, I have no pity and a hundred bridges to sell. And for the second...

Well, let's say that for the second sort I had thoughts of a not entirely bestial nature. Someone, I felt, needed to look out for them that got done sour by those that never count the cost. Some good man to lay his warrant on the protection of all the world's soft-heads and flipper-babies and such.

Not *me*, of course. Were you thinking it was going to be me?

No, I began this tale as a liar in a dead man's shoes and will finish it more or less the same way. But the Captain? *He* was a good man, after his fashion. Couldn't help but love a stray.

So while I watched out for the soiled doves, the rum-runners, the flimflammers and deserters and horse thieves, he made finer use of his days. The Captain was a man who left the world a better place than he'd found it. Sometimes burning, occasionally wracked, now and again littered with the bodies of bad men, but always improved on balance. Leaning (even if only slightly) in the direction of goodness. And I'd like to think myself at least slightly bettered by his company.

So... Do you believe me?

Yeah, you should be careful with that.

A few minutes later, I heard the little plastic window in the blast glass that separated the truck's cab from its bed rattle and slide open. The Captain was turned half around in his seat and he shouted back to me.

"You seem to be enjoying the ride," he said.

"Oh, you know how it is. Any day out-of-doors and whatever."

The Captain has this smile he wears when he knows someone is lying or bluffing or trailing the buck, but doesn't feel like diverting the wind of a conversation by pointing it out. It was the look of a boy who'd been bet a dollar he wouldn't eat a worm, ready now to go double or nothing. Of a cardsharp with an ace in his sleeve and two hearts in his boot watching a natural straight come floating to him on the river. A knife-sharp and cold smile that said, *it's not just that I'm smarter than you, but I'm better, too.* It was the kind of thing that would've gotten him punched in the face every day if not for the amount of firepower regularly hung about his person.

Because of the class and quality of the characters with which the Captain traditionally surrounded himself, he about wore that smile out at the corners, but that day riding on Marlene's back was the first time I saw it. And then he asked me whether or not I had a gun.

"I do," said me, and flapped open the wings of my tweedy jacket to show him the butt of the service automatic I'd walked off with. "Castle-made, tried and true."

"Do you have another?"

I allowed that I did not, steadied myself as Jemma rounded a corner and rallied off into another neighborhood that was more ash than plaster. "It occurs to me that a man is having a certain kind of conversation when he intimates that a man with no guns needs one, but a very different kind when he tells a man with one gun that he needs more," I said. "Mr. The Captain sir."

The Captain nodded, turned around to fuss around in the cab a moment, then turned back again and passed out to me a big thumbcracker—a six-shot smokebox that looked to have last seen service when Custer was a corporal. "We are two men," he says to me. "And we are having that conversation."

I rolled out the cylinder of the thing, checked its load, its action, then snapped it back. And all the while, the Captain is watching me with an appraising eye.

"You know your firearms?" he asked.

"Acknowledge the corn, friend. I've sold plenty of them in my day."

That smile again, the tips of his pearlies scraping his bottom lip. "Okay, well you make sure the hammer's down and put that in your pants where everyone can see it. Do you have a phone?"

Of course I had a phone. Had three of them, actually, of varying vintages and levels of functionality because, seriously, what was this? Nepal? The West was having itself a nice, *civilized* apocalypse, thank you very much, with coffee and thick steaks and cold beer and pretty girls and of course cell phones.

"No," I said. "Don't like 'em. Filthy things'll give you ear cancer. Why? You need to make a call?"

"No," said the Captain. "You do." He turned around again and poked Logue Ranstead in the shoulder with all the effect of slapping a rock, then snapped his fingers. Logue produced from his pocket the two phones boosted from the offices they'd so quickly ransacked.

The Captain turned to Jemma. "Whose is this?" he asked.

"Thewlip," she said.

"Nice. And the other?"

"Don't know."

"Then why'd you take it?"

"Thought it was pretty. Also, it's a lot nicer than mine."

"Fair enough," said the Captain, then turned back to the little window and handed me a sleek handset like a slab of mirrored obsidian.

"Audition time," he said. "You're Chester Thewlip, social secretary to the King. You speak seven languages fluently. They won't know that Techny isn't one of them. You have a slight lisp, one wife, at least two girlfriends, and a sincere dedication to one of the bar girls at Lucky Lucy's. You've also been pawning off the royal teacups and silver for years. None of that is important though. Unless it comes up. Which it probably won't."

I swallowed hard and scratched at a bit of muck on my trousers.

"Don't tell me you get stage fright."

I have a special smile, too. Maybe not so pretty as the Captain's and maybe not so affecting, but it's mine. I plastered it on as Jemma brought the truck to a rocking halt in the middle of a greeny traffic circle which sat like a lost island amid the pavement. "Course not," said me. "Remind me to tell you some time about the night I played Willy Loman with a bunch of traveling actors when their lead came down with the backdoor trots."

"I bet you were a wonder."

"I was fucking transcendent."

"I believe you. Now make the call."

I stared at the face of the phone. "A lisp, you say?"

"Bit of one, yeah. Not so you'd notice. Chester's got him a missing tooth or two."

I ran a thumb over the screen, enlivening the thing. It came to with a jangle and called me by Chester's name.

"Ladies man?"

"He is."

I stared at the phone, then looked back at the Captain. "I'm getting paid for this, right? I mean, I know we're doing the Lord's work and all, but..."

"You're stalling, Duncan."

Which was, of course, completely true. And also the third time he'd called me by name.

"Am not," said me. "Just getting in character. Your friends, they expecting this call?"

"Surely not. Not the types who regularly get calls from the Castle. Use that to your advantage."

"And I am . . . ?"

"Chester Thewlip."

"No, why am I calling?"

"Making an appointment for some of the King's men to visit with them."

"What kind of visit?"

"The soft kind, is my fervent hope."

"How soon?"

The Captain looked back at Jemma, who shrugged.

"Let's say ten minutes."

"And what's the visit for?"

"They'll know. And if they don't know, they're lying."

"Shouldn't I know?"

The Captain shrugged. "You know what you know, Chester. And you don't know what you don't. Now get on it."

He gave me three numbers, written on a scrap of paper in pink ink. I clambered out of the truck so's I'd have some privacy and pacing room, then punched in the first.

Disconnected.

The second rang and rang to no avail. And I was beginning to feel that luck was, perhaps, on my side after all and that none of the numbers would work and I would be spared the embarrassment of being caught in something a little more than half a lie. I poked in the third number and it rang, then rang some more. I was about to switch off when I heard a click, a gargle, and a shout, followed by a storm of clamorous nonsense.

"Miksi kutsut crash ten? Whois? True vernor, muthafuka, on meshin ruokin sysdimesi weasels!"

And that, my dears, was Techny. I looked back to the truck, smiled, and gave the Captain a thumbs-up.

I was fucked.

Here's the thing about Techny: It's a cant. A trade language. Like if you've ever heard short-order cooks talking while they're slinging their hash, you get me. Or bankers. Or mechanos. Every serious job develops its own specialized argot which acts as both a kind of verbal shorthand for them as want to get across complicated notions in the fewest possible words and as a deliberate barrier against understanding to them that aren't part of the tribe. The vernacular can be simple or complex, encompassing or merely flavorsome. Point is, they're nobody's *first* language. They function as addenda to a traditional lexicon.

Techny, though, was different. Somewhat. Because it was a tongue spoken exclusively by those what spent most of their wakey-and-worky hours speaking to machines, it was, in effect, a primary language—just one that was uniquely incapable of expressing anything that might be useful to the Lord's squishier critters. It was a perfect vernacular for discussions of register operands and load values. Less so for asking for a sandwich. And so, should a Techny-speaking engineer find himself in need of a sandwich, he would have to fall back on some human tongue in order to ask for it.

Everyone who spoke Techny spoke something else as well. But they spoke it in the *flavor* of Techny, if you follow. They spoke through mouths sticky with jargon, slang, the cant. Everything filtered through it. Whoever I was talking to, for example, spoke Finnish—which I knew because, like I've said, I had the ear. I didn't *speak* Finnish, of course, but I did have in me some things that were like Finnish. That were thick-tongued and fishy in the same kinds of ways. So I could infer that the man on the other end of the phone was upset. Knew for a fact that he'd suggested a distasteful Oedipal act. Was ninety percent sure he'd asked me my name and rather less confident in the rest of my translation.

He'd said something about weasels, though. And no one who's happy talks about weasels.

"Cha," I said. "Inita input?" which was some little bit of Techny I was sure of. It meant, more or less, *Hey, can I talk now?*

"Tekee puhua Technya?"

"I do," said me. "A-firm. Low calls." *Sure do, pal. Affirmative. Just go slow, and we'll do fine.*

"Go. Sig and serve."

"Sig Chester Thewlip," I said. "Sta...um..." I closed my eyes. Having used up my polite address and my initial apology (the two things that anyone who knows any language learns first), I was now at sea, desperately scraping around the old vault for contextuals or modifiers and feeling the sweat prickling my forehead as I found none. "I'm uh..."

"Speakin' English, butcha. Before you hurt you."

"Really?"

"Burning cycles, man. And calling fuck early. So jump-jump."

The best thing about the trade language is that knowing even a little of it is proof of belonging. Better than a union card or a company brand. Breaks ice like an alkie's teeth.

"Sig Chester Thewlip," I said, with just the slightest touch of a lisp. "And I am social secretary to the King."

The Captain was standing in the cab, the upper half of him sticking out Marlene's sunroof while he smoked a cigarette and watched me do my little dance. Logue was sitting on the hood, daring the truck's suspension to fail and picking at something on the side of his neck. Jemma stood a few paces off with her eyes closed and her face turned toward the sun.

When I'd hung up the phone, I'd left it pressed to my ear for a moment, breathing deep and smiling with my back to the Captain's crew. We'd made ourselves understood to each other, myself and Mr. Nils Sorenson, chief engineer of the Green Willow clave. In three or four or five different cobbled-up languages, we'd made the most basic sort of human connection: Had exchanged names and titles and made a date to meet in order to further our growing détente. I'd explained that he and his people were in possession of something that the King's men would very much like to get their hands on, and, as the Captain had said, Mr. Sorenson had seemed to know exactly what I was talking about. I'd said there was a lot of money in it for him if he was willing to meet and discuss terms, and he'd laughed with a cruel and rapacious booming that the phone made sound flat. He'd said he would be very happy to meet, of course. He'd agreed quickly. Almost anxiously. *Too* anxiously maybe. All he'd asked was for twenty minutes rather than ten.

My smile faded. I lowered the phone and walked back toward the truck.

"Twenty minutes," I said. "Your friend wants to lay out a spread."

"No friend of mine," said the Captain, squinting. "You talked to him?"

"Mr. Nils Sorenson, chief engineer of the Green Willow clave. Had a nice chat, him and me. Right neighborly."

"See, then? That wasn't so hard, was it?"

"Not a bit."

"And you were so nervous."

"Hardly. He seemed rather chummy, though. Your man among the savages."

"Did he?"

"Seemed awfully happy to hear we were coming, know what I mean?"

"Not a bit," the Captain said.

"Too happy. Like maybe he's planning a bushwhack."

The Captain sucked in a deep lungful of smoke and let it out through the narrow gaps in his smile. "I'd think less of the man if he didn't try something," he said.

Shrugging, I hauled myself up into the bed of the truck, stubbing myself in the belly with the butt of the pistol in my belt and tearing my pants on a twist of barbed wire hung off the side panel and meant, I assumed, to discourage boarders. Tumbling in, I banged the back of my head on Marlene's grenade-launcher-looking-whatsis and cursed in three languages while kicking it, all to little effect.

"Really, Captain, it's the accommodations that make me feel so welcome," I said, speaking up at him while rubbing my head.

"There's steps on the other side."

"Really?"

He looked down at me for a second longer than was comfortable, seeming to weigh me by eye.

"No," he said.

The Green Willow clave kept place deep in Cherry Creek, a formerly high-hog neighborhood that'd seen an arrhythmia of boom-and-bust cycles under Denver's various lords and absolute monarchs. With the ascension of King Steven the Uneven (so called on account of his missing arm, in case you didn't get that earlier), it'd been coming back again nicely, with many proper shops offering frillery and knickknacks to those un-oppressed by taste, cafes with something better than sawdust bread and vat meat on the menu, and several apple pie boozers made for them that could appreciate glass tumblers and ice over tin cups and none. On its goodest days, mobs of the Quality had walked the broad sidewalks of the Creek with their tiny dogs, shimmering veils of nan-stuff and sword canes tapping the sparkling pavement. Here and there they would stop to overpay for tiny thimbles of Italian coffee or pastries made with actual butter and fruit that'd once known the kiss of sun. They would sit and listen to fiddle players who didn't know a single song about pickup trucks or whiskey, or discuss among themselves the weighty issues of the day. It was a regular Paree of the plains.

Then had come yesterday's war and Cherry Creek had took it square in the neck. Too far from the Gray Castle to be reasonably held and altogether too poncey to defend itself, it'd become a raper's and a looter's paradise.

Were I a younger man (or perhaps just hungrier or more vicious), and had I for some reason found myself still in the Queen City once the siege lines closed up tight, to the Creek was where I would've gone. Would've raised up a gang, me. Colors and all. To pound down doors, riffle the finery, and relieve the swells of whatever they reckoned less valuable than their lives until every jack and jayhawker around would've known me for the man stepping out in two minks, a silky necktie, rings on every finger, and three fine Stetsons stacked up on my head.

And more's the pity that I didn't, because others had. Plenty. And I would've cut a more dashing figure than the whole lot of them put together. But I digress.

Eventually, the booty had run out and all the pirates had sailed on. Cherry Creek was abandoned, cold and dark; became briefly the home base of some minor reaver called Snake or Python or something elsewise clichéd, who held down two blocks of 1st Street like an old-timey highwayman until the Kansan air force decided one afternoon to plaster him with homebrew mustard gas and brand-name napalm dropped from drones operated out of some basement in Copeland or Altoona. Viper or Cobra or whoever was never heard from again, and King Steve the Grateful allegedly sent a muffin basket and a handwritten thank you note to the zoomie major who'd given the order, which was just the sort of odd stick he was.

After the fires went out, things were quiet again until the once-quite-splendid shopping mall there became one of the final strongholds of the retreating Kansans—a coordinated defense meant to delay the pursuing Western Confederacy forces so that the surviving jayhawker elites, commanders and supply ships could make an orderly withdrawal onto the plains and live, maybe, to fight another day.

The Captain talked as we drove, explaining how the mall had held for three days and two nights. There were 400 Plains Militia hunkered down inside Urban Outfitters and Let's Talk About Sox and JC Penney's and PJ Flannigan's Good Tyme Foodateria, living on bagged soy chips and melted Orange Julius, skittering about the promenades that glittered with a carpet of shattered glass and shredded silk, and swallowing a million dollars in bling after a high-explosive shell punched down through the roof and cracked open a safe at Esterhase Jewelers—hoping just to keep it inside themselves long enough to shit out tennis bracelets for their Confederacy captors and thereby buy their freedom once the inevitable end came.

"No one inside the Cherry Creek Mall had any illusions about how things were going to shake out there," the Captain said. "Every man among them had Last Wills, love notes and letters to their families tucked inside their war bags."

Still, say this about a Kansas man: He is stubborn. The apex of obstinacy. And none of these 400 gave up easy. They had among their ranks a certain number of sharpshooters with rifles all named after apple-cheeked Midwestern girls, a jetpack squad of near-suicidal cornpone rednecks who'd range out along the flanks of the Confederacy lines, disrupting supplies of ammunition and ice cream sundaes, then come home again to gas up, smoke a little crazy-dust, and fly back out again through the mall's shattered skylights. More important, they had two of Lord Phillip's three surviving Type IX's—the same sort of death-spitting, sky-scraping kill-mo-trons that had spearheaded the charge against the Castle. Towering ears and hats above the tallest buildings in the Creek, their every footfall was an earthquake powerful enough to bust glass, their lines of sight nigh on to a nosy god's.

A day and a night and a day they spent stomping, machine-gunning, flame-throwering, and just generally killing the ever-loving shit out of anything they could see, forcing the King's men to keep to hard cover until sappers could be brought in to swarm at the robots' ankles like ants. They burned the heavy armor away with the bright, cutting arcs of plasma torches, scaled the legs like terminal mountaineers, stuffed shaped charges into the joints while they hung from improvised harnesses of clothesline and nylon climbing rope and, occasionally, exploded themselves for the cause.

Once the robots were immobilized, the artillerymen took over, attacking from just a mile off with fire and acid and harsh language. Degaussing beam head-shots wiped chunks of data from the processors of the warbots as neatly as performing a coat-hanger lobotomy, making the huge machines schizoid, mental and trembly like spastics. Shells from the cannon batteries came screaming in on dead-flat trajectories, dragging tails of wind-whipped dust behind them and splattering the 'bots with radioactive dye packs that blinded their sensors or just plain exploded with the shattering force of Volkswagen Beetles stuffed with dynamite.

On the second night, one of the 'bots fell, taking down half an office block with it and bringing a cheer from the Confederacy lines that could be heard all the way to Hoth.

On the third morning, the second surrendered—72 hours of unending punishment becoming finally too much for the machinery to bear. The giant thing was completely insane at this point, firing wildly at clouds and ghosts, its insides making a howling sound like a belly-shot mastodon weeping for knowing that its end was all too near.

All of this data, this *detail*, I got from the Captain as Jemma wheeled Marlene through the wrecking field the place had become, grinding her way in low gear through narrow channels that'd been cut, cleared and blasted through hills of debris. He pointed out places and made *pewpewpew* noises at the appropriate moments, all as though he'd been right there for the whole of the show. And who knew? Maybe he had been. I never thought to ask.

"The second one was right there," he said as we rolled past a crumbled and pancaked parking garage which had, as a kind of grave marker, the skeleton bodies of three high-lift cranes around it and one massive leg that, itself, stood near forty foot tall.

"When the end came, it shrouded itself in defensive smoke and went into suicide shutdown, frying all its own internal whatevers and detonating what was left in its magazines. The engineers weren't quick enough to get in and stop it. The gas stank like the devil's bathroom after chili night. Bad enough to make you lose your lunch and chase it with breakfast. And the 'bot was all arcing with lightning bolts and fire." He shook his head. "In the end, there was nothing to salvage, which was unfortunate, you know? Machine like that can be worth a lot to the right people. Even in pieces."

There wasn't any cheering this time. The way now clear, the King's troops had stormed the mall with grim faces and the stolid dedication of working men who just wanted to get home in time for supper. Most of the Kansan militia surrendered on the spot, according to the Captain—laying aside arms and breaking into a ragged chorus of "Colorado" by The Rentals, which his Stevenness had, as one of his first official acts, made the official song of the capital of the Western Confederacy (followed close on by declaring donuts the official breakfast food, the entire actinide series as official elements, a kind of orangey-gold like aspen leaves turning as the official color, and Fridays an official part of the weekend, particularly during the summers).

There were still hard fights had in the food court and the ladies unmentionables department of the JC Penney's, but the worst was over. The song, I thought, had been a nice touch. Maybe even true. And the Captain sung a bit, quietly but with a sweet voice, as Jemma skirted a space-suited 'dozer crew like something out of a bad Saturday matinee and Logue grumbled like a mountain with the itis.

"Hate that song," Logue said.

"You are a traitor, sir," the Captain barked. "What song would you have had our wise and benevolent monarch choose?"

Logue opened his mouth, but the Captain raised a commanding finger and interrupted him. "You say the Flying Burrito Brothers, I swear I will make you walk the rest of the way, you lump."

Logue shut his mouth again. Jemma laughed. Marlene rolled on and on.

The first Type IX had fallen clear of the mall, coming to rest beneath the rubble of insurance agencies, content design studios and an orphan's benevolent association—all of it like grave dirt for a postmodern giant.

"Second one died with one foot crushing a shoe store," the Captain said, smiling. "There's something about that I just love."

And in the meantime, Kansas had slipped back into Kansas and, for the moment, peace in the realm had been restored.

"The King, he offered an amnesty to all jayhawkers left behind. All the surrendered militia, all the stranded units, whoever. He told them, anyone willing to stay and work at cleaning up their own damn mess was welcome so long as they took off their uniforms, swore allegiance to the Western Confederacy, and quit being such dicks—his words." The Captain paused, scratched at his bottom lip with a thumbnail. "Didn't mention the cortex bombs 'til *after* they'd sworn, which I felt was right Kingly of him."

And Cherry Creek, like Cheesman Park, became a resettlement zone for refugees, deserters, widows, abandons and those displaced by the late unpleasantness. Most of the POWs lived in the mall, no guards required. Those with useful skills (or who'd learned to crap fine jewelry) were moved into the houses of the Quality which, even half wrecked-up, overcrowded, and occasionally marked with grisly reminders of why it is sometimes not wise to be rich in a poor place, were still fine as cream gravy by comparison.

But the best places were, as always, reserved for them that could both take and defend them, and who had the kind of freedom of movement granted by not having to worry about your head exploding if you stepped wrong. And it was to one of those best places that we were now traveling.

"There," said the Captain suddenly, pointing ahead to a street-corner mound of rubble and kak that looked exactly the same as a dozen others we'd passed until we were right up on it. Only then did I notice the crashed and bullet-holed sign, which, in once-lovely curlicue letters, read GREEN WILLOW SALON AND DAY SPA.

"Roll slow, now, darling," said the Captain to Jemma. "We're almost home."

There were no guards. We were watched, that was sure, but not by any warm, meat eyes. Marlene's engine grumbled and growled as Jemma eased her around tank traps welded together out of jagged swatches of blackened steel and over too-perfect ditches cut in the pavement and too-freshly patched with tar-sand, which undoubtedly were home to pneumatic tire spikes and remote-detonated explosives. There were coils of razor wire and hurricane fence anchored by pillars of tires stacked around cores of cement parking blocks set on their ends that made a path narrow enough that it scraped the flanks of the truck as we passed. Beyond them were beds of tanglefoot and emplaced area immobilization cannons—booger guns that could net a ten-by-ten area in stretchy fronds of carbon polyurethane like a giant sneezing.

When we turned into what had once been the parking lot for the Green Willow Spa, I caught the sun gleam over the doors and windows where screens of organized nan-stuff (a trillion-odd atomic-scale machines, all working in delicate concert) shimmered like falling water as they fought to hold position in the gentle breeze stirred by our passing. Like the ladies veils and security shields of importantish peoples, these would act as screens against toxins, biological agents and environmental poisons. Also as shutters that could stop some certain amount of violence before failing. Also as a very effective means of keeping unwanted people out or wanted people in when you considered that, at a command, they could turn themselves into a hundred thousand razor blades or a billion microscopic bullets. Might that they could do different tricks, too, these nana. One never knew. These was still early days then, and the minds of them that toyed with the building blocks of reality were strange and shuddersome places.

"Cap," Jemma said. "We aren't ever getting out of here if things go poorly. Not in one piece."

"Then we'd better make sure that everyone keeps on smiling," he said, staring forward through the windshield as Jemma brought Marlene to a scrunching halt in the middle of the parking lot. It was clear, the lot. Almost seemed swept. Palisades of rubble rose all around it, packed and wired thickly together in a way that appeared hasty and random but was truly neither. One way in, one way out. Wasn't even anything like a gate, which showed either a shocking lack of foresight on behalf of the Green Willow clave or a frightening kind of confidence. If I was a betting man, I would've put money on the latter. And I am very much a betting man.

"Oh, yes," said Jemma. "And smiling is so often the way you leave people."

"Set the brake," he said. "Drop the gate. Logue, you're gonna stay with the truck, okay? On the gun but not, you know… Not *on the gun.*"

"What's that mean?" Logue asked. He shouldered open the door and slid out.

"Just stay with it, okay? Stay close. But don't shoot anything unless you have to shoot something."

Logue blinked. "I don't like talking to you."

The rear gate dropped with a resounding clang. I scooted out and Logue climbed in. He thumbed off the locks on the hard mount without looking, then sat on the side rail with a look on his face like a man staring at a very dull wall.

The Captain slid out Logue's side and closed the door. Jemma hopped out the driver's side. They stood together by the front of the truck, not moving, not rushing. Jemma had her hands in her pockets. The Captain had his propped on the hood, leaning back against them as though doing exercises. I walked up and stood nearby—close but not intimate. Polite distance. I was still a stranger here, after all.

For a minute, no one talked. I watched doors and windows, keeping eyes on everything at once. Jemma watched the clouds.

"You saying I'm not friendly?" the Captain asked suddenly.

"What?" Jemma asked.

"You said that I don't make people smile."

"I said that you don't *leave* people smiling, Cap. That's two very different things."

"That's not nice."

Jemma shrugged. "It is what it is. I've known you a long time."

The Captain looked at her, watching the side of her face. Eventually, she closed her eyes. He continued watching her until, apparently, he'd had enough.

"Chester!" he shouted. And it took me a second to remember that he was talking to me. "I seem like a nice man to you?"

I told him that was tough to judge, seeing as I'd just met him and all, and because I'd essentially been shanghaied out into the pillaged lands by strangers, told a story about large, stompy robots, and delivered to what appeared to be a ruined massage parlor with very little chance of there being an actual massage in my future. "Still, you haven't killed me yet."

"Politic," he said to Jemma. Jemma said nothing in return. He turned back to me. "Do I have a pleasing aspect? A generous nature? A comforting and easy way about me?"

"You kissed me on the face and give me a pistol," I said. "That's neighborly. And I certainly been treated worse. On the other hand, you made me pay for the coffee."

The Captain smiled, turned back to Jemma. "See? Chester likes me."

"You're sweet as summer wine, boss."

"I am," he said. "I smile and a hundred puppy dogs get born."

Jemma bit off a smile, teeth raking at her lower lip to keep it in line.

"Children like me. Girls like me. When I get the wind, rainbows shoot right out my—Oh, here we go."

There was a ripple in the sheet of nan sealing the front doors of the Green Willow Spa. A parting of the not-quite-waters.

"Logue," said the Captain, turning to look at the big fella who sat now with his elbows on his knees, carefully hand-rolling a smoke with fingers the size of jointed hot dogs. His hands were dripping with smudged tattoos. More crawled out of the neck of his shirt. He nodded, but said nothing.

"Good man," the Captain said, apparently content with whatever psychic messages had passed between them.

There was most of a sign still hanging beside the front door of the clave's home place. It'd once been neon green. The walls were spackly. The front doors were glass, with fake bamboo handles, and three men stepped out, eyeing the Captain and Jemma and the Captain and Marlene and Logue and the Captain and barely cutting a glance at me. Forgettable, forgettable me.

One of them was tall and straight and bearded, with a shaved head and a pale, bare chest and suspenders holding up his pants. The other two were smaller. One wore a conglomeration of doodads on his head that came down over his eyes with a variety of lenses and eyepieces and dangling wires. He kept a hand on it because it appeared to be too big for him and was in constant danger of falling off. The other carried a gleaming, wire-stock assault rifle with the barrel down and one finger on the trigger.

"Welcoming committee," said the Captain, "One with the hat is their security chief. His name doesn't matter. The other is Nils's bodyguard. His name doesn't matter either. Jemma, you know what—"

"I know."

"Okay. Chester, if things get complicated, just...I don't know. Go with it."

"Go with it?"

"Yeah. Go with it. You know, just hang loose. Don't do anything stupid."

And then the Captain spread his arms as though to embrace them all. He took a step forward and the man with the gun twitched the barrel. The man with the face-whatsis focused its optics on him. The big man in the center just stood. He raised one hand, signing stop. The Captain did not.

"Alright!" he shouted, a smile on his face and his arms wide. "Wouldn't have killed you to get a couple pretty girls to meet me at the door, but whatever. Maybe you three are as pretty as your kind gets. So tell me. Which one of you robot-talking idiots has my gadget and how much is it going to cost me to drive out of here with it?"

He never stopped walking. The man with the gun looked at the big man as though hoping for guidance. The man with the eye-pieces started chattering excitedly in Techny but was too far away for me to hear and talking too fast for me to follow anyhow. The man with the gun half-raised it, lowered it, stepped back, half-raised it again. Goggle Face reached out and actually yanked on the big man's arm, still talking, but the big man said nothing. Just stood. Lowered his ineffective hand. Crossed his arms. The Captain was halfway across the parking lot already. Then three quarters of the way. Jemma sighed and ambled after him. I kept pace with her.

"Just follow his lead," she said to me under her breath. "Maybe he has a plan."

"Maybe?" I asked.

"Yeah," she said. "Maybe."

"I might be new here, but this seems to me like the kind of situation where *absolutely* having a plan might've been a good idea. Maybe something deliberated by a committee? Approved by all parties?"

Jemma sniffed. "Not the way we do things, Chester. Captain knows what he's doing. Most of the time."

The Captain was standing at the edge of the walk in front of the door now. He was laughing, still talking. Not sure what else to do in the face of a fella who would willingly walk into a gun, both Mr. Machinegun and Goggle Face had retreated inside. The big man stood his ground, though. An amused smirk on his face. He was speaking and I knew the voice. This was Mr. Sorenson. As Jemma and I approached, I caught some of what he was saying.

"...sinum calls ten olla ne. Joka false, non? Tule sisaan. Gotsa lunch and stuff. All parity."

"Chester?" the Captain said out of one side of his smile. "Fucking translate."

"I think he said something about lunch."

Inside the Green Willow Spa there were no massage tables. No lattes or steam rooms or mud baths or little plates of finger sandwiches. There were barber's chairs, but they'd been turned into workstations with vboards on swing arms and flatscreen monitors cleverly suspended from the ceiling, showing a variety of views of the approaches to the clave's homeplace. The walls had been stripped back to their lathe and lined with aluminum shelving units where lived all the stuff of our unusual present. There was a tin bucket filled with buttons. A plastic bin the color of an Easter chick held spools of insulated wire. Paperback books were stacked like mud bricks, sharing space with ranked cans of Barbasol shaving cream, a plastic box full of hex bolts, a radiator coil, a stack of ceramic insulators, and a Nintendo Gameboy so used that the finish had been rubbed off the buttons. I could smell hot plastic and lubricating oil. From somewhere I heard the chuddering of an ancient dot-matrix printer chewing through a roll of paper. And on what had once been a reception counter there was now a 2-kilowatt blue-light laser bolted down into the scarred black marble, a beam splitter, and six coffee mugs of varying designs on the target platforms. On his way in, Mr. Sorenson had picked up a thumb-plunger trigger and pressed it. If it'd been a bomb, we would've all been chewing shrapnel. Instead, the laser pulsed for a flaring instant and steam rose from the cups.

"Kaf," he said. "Terveydeksi," and he took one himself, hooking it from its platform with one thick finger. "Make careful. Is hot."

"He made us coffee," I said to the Captain, then reached out and took a cup.

"I got that," he said.

"Tea, actually," I added, looking down into my mug. "Black tea. Smells nice."

The little man with the scanner eyes lingered around one of the barber's chairs, watching us and fiddling with the fit of the tin pot on his head, which made little dings and whining noises every time he got some bit of it to work. Mr. Machinegun had scurried off into another room.

Mr. Sorenson sipped his tea and looked from the Captain to me to Jemma. "Stoy loop here, div div minutin, and upload some kaf. Progs cycling inna boardroom."

Gobbledygook. Mostly anyhow. It was like watching a dog talk. Or like a refrigerator, in whatever tongue of whirrs and rattles a refrigerator would've spoke. But I looked at him and nodded. I could feel the Captain's eyes on me, expectant. I sipped at my tea and it tasted like burning, but also of peaches and orange and something tropical. I nodded again, made lip-smacking noises, and looked up at Mr. Sorenson.

"Good," I said. Then, like an idiot, added, "Mmm..." I stopped short of rubbing my belly, but only just.

Mr. Sorenson smiled. "Pullin' null sectors, butcha? Lookin' void, you."

When muddling through an unfamiliar language, context is key. If you're standing in a kitchen with someone who burns their hand and they start popping off in Italian or Tagalog or Barksy, you can guess that they're not talking about the weather. The kink of an eyebrow, the twist of a grin—all of these are clues. Instinct counts for a lot. Lucky guesses. When all else fails, you can just repeat the last thing that anyone says back to them as a question. It's not conversating, precisely, but it makes you look smarter than you are.

I turned to the Captain and said, "Mr. Sorenson is implying that I don't understand a word he's saying. And he's not being polite about it either. Got a pine-top tone that I don't much appreciate."

What was important here? Was it that I convince the Captain, who didn't speak Techny at all, that I did? Or was it to convince Sorenson, the native speaker, that I spoke a little? Both were crucial. The trick was to disappoint neither party. And to walk out of the Green Willow clave un-holed, with all my blood still inside me where it belonged. Tomorrow, I figured, I could start kicking around for some new employment more fit for my unique skill set. Whiskey taster, maybe. I could also cook a mean frittata.

But just then, I was where I was, and I turned back to the chief engineer, sipped again at my tea and said, "Lookin' void? No. Receiving clear, chief. No nulls. Ya punyimayo sinut taydellisesti. Sta trans gigo."

I looked him straight in the eyes, slid my free hand into one pocket and rocked a little on my heels, trying to look as cool as a cat. Like I had everything here under control. Didn't matter that my smile was plaster, just a pinch from cracking. None but yours true could feel the prickles of sweat starting behind my ears or the flutters my heart was making. None of the company knew that I understood maybe a short third of what Mr. Sorenson was saying (probably not the most useful third either) and none needed know that what I'd said back to him was just jabber, lampshaded with a little Russian and a lot of bullshit. "Ya punyimayo sinut taydellisesti." *I understand you sure as shootin'.* "Sta trans gigo." *Stop talking shit.* Techny, I knew, was a highly pliable language. The kind of thing that might change clave to clave, camp to camp. Who was to say I'd learnt Sorenson's version of it?

"Thewlip?" he asked.

"Sig and serve," said me. "Chester Thewlip. Secretary to the King."

"Sorenson," said Sorenson, slapping his own bare chest. And then he launched into a long bit of prattle with Goggle Face in the corner before turning back to me and bobbing his head.

I felt the Captain's hand on my arm. "Ask him why he's bald," he said to me, leaning over and hissing loudly into my ear, plainly loud enough for Sorenson to hear.

"What?"

"Ask him if it's cancer or if he just wanted to look like a testicle with that beard and everything."

I watched Sorenson, waiting for him to raise snakes. The Captain watched Sorenson. Jemma pretended to be interested in a broken stamping press in one corner with a plastic Hulk figurine stuck between the plates. She turned away so neither Sorenson nor Goggle Face could see her pop the snaps on her holster with her thumb.

But Sorenson's expression never changed. He didn't understand enough proper English to follow a nonsequitur, which was what the Captain was testing. Likely, he spoke about as much of the King's as I did Techny.

As I said, context is everything.

I took a breath. "Pomo liksa kaf," I said. "Zot, leet kaf." *Bossman says he likes your tea. Nice and hot.*

"Drink you tea," he said. "We standing."

"We standing," the Captain said, his own smile blooming and reaching so far back it looked like he was trying to bite his own ears. "That is absolutely what we are doing."

And that was the end of the talking. A minute or two later, Goggle Face cleared his throat, nodded, and Sorenson pushed open a door in the back of the room, gesturing for us to follow.

There were rooms and there were rooms. The Green Willow engineers had knocked out walls, reinforced ceilings, likely dug out a complex tunnel system below Cherry Creek where they bred and kept all their unicorns and atomic super-monsters, too. They'd colonized the entire strip mall complex in which the spa had once lived, punching through the cinderblock and shimming arches with extruded plascrete blocks, sealing some of them with pressure doors that appeared scavenged from a submarine.

Most of the places we passed through had all the slazy and slap-bang charm of steerage class aboard a rust trawler and were ripe with the stink of genius and close-packed nerdity—like sweat and ozone and glue and wet beards. Others, though, were passing fine in ways I couldn't reckon. There was, for example, a whole run of clean rooms that we passed, glaring white in the otherwise dim skeez. What appeared to be a bedroom decked out in silks and furs and carefully hung art prints of Paris by night, before the dome, and water lilies in a pond without tentacles in it. A workspace where a dozen scrawny, lank-haired mechanos in face shields and softwired waldo rigs worked over a piece of something hung from six chain-lifts like a side of giant metal meat.

As the Captain had explained, the Green Willow clave were war engineers and refugees. What they really were, were scavengers— parasites on a weird-wracked world, which is as noble a profession as any other. More so than some. And likely quite profitable besides.

It took me a minute to sabby what the mechanos in the workroom had been cutting on, but then it came to me. It was a hand. A really, really big metal hand.

Sorenson led us to the boardroom, which had been done up fine despite having once been a 7-11 or something similar, with mismatched chairs and a cacophony of lamps and a plank table set with a Lord's feast of black bread, pickles, rabbit, rat and ruckus juice still warm from the still. You could see on the walls where ragged flags and banners of the Western Confederacy had been hurriedly hung. And if you chose to see close, you could notice how they'd been hung right over the colors and pennants of the Kansan secessionists. For convenience's sake, I thought. Far as they knew, we were an honest deputation from King Steve. But if the Captain was to be believed, we were maybe not the only visitors they were expecting that day.

Speaking of himself, the Captain hesitated not a minute in making new friends. As soon as we were inside, he strode up and began pressing the flesh. There were four other big chiefs waiting on us, holding down one side of the table, which made five all told, plus Goggle Face, who'd followed us in, scampering along behind, and Mr. Machinegun, who stood alertly in the far corner, trying (and failing) to look harder than the gun cradled in his arms.

Jemma leaned in close. "He's checking out the English on the rest of the company," she said. "Go act like a translator."

Which I did, putting on the airs I thought appropriate to a King's secretary, and making my respects to the President of Rats, the Prince of Thieves, the Lord of the Dance, or whatever-all the puffers wanted to call themselves. They were young men in greasy jumpsuits or polo shirts and khakis or, in one case, a tailcoat and top hat over a faded tee shirt with a logo on it for Network 23. They were poorly shaved and worse washed and as pale as donut sugar, all.

To each of them, the Captain was *Pomo*—the boss—and the boss said this and the boss said that, all very friendly-like when coming out of my mouth while, in actuality, the boss was insulting them fantastically and reciting the lines of a dirty limerick about a young whore from Kilkenny and how much she charged for her best services. None of the big hats seemed to notice, though, honest, they might've been playing the same game in reverse and I might not have known it either. All that mattered in the moment was not letting either side know just how much at sea I really was.

After introductions was lunch, handled with a strange, almost adorable formality. Dishes were passed right-way-round. The plates and silver were all mismatched, but laid out in a rigid, Frenchified style. The black bread and pickles were tasty. The rabbit stew likely would've tickled a Geiger counter, but I shoveled it down, as did Jemma, who attacked all with an appetite that made our hosts smile and jabber away and me invent translations out of thinnest atmosphere. The Captain didn't touch the white dog, but Jemma allowed the man in the top hat to pour her a splash into a champagne flute and I myself had a couple of anti-fogmatics as well. Just to be polite, mind. And because my brain works that much better when properly lubricated.

"Eventually we're going to get 'round to talking," the Captain said to me. "You'd best be bright-eyed when we do."

And "Ah," said me. "I'm bright-eyed when jury-sober. But a couple drinks will just make me the more charming."

The Captain grinned. "Ask them if they're ready to negotiate now."

I did, but they weren't. Goggle Face (who was not allowed at table, it appeared, so stood twitchily in the rear) leaned down and said something to Top Hat, who giggled in a way I found peculiarly disconcerting, then turned and said something else to Sorenson.

"Stoy set here aseellisten," Sorenson said. "Heavy load and set, na? For lunch? Now me, Pee Oh Aitch, true. Skolot juzver wit you bangs and what." He slapped open palms on his bare chest. "We polite. Drink you. You adstoj."

The Captain looked at me.

"I'm pretty sure he just called us assholes," I said. "Possibly because we all brought guns to lunch."

"So did you," the Captain said to them, nodding his head in the direction of Mr. Machinegun, who seemed to take the gesture as an assault on his person and waggled the barrel of his chopper nervously in our direction.

"Bounce," translated me. "Rept usey." Which was the Techny equivalent of *I know you are but what am I.*

Because that was where we were just then. Calling names and talking smack over our bread and rat and bowls of glow-bunny stew. Everyone was still smiling, though. Least for the moment.

After lunch was more tea.

After tea was vodka, from an actual bottle of Stolichnaya walked the long way round the table by Goggle Face. The Captain now deigned drink with the savages, for politeness' sake, and so made the first toast and took the last swallow.

After vodka, Top Hat took the floor. He made noises which, I guessed, were more or less welcoming, and I said so to the Captain and Jemma.

"He's telling us he's happy we're here," I said. "Complementing us on our grace and carriage and fine appetites and whatever."

"You sure?" asked the Captain.

"More or less," said me.

One of the other Green Willow bosses talked next. Seemed to be a history lesson of some sort. Not a lot of jokes in it at any rate, and I allowed him to speechify while inventing translations from the whole cloth, embroidering freely and fastly until the man had finished airing out.

After that, it was Sorenson who spoke. And he, I was pretty sure, was just making sport of us. There were mean smiles blooming on the other side of the table. A few rough chuckles. Where, previously,

I'd been catching about one phrase in three, I was now faring worse as, I figured, the engineers were basically jawing for each other's benefit. Making jokes in deep jargon that only they understood. Pushing what they saw as their advantage.

"You need to say something now," I said to the Captain. "The conversation is getting away from us here."

Laughter burst from the other side of the table, and I continued. "He's playing to the gallery. And I can't really—"

"Tell them I want to see the gadget now," he said. "Ask politely."

"What gadget is that, exactly?" I asked. Because, to this point, no one had thought to enlighten me as to the exact nature of our dealings.

The Captain turned to me. "They have a machine brain here," he said. "Took it out of the head of the Type IX that didn't blow itself up. The one that fell into the building where I showed you. Baldy and his friends here have been picking that corpse clean since before the last angry shot was fired. Booby-trapped the whole area. Digging it out a bit at a time. No one can get near it, but we are not leaving here without that brain." He sniffed and, under the lip of the table, I saw him pop the suicide loop off the hammer of the Colby. "You should say something like that to them. Make it sing."

A machine brain, for them among you not technically or historically inclined, was what we had before cloud minds and evolved intelligences. In my time, they were the thinky-piece of any complex platform—of which a hundred-foot-tall war robot is an excellent example, but not the *only* example. A machine brain, properly motivated, might run an automated factory, say. A skyscraper. A whole ensmartened neighborhood. It might be convinced to crack codes or genomes or conn a shipping line or run a distributed network in the absence of any meat bosses wanting to make meat decisions. They were purely artificial intelligences, a bajillion-bajillion logic gates, heuristic algorithms, and chained processes, organized into Bayesian networks and cells of modal logic, all governed by a limited form of hierarchical temporary memory.

Simpler? They were like a fat bundle of emotionless, single-minded, and wholly dedicated boff Einsteins all rendered down into a soupy goop of electrificated liquid smartness, held in a case about the size of a gentleman's valise which, when asked nicely (and *properly*, by someone who maybe spoke its language) could do just about any damn thing under the sun, moon and stars. Didn't always do it well and didn't always do it fastly, but they were precious close to miraculous nonetheless. The first of the true thinking systems.

On the Big List Of Valuable Things, a machine brain would rank in worth somewhere above silver, above gold, above a cherry Cadillac with new black gumballs, or a long whiskey at the end of a terrible day, but below, perhaps, the lasting forgiveness for one's trespasses or a virgin's love and trust. In the day, machine brains were what a king's worth could be measured in—and often were. They weren't rare, exactly. The Western Confederacy had about a hundred of them, as far as I knew (and I do know far). Or rather a hundred less the six that Kansas had taken and stuck into the big metal heads of its war robots when it seceded. Three had been recovered from dead 'bots at the Castle. One had been fried at the mall. One had escaped back to Kansas in the head of Lord Phillip's last surviving murder machine. And one, apparently, was here, in the care and keeping of the Green Willow engineers.

I thought about the big hand in the workshop, the polished clean rooms. The fact that there was space here at the Green Willow Spa for fifty engineers to live and work but that we'd only seen a dozen. Made a man wonder where the rest of the gang was while the big hats were taking meetings. Defending the claim, no doubt. Keeping the wolves away while they did their butchery.

"Machine brain?" I asked.

The Captain nodded.

"Machine brain." I repeated. "Excellent."

I have seen men killed for the change in their pockets or the chips in their pile. I have known good men gone bad over a girl, a cross word, the turn of a card. In other times and other places, I'd dealt in gold, heroin, guns and powder, gears and contracts and cans of cat food. Some transactions had gone well and some had gone otherwise, mostly owing to the greed that hums in all men but takes some certain few like lightning in the blood. So what would a man do to have one-sixth the worth of a Lord? One-hundredth the power of a King? I squirmed in my seat as though suddenly roused by an inconvenient need to piss a gallon and felt the smooth butt of the heavy pistol the Captain had given me scraping across my belly.

"Talk to the gentlemen," he said. "And stop sweating so much."

And so I talked to the gentlemen. I muddled through asking if they could produce the gadget, and they said of course they could, but preferred not to. Not at so early a juncture in our negotiations. I got this not from any of the squawking or lip-flapping they did, but by Top Hat waving his hands at me like I was a pesky insect and Sorenson giving me the finger.

I asked why they were being so recalcitrant. They looked at me with blank expressions, like my mouth was moving but only bubbles was coming out. I tried again, with a different construction, different words, and one of them (a dark-haired and portly sort who had, thus far, been too busy eating and drinking to speak) hit me with a rip of word-noises that sounded to me like the kind of dirt music you get from thems speaking in tongues at a tent revival.

"Low calls," I said. *Slow down.* "We just want—"

Soreson was looking at the Captain. He gave Goggle Face a come-along gesture and pulled him down close by his shirtfront, speaking without looking away from his Captainness's blues. He said some words, then shoved Goggle Face off, sending him scurrying out a door on their side of the boardroom. He reached for a piece of bread then and tore into it with teeth like searchlights.

This, apparently, displeased some of the other members of the clave. Not the bread thing, but Sorenson sending his man skipping off to fetch up the brain for us to ogle on and drool over. Fat Boy loudly said something about Sorenson's penchant for selling his tenderest hole to anyone with a nickel to drop, and Sorenson looked away long enough to throw a spoon at him. Top Hat shrilly snapped an order at Mr. Machinegun—"Mene fetchim! Stat return!"—and Mr. Machinegun didn't budge from his place in the corner. Hands were thrown up in outrage.

"It occurs to me that your friends might not be of one mind when it comes to making a deal here," I said.

Jemma casually lifted her chin. "Check the guy in the corner," she said, meaning Mr. Machinegun, who had settled the wire-frame in his shoulder and half-raised his namesake—but was not showing us the business end, so to speak. He seemed more concerned with his own people. With the tumult on the Techny side of the table, which now involved a lot of slapping and drink-spilling. And then I had a thought.

"One of these men is yours, isn't he?" I asked the Captain, whispering to him, though I could've shouted and none of the other side would've heard.

The Captain just kept smiling. "You shut your mouth on that now, boy, and you keep playing it the way I tell you. Tell them that the King has personally authorized me to make them a payment right now. Two million in gold, drawn on the name of the King. Wind 'em up a little more."

I did this. I had to shout. And say it twice. Then make the thumb-brushing-fingertips sign that means the same thing in every language on earth. Fat Boy shook his head and folded his pasty arms across the soft rise of his belly. Sorenson was out of his chair, trying to bring some semblance of calm and order to the proceedings, which he did by grabbing people by the backs of their necks and shaking them. Top Hat slapped an open palm on the table and yelled for anyone to go and bring back "Sorensonsai pelortka golova." *Sorenson's little cunt-head.* A charmer, him.

The Captain tugged me close. "You made a mistake," he said. "Tell them you made a mistake and that King Steven has personally authorized me to make a payment to Roger Whitaker."

"To who?"

"Whitaker," he said loudly. "Ro-ger Whit-a-ker. Say it now."

I almost didn't have the chance. As soon as the other side heard the Captain say that name, they all turned on Top Hat, who looked momentarily stunned.

"Whitaker?" I asked across the table. "That you? True vernor Roger Whitaker?"

There was a quiet. A dead breath of silence.

"King Steven...uh...Init pos asset for you, Roger Whitaker. Um..." I made the sign again, thumb and fingers. "Two million," I said. "For the brain."

"Fucking brilliant," I heard the Captain say from beside me.

Sorenson turned to Top Hat. "Rog?" he said. "Read true?"

"No!" Top Hat said, his voice high and boyish with sudden panic.

Sorenson's hands hung by his side, opening and closing. His face squirmed with confusion. Slowly he inclined his head in our direction and asked, "How them know you name?"

"Nils. Readme, butcha. Ese False. *False*-false. Ya ponyatiya ne imeyu, o chem on govorit o."

That last bit was in straight Ruska. I got every word. *I have no idea what he's talking about.*

At which point everything happened very fast.

Sorenson was big. Not broad, but tall and with a ropy, furious strength. And he was *quick*.

He shoved his way clear of his side of the table, knocked Fat Boy right to the ground, and half-scrambled over the short end of the table, his eyes on me.

Jemma and the Captain were already up out of their chairs, hands held out, shouting. But Sorenson never slowed.

He clubbed Jemma down, his forearm like a bat, and bulled straight past the Captain, shoving him sideways into the table, which rattled with the impact.

I was halfway up out of my seat, the chair skittering away behind me and my feet trying hard to follow it before my knees had gotten the message. Sorenson helped me the rest of the way up in the quickest possible way—by gathering up a fistful of my shirt and jacket and lifting me with one hand.

I felt, but did not see, his other hand as it shot down in the direction of my manly tackle. I turned my hip into him out of reflex, but he already had what he was after: my pistol. The one the Captain had given me.

"Say you liar!" he bellowed. His spit flew into my face and he shook me like a kitten. Behind him, Jemma and the Captain were dragging out their iron and to my eye, it seemed like they were pulling molasses.

I saw the big revolver come up. I felt Sorenson drop me onto my stiff legs and then one arm was snaking around my neck. I was bent double, stuck in a headlock. Sorenson banged my forehead on the table, making the plates and glasses dance and the stars come out in my eyes. He ground my nose uncomfortably into the planks, and when something poked me in the back of the neck, I knew it was the gun. My gun.

"How you know him's name?" Sorenson howled. "Say you lying liar!"

I started to speak. I started to say that I was *absolutely* a lying liar and sorely regretful that I'd caused any ruckus among such a fine and level-headed company as was gathered there. That I'd never seen Roger Whitaker before, nor spoken the name. That I knew nothing of machine brains or money from the King and had, until very recently, been a consultant in the laying of roads and not even very good at that. I started to say all of that—all the words at once bubbling up on my tongue like a seltzer—but the gunshots stopped me dry. There were three of them, quick and rattling, loud like the end of the world in such a closed room, and they gave premature and final punctuation to my confession. For a second, I thought for sure that I was dead.

Nothing flashed before my eyes.

There were no joys or regrets. No white and glorious light. No one waiting for me, smiling on the other side.

But on the upside, I did not piss myself either.

Jemma yelled, "Don't move! Don't move!"

"Everyone *stop*!" I heard the Captain bark.

Then Jemma again. "Who do I shoot first, Cap?"

"Rog?" I heard Sorenson ask.

When I felt the arm around my neck loosen and fall away, I turned my head—the gun barrel still scraping along through my hair—until I could see a little of what had happened.

I could see Mr. Machinegun on the other side of the room, standing with his rifle raised above his head in both hands. I could see Top Hat near him, though he was no longer wearing his topper. He was sitting, hands in his lap. Three neat holes in the front of him and a good portion of his insides blown out the back of him in ragged streamers now decorating the wall and smeared all the way down. He died while I watched. There was no sound. One of his feet kicked up a little on the floor and then he just drifted away.

Seeing a little was enough.

"Killswitch," Mr. Machinegun said. He looked around the room. I felt the gun barrel leave the back of my head like a threat departing and Sorenson jig a half step back, tottering on his pegs.

"Killswitch," he said again. Fat Boy's hands were fluttering around his greasy mouth like a couple of pale birds. The smell in the room was of gunsmoke and shit and fresh meat and rabbit stew.

"Autoguns inna roof. Killya holding." He jerked his chin toward our side of the table, his rifle still held high. "Nils, ya holding."

I heard my pistol hit the table. *Saw* it hit the table, beside my head. I pushed slowly upright and saw Jemma with a gun in both hands, sweeping it slowly back and forth across the other side of the table. The Captain had a pistol in each. The heavy Colby and a .45 automatic. His arms spread in a V like he was waiting to hug someone.

The Green Willow bosses apparently had a security system built into their boardroom: computer-controlled drop-guns in the ceiling on a killswitch. Hit the button and out they come, ready to make haze out of anyone touching iron on the wrong side of the table. That was why we'd been allowed to carry our heaters into the boardroom in the first place. The Green Willow bosses figured that their machines could skin their guns faster than us on the quick-draw.

Top Hat had made a reach for the button when things went all agee, meaning to air out me and mine. Only Sorenson had been on the wrong side of things, too. And holding my gun besides. So Sorenson's gunsel, Mr. Machinegun, had ended him. Saved the chief of the Green Willow clave at the expense of one of its bosses.

"And now," said the Captain, "everyone is going to stay well away from that button, got it?"

Blank looks all around.

He sighed. "Chester, if you please?"

I shook myself. Looked around. Top Hat was staring glassy-eyed off into the great beyond. Fat Boy was chewing the tips off his own fingers. Sorenson was standing slackish like he'd been cashiered himself but hadn't yet come 'round enough to fall. "Stay the fuck away from the button!" I shouted, then picked up my pistol and pressed it back into Sorenson's hand. I had to curl his fingers around it myself. He only had eyes for the meat ripening in the corner. "Tell 'em."

"Stay fuck away from button," Sorenson said quietly.

"Sit," I barked.

Sorenson sat.

I wheeled on the Captain. "Can we go home now?" I asked, still shouting.

"Not quite yet. We still have some business to transact."

Which was when Goggle Face came back in, empty-handed. He looked around, saw Top Hat and three pistols pointed in his direction.

"Mosk zero inven," he said. "Brain gone."

There was more shouting, but it was half-hearted and passed quickly with everyone's eyes darting briefly over the mortal remains of Top Hat. The resigned, silent consensus seemed to be that the dead man had somehow played them all false. Had absconded with their treasure somehow, tried to sell it off himself, and left them dry. Top Hat himself was in no condition to protest his innocence, which, later, struck me as passing convenient.

Standing there, the Captain kicked me in the ankle and told me to look confused, which was the easiest order I'd had to follow in a day where just fetching morning coffees had nearly gotten me axe'd by a little girl.

"Tell them that there's been some kind of misunderstanding," he said. "A translation problem."

At the sound of his voice, the remaining Green Willow bosses all looked at the Captain and he shrugged, shoved me. "Tell them that you fucked up, Chester, but you think you can make it right."

I made it clear. Eventually. Mostly to Sorenson, who then translated my translation to his companions. The Captain nodded along. At one point, mugging for the crowd, he said "Idiot," and slapped me in the back of the head, which I appreciated not at all. Snapped at him, I did. Intimated that his mother might've done favors for sailors behind certain establishments of low repute.

"Tell them we already *have* the brain, Chester," he said. "Make it clear. Roger Whitaker delivered it to us last night."

I tried. "Mosk inven...um...us," I said. I patted my own chest. "We have. Roger Whitaker trans mosk...to us...viime yona, da?"

Sorenson shook his head. He ran his thumb along the scarred finish of my pistol's cylinder, tinking at the metal with his thumb. "Da," he said. "Fucking da."

The Captain nodded, as though this was good enough for him. "We're just here to pay Roger his other half, understand? As agreed. King Steven is very generous and very thankful for their cooperation. Tell them."

It took three attempts, but I managed it. Fat Boy perked up. So did the other two Green Willow bosses. Even Goggle Face pushed forward a little. Mr. Machinegun had laid aside his rifle like a hungry snake whose loyalty was seriously in question and was sitting in a chair with his face in his hands.

"Everyone get ready to leave," the Captain said to Jemma and me. "Chester, tell them that we're very sorry things went the way they did. We meant no trouble. We didn't know Mr. Whitaker was trying to cut his own deal, but are glad we were able to conclude our business successfully."

I said something. Might've been the right thing. Might not have. Beside me, the Captain dropped his Colby into its holster and reached slowly inside his jacket with his free hand. He came out with a single slip of paper, one edge of it roughly torn. Leaning forward, he laid it in the middle of the table.

"One half of a draft for 2 million dollars, signed by King Steven himself, to be paid in gold, as agreed," the Captain said. "Whitaker got the other half last night."

No one needed me to translate that at all.

We made our own way out of the Green Willow Spa. Past the giant hand, which was the hand of the Kansan war robot that'd died beneath an avalanche of cement, steel, insurance papers and toys for orphans. Past the quiet, white clean rooms. Past the sleeping places and eating places and workshops of the Green Willow clave with their old, unwashed smell.

In the lobby, the monitors over the barbering chairs flickered with visions of the outside world. I wondered how much effort it would take for them to activate their defenses. To burn us, explode us, spike us, or immobilize us as we hightailed it out of there. The Captain held out an arm and said for us to hold up, then gestured with one hand to Jemma, who filled it with the other phone she'd taken from the Castle offices. He punched numbers, held it to his head.

"Logue? We good?"

A muffled grumble in response.

"Good. Hit the door. We're coming out." And then to me: "Might want to cover your balls, Mr. Thewlip."

He turned his back to the door and cupped both hands over his own package. I hurriedly did the same, not knowing why until I felt the static sizzling on my skin and tasted tinfoil in the back of my throat. The monitors over the chairs all fizzled out to snow, then dead-glass darkness.

Jemma pushed open the door. We stepped out into the dazzling sun, bootheels crackling on a billion-billion dead nanites mounded up like black ash in a line on the ground and Logue standing in Marlene's bed, behind the trigger of what I'd thought was an alien grenade launcher but was actually an EMP cannon. The Captain dropped the phone as he walked and smashed it with the heel of his boot. I fished in my jacket and did the same with Chester Thewlip's. They were perished, the phones. Pretty as they were, they'd done their service and no one mourned.

Jemma made for the driver's seat at a half-trot. The Captain and Logue for the cab. It was the hard ride for me again, but not wanting another jab in the belly, I tossed my loaned pistol (which I'd recovered from Mr. Sorenson's hand on our way out of the boardroom) into the bed of the truck before attempting to climb in and heard it spang off something. I looked in and saw a case about the size of a man's valise laying there, all gray impact-resistant plastic and slashing red stripes.

"Get in," the Captain snapped through the open window. "It ain't gonna bite you."

Twenty minutes later, we were back in Cheesman Park, stopped in a bower over which grew the linking canopies of a copse of Norway maples. The Captain had the pistol he'd loaned me in hand and was pointing it at my face.

"See?" he asked.

"Convincing, yes," I said. "Can you put it away now? Once a day is generally my limit for having guns pointed at me. Any more than that and it makes me feel greedy."

He gave the gun a twirl, stopped it barrel-down, and snapped out the cylinder—extracting a single round and under-handing it to me. I caught it and touched the tip of the slug. It was wax. Gray-black wax, soft enough to groove with my fingernail.

"So then it was Sorenson," I said.

Jemma was standing beside me, watching the cracked path in one direction while Logue lay in the raggedy grass, watching the other.

"What was?" he asked.

"Sorenson was your man inside Green Willow."

He shook his head. "Nope."

"But he knew the gun I would be carrying would be loaded with blanks."

"No. He knew you would be carrying a gun and that he was supposed to grab it and hold it on you, but he didn't know it was loaded with blanks. He also didn't know about Roger. He only knew that someone inside his gang was a mole."

"Someone other than him, you mean."

"Well, yeah."

"So then it had to be Mr. Machinegun."

"The shooter?"

I nodded. The Captain shook his head. "No."

"Give it up," Jemma said, bumping my shoulder with hers in a companionable sort of way. "You're not going to get it."

"Well, how'd you end up with the brain in the truck?" I asked.

"We paid for it. Fair and square. Just like I said we would."

And me, I open my mouth to argue that no, actually, he hadn't. That he'd given a half a promissory note, which was worth exactly as much as anyone might pay for the autograph of King Steven, but no more. Only Logue interrupted by throwing a rock at the Captain.

"Coming," he said.

Logue stood. Another pickup truck (this one once-white and fine, but battered now, with missing hubcaps, scabs of Bondo, and the scars on her of long and noble service) rattled and squonked down the shattered path on springs that shrieked at every bump like tiny birds having something terrible done to them. There was a driver in the cab, wearing sunglasses with arms made out of dinner forks. One passenger. In the bed, four men in gray-green kit, boot gaiters and balaclava neckerchiefs that made them look like angry, overgrown Boy Scouts. Or cavalry officers from the poorest army imaginable. One had dirty, gray rabbit ears, which I thought was a hat until I saw them rooted biologically to the furred side of his head.

The white truck rattled to a banging stop next to Marlene and the Captain approached the passenger side. He waited for the window to come down, which it did only after the man sitting inside pulled at it and jerked it down into place.

"I'd say you should be embarrassed about your ride, but the fact that you're rolling around with a sack full of my money makes me overlook its more obvious flaws." The Captain smiled. "How you been keeping, Charlie?"

"Good, James," said the man inside, in the patrician tones of landed acreocracy. "And you? Your people?"

"Fine. Just fine."

I sidled around, trying to find an angle to see into the truck, but couldn't. Not without looking obvious about it. "This doesn't exactly strike me as a government operation," I said to Jemma. "Nor Royalty, for certain,"

She shushed me.

"But didn't the Captain say—"

I felt a heavy hand come to rest on my shoulder with all the delicacy of a wood vise.

"Help me load," Logue said. And he pushed me in front of him, around to the back of Marlene where we slid the machine brain out across the bed and dropped tailgate, carried it to where the four Boy Scouts were waiting, and handed it over so they could lay it in their own truck. They had a tarp to throw over it. A padded mat on which it could sit. Fine accommodations all around.

I heard the Captain's voice. "...not part of the revolution, friend. I'm just a man who likes helping out his pals."

I watched him reach out a hand. Another hand came out through the window. The cuff of a white jacket out of which protruded coarse tufts of fur. A black glove that seemed stiff and artificial. They shook. "You be careful with that now," the Captain said, smiling and winking one clever eye. "Don't do anything I'd ever have to come after you for."

From the back of the truck, four large nylon duffel bags were dropped to the ground. A smaller, heavier bag was thrown on top of the pile.

The white pickup rolled slowly and loudly off. Logue started transferring bags into Marlene's bed. I looked at the Captain.

"Who was that?" I asked.

He looked at me and laughed. Shook his head.

"Just saying that they didn't look much like O-men to me," I continued. "Because that's what you said, right? That you were with the OSS?"

The Captain had started to walk away, but then seemed to think better of it. He turned smartly on one stacked heel and stalked back over to where I was standing. "If I'd just given the brain back to the proper authorities, where would the fun be in that?" he asked, then threw an arm over my shoulder and turned me away from the truck, forcing me to walk with him, bent so that my ear was near his mouth. "On a scale of 1 to 10 with 1 being a nice day at the beach and 10 being the end of the fucking world, this was a 3. Maybe a 2.5. No one died. No one got blown up or stabbed or poisoned or eaten by monsters or turned radioactive. Everything went precisely according to plan, we walked out with the gadget and came away rich as goddamn lords. And that, boy, is a good day. Enjoy it because not many of them are."

He released me, spun me to face him, slapped me on both shoulders—sprucing me up like I was an old couch.

"Who was your man at Green Willow?" I asked again,

And the Captain tilted his head one way, then the other, looking me over. He straightened my jacket. Smoothed my lapels.

"You have anyone who can give you a ride?" he asked. "Family? Friends? No?"

He knew the answer to that. He'd always known the answer.

"Anyone you can call?"

I said nothing.

"No? Hmm."

He turned, stepped away, turned again, stepped back, and leaned close. "You did...not terribly today," he said, looked me up and down again—his motions jerky like a lizard's. And then his head was next to mine, hands holding me in place, and he was speaking.

"They were *all* mine, Duncan. Every single person in that room was in my pocket. All except Whitaker. And not one of them knows that any of the others are turned. I would've never walked into the room otherwise. Because I don't play games that I don't know I'm going to win." He danced back away from me. He had the big thumbcracker pistol in his belt now and his hands on his hips like the Son of Captain Blood. "Ask me one question and I swear to the Flying Spaghetti Monster I will answer it true."

Thinking back now on all the things I could've asked him—all the things I could've known so much earlier than I'd eventually know them—makes my heart ache for my own youthful dimness and ignorance. My own narrow vision. For the simpler, stupider man I was then who stood so on the cusp of so many great things and couldn't even see the drop before him. I should have, if anything, asked to be paid.

But I didn't. I asked him, "How did the brain get into the truck?"

"Larry brought it. The guy with the weird hat and goggles. Or brought it to Logue, anyway. That was his part in this. And I paid him $50,000 for it. Just like I said I would. Like a goddamn gentleman."

And then he turned away a final time.

And then he was climbing into the cab of the truck.

And then he was gone.

For a minute, I assumed it was a joke. That of *course* he was going to come back for me. That we would all have a laugh and pile in together to some boozer somewhere to celebrate with them bags full of whatever. But that minute passed. Then so did its sister. And then I was only a man standing alone beneath the trees in the green heart of the Queen City.

I turned in the direction of the Castle, put my hands in my pockets, and started walking.

A Brief Intermission for Music,
Some Drinks, and a Chat

It took me better than three hours to wend my way out of the pillaged lands and back to civilization. Would've been a bit quicker save that I stopped for lunch along the way. I've found that nothing speeds a man's appetites quite so fiercely as cheating Death out of his fair reward. Which is why it's a wonder I haven't been found fat, drunk, and dead a'tween the hams of a kindly girl a dozen-dozen times over.

Anyway, burning leather to travel was no novel concept for me, and I did it mostly with my head down and my mind on the doings of the day. Had plenty to cogitate upon, me. Not the least of which being how I now found myself once more disemployed and possessed entirely of the clothes on my back, the shoes on my feet, the gun under my arm, and the contents of my case, which I'd hooked out of Marlene's bed before the Captain set to educating me on the nature of the pistol which had so recently been pressed to my head.

As has so often been the case in my wanderings, at a certain point I ended up more or less back where I'd started. I walked the greenways that fronted the Castle, took a moment to look for the shark-mouth coffee girl Katarina in hopes of perhaps talking with her a bit more, but she was gone, so I skirted the sweeping arms of the old City and County building (which was now the offices of the Royalty council, land assayers, honorable lawmakers who didn't rate Castle real estate, and the local acreocracy), and slipped through the crumbling stone of the Greek amphitheatre in the park, thinking it likely that that was where I was going to be sleeping that night, the next, and on all nights following since one of the best advantages of my position at the Castle had been the bed and board it'd come with, which was now just another thing lost to one rash decision barely six hours old.

Unfortunately, even sleeping in the amphitheatre was purest skylarking. Whole families had staked out turf there, erecting fortifications and hardscrabble defenses, always leaving at least one uncle or cousin or nephew behind to secure the homeplace against invaders while the rest was out making a living in whatever way they could. Where there wasn't families there were gangs, and where there weren't gangs there were the hard sorts who could hold out singly against both gangs and families either through toughness or plain insanity. The whole amphitheatre smelled of piss and worse. I spent most of my time there with my hands up in a placating gesture, apologizing and tap-dancing amid the bedrolls and palisades of them that had so suddenly become my kind. The best I could hope for, I thought, was to marry myself into one of these gyppo clans as fast as possible. That afternoon, if I could manage to make a lass fall for me so quick. Failing that, I could simply sleep out in the grass where the wolves and monsters would find me, at best, a sour and troublesome, snack.

Depressed by the possibilities laid out before me, I decided that the best course of action was to have a drink.

"Give me a fucking long whiskey, Hippo," I says to the barman, Hippolite Smith, as soon as I come through the door of the Nob Hill Inn. Hippo stood in the well of the horseshoe bar concentrating hard and trying to light a wooden match with his mind. He'd been trying for two years. Had bought some magic beans or snakeoil infusion from a wandering bird-man who'd promised him the power of pyromancy if only he worked at it hard enough, and then had sold dear Hippo a phial of god-knew-what and told him to drink it and then start small—with matches—and see what happened.

What happened was Hippo bought himself a box of Lucifer matches and the bird-man absquatulated with Hippo's pesos, likely back to the Nations and laughing all the way. Now it was two years later and I could personally attest to the amount of work Hippo had put into his dream of being able to light a lady's cigarette from across the bar without his hands. As yet, he'd seen no results.

I liked drinking at the Nob because it'd been there since before the world went wrong. It had history the way old men and some furniture did, the passage of years scraped and sketched into every surface as though each going year had kicked hard in passing and drug a heavy chain behind. Bob Dylan had laid a drunk on one night at the Nob, pining for something that was never made clear. It'd been there when Neal Cassady painted the city red and when Tom Waits had played for warm beers with no egg in 'em.

In its time, the Nob had been a refuge for lawmakers and law-breakers, bag-eyed journos lamenting the oft-reported dying of the Word, working girls needing a warm place to sort their regrets, hustlers on the down-slide, lawyers, mayors, cops, robbers, and always, *always* the neighbors who were known by name and seat and poison at the Nob and remembered, here in the nicotine-stained halls of the tramp's Valhalla, both longer and better than they ever were outside it once they'd gone.

I liked the Nob because it was *dim*, not dark—which is a vital difference. Because they stocked my favorite brand of bourbon whiskey: cheap. Because to drink and cheat here at cards or dice or a hundred small bar games was to do so in a place where I was liked well enough to be given a three-step lead when it inevitably came time to throw me out. And because every now and again, on the tiny stage at the back of the big-small room, Banjo Oblangata would get up, plug into a nickel combo amp hung on his belt, lean into a birdcage mike hooked to the house's ancient PA, and play something that would make me want to pull my own heart out from the beauty of it all.

Hippo asked to see my money first, which, nothing against him, was wise. I had a tab at the Nob that, while not epic by any stretch, was still notable in its ups and downs. Unwilling to part with what little folding money I had about my person, he and I quibbled for a bit and finally came down on a suitable solution which, once more, had me thumbing out Castle-made bullets in exchange for refreshment. Two bought me the house's mercy, a third its grace, and I settled in behind a polished glass decorated by a generous two inches of Devil Eyes, its fumes strong enough to peel paint.

I nursed at it slow and did not go blind, which I took as a sign of my luck turning. The Nob was quiet. In the back, a few hardy souls had already started working the card tables, and the games still sounded civil. Two old men held down the horseshoe bar's distant flank, pulling at heavy steins of homebrew with sediment thick enough to hide gold nuggets. A lady of sorts held the point. Her name was Abigail and she'd once been a beauty, but long ago. She wore a balding fur wrap around her shoulders and her lipstick was the color of a fire engine, though it appeared she'd applied it with a trowel. For the price of sitting a bit closer and holding her hand while she told me of better days, she bought my second drink for me and called me a beautiful boy. A fair trade all around.

Hippo fiddled with the marconi and, in time, coaxed it into operation. Knowing my tastes (and the lack thereof of all my assembled companions), he jammed in a bootleg DAT of Banjo playing with his band, the Critical Malfunctions, and spun up the volume to a sweet and room-filling level.

The tape opened with Banjo's cover of "Shadow of a Doubt" by Tom Petty, slowed down to about half-time, and I remembered the night it'd been done live—about a week before I'd fled the city, when every moment had seemed fat with premonitions and prophecy. Cigarette smoke thick as antigravity milk had wreathed the ceiling at the Nob and swirled down the dark, paneled walls.

Hippo was pouring two-for-ones in anticipation of the bar's stock being nationalized at any moment. Laughter punctuated with sobs rattled around the room as the Malfunctions ripped through one song after another—Banjo blistering the paint and making the bottles in the well jangle and jump. They'd done "Machine Gun Blues." They'd pounded out "Let's Have a War" by Fear, then slammed straight into "I Love Living in the City." In the ringing silence that followed the last crash of the symbols and Banjo's guitar, East Coast Dave, the Malfunctions' keyboard player, had hit and held a chord that'd made Banjo smile. He'd slung his guitar, pulled the mike to him, and, together, the two of them had slow-walked through Petty's tune about a girl and a boy and the distance between them.

Just a shadow of a doubt, she says it keeps me runnin'.
I'm trying to figure out if she's leadin' up to something.

It'd cooled the room. Right up until Banjo unslung his six-string for a solo that could've killed you to hear it. On that night, anyway. In that place. I'd known Banjo from back in the days when he used to strum a scratch-built bouzouki out by the monorail stairs and sing songs about salvation and whiskey drinking for beer chits and shards of glass. He was a talented kid, but only found his true calling when he first strapped on a Gibson hollowbody classic, and he was never better, never sweeter, never sadder than on that night before the war arrived.

Wasn't bad on tape, either. I patted Abigail's hand and kissed her cheek, begging her pardon as I excused myself.

"There are some gentlemen in the back wanting an education in odds and probability," I said to her. "And I feel like you've brought me some luck by your company, darling. Be a shame to waste it."

The next song that night had been an original called "Bar the Doors." A dancing song, and I had. But on this afternoon, I just begged a courtesy top-up from Hippo, who was flipping silver eagles now with the old men, and eased my way into the back room where I planted myself at my customary table, laid a dollar in scrip down on the scarred plank, and asked a deal.

"Tell me we're on a nickel bet, please," I said, my eyes on my whiskey as I tipped the glass to my lips. "I am just a poor country boy and I don't rightly understand these big city games."

The voice that answered me was damnably familiar. "Then maybe you shouldn't play at all, Duncan. Wouldn't want you to find yourself in a bad spot after the day you've had."

It was the Captain. He had his chin down, a derby bowler cocked low, and a musty serape piled around his shoulders, giving him the look and slump of any one of a thousand bad luck refugees just in out of the sun. But he looked up when he spoke, and pushed up the brim of his hat with one thumb.

"Don't do anything foolish now," he said, his voice low. "Just sit. Drink your drink. And we'll have a full table before very long."

So I sat. I drank as ordered. I knew three ways out of the Nob, but all of them would involve running. And truth be told, I was more than a bit happy to see him again. Since I hadn't the quick tongue and presence of mind to ask about a day's generous pay for a day's dishonest work before he'd up and left me raw in the middle of a refugee camp, I felt that this might be my best chance at touching fingers to a bit of that payday he'd seen.

"Could've given me a ride," I muttered. "Since you was coming here and all."

"Shh . . ." said the Captain, one finger held to his lips.

"I mean, it wasn't a pleasant stroll, really. Footsore, you might say. And long besides. So when it comes time for you to figure on my cut for this afternoon's caper, maybe you take that into account."

"Shh," the Captain said again, shorter and sharper this time.

"And have you been here the whole time? Didn't notice you walk in, is all, and I fancy myself an observant man."

The Captain looked quizzically at his shushing finger. "Why is this thing not working?" he said, then looked back at me and gave me a third. "Shh."

The door to the Nob's back alley lot opened and Logue filled it all up. When he came in, the floorboards creaked under his weight. He sat down beside the Captain and I wondered at the fortitude of the chair.

"This is what I mean," said me. "Noticed your ox, didn't I? Right off, too. Said to myself, 'Well, if it isn't the Captain's pet mountain come to visit.'"

The Captain turned to Logue. "I've said 'Shh' to him three times but he's still talking. I think my finger might be broken."

"Want me to try?" Logue asked.

"No. When you shush people they tend to stay that way forever. And we have some words we need to say to our friend here. Oh, look. Here comes beauty."

I turned and saw Jemma Watts float across the front room, the door sighing closed behind her. She'd changed, too—into a white dress and sensible shoes, her hair pulled back into a tight braid that swished like a tail. She couldn't have drawn more eyes if she were afire, and the Captain stood when she approached, pushing a chair out for her with his boot.

"Lovely," he said.

"Your dime," she replied.

"Worth two of them, at least," he said. "So did you get it done?"

"Yup," she said. "It'll take two days or so, but we're begun." She handed over to the Captain a folder full of papers that I hadn't even seen her carrying. But in my defense, pretty as her fingers might've been, no one else would've either. "This is just the top-level stuff. Everything that was available at hand."

I had no idea what they were on about and didn't rightly care. Standing close, Jemma smelled of vanilla and hot leather. She settled into her chair, scraped it up to the table, and favored me with a smile that was full and completely without guile. "Pleased to meet you, Duncan," she said. "You were quite the surprise."

"Not to me," said the Captain. He was scanning through the papers in front of him, separating and collating them on the table. "Knew this one the minute I spied him."

I made my manners to the lady, then turned back to the Captain. "Thought I was just the right man in the right place when you needed one," I said.

Papers went here and there. "That's assuming that this morning was the first time I ever seen you," said the Captain.

"Wasn't it?"

He shook his head. There was suddenly a nervous lump in my throat. I splashed it with whiskey and hoped it drowned. "And you thought you knew me sometime previous?" I asked. There was a rasp in my voice and it wasn't all from the Devil Eyes.

"Did and do, Duncan Archer. Or should I call you—"

"Oh, no need for that now," I said, far too loudly, interrupting and tapping my glass on the table. "Duncan will suit just fine. I mean, what's a name or two between friends?"

The Captain had a glass by his hand, but it was dry. He moved smoothly among the papers. There was a deck of greasy cards on the table. I knew every mark and dog-ear and crease in them like I knew the lines on my own hands. I knew the table and the rattle of the rickety chairs. I knew most of the few people huddled around the tables, too, though when I raised up my head and looked around, all I saw was their backs. Them as weren't slowly fleeing in a shambling stream for the front room or the jakes were sitting frozen and hunched over—something about the aura of our table filling the place with the kind of bad juju that a good card player can feel in his bones. Mine, for example, felt about to turn to liquid. All of them at once.

The Captain looked up at me. "You know what this is?" He tapped a finger on the papers now spread before him. There were three stacks. A thickish one in the middle, flanked by two that were much, much thinner.

"Love letters?" I said to him.

"Hmm. Of a sort."

"Pretty man like you. Sure you collect your share."

The Captain laughed. He looked at Logue and then at Jemma and then back at me. "Pretty man!" he sniffed. "That's good, Duncan!"

I nodded at his appreciation. Beneath the lip of the table, my hands were fists. My legs were bunched for running. All I needed was a distraction. A three-step head start.

But then the Captain's face hardened. "I know what you're thinking right now. Don't do it."

"Why?"

The Captain said nothing. After a few long seconds, Jemma answered. "Because you'd never make it out of the chair," she said. "Because Logue'd bring you back anyway, but not nicely. And because the Captain has some things to say that you want to hear."

And then it was my turn to say nothing—a state which came neither natural nor pleasantly to me. To make the back door, I'd have to get past the three of them. The front would involve getting out of my chair and turned around. There was a side door most people didn't know about. Had to go past the office, storeroom, out a fire door. It let out into an alley—narrow but open at both ends.

"He's counting exits," said the Captain. "Look at him."

"This is your official file, Duncan." Jemma laid a hand flat on the tallest stack of paper set before the Captain.

"Supposed to be private," I said. My mouth was dry. My tongue a stropping leather.

"Can't go out the back," said the Captain, stroking his chin in a mockery of thoughtfulness. "Not without going through us. Can't get turned around quick enough to make a dash for the front…"

"It is private," said Jemma. "But it's just us friends here."

"Is he considering the side door, do you think? I'm just saying, if it was me and I was of a mind to rabbit, I'd be thinking the side door."

"How did you get it?" I asked Jemma without looking away from the Captain. Out of the corner of my eye, I saw her purse her lips and raise her eyebrows, pulling a face that said such questions were above her pay grade.

"Didn't I tell you we were the OSS, Duncan?" he asked me. "Did that slip my mind?"

"No, you mentioned it," I said. "Just figured you was lying."

His Captainness shook his head. "Now that hurts my feelings," he said. "To be called a liar to my face. Do you know anything about psychology, Duncan?"

I said that I did not.

He said that he did. A fair piece, too. He said that there is, among doctors of the cranial arts, an understanding that a guilty man will often see in those around him evidence of the same wrongs that he, the sinner, had done. Whether they're there or not, he'll see them. A killer of men will see murder in the eyes of everyone around him. A thief will fixate on the pilferage of others.

"Transference," I said, and the Captain slapped a hand down on the table then pointed a finger at me.

"See? You *do* know a little bit of head-shrinking, don't you? I mean, you'd have to, being who you are when you're at home. But I do understand that you're a humble man and maybe you just didn't want to...toot your own horn." He set about straightening the papers that'd been disturbed by his exuberance. "Transference. That is the word, Mr. Duncan Archer. And what I'm thinking is that you're suffering from a bit of that yourself."

"How do you figure?"

"I figure that, being a liar, you assume everyone else is, too. Having spent so long lying, you assume that I'm a liar, too. And Logue here. And sweet, innocent Miz Watts. And you *call* me a liar without even thinking about it." With his tongue and teeth he made a *tsk*-ing sound like a mother hen clucking. "But I am not a liar, Duncan. I'm a captain. Office of Special Services. Logue is my lieutenant. So is Jemma. You know how she got your file? She walked into the big building down the way there—the City and County building it used to be—and she *asked* for it."

"Well, almost," said Jemma.

"Shush," said the Captain. "She can do that, Duncan, because she is an officer of the OSS and all the petty, small, officious men in this kingdom, they quail before the threat those three letters imply. Them as know what the OSS is capable of go blind when they see us coming. Go deaf. Leave open any door we ask after. But you know that, don't you?" He tapped the papers before him. "This isn't your whole file, of course. That's going to take some time. But it's enough."

"Enough for what?"

"Enough to know you," he said.

I shook my head. "No. It's not."

"It's enough to know where you come from," said the Captain. "Enough to know that I was right in recognizing you. Enough to know that you weren't joking when you said they were love letters. Because they are, what we have of them. You were good, Duncan. In your time, you were *very* good. Linguist. Translator. Field asset and scalphunter. A sworn and bonafide OSS man. The paperwork gets a little thin once you came out West, but it's got a...a *scent* on it."

Oh, my dears, my dears...Did I not mention yet that I used to be an OSS man myself? You can, I hope, forgive my reticence. I was young then. Impressionable. Still swayed by the snap of banners and the trill of the pipes or some such. They found me when I was a boy with nothing. An empty vessel, cracked nigh onto breaking but just aching to be filled up.

But just between us, who among you hasn't done some things in the blooming of youth that you'd rather not dwell upon in the fullness of manhood? Drunken shenanigans, circle jerk, smoked a little something, maybe did a bit of nail-pulling and wet work for the last remaining effective agency of the government-that-was?

I ain't proud. At the time, I was well and fully ashamed. I run fast and far to get away. But it is what it is and now you know what you know. No one gets to outrun their past, no matter how hard they try.

Which is something I'm sure you understand.

"I know what you're thinking," said the Captain. "You cannot make it."

I looked at him, my heart pounding in slow, booming time, lungs like balloons filling.

"You going to sit still?" he asked.

I cut my eyes at Logue. At Jemma. Then back to the Captain. "No, sir. I aim to run."

Three steps was all I needed. The side door was what made the most sense. So I was going to go out the front. Flip the table. Kick out of the chair. Logue would be waiting and would reach on me the minute I moved. He would get the last mouthful of my whiskey in his eyes, followed on fast by the glass. Blind him. The table would take Jemma and I could run straight over her. Hope to break something and hobble her. No time for a pistol, so the Captain would be trouble. But I was fast. Wicked fast. He'd have to catch me.

"I'll make you a deal," he said. "Stay in the seat long enough for me to tell you a joke, okay?"

I said nothing. I breathed deep and evenly.

"Good. Stop me if you've heard this, okay? So in the OSS, they give every agent an intelligence test. Give you ten pegs that need to be fit into ten different-shaped holes, right? You have all the time in the world, but still half of the agents fail the test. Half! The examiners are flummoxed by these results. The consultants are horrified.

The results are passed up to management, and do you know what management says, Duncan?"

"They say, 'Half of our agents are morons and the other half are very strong,'" I said to him.

"That's right," the Captain said.

He leaned back in his chair and I was never going to have a better chance. He would go straight over backward. I lifted my glass and tipped all that was left of it into my mouth. Held it there.

"So which one were you?" the Captain asked.

Logue looked at me with his flat, dead eyes. Jemma had both her arms laid on the table, her weight on them, and she gave her head the slightest of shakes—one degree this way, one degree the other. The Captain raised up his arms like to put his hands behind his head and I twisted my heels into the floor, ready to jump, but then he did something. Shook one hand sharpish. There was a hiss like fingernails dragging on cotton and a snap of well-oiled mechanisms and his Jesus gun—the one that lived in his sleeve—leapt into his hand of its own volition. *A spring holster*, I thought. *That is just a special kind of cheating right there.*

"So which are you, Duncan?" He asked. "Are you dumb or are you strong?"

I relaxed. The tension drained out of me like water down a hole. I swallowed the whiskey in my mouth and said, "Neither. That's why I left."

"And that's why I am bringing you back in, old son. You game?"

Somewhere behind me, Abigail was drinking her way back to youth and vigor and Hippo was trying to light fires with his mind. Banjo sang Tom Waits, a song about not wanting to grow up, which, really, is what every great rock and roll song is about. It's what makes rock and roll different from the blues. The blues are what you sing after you've made all the mistakes you can never take back.

"How 'bout the Company pays for the next round and we can talk about it?" I asked.

EPISODE

2

A Boy and His Dog

I WOULDN'T HEAR FROM THE CAPTAIN AGAIN FOR ALMOST A MONTH.

After our moment at the Nob (after the guns had been put away, after he'd sent Logue to fetch the asked-after drinks, and after we'd put them down with companionable speed), we spoke of many things and told stories and shared secrets. Mine had been living in my belly like a cancer for more years than I care to mention and they came out of me like purgation. Angers and shames, blood, money, old resentments, humiliations and worse. The man had said he knew me. Had his papers in front of him, but the papers didn't tell even a whisper of the story. Not the true one or the best one. There weren't no papers that could. I mean, if there were, I wouldn't be here talking to you, would I?

None of what was said that afternoon is important now. Some was lies and some was truths and wouldn't none of it make any kind of sense anyhow, were I to tell you. But parts of it will become important later. There's a time for things. And each thing's time will come.

At a certain point—two, perhaps three drinks on, in the midst of a storm of laughter and the slapping of hands on the table—I rose and left to give back some of the firewater I'd drunk. There's a trough at the Nob for pissing, but it's inside so that made it classy.

Standing there, my dick in my hand, I recall thinking placid thoughts. The Captain, so you know, was a funny man. *Is* a funny man. Can tell a story, a joke, far better than me. Got a way of talking, him, that just . . . I don't know. *Draws* you, I suppose. He doesn't wear the high hat. Doesn't sermonize. He's quick, so can talk to two and three people at a time without losing himself, his hands always in copacetic action. Born to a barstool, my mom would've called him. A man meant for keeping company.

Anyway, I recollect being happy and smiling at the tiles. Had me drinks and a table full of like-minded villains with which to share them. More important, I had the promise of more to come. "I've got big plans for you, boy," he'd said, promising gold, fireworks, pussy, laughs and lord knows what-all-else. James the Pleaser, he's been called before, the Captain. And he didn't earn that name light. I liked the man. Liked Jemma. Even Logue, the big ape, had an air about him. And that was important.

But what was more important was . . . Well, you know what was more important, don't you? You all sitting there, you know what I was truly about. I tell you these stories as though my own joy and sweet feelings was paramount, the most vitalest element in our coming together, and while they was influential—while they *flavored* what was to come—I think you know that there was more to it. Had a job to do, me. For the Captain, clever as he was, hadn't been the first OSS man to find me, had he?

I finished up with the pissing, shook off, zipped up, splashed some water from the basin, and tried to fix a face on that weren't too needy for the right good times. Then I walked back out into the room.

The Captain was gone. Logue was gone, Jemma was gone. They'd left me behind again.

He did this a lot, the Captain. That's something you need to understand. Matter of fact, he's going to do it again at the end of this story. Then, for a while, he won't be able to get shook of me quite so easy. But later on, he'll do it again and again and again. These are his stories, but in many ways, the story of him is the story of his absences. Of the holes he left in the shape of him.

It was his way. It was deliberate. Everything to him was a tool. A drink was a tool. A gun was a tool. A knife, a word, a hammer, a smile. All tools.

People. All of them, tools. To be used and then, when their moment of usefulness was over, set aside.

Not *cast* aside, mind. He was too caresome a craftsman for that. Nothing he ever laid his hand to was cast away or wasted. He never lost anything. That machine brain he gave up to the furries with the ears and Cub Scout outfits? You ain't gonna hear about that again for a dog's age, no. But it weren't lost. Nor was it forgotten. Was a long game the Captain was playing at. Longer'n long. He was a smart man. Smarter than me. Damn sight smarter than the lot of you, obviously. Everything I knew, and he foxed me time and again. Foxed everyone, because he was a man who knew what he was about and didn't brook no distractions.

So you gotta trust me a bit here in the telling. Like I said, each thing's time will come. Just wait and see.

When I stepped to the bar and asked after my friends, Hippo shrugged and said they'd lit out. Paid the tab. Fine tip. "Better'n you ever leave," he sniffed.

And once the Captain was gone, he was *gone*. I didn't see hide nor hair of him or his for three weeks, four days, and a handful of hours. Some of those I spent telling myself that I was lucky. That, while in his company for less than a day, I'd nearly been killed. Had been threatened, lied to, cajoled, bushwhacked, blusterated, manipulated, and, ultimately, abandoned (twice). And all for the price of a couple long pours of Devil Eyes.

Count yourself fortunate, man, I said to myself. *You walked away unholed, unkilled, free, and at leisure. And what more have you ever asked of a day?*

But as the days became weeks and the weeks began to stitch themselves end-to-end, I began feeling a bit apostatized. More than a touch. Like some unbeliked little fat kid left behind while the big brothers were all off adventuring.

I mean, he'd called me up hadn't he? Hadn't those been his words? *Called me up*? Or maybe it was *bringing me back in*, as in to the fold. Back to the company from which I'd run. He'd knowed me from the moment he saw me, he'd said. He'd seen something in me, as was intended. Had recognized something, as was also. I'd been laid in his path deliberate, and he'd picked me up like a found penny. But this was the most delicate time. And were he to disrecall me now, whether of a purpose or through inattention, it would all be for nothing.

Wasn't no bad man, me. A little rough-and-tumble, perhaps. Had some things about me past-wise that I'd just as soon not come out in daylight. But who didn't? And no straight arrow would've walked the path that I had in my darkest days when *bad man* wouldn't have even been fit to describe my shadow.

So there was some terrible small hours where I lay in my sagging charpoy above the whore's cribs at Miss Kitty's, just staring up into the dark meeting place of the rooflines and asking myself what it was that had gone wrong. How was it that I was so fouled that even himself couldn't find some small use for me?

I'm sorry. I'm getting ahead of myself. It's time that hobbles me here. Time, which I've been thinking on quite a lot lately. The way it speeds and slows. The wounds it heals and the ones it makes worse. It's just that I know where the tale is going and have a habit of trying to race it all ahead.

I say that I was sad. That I was thinking on the man and missing his company, but, honest, I am not sure that that was the way of things.

It might've been that I was joyous then. I don't think so, but it's possible. I certainly had enough and more with which to occupy me. It might be that I was sad about other things. And I was, but in my mind, they are two separate things—one which turned the other into anger.

It might be that time is twisting the way I recall the days. That I came to know the Captain and like him—that I came to know his crew, too, and like them and trust them and swallow their Kool-Aid, down to the last drop—might be making me misremember how I felt in those early days. I might be lending a weight of seriousness to my thinking that was not, in actuality, there. Because I hardly knew them then, did I? Any of them.

It's like knowing a girl and falling in love with her and giving time to her and then losing her in a hard way. You look back and, even in its first, raw moments, you can taste predestination in the relationship. You see it in its completeness, from the beginnings on to the end. You can't think of yourself as getting to know her because, while you're thinking about it, you *already* know her. Your memory of the first day is warped by memories of the last.

And that's the way of time fucking with you. Making a lie out of every thought you think. Deforming truth with the certainty of retrospect.

Ain't none of us can be sure of anything anymore. Of the private histories we spin, least of all. But I am trying. And if I don't get the actualities of things down proper, I am at least trying to fix the notion of them. To be true to my recollections of them. That's the best I can manage.

This is what I know: There was our afternoon at the Nob and then there was what come after. Having nowhere better to go, I stayed on after the Captain, Logue, and Jemma left, nursing drinks bought on kindness and credit, then talked sweet to Hippo until he agreed to let me sleep the night outside the back door, in the little alley yard there. The man even gave me a blanket, which I found quite neighborly, and once I'd buried myself down beneath flattened, wet cardboard and a bit of broken-up shipping palette, I was snug as a tick. He told me that if I died in the night he would consider it the same as running out on the tab I owed and would refuse my ghost service at the Nob forever after, so I promised to take care and slept with my pistol in my hand.

Come the morning, I woke achy and smelling of alley, but helped Hippo open the bar anyway because it seemed the proper thing to do. I swept and polished, watered bottles in the well, and even made myself useful with a toolbox by fixing one wobbly table and the fuzz in the house PA. For this, Hippo gave me coffee with no milk or sugar, permission to take a bath in the men's room sink, and enough pocket junk to trade for breakfast—provided I found it, at his insistence, somewhere that wasn't his bar.

"Only two kinds of men end a night and start the morning at the same bar," he told me. "Alkies and bartenders. And since I'm the bartender and I don't want to think poorly on you by assuming you're the other sort, it's time for you to move along."

The man had a sort of unassailable logic there, and so I was off. My pockets were a-jangle with coin and kind and, being ever a resourceful man, I managed to parlay the two AA batteries, one 12-gauge shotgun shell, half an eagle, and the twist of copper wire that Hippo had paid me with into breakfast, lunch, regular employment plonking away at a whorehouse piano, and a backstairs room above Miss Kitty's cribs by the end of the day. I was proud of myself, but not overly. When finding night work in a hook shop marks the high point of a man's accomplishment, he might want to take a look back over his shoulder and see how low the bar was set.

The details of how I done it are dull. Pedestrian, really, and in the truest sense of the word. It was all a trader's game—just knowing who wanted worst for what thing and being willing to walk a piece in order to make the best of every little movement of junk through the system. It started with batteries for eggs and eggs for my breakfast, and many hours later ended with an un-smartened prosthetic leg for piano wire and a fine Stetson hat. The hat stayed with me. The wire went for the piano in question—which I knew how to fix both because I am a tinkery sort of man when I want to be and because I'd once long ago kept a piano not unlike the Regent upright in the parlor at Miss Kitty's and so was accustomed to its particular needs.

When I was done with the fixing it was the waning of the afternoon and I'd sat down and tickled a little, running a few bars from Fats Waller's "Honeysuckle Rose"—easy ones, but with a lot of bounce and flourish enough to make me seem a wicked talent. She wasn't in perfect tune, that Regent, but she was alright, and there was something in the worn keys that just fit my fingers right.

So even though I was satisfied that my work had been on the level and by the square, I just couldn't let her go yet. I pushed back on the bench, gave that Regent a little juice, and ran through "Tore Up" by Sleepy LaBeef to the great amusement of the assembling working girls and drowsy floormen who gathered up at the bar to listen to me work that old 88 while they had their breakfast or begged an early pop of shine or norepinephrine catalyzers from Madam, who was standing behind the long oak listening to me work with a peculiar sort of concentration.

I truly believe Madam had made up her mind on me before the tune was done, and it isn't a wise man who says no to her. I made a show of haggling some, but opened that night as the musical talent that lent Miss Kitty's downstairs parlor an air of class. And when I was done, I dragged myself up the stairs to sleep up under the rafters in a room as small as it was mean, but which kept the rain off, mostly, and the night's grosser creatures well at bay.

Of my time at Miss Kitty's, I have a few recollections, mostly out of order.

I remember the chipped paint on the nails of a girl called Sugar Magnolia as she sat on the lap of a fat man, sipping at the pink martini he'd bought for her. The drink was made of quinine, strawberry-flavored vitamin tonic and a dash of broad-spectrum antibiotics. It was what all the girls drank, overpriced as hell, and none of them retired from the tables in the downstairs to discuss Planck's Law or the fine points of Eliot and Whitman upstairs in private without first getting their trick to buy them two at least.

I remember eating toast for breakfast at three in the afternoon; learning how to play a nice, tinkling run down the Regent's keys one-handed while I drank with the other; a working boy named Leon weeping in the quiet of the kitchen stairs; the tink of coppers against a cement wall; the smell of Royalty scrip wet with beer; the smell of cheap lye soap; the smell of cold morning rain on pavement still hot from a night when the heat just wouldn't leave the world.

The spray of blood on the polished bar from a broken nose.

The taste of peppermint lipstick.

The play of the parlor lights along the blade of a famous knife.

The tickling heat of marijuana smoke deep in my lungs and trying to play while the keys swam under my fingers.

The ridiculous, breathless laughter of girls and boys and men and women all acting the fool on the night a bat somehow flew into the main room at Miss Kitty's and made a terror of itself until the chef went after it with an old tennis racket. No one knew where the racket had come from. Or the bat. Or what might've happened had the chef actually managed to hit the thing, which he never did.

Falling to sleep to the clatter of knocking headboards and the spirited acting of Madam's girls and boys humping the last coins out of the dregs of the horizontal trade.

The quiet of a morning, sitting over some sewing that needed doing, and the growing sense that things were slipping sideways on me but not knowing how to stop the slide.

I never knew Madam's Christian name. She was just Madam. Always had been, except for the old days when she was Madam Mayhem and would hear her name announced over the screaming of a roiling sea of bloodthirsty fans.

She had, in her youth, been a champion knife fighter with 22 wins on her card and no losses—as proven by the fact that she was still above snakes and breathing without the aid of a respirator or someone else's lungs.

But Madam as I knew her was a vain creature with Barnum notions on doing her business and an up-stuffed way of comporting herself. She was somewhere between 17 and 900 years old (depending on the light and the time of evening at which one encountered her), and whatever scars she'd carried away from her first career were long gone, buried beneath the infrastructure of successive plastic surgeries done over the years in contraction zone clinics of decreasing quality. But she still wore a fighting knife in a cross-draw sheath on her left hip and would, when properly motivated, draw it out slow as dancing and let the light catch in the toothed angle of the point and the blood gutters that notched the spine.

The money Madam won by burying that knife in willing meat 22 times all counted had gone into the maintenance of her visage and illusions of youth, and to the purchase and upkeep of Miss Kitty's. She'd had visions of her cat house as a salon of sorts—a calash establishment on the frontside where educated girls and boys in fashionable dress could sit with their johns and jills playing backgammon or bridge, listening to a tune or two and discussing poetry, particle physics, and the news of the day. A customer could dance a box waltz or jitterbug, could ask up a feed from Madam's well-stocked larder and have it prepared by a chef who could make pate de foie gras and grilled cheese sandwiches with equal pomp and facility. He (or she) could drink good wine or awful choc and smoke a two-dollar cigar while the working girls laughed at their jokes and sipped their pink martinis.

Upstairs where the cribs were, the illusion of fineness grew thinner, but was maintained somewhat by an emphasis on bathing (included free with every genital-based transaction), polite flirtation, and a rigid pricing structure that brooked no haggling. You wanted just a warm hole or a stiff pole? You took your trade down to the red-lights in LoDo—to the White Dog or Sally's or Lucky Lucy's where the girls were so wore out that if you shouted at 'em, they'd echo. Miss Kitty's aspired to something finer.

But despite the music and food and pleasant conversation, the lads and ladies in Madam's employ would still be out of them bolshy clothes and hard at work with their heels up or their knees down in a minute once the money came out because, really, a cat house was a cat house no matter how many doilies it had.

While waiting on the Captain's pleasure, I spent my evenings down on the main floor, playing a little Scott Joplin and a little Jerry Lee. When I got bored, I'd noodle out half-remembered jazz compositions or stitch together bits of six or a dozen different songs so that "Take On Me" by A-ha and the theme from *Night Court* would blend into "Fernando" or "Down in the Park" and it would all sound of a piece so long as you were paying more attention to the girls than you were to me. Sometimes I took requests at the piano and sometimes I didn't. I even began to attract a short list of regulars who, on a good night, might number as many as two. Most of the crowd was still there for the fucking. I didn't have no illusions.

When things were slow and the whores felt like dancing, I'd burn up some Harlem stride like I was born with fourteen fingers. And when, after about a week of working that Regent and taking my pay in cold beer, half-eagles and six meals a day, I broke the arm, nose and face-bone of a man I saw raise a hand to one of Madam's good earners, I became a Josey as well—escorting her angelicas on outcalls, giving them a respectable arm to walk on and making sure the money got paid.

I killed a man on Pennsylvania Street and 14th in this capacity. Left him bubbling in his own claret, his back up against an arrow-straight maple tree scabbed with the sticky scars of burns and the gray plague. And he died wondering, no doubt, how his life's story had come to such a cheap and early end.

There was nothing to it but that he had it coming, and yet it pained me. Upon giving me the position (which she'd done right over the bloody smear where I'd bounced that first felon's head off the curled rosewood of the bar), Madam had said that she was offering it because she saw in me a certain naff but irresistible savagery. That I wasn't a big man or a quick man, which was true. That I wouldn't be able to intimidate a nickel out of a child. But that the girls could always use someone dumb enough to scrap on their behalf over transgressions only offensive to them that had a short fuse and a weakness for girls even when they had their mouths and legs both closed.

When I wasn't playing, I rolled dice with the floormen and gun hands and pitched coppers with the derelict wrecks that Madam hired to haul her trash and run her laundry; ate cheese sandwiches, green beans, the good parts of half-rotten apples, and bowls of congee with pink shreds of shrimp protein in the Kitty's rattle-trap kitchen. I collected rumors and told jokes and bid along with the girls and the boys for the best leavings from each night's lost-and-never-found box. When it was required, I walked the streets, arm-in-arm with Glinda or Leon or Clementine or Sugar Magnolia who, with or without me, couldn't step ten paces in public without someone falling in love with her because she was small and devilish and cute as a button polished to a high shine.

Occasionally we rode in Madam's car—an ancient Mercedes that'd once been black and smart and elegant, but was now scratchedy, loud and dumb as rocks—but not often. Fuel was expensive, its supply undependable. Walking cost less and was, on the whole, safer. I held the money, did the negotiating, and learned how to smile with my mouth even when my eyes were cold with the knowledge that every night was just one bad decision away from being the worst one since the last one.

I took to wearing my gun everywhere. One day I stayed up to sit over a table in the main room, humming to myself some snatch of a ballad and picking apart the stitching on the shoulder rig that'd come with my gun and Castle employment so that I could sew it all back together again properly and in a more aesthetically pleasing fashion, giving it a lower hang and a loop for an extra magazine that I'd made Madam purchase and fill for me. This was more so that I'd always have something to trade with and less for thinking that I'd someday need be involved in a shooting match that would involve me trading 28 bullets with anyone, especially when each one of those was worth as much as dinner.

Coming home in the cool of dawn after a long outcall, I would sometimes hear birds singing and smell breezes that didn't stink of rotting meat, ash or long-chain monomers, then sit in the quiet bar for a cup of chicory that I'd made myself and maybe a shot of vasopressin or half a Blue Monday, depending on whether I could pay and if I wanted to stay up or go way down. I would twist the dials on the bar's marconi and listen to the pirate radio feeds that came in from out of the gray places—DJ Logix, the Rawhide Kid (who played country and bluegrass and passed messages for bounty hunters and Regulators), Radio Free Georgetown, and Power Hits 103.3 The Voice Of The Revolution, which was my favorite, mostly because its DJ, Hard Harry Henderson, demanded an uprising of all the world's vegetables, believed in the coming of space aliens and of doors in the mind that let in on other dimensions, espoused the merits of Buddhism, anti-dogmatism, biological impurity and peyote eating, and sometimes even played music from the days before the end of the world.

When at my leisure, I would sometimes walk and pretend that I wasn't looking for Jemma Watts. That I wasn't listening for the low-gear rumble of Marlene on the streets of the Queen City or the chatter of the Captain's urchin army in the blocks around the Castle. And sometimes I really wasn't.

But most of the time, really, I was.

And when, come a morning, I curled into the sagging resignation of my bed, I slept with the ghost of the man I'd beefed on Pennsylvania Street. With his eyes on me and the bubbling sound of him drowning in his own blood in my ears. He'd been a fool. He'd drawn down on me even though he'd been so drunk he could barely stand and was holding his pants up with one hand as he came charging out the front door looking for a whiskey-dick refund that just weren't never gonna happen.

I didn't know his name, and when he came to visit me, he never introduced himself. Didn't matter, though. After two weeks or three, we were well acquainted, my ghost and me. And honest, I thought it another visit from him in the gray dawn when Captain James Barrow and Logue Ranstead finally came back for me.

I found myself roused from the beginnings of sleep by the sense that my aloneness had been somehow compromised. It wasn't the groan of the floorboards or the soft rasp of things being moved about that did it. In my weeks of comfort in Madam's attic I'd lost a bit of the edge of paranoia that comes from sleeping rough in wild places. It really wasn't no specific thing at all that shivered me awake, but rather just the electric knowing of a solitary man that he is being looked on by someone or something that's come a'wanting.

"Not tonight," I mouthed, my tongue cottony and my throat raw from the clinch mountain I'd been drinking and the handrolls I'd taken to hanging from one lip while I played. I had, somewhere, acquired a thin pillow for my charpoy, and I pulled at it 'til I could put the cool side over my face. "Not tonight . . ."

"Night," said a voice, "is really a foregone thing at this point, Mr. Archer. It's morning if you can see your dick to piss with, and morning is time for a man to turn his hand to the Lord's work."

It was the Captain, of course. I breathed out the stink of three weeks waiting into the smothering blackness of my pillow and said, "Finally" in a voice far too soft for anyone to hear.

They'd already been halfway through the search of my room—had let themselves in, tossed my drawers and pockets and most readily accessible piles of what-not without disturbing me—and now were continuing on with their shameless rooting while I pawed at my eyes and coughed myself full awake.

The Captain sat in my room's one chair with my briefcase open on his lap, gently stirring the contents with the capped end of an ink pen. He was dressed, near as I could tell, exactly the same way he had been when I saw him last—the only additions being a haze of dark whiskers framing his cheeks and chin and enough bags beneath his bloodshot eyes to hold him for an intercontinental voyage. He had Logue with him, wrapped in some kind of jumpsuit big enough to tent a small house for roach spraying, and damned if I wasn't happy to see him as well, despite the fact that he was pawing carelessly through the sad stock of worldly possessions I'd acquired in my time at Miss Kitty's.

"Seems you've come down a bit in the world since last we met," said the Captain.

I yawned. "Went from working for a King's councilors to working with whores. I rather think that's just finding more honest employment."

The Captain nodded. With his (my) pen, he lifted the corner of a paper copy of *The Westward*, the only newspaper still printing in this part of the world—useful mostly to anarchists, smugglers, funhogs, conspiracy theorists and them as might be looking for a quick handjob, a used futon or a cleaned ounce of skunky Mamasan at a fair price. "Working here," he said, "I'd think you wouldn't have to go calling around for a tug."

"I read it for the horoscopes," I said. "And the Sudoku."

Logue had to slump just to fit in my room unless he was standing directly beneath the peak of the roof. I watched as he picked up my wallet and put it down again before the alarm went off then swirled the small pile of silver eagles and coppers I had on the upturned steamer trunk I used as a wardrobe and added to it the thin fold of Royalty scrip and American dollars, worn to smooth, linen softness, that I'd had hidden in a gap between a roof joist and its sheeting. It was all I'd managed to put away since I'd first played "Tore Up" in Madam's parlor. The tips at Miss Kitty's were not great, but they were all mine. And I collected five percent of all trade while joseying. It was the kind of thing where, if I'd kept at it for a hundred years, I might've gotten myself rich.

Beneath my thin sheet, I suddenly felt the need to scratch, and did so ferociously with one hand while, with the other, reached for the roach-end of a joint balanced against the mason jar lid I used as an ashtray. Among her many other pursuits, Madam grew her own rococo strains of high-powered weed in a lab below the parlor, juicing them at the molecular level with adrenocorticotropic hormones, nine-amino-acid peptides, phencyclidine, and NMDA receptor antagonists. It was her hobby—something akin to fancy ladies cultivating orchids, but with higher profit margins—and she was good at it. Her girls did most of the selling, upstairs or out on the streets. The rest went out right across the bar or to her employees as occasional pay, all weights carefully calculated against street value.

I stopped scratching long enough to touch a coil lighter to the charred tip of the joint, then went right back to it.

"So you've been keeping busy," the Captain said, nodding in the direction of my manly issues.

"Crabs," I told him, which was true-ish. I'd borrowed a nasty bunch of them from Big Libby one night after we'd both had a few pops following a long night's working. I'd weighed my thin finances against another dawn spent with my ghost and had wound up riding her like a horse bucking just so's I'd have the mercy of warm company. I'd hobbled away with bruises and the bugs, both. Like a lady, she'd apologized, of course. Even offered to refund half my money (which, being a gentleman, I refused). But such troubles were easily remedied with a quick shave and some chemical defoliant. It was the five o'clock shadow that itched like the devil.

"Hazards of the work, I'd imagine. You ever hear of a guy named Bennie?"

"No," I said, wondering if maybe that was the name of the man I'd killed. If maybe the Captain knew about that as well. I pecked at the joint and held the smoke deep in my lungs. "Friend of yours?" I squeaked.

He shook his head. "He was a piano player, too. Liked the working girls. You just remind me of him is all." He closed my case and set it aside.

Logue had picked up my coil lighter and was turning it over between his sausagey digits. It had a dust automata built into it—a pin-up girl who'd masturbate frantically when woken by the heat of the mechanism being triggered, her squeals like the peeping of tiny gears in need of lubrication. When she was done, she'd insult you for watching, then turn away coquettishly or read a tiny magazine. I called her Darlene.

"I have this?" he asked.

"Best just to say yes," the Captain advised.

I shrugged. "Sure, Logue. My gift to you. You can see how much I have to give."

He put Darlene in one of the pockets of his jumpsuit and went to stand by the door. The Captain closed up my case, stood it beside my bed, and rubbed his hands together.

"So if you're done playing with yourself, you should get up and get dressed," he said. "We've got a job to do. Vitally important to the safety and security of the Kingdom and whatever."

"What, like this isn't?"

The Captain pursed his lips and rubbed at his red eyes. "Enough jokes now, Duncan," he said. "But come on. You'll like this one, I promise. It has to do with roads, so maybe you can learn something."

I wanted to ask him where he'd been. I wanted to ask him what he'd been doing that was so important and why he'd just vanished, set me aside and put me in this place where I'd had to kill some dumb, drunk man with his pants half-down for a few dollars out of a whore's pay.

I wanted to tell him to take his roads and his judgements and his insinuations and to bang them right up his ass crossways. That maybe Logue could watch. Or that there were girls and boys below who'd be happy to help if he was happy to pay.

Fuck you, Mr. The Captain Sir, I wanted to say. Or maybe I just wanted to thank him for finally coming back. For ending my waiting on him to come back. I don't know. It was a strange time and, as I said, telling the story now is like thinking back and trying to remember how you'd made a friend that you'd had forever and a week.

But none of that mattered anyhow, and the Captain certainly didn't care. He was already slapping hands on his knees and standing, casting a look around the poor quarters of just another one of his occasionals as though knowing that he was seeing it this once and maybe, probably, never again. He was turning for the door that let out into a narrow passage that bragged by calling itself a hallway, and then the stairs. Was making, again, to leave. And wasn't a man to look back, the Captain. Not once or ever.

So "Hand me my hat, would you?" I said instead, to delay him and distract him. "And that bottle of shine there on the chest-of-drawers, too."

And he did both. The hat I planted on my head while pinning the last of the joint between my teeth, then whipped back the sheets and poured a triple shot 160-proof base burner onto my shorn privates—which scorched 'em up like hellfire but would take the edge off the itching for a time. It was a trick I'd learned from the girls (who normally did it with tincture of witch hazel after their own depilatory treatments began giving way to nature), so one surely can't say that I hadn't at least gained a bit of wisdom in my time among them.

I stepped into my best blue jeans as they were going out the door, Logue and the Captain. Loaded my pockets in a hurry, found a button-shirt with a fat necktie still looped 'round it, my holster, and even as I was stamping for the door, was pushing bare feet into a pair of stack-heeled roper boots that I'd won out of the left-behinds box. I hooked my briefcase on the way, catching it as it fell open just in time and snapping fast the latches.

Outside in the hall, I saw Logue and the Captain headed the wrong way and hissed at them—trying to keep quiet for the benefit of all the good girls and boys trying to sleep below—saying, "This way, gents. Only one set of down-going stairs here."

The Captain turned, saw me there all come apart with one boot flopping half on, my Stetson all crook'd and my shirt still unbuttoned. He smiled. "We're not going down, Duncan. We got a ride waiting this a'way." And then he pointed up toward the rafters and the dark sky and all the morning stars beyond.

Logue reached up and punched out a hinged hatch that let out onto Miss Kitty's peaked roof. Light spilled in like gray water. And the sound, distant but approaching, of humming turbine engines.

"You're not afraid of flying, are you?"

The Osprey must've been hanging at altitude, just waiting for the Captain's call, because it was dropping from the gray sky like a terrible bird, blowing downgusts of morning air and dust and dead nanites and bugs and dew and crud through the roof hatch even as I turned to walk toward it.

Even as I turned to walk toward it . . .

There was a monstrosity about the scene. The sense of a doorway having been torn open between the quiet world of a whorehouse attic's dawn and some howling, windblown plane where all was furious noise and violence. The Captain and Logue hunched under the onslaught, turning away to give it nothing but their backs while they scrabbled at pockets for sunglasses and cupped hands over the backs of their necks to keep them from the stinging crap-spray. I can only imagine the consternation all that racket must've been raising downstairs among the girls and the gun hands. The tiltrotor's roar. The hail against the roof. The thunk and clang as a bright yellow penetrator on a steel cable came dropping through the open hatch like magic.

And I walked *toward* it. Like an idiot or a puppy-dog chasing after its master, I walked away from the dimness and calm of my room and rented bed and toward the howl of wind and machinery. At the end, I might've even ran.

The Captain stepped onto the penetrator's footring, clipped himself onto the cable, and was zipped up through the hole and to heaven beyond like a rabbit disappearing upside-downsy.

I stomped my foot into my boot. Logue peeked up through the hole into the sky and snapped his head back as the penetrator came down again, spanging this time off the frame of the hatch and spraying wood splinters. I crouched down, shoved my gun and holstery into my briefcase and snapped it tight closed again. I tried to tuck down the flapping tails of my shirt and tie and, when I stood, Logue pressed a pair of goggles at me—round things, made of blue glass and leather and copper fittings—and I put them on, looking, no doubt, like some crazed aviator just back from strange lands. Next was a harness to step into, closed with a D-ring, used then by Logue to drag me forward as he snapped it fast around the cable.

"Feet!" he bellowed over the rush of wind and morning breaking in all over us, pointing to the footring onto which I stepped. He glanced over my shoulder at something down the hall, and I tried to look, too, but there was no time. He reached out, shook the line fiercely. "Watch your head!" he yelled, then jerked a thumb skyward.

There was shouting I could barely hear. Above me was the gray body of the Osprey hanging against the gray bellies of iron clouds, the black blur of rotors, the maw of the rear hatch hanging open— an impossible second door in the sky.

And then, of course, I was flying. Being reeled in fast like a fish on a hook. There was a part of me that hoped all the girls and all the boys was up. That we'd roused up all of Miss Kitty's with our clatter and that they was all hanging head and shoulders out of their windows to see me lifted up like Jesus, off onto some great and glorious adventure from which I mightn't ever return. There was a part of me that knew I'd be all the talk at breakfast, at the tables, and down the bar that night. *Flying*, they'd say. *They done sent some kind of helicopter for him. Not even just a car.* And all concerned would wonder over what important business Mr. Duncan Archer was at. What the bawdy house piano player could possibly have going that would require him floating off to

Lord-knows-where in such a hurry that he hadn't even stopped to say goodbye.

At the top of the ride I was roped in and wrestled aboard by the Captain and another man, dressed in a jumpsuit like Logue's and a flight helmet with a matte face shield that spoke to bolshy and expensive things going on behind it. They unclipped me, handed me down onto the decking, then bid me get fastly out of the goddamn way while Logue was brought up and all was secured for travel. I asked whether or not they was going to drop two ropes or maybe bring in a second whirlybird to reel up the enormous article, but no one laughed. I can still recall the feeling of standing there, on a floor but in the sky, as being one of the strangest things in a world full of strange things. But who knows. Maybe I was just easily impressed back then.

"You gonna bullseye it this time, Holcomb?" asked the Captain.

"Sure am," said the man, who was apparently called Holcomb.

"I'm just saying that the last time . . ."

"Your jawing certainly ain't helping my concentration none, Cap'n."

"Don't want to have to pay the lady of the house for any more damage to her roof is all I'm saying. So if you could—"

Holcomb pulled a lever. The penetrator fell like a dart. The Captain leapt for the edge of the open ramp, disdainful of falling, as though something so common as gravity could never affect him. He held loosely to a short drape of cargo netting and leaned out like a child afraid of nothing because he'd never known no pain.

"Oh!" he shouted. "Oh ho ho . . . Right on the button. That's two for three on the day, Holcomb. That's not bad. I mean, it's not *perfect*, but in the wind—"

"Yeah, s'windy up here, sure."

"In the wind and the poor light?" He slapped the man on the shoulder. "Two for three is *completely* respectable."

"It is."

"By the way, how many kids you have now?"

"Three. I have three."

"Hmm. I mean, I'm just asking, but if this was a fire and you pulled two of the three of them out? That's a passing grade, isn't it? That's better than half of them saved."

Holcomb turned the blankness of the visor on the Captain. The Captain stared back into it like he could see the man's eyes behind it. "Two out of three? That's close enough for government work. Right, Holcomb?"

And the other man, Holcomb, seemed about to say something when the cable rattled in its cradle. "Alright," said the Captain, looking away. "Here comes the big man. Let's get this show on the road before we attract any more attention."

The winch squealed as it dragged in the cable and lifted Logue Ranstead into the sky, but it didn't struggle a bit, likely because it was a machine accustomed to lifting tanks and such-like, and Logue, despite his mammothness, was still only made of meat.

We flew north, twining out around the edges of the city's core—skirting the shattered skeletons of dead, useless skyscrapers and the twisted fingers of the airline rails—then surging out past the reach of the city in a blink. We climbed out over the suburbs of the Queen City, the sound of the engines inside the cargo compartment where we sat just a gutty throb, and below us, Denver fell away.

I watched her go myself, from a small round window in the barreled body of the Osprey, sitting in a fold-down seat that wasn't more than an uncomfortable shelf for my ass, with all manner of tubes and bundled wires and clutterment dangling above my head. Even in the thin light of dawn, the endless runs of houses and development tracts with their war scars and stomp-holes went from green and brown and red and living to gray and dead as we reached the limits of habitability—of the power grid and the feed, the protection of the Castle and the King, the civilizing influences.

In the contraction ring, acres of dead homes rotted or went feral, making strange, semi-intelligent molecular war on their neighbors. Ripples of spent matter like waves marked places where freaked constructors, frantic for atoms to process and operating on garbled, nth-generation programming, had eaten the earth and trees and fire hydrants and abandoned cars and wild cats and weird loners who'd scavenged in the ring before being snuck up on by a pop-top ranch or semi-detached garage driven insane by starvation and loneliness.

There was life in the dead zone, for sure. Plenty. Meat and mechanical both. Apocalypse nerds wore pith helmets and cargo shorts, slung rifle-format rail guns across radiation-burned shoulders, and stalked the dusty, weird, silent streets for bears, 'bots or city busses gone wild. Cults and compounds sprouted like weeds, growing up out of the abandonment to worship bombs, grow plagues, dance with snakes, commit ritual suicide or wait for the alien mothership to come for them. Sometimes all of that at the same time.

Black manufactories hidden inside ruined strip malls or buried underground churned out consumer goods both smart and dumb, both legal and not so. Chemists cooked drugs and grew monsters down there, in the gray wastes. Moonshiners and ethanol barons ran their stills in basements the size of aircraft hangers and secured like the Mint. And some people just made tee shirts or sandals or antibiotics or art. There was clinics where science with terrible, unknowable consequences was practiced, and there were fields, shrouded beneath heat-reflective covers, where rebel farmers with scatterguns and packs of biogen dogs kept close to heel eked life out of the exhausted, poisoned soil, growing melons and rice and marijuana and blueberries and soybeans where they could, microchips and children's toys and televisions where the ground was so saturated with heavy metals and radicalized elements that no natural seed would take.

I felt it in my belly as we banked west, saw only clouds out my window until we leveled, and thought that we must be following a road or maybe one of the airlines. Looking for something, it felt like.

"Where we headed, Captain?" I asked, but he didn't hear me. Or was ignoring me. Tough to tell. He sat with his hands on his knees, whistling and tapping one foot on the deck plates. I asked him where he'd been keeping himself and where he'd laid hands on such a sweet ride and got the same response.

Logue had his eyes closed, a greenish cast to the skin beneath them and a paleness around his lips. The man did not like flying, I would come to know. But he felt that not telling anyone would just make the fear up and go away one day. I rolled my head on my neck and went back to staring out the window, waiting out the quiet time and chewing away at my own smiles, trying to swallow them before they bloomed.

Denver during the expansion had been huge. That's just history. When it was still part of America it grew like a living thing. Like an amoeba, sending out tendrils along roads that'd been first cut by Indian scouts and wagon trains and wild ponies, colonizing the wide, rich, flat lands like a bacteria that'd found its ideal biological niche.

At its height, it went big until its gravity was enough to suck in anyone looking for action, fun or a fresh start. It had as many wind turbines as some small towns had people. It sucked water like a sponge and devoured resources as though there was a massive, hot fire burning in its heart that had to be fed morning, noon and midnight. It was the kind of existence that was only tenable at the apex of the expansion. In a world that existed like a race to see how fast it could eat itself hollow.

It couldn't hold, of course. Nothing could. You know that. I mean, look at where we are. But you look back sometimes and you think to yourself: Where did everything go wrong? Where, precisely, did our things get the better of us?

Maybe you have to be older. The world now, everything is new, isn't it? Every day, everything is new. And even then . . . I mean, folk talk about it like it were the end of days, but it wasn't. It was just the end of the old. And the old, it didn't go quiet. It had to be *shook*.

But still, there was a moment. Some point in time. And maybe you get to an age where you start thinking on such things and it comes to you in bed one night, or over a fifth pint down at the boozer. You think you've found that place where everything kind of turned.

For me, everything in the whole-wide-whatever became unhinged on the first day your phone started talking to you without there being no person on the other end of the line.

You wouldn't know this. You all weren't there and couldn't know the feeling of it—the strange sense of the future arriving when you was looking elsewhere. This dim, giddy flutter in the belly like standing on the edge of something and looking down on the world from great height.

But trust me. It seemed so whiz-bang at the time. So fucking clever. A gank that didn't really feel like a gank. But at that point you were talking to a ghost, communing with hoodoo spirits, and supplicating yourself to an intelligence far vaster than yours. Even if you were just asking where to find some frozen yogurt, it was making a deal with the machinery. Giving something up to it that you'd never get back. You accept that shit and everything else is just a slip-n-slide down into weirdness and giant robots and joyous, fuck-it-all ruin.

That's what I think anyways. My opinion, take it or don't. It wasn't the day I watched one of the great cities of the East crumble around me. When it rained concrete and melted steel and I breathed poison and hid in the dark from glow-eyed monsters and them that kept them. It wasn't the smoke and the flames. It wasn't what I lost or what I gave up that marked the hot, fast death of one world and the borning day of another. It was asking a slab of plastic in my hand where to find some froyo on a sunny afternoon and having a voice from out of nowhere answer me. It was *believing* that voice.

It was finding nothing terrifying in it at all.

I saw the bones of a dragon out the window as the Osprey hauled up, shot her tail, and started to spiral in toward the solid ground.

They were black, those bones. Big carbon fullerenes, shot with traceries of silver that was either titanium or aircraft-grade aluminum. The teeth were ceramic knives. The head was a giant wedge of bone, stained a wet pink but already scoured nearly clean. There was a spot in the massive cage of her ribs where they'd been broken and blown inward, likely by the rocket that'd brought her down. The insides had already gone to liquid. The skin was whipping off in flaps, torn by the breeze and blown off like paper in a fire.

"It ate three of the engineers before their security detail found a rocket that would actually fire," the Captain told me. He had squeezed in next to me and was sharing the window, our foreheads touching the smooth, rounded frame. "Big thing," he said. "Big, beautiful thing . . ."

The dragon had come down on them in the night, attracted, they thought, by the worklights. Or the chug-and-stink of the ethanol generators. Or maybe just the chance at a warm meal. It must've been starving, the poor thing. Lost out in the Big Weird.

It was an escapee, near as anyone could figure. From one of the gene labs or clip joints—the black places where confounding the Lord's plan for a natural human biology was their bread and beer.

Or maybe it was a guard dog that'd gotten loose. Dragons were a perennially popular product in that respect. Something about the deep, mythic memories they stir across virtually all cultures. Though usually they came in smaller varieties. Less likely to eat them that had purchased them.

But this one had been a monster. Better than seventy feet long, with a head the size of a minivan and weaponized besides.

"Teeth. Claws. A powerful hunger," the Captain said. "Could breathe flame, too. That's what the survivors say. And not from gel-fire tanks, either. Grown-in biological system."

That kind of thing didn't come cheap. That kind of thing came, as a matter of fact, pretty motherfucking dear. Someone, no doubt, was missing her fiercely.

It'd come up on them walking, to hear it told. Limping, really. But definitely not flying. Something wrong, maybe, with one of its wings. Already hobbled and paining when it'd come hoping to scare up a snack.

It'd smashed one of the road crew's trucks, eaten one man who'd froze up in her path, then two more who, apparently, had underestimated the speed at which the big lizards could move when hunting and jacked up by warm blood and adrenaline. Fast like a snake striking when their dinner depended on it.

The crew had been out on an extended road project—trying to reopen the King's Road between Denver and the Free Republic of Boulder, where it'd got the wreck-up by wastelanders and FRB citizenry both who'd thunk that when Denver fell to the Kansans, Boulder might could be next.

In anticipation of this potentiality, they'd cut all the roads in. Blown bridges and passes. Laid in barricades and poppy fields of landmines that would go boom sometimes at the slightest prompting or, sometimes, not at all. And ever since Denver *hadn't* fallen, the Royalty road crews had been laboring to get all the mess clear— a thing I ought to have known since, ostensibly, I'd been helping in the planning when the Captain had found me and whisked me away to this life of whiskey, women, and wild adventure.

The crew traveled in a gang. Twenty Royalty road engineers and a mob of wet-brain laborers for the ditch-digging and such, carrying their own supplies and their own machinery and rolling with a tin-can APC full of their own security who were good and well-blooded after weeks of sniffing after IEDs and scrapping with the residents of the gray places, almost none of whom care for unannounced visitors wearing the sigil of the Kingdom of Steve.

True, they weren't rightly equipped for acts of Medieval heroism, so to speak, but then who is? They had not a lance, not a shield between them, so when the dragon had showed up, they'd gone with anti-tank weapons instead. Wise, save that their RPG-7's were firing Castle reloads with shit primers and worse fusing that either jammed in the launchers or simply bounced off the howling critter's hide and went loudly corkscrewing off into the night. But the HAWS tubes were aces. One in the haunch had got the beast's attention, made it kick up, curlicues of flame drooling from her asbestos nostrils, and look about with half an engineer hanging from her teeth. A second shot high in the body did for her complete, bedding her down with a roar and a gout of fire as her triethylaluminum sacs ignited.

The impact had almost severed the neck from the body. Everyone on the crew still living laid claim to a souvenir. Teeth, mostly. Or hanks of skin to make boots and belts out of. The man who'd fired the fatal shot would get the head, of course. He already had in mind a bar where he could trade it off for free drinks for life. And with the chemistry kits and heavy tools carried by the crew, the butchering had gone fast.

Funny thing was, the dragon wasn't even what we were there for. It was what had been *hunting* the dragon that concerned the Captain and had scared the chief of the road crew bad enough that he'd called in to the Castle for a specialist.

"Lucky for us, we were listening in," the Captain said.

The Osprey had leveled out at about fifty feet above a flat piece of road, just outside the ring of lights cast by the crew's camp.

"And double-lucky that I just happened to know a man who knows everything there is to know about roads," the Captain continued, patting me on the shoulder.

"Me?" I asked, incredulous and wanting to remind the man that the reason I'd ganged in with him in the first place was precisely that I knew sweet fuck-all about roads and was in kind-of-mortal danger of that being found out when he'd arrived.

And he says, "You," then stands up and punches the control that opens the ramp back up. There is a klaxon honk, spinning warning lights, howling wind and stinging dust. I clutch at my hat with one hand and drag my goggles down with the other until they're covering my lookers most-ways, and then I have to shout at him again.

"I don't know anything about roads!"

"You know enough to pretend!"

"I'm not really sure that's true!"

The Captain grinned. "Too late to worry about that now. You remember your insertion training from super-spy school, Duncan?"

I did not. But apparently, in the Captain's mind, knowing enough to pretend was also good enough for falling out the back of an aircraft. Logue went first, shoving past me, clipping onto the line, and going out rappelling-style without the least word of complaint. Then it was my turn. Once I was clipped in, the Captain pulled me close so's to yell in my ear and be heard over the roaring whatnot. "We're about an hour ahead of the Castle's real experts," he said. "Maybe less. But we do *not* want to still be here when they arrive, understand?"

I nodded.

"Which means we have to be fast. As far as those men below know right now, *you* are the Castle's road-man and Logue and I are bomb specialists working for you. So we'll all just march in there, you'll throw some road-engineer talk around, shout at some people, act all official, and get this settled toot sweet."

"So what's down there?" I asked.

"Dead dragon. Bunch of idiots," he said. "Some other stuff."

"It's the other stuff that's got me itchy."

"It's nothing. Everything will be fine."

"Yeah, but if we're not collecting dragon bones or pieces of dead road engineer, why are we here?"

"A dogboy," he said, eyes sparkling with the mischief of even just saying such a word out loud.

I told him no way. That he was spinning fibbery just to mess with my already jangled head.

He raised a hand. "Honest injun."

"You're serious?"

"Rarely, but I ain't lying about this either. Somehow these roughnecks got one caught down in a hole somewhere that it can't get out of. And do you want to die before seeing something like that? Just follow my lead, do as you're told, and everything'll be fine."

"You keep saying that!" I shouted.

"Haven't been wrong yet!"

And then he didn't exactly *push* me, but let's say gave me a very enthusiastic pat on the back.

Fifty foot of falling feels like a lot less than it is when you're doing it. Nevertheless, I screamed the whole way down.

Later—much, much later—the Captain would be standing over me in a hospital bed and I would be on the fence about dying, half of me wanting to go but half of me wanting pretty badly to stay. I'd been tore up good. Enough that I was shitting teeth and had ruined more than one set of sheets from bleeding.

The Captain, he had the movie-of-the-week look about him: unshaved, eyes bloody and sunk. The look of a man who'd been sitting uncertainly by a bedside for a long stretch without interruption. But when I roused, he was standing like he'd just arrived. He looked down at me and grinned.

"You happy?" he asked.

Not quite so late as all that, in the bunkhouse, we would cross paths in the long reach of a bad night. Just one in a whole, long train of them. I was fighting with the coffee machine and losing. Throwing things. All of a sudden, he's just there.

He asks me, "You happy, Duncan?"

He asks me once in the middle of a gunfight. He asks me once on vacation with the team—us painting our tonsils and carrying on like toffs in the streets of some hell-rousing nowhere of which I recall only the green smell of river water, humidity like breathing hot soup, and a midnight rain that burned like bacon grease spattering from the pan. He comes at me out of the darkness with this three-by-nine smile and he asks, "You happy?"

And I was. Lord, I was. Because when the Captain asked, "Are you happy?" what he was really asking was, are you happy-*er*. What he meant was, *Look around you, boy. Think about where you are and what you seen. Think about your day or your life and what it would've been if, on the day of your calling up, I had passed you by.*

Are you happier with me than you would've been as just some schlub? That was what he was asking everyone to whom he put the question. Happier than if you'd slept in today. Called in sick. Happier than some fat, cuntish chucklehead in chinos and a polo, just spending all day barking at a knot. Happier than if you was perished already and gone on to your reward.

I hit the pavement hollering and near bit my tongue off. Logue pulled me clear of the line, jammed my hat down tight on my head, un-sucked the goggles from my eyes and handed me my briefcase, which, apparently, he'd carried with him while roping down.

The Captain came down almost on my heels, threw the line and said something into the sleeve of his jacket that didn't have the snout of his Jesus gun poking out of it. Orders to the Osprey, I assumed. Then he looked at me.

"That was fun, right?" he asked.

"No," I gasped, bent over a bit, hands on my knees and hoping not to air my paunch right there on my boots. "It was not."

"Bullshit," he snapped. "Duncan, you just fell out of a plane and hit the ground living. You seen a dragon's bones, caught a dawn ride off a whorehouse roof and flew away like a hummingbird. If we hadn't come to get you, what would you be doing right now? Sleeping? Scratching your balls? It's adventure time, you ungrateful motherfucker. So tell me, you happy?"

I straightened up carefully, dragging the back of one hand across my mouth and wanting fiercely for a cigarette. "Am I happy?" I asked.

"Yes. Are you happy?"

I thought about it a tick. Examined my internal whatevers. Weighed this and that.

"Yeah, Captain. I am. Happy I'm alive and all in one piece, anyway."

He grinned then, took me by the shoulder and shook me like rug-pissing dog. "Goddamn right you are. Now it's showtime. Look up. Wave off the bird. You're the boss here, so make like the big figure."

So I did, shielding my eyes with my briefcase and waving in what I hoped looked like a bossish and commanding fashion. In response, the Osprey dipped her nose, rotated, and moved off slow, taking her wind with her.

"Good work," says the Captain. "See how easy this is? Seems a shame we even get paid for it."

"You say that like I been paid yet," I said, but the Captain ignored me.

"Quick, now. Let's go lord it up and get this done, huh?" he said. "Happy as clams, safe as houses, every one of us."

The chief of the road crew was, thank god, not any fella I'd ever run across while doing my business for King Steven. A big man with hair like a wire brush and a table muscle like he was smuggling flour in his shirt one sack at a time, he saw me and the lads coming and seemed to sag with relief.

"You the special men, I reckon," he said.

"Special is sure what we are," I said. "Dexter McThorphan, that's me. Lead engineer from the King's roadways and infrastructure working group. I hear you've been having some difficulties here?"

"To say the least. You seen the dragon coming in?"

"We did. Looks like you all settled her hash right nicely."

"Cost me three men dead and a five wounded."

"Them things that are precious are saved only by sacrifice," I said, quoting a line I keep saved up like a bullet on my tongue for them moments that find men in states of emotional upset and me not caring overmuch for their perturbations.

"What's that now?"

"Not important." I waved a dismissive hand at him. "Now the dragon, you took care of. And you sure didn't call at some godawful hour and rouse the Castle just to report one dragon, dead."

"No. Course not."

"Which means . . ."

The man looked at me blankly. I rapped knuckles on my case. "Which means that you called about something else, yes? Some other terrible thing come up out of the night?"

"Yes!" he said. "Yes, the dogboy."

At which point then I reached out, hung an arm over the chief's ample shoulders, and steered him away as though meaning to keep our conversation more discreet.

"Chief," says me. "That is *not* something you want to say too loudly now, you understand? Because finding a live dogboy? That would be impossible. There are no such things any more. And if there were, probably just *seeing* one would be a war crime. I mean, I don't know for sure that you'd be taken into custody and beaten with a hose until you called your own self a liar, but it might happen. I'm not saying that I've seen such things. But maybe, just between us, you can say that what you seen was a real ugly fella, right? Got him some kind of messed up face? Maybe looked a little like a dog, maybe he didn't, but you was suspicious. A little bit rattled after fighting off Bahamut there. So you made the call. No one can blame you for that."

The chief engineer nodded. "Yeah, but what we got down in the hole there sure as shit looks like a—"

"Looks like a plug-ugly sumbitch maybe wearing a bomb vest? A terrorist, right? Everyone loves catching a terrorist. Maybe wired-up with cyclonite? You know what they call a man who catches a terrorist? They call that man a hero, chief, and don't even *think* about cutting off his fingers with tin snips in some stinking cell beneath the Castle."

He seemed to chew on this a moment. "Sure. If you say."

"No, chief. Isn't *me* saying. It's you saying, understand? You got a man in a hole got blown in your road and you're worried that the man in the hole has a bomb. Big bomb. Big, dangerous bomb. And that's why you called the pros from Dover, right?"

"Okay."

"Okay!" I slapped him on one beefy shoulder. "Now why don't you point me in the direction of this unfortunate soul and the hole he's down in so's we can settle your difficulties and get you men working again."

The chief pointed off beyond the main reach of the night camp, out toward the flatlands and the foothills beyond where the morning sun was just beginning to flare against the smooth arc of the Free Republic dome and the little soap bubble arcologies that ringed it. "They's a big crater 'bout three hunnert yards off. Sections the entire roadbed, blows down through the aggregate base. Got a helluva ejecta ring, too. We think he's laid up in there."

"That way?" I asked, pointing in the way he'd pointed.

"Yup. And mister McThorphan, you can say what you like about what-all you find there, but this . . . this *thing*, it was hunting on that dragon, I'm sure of it. And it weren't happy when Larry put 'er down.

That's Larry Gould, from the security team. The one that put the rocket into her."

"Larry Gould," says me. "Got it. And how'd the thing end up in the hole then?"

The chief looked at me like that was the stupidest question he'd heard all night. "We shot it," he said. "And the hole was what it fell into."

Standing at the edge of the hole, we can all plainly see the predicament that both the chief engineer and the dogboy have found themselves in.

The dogboy's problem was that it was a dogboy, and therefore shouldn't ought to have existed at all. Further, it was hurt bad, crippled and stuck in the wet and muck at the bottom of a big-ass hole, from which it stared up, snapped its jaws, and told all three of us to fuck off in a voice like Barry White drowning in pudding.

I could see the mess of him, even from the lip of the crater. The ratty mane of hair that fell in lank mats from his head and down across his shoulders and bare back. The exposure sores on his long, ropy arms and strange, strong, clawed hands. The twisted hitch in one hip and gleam of wet metal where something had obviously gone terribly wrong with one of his cybernetic legs. There was blood on him. Maybe his, maybe not. Maybe old, maybe not. We couldn't tell for sure. Not from that distance. He rolled onto his back, watching us until, after a moment, he just leaned his head back and closed his eyes—swollen tongue poking out of his snout a little as he panted.

The chief's problem was simpler. He had an actual, honest-to-Jesus dogboy in the bottom of a big-ass hole, which was impossible for a dozen reasons, but was nonetheless true. The complication was what to do with it.

"I can't believe it," I said.

"Says the man who jumped out of an airplane and landed beside a dead dragon," said the Captain.

"This is different," I said. Because it was.

You have to understand, there was something just so horrible about it laying there in the seeping water and muck. So awesome. Like tramping through the pinewoods and finding a Bigfoot just setting on a log. Not a fake one. Not some mooncalf who'd got himself tweaked to grow Chewbacca hair. But an *actual* Bigfoot. A thing like you'd heard about all your life but never, ever expected to see.

Dogboys were nightmares come to life. Like proper, serious monsters in a world just full-to-bursting with half-assed ones. They were recursion hybrids—part human, part mutt dog, all full up with a stew of genes, randomly expressed, broken ladders clumsily thrown together in horizontal transduction processes, lab-grown teeth and eyes that could see into the far infrared. Roped down on Frankenstein slabs in Houston and basement labs in Beaumont and Galveston where the Texas secession had been plotted and born, all dogboys had begun the transformation as teenage "volunteers"—all boys, young as 12 but no older than 17, and all rabid for blood or violence or Texas. I imagine some had some pretty serious second thoughts when the doctors came at them for the first time with the bone saws and infusion serums crawling with customized viral phages full of Doberman and pitbull RNA. I imagine they fought hard against the restraints and argued eloquently that maybe Texas maybe ought to just stuff it up and quit bellyaching about freedom and independence if they was going to be the cost of it. But that's just the way of things, isn't it? Sacrifice always seems more noble when it's someone else on the slab. And anyway, there was no going back. Once you'd given your body to the cause, the cause would do with you what it would.

A year it took to turn a 15-year-old boy into a panting, long-jawed, rape-and-murder machine. Success rates ran to about eighty percent in the latter days, and nothing was wasted. The failing twenty percent were used as food for the survivors.

Dogboys had been the shock troops of General Kang and the Lone Star Rangers during the war for Texas Independence. They were strong, fast, had powerful senses of smell and hearing—synesthetic channels of input no human brain was meant for and which drove most of them insane before that first year was up. They could fight a garbage truck and win, jump through a second-story window from the ground, had all the gentleness of a whipped hound, combined with the wisdom, social grace and moral restraint of a teenaged boy.

Kang used them as scouts and stormtroopers, as minesweepers, as human bombs because each one of them went into the field with a dead-man's switch snugged up against his heart. If they died, they exploded: their bellies stuffed with tumors of Tovex blasting compound in caul fat sacks.

By the time the war was winding down to its bloody conclusion, Isabella Kang had thousands of dogboys in her army, all brave sons of Texas. Had factories that she called military academies which turned them out like sunglasses. They fought in the trenches in the North. In the swamps and bayous in the East. In suicide waves, bounding and leaping across the sands in the West.

They would turn on their own side sometimes, but that was fine. They could be detonated on the spot by remote, and there would always be more to take their place. Handlers would chain two dozen of 'em down in the back of a semi, drive it into Tucumcari or Lawton, Oklahoma, then let 'em loose in the dead of night and run without looking back. The screams carried on the cool night air would be proof enough that they were doing what they were made for—killing and raping and eating everything they saw and, if you were lucky, remembering to do it in that order.

At the end of the war, part of the terms of settlement were that every single dogboy be destroyed. General Kang was only too happy to comply. They were monsters, she said. Unfortunate horrors that would be the shame of her life, but whose memory, she hoped, would remind a rapidly fragmenting America of the lengths to which the people of the Lone Star Republic would go to preserve and defend their freedom and autonomy. There'd been a weight of threat in those words that no one missed.

She signed the execution order herself. In a lovely gown of executioner's black, she stood as witness to the destruction—watching her fiercest weapons driven with shock rods and water cannons into blast furnaces or detonated in open fields and then plowed under by robot bulldozers. For that, General Isabella Kang won for her people all of Texas south of Plainview and east of Fort Stockton. A republic of their own—soaked in blood and charred around the edges, but powerful, proud and rich in a way that didn't bear counting.

How this one down in the hole had survived the executions, didn't none of us know. How it'd lived so long (ten years, at least) without being found and destroyed was something either miraculous or deeply frightening, depending on your particular memories of the Lawton Massacre, the Battles of Tishomingo and Sandy Creek, or whether you saw the vids from Shreveport as it fell—the barricades being overrun, the flood of dogboys like a wave crested with teeth, crashing against the backs of the fleeing defenders with nowhere to run as the rockets rained down and the Red River caught fire afore them.

"This is different," the Captain echoed. "It is."

"Gotta kill it," Logue said. "It's hurtin'."

We stood close to the lip of the crater, all in a line. Had the dogboy below been healthy, it could've leapt the distance easy and I wouldn't have given odds even on big Logue Ranstead surviving the ten following seconds without choking to death on his own blood or something worse.

The Captain nodded, but said nothing. He reached into his jacket and pulled out what appeared to be an old-timey pirate's spyglass—snapping it open and cradling the front lens of the thing on tented fingers.

"Oh, baby . . ." he said quietly. "What did they do to you?"

I looked back over my shoulder. We'd left the road crew standing in the arc of their own lights, which were just a glow behind us, becoming less substantial as the minutes crept on toward daylight. It was gonna be a warm day. You could tell. Even in the gloaming of the morning, there was a brittle dryness in the air.

The Captain was quiet. He leant forward, as though straining his own eyes out of his head to see. Runnels of dirt and gravel trickled from under his boots and ran down the side of the hole. Logue stood with his hands at his sides, slowly curling and uncurling the boiled hams of his fists.

"'S'unnatural," he said.

"It certainly is that . . ." said the Captain distractedly. He straightened up suddenly and handed me the looker. "I want you to take a close look," he said. "Then I want you to chat a moment with Logue and me. Then I want you to go back there to those boys and tell them they have to stay well back. That we're going to blow the thing up ourselves and that it is going to be very dangerous. Got it?"

"Got it."

"Now look."

So I did. The Captain's spyglass wasn't exactly what it appeared—the brassy case of it having been packed with a King's paycheck in gadgets and electromacallits so that when I put my eye to the oculus I was suddenly staring straight into the Dogboy's face like I was close enough for kissing. The thing read heat and contrast, had tiny little flaring numbers and sigils in the corner like that might've been heartbeats and respiration, distance, drop, windage, hat size, and what the monster'd had for supper last night. Who knew?

I startled back a bit at the intimate closeness of it and started a minor landslide of gravel. This was enough to rouse the thing, which opened its eyes. Looked straight up and into me over the bulldog cast of its scarred muzzle. Its dog teeth had worn black grooves in its lower lip. Its pugged nose was dark and trickling blood.

From beside me, I heard the Captain's voice. "Look at the hip," he said. "The break."

And again, I did, seeing the mangled flesh there, old scars where the hair had burned away and left the skin below mottled black and rough. The silvery gleam of broken microhydraulics bleeding fluid across the skin.

"He's dying," I said. "And slow."

The Captain took the looker from me, collapsed it, and tucked it back into his jacket. "Survived this long all on his own, and now he gets put down by these idiots? That just doesn't seem right, does it?"

"Nothing about this is right," said Logue.

"The question is how did he survive at all?" I added. "All the dogboys were destroyed."

Logue rumbled like a grumpy volcano.

"Those burns on his hip," the Captain said. "Toward the end of the war, the factories were running short on supplies so started using cheaper explosive compounds. Homebrew, mostly. Chemical dynamite mixed with old motor oil, polystyrene packing peanuts and house paint. Didn't always fully detonate, but most times it was enough. Even if the boom didn't kill them, having a belly full of poisons surely would. But Spot here . . ." He cast another look down into the hole. The dogboy snapped weakly. "Looks like he got a particularly shitty batch. It burned him, but never blew. Or maybe just blew out that joint in his hip, though that might be new. I don't know."

"Lousy way to go," I said.

"Ain't no such thing as a good way to die, boy. It all ends the same way." He straightened up, yanked down on the short front of his jacket to straighten the seams. "You remember what to do?"

"Push back the rubes," I said. "Wait for the boom."

"You got it. We're gonna call the bird back in and nuke Spot from the air. Logue?"

The big man turned to look at The Captain.

"You go up with Holcomb and what's-his-name. The pilot?"

"Lemming," said Logue.

The Captain tilted his head. "Seriously? Our pilot's name is Lemming?"

Logue nodded.

"Jesus . . . Anyway, you're up in the air. I'll call the shot from down here."

I turned and started to walk back, but the Captain called out. "When it's done," he said, "you bring that chief and some of his men in to check the site, okay? Have a nice close look and see that we done our job proper. I want them to see everything."

I nodded and said I would. I heard the Captain talking to Logue as I walked off. "A minute of your time, Mr. Ranstead, if you would . . ."

I explained to the chief engineer what was going to happen next. Told him that when my boys were done in that hole there weren't gonna be nothing left that would look like dog, boy or anything else.

"Gonna be dust," I said. "Maybe a puddle. Road's gonna be tore up something awful, but you and yours are just going to forget what you saw completely and get on about your business. Clear?"

"I get ya," the chief said.

I told him to pull all his people back to the opposite side of the camp and to put them under cover if there was any to be had. "One helluva boom coming," I said. "We don't want any more of your people injured."

They went to ground behind the container trucks and the security team's APC. The Osprey came in over us, went to hover in the vicinity of the hole, then came down to pick up Logue. It stayed on the ground for a bit while, I assumed, the Captain gave instructions to Holcomb and Lemming, the pilot. And then it stayed on the ground a bit longer still.

The chief was sitting in the dirt beside me, his back up against the skin of a mobile lab unit. He leaned out to peek around the edge and asked me, "There a problem, Mr. McThorphan?"

I turned to look down on him where he sat. "If there was a problem, my radio would be going off, chief. Do you hear my radio going off?"

"No."

"Then what does that tell you?"

I did not have a radio, but he didn't know that. And not having a radio did not change the fact that my radio was not going off. "My men know what they're doing," I continued. "Just sit tight."

After another couple minutes, I saw the whipped dust and heard the thwopping of the rotors as the Osprey lifted. It withdrew to hang just short of our position, slid a little this way, then a little that way. Rocket pods hummed out from hatches in the wing-pits and locked into place as the Osprey dipped its nose.

"Fire in the hole," I said. Everyone ducked and looked away.

The firing of the rockets was like a sibilant *Sssss* beneath the pulsing of the twin props. The crumps of their impact was something we all felt in our feet and bellies more than heard. And then there was a secondary explosion—a sharp, percussive *pop* that rolled and echoed across the flatness. Dust bloomed. A scratching hail of pulverized stone rattled down like a sudden burst of summer rain.

And then it was done. Simple as that.

"Is that that, then, Mr. McThorphan?" asked the chief.

"I believe so," I said. "Have a feeling you might have a bit more repairing to do now than you did this morning."

The chief stood, slapping palms against the thighs of his dungarees. "And getting a late start, too. You'll tell the Castle we was inavoidably delayed or something, will ya?"

I assured the chief that I would, then told him to gather up a couple of his top men so's we could all get out to the hole and have a look at what remained. "An assessment is what's needed, Chief. Have to account for myself to the tops-and-tails back at HQ, too, don't I? So they'll know I've been about the kingdom's business and not just skylarking and taking in the scenery."

Above us, the Osprey was flitting about somewhat wildly. Tilting this way and that. Bucking its nose around. I tried not to make a big thing out of looking, but something seemed not entirely right.

The chief brought four men up, three senior engineers and his road boss, and we walked the distance between the night camp and the hole (which was now significantly more hole-y) in silence. Gray dust and tendrils of stinging smoke clung to the ground. Everything was crunchy with debris. No one figured anything could've gone wrong until we were nearly right up on top of the hole.

It was one of the chief's men who called the first halt, holding up a ragged scrap of gray-green cloth that looked like it might've been a sleeve cuff, bloodied at the tear, though the blood was dust-colored from being snowed upon by all that'd come up out of the hole.

"That thing in the hole," said the chief. "Wasn't wearing no clothes, was it?"

It was not. Or certainly not a field jacket, stitched over with patches and insignia from a dozen-odd services. I suddenly had this terrible feeling in my belly. And it only got worse when we got near to the crumbling edge of the hole and found one boot, badly damaged but with no foot in it, that was most assuredly one of the Captain's tankers.

There was goo. There was more bits and scraps. I expected to trip over his head at any moment, but didn't. I was thinking that, of all the thousand ways to die these days, this one would've been on no one's list. Blown up by one's own airstrike while trying to kill the world's last dogboy.

There was, behind us, the thwopping and roar of the Osprey coming down, blowing grit and badness up into a storm of shit to which we showed our backs, cupping hands around our eyes to keep from being blinded. The chief was talking, but I could not hear him. I was just standing there, staring down at the boot by the edge of the hole. I shoved at it a little with my toe, scuffed at a smear of something that looked a bit like strawberry jam all chunky with gravel near to it.

Logue came. Bulled through the milling crowd of engineers. There wasn't no dogboy in the hole, of that they were sure. And the damage that they were going to have to repair was extreme. But no one was complaining. Not at the moment. Not with another man missing, probably exploded. Or not where I could hear them, anyway.

"Your man . . ." said the chief.

I said nothing.

Logue took me by the shoulder and shook me. "Gotta go," he said. "Cap called the coordinates short or something. Got blowed all up."

I said nothing. There was something about the boot. That there was no foot in it, for certain. That it was so *close* to the hole, not blown half a mile away like it would've been had there been a man filling it at the instant of badness.

Logue shook me again. Harder this time. Enough to rattle my molars. I looked up at him and he met my eyes without blinking, angling his head in the direction of the open and waiting Osprey.

"Gotta go, boss. *Now.*"

"Right," I said, then "Right. Gotta go. Chief!"

"Yeah, Mr. McThorphan?"

"We have to go. Back to the Castle to report this. I think you'll have no more trouble here, and you boys know what to do."

"Yessir. We do. And I'm sorry about your man."

"As I am about yours," I replied. He reached out to shake my hand but I slapped him on the shoulder instead. There was a strange moment. Two men whose gestures on manly condolence had all been used up and done wrong. I looked away, watched Logue retreating up the ramp, which had been angled away from the hole on landing.

"Fuck it," I said and took off after him at a speed walk that likely didn't have much dignity to it. The Osprey's engines were already powering up. I screwed my hat down tight on my head. My goggles were around my neck again and the propwash made my eyes sting in a way that nearly looked like I was crying.

Holcomb was closing the ramp even as I ran up it. Logue was inside the main compartment, his arms crossed and his back pressed up against the forward bulkhead. On the deck of the Osprey, held down with levered cargo straps and obviously heavily sedated, was the dogboy.

The door to the cockpit was open and Lemming was yelling back. "Ten minutes out, max. That's cutting it awfully fucking close, guys."

The copilot turned, too. "Yeah, seriously, Duncan. What'd you do, crawl?"

It was the Captain's voice and the Captain's smile and the Captain's face when he snapped up the visor of the helmet he had strapped on. The Captain in shirtsleeves, his jacket missing. And with one bare, pale foot.

"Thought you'd gotten yourself blown-up, Captain," I said.

"Did it convince the yahoos?"

"I believe that it did, yes. Thought they might throw a funeral for you right there on the spot."

He nodded. "That's a successful day's work, then."

I looked down at the dogboy, laid down on its side with its paws curled tight against its broken body. Its tongue was hanging out. It was panting gently. "We're taking this with us?" I yelled over the sound of the clanging gate and the engines cycling up.

The Captain nodded and gave me an enthusiastic thumbs-up. I felt a lurch as the Osprey left the ground and reached out to steady myself on one of the seats.

"So you found yourself one of the most dangerous creatures ever made by man. Something that was supposed to not even exist anymore. And you, what? Decided to bring it home with you?"

"Absolutely," he said, grinning so wide it was like he was trying to bite his own ears. "I've always wanted a pet."

I nodded as though this made perfect sense. As though there was nothing suicidally ridiculous about it at all. The Captain squeezed his way out of the cockpit and walked unsteadily back with one boot on and one boot missing. He passed Holcomb, who took the copilot's seat, then came and squatted down to stare at his prize and fret.

"What'd you put him down with?" I asked.

"Ketamine and ether," he told me, picking at a bit of plastic film on the back of one of the jumpseats. "Didn't take much. Any more might've killed him."

"What happens if he wakes up?"

The Captain thought about that a moment. "Don't know," he said. "Maybe we'll die. Or he will."

Intermission: A Brief Tour of Historical Battlefields of the Early 21st Century

The sun came full up and we flew under its glare, close to the ground and on no rational course. Holcomb called the Captain forward, then he came back and said to Logue, "It's all over the air now but the descriptions are no good. 'Three men in a stolen tiltrotor aircraft masquerading as officials of the King's civil council?' That could be anyone."

"Told you," Logue said. He was sitting as far forward as he could get—on the floor with his back against the bulkhead. He kept an eye on the dogboy, aware of every twitch and groan. "There are easier ways to fake dying."

"But the jacket? The boot?"

Logue shrugged without looking at the Captain. "If they sniff around some, word'll get back. He might believe it. Might not. A body would've been better."

The Captain looked at me. "It was briefly discussed, using your body as a double for mine. Pieces of it anyway. Logue was all in favor."

When I looked at him, the big man was staring at me, eyes flat and guiltless. Then he looked back at the dogboy.

"I voted no," the Captain continued. "There is no part of you pretty enough to pass for any part of me. Even my spleen is prettier than yours, guaranteed."

Holcomb was passing rearward, edging his way carefully around the dogboy, and he added, "Plus the DNA, blood type, structure and markers are all different." He stooped to look for something in black shock-proof case that'd been lashed to the decking. "Hair color, eye color, height, age, scars, dental records . . ."

"Yes, but I voted no on the prettiness factor alone," said the Captain.

"So why are you faking your own death?" I asked.

"For the drama," Logue answered. "Does this every six months or so."

The Captain gave Logue the finger and crouched down, holding onto a seat with one hand. "Don't listen to him," he said. "I did it so I could come back to life at an opportune and dramatic moment and confound the plans of my opponents."

"See?" said Logue. "Drama."

Holcomb edged around the dogboy again and set down on his hunkers near its head. He had some kind of gadget in his hand that looked pistol-y and expensive and he spent a moment fiddling with bits of it while the Captain talked.

"That's how it always works in the soap operas, isn't it?" he asked. With his free hand, the Captain reached down and laid his fingers in the divots between the dogboy's ribs. The skin was gray-brown with filth, but hairless. He watched his own hand rise and fall with the thing's fast, shallow breathing, then looked back up at me. "You remember soap operas, Duncan? *General Hospital*? *All My Children*? That one with the doll that came to life? You're of an age, aren't you? A lot of what I know, I learned from soap operas."

"I'm pretty sure you're the first person that's ever said that, Captain," I said.

And he just laughs a little, gently pats the dogboy's side, and watches as Holcomb does something with his gadget—poking it into the creature's slack mouth and scraping it around.

"Anything?" the Captain asks.

"Patience," says Holcomb.

"Not something I have in spades right now."

Kevin Allen, if it matters. That was his name. The dogboy.

We know because he told us. One of those things that everybody forgets is that dogboys could talk. That they were, firstly, *boys*, with a boy's brains and a boy's ways. Got them a terrible kind of accent, what with their mouths being all doggish, but they could talk.

So Kevin Allen was his name, but we never called him that. Way the Captain looked at it, he was unique, so's we just called him Dogboy. Kevin seemed fine with that. And in all our wanderings, we never saw another, nor heard of one. Near as I can say, Kevin was the only one that lived. He was the last of his kind.

We flew for a while and a while.

Eventually, we settled down onto what seemed a different earth. When Holcomb opened the flank door, dusty sunlight poured in. The smell of warm dirt and living things. I looked out and saw a razed field, burn-scarred here and there, but otherwise golden and wild. There were giant rolled hay bales gone green from rotting and a cacophony of buzzing and clicking and whistling which was the music of the natural world performing its symphony to no human ears.

The Captain clambered out, followed by Logue. Holcomb (who, I would later learn, was actually Doc Holcomb, though he was only a tooth doctor and not the cut-you-open kind) stayed near to Dogboy because he seemed to be maybe coming around. Or maybe just dreaming of rape and killing. It talked, though none of us could then make out what it was saying. Perhaps that was for the best. Holcomb had sealed the worst of the leaking holes in Dogboy while he slept. Had cleaned them, filled them with liquid meat and sprayed them with knitters. He'd shaved a patch of skin clean and thumbed on a rainbow of sticky dermal patches: sensor mites, analgesics, antibiotics, blood purgatives, tiny doctors. The white bandages looked like flares burning coldly against the dirty brownness of the rest of him.

I followed Logue who followed the Captain who wandered out into the sunlight and the field like it was an ocean, his arms held out to either side, palms down, as though patting imaginary wave tops.

"Where are we?" I asked, but no one answered. There was no road. No homes. No man-made thing broke the table of the land for as far as I could see. A city boy, me, I felt the sudden urge to cower under so much sky. To go to ground, snuffle the soft earth, and listen for the distant approach of unseen dangers.

The Captain stopped and turned in a circle, eyeing the small rises and falls of the landscape, the way it folded into a roll of hills off in the middle distance and how the eye leapt the reach of a shallow valley to catch on a stand of tall, straight pines that'd never known the touch of plague.

"It's not here, Cap," Logue called, but the Captain pretended not to hear him. He began walking in widening circles, kicking at clumps of dirt with his one boot and tufts of prairie grass that'd sprung up where wheat or alfalfa hay had once ruled.

Logue scuffed at the ground with his boots. He stepped up to one of the fermenting bales and pushed at it until it began to fall to pieces. Then he repeated, "It's not here."

"It is," said the Captain, chopping a hand at the ground. "This is Theta FMU."

"Is not."

"Is. I have a map."

"Where?"

The Captain sneered. "Here," he said, pointing to his head. "You think I'm going to forget?"

"Your map is wrong."

"It's here."

Logue stopped and put his hands on his hips. "I will bet you one thousand dollars that it's not."

"Really? A thousand dollars?"

Logue nodded. The two of them started arguing over terms and I grew bored and walked off a bit, my hands in my pockets, just enjoying the day until I happened to snag a foot on something buried under the matted duff of the field. It was a cable of braided steel, about as thick as my finger. I called out to the two of them and both shouted at me to freeze. Not move. Not even breathe.

"Booby traps," said the Captain, coming at a limping jog in his one boot. "Sometimes, but not always. Just stay still."

Logue squatted down and took the cable between two fingers. It was slack, so he lifted it off my foot and pushed me back a step—one big hand flat on my chest. The Captain looked in both directions that it ran.

"There," he said, pointing to just another hay bale, sitting about fifty feet off. "Right under there. Go look, ya big lump."

"Why me?" asked Logue.

"Because you didn't believe me and I can't abide faithlessness. Also, my foot's cold."

"Your foot."

"Gave up a good boot for the defense of the realm today, didn't I? What have you done other than get up early?"

Logue grumbled, but he went, stomping off in the direction of the bale, then kicking it hard.

"No booby trap," he yelled back over his shoulder.

"What is it you're looking for?" I asked the Captain.

"Theta FMU," he said. "Field Medical Unit. There's a few of them buried around here." Then, to Logue. "Is it there?"

Logue nodded.

"You owe me a thousand dollars, son!" he yelled.

"No, you owes me a thousand dollars *less*," Logue yelled back.

"Come on now," said the Captain. "Let's go see what kind of treasure we've unburied."

☢

It was a hatch. A metal hatch, bunkered in a concrete slab, covered over with the hay bale that Logue had kicked up. Beneath the hatch was a metal staircase with a stretcher lift built in. At the bottom of the staircase was a small, white room, pocked with bullet holes and smelling of plastics kept too long under cover. And then there was a door.

"Surgery in there," said the Captain. "Robots. All automated. Which I think will give Dogboy a better chance than he has in the hands of a former tooth mechanic like Doc Holcomb."

Dogboy was fetched out of the Osprey. Logue carried him the way he would a babe, cradled in his arms with Dogboy's head pillowed against one massive shoulder. The monster's jaws snapped. His tongue lashed out over his nose. He was talking again, but so quietly it just sounded like breath.

Holcomb and the Captain busied themselves in the surgical suite. The lights were dim and flickered. There was a lot of buzzing and, once, a shower of sparks. The surgeon was a tangle of articulated limbs tipped with tools and needles and probes, all dangling from a central nub in the ceiling. The bed on which Dogboy lay was a wafer of white plastic three inches thick and layered with electronics like a parfait. There were drumheads of sensors built into the walls. Panels full of buttons and touchscreens and monitors, some of which were lit and some of which remained dark like dead eyes in white plastic sockets. In the keeping room, Logue stood tirelessly, holding Dogboy, stroking thick fingers down the filthy mats of his fur and watching the progress. I sat and began rummaging through cabinets built into the white plastic walls—finding nothing in some of them, but some things in others. And then I amused myself by poking fingers in bullet holes and wondering to what violent uses this place had once been put.

In time, there was an argument between Holcomb and the Captain. Holcomb stomped up the stairs past where I was standing and, shortly after, I heard the door to the surgery hiss and suck itself closed with a sound like a switchblade knife snapping open. I peeked around the edge of the wall and saw Logue and the Captain both standing with their heads together, looking in through a tiny observation window.

"He gon' live?" Logue asked.

"Yup," said the Captain.

"You know that or you just guessing?"

"This is one of the things I know," he said.

The day wore on. I climbed back up to the surface at one point to smoke a cigarette and no one moved to stop me. From the base of the stairs, the sky through the hatch was a rectangle of pale blue into which I climbed, only to find myself once more treading upon the earth with the sky above me and hidden things below. In the distance, Lemming and Holcomb were netting the Osprey and garlanding it all over with greening clumps of hay—trying to make it invisible from the air or any reasonable distance.

They played like children, the two of them. Throwing clods of dirt, chasing each other around the aircraft, colliding and falling and rolling in the dust.

There was no wind. My smoke rose straight into the sky like a post. And when I turned to go back down through the hatch again, it'd become a black mouth in the ground. A door into night. It looked, if anything, like an open grave.

In the keeping room of Theta FMU, Logue Ranstead had fallen asleep.

The Captain had produced a deck of cards and bid me play a game where the pairs and straights and flushes didn't matter but points were gained for catching the other man cheating.

He was good but I was better. This was because the Captain had never had to play for his next drink, his next meal, or his life. A game could just be a game to him. Even the important ones, he still played for fun.

"There is nothing in this world worth dying for," he would sometimes say. "Because if you die, then all the fun is over."

He didn't live that way, but that was how he talked. There were times when I'd think that all he was about was finding something to die for. That searching after martyrdom was the wholeness of his being. But for some reason, death kept missing him. Sometimes closely. Sometimes by a mile. Some men are like that, you know? Slippery. And the Captain surely was one.

"How'd you know this place was here?" I asked him.

"I have a map."

"In your head, yeah. You said. But how'd the map get in there?"

He looked at me across the upturned crate we were using as a table and I took the opportunity to slip a jack of hearts. "Now *that* is the question, isn't it?" he asked.

"It's the one I'm asking."

"Hmm . . ."

I called him out for palming a three. Then caught him dropping a nine of clubs.

"Well?" I asked.

"Oh, you expected me to answer? That's funny."

He dealt a fresh hand of five cards each and I noticed that the deck was growing thin from all the drops, pulls and snatches that'd gone uncaught.

"You're bottom-dealing," I said.

"Did you *see* it, or are you just assuming because of the evidence before you?"

I picked up my cards. Between my hand, my sleeve and one boot, I had the makings for a jack-high straight. The only trick was outing it together.

"Look around you," the Captain said to me. "Tell me what you see?"

Just a small room, I told him. Cabinets. Medical supplies. Himself, myself, Logue asleep and snoring. And on the other side of the sealed door, a monster.

"More," he said. "What else?"

Playing cards, I told him. A collapsible pellet stove upon whose altar we had burned some coffee earlier until it'd tasted like tar sweetened with powdered milk. The cups from which we'd drunk. The spoons with which we'd stirred. Bullet holes.

"Yes," he said, snapping his fingers. "Holes. And above us, the earth. Stripped of trees, scarred from fire. Walk north a thousand meters and there's a creek. Not a big thing, but handsome. Laying down in a fold in the land deeper than a man is tall. Kick around enough and I bet you find some shell casings, bits of this and that. Pretty sure there's still half a Sentinel body buried a ways up, too. Fell right where it got cut in two."

He spread his arms then, looked up at the rough cement nothing of the ceiling. "This back here? All of this was behind the lines. Had exfil. A machine pit. Motor pool. We laid in six of these field medical units and they were beautiful, man. See, you set off a sonic mine, and it does this thing where it basically turns the dirt to liquid. Does it with sound waves. Just jiggles everything up until its like pudding. So we do that, and then we just have the FMUs choppered in, dropped right in the middle of the soup. Switch off the mine and the ground turns back into ground. Just locks up tight. It's a cool trick. Kind of thing we could do back when there was all the money in the world and wars enough for everyone. Nowadays, OSS gives you a shovel and a box of band-aids and tells you go bury it in the backyard. Bingo: FMU."

His cards were on the crate, lying facedown. Untouched until he laid a finger on the first of them and held it there. While he'd been rattling on about Sentinels and sonic mines, I'd coughed, scratched the back of my neck and gone searching for more cigarettes. Thus,

I had all my cards mechanic'd up nice and right where I wanted them. The Captain, I'd thought, was hardly even paying attention anymore.

"So anyway," he continues, tapping now with that one finger on his first card, "you take all the evidence and what do you think happened here?"

And "A battle," says me. "Big one."

"Exactly. But you didn't see it, did you?"

Of course I hadn't. Matter of fact, I hadn't even seen the creek he was talking about, nor any of the other of it neither.

"So, then, did it happen, or am I lying."

I went to speak but he stopped me.

"And remember," says himself. "I *did* know where this place was."

"Did not," muttered Logue without opening his eyes.

"Tell you what, Duncan," said the Captain, ignoring Logue. "This hand before us? If you win it, I'll tell you the truth of what happened here. Which, I might add, is something I've never done. But if my hand beats yours, my secret stays with me. Fair?"

No, I thought. It wasn't fair at all. I was holding a jack-high straight. The odds of him beating me on a natural draw were, what? One in a million? In ten million?

He tapped his finger on his first card again. "Also, I win, you have to give me one of your boots."

It never occurred to me that he hadn't turned over any of his cards. That he hadn't even looked.

"Deal," I told him. "Show your cards."

Yes, I know it was a sucker bet *now*. Everyone is a genius in retrospect. Isn't that what they say? Or everyone is a genius on the day after? No, that doesn't sound right either . . .

Anyway, shut up. Sitting in that hole with the Captain, I had a jack-high straight. And if you're not going to bet it all on a hand like that? Then son, you got no business playing the grownup's game.

The Captain flipped over the deuce of clubs and I smiled at the tickle as my odds jumped.

Then came the deuce of hearts. And of diamonds. And I was no longer smiling. He flipped the deuce of spades and I laid my cards down.

He asked me, "What were you holding?"

"Straight. Jack-high."

"Gotta bet on that," he said. "No choice but to." He laid a finger on his last card now. "What size boots are those?"

"Ten," I told him.

"Perfect." He turned his card. It was a deuce of hearts. An *extra*. He had five of a kind.

"Where are we anyway?" I asked him.

"Nowhere," he said. "Place called Jackstraw Creek."

Logue woke, rummaged, found food and cooked it. Holcomb and Lemming remained topside, even when the smell of frying corned beef hash and powdered eggs drifted up and out of the hole.

The Captain peered into the surgery through the little window in the door but did not break the sterile seal.

"Doc Holcomb's angry with you over this, you know," Logue said.

"No, he only thinks he ought to be." The Captain tapped on the glass lightly with one knuckle. "This was somewhat beyond his capabilities. Deep down, he knows that."

"He's pouting in the bird with Lemming, though."

The Captain shook his head, chuckled gently. "Pouting ain't what they're doing in there, Logue."

I thought about the two of them chasing each other in the dusty sunlight, dodging and ducking and falling to the ground together, and smiled.

Eventually, I fell asleep.

I woke to a quiet like the grave and thought that I'd been abandoned again. The keeping room was dark, as was the surgery beyond. And both were empty now, touched only with the leavings of temporary residence and the lingering smells of scorched coffee, canned hash, antiseptic spray, and the hot, sour, tinny smell of sterilizer lamps and medical nanolithography.

It was one of those moments where, like in one of them old movies, someone would pass out during a party, or get knocked down somehow, and the next thing he knows he's waking up in the afterclaps of wrack and ruin and he says, totally confuzzled-like, "How long was I asleep?"

This was just like that. The coffee cups was cold on the crate table. The plastic plates and eating irons was unwashed. The cards was still laid for a losing hand of solitaire. And the only difference was, I didn't say that stupid thing, but sat up and said, "Motherfucker done it to me again."

At which point I hear a scuff and a rattle from up the top of the stairs and a sound like a dinosaur choking on a chicken bone, which was Logue clearing his throat.

"If'n you're awake down there, princess, come on up now."

I found a slick plastic bottle of purified water, cracked the foil seal with a thumbnail, poured some over my head, and scrubbed fingers through my hair. Wiped my face with a towel that drank the liquid away and used the hydrogen and oxygen and the oils from my skin and dead cells to thicken itself and grow. Then I sucked down the rest of the bottle myself and let my body perform the same trick, though it is somewhat more impressive when done by a towel, I guess.

"I'm coming," I yelled, limped to the base of the stairs in my one boot and one stockinged foot, and looked up into a soup of stars. And *then* it was my time to say, "Jesus, how long was I asleep?"

"All the dregs of the day," Logue said. "And you was scratching so damn much, I finally come up here just to leave you to it."

I walked up into the night and found Logue standing alone, limned with moonlight like a small planet in imperfect eclipse. The wind was fresh and cool on the land and it carried nothing but the smell of living things going on about their green business, unconcerned by the tribulations of man.

"No Captain?" I asked.

Logue shook his head.

"Dogboy?"

Logue shook his head again.

"Don't figure they left the Osprey for us to toodle 'round in?"

"You know how to fly one?"

"No."

"Neither do I."

"Well then . . ."

We stood in silence a moment, then Logue said, "Three things you gotta know. One, don't talk about what we do. Two, don't think about it too much. Thinking makes for questions and questions won't do you no good in the long run. Three, everything is disposable. Especially you."

I nodded. "You give this speech to everybody?"

"When I'm told to. Most don't never need it as they's here and gone without never knowing what they was on about. But the Captain seems to find you fetching, so you get the speech. There's a longer version. You wanna hear it?"

"No. I think I'm good with the abridged."

He raised up then onto his toes, stretched, rolled his head on his shoulders, yawned hugely. "Home is that way," he said, pointing off into the moonlit dark. "Just start walking and you'll do fine once you hit the road."

"Walking?"

Logue nodded.

"How far is this road?" I asked, and Logue considered this a moment before saying, "Far."

And then he turned and, aiming himself in the opposite direction, walked off into the night.

"Where you going?" I called out to him.

"Business," he said, his voice fading.

"Well, can't I just come with you?"

"No."

And then Logue was gone, too, and I really was alone.

So I walked fifty careful paces off in the direction he'd pointed and then went to ground. I waited and I watched and when I was reasonable sure that no one was doubling back to the hatch—that the whole bunch of them wasn't just hiding out in the bushes and waiting for me to get myself gone so's they could have a party without me or something—I went back, stuffed my pockets, my briefcase and a sack made from a pillowcase with all the medicines, tiny gadgets, freeze-dried food, and sealed water I could carry. Theta FMU was like a goldmine to a scavenging sort, and who knew if I was ever going to be back.

The going was not easy. One boot is worse than no boots for walking, so I took off the one the Captain had left me, wrapped both feet in strips of bed sheet padded with foam, and set off walking.

Logue had been right. The road was far. But I caught the glow from it after about an hour's stumbling through the dark and, after two, came upon its crumbling apron and mounted it like a man discovering a new land.

And there I sat, under the cold haze of the highway lights, waiting and just knowing that I wasn't going to be doing no more walking that night. There was someone coming. I knew it. I knew somehow that this had been *intended* on the part of the Captain and that, were I just to sit long enough, some new opportunity would present itself.

Around me, the night was dark and, above me, the sky aswirl with stars. I lit a cigarette and quietly smoked it, feeling with my feet on the pavement for the distant rumble of approaching traffic. I had the spooney notion of laying my ear to the ground like an Indian guide, but didn't. There was no need. As I had during certain moments while in Madam's employ, I felt watched. As though an entire complicated architecture of things and people and events were rotating around me, some of them hinging on me, others constantly informing the Captain as to my whereabouts and well-being.

It was a ridiculous, giddy feeling. Totally mad. But that didn't mean it weren't also true. And that night, I meant to have the proof of it, one way or another.

In the far distance, a bank of lights crested a rise and began to draw in toward me. I heard the rumbling of a powerful engine grinding along in low gear and felt the thrum of vibration in the roadbed. I smiled into the night, squeezed the ember off my handroll, and tucked the dog-end behind my ear. This was my ride. I was as sure of it as I ever had been of anything.

I stood. From out of a clever, hollow place in my briefcase, I drew one of my dumb-phones. The satellite signal was weak, but there was one, so I dialed the only number in the phone's memory and held it to my ear.

It rang as the growl of the oncoming vehicle grew louder. There was a click. The call went to the voice mail of Pork Chop Express Carting and Haulage.

"Leave a message," the phone said. "Or don't." I waited on the beep.

"I got the speech," I said. "I'm in."

I snapped the phone closed and shoved it in my pocket. The machine had drawn close—treads clanking, engine huffling like some live thing. It was a tank, covered in blown plates of reactive armor over slabbed Chobham, its main gun covered in a skin of bright, looping graffiti. Crude teeth had been painted onto its front glacis, cavitied with the spangs of bullets. Buddhist prayer flags and banners of the Western Confederacy flew from the whip aerials that sprouted off the back deck.

The commander's hatch opened with a clang and I was blinded by the beam of a spotlight pointed directly in my eyes. But I could hear a voice. A girl's voice. And she was hollering down to me because there weren't no one else there to holler at.

"Hey, you are in the middle of fucking nowhere, man! You need a ride or something?"

EPISODE

3

The Perilous Life of Miss Holly Bright, Part 1

THE NAME OF THE GIRL IN THE TANK WAS MISS HOLLY BRIGHT—late of Bowie, Sweetwater, Last Chance, and even worse places in between. She was young and smart and fast and pretty as a summer peach, with short hair the color of cinnamon candy and bare legs, skinny and bug-bit, sticking out of a pair of cut-off fatigue pants in a big man's size. The shorts were cinched around her hips with a length of parachute cord, tied in a neat bow. She wore rodeo gloves with rope scars on the palms, a grease-stained white tee shirt with the neck and sleeves torn out and big, black boots with steel plates strapped onto the shins.

"It is hotter'n a motherfucker in here," she said by way of, maybe, explaining herself, but maybe not. "Thing's pro'lly got an air conditioner somewhere, but I'll be *damned* if I can find which

149

button it is. I stole'd it, you know? This tank? Well, kinda I did. So it didn't come with no . . . whatchacallem."

"Owner's manual?" I offered.

"That's it, bud!" she yelled over the growling of the engine, a smile blooming on her face with the joy of a fresh dawn as she reached out and punched me on the shoulder. "Course I taught myself how to drive it. 'Ventually, anyhow. And I'm doing good, right? Can keep her even mostly on the road."

I loved her immediately. Who wouldn't? She was a car thief and a getaway driver. An expert, she swore, in anything with wheels and an engine. An orphan. A runaway. A deserter from a youth camp in Enid or the Arkansas Home Guard or maybe both. She preferred chopsticks to a fork. Had once stolen a small airplane and driven it, on the ground, for forty miles before getting bored and lighting it on fire. Knew every word to every song Public Enemy and Metallica had ever done. I learned all this in my first five minutes with her, all the while just trying hard to maintain a gentleman's demeanor and not stare straight at her tits or to bang my head on any of the hundred different hard and sharp things protruding from every angle of the crew compartment inside her maybe-stolen tank.

"What happened to your shoes?" she asked.

"Lost one of them gambling," I told her.

"Just one? That's a strange bet."

"I was playing against a strange man."

She did something with the controls. There was a bang and the tank lurched forward like it'd been bee-stung. She laughed as she fought to keep it going the direction she wanted.

"You going to try to rape me?" she asked. "You some kind of weirdo or sex pervert?"

I assured her that I was not either of those things. She turned and looked at me, eyes jumping up and down the latitude of my less-than-handsomely-put-together self and then staring straight on at me, her face briefly serious.

"I don't want you to take the impression that the way I'm dressed is some kind of comment on my morals or my character," she said. "The way I'm dressed is just the way I'm dressed. It is not a . . . wha'dyacallit. A signifier of my womanly weakness or desire to be possessed by any fella. Can you get your head around that?"

I told her that I thought I could. "How's about I don't judge you on your lack of pant legs or a bustle and you don't judge me on my lack of shoes. That fair?"

And she smiled. "Eminently," she said. "But just in case you change your mind, I got me a dentata. Big fucking teeth down there. Bite your dick clean off."

"I will endeavor to restrain myself, ma'am. Honest, I'm just thankful for the ride."

She turned her eyes back to the road before her and the straight shot she had through the ocean of the night. "Then we're gonna get on just fine, bud. Gonna be about four hours 'fore we see civilization, so wha'dya wanna talk about to pass the time?"

We talked about where we'd been and what we'd seen there, where we were currently and where we were going. In all cases, I lied smoothly and skillfully and so did she. Or I assumed she did. When that was done, we talked about the roads, the various dangers that walk upon them, and how all but the most scarifying creatures were made significantly less so when you were rolling around with a 120mm smoothbore canon on your back. And when that was done, we talked about the weather.

She told me that, back home, she had a garage full of cars she'd collected. All classics, but her favorite was a 1969 Chevy Camaro, tuxedo black, with the 302 factory small block and Hurst shifter. She told me that she'd worked as a coyote along the Texas and Arkansas borders (which I found doubtful for my own reasons), moving them that wanted to be where they weren't back and forth across the line until they were where they thought they wanted to be. Sometimes she did it for pay and sometimes she did it because she didn't cotton to things like borders or them that saw to enforcing them. She'd also run guns and drugs and tech and 'shine, done a little chemical bootlegging when it suited her, and had been all the way to California and back on one mad-cat jag, all tooled up on red-eye and military-grade stimulants and not sleeping a wink for forty-odd hours. If it was true, it made her one-in-a-million. "Seen the ocean and everything," she said, hand over her heart. "Looked like nothing special. 'Course it was nighttime."

Somewhere in the long dark, we passed a convoy of trucks moving with no lights and she had me get in the loader's seat to check them out through the periscope. By the time I figured out where to sit and how to raise the gadget and which buttons worked the infrared and light amps, the trucks were long gone. I apologized, then asked if there were any shells for the main gun and she just laughed at me. "Just keep your trigger finger away from the big red switch, okay cowboy?"

Later, she told me that the tank wasn't really stolen. That it had been more or less abandoned and that she'd been watching it for days, from a hide-out on the flats. Just her, a couple gallons of warm water, a pound of venison jerky, and nothing for company but the first two fingers of her right hand. She was waiting to see if anyone came back to claim it, that tank. And when no one did, she got to thinking that such a lovely and powerful machine must get terribly lonely just sitting around without no one in it making it do what it does best. So she'd stolen it mostly because she couldn't stand the thought of it being sad.

"That's sweet of you," I told her.

"Machines ain't meant for sitting still and neither am I. That's why me and them get on so famously."

We drove through the night and on into the morning and, all the while, I managed not to behave in any untoward or ungentlemanly fashion. Wasn't that I wasn't thinking about it, but still. Girl had a *tank*. And pretty much, if you're the one with the tank, you're the one gets to make all the decisions.

When she'd gotten me as close to the city as she reasonably could without raising the hackles of them who might wonder at what a tank is doing in their neighborhood, I dismounted, offered my thanks, a tip of my Stetson, and said goodbye. She smiled and told me she liked my hat. Told me to stay safe. Told me that if I just walked thataway for a mile or three, I'd likely run across someone willing to haul my shoeless self back to civilization, provided I was able to pay. Leaning out across the commander's hatch of her tank with the sun in her hair and sweat beading on her bare skin, she was one of the shiniest and most purely beautiful things I'd seen in an age. An image of all that is raw and fearless in womanhood. A tiny piece of the divine.

I had to turn away—to shade my eyes with one hand and gauge the arc of the risen sun—before the effect of her became apparent south of my belt buckle.

And then she buttoned up.

And then she was gone.

"It's alright," I said to myself and the wind. "I'll be seeing you again soon enough."

I watched after her dust for a time, then shouldered my sack of pilfer, picked up my briefcase, and got to walking. My foot-wraps held for a time. I walked on grass where there was some, or the poison ruin of the earth when there was not. I strapped on my gun to discourage bad men, avoided all signs of life and habitation, was briefly menaced by a brain-damaged household 'bot that'd been holed through the middle by what looked like a cartoon canon but had dragged itself across the wild lawn of a ranch house offering me a haircut or a nice ham sandwich and called me a pussy-faced communist when I politely refused.

"I'll find you, mister," it said, vat-grown eyes rolling in its ceramic sockets, dirty and shredded fingers clawing at the tufts of HiGro in what had once been the front yard. "You think I won't, but I will. I've got a knife and I will find you and I will end your pathetic, filthy meat life, mister. Mister!"

A few blocks later I found a pedicab driver sitting in the middle of a four-way intersection, staring up at a swaying, broken traffic light and picking distractedly at the sprung corner of a light tattoo on his shoulder. I traded him a blister pack of antihistamines for a pedicab ride back to Miss Kitty's. Bought myself a bath, one joint, and a hot meal of fried eggs, crumbled vegetable protein and last night's noodles served across the bar (during which I deflected all questions as to where I'd been, what I'd been doing and what had happened to my shoes), then retired to my room and slept until the sun went down.

That night, I played piano. I rousted drunks. When folk asked what had happened with me, flying off the roof and all and disappearing for a day and a night and most of a day, I told 'em that I'd had a wedding to attend, that Banjo Oblongata had called me away to play with him and the Malfunctions at Red Rocks at the last minute, that I'd gone to consult with the President of America on vital issues of state.

My regulars had missed me and worried over me, which I found heartening in a way I didn't expect. Reggie (who Madam called Colonel Happenstance because he was, in fact, a retired Colonel, and was the sort of man who was always just happening by when interesting or embarrassing things were happening) was already sitting there when I settled in behind the Regent for the night. He shook my hand, bought me a tall glass of beer and asked me if I'd had myself a suitable adventure. One-Eyed Annie kissed me on the cheek and asked me to play "Hard Luck Blues," which she sang in a soft, husky voice only loud enough for me and the Colonel to hear.

When, near on toward dawn, Madam corralled me at the bar and put the hooks to me, asking the same questions I'd been dodging all night, I told different and even less believable lies. And when I was sure she wasn't believing me a bit, I handed over a middle quarter of the medical supplies I'd hooked from Theta FMU (not the best of my plunder, but not the worst neither) by way of apology for my unexpected absence and to buy my way out of any more interrogating.

"I'm a resourceful man, Madam," said me. "And sometimes I'm of a mind to spread it around some. That alright with you?"

But she was already making the spoils disappear behind the bar and, after that, didn't seem to botherate much over my comings and goings.

Of all the things Miss Holly Bright had claimed she was, the one thing I *knew* she was was one of the Captain's crew. She never said so during our ride and I never asked, but I knew it. To be her and to be there, in that place, at that moment? It was impossible that she was otherwise, wasn't it?

Thus, I decided that I'd keep an eye on her—a decision made, really, in my first minutes of knowing her, but firmed up during my constitutional walk across the contraction zone. Because if she was the Captain's girl, I figured, and operating under the Captain's orders, then she was also my way back to him. And I had no intention of waiting another month or more for him to remember me again and come looking. I had a job to do, me. I had orders. I needed to know what the Captain was about. I needed to know where that machine brain had gone and how Dogboy was fairing and why he'd needed to fake his death and a hundred other things. Also, life was just more interesting with him around.

True, I didn't know how I might manage finding Miss Holly Bright again, exactly, but as I'd said to Madam, I was a resourceful man. Had once been moreso, but the basic skills were all still there. And just thinking on it—planning out who to talk to, what questions to ask, what holes to poke into—was like old habits and long-quiet muscles coming suddenly back into smooth and uniform action like a bunch of old geezers rousted up and stuffed back into their uniforms and asked to march for a Veteran's Day parade. I suddenly felt vital again. All kedge and hot-fired and, well, not young, maybe, but . . . I don't know. *Energized*, let's say. On my first morning back in my old room after my first night back behind the old 88, I made a list. First this, then that. Research the name. Find the youth home. The Home Guard commander. Anyone in Denver who might be in the market for one hot tank, slightly used.

But as things turned out, none of this was anything I had to worry much over because, for a time, it seemed that everywhere I was, Miss Holly Bright was, too.

Okay, not *everywhere*. But most-wheres, for certain. I saw her one night leaning up a post and jawing fit to break a bit while I was out joseying with Maggie on my arm. I saw her one night at Jezebel's in the Five Points where I'd gone to sit out a long watch and listen to the great juke there that'd survived already so many years of strange unpleasantnesses but still played Creedence and Lou Reed and the Mercury Brothers like they was new.

Holly never showed her pretty face at Miss Kitty's, nor at the Nob, but down on the Avenue one afternoon, while I was hauling up a load of top hats and coats I'd liberated from the cloakroom of a bougie drinking place outside of the red-lights and meaning to sell them at a neat profit, I saw her blusterating at a couple of beeps who had apparently committed some sin against her person. They was smiling down upon her with all the benevolence of unchecked authority, and because they wasn't busting her teeth out on the curb, they obviously found her more than a little cute, so I did not intervene. Had my hands full, anyway, didn't I? And the money on them coats and hats—even after kicking back twenty percent to the cloakroom girl who'd let me in to get the best pickings—was good enough to eat on for a week.

Anyway, yes. All of that could have been coincidence, true. Denver, big as she is, was still a small place where making enemies one night was dangerous simply because you'd like as not end up shoulder-to-shoulder at a piss trough with 'em the next day or the next.

But when I saw Miss Holly Bright knocking the boards of the high street in Golden (where I'd gone on a short jaunt with a couple fellas to be their Fourth Man in a running cartage scam they had working), it was enough to make a mash on me—to prove, at least in my mind, that she'd been put on me deliberate. That she was the Captain's eyes into my doings while he was away and, therefore, my way back into his good grace and company.

That's what I thought. I was dead wrong, but that's what I thought.

Just one day in Golden had fixed me up nicely, and the lads who'd brought me in on the cartage game (irregular upstairs customers at Miss Kitty's, them, called Jack and Asa and Julio Reconquista De la Teja, who everyone just called Julie) were right scoundrels with good eyes for money and fast hands for spending it. I liked them and they liked me—at least well enough that, when a fresh business opportunity presented itself, they come to me and asked if I'd care to throw in with them again.

It was the sort of proposition which first required the finding of a red-nose establishment of the proper bad reputation and quiet temper in which to discuss it (which we did by gathering at a place called El Cielo off Broadway which, aptly, was situated underground), then procuring for ourselves just the right back-in-the-corner-type table appropriately wreathed in deep and beer-smelling shadows even at the crack of noon (which we got by dint of comporting ourselves like gruff and no-nonsensey types and then, when that failed utterly to impress the axe-faced maiden ministering to the gathered lushes, asking pretty, pretty please).

And even once the preliminaries of atmosphere had been rightly seen to, there was still buckets of swill beer to acquire and appreciative noises to be made over the various accoutrementation that'd been acquired by each of us since last we'd split, our pockets all a'jangle with coin. I, for example, had paid honest money for a new pair of justins—tooled leather the color of milk chocolate and honey, with high pipes and low heels, and new, soft socks to wear them with. Jack had got a dust tattoo done. A glossy black snake that shimmered like oil as it slithered up and down his arm and, on command, would curl into his palm and turn into a dollar sign and the words, EVERYONE PAYS. Asa had four arms and had bespangled near every finger of his second set of hands with fine rings. And Julie had gotten one of the two breast implants he was chomping after and proudly opened up his shirt to give everyone a look and a feel.

It was nice work, I'll give him that. But as he well knew, it was fixing the downstairs plumbing and tackle that was really gonna cost him. Which was why the boys was all so hot on this newest scheme.

"Horse cum," said Asa with a grin when it finally came time to get down to the business at hand.

"Did you say whore's cum?" I asked. "Speaking as an expert on the subject, I'm fair positive there ain't no money in that."

"Asa, you speak politely now, bru," Jack insisted, rattling his pint glass on the table, his wildcatter's accent and strange, up-jumped slang growing thicker as he drank. "We's gentlemen here and will, perforce, talk as such."

"Not whore's, Duncan. *Horse.* As in . . . uh . . ."

"As in horses," said Julie. "Like giddyup, you know? Horsies." He had one hand inside his shirt and was scratching delicately at his surgery scars.

"Horse *semen*," added Asa again, glancing at Jack, who nodded happily at his use of the medically correct terminology. "Like from horse cocks."

I held up both hands in protest and was about to say something hilarious when Jack leapt into the conversational breach.

"We's got a man," he said. "Knows him another man who works up north of the nationals at one of the Mountie stations, right? And this man—"

"Which man?" I asked. "First one or t'other?"

"The second man."

"Caleb," said Asa.

"Asa . . ." Jack whined. "I like Duncan, too, but that don't mean we tell him ever'thang about our business. No names. We agreed."

Julie laughed, then rubbed at his one boob with his wrist.

"Sorry, Jack," said Asa. Then, to me, "Forget I said that, okay, Duncan? Ain't no Caleb."

"Got it, Asa. And Julie, you keep picking at that it's gonna get infected."

"Itches like the goddamn dickens."

"Next time you come by Kitty's, I got something that'll help. Just remind me, alright?"

Julie smiled. "Thanks, Duncan. You're a pal."

I raised my glass to him and Jack cleared his throat.

"Can we get back on the business at hand now, boys? So this second man . . ."

"Caleb," said Asa.

And then Julie laughed so hard that he upset two of the glasses on the table and Jack couldn't help but laugh, too. And then we needed new drinks. And then had to drink them. And this all went on for longer than it ever ought to have, but that was the way with Jack and Asa and Julie. Like the Three Stooges, them, only heavy-armed and crake-smart and criminally minded in the way of men who can make a living off it without no one ever catching on.

Anyway, what it all came down to was that they knew a man who knew another man named Caleb who worked as a groom and smith at one of the Canadian Mountie stations up along the border near Wild Horse and Milk River Lake. And this man Caleb, he owed money to the first man who knew Jack and Asa and Julie. Quite a lot of money, though how anyone could get so in hock to anyone in such a place as the trees outnumbered the people ten-thousand-to-one I have no earthly idea.

Caleb's notion of getting square? Collecting about a hundred ounces of prime horse semen and handing it over to the first man. The first man was then going to sell it to Jack, Asa and Julie for about twice what the debt was, then Jack, Asa, Julie (and, presumably, me) could re-sell it for about a hundred times that, with the understanding that we were still taking a fat loss. The kink was that Caleb knew how much the stuff was worth (and would be taking a healthy percentage of the profits after his debt was cleared) and *we* knew how much the stuff was worth, but the middle man? He was apparently not that bright. Vicious by reputation, easily goaded to anger and not so good at taking a joke, but just dumb as a cold hammer. They were bringing me along as a fast mouth and a spare gun. All's I'd have to do was stand there and be clever.

"We don't have to actually . . . uh . . . milk the horsies ourselves, do we?" I asked.

"Nah," said Jack. "That's Asa's department."

Julie made blowjobbery motions with his hand and tongue and Jack flicked beer foam in his eyes.

"Savages!" he snapped. "The bunch of y'all."

I took a long swallow of my beer. "If you can't laugh at jokes about sucking off horses, Jack, what can you laugh at?"

"And ain't a *one* of them horses ever complained," said Asa.

"Tell him you was a veterinarian, Asa," said Jack.

"I was a veterinarian," said Asa. "And the horse cum—"

"Semen."

"—has already been harvested. It'll come frozen in a cryo kit. Just like a bunch of popsicles."

"Horse-flavored," said Julie.

"Delicious," said me.

So with a hundred ounces of liquid horse in our possession, we would be rich. Actual meat horses were rare and valuable things in the West then. Desirable, for certain, but fairly delicate creatures who didn't fare well walking through fire and eating poison and whatnot. Automatic horses were more durable, sure, but didn't have that vaquero cachet of the real thing, you know? So we could piece out the horse spunk to breeders with mares in season and make a couple large fortunes. We could bring it to a clip shop, let it go by the milligram to them that just wanted the ladders to tinker with, and make a whole bunch of tiny fortunes. Or we could take it out into the zone, to any one of a dozen black clinics, and have actual meat horses built for us, straight up from the genes. They'd be clones. They'd be sterile. They'd take a while at growing. But they'd be horses and we would have, depending on the fail rate, a virtually inexhaustible supply. We'd be horse barons. It was one of those plans that was so good, something just *had* to go wrong.

And soon enough, something did.

There was no honest reason why Miss Holly Bright would've been in a place like El Cielo save that she was following me. But when she came down the stairs and through the door and saw me seeing her she got this look on her face like it was *me* that was doing something wrong. Like what honest reason did *I* have for being in a place like El Cielo save that I had obviously fallen in love with her and was following *her* all over the city with certain stalkery notions of collecting up all her used napkins or mailing her my ear or something.

But I was there to drink beer and talk about horse semen with my friends, so's I was the one with the reason for being there. Plus, I'd shown up first. So it was her that was plainly following me.

I mean, that's what it looks like, right? I wasn't being crazy?

Anyway, the minute she comes through the door, she spots me and gives me this look like to wither me from the inside out. A look of pure, furious shock, settling into anger, then resignation—like I was banjaxing some carefully calculated plan of hers merely by existing.

And maybe I would've thought that and gotten out of her way if she had done something or said something, but instead, she did *nothing*. She just shakes her head, makes a very deliberateish show of turning her whole back on me (which, anyway, was my second-favorite view of her), gets herself a single beer and a single joint from the bar, sets down the one, lights the other, and falls onto a stool in the middle of the long oak with her shoulders hunched and her head hanging down. Does not look at me. Does not say a word or give a sign or nothing.

And as a matter of fact, she is *still* sitting that way when comes through the door four men of less than savory aspect, who seem to have eyes only for her.

Snake-eaters, them. Hard-road men in leathers and iron who looked to have been many miles without a bath or civilizing comfort. There was a fat one and a skinny one. The fat one had a beard that did nothing to hide his hungry smile. The skinny one had a twitch, slow, dull eyes and a bad case of the morning shakes. The third one was older. Wiser, perhaps, as he'd come through the door last, or perhaps was just slower. And the fourth wore a bowler, a pair of pince-nez that gleamed with enlivenment, and the remains of a once-fine gray suit over a boiled shirt going yellow with sweat and grime.

They were bad men. Worse, they had the stink of artificial law all over them. And even though Asa was, at that moment, laying out the plans for the handover of the liquid horse—using all four hands to move glasses and napkins and half-eagles around the table like a mutant Patton—I'd stopped paying attention and knew from my guts up that things were about to go badly. Probably for me, as that was just the way of things. Knew that much going in, me. I was, as they say, accepting of the ways that fate was going to have with me because coming four-through-the-door with mean eyes for a girl alone at a bar? That was no way for a gentleman to behave. And I was not the sort to let that stand.

They clustered up just inside El Cielo's door, the four of them, and made their battle order—Glasses in front, Fatty and Twitchy at his shoulders, and the old man hanging back with one hand up under his duster in such a plain "I have a scattergun here" kind of way that I doubted if he had one at all.

Was wrong about that, too, as things turned out. Guess it just wasn't meant to be my day.

The three of them approached Miss Holly Bright who, outwardly, made not the least sign of having noticed bad things approaching, though I could see her hands bunching into tight little fists and the way she unhooked the heels of her boots from the rung of the stool.

Asa was droning on. There was a clap of laughter from the lads, loud enough to temporarily grab the attention of the advancing party. Glasses looked in our direction for a long second and I made a show of just pulling at my beer, paying no one no mind, while Julie said something and Jack slapped a hand down on the table, trying to draw the meeting back once more to some semblance of order.

Glasses dismissed us. He and his lined up behind the girl and he said something near to her ear I couldn't hear. I saw Holly draw hard on her joint, could almost hear the ember crackling as her cheeks puffed out and she let the smoke leak from her nose.

"Lads," I said, pushing back slowly from the table. "You're gonna have to excuse me a moment. I think I'm going to go get punched in the face right now."

Glasses reached out and laid a hand on Miss Holly Bright's shoulder. She spun fast on her stool and expertly flicked her joint into his face, exploding it in a shower of sparks against one lens of his pince-nez. I was already up and moving then, half a glass of beer in one hand, wrapping the other in a towel I'd filched from the far end of the bar as I came on.

Glasses jerked back. Holly pushed him and he tangled with his two friends.

"Don't you lay your goddamn hands on me," she shouted—loud enough to get the attention of everyone in the bar who wasn't already paying very close attention—and followed up with what appeared to be an exceedingly weak slap in the direction of Twitchy. When she saw me coming, I could swear she shook her head at me. I could swear I saw her mouth the word "No."

"Gentlemen," I said—meaning to launch into a whole *The lady doesn't seem to appreciate your attentions* kind of speech, but never had the chance. No one, in real life, ever does. I got exactly as far as "The lady—" when the badges started coming out.

"We're Regulators, Lancelot," said the fat one, opening his voluminous jacket to show me the silver badge clipped to an ID wallet shoved in his shirt pocket. "Back off."

"I appreciate the literary reference, sir," said me. "Do you prefer the Malory or the Tennyson?"

"The what?"

I smiled. "That's a pretty tin star you got there."

Which was the point where Miss Holly Bright screamed and the skinny one tried to hit me and she lashed out a wicked kick in the direction of Glasses and I swung the beer glass (now transferred to my towel-wrapped hand) in the direction of Fatty's head, connected with his shoulder, and sprayed everyone liberally with cheap beer and broken glass.

I heard chairs banging over, which was likely my boys coming to join the ruckus, but knew already that they'd be too late. I was hit from behind and saw stars, allowed myself to stagger forward into Fatty's enveloping, beefy arms, put my hands up and got in a head butt that took him in the teeth hard enough that blood ran into my eyes.

The hostess and the bartender were shouting. I saw Miss Holly Bright jink under a wild punch from Glasses and him snap an arm down, throwing out a telescoping shock rod to its full extension.

Fatty hit me with both hands in the middle of the back, slamming them down like he was swinging an axe. I had my face in his beard and it did not smell good, so I pushed with both hands, not moving him in the slightest but bouncing myself back to get a little swinging distance. I heard Holly scream. Saw her hit the floor, all stiff and spitty and curled up around where Glasses had stroked her across the belly with the shocker. And when I looked back, it was to see one big fist coming my way with bad intentions.

I stepped into it, taking the worst in my forehead and didn't really feel it when Fatty's big hand connected. He did, though, and started jumping around with his (hopefully) broken hand held between his knees. Frankly, I was just glad to finally have an excuse to go down—falling face-first with my hands beneath me.

The boom of the shotgun in such a confined space was enough to command the attention of the room. For my part, I pretended to be asleep.

When the echoes of the shot had died, the old man spoke. I couldn't see him from where I lay, but could hear him just fine.

"Everyone cool out now," he said. "Everyone just cool out. We are Regulators, executing a lawful warrant for the apprehension of this woman, and I got five more sandbags in this here gun for anyone who feels like playing the hero. They won't kill ya. Probably. But I've every intention of aiming low and making it so none of you drunks ever breed again."

There was nothing but a ringing quiet. I felt hands on my back, but they were gentle—shaking me and trying to see whether I was dead, not going after my watch or wallet.

The old man spoke again. "Rufe, bag that little cunt so's we can absquatulate these premises please. And Harold? Harold!"

"He broke my goddamned hand!" said Fatty.

"No, *you* broke your goddamned hand on his goddamned head. Now stop hopping around like a fairy and get the fuck outside."

I knew I had a kicking coming and so tensed up waiting for it. But apparently, Jack and Julie and Asa had formed up around me and wasn't about to let that happen.

"You already put him on the ground, big fella," I heard Jack say, his voice eminently reasonable. "Ain't no cause to be nasty."

"And I ain't making much use of my fuck stick these days, so I'm happy to take one a'tween the legs if it means I get me a piece of you."

That was Julie, and I had to bite my own lip to keep from grinning.

There were groans. Scrapings of furnishings and the crackle of boots on broken glass. The door creaked open, slammed closed, creaked open again, then the old man's voice once more.

"There's no cause for rousing the beeps on this, y'understand? That's a bad woman we're taking off, and we're only doing our job." Pause for effect. Perhaps a tip of the hat. "Pleasant afternoon to y'all."

And then the bang of the door one final time. Footsteps on the stairs. Regulators were not law in any formal sense. They were man hunters, trackers, private investigators with cereal box badges, and guns for hire that anyone with the silver could put on like a suit of artificial muscles. A Regulator had all the legitimacy and loving kindness of a hot pistol or a midnight repo man on the prowl. The righteous law hated them, as did their own mothers, most like. A public brawl, a daylight kidnapping, the discharge of firearms in public—none of these was unusual activities for a Regulating man, but they would still be in a great hurry to get quit of the area afore they was noticed by them as might like to feed those stars to them slow in a windowless cell somewhere.

I counted five Mississippis, then rolled over and stood up, a bit bloodied and achy about the back, but feeling all aces otherwise. My brain was going ten miles a minute.

Jack said, "You okay, Duncan?"

Jack said, "Who was that girl?"

Jack said, "Duncan?"

I turned to him and slapped him on one shoulder. "Right as rain, Jack," I said. "Right as rain. And thank you boys for throwing in and backing my play."

"Got yourself beat down pretty hard there, boy. Going three-to-one didn't seem fair," said Asa, who was rubbing at his belly with his extra set of hands and breathing a bit crook-wise.

"Might not've looked like it, but I won that fight," I said. Julie laughed. So did the barman, who'd been cowering behind his long oak through the whole thing. "Son," he said, "that was the losingest fight I ever seen in here."

I whirled on him. "Must've been tough to see from down under the taps, friend. So perhaps you missed the best bit." At which point I turned back to the lads and lifted my hand to show them the badge and wallet I'd stripped from the pocket of the fat man called Harold while he was busy beating on me and taking a bite out of my forehead.

"That girl was a friend of mine and she done me a service once. I mean to go and rescue her. You fellas fancy an adventure?"

It took a debate and vote amongst the fellas, but it came out two-to-one in my favor, with Jack being voted down and apologizing after.

"We got us a chance at some real money with this horse deal, bru," he said. "I'm just concerned that this will get in the way of that."

"I understand completely, Jack. But I'll promise you this: If this bosh ain't resolved sweetly in a day or less, it won't matter a damn and we can part friends or throw in for the horses or whatever you choose. Fair?"

He shrugged. "Fair enough. I ain't one to let down a friend."

"Least not when outvoted," said Julie.

"So what do we do next, Duncan?" asked Asa.

And "Don't worry," said me. "I've got a plan."

I did not have a plan.

What I had was an absolute understanding that Jack, Asa, and Julie needed to *think* I had a plan lest we lose the comradely momentum of the moment, and the firm belief that a plan would come to me so long as I could have a moment or two to cogitate upon this newest predicament.

So to give myself that necessary space, I did what any wise commander of men would do in a similar circumstance and sent Jack, Asa, and Julie up onto the street to talk to anyone who might've seen the Regulators making their getaway while I sat back down at our table, drank all the un-upended glasses of beer still sitting there and pretended to talk on one of my cell phones while waiting for inspiration to light upon me.

Eventually, it came. Not inspiration so much as a dog-dirty trick from my younger days, but it was a start. The idea sparked in me while I sat running my thumb over the badge of one Harold Lartner, aged 32 years and working agent of the Eastern Plains Regulator office. Harold Lartner, whose licensing papers and ID were full of identifying material like his thumbprint, retinal and helix scans, but did not include a picture. I smiled as I drained away the last inch of the last glass on the table, wiped my mouth, and dropped two eagles to cover our tab and damages.

Might not have no goddamn flying cars nor clean water nor cures for the common cold, but thank the good Lord for us living in a science-fictionated future, is what I thought. Because technology, no matter how smart, can be got the best of by the backward man nearly every damn time.

Up on the street, the boys were running harum-scarum like herd dogs trying to keep spooked stock in place. They'd grabbed up everyone they could lay hands to and asked them all the basics: *What did you see? How many were there? What were they driving and which way did they go?*

Them as were reluctant to answer got their cogs greased with half-eagles and kind words. And them as were thought to be holding out deliberate got threats, shouted up one side and down the other, or worse. The boys were loud and they were thorough.

Most of the street creatures was let go directly. But some few the lads had corralled up near on a crumbling wall which had once been the front of a music store, and there they were holding them to await my pleasure.

"So, Jack," I says. "What did we find?"

And he ran through the assembled, pointing and poking where necessary, showing me how this one said there'd been four men and a girl and this one said it'd been five, how this one said that they'd left in one car and that one claimed two.

I nodded thoughtfully, a thoughtful look upon my bloodied face as I dabbed at my forehead with a borrowed handkerchief. None of this was important to me as I already knew how many there were and what they looked like. It was the *details* which concerned me just then, and the choosing of the most trustworthy source.

"The girl," I said. "Did she walk or were they carrying her?"

Carrying, it was agreed. Between two men, with her head in a bag and the toes of her boots scraping the road.

"So unconscious then?"

Or dead, sure enough.

I asked about the vehicles, and this was where the argufying became strident. I was walking an eagle back and forth across my knuckles then. Holding it up between my fingers. Making it appear and disappear. It was for the hand of him or her that gave me the information I wanted. It and more of its friends. That was plain.

They had one jeep—open-aired and roll-barred—insisted some.

But no, said others, because they was yelling over who ought to be riding where and, anyway, no four men and one lady would fit in any one jeep anyhow.

Two arguments became four, became six, became eight. Hands were waved and voices raised, all to get my attention. None of it worked. I saw the crowd as a single body with many shouting heads, all of them stupid and wrong. All save one.

"There was one jeep," claimed a youngish man, his eyes hidden behind black sunglasses, hair sculpted into twin fins running at angles down the crown of his skull and hung at the back with the shredded remains of seagull feathers. He squatted against the rubble and sipped at a beaker of something blue, swirling with heavy elements like ribbons of mercury. His fingers were black with filth.

"The men," he said, "planned poorly. Dumbshits. One jeep was too small. Two of them—the old one and the fat one—go in the jeep with the girl. The others, the thin one and the mad one, they take a hansom."

The chattering mob ceased to interest me. The other faces, the other voices, all faded to static. "The mad one?" I asked.

And the man, he sets down his beaker and makes two circles with his fingers and holds them up to his eyes like glasses, bares his teeth, which are weirdly white and straight and perfect, and waggles his tongue.

"Glasses," I says.

The man nodded, picked up whatever magic potion he had in his Erlenmeyer. "Wanted to kill the girl, him," he said, taking another long, slow sip. "Cut her. Tie her to the hood like a buck deer."

"The jeep," I asked. "Was it heavy loaded? Have a bunch of *things* in it like packs and cases and gas cans?"

"Nope," said the man.

"Okay," says me. "This'n's the important one."

"You're gonna ask if I hear the mad one say where he wanted the hansom should go?"

"That's the one, bru. That's the nut."

"Then that's the one's gonna cost ya," he said. "Bru."

I told the lads to cut everyone else loose. Thank 'em, pay 'em, shake their hands, whatever. Just put 'em in the wind. And then I squatted down to look at the young man sharp, the wanting in my eyes reflected back to me in the black lenses of his glasses.

"Your lucky day," I says to him. "That girl? She's important. Name your price."

"Million eagles," he said with no hesitation.

"That's funny."

"Suck my cock then."

"Also not gonna happen."

"Then how bad can you really want her?"

"Look, if that's all you're after, I can set you up fine with one of the working boys at Miss Kitty's. Suck you inside out, from what I hear."

"Girl?"

"One of each, that's what you want."

He waved a hand at me. "Fuck that."

"You're stalling," I said.

The man sipped. The man rolled his head on his neck without ever taking his eyes off me. "I am."

"So what do you want?"

He watched me. From behind me I heard Asa say, "Time's running, hoss," and I ignored him. My knees ached and my back hurt, but I held to the strange man with my eyes.

"Be my friend," he finally said.

"Your friend?"

And he nodded. "Yup. Ain't got no friends here now and I'm tired of talking to myself."

I could've said yes, shook his hand and been done with it. Get what-all I needed and never see him again, sad little thing that he was. But I didn't do that because . . .

Well, I honestly don't know why I didn't. Just something about the fella, 'tween hay and grass as he was, that made me consider seriously his ask.

"What happened to your friends?" says me and, "Dead," says him. "Come up for the war, my crew and me, and by the time I turn around, the war's all done and all my boys is chewing dirt. So now I'm alone. Low man in the city. Got nobody. No action. Just walk around all day sucking my teeth."

"What's your name?" I asked.

"Don't matter," he said. "Ain't no one around to say it."

"What's your name."

"Some people call me Injun Joe."

"Your real name," I said.

He hesitated, then said, "Clarence."

I stuck out my hand to him. "Duncan," I said. "Pleased to meet you Clarence."

And Clarence shook my hand. Said my name. Smiled. "We friends now, Duncan?"

"Help me out and you are my man, from here to the end of the end."

"Broadway and 17th," he said. "Brown's something-or-something. That help?"

The Brown Palace, finest of the remaining fine rooming places left in the Queen City. Staying on the company dime, of course that's where a gang of road-dirty and repugnant sons-of-bitches would be.

"That helps, Clarence," I said. And Clarence smiled, those weird white teeth flashing again in the haggard mask of his face and a sudden age descending on him in a network of fine wrinkles around his eyes.

"That man, the one with the glasses? He gonna kill your girl 'less you get him. You like her?"

"I owe her," I said.

"She you friend, too?"

I grinned. "No, bru. Just a girl I know. If she was my friend, them motherfuckers never would've laid a hand on her."

I told Clarence to go to Miss Kitty's, to ask for Madam and get himself a bath and a bed and a hot meal and a tumble, all on my tab. "In that order," I said. "It's a class joint, so do it right." I said it was the least I could do, on the off chance that I got my damn self perished in the next few hours. But if I survived, I'd see him back there tomorrow night, down in the parlor, playing at the piano. "My friends get the good seats. And since I ain't got so many, there's always plenty of room."

He took the eagle from my hand and clamped it between his teeth, stood, looked around him at me and Jack and Julie and Asa, then tucked his hands into the back pockets of a pair of black jeans so dirty they shined with grease.

"I see you 'round, Duncan," he said, speaking around the coin. "You promised."

And then he was gone, strolling like a man with a steak in his belly and a hundred dollars in his wallet, ratty feathers bouncing against his shoulders.

After that, I gathered up Jack and Asa and Julie and told them I had a plan.

"You said before that you had a plan," Jack said.

"Yeah, well before I was lying. Now I have an actual plan."

"'Preciate the honesty, I suppose," said Julie.

"I feel less bad about voting against you now," said Jack.

"Democracy is a motherfucker," I said. "But this plan is a good one. Trust me."

I laid out the particulars. Right now, somewhere in the vicinity of the Brown Palace, I said, the Regulators were loading up their gear and making plans to get the hell out of Dodge, post-haste. They were long-haulers, these four. Out-of-town talent, brought in special by someone, and like as not in a hurry to get pointed in the direction of home. The Eastern Plains Regulators office was a long ways off—two hundred miles, maybe a little less—and if they were bringing Miss Holly Bright back in that direction, they weren't going to do it with the fuel in their tank and the junk in their pockets. The fact that they had no gas with them on their jeep, and no bags, made me think that they'd left their ruck behind when they'd come in for the capture. That they'd come in the daylight made me think they was in a hurry, too—had maybe just taken the chance presented to them and been hoping for the best. And that they hadn't thought about how they'd fit everyone in one unsuitable vehicle made me think that they likely had another one back at their hotel, and also that they weren't very smart neither.

I could've been wrong about any one of these things. As it turned out, I *was* wrong about several. But alls I had to be was right on one and we might have a chance at catching them.

"And what do we do if we do catch 'em?" Julie asked.

"Well, actually, we don't want to catch 'em precisely," I said. "I don't particularly like guns and I certainly don't like them pointed at me, so I ain't fancying on a throwdown in the middle of the street or the lobby of a fine hotel. All's I want right now is to know where they are and where they're headed."

"So's we can bushwhack 'em," said Julie.

"That's right. Gently if we can. The other way if it comes to that. But we're getting back the girl one way or t'other."

"Regulators ain't precisely known for bringing a lot of their bounties back alive, Duncan," Jack said.

"Then that's why we need to be quick. Any of y'all ever done any acting before?"

They had not, but they fell to the craft with a passion, my lads.

The gimmick was that with Harold Lartner's badge and ID, I could masquerade as a Regulator asking after them that had taken off Miss Holly Bright. I could get a room number, where their wheels had been laid up, perhaps where they was off to. I could bluff and bluster and bullshit as much as was necessary because a badge in hand is license to act as poorly and as rudely as one wanted. It was just what everyone without a badge expected of someone with one.

And the boys, they would be Regulators, too. My backup. All's they had to do was stand there and look mean, I explained to them. Wear guns. Look filthy and none too bright.

"Supporting players," I said to them, "are vital in laying the scene, you understand? Me alone is just one man with a tin star. But me and a tin star with you lot being all menacing behind me is a small army, capable of causing all manner of trouble for them as don't jump when I say so."

They all nodded. At which point we lit out for the Brown Palace with a whoop and a holler, meaning to be flat-out movie star heroic and, of course, couldn't find a cab.

"We could just go get the truck, Jack," Asa said, after ten solid minutes of him walking backward and fruitlessly waving all four of his hands at every hack, hansom, pedal-cab, and rickshaw that passed us.

"You have a truck?" I yelled. "And you couldn't have mentioned this earlier?"

Jack raised his hands. "We have a truck, yeah, but it's in the lockup."

"Where is the lockup?"

"Up in the Five Points. By the old water factory."

Which was in the direction we was walking. Kinda. Only a couple or three miles further on. Precisely zero help, in other words.

"Also, it ain't exactly meant for city driving," he added, but I just waved him off, quickened my pace, and told Julie that maybe he ought to start flashing his one boob at passing cars.

"That's hurtful, Duncan," he said. "You shouldn't ought to treat half a lady that way."

I apologized, shook my head, and we walked on.

The first hack that stopped for us was another twenty minutes later, when we was close enough that I could read the curlicued sign on the front of the Brown Palace's wedge-shaped, red-stone grandiosity. I scrubbed the sweat off my face with my now-stolen handkerchief, gave the driver the finger and told him to roll away 'fore I offered him worse. I was in a sour mood, but attributed it to my getting into the character of a fat, lunkheaded kidnapper of innocent(ish) women.

The Brown was a long and low-slung triangle of a building with a front corner like the prow of a stone ship cutting the waters of commerce that ebbed and flowed around 17th and Broadway. Surrounded by the broken fingers of arching, once-gleaming skyscrapers that'd previously been temples of money, power, and pulsing enlivenment, it'd survived the worst of the late unpleasantness simply because these all had made far better targets for the Kansan gunners to zero in on when they was lit up and looking to break some windows.

Still, there was a gouge taken out of the Brown's top point. And because the top floors had made excellent (and classy) nests for snipers, some windows still had graying boards up over them and the stone showed the scars of heavy calibers fired in anger. But all along the ground, flowers in a dozen colors burst from the pots; victory flags with the sigil of the Western Confederacy and the seal of the great kingdom of Denver fluttered from white-painted poles; and housemen in formal livery, with muscles on the twitch-cycle of store-bought implants, stood straight as sticks by the grand front doors.

We bulled right up to them, the boys and I. And like robots, they stepped aside and swept open the doors for us. In the grand lobby, handsome men and beautiful ladies of the Quality sat rigid over tea and toasts, their nanite veils parted within the comforting embrace of veined marble and armchairs made when the world was still young. In the bar at the Brown, Winston Churchill had smoked cigars and Dwight Eisenhower had plotted the Allies' western strategy. The Beatles stayed there. And Sun Yat Sen. Now birds fluttered around the bright dome of the atrium, having flown in through the shell hole and unable now to find their way out again. In a panic, they shit down nine stories and spattered the hats of fancy ladies and the thick Oriental carpet.

"There," I said, pointing to the reception desk. "That's the man we need. Stay close, gentlemen."

I took out the badge and led with that, affecting a thin blade of a smile and stalking menacingly toward the long expanse of polished wood behind which sat a single attendant in a spotless gray suit and a smart monocle. *Pushover*, I thought.

But then a tall, lithe woman in swirling silks, leading twin biogen greyhounds on gold chains, stepped thoughtlessly ahead of us and, without so much as a glance in our direction, started in on haranguing the concierge about whatever it is concerns fancy ladies and their dogs.

I was loath to just shove ahead of her. A real Regulator would've, for certain. Then grabbed a handful of rich ass besides, spit on her shoes and clubbed and eaten her dogs. But an act goes only so far and some niceties are burned in so deep that they can't be easily shook.

So we waited, me rocking on my heels and trying to look bemused, the lads idling behind me, as she did her business and three shuddering drays full of her luggage were wheeled past, pushed by stout men straining at the physical weight of such luxury.

In time, the woman finished. She turned away and, in the flutter of her veil, I saw the livid scars of closed staph aureus abscesses freckling her pale skin and the black bruising around her sockets where she'd had new eyes installed to replace those eaten away by infection. I wondered whose daughter she was that she'd survived that. Whose wife.

I tipped my hat as she passed and quietly clucked my tongue at how the terrible things of the world don't always discriminate in favor of beauty, wealth and grace.

At the desk, I showed Harold Lartner's badge and asked after my presumed friends.

The deskman gave me a long look through his monocle. "You're with them?" he asked.

"Not at the moment, no. And that is my difficulty, you see? We're supposed to meet them here. We've some business needs doing."

"Yes . . ." said the man. "I'm sure you do."

And then he said nothing.

And I said nothing.

He stared and I stared.

And then, from behind me, I heard Asa pipe up shrill—him being the one what was most excited about this opportunity at play-acting. "We're capable of causing all manner of trouble for them as don't jump when he says so!" he barked, running all the words loudly together and talking like no natural man ever has.

I smiled dazzlingly at the deskman, turned slowly around, gave Asa a blazing look, and calmly said, "Relax."

"Sorry," he said, looking about at the curious stares and the sudden quiet he'd caused.

"You okay now?"

"I am."

I patted him on one shoulder. "Good. Just . . . stand there, okay?" I turned back and, to the deskman, said, "Excuse my partner. He's a touch excitable."

"I feel kinda sick," Asa muttered behind me. I heard Jack and Julie stepping tactfully away. Saw the man before me's eyes widen.

"Your friends are already gone," he said quickly. "Perhaps you should follow them."

"Gone?"

"About fifteen minutes ago. They assaulted one of the bellmen, *ruined* the afternoon tea. Took their bags and left. As you should as well. Your friend, he doesn't look—"

"Did they have a girl with them?" I asked.

"They did," said the deskman, then leaned forward three millimeters—which appeared to be about as confessional as the man ever got. "And she did not appear to be looking forward to the trip."

I swore under my breath. "Don't suppose any of them mentioned where they was headed, did they?"

"No, sir. They did not. But if you could inform your superiors that your sort are no longer welcome—"

"Yeah, sure. Where were they parked?"

"Sir, I've already told you that your friends have departed the premises."

I stepped forward, laid my hands on his polished counter. "They didn't go walking and they're not my friends, pal. Not in the least bit. Now how 'bout you tell me where were they parked afore my partner here makes a mess on your rug?"

He squared his shoulders, the deskman. Looked cross at my ugly hands laid on the prettiness of his world and told me that I'd have to talk to the head valet. At my urging, he told me where the valet could be found, then shouted after me as I turned on my heel, took a rapidly paling Asa by one of his lower arms, and started to walk off.

"Sir, there was substantial damage done to their rooms. Would you be in a position to make restitution?"

"Call the Eastern Plains Regulator's office," I said without turning around. "Try your luck with them."

After Asa had caught his breath and re-swallowed his liquid lunch, we found the valet standing near to the mouth of an underground parking garage. He said he hadn't heard anything, but referred us to the man who'd brought up their vehicles—pointing down into the lamp-lit dark.

The man who'd brought up their vehicles saw the badge in my hand, immediately turned whiter than Asa, and rabbited. Jack and Julie gave chase, but only caught him because the man ran into a post while looking back over his shoulder at the closeness of their pursuit. When he came to, he wept until I explained to him that weren't none of us really Regulators, but just concerned citizens who happened to be in possession of a Regulator's badge.

After that, he called us all assholes and refused to speak until Julie poked a thumb at the goose egg on his forehead. Then he called us all a few more names and said that the *real* Regulators had said they were headed north for the old border, but that they hadn't said where.

"Just kept saying they was going to have a great time," said the car-parker. "They had a girl with them. She didn't seem like she was having a great time. But they were all laughing and carrying on."

"Carrying on," I repeated.

"Like they was on a frolic."

I asked after details—how many vehicles, how many men.

Behind me, Jack said, "Great Times."

Asa said, "Really?"

Julie said, "You think?"

The car-parker said four men, no more, and two vehicles. A jeep and a truck. Truck was small. A road truck, not a work truck, but loaded heavy for a long trail.

Behind me, Jack said, "Yeah, they would, wouldn't they?"

Julie said, "If they was headed north? Maybe."

"Which vehicle they put the girl in?" I asked.

The jeep, he said. She was cuffed. Gagged. They had a leash on her like a dog's and just kept talking about having a great time.

I felt Jack lay a hand on my shoulder. He said, "We got an idea where they might be headed, Duncan. Maybe let the man stand up."

"Stand up," I said to the man. Which he did, casting about with a wary eye.

"Y'all really ain't the beeps or nothing like it?"

"We really are quite the opposite," I assured him.

He looked us over, raised a hand to his head, rubbed fingers across the spot where he'd met with the post and spit.

"Why'd you run like that, boy?" Julie asked him.

"When you ever know a man with a badge to be bringing glad tidings?" he replied, then turned to me. "The girl," he said.

"Her name is Holly," I said.

"Yours?"

"Just an acquaintance. But I like her a lot more than I do the men who took her."

And he said, "Hmm," and then "Well . . ."

From behind me, Jack said, "Think we got us an idea, man."

"Great Times," said Julie. "Shit."

"They're bad men, them that took your girl," the car-parker said.

I nodded. "They ain't Samaritans."

"Straight buckra. And they got the wild eye on 'em, too, you know?"

I said that I did, hooked thumbs into the pockets of my blue jeans and rocked back on my heels. "You sound like a man trying to convince hisself of something."

The car-parker said no and scratched at one cheek. "It's just that, them men? I ain't altogether sure they was Regulating, if you know what I mean."

"I surely do not," I said.

"I mean they wasn't working. That girl, she wasn't a bounty. Or maybe she was, but not one of the ones they was here to be hunting after."

"How do you mean?"

The car-parker looked off into the dimness of a corner of the garage. "I walk over that way, y'all gonna chase me down again?"

"What's over there?"

"Just something. If them men are of interest to you, I might have something you'd like."

"Where?"

The trunk of the back half of a fine town car, he explained, of which the front had been crushed completely by a falling piece of ceiling. He had the lid of it booby trapped with a screamer alarm and a 12-gauge side-by-side with its triggers wired together, the barrels cut so far down that they were shorter than my thumbs.

"Impressive security system," I told him.

"Yeah, well you can't trust no one 'round here," he muttered, reaching in under the lid to carefully detach the cord that would drop the hammers on the scattergun were the trunk popped indiscriminately. "Criminals, all of 'em. I ain't never seen such sorts."

Inside the trunk were a dozen purses. A plastic bag full of cigarette lighters. Another one full of phones. Fancy shoes. Sunglasses. Hats. Dozens of owner's manuals, all stacked and bound with fat, red rubber bands. There was a garland of air fresheners, a small cardboard box half-full of loose cigarettes, another one of pistols, another one of pill bottles and pharmacy vials and rolls of derms and a sticky paper bag stuffed with weed. Two assault rifles, a Winchester repeater and a shock-rod were bungee-corded to the inside of the lid and there were papers everywhere—in stacks and folders, stuffed in sacks, bound with string.

"We warn folk not to leave anything in their cars," he said. "That we ain't responsible for any items lost or stolen while the vehicle is in our care. Some people just don't listen."

I whistled low. Asa craned his neck over my shoulder to look and said, "Respect. Nothing but respect, bru. For serious."

He shrugged. "Yeah, well, this is for you, then." He took a plain folder from the top of one of the stacks and handed it to me. "Was right in the glove box of the jeep. I mean, the glove was locked, but then I had the key, didn't I? Seemed wrong *not* to take it."

I opened the folder. It was a thick sheaf of forms—bounty announcements with names, descriptions, aliases, capture and delivery details, last known addresses. The paper was cheap and slick. Some of the forms had more information than others. They all had smeary black-and-white photos. I flipped through, glancing at the names: Daniel Barnum, Lud Margate, Seth Holcomb, Gerry Strange, Jemma Watts, Roland Oates, Marcelo Baird, Logue Ranstead, James Barrow—a.k.a. James "The Captain" Barrow, a.k.a. Jack Tenrec, a.k.a. Harry Tuttle, a.k.a. John Smallberries, a.k.a. Tom Cody. His file was marked POSSIBLY DECEASED, written in ballpoint with a scrawling hand.

"Look at that," I said. "Guess it worked."

"Five dollars," said the car-parker. "Take it or leave it. And in the meantime, since the store's already open, any of you gentlemen have need of some cigarettes or barking irons? Or them purses are all for sale, too. Genuine pre-contraction, all of 'em. If'n any of y'all got a discriminating lady at home, they's a fine purchase."

I paid the man, wished I'd thought to bring my case along, but creased the folder longways and stuck it in the back of my belt. It stands, of all the purchases in my life, as the best five dollars I ever spent.

Best by a long stretch.

Jack, Julie, Asa and me strolled our way back up out of the garage and toward the light.

"Great Times," Jack said. "I think I know where they took your girl."

And Asa said, "We," and Jack said, "What?" and Asa said, "*We* think we know where they took Duncan's girl, Jack. Ain't just you's the smart one. We're a team."

Jack rolled his eyes. "Alright then, *we* think we know where those Regulators might've taken your girl, Duncan. Place called

Great Times, up near the old Montana border. It's a . . ." He trailed off, as though at a sudden loss for descriptive flourish.

"A party town," Julie added.

"Not really a town," said Jack.

"A party outpost then. For all the cops and long riders and Confederacy military in the area. Got a couple of shanty bars. A hot-sheet joint that does mostly hand business, but not always. Lotsa freelancers making their dimes. Got a store or two, work on trade. Gets its fair share of crooks, too. It's a kind of . . ."

"A sanctuary," Jack finished.

"Hell-hole, was what I was gonna say," said Julie.

"A hive of scum and villainy," said Asa, waggling his fingers and speaking in his most foreboding voice.

Jack turned to him and said, "Really?"

Asa grinned. "Lighten up, Jack. How often does anyone get a chance to say that and really mean it?" Then, to me. "They also got a store there sells ice cream. Made from goat milk, but it ain't bad. Once you get past the goat taste."

"So y'all have been there?" I asked.

"Once or twice," said Jack. "Most times, if we're running in that area, we try to avoid it because, you know . . . cops."

"It's the gunhands that are more dangerous," Julie said. "Whole place is built like a hacienda. Walls all up around it and security and what-not. Just to keep the peace. Don't often work out that way, but there's enough guns up in there that trouble often as not works itself out fast."

We came out onto the street, into the glare of hot sunlight and the confusion of bikes and cabs and carriages and the few clattering cars run by them as could afford the fuel. There was music thudding from somewhere down the way, and when I turned to look, I saw a passel of little scrappers on the sidewalk talking with an old man.

I spied them right about the time they did me. There was a half-dozen. Maybe eight. Scrofulous things, but passing familiar. Wouldn't have sworn to it in the moment, but I was pretty sure I saw one of the girlier ones passing a pink-headed ice axe back and forth from hand to hand.

"Hey . . ." I said.

One minute they was talking with the man—who, my second thought was, also looked familiarish. Then I saw them and they saw me, and the next instant one of the little monsters was kicking away the stick the old man carried while another pushed him into the waiting arms of a third.

"Hey!" I yelled, beginning to move in the direction of the half-pint affray. "You shits! Lay off that geezer!"

The little beast who'd caught the old man held tight to him a moment while another leaned in and appeared to be biting him. I shouted again, but they were already scattering. One or two hesitating long enough to eye me up and down, give me the finger, or laugh. When there were only two remaining, I was nearly positive one of them was Tuesday—the Captain's moppet chief of security or whatever, who'd been tasked with keeping an especial eye to my welfare. Hadn't seen her since that moment, but now here she was. I was nearly sure.

She was the one doing the biting, though, and before I'd managed to push my way through the crowd on the sidewalk and draw close enough to spec her for certain, she'd bolted. The last urchin let the man go then, appeared to pause long enough to give a quick, sweeping bow, then jumped up, turned in the air and was gone fast as a handclap. Little thing had a tail, he did. Long and whip-thin and with a spaded point like Ol' Nick himself. Something about that, I recall, disturbed me an inordinate amount.

The old man turned 'round in a bewildered circle. He seemed half of a mind to take off after the urchins, but didn't. And when he turned to face me full (though not appearing to notice me coming his way), I knew him for sure.

He was Arthur Reginald Molesworth. Reggie to them that knew him as a civilian and a reconstructed man. He was one of my regulars at Miss Kitty's—one of the two or three music-loving souls who came for the choc and the company, tolerated my plonking attempts at entertainment, and mostly left the whores alone. He was also a former Colonel of the Western States Militia who'd seen action as a cavalry officer during the Amiable Separation and formation of the Confederacy.

"I amiably blew bridges in Atchison and Joplin," he would say. "Amiably looted and burned arms processors and supply fields in Maryville, Blue Springs and Fort Smith. I amiably took my men against the Okie guardsmen before the Demarcation, the 102nd infantry division in Lebanon, and Skip Harding's Avengers in an Oklahoma corn field where I amiably killed eleven men in close action and took my sweet Persephone against an early third-gen exo and won."

Persephone had been his horse. He missed her every day—a fact he rarely failed to mention three or four times in any conversation.

Reggie was white-haired but hale, with a younger man's barrel chest, an enormous, walrus-y mustache, and a fancy chrome-cased prosthetic arm with a hinky nerve splice that made him twitch like Dr. Strangelove.

"Reggie!" I called to him, waving a hand to rouse his attention. "Over here!"

He saw me, bent to recover his stick, stood, straightened his traditional ensemble of short pants, garish Hawaiian shirt (pineapples this time) open over a mismatched t-shirt (a souvenir from the 1984 Yoyodyne Propulsion Systems company picnic), and a boonie flop hat onto which he'd safety-pinned one of his Colonel-y eagles, then began hoofing it in my direction.

"Ruffians!" he barked. His excitement enough to make his lip-broom wobble. "Did you see that, Piano Man? I was accosted by ruffians!"

"I saw that, Reggie," I said, taking his metal hand to shake it. "Are you in all ways well?"

"In broad daylight!" he blustered. "Why, if I had been astride my sweet Persephone—"

"Are you *harmed*, Colonel?" I asked. "I think I know them urchins and they're not the most pleasant of God's shorter critters."

Reggie fumfured and hucked. "What? No. Those lot? Never seen them before. Knocked me about a bit is all. Nothing hurt but my pride, I suppose. Though if you hadn't come along when you did, I believe I might've had to teach them a lesson in manners."

He laughed then and so did I. The boys had hustled up to meet us on the walk, and the crowds parted around us as up to the curb pulled a fine phaeton done up in metallic flake blue under polished white trim like a big-wheeled lowrider, pulled by an automatic horse stripped down to its frame, buffed out in gleaming silver, and decorated with flames about its fetlocks and Von Dutch pinstriping along its flanks.

"We've got a couple errands to run, Reggie, but one of them will put us at Miss Kitty's. You need a ride?"

"A bit early to start fooling with whiskey and whores, my boy."

"You might could get a bite of something," I suggested. "Lay a hand of cards? I'd feel bad just leaving you on the street."

Reggie shook his head. "No, no. I'll just be on my way, I think." He twirled his stick once, artfully, tapped its ferule on the cement, then slapped down his metal hand when it leapt up as though snake-bit. "Be a damn site easier traveling if I still had my Persephone," he said, then touched the brim of his hat to me and the boys and began to toddle off.

The boys and I, in turn, compared pocket change for the cab's fare and set in to argufying over where we ought to head first.

"You know . . ." I heard Reggie say, and turned back to see him standing just a few paces off. "I do owe you a debt for hustling off those hooligans, Piano Man."

I said, "Don't give it a thought," and waved a hand. "Lay an extra eagle on the Regent the next time I play you 'Half Jack.'" And then I went back to the haggling.

But the old soldier would not be put off so easy.

"Nonsense," he said. "You men seem to be all aflutterated about something. Perhaps there's some way I could be of service?"

"We're going to rescue his girlfriend," said Asa, and I closed my eyes and shook my head.

Jack said, "Dammit, Asa. What'd we say about talking without thinking?"

Then Asa pushed Jack—all four hands thudding into Jack's body, his face lit scarlet. "I ain't your child, Jack, so don't treat me so. You telling me we couldn't use another hand in this?"

Reggie stepped back in among our company. "Seems that you're already overdone in the hand department, son. But I am happy to help."

"Don't talk to strangers!" Jack shouted at Asa. Julie, meanwhile, was moving to step a'tween them, but not being quick about it.

Reggie inclined his head in my direction and said, "Anyway, I didn't know you were so fixed, girl-wise, Piano Man. Not the way you carry on with the trade at Kitty's come the end of the night." And then he laughed grossly.

"Not my girlfriend, Colonel. Just a girl who has found herself in the company of unpleasant men."

Asa yelled, "He ain't no stranger, Jack. Look. Duncan knows him."

And Jack shot back, "Oh, and is Duncan running this gang now?"

"I've never truly thought of us as a gang," Julie mused, moving gently about them until he was separating them with his body and reaching out to touch them each—laying his palms flat on their chests. "We're really more a mob."

Jack whirled on Julie, knocking his hand away. "Three men don't make a mob!" he shouted. "We're a gang."

"A syndicate?" suggested Asa.

"No, a syndicate is bigger'n a mob."

"And more organized," added Julie. "Which we ain't. I thought mob best captured the generally anarchic flavor of our doings."

"So you're going to rescue her?" asked Arthur Reginald Molesworth, Colonel of cavalry, retired. "That's fantastic! I honestly never thought the life of a cat house piano player to be all this exciting, but how can I help?"

"Well . . ." said me, thinking fast. Or fast as I could, which, as it turned out, was not fast enough to come up with a reasonable excuse to not bring along a senior citizen to a gunfight.

"Oh, never mind," said Reggie. "I can find ways to make myself useful." At which point he turned to the boys, who had fallen now to shoving and headlocks in their semantic dispute, and said, "Gentlemen, I believe the term you're fishing for is *outfit*. You. Jack is it?" Jack nodded, but did not release Asa, whose head he had tucked up neatly under his arm. "What's your last name, son?"

"August," said Jack.

"Mine, too," said Asa as he reached down and tried to grab one of Jack's legs. All around their tussle, a scandalized crowd looked on. The cab driver watched from his bench with a look like he'd seen this all before.

"Man didn't *ask* you, Asa!" Jack bellowed, and Julie had to reach in and grab Jack's arm before he choked Asa clean out.

"They're brothers," said Julie. The August brothers. I'm Julio Reconquista De la Teja."

"That's a mouthful," said Reggie.

"That's what he said," said Julie, grinning.

"Right. So, anyway, you'd be the August-De la Teja outfit, then. Which, if you don't mind me saying, has a nice kind of ring to it."

"Huh," said Jack, a bit of the fire draining out of him. He repeated the name, as though trying out the size of it on his tongue. "I like that."

He released Asa, then and stepped back quick with his hands up. But Asa just stood there, bent double, hands on his hips and knees, shaking his head to clear it. "Dammit, Jack," he said. "You gotta *wash* more, bru. The smell of you damn near killed me."

"Shut up, Asa."

"No, *you* shut up. And when they say August-De la Teja, they mean me first, understand? Asa August *then* Jack August."

Julie stepped back in then, steered Asa clear. Reggie grinned and said that he was pleased to have helped them settle their disagreement, then turned to me and spread his hands as if to say, *Ta da!*

"You see, Piano Man? I'm already being helpful." Then he locked his hands behind his back and looked over our assembled selves. "Now then, if the August-De la Teja outfit would kindly load up alongside Mr. Archer and myself in this fine vehicle, perhaps we can all take a ride and you can explain to me the particulars of this mission of mercy. Our assets and liabilities, such as they are. And where-all we might be headed in pursuit of Mr. Archer's fiancé."

"She ain't my fiancé, Reggie," I said. "She's just a girl."

And Reggie smiled. "Not many men go about raising up an army for 'just a girl,' son."

There was more to it, of course, but none so much as I felt like explaining. If such romantical notions suited the circumstance and kept things moving along, I was happy to let them lie.

But anyway, that's how Reginald Molesworth ended up coming along with us to rescue Miss Holly Bright.

How we ended up bringing two prostitutes as well is a different story entirely. But Big Libby and Clementine? They owed me, each for different reasons, and we wouldn't have lived five minutes without them once things kicked off up among the dust and summer lightning, in the Plaza de Cono at Great Times.

Yeah, I understand what I was doing. Do you understand what I was doing? Jack and Julie and Asa, Clarence with the seagull feathers in his hair, the car-parker at the Brown Palace, Reggie, Big Libby, Clementine. I was doing what I always done—what I did every day and every night, without thinking, without most of the time even realizing I was doing it.

I was building a team. A network. Though it did not occur to me in the moment to lay a technical language on it, I was doing like I'd been taught once upon a time. I was *assessing and acquiring assets in the field.* I was *utilizing local and available resources in a fluid operational environment*, each of them with a mission-specific usefulness. They was planners and disruptors, diversions, mobility, logistics, fallback, and them as could bring guns to bear should guns be required. All of which was a polite way of saying that they was warm meat to stand between me and any harm that might come my way.

No, that's not cruel. That's *facts*. That's the way of remaining a living man at the end of the day when the world about you has gone all agee. We could talk up and make jokes and squabble amongst ourselves. We could whoop and holler and act the big figures, dashing off into the night to rescue a lady from bad men. But we was running toward badness. And what I was truly doing was nothing more than gathering bodies to take the share that ought rightly to have been mine.

That was what the OSS had taught me to do best. And I was recalling it in my bones.

In the cab, headed in the direction of the August-De le Teja outfit's lockup in the Five Points, we did as Reggie suggested and discussed our assets and liabilities.

To our detriment was the lead that the Regulators had on us, the distance between Denver and Great Times, the walls around Great Times, the unknowable number of gunsels, smugglers, reavers, Regulators, border riders, militia, battle police, galvanized Westerners and manhunters who might be recreating in and around Great Times. The equally unknowable depth and methods of security that might be employed at Great Times. And the fact that we didn't know for sure that the Regulators had actually taken Holly to Great Times.

"Do we have another equal or better assumption?" Reggie asked. I admitted that no, we did not.

"Is there another source of intelligence that might be tapped in an amount of time that would not cause our current assumptions to stale?"

Again, no. Not as such.

"Then we go forward, Piano Man! Because in the absence of perfect intelligence, acting on the available information has a better chance of resulting in success than doing nothing at all." He slapped me on the arm and grinned like he was trying to bite the ends of his own mustache. "Now what are our assets?"

One truck, I told him. The five of us. One Regulator's badge, slightly used. Our wit, charm and fine looks.

"Do you have air support of any kind?" Reggie asked.

"What? No. Of course not."

"What about artillery?"

"Where would I keep artillery, Reggie? In my pockets?"

He frowned. "It's not so ridiculous, you know. You are the piano player who was lifted off the roof of Miss Kitty's by an unmarked Osprey and whisked away to some mysterious destination. Do you have any idea how many favors Madam has called in trying to figure out where you went? Any idea how much she has already paid *me* to try and find out?"

"Really?" I asked, surprised more than a bit, and Reggie nodded. "Could've just asked me, Colonel. We could've split the fee."

"Would you have told me the truth?"

"Of course not."

"Well then."

He was quiet for a moment, then said, "So, do you have access to—"

"No, Reggie. No artillery. Sorry."

"Excellent," he said. "That would only complicate things."

"I'd take a cannon if we had one," I muttered.

"We got surprise," Asa offered, leaning in from the jumpseat. "They don't know we're coming, do they Duncan?"

"I don't reckon they do, Asa. No. So there you go, Colonel. One more point to our advantage: surprise."

"Well that's something, too," said Reggie.

The cab joined a snarled knot of traffic all balled up at Champa Street where the King's civils had three gengineered war elephants working at tearing down and clearing the wreck of a collapsed apartment block. Huge and stinking things, they were twice the size of your standard-issue elephant, with the brains of a sponge and the loyalty of golden retrievers. These ones heaved and trumpeted in the traces of a complicated winching system with tiny little men riding high up on their massive shoulders and directing them with shock rods that would've killed a good-sized house.

Our driver, though, was slick and fearless, with our lives as well as his own. He jumped a shattered curb and passed close around the beasts—scooting actually beneath the feet of one that reared in the heave, and then laying the virtual whip into his automatic horse to get us yanked clear of those stompers before they came down again and mashed us flat.

Passing so close, I could see how the double rows of scything tusks had been removed. Cut off, it looked. Likely with chainsaws. All three beasts showed the scars of violent natures. They were elephants who'd seen the elephant, to be sure. Who'd danced with tanks and tangled with robots and broken the lines of the Kansans in the charge, leaving only smears and small chunks where once there'd been men. They were survivors turned now to more domestic chores.

"Poor creatures," said Reggie, looking out over the work site as the phaeton lurched around a run of hurricane fence and bumpily mounted a plank bridge thrown over a grave-deep gouge that'd been torn in the roadway. "Bred for war and now being used as common labor."

"I don't know about that," I said. "I'm fairly sure that any animal is happier turning itself to work which don't involve killing and dying."

"Speak for yourself, Piano Man," Reggie told me.

And "I am," said me. "Most directly."

Reggie looked at me with an odd, bemused expression, then shook his head and caught his arm again as it flopped in his lap like a fish.

Jack's truck was itself a beast—some strange offspring born of a light infantry transport mounted and roughly put with child by a monster truck. It had six oversize tires, knobbed for driving upon tailings piles and nitrogen ice, an armored cab, a flat nose like a bus, an open and roll-barred bed, and a massive, banging heart that could run happily on anything from jet fuel to kerosene to pure ethanol to electricity.

"Truck," said Reggie, nodding appreciatively. "Definitely an asset."

The distance between Denver and Great Times was not a detriment, Reggie insisted. The more lead the Regulators had on us, the longer they would have to behave poorly, get drunk, get separated, get tired and slow and forgetful. Great Times was, by the boys' description, a place made for the severing of a man from his senses and wise judgment.

"They want to do themselves harm? Let them," Reggie said. "They want to make themselves bleary and clumsy and foolish? We should give them all the time they like and just stay out of their way. Jack!"

Jack poked his head out from the other side of the truck.

"How long is it to Great Times from here?"

"On roads or not?"

"Is it faster running overland?"

"In some places, yeah."

"Best case then."

Jack thought a minute. "Ten hours if we meet with no mischief."

"Call it twelve then. And Great Times keeps the lights on all night, I assume?"

"And all the day, too."

"Perfect. We'll leave in about an hour then. Aim to arrive around 4AM. Ambush hour."

This, Reggie insisted, would also minimize the effect of Great Times's security and the random gunhands, assuming that even the greatly debauched had to shut eyes at some point. It would also maximize our element of surprise. Unfortunately, his plan, for all his military blusterations, was ridiculous. He wanted a full frontal assault—to charge the gates and win through on grit or something. All blazing guns and bloody mayhem. Him being a cavalryman, I don't know why I thought he might come to any other conclusion. But as for me, I was anxious about keeping all my blood inside me where it belonged.

"The essence of a good battle plan," he insisted, "is to neutralize as many of our liabilities as possible. Or to turn them into strengths. That and simplicity. And glory, of course. There must be glory."

"What about not dying, Reggie? That's high up on my list of earmarks of success."

"Because you'd like to see your girl again?"

"Because I'd like to see morning. I appreciate the simplicity portion of your scheme, but we're four against the world up there."

"Five," he said.

"Do you even have a gun on you?"

He pursed his lips. "I may need to make a stop before we leave, but it's still a good plan. We crash the gate, charge the main building. Fast entry. Shock and awe. Grab the girl. Home before supper. Easy."

"Ain't no main building," said Asa, walking past with a pole across his top shoulders laden to bending with jerry-cans of truck juice, and two more cans in his lower hands. "Just a clutter of little ones and then the posada with the big bar, the benzineries around it. The bed-houses for the working girls."

"It's a bad box, soon as you're through the gate," added Julie, who'd been sitting cross-legged on top of the truck's cab itching at himself and listening to Reggie and me argue. "Lotta holes to go to ground in, but nowhere really to go."

"And crashing the gate isn't an option," Jack said. "Even if I were willing to give up my truck to this, which I ain't—sorry Duncan—it's ten-foot walls with bedded posts and a steel rollaway gate on a winch drop. We'd bounce right off."

Reggie furrowed his brows and grumbled into his mustache. Something about his horse, most likely. Because it was always something about his horse.

"Prostitutes," I said.

"Yeah, they got them, too," Jack said. "But the truck would pretty much roll right over them." He laughed and went back to lashing down supplies in the bed.

"No, that's how we get in. Prostitutes."

It took me thirty seconds to explain my plan to Reggie. Then I called over Jack, Julie, and Asa and explained it all again. When I was finished the second time, Jack shook his head and asked if anyone wanted to change their vote. But Reggie narrowed his eyes and nodded sharply.

"That's not bad, Piano Man. Lacks for glory a bit, but has the added benefit of maybe actually working." His hand jumped and he caught it, poked me in the chest with one of his metal fingers. "But if you'd listed a brace of whores among our assets in the first place, I might've come to the same conclusion."

I smiled. "We do it right, no one needs to fire a shot."

"Well where's the fun in that?"

We did not do it right. How could we have? There were too many unknowns and unknowables. Too many uncontrollable elements. Far too much that ain't none of us knew walking in.

But none of that mattered until the moment when things started to slip, and that moment was still a long drive off. I remember wondering briefly what the Captain was about at that precise moment. How he would feel when I pulled off the rescue of the girl who was supposed to be watching me and delivered her, whole and unharmed, to his door.

I didn't know where his door was, of course. But she would. And she would take me there because she would have to. She was his eyes. A perfect watcher. I was so sure of it that I could've squirmed with pride at my own cleverness.

I imagined how grateful she would be to see me. Her laughing with relief when our ridiculous plan went off without a hitch. Three semen thieves, two whores, a retiree, and a cat house piano player? No rescue had ever been less likely. But I sat in the lockup, checking tire pressures and helping Asa to glug fuel into the auxiliary tanks until my head swam with the fumes, and I imagined how she would tell the Captain about my remarkable heroism. *This one, Captain, is one that ought to be taken immediately into your confidence and told all your deepest and darkest secrets.* That was what she would say. I couldn't conceive of it going any other way.

Why? Because I was a fool, that's why. Because I didn't even know enough yet to be dumb. Because for all the confidence and fattened sense of gallant purpose I was feeling, I was really a hundred miles out of my element and walking in completely the wrong direction.

Just wait. You'll see.

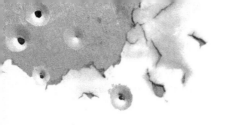

EPISODE 4

The Perilous Life of
Miss Holly Bright, Part 2

BEFORE WE GO ANY FURTHER, I NEED TO TELL YOU A STORY FROM my earlier days. It'll just take a minute, so sit tight and listen. It's important.

When I was a younger man, I had me this partner.

Well, not a *partner*, precisely. More like a colleague, I guess you'd call him. An associate. Wasn't like the movies where we'd buddy around together, eat casserole made by each others' wives, get involved in hijinks and realize we was fucking the same lady. Nothing like that. We had a drink together now and then when we was off the clock. Spent a fair piece of time too close together—smelling each others' farts and bad breath and telling the same bad jokes a hundred times. So, yeah, in that way it was like the movies, I guess, but not, you know, a *good* movie. Not one that anyone wise would pay honest money to see.

His name was Gordon Navarro. He'd go right after your eyes if you called him "Gordo" because gordo is Spanish for fat and he was greyhound-skinny in his day but, apparently, had been a round little fat boy when he was a child and caught all manner of hell for it. The end of the world cured him of that. As it had so many survivors of the weird. So, you know, the apocalypse wasn't all bad. Had some silver linings if you were the sort who cared to look for them.

Gordon Navarro was called many things, but the one he was called most was La Canalla, which, when used gently, almost affectionately, meant something like "scoundrel" or "rascal." The kind of man who'd flirt with your grandmother to get an extra cookie.

But no one ever used it gently when they were talking about Gordon.

Gordon was La Rata. La Puta Canalla Periodista. A blackleg opportunist and working journalist, which, even in the bad ol' days, was still the near perfect cover for a field asset reporting to an OSS handler. Which, at the beginnings of things, was what I was when I met him. It was my first solo flight and Gordon was a source I'd inherited from the man who'd had him before me. That fella had died with his service automatic in his hand, I'd been told. Didn't find out 'til later that it was on the toilet, of a single bullet to the head.

Anyway, I was scalphunting then, me. Recruiting out of a one-room office in Magnolia, Arkansas. On Jackson Street, right near Hospital Park. And Gordon was my man in the titty bars and trailer parks, among the Texas expat community, the angry dispossessed, the smugglers and coyotes and Mexican instigators and methamphetamine enthusiasts and armed maniacs who were plotting insurrection in their garages. We had a good thing going, Gordon and me. Once a week, maybe once every other week, he would call upon me at my office or meet me in the park—flopping down aside me on a bench in broadest daylight because things was loose back then and it didn't matter a damn. He'd come to me with a list of possibles. Names and last-known-locations on a half-dozen people who he'd run across while writing his stories on border politics and government corruption, and who might be of some use to the government of the United States of America should said government ever feel the need to start uniting them states all back up again.

For this, I would pay him. Sometimes cash out of my maintenance fund. Sometimes heroin, straight from a courier who was Uncle Sugar right down to his O.D. underwear. Sometimes other things that I'd have to acquire all by my lonesome, often requiring adventures that aren't germane to this tale I'm telling. I always took a skim. Was a bad man even when I was supposed to be a good man, me. And Gordon, for his part, always padded his lists with a couple make-believe names. Sometimes all of them were skylarking inventions. But sometimes not. Gordon, he knew some strange people.

I'd take the list and do what I did. Background checks and whatnot. Research which could be done by lamp when there was electric, and candle when there was not—which, not for nothing, was kind of romantical and spoke to the literary man in me.

Better days and all that.

I had me a computer then that still spoke to the Internet when it felt like it. Used it to access the information network that the OSS maintained, so I could check mail and cell phone records, past employment, known associates, all legal paperwork. On a good day, I could have your date of birth, gene markers, dental records, place of work (legal or not so), dealings with the law, height, weight, shoe size, sexual preference, the names of all your friends, aggregated loyalty levels, birthday wishes, favorite animal, last night's dreams, and current location to within fifty feet, all within about an hour. But none of that was worth anything. Not really. What mattered was the man. Or woman. Or whatever. What mattered was them that I choosed to go have a look at in person.

Gordon and me would go together. He wore a bulletproof vest everywhere he went. Carried a hook-bladed pumpkin knife, a .25 caliber pistol so ice-cold it left frost on the palm, and a recorder in his head good for twenty-eight hours of sound and optical-quality video. I wore a black suit and a white shirt and carried a small notebook and a pencil. My fervent hope was always that if there was violence, they'd shoot Gordon first while I ran.

Yes, all of this is important. Just *listen*.

This one time, Gordon got me a lead on what my elders and betters would've called a "hot touch." A man who was actually in the midst of doing terrible wrongs and was having second thoughts. He calls me—one, maybe two in the morning—and he's a mess, is Gordon. He's yelling. He's whispering. I can almost taste the smoke of his brain cooking over the phone. Can hear him grinding his teeth together as he tries to get out what he needs to say.

"A big one, Jimmy," is what he says to me. Because "Jimmy" is what he knew me as then. Jimmy Fields, friendly neighborhood O-man. "A big one. *The* big one. Jimmy, you listening? You listening to me? I got this . . . this guy. Oh, man, you got to find me now, Jimmy. I don't know where I am, man. But I got the guy. The guy the guy the guy. You hearing me? Fucking phone . . . You listening to me, Jimmy?"

"I'm listening, Gordon. What guy?"

"*THE* guy, motherfucker. You're not listening. You're not *listening*. Fuck you, Jimmy. Who's your boss? Gimme his number. He'll listen. Gimme his number right now."

I says *no*. I says *calm the fuck down*. I says *try speaking in complete sentences, Gordon. Give me a name. A location. Anything.*

"Castillo, Jimmy. Roger fucking Castillo. Of the Castillo brothers, right? Oh, man. I can't talk about this now. You have to find me, Jimmy. You have to find me and get me. Send the cops. Send your spy buddies. Send anyone. I just, uh, have to get off the streets right now. So can you get me, man? Please? Can you just . . . Can you just come and get me?"

As it turned out, Gordon was about two blocks away. He was staring at the front door of my office while he was talking. And he was so tweaked on dirty trailer meth that he had no idea.

Just listen, okay? There's a point. I'm getting there.

The Castillo brothers were mechanics. They ran two or three car lots in and around Magnolia, keeping used cars (which were the only kinds of cars left) running and the people of Arkansas mobile. Because of this, they were also bankers, who held loans and markers on half the region. They were also import/export barons, with a steady supply of parts coming in and cars going out. And, of course, they were also smugglers, bankrollers, and heavy operators in the Free Arkansas Militia—the most trig of the rebel factions operating in the borderlands, and also the most accepted. The FAM handed out a lot of hams and helped rebuild a lot of barns. Their public relations were excellent. The mayor of Magnolia was an honorary colonel.

But in its darker humors, the militia was heavy-armed and serious about keeping Arkansas free of Texans and the United States government, in that order. Arkansas herself hadn't seceded yet, but that was only because what remained of the central authority in Washington D.C. had degraded to a point where most living politicians couldn't hardly tell you where Arkansas was anymore. It'd been pretty much forgotten by all save the OSS. Which would seem a strange thing to happen, an entire state of the Union simply being forgotten about—but seriously, disregarding Texas, name for me the five other old states that Arkansas touched.

Yeah, that's what I thought.

Of the two Castillos, Roger was the younger and the saner. He was the businessman of the family, kept the books, watched the cash, dealt with the legit hands working the yards and the numbers side of their dealings with the militia. I knew enough then to know that he was making a mint doing so. Literal *bales* of old states dollars, gold and product buried in marked plots in the car yards. I'd seen them.

Joe Castillo was the older brother and he was bad medicine. A rusticated maroony who hated on everything and everyone what wasn't of his brand and kept precious-close a ring of broke-headed thugs and gunsels who shared his dim and backward views on modernity, exigency, courtesy and the gentler human emotions.

The two of them did not get on peaceably. They mostly did not get on at all. Roger was the brains and Joe was the muscle and they both had enough men between them that there was scarce need for the two of them to meet eye-to-eye. But then, they were brothers. They had common cause, common politics and, most important, common blood.

That was what I did not understand when I went to collect off the street the bundle of twitches and vile language that Gordon had reduced himself to. It was what I did not understand once I got La Canalla cooled out and talking sense. I'd never had a brother of my own, so brothers and the doings of brothers was a mystery to me, and, in that way, I was uniquely ill-suited to comprehend the weight of it when Gordon told me that Roger, in his cups down at the Main Street Saloon, had admitted that he was ruminating upon the wise-ness of cutting out of his brother Joe over a bridger's shipment coming in out of Texas—a trailer box full of fifty cooled-out souls that Joe had bought from an overcrowded prison camp in Kilgore, Texas.

"*Bought*, Jimmy," Gordon said to me. "Had 'em temporarily lobo'd by a doc there, bound down, thrown in a box trailer and brought across the border last night. Roger found out about it by accident, so he doesn't know how long this has been going on. But Joe is buying people, man. Slaves."

They were brothers and, seeing only the opportunity to flip a big figure in the FAM, I didn't waste a moment considering the complications of blood. The way that hatreds and love can look so damn similar in them as are bound by bonds of family.

Roger was the classic hot touch. I had him in my pocket before the sun came up and was an instant hero to my controller in the Bentonville state office.

For six months, I had Roger and for six months he fed me everything his brother did—and Joe was dirty as a six-foot shit trench. He ran slaves, guns and genetic material, owned drug labs of both the black and white flavors, sold bodies as organ farms, contracted out muscle to various small-time gangsters, organized hijacks and bombings and acted as a mid-level financier to both rebel and loyalist groups in Arkansas, Texas, and Louisiana.

I had Roger for six months and for six months I milked him dry. For six months I passed him around like a bought whore, handing him off to every company heavy they could pass into Magnolia, every two-bit unit commander in the five-state region, every agent runner they could slip over the border at Texarkana or 4-Eyes. By the time it was done, my little one-room, one-man office had seventeen agents attached—two full-time pavement teams, three listeners working 'round the clock, two agency fixers, an exfil specialist, a database and IT specialist just to handle the mountains of cross-referenced data produced by my growing source list, an interrogator who lived in a trailer down by the railroad tracks, and a three-man security detail.

For six months we all ran around like our tails was afire—investigating, snooping, moving paper, infiltrating brother Joe's operations all over the state and passing vital information back to the Big Hats in Bentonville and elsewhere who were running the board. Recalling it now, it feels as though I didn't sleep one minute in six months. I remember myself, young and confident and in command, managing men who ultimately did me no good at all except, in their dying, to teach me of the ferocity to which betrayal can drive a man when Joe Castillo finally came to call.

He did not come in the night nor in any bushwhacking way. It was raining fit to drown a snake, but I don't think that was anything more than a dramatic convenience for Joe. He called on me in daylight, at my office, which was either brave, foolhardy or insane, depending on your point of view, and he brought with him eight of his hard men. They were killers, all. The mean sort, mostly, and not at all skittish of the bang and blood and clamor. All eight of them got put down in getting Joe to my door, and that, I believe, probably seemed a bargain to him.

In all, he and his killed nine of mine in a fight that lasted about 45 seconds, start to finish, as is the way of these things in the real world. And according to the butcher's count, when Joe came kicking through my door, he had six bullets already in him and nothing but blind hate keeping him vertical.

There was no drama to it. No big last words. He got off one shot. I aired him out with a scattergun and it was done. But that's not the important part.

Later, as I was setting in to a bit of necessary housekeeping in light of my network being blown and me being soon for the wind, Gordon shows up. I'm standing there in a strap shirt and dungarees, the whole office hazy with gasoline fumes, a Lucifer match in my teeth, and suddenly there's La Rata the Unkillable slouching in my doorway.

He tells me that he'd spent the past day holed up in what passed for a Champagne Room down at Misty's, a local gentleman's club. He'd had a hatful of meth, a couple of low-rent bar girls, and a pistol in his hand, just waiting for Joe to come for him, too.

But Joe had never come. Nor any of Joe's hard men—most of whom had been in my pay at that point anyhow. He'd been expecting it, Gordon had. He'd prepared for it in the only way I think he knew how. But he'd been left cold.

This, of course, had offended Gordon's sense of an orderly universe, so once word had gotten to him about the shootout at my office, he'd crawled out of his hole and gone sniffing around. He was a journo, after all. In his more lucid moments, he was. He had that disease of always needing to know what had happened. The truth, or at least something close to it.

Joe had known, Gordon says to me. About Roger and his perfidy. About me, about the OSS and my crew and all the hundred betrayals. For a couple days at least, he'd known *for sure*.

So he'd killed his brother and done it slow. Taking back from Roger in 12 or 14 terrible hours everything he'd given us over six months.

He'd killed the men who'd turned on him. Who'd informed on him to me. Not all of them, but a lot of them. "Enough," says Gordon. "More than."

It'd been matter-of-fact at first. Questions, answers, apologies or begging or both, then the bullet or the knife. But when that became dull or too slow or somehow insufficient for slaking his rage, Joe'd had his enemies herded up onto a scaffolding in one of his car lots and pushed into a compactor.

When he was done, Gordon says, he had perhaps a dozen men left.

"Eight," I tell him. "He had eight."

"Okay, eight. And then he came for you."

It was ridiculous, of course. Since Joe had known we were onto him, he could've run. He had the jump on us. He could've rabbited, holed up somewhere. He had friends everywhere.

Well, not *friends* exactly. He had folk who owed him. But it amounted to the same thing. He could've skipped and the OSS—meaning precisely me—wouldn't have even bothered chasing him. After six months, I'd turned Joe's operation inside-out, thanks to Roger. Joe Castillo was already a dry hole. Chasing him wouldn't have been worth the resources. He might've known that. Might not have. Either way, it didn't figure into his calculations.

Because Joe hadn't run.

And Gordon asks, "But *why* didn't he run?"

"Because he couldn't run," I tell him. "Because Roger was his brother and I'd fucked with his brother. Because it was me that'd forced this. Made him kill his own brother. There was no way a man like Joe could let that go."

Then I'd popped the match on the zipper of my blue jeans and thrown it into the puddle of gas on the floor of the office. The fire was beautiful.

This is what I thought about once we finally had made it to Great Times—once the drive and all its complications had been put behind us, once the rescue had been botched and all my careful plans come to nothing.

I think that maybe it was the heat that reminded me—the licking waves of it coming off the posada as the flames started to eat their way into the heart of the first floor and pop the bottles in the well of the bar. Or maybe it was just circumstance. But as I stood there in the dirt square of the Plaza de Cono, staring down at Jack's body and Asa holding him, scooped up in all four of his arms, I was thinking about Magnolia. While I watched Asa rocking and keening as bits of Jack's brain fell out into the dust and the smell of dead man spiked the dawn air, I was thinking about Gordon and the gasoline flames curling into the damp night air and the Castillo brothers. I was thinking about Roger and how his body was found in the room that the two of them had shared as children, in the house that Joe still kept. I was thinking about how he'd been found curled into the bed there as though asleep and how the local police, dim as they were, had figured that he'd been carried there alive, laid down gentle. That someone else had lain down beside him, close to him, and held onto him while he died.

I was trying to remember who had told me that, but couldn't quite recall. I was thinking how that was one of those things I wished I could un-know.

Anyway, point is, brothers can be strange. It was something I should've thought on before bringing Jack and Asa to Great Times together, but didn't. Not until it was too late. Lightning flashed. The rain refused to come. And standing there with men and death and fire all around me, I took a step back from Asa and his brother and made sure my pistol was loose in its holster.

Thirteen hours before Jack died, I was at Miss Kitty's. I was fetching down my briefcase and stashing the papers I'd bought from the car parking man at the Brown Palace—closing my eyes when I tucked them safely into my best hiding spot so's I wouldn't be tempted to look and telling myself that there would be time to read them later. Always plenty of time.

Twelve hours and some before, I was standing at Madam's bar, trying to talk Big Libby and Clementine into coming with us to Great Times. Both of them owed me for different reasons—Libby because she'd given me a case of the crabs that'd required heroic measures to defeat, and Clementine because it'd been her I'd been joseying for when I'd had to drop a pistol-waving man who'd come out chasing after a refund—but both were being obstinate. It has always been my experience that men understand the seriousness of debts owed better than women do, but that women are better judges of their burden. Which is to say that, among good and moral men, simply saying "You owe me," is enough. But women will haggle.

For my plan to work, I needed them. One might've been enough, but two felt righter. As I'd explained to the boys earlier at the Brown Palace, supporting players are essential when trying to lay a convincing scene. And I needed my scene to be powerfully convincing if we wanted to get in and out of Great Times quiet and without undue consternation.

Luckily, I am a very persuasive man.

Twelve hours before, we was waiting on Colonel Arthur Reginald Molesworth, retired.

He'd tried to leave us at Miss Kitty's, claiming he needed some things for the trip and would be right back, but I'd said no, not wanting any of us to get separated just now that we was all finally together and moving forward in a productive fashion. In his old man's way, he'd gotten hot over this—harrumphing into his moustache and whatnot and fussing about then with a beer bought on my tab at the bar.

Once we'd collected the girls, he'd insisted that we make a stop to visit a friend of his. I pled haste and told Jack to drive on.

"Piano Man," he said to me, "Do you have any idea what we might be walking into once we get where we're going?"

I allowed that I did not. That none of us rightly did.

"And does it occur to you that I am a former military man who might, perchance, have stowed away among my things some bits of this and that which might help square the odds for us, should things go awry?"

I considered this briefly, weighing want against hurry.

"How long will this delay us, Reggie?" I asked.

"A minute," he said. "Five, tops. Maybe ten."

So we stopped. His friend was not about. So then we went to Reggie's home, which by all appearances was a tin shack in a rubble lot poisoned with mercury puddles and ferocious gray kudzu. It seemed currently in the process of falling down, his house, but he scuffed his way straight up to it and disappeared inside. "Just have to make a call," he'd said. "Back in a minute."

Jack and Asa were arguing over our route. Clementine and Big Libby were in the back of the truck, laying about and trying to make themselves comfortable for the drive. Julie was with them, bobbing about their perimeter like a small, strange fish. Like a little girl arching for the attention of her big sisters.

Clementine asked if we could go back to Miss Kitty's so she could get a pillow. I said no. Big Libby rummaged around in her purse looking for a magazine. I watched the door of Reggie's house and, when more minutes had passed than I could rightly countenance, I picked my way across what passed for his yard and stepped up to his falling-down wood steps.

I called his name and he did not answer. I pushed at his door—being careful not to knock it clean off the frame—and it swung inward onto a bare, empty room with a bowed wood floor, the corners mounded with trash, not a stick of furnishing in evidence, and nothing to distinguish it but a rather remarkable smell of shit and animal funk.

And yet I could still hear Reggie's muffled voice from somewhere, saying, ". . . raise him, tell him that I am traveling now, but I've got his laundry."

Then a pause.

Then: "Well, when do you expect him?"

Then a pause.

Then: "I understand. Just pass the message and give my best. I expect to be back by tomorrow."

Then nothing.

Then more nothing save a creak and a scrape from below.

And when the cleverly fitted panel in the floor popped up, spilling light into the dimness of the shack's interior, I was squatting in the doorway, waiting. The panel slid aside and I stepped quietly away, letting the sound of it scraping the boards cover the noise of me hopping down from the top step and retreating five steps back across the lawn—at which point I stopped, turned and hollered for Reggie to hurry, please, as daylight was wasting.

"Hold your horses, Piano Man!" came his voice from inside. "Let an old man take his time."

He was, I knew, fitting back the panel. Securing it in whatever way he did. Standing in the center of the room and turning in a slow circle to make sure that nothing—no footprints, no drag marks—were in evidence that would give away to a careful eye the truth of his little house. I could imagine him doing it because it was what I would've done.

And then he was outside, leaning heavy on his stick and wearing, slung across his ample body, a black and yellow nylon satchel which appeared so foxed and fire-new that it seemed to glow against the remains of all the rest of the world.

I held my ground and let him walk to me. I asked if he needed a hand with the bag, as it looked heavy and he seemed winded.

And he said, "I was kidding about that 'old man' shit, you know. I'm fine."

And then I said, "Whose laundry are you carrying, Reggie?"

He stopped. Cocked his head. There was a sudden flutter in Arthur Reginald Molesworth. A flickering of hardness and coldness like a sudden chill draft moving the curtains in a warm room. It was a scant glimpse of the man beneath the man, if you know what I mean. The heart of him peeking out for just an instant before going down to hide again beneath the mustache, the flop hat, the preposterous shirts. "You heard that?"

"A piece of it," I said, then repeated myself. "Whose laundry are you carrying, Reggie?"

He stared, his aspect no longer quite so bumptious, and I met his gaze coolly. His eyes flicked over my shoulder to where Jack and Asa were roughhousing and Julie and Clementine were listening to Big Libby tell a story, and then came back to mine.

"Laundry," he said, patting the bag hung across him. He lifted the flap and pulled it open just enough for me to see the gray blocks of Composition 4 in their waxy skins, the clear plastic box of detonators, the loops of fusing wire and detcord and the electric arming box, each nested in its own compartment in the way that things only do when they are new and untouched. "I'm borrowing it from a friend and he would be quite put out if he were to come home and find it missing."

"If he comes home to *your* house," I said.

"Yes," said Reggie, closing the bag again and brushing the flap down smooth with the palm of one hand.

"Your shack right here."

"Yes."

"And finds his brand new bag of explosives has walked off."

"That would piss him off, yes."

"So you . . ."

"Called him to let him know."

"But he wasn't in?"

"No."

And then we stared at each other until staring became uncomfortable.

"Did you at least remember to get a gun?" I asked him.

He looked back toward his shack. "Shit. Do you mind if I—"

I threw up my hands. "Dammit, Reggie . . ."

"Anyway, I thought you said that if your plan works, I wouldn't need . . ."

"Just go, Reggie. Go."

And once again, his crooked grin split his face below his mustache. "I'm kidding, Piano Man!"

"Kidding? You're . . . You're kidding."

"Of course."

"Okay."

He reached out and squeezed me by one shoulder. "You really need to lighten up a little. Come on, now. This is going to be fun."

Eleven hours before, we were passing through the contraction zone with Jack behind the wheel. Julie, the girls and Reggie were all in the back, bedded down among the gear and the bench seats, laughing and sipping at warm beers in unmarked brown bottles taken from a picnic cooler lashed down with bungee cords. The truck had a radio and Asa had it packed with death metal and Johnny Cash and some deep, raw country full of lonesome fiddles and accents so thick and ripe that they sounded like an alien language spoken by lightning-struck stones and the blind roots of trees.

We drove through cinders and ashes. We drove through a place where the lawns had become jungles full of emerald grasses and twisted, thick trees and flowers that grew as tall as a man and seemed to turn their heads—following us with some hungering menace as we passed. We drove through neighborhoods full of skeleton trees and dead houses where it seemed as though we'd accidentally fallen into a black-and-white movie and I found myself staring at the lights of the dashboard, rings on Asa's fingers and the red stitching on his cowboy shirt just to give my eyes a break from the strange, flat monotony of the world.

At one point we were chased by two Mad Max–looking addle-brains on dirt bikes, but we quickly outpaced them because they both crashed before they'd made it a block.

At one point I thought I saw a gargoyle sitting crouched on the roof of a Chinese restaurant called Joy Fun Buffet and I thought it strange until I saw that it was only a girl, her skin the gray of stones, and I watched her stand up, spread her wings and take flight.

At one point we passed an old woman in a housecoat and an oversized bulletproof vest, pushing a gimpy shopping cart full of domestics and dripping pieces of domestics, their arms and legs hanging out over the edges of the cart. She left a smear of hydraulic fluid, lubricating oil and processing gel behind her and it looked like she was casting a wake of blood.

At one point we crashed through the burned remains of a road-block garlanded with skulls and blackened bones and crucified bodies dressed in the remains of Western Confederacy uniforms.

"Those are fake," Jack said just before we hit it.

"How'd you know?" I asked once we were through.

"We been through this way before," Asa said.

"Yeah, we know these guys," said Jack.

I shrugged. "Well, fake bodies and all. They must be friendly."

Jack chuckled. "No. No, they're really not."

Asa said, "You don't want to know what they do with the real bodies."

Ten hours before, I was watching a blimp chain in the distance, cutting across the glow of the setting sun at a sharp angle, headed for the western borders in a powerful, slow hurry.

They were massive things, their translucent gasbags packed with superheated noble gasses and a million billion microscopic lifting engines, their cargo containers the size of a dozen tractor trailers. The ones I watched were traveling under wind power—billowing mile-wide sails of carbon-fiber cloth just a few microns thick that were also solar collectors to power the maneuvering fans.

They glowed—the sun heliographing off their cables, their bags shooting out rainbows like artillery fire—and they were gorgeous. Sailing free of the airlines, they were obviously smuggling, and I silently wished them good winds and the mercy of nightfall.

Nine hours before, we had snacks. Everyone complained that there was nothing but buffalo jerky, stale cornbread, two cannoli, and a paper sack of fried shrimp puffs that smelled like dirty feet, then complained more that there was so little of everything.

I drank half a warm barley-pop and stayed out of the bickering. Jack had left the roads miles back and had parked the truck in a stand of live birch trees beside a trickling creek that ran clear and cold. The earth was padded with seasons of leaves. The creek's bedding stones had been worn smooth by ages of water rubbing them clean of all imperfection. It was one of those places that seemed almost untouched by weirdness, decay and the foulness of man. A place where the end of the world had come and gone unremarked.

And I hated it.

I missed the city, Miss Kitty's, the Nob, the Castle, and all the rest of it terribly, and didn't feel right again until we were back in the truck, its big tires tearing like teeth into the vestal earth, and Asa had dialed up "Die with Your Boots On" and turned it up so loud that it made my balls itch.

Nature, for all its wonderments, looked like nothing but a threat to me. Any piece of the land that had survived whole and healthy through all that had become of the wrecksious earth had done so only because it was mean in a way that you never saw until it was too late. Lovely, maybe. Peaceful. Refreshing. Whatever. The minute you started to believe it, then BAM! You'd get killed by a falling tree or eaten by a lion or catch some fungus disease that would chew your skin away until you were nothing but damp bones and regret.

Eight hours before he died, Jack and I were laid out flat and belly-down on a stony ridge overlooking the last of mile of Colorado, Asa and Reggie to either side of us.

"Asa?" said Jack, speaking over my back.

"Yeah?"

"You're a damn fool."

"Am not."

"Y'are, and shut up besides."

The sun had lit a purple fire on the horizon that looked like a livid bruise, and we were trying hard not to break the smooth silhouette of the land as Jack and Asa argued and we passed a pair of binoculars from hand to hand to hand.

"Did I tell you I would get us here, Jack?"

"Haul north in a straight line and I could've gotten *myself* here."

"Yeah, and that's pretty much all you could do."

"So are you claiming that this was deliberate, then?"

Asa thought for a minute. "I'm saying that it wasn't *un*-deliberate."

"That's not even a word."

"You'se an unhappy man, Jack, and you shouldn't ought to lay it all off on them as are trying to help you."

Below us and not but a mile or so off was the Colorado/Wyoming border. And where we'd come up upon it, it was lit like high noon under the sulfurous, yellow glow of pole-mounted flood lights.

There were two major, legal crossings east of the mountains—Interstate 25 and the cracked and pitted remains of route 287—and

Asa had brought us in between them, though just barely. What we were looking over now was the border control point at route 287, and when it was my turn with the glasses I panned them over the bunkered gatehouses with their field laser emplacements and booger guns, over the bedded nets of monofilament wire that could be sprung up with the push of a button and make crashing the line like running headlong into a sieve—nothing left of you on the other side but a thousand perfect, squishy cubes of meat and shiny metal filings.

The crossing itself was manned by battle police, lumbering around thickly in their chubby armor, checking papers and cargos and shining their flashlights in people's eyes. But the Colorado militia had two army surplus exo's flanking their side of the road, their armor slashed in the battered colors of King Steve. Their poor cousins, the Wyoming Volunteers, had Ogres on theirs—nine-foot-tall heavy construction robots, re-fitted with flamethrowers and chain guns and giant chainsaw hands, operated remotely by pimply teenage boys with hacked PlayStation controllers, doing 14-hour shifts and sucking away at camelpacks filled with home-brewed energy drinks laced with phenotropil, distilled taurine, and dextroamphetamine.

There was a motor pool with a couple of decrepit V12 inter-ceptors that burned pure alcohol and, occasionally, exploded for no reason. I counted three shuggoths shivering along impossibly through the darkling sky, their bodies filled with strange bio-logical magic and complex arrays of sensors that could hear a squirrel fart from a thousand yards off. There was a fair tangle of traffic backed up on both sides of the crossing, including one smallish blimp that hung at stays, trailing the banners of one of the rich mountain strongholds. And when I handed over the lookers to Jack beside me, I rolled onto my back and thought about those black interceptors, the way they seemed to suck the light out of the world like holes, and about Miss Holly Bright. I thought about how much she would've liked one. How much she would've liked *stealing* one. How she would've laughed as she burned, deathless, out of the lot in a rain of lasers and boogers and lead.

"So how do we cross it?" I heard Reggie ask.

"That?" said Jack, and laughed.

"We don't," said Asa. "Jack and I ain't crossed a legal border in a dog's age."

"But Asa needed to see it, din't ya, Asa?"

"I did. Need to know how the traffic is stacking up and how bored or busy all the fellas look. Needed to see how they were ganged up for the night. How the line looks."

Reggie again: "And how does it look?"

Then Jack and Asa both together: "Bad."

"*Bad*-bad," Jack added.

"Really not even a little good," said Asa. "They must be expecting something bigger'n us coming through, and they's gonna have all their ears up, besides."

"So do we go home then?" Reggie asked.

"No," I said, linking my hands behind my head. "We don't go home."

There was a pause, and then Jack said, "Begging your pardon, Duncan, but I believe that's my brother's decision to make. Not yours."

Asa, apparently, was the border reaver in the family. The one with the coyote blood.

"He's got the luck of it," Jack said. "Ain't no one gets across lots and under brush like Asa does."

I sighed, made my apologies for being presumptuous and saw Asa show tooth in the last gentle glow of the sunset. "That's alright, Duncan. You couldn't of knowed that I was both the handsome *and* talented one in the family."

He pushed himself up with all four arms and squirmed backward until he was below the sightline of the ridge. Jack and I did the same.

"We'll go," said Asa. "But not here. We're gonna have to eat some dirt first."

Meanwhile, Reggie had the lookers and continued glassing the area, as though if he only waited long enough, the view would get better.

Seven hours before, we made our crossing. We did it blacked-out and slow, with Asa and Jack in the cab and everyone else bedded down flat and quiet in the rear of the truck, heat-reflective sheets strung from the open ribs of the roll bars and only the purr of the electric engine to move us.

Asa navigated in the green haze of nightvision—a complicated single-occulus rig strapped around his head like the sort that night-drop helicopter pilots wear—and with Jack whispering in his ear.

Asa threaded the truck through deer trails and rabbit paths, took it up and down inclines that felt like 89-degree slopes when we were all laying there, clutching at the seats and packing straps to keep from tumbling out the back of the truck's bed. There were times when Asa seemed to be racing the wind. There were times when we didn't move at all. Just sat in ticking silence in the black-on-blackness of full night under thick canopy forest. The girls whispered to each other. Julie's scratching at his stitches sounded loud enough to bring the whole of the world crashing down. Reggie hissed in my ear, "If I had my Penelope still, none of this would've been necessary."

There came a moment when the truck lay still and seemed to strain against its own stillness. I heard crickets and the whispering of the breeze through the clattering needles of the pines.

Then suddenly we were dashing, bouncing crazily, diving down into a canyon—a midnight abyssal of knife-bladed stones and dry trees that broke against our progress with cracks like thunder—and skidding like slewing across glass with that sickening feeling of a machine slipping beyond the physical boundaries of control. There was a flash of light. Then another. The truck straightened out. It surged forward even faster. Another flash. It climbed a mountain. Smashed through boulders. Leapt a hundred feet in the air and dropped like a comet. Then stopped. Sighed. Rocked on its massive springs. Was quiet.

We all heard the cab's doors open then thunk closed.

Someone stripped back one of the panels of heat-reflective fabric. It was Jack.

"We're across. Everyone unbutton and stow this canvas."

We did so. Above us, the night sky swirled with a milk of stars, but there were clouds coming in. There was a breeze, charged with the electric smell of lightning. I lit a cigarette and shared it with Big Libby, and when I climbed back into the bed of the truck, I fell asleep like someone flipping off a switch.

Six hours before, I was sleeping. Five hours before, I was sleeping.

Four hours before, I was sleeping but came awake from a dream I still recall for its patent ridiculosity and cold, gnawing strangeness.

In my dream, Clarence and me had been walking hand-in-hand through the streets of a dead city which was the apotheosis of all dead cities—one that stretched corner to corner and end to end across all that remained of the world. We'd moved through canyons of warped and fire-blacked skyscrapers that curved inward as though reaching for each other until they became like rotten, hooked teeth in a giant's mouth.

In the dream, my good, new boots had grown old, worn down at the heels from walking many a weary mile. The feathers woven into Clarence's hair were no longer seagull but eagle, fresh and new and powerful. And from somewhere, a woman had been singing in this beautiful, pure and shining voice.

"That's 'Duo des fleurs,'" he'd said to me. "'Sous le dome epais.' The 'Flower Duet' from Lakmé."

"I know that," I'd said to him, though I surely did not because while my education has been broad and varied, it does not stretch to the knowing of French operas. And then I told him that I did not like it, which was also untrue because it is quite a beautiful tune and I thought the way it boomed and bounced 'round the husk through which we strolled—echoing down like the voice of God or his angels—was lovely in a way that not much else in all of my memory ever has been.

In the middle of the street, Clarence stopped. Smiled at me. Around us, there was a rumbling. A tinkle of falling glass. Behind him, down in the direction that we'd been headed, the façade of a crumbling building slid free and came crashing down in a gout of dust and brick.

"You don't like it because you know what comes next," Clarence had said.

From behind me there'd been a groan of metal. A terrible rending and screeching. And a building that looked a lot like the Chrysler Building had slewed in its foundation and begun to topple. Behind it, the Cira Center shuddered and all its glass blew out at once like a bomb had gone off in its heart. Smaller buildings began to crumble everywhere, flowing into the street like they'd been turned to liquid, and the bigger ones—the Petronas Towers, the Burj Khalifa, the Sears Tower, 1818 Market, the Jin Mao tower, Sears Tower, the Twin Towers, the Nakatomi building, the Tyrell Corporation headquarters—all died and died as the music swelled and the voices soared over the grumble, crash and shatter. And then Clarence had leapt into the air and turned into an eagle, flapping upward into a rapidly shrinking window of perfect blue sky.

I woke in a sweat, feeling sticky and cotton-stuffed with the "Flower Duet" still ringing in my head and my tongue laying like a piece of leather against my teeth. Asa was pulling the truck over to the side of a narrow, unmaintained road which cut arrow-straight across a flat plain. There was nothing out there but darkness, monsters and, in the distance, the crackle of heat lightning stabbing down from the sparkling bellies of low clouds.

Jack climbed out of the cab. He banged on the panels with his fist.

"Piss break," he yelled. "Ladies to one side, fellas the other. Julie, you're dealer's choice, I suppose."

I yawned, stretched, and rolled out into the cool and dark with tatters of dream still hanging on me like cobwebs and my feet not seeming to fully contact the earth. My legs were half-asleep. I hobbled off the road and into the flatness beyond and found it a field, twined with thick, heavy vines and lumpy with what looked like pumpkins. I took a breath.

And before I'd even unlimbered my timber, I heard Jack yell, "Jesus Christ!" Then a scream from the other side of the truck. Running footsteps—bare feet slapping on pavement. Julie yelling, "Lights, Asa! Lights lights lights!" and another scream.

Still muddled from sleep, I fumbled for my gun but wasn't wearing it. I dropped into a crouch.

"Where?" shouted Asa from the cab of the truck.

Then many voices. Then a sweeping cone of light from a hand-held lamp.

"Where?" Asa again.

Julie's voice: "Over here! Over here!" And Jack, in the darkness, "Here, Asa! Right here!"

The field was full of heads. Both sides, all heads. Or rather, it was full of thin shells that looked like pumpkin skin or melons, but inside were heads—girl heads and boy heads, the same half-dozen faces repeated over and over. Some shells had broken open and the faces were rotted away. Some of the skulls had split or been broken open, showing the twinkle of gold connectors, diodes, Peltier coolers, thyristors, supercapacitors, and the fur of hair-fine wires. Some shells, obviously ripe, had opened to the moonlight, the skin glowing waxy-smooth, the wet eyes blinking, rolling in their sockets, the faces opening and closing their idiot mouths.

"Back in the truck!" Jack bellowed. "Asa, kill the lights!" And from where we had all so recently debarked, now we tumbled like kittens over one another in our rush, scrambling to be clear of those faces, the perfect teeth, the smooth, bald heads.

The light danced crazily, then switched off. The engine growled in low gear. Jack was yelling at Asa to go—*go, go, go*—and then we were going, the tires biting, everyone touching everyone else to make sure no one was left behind, and me wondering if we'd been on the road the whole time or if Asa had cut across that field, popping heads beneath the wheels like ripe melons while I slept.

Everyone watched the sky. For drones. For vengeance. For the twinkle of a falling star which would be the exhaust signature of a liquid hydrogen missile locked on to the truck's heat and weight and shape or the smell of our sweat as we lay, panting, in the bed.

"Operation like that," Julie said, his fingers knotted together atop his head. "I can't believe they don't have security. That they'll just let us drive away."

Big Libby chewed on her bottom lip. Clementine hid her face. Reggie was massaging his twitchy arm. Jack crouched with his back against the rear wall of the cab, his head down between hunched shoulders as though expecting a blow, eyes wildly searching the sky.

But there was no drone. There was no missile. There was nothing but wind and the night, the lightning drawing closer and the quiet, nervous talk—all of us wondering then if we'd just imagined the field full of heads. If it'd all been just another dream.

Eventually, I stood and pissed out the back of the truck, holding to the roll bar with one hand, myself with the other.

Clementine asked, "You want me to hold that for you, baby?" But her heart wasn't in it. Her voice at once both small and too loud, like she was trying to spook her own fears away by shouting.

And I said, "No, Clemmy. I think I'll be alright," then finished, tucked it away and stood, watching the clouds dance on a hundred electric legs.

Three hours before, we were lost. Inside the cab, Jack and Asa were laughing, holding mini-flashlights in their mouths and puffing out their cheeks like children. Julie was sitting beside me on the siderail of the truck and he smiled.

"Them two," he says, shaking his head. "I don't know that the one could breathe without the other."

Two hours before, we'd gotten ourselves found again and were easing once more overland. The girls had gone quiet and were sitting close up on each other, holding hands and staring silently out the back of the truck. Julie'd climbed into the cab with Jack and Asa. Reggie was sitting cross-legged, poking through his bag.

"How do you know this girl, Duncan?" he asked me all of a sudden. He spoke without looking up from his work—smoothing a thumb over one of the bricks of explosives, pushing and un-pushing a button on the arming box.

I was chewing distractedly at one of my thumbnails and wanting badly for a cup of Castle chicory. "She gave me a ride once," I said.

Reggie huffled out a chuckle that made him sound like someone's doting grandpa. "Gave you a ride," he said.

"I mean that in the literal sense. As in she picked me up and took me from one place to another."

"She must be very pretty, this girl."

"She is."

"Smart. Joyful. Suffused with grace."

"She is," I repeated. "Least I imagine she is."

"You imagine."

I could feel the girls' eyes on me. Curious, perhaps, at the strange motivations of my alien sex. "Are you saying I wouldn't be doing all this for an ugly, dumb and clumsy girl, Reggie?" I asked.

He pursed his lips and nodded his head, clucking like a hen over one of the detonators and blowing off an imaginary bit of dust. "I'm saying that you intrigue me, Piano Man. I'm saying that if your motivations are as pure as you claim them to be, then you are the rarest man I've ever met." He looked up, his eyes flat and black. "But I don't believe it."

I said nothing. Neither did the girls.

Then Reggie shrugged. "Not that it matters," he said. "A battle is a battle and a girl is a worthier prize than land or revenge or anything I ever rode for."

I turned away from him and stared out into the dark, thinking my own impure thoughts and keeping my mouth shut about them.

An hour before, we were there. Or near enough. Asa had stopped the truck about a mile off, in what he recalled to be the last blind spot before the approach to the front gate.

Reggie lobbied again for a bloody and glorious frontal assault. I demurred, in a gentle and politic fashion considering the hour, and by good rights, drew together my company and explained once more the order of how things was going to go.

"Remember," I said. "We're not walking in there looking for a fight. Jack, Julie, Asa, you're just yourselves, okay? Weary travelers wanting an eye-opener and too tired for any complicated amusements. Hold your tongues. Be as invisible as you can. Spread out about the room if you're able. Ladies, you will be with me once the Colonel and I get ourselves fixed up. Either one or two or three men should ought to be left with you in the room once this kicks off. If it's three, do nothing and we'll come for you. If it's one or two, do your best, alright?"

Big Libby, with a fiercely piratical grin and a generalish black-hand look about her, nodded. She was dressed for battle in her best heels, her shortest skirt, and her liftingest underthings. She would be first through the door. Clemmy would sashay in behind, in her easterns and nothing more. Both ladies had worked at jack-rolling before, so taking men at their weakest and most unwise was no new thing to them. And for the moment, they seemed to be taking no small delight in the itching, sour nervousness of the men around them.

"You're armed?" I asked them.

"In the best way possible," said Libby, saucily cocking one hip and winking at me. "But we got tasers, too."

I didn't feel comfortable asking where they were carrying them.

Reggie would be with me until we got situated. He'd wrapped his bag in a ratty scrap of cloth he'd found in the truck's gear box so it didn't look so new. He had a pistol in his belt, Asa's nightvision rig around his neck and a compact little submachine gun besides. He would cover our retreat and be our reinforcement should things inside go all agee. I'd also placed him in charge of taking Miss Holly Bright in hand and hustling her to the truck. Colonel Arthur Reginald Molesworth was, essentially, in charge of every-thing, the rest of us just there to play-act and yell real loud and run like the devil was onto us once all was said and done.

I looked every one of them in the eyes and nodded and smiled at them because they were, in that moment, my true and boon companions—following me into nonsense, walking boldly into danger just because I'd asked them to. Wastrels and whores and thieves and crazy old men, all, but just then, they was also my army.

"Thank you all," I said to them. "This goes right, we'll all be home and safe and drinking toasts to our gallantry before sup-per. Everyone does their part. No one gets hurt. Them's the rules, understand?"

Everyone understood. They were good ones, them.

"Alright then, Asa. Let's load up and go have a drink, eh? I hear Great Times is just the place for it."

Thirty minutes before, all was set-and-settled.

From a distance, we could all see the stain the place cast against the sky in a great and greasy sheen of yellow light that put me in mind of the crackle of fat over a fire.

I imagined I could hear drums pounding though I could not. I imagined I could smell the sick, sour sweat of them as had given themselves over to all that was broken and wrong in the human character though, plainly, I could not. And even though, in that quiet, eternal moment before the quickening of the action, I sat my inner self down and gave him the gad, explaining how we had been in a hundred places worse than Great Times could ever dream of being, me and me, and had come and gone happily and in all ways unperished every time, my imaginations and bitterest humors were nonetheless running south with me.

I saw walls a hundred feet high, crawling with stone-faced screws and giggling psychopaths. I tasted the heat of sacrificial fires, imagined iron doors and death rays and mean dogs and loud-headed girls with razor-edged smiles working over a crowd of vicious drunks, junkies, sneak-thieves, murderers and savage night creatures. I saw men rolling like pigs in the filth of their own making. A bloody, fire-touched nightmare where babies fought monkeys with knives and fat men danced shirtless to a doomed bar band playing "Rock You Like a Hurricane" over and over again forever.

"Well here we go then," I said to myself as Asa bumped the truck up onto the road and we began the long, flat approach to the gate.

In all of its actualness, Great Times was nothing like any of that. The faux adobe walls were ten feet high, not a hundred, and were crumbling besides. The gate was daunting as a jaw filled with iron teeth, but it stood open as we drew near and had nothing but a single man on it, and him asleep behind a bottle of popskull.

There were no guards. There were no monkey-baby fights. There were fires, but they were small, smudgy things, tended mostly by red-eyed women brewing coffee or wash water and who watched us pass with flat, disinterested eyes.

Inside, a scattering of vehicles was parked all higgledy-piggledy and looked, mostly, to have simply been abandoned where their drivers had left them. There was a central square, lit weakly by pole-mounted lights run off a chugging ethanol generator, with a wooden sign that said Plaza de Cono in sloppy red paint and had a stuffed Mickey Mouse nailed to one corner, black X's of electrical tape covering its eyes.

The borders of the square were demarcated by a mess of falling down shacks and weather-stained tents raised up off the ground on wood platforms growing beards of windblown trash. The store where Asa had bought his goat-flavored ice cream was dark and looked to have recently burned half down, but there was signs in the spider-webbed windows offering fuel by the liter, ammunition of all calibers, plates of shrimp and goat-meat tacos. There were no death rays, but from a couple of the more lavish hovels sprouted tinfoil-and-chickenwire satellite dishes all asnarl with patch cables and extension cords. And what few apparent seekers after the legendary hospitality of Great Times we saw were either skittering furtively through the cluttered and laundry-hung dark between shacks or stumbling 'round the Plaza in directions determined by the whiskey compass and not no kind of rational thinking.

Great Times, for what it was, looked more like a decaying summer camp for old drunks and retired pole-dancers than any den of terrible iniquity. And in the center of it all, all the way down at the head-end of the Plaza de Cono, the posada rose like two stories of rattletrap slowly being sold off for scrap, with loose-hanging batwing doors, a collapsing veranda, more gaps than shingles on the roof, and dull, cold neon in the filthy front windows advertising COLD BEER and PUSSY PUSSY PUSSY.

"This is it?" I asked Julie. "You sure we're in the right place?"

Julie chewed on his bottom lip. "It seems to have fallen on hard times of late, don't it?"

The original plan, when I'd imagined Great Times to be a vast and sprawling metropolis of sin, was for Reggie and me to hop free of the truck just inside the gate (perhaps performing action hero combat rolls to impress the ladies and give our later retellings of events a certain Rambo-ish flavor), then to reconnoiter out among the twisting alleys of Sodom until we'd clapped eyes to the vehicles driven in by the Regulators so we could know where they were at.

I'd been concerned that I wouldn't recognize them. I had descriptions both from the car-parking man and the bystanders outside El Cielo, but I hadn't known if it would be enough. A red jeep, open and road-broke. A street-driving fuel-cell pickup, blue over Bondo, with a loaded bed and a fancy gearbox. To find these two vehicles among the hundreds of *other* jeeps and *other* pickups and deuces and four-bys and monster trucks and lowriders and hovercars and saddled unicorns and Millenium Falcons and all else I'd imagined being gathered there in Great Times's heavily guarded parking zones had seemed unlikely bordering on impossible. This was, of course, a concern I had not shared with my army. No sense fretting them unnecessarily, I'd thought.

But what I hadn't counted on was the general squalidness of reality and the mournful look of the dozen-odd beaters parked in the dust, the few work-model automatic horses standing barded, their eyes blinking red with anti-tamper electronics, and the one sickly-looking bandersnatch coughing worm-flecked vomit into the dirt beside the post to which it was chained. It took all of a second to pick out the Regulators' whips. They were parked side-by-side in front of the posada, still loaded down with gear, and with another bonus as well: Harold Lartner himself. The fat, bearded Arthurian scholar who'd broke his hand on my head back at El Cielo now lay like a beached whale in the space between the two vehicles—his filthy snap-front riding up over the pasty white hummock of his belly, his right hand encased in a cocoon of bluish sprayplast, a constellation of empty brown longneck bottles arrayed, halo-like, about his head.

I pounded on the cab with my fist and told Asa to stop the truck. Then I asked Julie for the loan of his knife.

"You're not going to kill him, are you?" he asked.

"Of course he is," answered Reggie, and I told him to get out of the truck, which he did with a harrumph.

"No, I'm not going to kill him," I said to Julie as I took the knife. "Take Jack and Asa and get in there. Stick to the plan. If there's trouble, holler out, but all's I need is five minutes. Maybe less. Hold the line, wait for the hot moment, and keep a hand near to Asa, okay? I don't want him getting nervy."

They went, acting the parts of themselves, but up to no capers. Jack had an arm thrown around Asa's shoulders. All three of them were laughing. If any of the Regulators were still up and in the posada's bar, they were to come back out fastly before they got recognized. Those were the orders. When they didn't come bolting immediately back out the batwings, I guessed we were golden.

"Reggie, you're on. Start making like a drunken pervert and peeping in windows."

"And if I am discovered?"

"Improvise."

He smiled. "Stellar."

"Don't kill anyone."

His smile snapped off like a light. "You have a funny way of operating, Piano Man."

"Just find the girl and I'll join you directly."

And then he was off, too—marching with his stick tapping and his arm on a twitch that unbalanced him with every other step. After that, it was down to me and the girls.

"Ladies, cuff up, if you please. But gimme your sparker first, Miss Clementine. I promise I'll bring it right back."

She was wearing hers on a rawhide loop inside the back of her dress—a thing meant for pulling out as the garment was being removed, when a fella was at his most distracted, which was clever.

"Everyone thinks we'd hide 'em in our cleavage," she said.

"Or up in our pussies," added Big Libby.

"Yeah, so no one ever sees it comin'," Clemmy finished, then turned. "I can't reach it 'less I'm taking my dress down, and you ain't paid for no show." She held up her hair until I'd fished out the dull silver tube, half-wrapped in insulating tape.

"How many charges?" I asked.

"Two," she said. "And you've got to hit him with it pretty hard to activate the discharger."

I hit Harold Lartner with it pretty hard. He pissed himself voluminously and the contacts burned a brand into the rings of dirt on his fat neck where I'd shoved it into him.

After that I slashed the tires on both vehicles—setting the knife point into the rubber and stomping on the nut end with my heel because cutting through tire rubber is always harder than they make it look on the TV. There was some noise, but not a lot. And anyway, no one appeared to notice. All about us, Great Times just went on about its sad, exhausted business.

Then I rehung the sparker for Clemmy, liking the way she shimmied to get it to lay just right. They both had zip ties hung around their wrists as though they were cuffed, but loose enough so that they could have their hands free quick as a twitch. I pulled the bags over their heads myself.

"Rudeness," I muttered. "Ladies, I am truly sorry for these tribulations."

"Hardly the worst position I've found myself in," said Libby.

"My bag smells like feet," said Clemmy.

"Breathe through your mouth, darling. I'll be back in one minute. Try to look . . . I don't know. Kidnapped."

Reggie was having troubles. There were windows letting in on all the rooms on the posada's first floor, but most of them were covered over with plywood or black plastic sheeting in lieu of the glass that'd long ago been smashed out of them. There were other windows, smaller and higher-set, that he thought were likely for the bathrooms, but he couldn't reach them.

"Boost me, Piano Man," he said. "Quick-quick."

"No, t'other way 'round," I said. "I know who we're looking for. You don't."

"Because you think there's going to be more than *one* kidnapped girl in these rooms?" he asked incredulously, then knotted up his brows when I spread my hands like to say *look about, friend.*

Then he nodded. "I take your point." He crouched and made a basket of his fingers—real and metal—into which I carefully stepped. He quivered and shook, but it was enough to get my eyes above the lip of the windows.

In the first there was nothing.

In the second there was nothing.

In the third, there was a teddy bear, brown and careworn, but near life-size and with wet and glistening girl-parts. It saw me peeking, and gave me a look of such sadness that it broke a piece of me I hadn't thought I possessed.

In the fourth, meth lab.

In the fifth, nothing.

In the sixth, a woman washing herself in a most private fashion. It wasn't Holly, so I quickly turned away.

The seventh window had been replaced by expensive louvered shutters, snapped hard closed. I considered forcing one with Julie's knife, but didn't. If necessary, I could come back. And anyway, there was a smell seeping around that window that I liked not a bit.

The eighth window was lit. I peeped in carefully and saw an empty bathroom—a broken sink, gravity shower, a disgusting toilet, everything white and tiled as though to best show and preserve its fascinating collection of human stains. There was a door. It was open. And beyond it, a lit main room that appeared to have no one in it, except that maybe there was a *feeling* of occupation. Can't explain it any better than that. I craned my neck around. Thought I saw some conglomeration of electronics set on a table pushed tight against the wall adjoining the next room. Thought I saw beer bottles and an ashtray twining with white smoke. Thought I saw the shadow of someone moving.

And then Reggie dropped me.

"One more," I mouthed once we'd gotten ourselves silently untangled and Reggie had fetched up his stick and screwed his hat back down onto his head. I held up one finger. He shrugged. Shook out his hands. Got in position.

In the ninth window was Miss Holly Bright. There was duct tape over her mouth but the bag had been removed from her head. Her cinnamon-candy hair was lank. Her eyes were closed. There was dried blood on her face and fresh blood running down across her hands from where she'd been fighting the steel handcuffs she was wearing, looped around the metal drainpipe of the bathroom's sink.

She was not sleeping. Who would be? I scratched a fingernail at the window. I tapped at it lightly but insistently. Eventually, her eyes snapped open and fixed on me. They widened in surprise, crinkled in a sweet, flabbergasted confusion, and then I expected a flood of joy, relief, intense sexual longing, something.

Instead, I finally got my death rays.

To which I responded by giving her a thumbs-up and a dumb grin. Then miming something blowing up. Then miming her covering her ears. Then Reggie dropped me again.

"She's here," I hissed in his ear. "Awake and of a piece. Chained to the sink pipe with police cuffs, about five feet back from this wall."

Reggie nodded.

"Can you take it down without killing her?"

He nodded again. He was already digging things out of his bag.

I rose up to my hunkers, began to move off, but then came back. "Can you *really* do it?"

"I can."

"Without killing the girl."

"Yes."

"Or yourself."

"Yes."

"You're sure?"

"Piano Man," he said, whispering as his arm twitched and made me highly regretful of leaving him in charge of a sack full of explosives. "During the Amiable Separation I—"

"Blew bridges and burned up buildings, yeah, I know."

He grinned and laid his chrome hand on my arm. "Go do your piece, Duncan. I'll get your girl out." His arm twitched and he cuffed me in the side of the head.

"You should really have that arm looked at," I said.

"Who says that was the arm?"

I went back to the truck and found the girls sitting where I'd left them. Big Libby was smoking a handroll with her zip-tied hands, the bottom of her bag pushed up just enough to clear her red lips.

"Ladies," I said.

"Duncan?" asked Clemmy.

"Live and in person," I said, took the smoke from Big Libby's hand and had a pull. "Y'all ready to put the cosh on some bad men?"

The haute decor and sense of lavish opulence did not change from the outside of the posada to the inside. Directly through the batwings was a wide barroom, lit gutteringly by slut lamps burning what smelled like cooking fat and two bare electric bulbs grafted onto a hanging cord that looked to have once supported a fine chandelier. The bar was long and lovely, made of knotty pine that'd been smooth and polished in another life but now was just a flat place for drunks to lay their swimming heads. At the far end, a broken Wurlitzer squatted darkly as though passing judgment on the poor taste of them as would let such a machine lay wounded. High behind the bar, a broken TV wore a hat and a frowny-face sketched right onto the screen with thick black marker.

Jack was at the bar, his elbows up and his head down. Julie had fixed himself at a window and made to be looking off mournfully toward the horizon. When Asa saw me come in, I saw him stop himself from waving, slap a fake scowl on his face, and stomp over to the cold juke where he proceeded to poke at it with his lower set of arms to no good effect.

"That's broken, sir," said the kid behind the bar—a little twist of a thing, thin and mean as a rawhide cord and dressed in a brushed black bowler, tweed trousers, a pocket vest, and fine shirt that all hung on him like he'd nothing beneath but bones. His eyes were puffy from the hour. His talk more than a little slurred from tucking into his own medicine.

Aside from us, the bar was lightly populated, owing to the hour, perhaps, and the fact that I couldn't imagine an ounce of fun having been had there since before dogs was pups. There was a card game going at one table with three sharps all trying to fleece the same sheep. A trucking man in a billed hat and a sleeveless shirt with his beddable pulled up close on the seat beside him and squirming like she didn't appreciate his smell. One man asleep in a corner with a bottle a'twixt his knees. Another dozer at the bar. Two men drinking at the seats nearest the door, sipping at beers in glass mugs that'd sweated rings onto the bar.

I had, then, a lighting-spark moment of pure genius where I thought that I might just take the whole place over complete. Storm in, announce myself King and holy sovereign of Great Times with my boys as muscle backing my play, and run the place like a proper Amsterdam of fun and cultured felony. I would get myself a crown and robes of finest ermine, fix up the roof, the window-glass and the chandelier, re-start the store, let Big Libby and Clemmy school the girls on the right decorum of them as make their money lying down.

It was an instantaneous fantasy, blooming full in my head. I saw Great Times rebuilding and then flourishing, with me swanning through the posada's bar in a fine suit with a good hat and a watch on a chain. I heard the clamor of the gaming tables and saw the hard, white glow of the crystal lights spilling down over men in string ties and polished boots. I saw bad nights and sweet nights and cool mornings where I sat up counting up my dollars with a cup of chicory steaming in the soft dawn light. I saw Banjo Oblangata and the Critical Malfunctions brought up to play sets in the Plaza and me growing old here, with Jack and Julie and Asa as my brain trust and aides-de-camp. I saw it being passed down peaceably to a son who carried my name. My *real* name.

It would've been nice, I think. Or maybe not. Maybe I would've botched it. Grown bored. Burned the whole thing down one night out of petulance and spite for lost chances.

But no matter what it was, it would've been better than what came next down the path that I chose.

I pushed the girls in ahead of me, tugged on my biggest fun-boy's smile, and called out loudish, "Good morning to you, gents!" I tipped my hat to the trucker's girl, said, "Ma'm," then clapped eyes to the barman. "Need to speak to a manager, me. There one about at this cheerful hour?"

"That'd be me, I s'pose," said the boy, slitting his eyes at me and taking in the girls in a single glance as well. "What'choo need, friend?"

Smile like the breaking dawn. Heart swelling with the sudden, sure, stupid knowledge that we might actually pull this off. Amid such squalor, among such dregs, how could we do anything but?

"S'not what I need, son. It's what some of yours is a'wanting. These two—" I prodded Big Libby a little to make all six-foot-something of her shimmy, then pulled the bags off of both of their heads with a right flourish. "—is a delivery. A special gift for Harold and Rufe and them."

Talk like you know what's what. Talk like you know everything there is to know. That's how you make this work. Talk like the other party knows just as much, is heir to every bit of knowledge, so that they feel strange in admitting that they're out to sea. And just never stop talking. Never *ever* stop talking.

I stepped around the girls and leaned in over the bar. The conspirator's pose. I lowered my voice so's the barman would have to lean close, too.

"Saw Harold outside, I did. Looks like he's had hisself a spree. How long they beat me by getting here?"

"'Bout three hours, maybe," said the barman, and I slapped him on the shoulder, adding even more watts to my smile. "Guess I am in a piece of trouble then, ain't I. Running late, me. On account of the girls, that was. Had to pick 'em up special. Rufe, he's got his tastes, huh?"

The barman said nothing.

"Well hell, boy! Don't just stand there. Pull us a bucket of your finest lager and then take these two back, will ya? Say they's from Elmer Stump, special delivery'd, and that Elmer would greatly 'preciate some company out here and someone to pick up the tab for all his troubles."

"You're who now?"

I pulled out Harold's badge and flipped it open to show the star. "Son, I am Elvis Stamp and you'd best put a wiggle on. Beer first. Girls second. Jump to it and there's the top part of an eagle for your trouble." I pushed the girls in the direction of the back door out of the bar—the door that led back to the rooms, I hoped—and bounced up sprightly onto a stool as the barman made a move toward his taps.

"Actually, you know what, son? Maybe take the girls back first. Depending on how pleased the boys is with their new friends, p'raps they'll stand a fella to something a bit more powerful."

He stared dully. I laid the badge, star up, on the scarred bar top.

"Git now. Elvin Stomp. That's what you tell 'em. And I'll watch your liquor for you. If you can't trust the law, who can you trust?"

The barman held for a beat, then two, then shook his head and made his shuffling way around the far end of the bar, taking both girls in hand and leading them off without another word.

I looked around the bar. Most eyes were on me. Except for the two men at the seats nearest the door, who were staring intently into their beers.

That's where the trouble will start, I thought. They'd be my first concern once the fun started.

What happened next was confusing. It was, and remains, all a jumble. A mess of surprises and oddness and things falling wrong in ways that no one could've expected.

I sat at the bar, laid my elbows down, hunched my shoulders and stared into the place where any proper bar ought to have a mirror but this one just had a crude sketch of a girl with her legs spread done right on the chipping plaster by what must've been either a mental patient or a small child with a dull pencil. The artwork wasn't my concern, though. Sitting that way put my hand as close as possible to my gun without me actually drawing it and waving it around.

Asa was by the juke. Jack had the opposite end of the bar. Julie still stood by the windows, but had turned now and had the sweep of the room.

At the card table, the game continued apace. I could hear the knocking of the barman on the Regulators' door, but no voices. A minute passed. A door opened. A door slammed closed. Coming back down the hall, I heard the popping of more than one pair of boots on the well-trod boards. I put my head down. All's I needed was for them to get into the room—clear of the door, quit of the hallway. That was it.

"Who in the fuck is Elvis Stump," said a voice, commanding but conversational. *That would be the old man*, I thought. I glanced sideways. Saw that he had the young and shaky one with him as well. Him as was called Rufe. Which meant that it was only Glasses, the mad one, left in the room with two hundred and fifty combined pounds of angry, determined prostitutes who didn't take kindly to men who didn't take kindly to women.

"That's me!" I announced loudly. "What? Y'all didn't like your gift?"

I stood. The old man recognized me fastly and stiffened, but the lads were already moving—guns out, shouting up the whole crowd like they was running cattle. I hopped back quick off my stool, my own pistol leaping into my hand with a will, and got some space a'tween me and the two quiet lads by the door.

"No one touches leather," said me. "Them as do get dropped."

Always keep talking. Always, *always* keep talking.

"This ain't no robbery. Leave your watches and wallets where they lay. We ain't after none of you. Just everyone sit tight now and wait for the boom."

There was a shout from back among the rooms—a raw and strangulated thing. Then a thud. Then a laugh that I knew as Libby's for certain.

"That's two of your four done, hoss," I said to the old man.

"You're gonna hang for this, boy," he replied. "I am a lawful man doing a lawful man's labor and you are going to hang for this."

"Maybe. But not today."

The explosion, when it came, was loud enough to startle the entire room. The walls shook. Plaster rained down. The lights swung crazy, rustling up shadows like unquiet spirits. The barman yelled and dropped to the ground like he'd been shot, though he hadn't been. I looked sharp to the two men nearest the door, but they were in a cower that confused me for just long enough to take my eyes from the old man, who dove away quite sprightly, hit the hard floor, and vanished behind the bar like a scuttling roach. Asa, with a pistol each in two of his four hands, was the nearest to him and began firing.

"Run!" I was yelling. "Everyone! We got what we came for! Get to the truck!"

The skinny one, in a plain, bewildered panic, reached for his iron and I shouted at him not to do it, but he wasn't listening. He had plaster in his hair and a look in his eyes like maybe he believed this, and maybe all the wide world, was just a piss-poor dream in which his starring turn was about to be cancelled. The girls came hustling down the hallway at a run, heels tapping like knuckles on the board floor, their cuffs (if they'd done right) now securing Glasses back in his room, one of their bags on his head. The skinny one heard them coming. He turned with his gun out and Julie fired on him, straight over the heads of the card players who'd gone to ground beneath the table. I did, too. Don't know which one of us holed him, but he went down.

"Run, dammit! All of y'all. Out the door and into the truck."

How many seconds had passed? I heard a second boom—smaller, flatter—and thought it was gunfire so ducked and crabbed my way backward until my back was to a wall beside the front door. Jack scrambled the length of the bar on his hands and knees hollering for his brother. When he reached the two silent men who'd been staking down the bar's far end, he climbed right over them.

"Go, Jack!" I yelled to him. "Start the truck!"

He went out the door.

The ladies were hugging the far wall, by the windows. Julie took them in hand and hustled them along until all three of them huddled in the corner. When I looked to him, I saw through the windows a body passing in the dark, followed close-on by a second. One of them might've been mustachioed and limping. One of them might've been pretty and smart and confusingly mean, but it was hard to tell. One of them might've been beating the other about the head and neck with angry, poundy little fists, too, but it was dark and I was busy, so I couldn't have said for sure.

"Go, Julie," I said. "Get 'em in the truck."

"Where's Asa?"

I swore. I looked. I heard nothing and saw nothing, so I hollered out his name.

"He's got a gun, Duncan," Asa yelled back.

"Goddamn right I do," hollered the old man from behind the bar. "What happened to my boy?"

"That Rufe?" I shouted back.

"Yeah."

"Might be that he could use some care," I yelled back. "He's bleeding, so you pitch your gun over the bar and you're free to see to him the moment mine walk out of here."

"You motherfuckers," he growled back. "You shot my boy."

"He was gonna shoot the girls," Julie said. "There was no cause for nobody to shoot nobody here."

I told Julie again to go and this time he listened. The girls followed. Then I told the old man to throw out his gun again.

"Fuck you, Elvis," he said. "Fuck you and them cunts and everyone you's rolling with. You's all gonna burn."

I stood up. "Asa, you shot?"

"No."

From behind the bar, the old man started calling for Rufe, but Rufe was not answering.

"Come to me then," I said. "It's time to go."

I heard shouting from outside. There was, from somewhere, a crazy dance of lights. I fired high into the wall behind the bar, just to keep the old man down and worrisome. Asa poked his head around the far end of the bar and ran hunched over, both his guns shot dry, their slides locked open. He skidded to a stop beside me and held them up, grinning wildly, "I forgot to bring spare clips," he said, then giggled sickly.

"Get to the truck, bud," I said. "Time to roll out."

"Throw out your gun!" I yelled again to the old man behind the bar. I fired twice into the dirty sketch of the girl, one bullet catching a bottle and filling the room with the Christmas tree scent of bathtub gin. I backed out the door, suddenly heard the rip of a machine gun firing, spun 'round quick and saw Reggie trying to cover both corners of the building at once.

"Time to fly, Piano Man! The natives are getting restless."

Jack came out from the side of the truck with a gun still in his hand. He ran under Reggie's barrel and darted to where Asa lay in the dirt. He'd fallen and I didn't know why. I saw firefly sparks in the darkness out across the Plaza de Cono and heard the pops of small calibers. From inside the posada came a howling. Jack and Asa rose before me, the two of them together, arm-in-arm, and laughing as they scrambled through the dust. In the cab, I saw the face of Miss Holly Bright. She was watching me and I felt the hero for it. I moved to walk toward her. Reggie had gone to the opposite corner of the cab and was firing clattering bursts into the night. I looked into Holly's eyes and I smiled.

I watched as her eyes grew large.

As she dove sideways.

As the bank of lights that ran along the front of the truck all blazed forth suddenly in a perfect titanium whiteness that dissolved the world into nothingness.

And then I heard the shots.

I was blind for five seconds. Maybe ten. I had somewhere misplaced my pistol when, in a sightless panic, I had hurled myself at the earth and tried to hug all of it at once.

As I later was made to understand, Holly had seen the old man—the last standing Regulator—come lurching out of the posada's batwings with a cut-down lever rifle in his hands. Having no other recourse to violence, she'd leaned over and punched the button that turned on all the truck's lights, blinding the old man just as he'd leveled the piece to back-shoot me like the scalish thug he was.

His shot went wide and I lived. He got off two more before Reggie turned the meatgrinder on him and took his legs off at his boot-tops. But as things turned out, he would live, too. Jack August, on the other hand, was the unlucky one. He took the lead meant for me, one bullet taking the top of his head off like opening up a can.

When my eyes cleared, the first thing I saw was Reggie with his hands up, peaceably giving over his little smig to some character dressed all in black like a cartoon ninja. Out by the truck's cab, there was another—a big one, with a pack on his back big enough to smuggle a small elephant in. He was hauling open the door from the outside and offering a glove to Miss Holly Bright, who took it and allowed herself to be handed down into the dust.

"Wait," I said. "No, wait."

Suddenly, the world seemed to be filled with men dressed for night-fighting. All in black. And masks besides. And carrying large and complicated firearms. There were lights. The rumble of engines and the smell of smoke. I saw Jemma Watts come staggering into my line of sight with her mouth hanging open and her hands over her ears.

I called out Holly's name and tried to push myself to my feet but was stopped by a firm hand between my shoulder blades.

A voice above me said, "Not a good idea right—" and that was as far as he got before I scissored my legs into his ankles and felt him fall half-atop me with a shout of surprise.

I kicked myself clear, drew Julie's knife, and went for him. Was stopped by many hands and many feet and put firmly back down on the ground. When I got a good look at the man I'd tried to stab, I saw it was one of the two men from the end of the bar. The quiet ones. Our eyes met and he grinned at me and shook his head as though I'd just told him a joke that wasn't quite worth laughing at, then stood and placidly batted the dust from his clothes as the knife was twisted from my hand—firmly, but not without care. None of my fingers got broke even though I was holding to it tight as death. From near to the truck, I could hear Asa calling his brother's name. I watched Holly being hustled away, and the man who'd taken her from the truck had taken off his black ski mask and it was Logue Ranstead. All the while, there was a look on my face like a dog asked to recite the Pledge of Allegiance.

"Let him up," said a voice from above, and all the hands and all the men attached to them did as they were told. But even when the weight was off, I stayed in the dust. I lay my forehead on the ground and closed my eyes. Because, of course, I knew that voice.

"Captain," I said. "Fancy meeting you here."

The Captain had gotten down on his hunkers before me and peeled the black mask back until he was wearing it like a hat. He was red and sweating beneath it. His breath had stunk of coffee.

"Duncan Archer," he says to me. "You are just born unto trouble."

And I said back to him, "As the sparks fly upward, I am."

He'd nodded, looked as though he were about to say something further, then didn't.

I was taken in hand after that, given back my pistol and Julie's knife and set in a line with Reggie, Julie, Big Libby, and Clementine. We were all told not to move. To stay rooted and quiet. I looked around for Miss Holly Bright, but saw her nowhere.

Asa had been let be—kneeling in the dirt with Jack's body in his lap, weeping over him, straightening up his collar and smudging the spatters of blood off his brother's face with his thumbs. Behind him, the posada burned, the fire sparked by the explosives that Reggie had used to blow out the back wall of the bathroom in which Holly had been held (and the pipe to which she had been attached) spreading now and chewing its way hungrily through the heart of the place. Unless it had been recovered, Rufe's body was getting a Viking's funeral, which was surely more than the little fucker deserved.

Harold Lartner had been scooped up. Glasses had been recovered from the room where Libby and Clementine had left him, but not before the flames had had at him more than slightly. He came out under a silver shock blanket, his pince-nez still clamped to his aquiline nose, one of the lenses cracked. The old man was doctored up on the spot until the flames became perilous, then was carried to the hood of a car where the saving of his life continued unbothered by little things like fire or guilt or want—the sickening, consuming want—of terrible vengeance.

And that, then, was the moment I thought of Gordon Navarro and the Castillo Brothers. Of the smell of gasoline, the story of a car crusher, a bed mussed by two bodies, and one brother bedding another one down to a long, cold sleep. I thought of rain but saw only the dry lightning stabbing heartlessly at the land from clouds that could not contain its rage and listened while Asa keened and rocked his dead brother in his arms down in the dust of the Plaza de Cono.

Intermission: In Which Old Friends Come Calling

We were taken, one-by-one, away from that place and to another place, out among the shanties that had become not just deserted but *remarkably* deserted. But for the fires, it looked like they hadn't been inhabited in a hundred years, and even then only by mole people who had no use for earthly things like televisions, blenders, or changes of clothing. We were told to sit. There were some of the Captain's ninjas there, but they paid us little attention. When I asked one of them if I could go get my briefcase out of the truck, he told me it could be gotten for me and asked me what it looked like.

"I'm just guessing, but I'd wager it's the only briefcase within a hundred miles of this place. So if you see one, likely it's mine."

Eventually, it was brought. It'd been sprung and riffled, but not expertly. Nothing important was missing.

Time passed. The sun began pinking the horizon. Asa was the last to be put among us and he didn't say a word.

Eventually, the Captain came—his head bare and a smile upon his face. No time for mourning, him. Nor a talent for it.

We all stood, save Asa, and his Captainness made courtly gestures to the ladies and kissed them both on the hand. Reggie he took by the back of the neck and shook. He was grinning, but there was an edge of meanness creeping into his teeth. He gave a look to Asa, but no more. For Julie there was a handshake and a gentlemanly exchange of names in which Julie gave his full one and the Captain gave a false one.

"Jack Tenrec," he said. "Any friends of Duncan's and suchlike and suchlike." And then he stepped back, surveyed the lot of us with his hands on his hips. "So," he said. "To the victors, then, yeah? An incredible thing you've done here tonight. Foolhardy." He looked at me. "Costly, I'm sad to say. But also amazing. *Inspiring*, even." He turned his gaze on the men milling about and snapped his fingers at them. "So medals, cash, cigarettes and whiskey and a ride home as heroes. All for my new friends."

"Thanks, but we've got our own ride," said Julie.

"Don't worry about that," the Captain said. "We'll take care of that, too. Got us some fine drivers. Certainly know the way from here to there."

"Duncan . . ." said Julie, looking over at me.

"It's fine, Julie," I told him. "We'll take a ride. No one's going to hurt the truck."

"Not sure if anyone *could* hurt that monster," said the Captain. "But he's right, Julie. Polish it for you, if you like. Gas 'er up. Just let one of these men know where it needs to go and, *poof*, it'll be there. And you'll be right behind if that's your wish."

"It'll be fine, Julie," I said. "I'll go with you to the lockup. You'll see."

"No," said the Captain. "Mr. Archer, you're with me. Everyone else, it's time to make like tumbling tumbleweeds. I have a . . ." His voice trailed off and he looked over both shoulders, turned all the way around. "Dammit," he said, then barked, "Barnum! Strange!" and the two quiet men from the bar at the posada appeared, coming up out of the shadows between two of the shacks.

"Stop sneaking up on people you weirdoes," he said. "Now take these good people away and find them the smoothest ride we have. They are kings and queens, you understand? They are to be taken wherever they like, given soda pops and ice cream if they want to stop on the way, and it all comes out of your pockets. See them home safely. Go. Now."

☢

Reggie was taken away by men still in combat masks and black gloves. He went without a word.

The man called Barnum took the ladies away. I thanked them and reassured them that they were among good people, but they gave me nervous looks over their shoulders as they were walked off into the breaking dawn.

Asa and Julie were taken away by the man called Strange. We never did become rich men or horse barons. Maybe in another life, though.

And then it was just me and the Captain and he walked a full circle around me, looking me up and down like he was deciding whether or not to buy me. I held my briefcase in front of me, all ten fingers knotted through the handle.

"Twenty-four hours," he said. "You did this in twenty-four hours."

I shrugged. "Had to."

"In twenty-four hours you tracked down four Regulators, assembled a team, organized logistics, and staged an assault and extraction on an armed compound."

"I did."

"Honest, I do not know what to make of you, Duncan Archer."

I said nothing.

The Captain explained that he and his had been planning their own operation for almost a week. That he had money, men, support, intelligence. "Both the spy kind and the kind actually lives between my ears," he said. "Both of which you appear short on."

Holly, he said, had been bait. He'd been trailing her around the city for days and nights and days, hoping that her path and the paths of the Regulators would cross because those Regulators had been causing him a pain for quite some time and he needed them removed from his landscape.

"She knew what she was doing, Duncan. Mine all do."

She'd never been out of sight or mind, Holly. The Captain had had pavement artists on Broadway when she went down to

El Ciello, his urchins watching the Brown Palace. Jemma Watts had been camped for days in the room next door to the one occupied by the Regulators, listening to every curse and snore and fart. Barnum and Strange had been haunting the bar for nearly as long.

"I had forty men," he said to me. "You had, what?"

"Two hookers, three semen-thieves, and a retired cavalry colonel," I said.

The Captain laughed.

"If Holly was your bait," I asked, "how was it she was following me?"

"She wasn't following you, idiot," he said. "I had her pick you up that night because she was in the area and available. After that, we thought you were following her."

"So who did you have on me then?"

He leaned forward. "Who says I had anyone watching you?"

"Because you did. Because you wouldn't *not* have someone watching me."

"Because you're so all-fired important all of a sudden?"

"No. Because if I was you and you was me, I would've had me under 24-hour solitary, rotating watch. One good man who . . ." My voice trailed off.

"Think it through," the Captain said.

I sighed. "Reggie."

The Captain smiled. "Of course, Reggie. He's been watching you since day one."

"I was the laundry."

"I have no idea what that means, but sure. You're the laundry, Duncan."

Holly and me, us bumping into each other had all been coincidence. She'd almost aborted at El Cielo, but then hadn't. The Captain's plan had been to take all four Regulators alive at Great Times, all in one rush. In and out in two minutes flat. Reggie's explosives had forced them to move early. Had deafened poor

Jemma. Barnum and Strange had thought the plan had changed and no one had told them.

"So what about One-Eyed Annie?" I asked. "She one of yours, too?"

"No, she honestly just likes your music."

"At the Brown Palace?"

"No one. Just the kids. They were following Holly and the Regulators. Reggie was following you. When they tangled, I guess they had to improvise."

"And Jack and Julie and Asa?"

The Captain shook his head. "No, but I like those guys. Well, two of them anyway. Somewhat less impressed with one the one who died."

I told him to shut up. He shook his head.

"What about Clarence? He had to be one of yours."

"Who's Clarence?"

"At El Ciello. Weird guy. Feathers in his hair. He was the one who sent me to the Brown and put me on the trail."

A single line appeared between the Captain's eyebrows. "No. Tell me about him."

So I did. Black hair. Young at first glance, but maybe older than he appeared. Talked a little funny. Kept drinking from this flask of blue—

At which point the Captain cursed, spat into the dust and shook his head.

"Injun Joe," he said.

"That's what he called himself, yeah," I said.

And "Brash . . ." said the Captain, then turned, pinched at his throat, and spoke into a radio link. Immediate dust-off, he said. Police up and fall back by predetermined escape routes. Wounded and all prisoners to the secondary evac under cover. "Send out the code to all irregulars and outriders," he said. "Assume we have been blown and behave accordingly."

Jemma arrived a moment later, driving Marlene with Logue crammed into the cab with her. She had clean white bandages over her ears.

"You're riding with us, Mr. Archer," the Captain said.

He ran for the passenger side door, yelled "shotgun!" at the closed window, then yanked open the door and shooed Logue out.

"That's not the way the game works," Logue said.

"Don't care," said the Captain. "Get in back. I need to talk with Duncan."

When the Captain wasn't looking, Jemma gave me the finger. But she was grinning when she did it. Then the Captain was yelling for me to get in and Jemma was racing the engine and all around us was noise and furious activity.

I took the passenger seat. Put my case down on the floor between my boots. The Captain reached past me to close the door.

"Take us home," he said to Jemma. "Shortest way possible."

And then to me. "Duncan, I need you to tell me every single thing that man Clarence said to you. Everything he did. Spare no detail, you understand? And don't lie to me or I'll know."

Which, of course, was the funniest thing of all. Because everything I said to him was a lie, wasn't it? From my name on down. Not one thing about me was true or honest.

And the Captain, smart as he was, never knew a thing.

The ride was long. Eventually it ended.

The Captain asked me everything about Clarence and then, when he was done, he asked me everything again. He didn't let me sleep. He was gentle about it, but he didn't let me sleep. There was never a moment to close my eyes because the Captain, he never stopped talking neither. He knew how these things were done.

For my part, I told him what I felt needed be told and didn't say a damn word further. And frankly, I was glad for the distraction of the talk and the questions and the focus required to keep every lie singing harmoniously with every other, for they kept me off of thinking on the one thing I knew I must not say to the Captain—mostly because it just made me look plain dumb.

Clarence knew where I worked. Knew I played piano, nights at Miss Kitty's. He knew where I lived because I had told him. I had told him I would meet him there when all this bother was done.

In the course of the questioning, I asked the Captain three times who Clarence was—hoping each time for an answer that would comfort me and cool the anxious fire burning in my belly, believing less each time that I would get it.

"Who is Clarence?" I asked him.

"Injun Joe," he said. "Now remind me, what kind of feathers did he have in his hair?"

"Who is he, Captain? I think I should know."

The Captain cracked his knuckles. He squinted down his eyes and fiddled with the radio until he picked up Power Hits 103.3, where Hard Harry was playing something weird and mournful by Silver Mt. Zion and talking low over the music about the coming uprising of the impure.

"He's not an Indian, you know," the Captain said. "A Native American? He's Greek, I think. Or was. Best I've been able to tell. But he *looks* like an Indian, doesn't he? And that bothers me. It feels like it's racist, him calling himself that. But I honestly don't know."

"It's racist," said Jemma.

"It is," I agreed.

"But what if he really is? Like, how *much* Indian would he have to be before it's not racist anymore?"

And it went on and on like that for miles.

We'd been quiet for a long time, the sun burning down on us like true vengeance, like remuneration for the evils we'd done under cover of dark. In Marlene's bed, Logue had crawled under a tarp to keep from burning. Whenever I looked back and caught his eye, he looked at me like he wanted to eat my lunch.

"He vexes you, Captain," I said. "So who is he?"

"Clarence Doolittle," the Captain said, sighing and scrubbing at his face with his hands. "He's an OSS recruiter. Or was, last time I heard of him."

I was confused. "What's the problem then, if he's OSS like you?"

"Like us, Duncan. *Us.* And Clarence Doolittle isn't OSS like us."

"How do you mean?"

"He's a bad man is all. And really good at it, too. And if he's been put onto you, then that is nothing but a world of trouble coming."

And that, of course, wasn't comforting at all.

For ten hours straight, the Captain talked and I talked and, in his ear, a radio hummed with news of his demobilizing operation.

I asked after Miss Holly Bright and he would only say that she was busy. I asked after Julie and Asa and Clemmy and Big Libby and he said they'd be taken care of, as he'd promised. "Never know when you might need them again," he said.

I asked after Reggie and the Captain chuckled. "How many times he tell you about his horse?"

"'Bout a thousand."

"Yeah, that sounds right."

I asked after Jack's body, too, and to that he had no response at all.

They finally dropped me on the street outside Miss Kitty's in the heat of the afternoon.

"Tomorrow," the Captain said, "I would like to see you at the Nob. Bright and early. Let's say noon. Do you think you can go a whole day without doing something stupid?"

"I doubt it," I told him.

"Try," he said. "Since you loose and on your own seems to cause me headaches, I think I have a job that will be perfect for you."

We shook hands like men and parted amiably—me with my gun, my briefcase, and Julie's knife still in my belt. I had to fight to keep from running inside and straight up the stairs to see what my stupidity had wrought, but stayed rooted to the pavement while Logue took my seat and the Captain complained of the smell of him and Logue threatened to twist his head off and Jemma got Marlene back out into traffic and headed off down Colfax Avenue.

Then I ran.

My room, of course, had been expertly tossed and I knew immediately that Clarence Doolittle had been there while I was off making a nuisance of myself and bringing a friend to his mortal end.

I stepped carefully through the scattered piles of junk. Everything that had once been inside something else was now lying out and had been picked through by someone who knew what they were doing, but didn't know precisely what they were looking for. What few clothes I had were piled on the floor. My bed was turned up against the wall, the thin mattress split. The cash, the medical supplies from Theta FMU, and other little things that I'd tucked away in various small hiding places were all carefully stacked up on the nearest horizontal surface as if him that'd found them had scorned even the bother of stealing such trifling plunder.

But really, there was only one thing I was worried about and that was the stack of papers that I'd bought for five dollars off the car parking man at the Brown Palace—the Regulators' papers on the Captain and all his crew. Those I had rolled and laid up in a hollow spot I'd made behind the wallboard right by the door, pushed up tight against the frame. It was my best hiding spot. One of a sort that I'd been using for years spent living on the bounce in temporary rooms subject to all manner of unpleasantness and peepery. And, of course, when I checked it, it was empty.

I sat heavily down on the floor and put my head in my hands.

"You looking for these?" said a voice, and when I looked up, there in the hallway outside my door stood La Rata the Unkillable, Gordon Navarro. He wore an eye patch now, covering the place where they'd dug all the sound and video recording gear out of his head, and a suit the color of dried blood over a white shirt buttoned all the way to his throat. He had the stack of papers in his hand. As he smiled down at me, he slapped them against the knuckles of his opposite fist.

"Gordo," I said.

"Took me two minutes to find these, you know? You were always so *predictable*, Jimmy. Or should I call you Duncan now?"

I said nothing.

"That other fella? He looked and looked and looked. Also, he pissed all over your bed so I wouldn't sleep on that 'til you have it laundered."

"Thanks," I said.

"Anyway, the boss wants to have a word."

I shook my head. "No, Gordon. I have been up for a day and a night and a day and I need to sleep."

His face rearranged itself into a mask of concern. "Oh. I understand, Duncan. You've had a busy couple days and you're tired." Then he stepped into the room, the heels of his fancy leather shoes popping on the loose boards of my floor, and dropped into a squat in front of me, his hands loose on his knees. He tilted his head until he could look me in the eyes. "But what makes you think that was a request?"

See? I told you that story was going to be important.

EPISODE

5

Last Man Standing

REMEMBER BACK WHEN I TOLD YOU THAT THE POINT WHERE everything in the world went wrong was the first time someone's cell phone talked to them without there being anyone on the other end? That it was me asking an ensmartened slab of black glass and plastic where to find some frozen yogurt and not finding anything to fear in it telling me?

So I'm wondering . . . Can I take that back? Can I have it maybe expunged from the record of this little chat we're having or whatever it is you all do?

No, it ain't a lie. When I lie, I tell you. Most times.

It's just that, I've been thinking on it since the last time we talked and I feel like it don't, uh . . . Like that story don't quite carry the *weight*, you understand? Because you're not hearing it in its rightwise context, it just doesn't fully explain how the world went sideways.

I mean, it does and it doesn't. It does for *me*. The phone, that's something I remember, and it sits in my brain like a bookmark showing the end of one thing and the beginning of something completely other. But for you it's like, talking phone? Voice-activated search function? Algorithmically parsed speech analog? *Pfft.* We got innertality and cities that fly through space, and this yack over here is saying a talking cell phone is the thing that pushed the world over the edge? Fuck that.

But I'm telling you, it is and it isn't. The Captain, he's got a different theory about how things went wrong. I've heard it and I believe it because his goes way back. Jemma had a story, too. Heard her's one night 'round a fire in Dodge City. Logue had a story. Lud had a story. Laszlo, Holcomb, Barnum, Strange. Ignatz, the Chemist. He has a story. Man, does he have a story. I dunno. I think everyone had one who lived. But none of them were the real story and, also, *all* of them were the real story at the same time. I'm no psychiatrist, Lord knows, but I think it's just because something in the brain needs to put a date to something, you know? Needs to find a moment where they feel like, if things had just gone a little bit different, everything could be put to right.

I fear I'm not making much sense.

Look. The thing I told you about the phone? That was true. That was true for *me*. For me, that was the tipping point—where our things began to stop being the servants of us and it kinda flipped the other way 'round which—again for *me*—is what I see as the sickness at the heart of the world-that-was. It's not something I thought of in the moment, but only came to me after. And the reason why I want to make it right on the record is because I don't believe anyone who isn't me will see it the same way.

So I want to tell you about the armless man instead. And the building that wasn't, and then was. I want to tell you about the Abjuration.

But first I have to tell you about the first time I died while working for the Captain.

☢

After returning from Great Times in the company of the Captain, finding my room at Miss Kitty's tossed by Clarence Doolittle (who was maybe an Indian and probably an OSS recruiter put onto me by mysterious men about whom the Captain resolutely refused to speak a word), and then having Gordon Navarro—my old source, my old asset—sneak up on me out of nowhere, I was having what you might call a day. I wanted sleep. Maybe a joint, definitely a drink, and then a patch of sleep like the kind children know—long and deep and untroubled by guilt-stricken dreams.

But La Rata wasn't going to let that happen. He had him some orders and was going to carry them out, no matter my opinions on the matter.

I had expected that Gordon would escort me right out of Miss Kitty's—maybe frog-march me straight through the parlor in the full view of Madam, all the boys and girls, and all the early trade who couldn't wait on the sun's setting to get their cocks into something or their tonsils painted.

I had expected that he would walk me out into some skeezy alley somewhere, or perhaps hand me gentleish into the backseat of a waiting car, because Gordon, in his ascension, was more than a little sweet on the *image* of himself as a covert man and had taken to living his life like it was a movie about spying rather than the real and actual thing.

"So how's this going to go, Gordo?" I says to him, knowing full and well how much he hated that name and wondering, in some dark place in me, how far I could push him before he'd blow his collar and just slug me. "You gonna rough me up a little first, sweetheart? Or do you have a whole 'we can do this the easy way or the hard way' speech all cocked and locked?"

And La Rata the Unkillable, he just winks at me with the one eye remaining to him and says, "Don't be so dramatic, Jimmy." And then he prods me ever so gently with the toe of one expensive shoe until I scooch fully inside my wrecked-up room, steps in with me, pulls closed the door, grabs my briefcase, pops its locks and snaps open the clever little compartment where I kept my dumb phone hid.

"Duncan," I says to him.

"What?"

"It's Duncan Archer. That's my name here."

And La Rata, he shrugs, says, "You'll always be Jimmy to me," then thumbs a number into the phone and hands it to me ringing.

"Aren't you worried the room is bugged?" I ask him. And he tells me, sure. It *was* bugged. All up and down and nine ways from Sunday. Sound, motion, video, differentiation. He'd even found an ancient video cassette camera hidden in the wall that'd probably been there since before Kitty's was a cathouse and before the Weird got weird. "Kept that one," he says to me. "I'm nuts for antiques these days."

The phone rings and rings. Finally, there is a buzz, a click, a buzz, an escalating scale of manufactured tones laddering up to a silent infinity.

"Secure," I says. And on the other end, the boss says, "Secure," and then we start our dance. Gordon, closely examining the moons of his fingernails, even steps away and turns his back to give me the illusion of privacy.

"So," says the boss. "You've been busy. Tell me everything. Start with the names."

And I give him the names because that is what I do for him. I collect names. Dates. Places. Details that would matter to no one else and maybe don't even matter to him, except that he demands them anyway because he is listening for things that are beyond my ken. Assembling a vision of things above my pay grade.

I start with the old names first. The classics. Captain James Barrow. Logue. Jemma. Then I start lavishing him with new ones and what details I have because, like he said, I'd been busy. I give him Arthur Reginald Molesworth, Western Confederacy cavalry colonel, retired. Known freelancer for James Barrow. Watcher and bodyman. Confirmed. Julio Reconquista De La Teja, a.k.a. Julie—pre-op transgender and street-level criminal. Asa August, associate of Julie. Trade same, but also a border runner of some skill. Jack August, brother of Asa, associate of Julie, deceased. No further associations known.

I give him everything I know on the four Regulators (which isn't much other than speculation, and the boss, he hates speculation like a poison), and list the one—Rufe, last-name-unknown—as deceased, probable. The rest are in the possession of the Captain and his people, again, probable, so I says so. I give him the car parker at the Brown Palace. I give him Clemmy and Big Libby, who, really, aren't even mine to give. I give him Barnum and I give him Strange.

"Wow," says the boss. "Those two . . ."

I give him a brief run-down of events since last we spoke. He knows most of it already, so I just try to give him the flavor, you know? A view from the inside, as I saw it, from my limited vantage. There was so much then that I didn't understand. A Bill show of noise and furious action that was happening like just a whirlwind around me. But the boss tells me that it doesn't matter. Tells me and tells me. *Leave the big picture to the wiser heads*, he says. *Just tell me what you know.*

I make a revision to a previous report. "Bright, Holly," I say, "is not a watcher for the Captain. Repeat: *not* a watcher. She is capable support for sure. A pavement artist. Possibly a turtledove and his coat-tailer, too. A baiter through-and-through. An irregular but not a freelancer. Confirmed all, by the Captain."

"James Barrow," says the boss.

"Right."

"So why was she following you then?"

"Apparently, she wasn't. It was coincidence."

"Hate that stuff."

"Tell me about it."

"But you brought her in?"

I shrugged. A particularly useless gesture to make over the phone. "I brought her *out*. Of Great Times, that is. But apparently that counted for something with the Captain. He seemed rightly impressed with my gumption and total lack of mother's wit."

"Barrow," says the boss. "James Barrow."

"Right," says me. "Last I saw, she was with Ranstead, anyway. He disappeared her pretty quick."

I give him Clarence Doolittle after that. Injun Joe. And the boss, he goes steely. Gets all by-the-book with me—asking for a complete description, length and nature of our contact, a word-for-word on our conversation—mine and Clarence's—and then another on mine and the Captain's, regarding Clarence.

"That was ten hours, give or take," I tell him.

"Do your best."

So I do, and even still, the whole debrief takes ten minutes, maybe fifteen, which is both too long and too short at the same time and I know it. Too long for a casual top-up, too short for a proper interro. This whole thing, it's just a refresher from the boss, right? Drawing me back down to earth after my jaunt and adventures. Reminding me of who I am and what I'm about and why I am where I am in the first place. Keeping me in the habit of playing the good parrot, him. Of remembering and repeating and reporting on command.

At the end of it, the boss asks the Three Questions. Same ones I'd put to a hundred different assets a thousand different times when I was the man on the other end of the phone.

"Have you, since our last contact, done anything that you feel might jeopardize your cover, your legend or your mission?"

"No sir."

"Do you feel like, at this time, you are under any threat of physical harm?"

"No sir. I'm right as rain."

"Is there any further information you wish to disclose regarding your mission or its principal which we have not already discussed?"

I look up and, from the other side of the room, Gordon is watching me. He has the sheaf of Regulator paperwork in one hand, folded double, and is slapping it against the knuckles of the other.

"No sir," I says. "Nothing. Early days and all."

"Understood," says the boss man. "We'll be watching."

"Yes, sir."

And then, a pause. A sound of breath being sucked in across teeth like the boss, if I didn't know better, was thinking on the wiseness of saying anything further. As if the boss ever let slip an un-meant word.

"Be careful of him, Duncan," he says.

I think he means Clarence, but I am wrong.

"Barrow will draw you. He'll bring you in. And from the inside, he's going to start looking sane. But you have to remember who he is."

"I don't really know who he is, sir," I say.

"I'm not entirely sure that I do either."

And I hang up. Bounce the phone lightly in the palm of my hand. Look at Gordon Navarro, who is looking at me.

"Do you feel like, at this time, you are under any threat of physical harm?" he repeats, half-smiling, and I'm like, "If you're gonna come for me, motherfucker, just do it and quit flappin' your lip because I am fucking tired," and he says, "That's not what I'm talking about, bud. I'm talking about all of this," and he gestures large, like around at all the wreck and ruin of my room. "You don't think this was worth mentioning?"

"Nope."

"And I notice you didn't tell him about these either," he says, slapping the papers one more time against his closed fist.

"Did you?" I ask.

"Of course I did," he says, because La Rata, for all his quirks and lechery, was always eager to please. "This is intel. The good stuff. And now the boss is going to know you're lying to him."

"He knew I was a liar when this started."

"He's going to know you're holding out on him, I mean."

I get up off the floor and brush my hands together. "You worked for me a long time, Gordon," I says. "You were a great source. Straight aces. I mean it. And for all your fucking around, you had your nose open all the time. Never held back. You gave me a lot of shit, but there was gold in it. Real gold. And you never kept any back because, I think, you were maybe not smart enough to. I loved you for that."

"Fuck you, Jimmy."

I yawn. Stretch. Roll my head around on my neck. "No, seriously, Gordon. It's the trick you never learned. Yeah, the boss is gonna know I'm holding out. And if I'm holding out on the papers, he's gonna start to wonder what *else* I'm holding out on, too. What I have that he doesn't know about. Just like you're going to start to wonder soon as we're done here. And that is what's gonna keep the boss awake nights and me alive and at liberty for as long as I need. That wondering. Now give me the papers."

And Gordon, he snatches them papers back like I made a grab for them, which I most surely did not. "What makes you think I would give these up?"

"Because the boss told you to."

"He tell you that?"

I shook my head. "He didn't have to. It's what I would've done when I was the boss. When I was *your* boss, matter of fact. Something like that is more valuable to the agent in the field than it is to management. And that's exactly what you were told, wasn't it, Gordo?"

"Don't call me that, Jimmy. You know better."

"La Rata," I say. "La puta canalla periodista."

And my old friend's one remaining eye darkens. He takes a step up on me, hands curling into fists. I lean back against an old trunk and smile at him. "You used to be a lot more fun, y'know that?"

Which takes the steam all out of him then, and when he grins back at me and kind of squeaks out this weird little giggle he used to have, for just a second he is a young man again. A junkie journo on the OSS dole, feeding me rebels and traitors and freaks of all description, sitting with me at the bar at Misty's while some daughter of the revolution with leopard spots and a slinky tail humps the chrome off the pole in front of us.

"Heavy lies the crown and all that," he says.

"No, heavy lies the *head* that wears the—"

"No, it's the crown."

"The head. The head is heavy that—"

"Heavy lies the crown on the head that does the . . . something."

We went on like that for a while.

Eventually, Gordon left. He gave me the papers as I knew he would and took my dumb phone (the burner he'd called in to the boss with), snapped it in two, pulled the sim card, and snapped that between his teeth. Then he left me a new phone in its place, again programmed with just a single number linked to a dead-drop voice mail system.

"Keep in touch, Jimmy," he said as he was going out the door. "I'll be seeing you."

I played piano that night. Reggie wasn't there, but I saw Clemmy and Big Libby both, which cheered me. There'd been a part of me that'd wondered if they'd just end up covered in lime in a ditch somewhere, their teeth pulled and their fingertips snipped off. I didn't believe that the Captain was that kind of man, but it was good to know for sure. I didn't have a chance to talk to them, and they seemed not of a mind to speak with me.

A lot of slow jazz was what I gave the crowd that night. Long, loopy runs on the 88 that twittered out into meaninglessness. No one from the staff said a word to me about my room, and while it was possible they didn't know (I was the only one lived up in the attic), that was unlikely. There's not a lot of secrets in a whorehouse. And none that stay that way for long.

I nodded off for the first time around midnight, but recovered with hardly a sour note. After the second time, Luke—one of Madam's fellas—came by and laid a china cup and saucer on top of the piano.

"Madam says that if the girls can keep it together after the night you gave them, then so can you," he said to me, and when I looked over at the bar, she was sitting there watching me, face as expressive as a snowbank.

"Tell Madam," I said without looking away, "that her girls get to do all their work lying down, but I thank her for her concern." Then I waved at her while playing a quick, dancing little run down the keys with my other hand.

On the saucer, beside the teacup, was a single red pill all full of uppity-juice of one variety or another. I ate it and was grateful. In the cup was black tea, briny with constructors and effectors, swirling with heavy elements and Lord knows what else. I drank it down with one pinky up as ever the classy man does, and then, for two minutes, felt sick nigh on to airing the paunch, but after that played for five hours straight with a concrete hard-on, twelve extra fingers, and the notes all swirling up and out of the old Regent in a tornado of colors and smells and strange, crystalline harmonics that only I could hear.

Come the dawn, I ate my pay in rhubarb pie and cold dumplings filled with cattail root and fried black squirrel, then went to the chawed-up remainders of my room, locked the door, curled like a cat in a blanket on the floor, and slept like I was dead for six hours exactly.

When I woke, I pissed toner until the toilet water was black with dead nanites, but I felt good, my life bar well into the green. After a bath I felt even better. I managed to go ten whole minutes without thinking of Jack August dead in the dirt at Great Times or of Rufe turning toward the ladies as they came down the hall behind him, his gun already coming up and my own iron coughing and bucking in my hand. We was of an age then when it was hard to tell an American story without a gun in it, and the natural result of that was bodies: Jack's, Rufe's, Roger Whitaker of the Green Willow engineers, and that dumb, drunk man on California Street, all beginning to stack up already in my memories and on my conscience. It was, I think—I *hope*—just part-and-parcel of the times we was in. But I honestly do fear sometimes that, like I'd said to the Captain, I was just a man born unto trouble as sparks fly upward.

Speaking of himself, he and I had a meeting at the Nob. Though never a punctual man, I could not countenance lateness in this case for fear of missing the man and him going missing on me again, so paid good money to a kid driving a pedicab who looked like ten sticks lashed together with catgut string. His feet were bare and dirty and ended in talons that gripped the pedals. On his back was an animated dust tattoo that showed a Tasmanian Devil forcibly violating a Teddy Ruxpin doll and, sitting behind him, I got to watch it cycle over and over again like the worst TV channel ever.

On the streets of the Queen City there was tumult and uproar. Farmers were marching on the Castle in semi-organized protest, demanding recompense from the crown for their lands that had been variously burned, stomp-holed, poisoned, salted, ate up or just generally befouled by the Kansans in their ill-starred march on the Western Confederacy. They shouted and carried signs and tangled in the green spaces with the street market sellers, their customers, them of the Quality coming and going on vital errands, and the King's own security for, as was his way, King Steven the Uneven always took it upon himself to go down among the angrified masses when they turned up in his dooryard and to argue with them man-to-man. It would take hours, shut down the whole of the Royalty, banjax the plans and schedules of ministers, lords, and the heads of state. And all this pleased King Steve greatly. It was precisely why he did it.

"What should be more important to me than the want of my people to be heard?" he would say and, by saying so, would win over 10,000 supporters of his kingship and then plunge into the roiling crowds to shout, point fingers, pass out cookies that he always claimed to have baked himself, and, occasionally, sign his own name to petitions calling for the dissolution of the Confederacy, an end to his monarchy or declarations of war on invisible enemies from beyond.

So the farmers hollered and shook their signs and hayforks in the air. The street preachers ranted and the day-hookers shimmied what they had for the prurient amusement of all assembled. The coffee-sellers jangled their bells. Water merchants with giant tanks on their backs screamed about the benefits of their water over everyone else's water, how *their* water had far lower millirad counts, viral transcriptase levels, and parts-per-million of rat shit than any other water in the state, and, in the center of things, the King's Housekarls tried to establish order with tower shields, shock rods and old socks full of nickels until, eventually, they'd carved out a kind of amphitheatre of the flesh into which King Steven the Quarrelsome could step with anyone foolish enough to try matching him, wit-to-wit.

"Lucky day," said my driver, glancing briefly back over his shoulder as he pumped the pedals and slid us in between a buckboard loaded down with scrap plastic and a luxurious phaeton being pulled by two pure-white unicorns. "Is very little traffic."

On the sidewalk outside the Nob, Hippolite Smith was sluicing down the pavement with buckets of water. He wore a threadbare tank top with more holes than fabric, and a transistor radio hung around his neck on a dirty string. The radio was playing Martha and the Vandellas' "Nowhere To Run," and I paid off the cabbie with two dollars in scrip and a half-full tube of Bacitracin ointment. He thanked me, glanced back down the hill toward the Castle yard, and pulled on a pale blue respirator mask that was hanging around his neck before pumping back out into traffic.

I looked the way he had and saw wispy clouds of white smoke twisting up into the air from where the protestors had been gathered. Tear gas.

"Might be time to go inside and fix a fella a drink, Hippo," said me, jerking a thumb in the direction of the commotion. "Someone must've gotten hands-y with his Kingness."

Hippo sighed, straightened up, kicked over the last of his buckets, then gathered them all together by their handles and went, clankingly, through the door. Down the hill, I could see clouds of gas rolling out into the street and people fighting the press of traffic to get clear. On the sidewalk, the water running into the gutters was pinkish and I stepped over it to walk into the cool dimness of the Nob and wait on the Captain's pleasure.

Inside, I had my pick of stools and so took one with a clean view to the door, stashed my briefcase on the floor between my feet, drank a morning whiskey and ate blueberries and pickled onions out of Hippo's garnish tray when he wasn't looking. He took the radio from around his neck and switched it off. Left the lights out. Barred the front door. From near the register, I heard the ripping of Velcro and watched him lay a compact little Skorpion machine pistol on the bar.

"I'm expecting someone," I said.

"They can knock," said Hippo.

We passed the time playing penny-a-turn hi-lo with a daubed deck from the card room, Hippo and me. In the end, no one came crashing through the windows of the Nob. No mobs descended, murderous in their lust for bathtub vodka and the butts of last night's cigarettes. And when it became plain that his bar was not about to be laid siege to by angry farmers, their eyes all capsicum-bright, Hippo heaved himself back out onto the floor, unbarred the door, and propped it open in hopes of catching a wisp of a breeze that didn't stink of CS. When he bent to put the Skorpion away, I thought I saw him sigh with relief.

Soon enough, some of Hippo's regular daylight drinkers began slinking in, all talking of oddities and improbable things happening in the streets, and Hippo turned the old radio back on—mostly to drown their blusteration—and dialed up a pirate station out of the flatlands that played whole albums by Buddy Guy, Joy Division, Hank Jr., and Nick Cave. As he began serving his customers their medicine, I rolled a cigarette with the slow deliberation of a fella with no other plans for the day, closed my eyes, and listened to "Red Right Hand," my head nodding slowly along.

It was a day and a day—lovely and sunlit without, but dim and whiskey-sharp within. Nick Cave sang "Stagger Lee" in an artificial twilight seasoned with the jittering, fragile laughter of drunks settling delicately into their true vocations. He sang "O'Malley's Bar" and I knocked a knuckle on Hippo's long oak and pointed to the bottle of Devil Eyes for a top-up. I told a long joke to a man called Pipsy and he laughed until his false teeth came out because I am, or was, a powerfully amusing man. And then, just as Cave was settling into "Song of Joy" on the radio—telling me how all things move toward their end, all things move toward their end—the phone behind the bar at the Nob began to ring.

"Shit, Hippo," I said. "You have a phone?"

And Hippo, he just looked bewildered, staring down in the direction of the dusty, jangling noise of bells like looking through a hole into another dimension. He glanced up at me and asked, "I have a phone?"

"You apparently do, man. That's what's ringing, isn't it?"

"But I don't have a phone," he said.

"No one has a phone," I replied. And now, save for Nick singing his song, the bar had gone quiet as everyone within it sat listening to the ringing with glazes on their eyes like they'd been hypnotized by a sound unheard in this world for an age.

I mean, cell phones was one thing. The networks could be patched and maintained by them as knew the ways of doing so—who could pull cable and cool the microwaves and talk sweet to the groaning machinery still chugging along on the backhaul—and that was what happened in civilized places because to *not* do so would be the end of the world complete. It would be Mad Max times, and no one wanted that. Phones, rebuilt and jailbroke, could cycle and cycle through the population of them as could afford their luxury and pay out their tithes to the warlords and bandwidth barons who controlled the systems. But a wall phone? The sort requiring poles and wires and all manner of old-fashionedy copper nonsense buried under the ground where the dead men go? Who had the time? Who, for that matter, knew the how of keeping them living?

The phone rang. And rang.

"Well answer it already!" said a fella down the other side of the bar who'd slunk in with the noon draft. He had a plastic cup full of Hippo's murky homebrew in front of him and a face like bad meat, with one half of it looking like melted candlewax that'd oozed down and mostly sealed one eye.

Hippo looked at me. The phone rang again. I shrugged and said, "A ringing phone does kind of want to be answered, Hippo. But I don't know. There does seem to be something . . ."

"Portentous," said Hippo.

"Exactly," said me.

"Fuck it," said Hippo, then reached beneath the bar, picked a dusty green receiver with a tangled pigtail cord off the jangling cradle, put it to his ear and said, "Nob Hill Inn. How can I help you?"

He stood awkwardly, his eyes cut over as if trying to watch the receiver in his hand lest it suddenly turn into a snake and bite him in the face.

He nodded. He said, "Uh huh," then looked at me and said "Uh huh," again. Then "Sure." Then "Okay."

Hippo took the receiver from his ear and held it out to me. "It's for you," he said. "Apparently you've won the lottery."

I came up off my stool and walked toward Hippo and the phone as if approaching a sleeping animal whose teeth I intended to pull. The receiver was heavy when Hippo handed it over, the cord having a tug to it like the whole machine wanted badly to be put back together again and forgotten for another hundred years. I pulled it to my ear, leaning slightly over the bar, and said, "Hello?"

The connection was scratchy and full of pops and weird echoes. I, of course, expected it to be the Captain, but it wasn't. It was Jemma Watts, her voice like sweet honey poured over popping corn.

"I need you to wait three seconds and laugh like this is all some kind of a bad joke, Duncan. You understand?"

I waited three seconds and then I laughed. All around me, the bar seemed to deflate, the air souring with the collective sighs of a near-dozen wigged-out rummies as all the Nob Hill glee club shook off the peculiarity of the freaked moment and got back to the important business of chasing the bottoms of their various glasses.

"Say, 'Dammit, Lori. How did you even get this to work?' But do it with some affection."

"Dammit, Lori. How did you even get this to work?" I said, with some affection.

"You're doing fine. Now look around. Is there a man there, looks like he's been in a bad fire? He wouldn't be the handsomest fella there."

"That's because I am," I said.

"Says you. He'll also have one hand kinda melted up. Like a claw."

The man who'd insisted that Hippo pick up the phone was staring down into his plastic cup of beer like he'd accidentally dropped a nickel in. The hand with which he held the cup looked perfectly normal to me. But then he reached up to scratch the side of his face with something that looked like a chunky flipper. A paddle of meat with a nub of a thumb on the downside.

"Yeah, Lori. I see what you mean," I said.

"That man has something for you. You're going to go talk to him. Make nice. But fairly quickly, I need you to say the words, 'Lori says she's coming. Let's go meet her on the corner.' Got that? Those exact words."

"Got it."

"He'll have a big case for you. Once you have it, I need you to just sit with it. Do not move. Once he's gone, we'll have someone come fetch you. Understood?"

"Absolutely. Anything else?"

"The man's name is Schuler. Carmen Schuler."

"Okay, then," I said brightly. "This was fun. Thanks, Lori."

"See you soon, Duncan."

She clicked off and I handed the receiver back to Hippo. "That was weird," I said.

"Who was it?"

"Friend of mine. Lori. She used to be a telephone engineer, back before. Does this kind of thing for fun. Anyway, looks like your phone works. Least for the time being."

I picked up my glass of Devil Eyes and drank down half, then looked up at Carmen Schuler who met my eyes across the well of the Nob's horseshoe bar. I stood, hooked my case up off the floor, and walked over to his side as the talk and the drinking continued around me unabated. There was a stool open next to him and I planted myself upon it.

"So how you been, Carmen?" I asked.

"Splendid," he replied, his eyes searching me. "Dancing girls and champagne. So much pussy I must to beat it off with a stick."

"You and me both, brother. That's the perils of handsomeness though, ain't it?" I peeked over at his drink. It was still mostly full. His cup had an advertisement for a Batman movie on it, mostly washed out by decades knocking around the Weird. "You got you a wounded soldier there in front of you, bud, so why not drink it down. Lori says she's coming. Let's go meet her on the corner."

Carmen said nothing. He looked at me for a long moment, then lifted his cup with his good hand and drained it down to the dregs without looking away. When I saw it was going to be a race, I shot mine down as well. We both tapped glass to the bar top at the same time.

"Let us away then," he said. "Wouldn't want to keep Lori waiting."

There are any number of things that a man might have for you when you're told to get something from a stranger you meet in a bar, and none of them are going to be something nice. No one is ever told to go meet a man at the boozer because he has something you need and then, come to find, it's the absolution of your sins, a medal for civic rightness, a pretty bunch of flowers, or a sackful of puppies meant for something other than eating.

There are any number of ways that kind of meeting can end, and none of them are going to be what you expect. As a matter of fact, it's nearly always going to be the one way you *don't* expect. There ain't no sense in planning because all you'll get is a headache and, when all is said and done, you'll still be surprised when the mimes all turn on you or you just explode for no reason. That's just wisdom.

So I was full-to-brimming with the Zen of the moment as I followed Carmen Schuler out of the Nob and into the street. I regretted immediately not having put my gun on this morning, but let it go. I regretted not even having a good knife on me, though I just smiled into the sunlight and faint whiff of tear gas still drifting on the afternoon air and let all my worldly cares float away like ghosts and resentments and recollections of days less fine.

"We walking far, Carmen?" I asked. "Not that I don't find the day passing lovely, but I'd just like to—"

"No cause for us to talk yet," he said.

I sniffed, wished I hadn't. "No cause to be rude either, friend. Just a question."

"Keep them to yourself, please."

He had a haze of an accent on him that I couldn't quite place. Something fading but Continental that I wanted to hear more of.

"I'm wondering if we should hail down a hansom is all," I said, digging my hands into my pockets and pulling up even with him on the sidewalk. "You know, arrive with a little class."

"Arrive?" he asked.

"Reach our destination," I said.

"I know what means *arrive*. But I'm beginning to wonder whether you understand what we are doing here." He spoke without looking at me, his eyes fixed forward like gunsights, and turned a corner with no warning, forcing me to jog a little to keep on his wing.

"I surely do not," I said. "I know you're supposed to give something to me, that's all."

And Carmen Schuler shook his head. "Good God, the man has a strange sense of humor," he said. "That is what it is, isn't it? Humor? He is playing the prank on you, yes? He doesn't expect you to . . ." His voice trailed off.

We were in an alley that let in on a maze of parking lots and the back doors of various homes and businesses. There were trash middens and the skeletons of cars, all manner of falling-down shacks, broken things and lost things and mantises the size of king crabs picking through dumpsters ripe and baking in the sun. Broken glass popped and crackled underfoot like walking through a Golgotha of lab glass and shattered bottles of barley pop.

"Who we talking about?" I asked.

Carmen stopped. He looked around at all the million places where bad things might be lying in wait. When he spoke, he leaned close. "The Captain. You are one of his men, yes?"

"Never heard of him," I said.

"Right, right. Of course." He leaned even closer. "But you *are*, aren't you?"

"You get any closer Carmen, we're gonna be kissing."

He reeled back. His breath had smelled like dark beer and not enough brushing. The roils and twists of his skin where it was burned had an odd sheen to them. A look like plastic rubbed with a thumb.

"Look," I said. "I just know that Lori told me that you had something for me. That's all. I say the magic words, follow you, and you give me the whatsis. Honestly, if things are going to get any more complicated than that, I'm really going to need a moment to prepare myself."

"You should prepare," he said.

"Wait, really?"

I'd been kidding. He was not.

"Really."

"Should I get my gun or holler for help right now?"

"No, but if you've a need to urinate, you might want to do it before we proceed."

"German," I said.

"Excuse me?"

"Your accent. German. You were born in Germany. Not Berlin, but . . . . Strasbourg or Stuttgart, maybe? Raised there, but left young. I've got kind of an ear for languages. I find the variability of the human tongue and the ways in which it betrays us fascinating."

Carmen Schuler closed his eyes and shook his head. "This is not going to be a good day for you," he muttered, then walked on with me following after.

☢

Twenty minutes later, I am sitting on a big black box. Hard plastic. Shock-resistant. Inside are nineteen glass tubes of gray goop that looks like Vaseline, stoppered and vented at one end, all of them nestled comfortably in nineteen holes in a thick foam pad. I know because Carmen Schuler had shown me.

The twentieth glass tube of goop is in my hand, my fingers wrapped delicately around it, and Carmen Schuler is wrapping my fist in one of those stretchy bandages just to make double-super-extra-sure that I don't, you know, drop it.

"So was I right?" I ask him. My voice is a little squeaky and I have to swallow three or four times just to get up the spit to talk.

"About what?" Carmen asks, carefully rolling the bandage over and around my hand.

"About Germany," I say.

"Please do not move."

"I'm not moving."

"You're breathing."

"Breathing is bad?"

"Breathe . . . I don't know. *Less*."

"Breathe less. Got it."

"Is live now, you understand? Active and unstable."

"Sounds like my kind of goop," I say, and when Carmen doesn't respond, I add, "Active and unstable. Get it?"

"A joke?"

"Yeah. A joke."

Carmen is on his hunkers in front of me. He looks up. "Please do not make joke."

He adds a final two turns to the bandage and affixes it with a plastic clip. He scrapes backward with his hands held out in front of him as if asking mercy. He stands up.

"Balingen," he says. "You were close. Viel gluck."

"Gluck ist nicht was ich brauche."

Carmen Schuler takes a step backward. "You will not follow?"

"I don't see how I can, bru."

He takes another step. "Good." And then he turns and is off like a spooked horse—running like a man who hasn't in quite some time but is determined to remember how in a hurry.

In my hand is one tube of Cyclot-8, one of the most powerful and quick-tempered military explosives I know of. It'll explode if you touch it, shake it, warm it up by one degree too many, look at it cross-eyed, or say something less than friendly about it near enough that it can hear you. There is no state in which it is stable, only things you can do to make it *less* stable than its already incredibly unstable natural state. I've known women who were the same way. Mean as some of them might've been, none of them were as mean as a few ounces of Cyclot-8 when disturbed.

In the case on which I am sitting are nineteen more tubes of the stuff. Enough, I calculate, to take down one medium-sized skyscraper if employed correctly. Maybe even if employed totally haphazardly. Except for one thing.

The tubes in the case are fake. Totally inert. The one in my hand? Very much real.

I'd tried to ask Carmen why he'd assembled nineteen tubes of fake boom jelly for this man, the Captain, and he'd said only that it was what the Captain had asked him for. That he didn't require explanations. That he did as he was told and that he would appreciate me reminding the Captain of this. I'd said again that I didn't know this Captain of whom he spoke, and Carmen had chuckled. I'd tried to ask what the Cyclot was for, and Carmen said nothing. I'd tried to ask why he'd only made one real one, and Carmen had said nothing. I'd asked why I had to sit here *holding* the one real one—that Lori hadn't mentioned anything about this particular wrinkle in the plan and that if she'd known about it and not told me, I was going to give her a stern talking to the next time I saw her.

"Is my security," Carmen had explained while wrapping the bandage around and around my hand. "This way, I know you will not follow me."

"Could've just asked nice," I said to him.

"Had to be sure. Is also the way that the Captain will know the real tube from the fake ones."

"Well, you know . . . Anything I can do to help."

The heat from my hand, Carmen had told me, was enough to angry up the Cyclot. To get it to a state where moving it around all too much (or even just a little) would be enough to set it off and make it (and me) explode in such a fashion that whatever was left of me would have to be shipped home to mom in several dozen leakproof sandwich baggies. And that's if any of me could actually be found. And if I still had a mother for my remains to be sent to.

Carmen had called the activation of the Cyclot in my hand *making it live*, as if there was a sentience and a damnably sour attitude inherent in the little tube of goo. Which, I guess, if explosives are your thing, you might really believe.

"TNT is like a friendly dog compared to Cyclot," Carmen had said. "C-series plastic explosives are as dangerous as an old woman in a coma."

"You're a weird cat, Carmen."

"The Captain must be making a point with you, I think. I've worked with him before. He would very much like me to work with him more, but I am not so much interested. Can you tell him that for me also?"

"Don't know the man," I'd insisted, though I was doing it then through gritted teeth, with my eyes fixed quite firmly on the tube full of messy endings in my hand.

"Not so much talking please. More with the listening."

If I move, the Cyclot in my hand will explode. If I stand up, it will explode. If I try to take the bandage off? Well, really that is for my own safety. Get nervous. Hand gets sweaty. Suddenly have to sneeze. Boom.

"Do *not* sneeze," Carmen had said. "Or cough. Or laugh."

"This might be easier if I was asleep."

"Do not fall asleep, please."

I should've taken his advice and pissed before sitting down. But I hadn't known. Carmen had told me nothing until he'd pressed the first tube into my hand. Then he'd told me everything. But only then.

Once he is gone, I expect the Captain and his crew to come rushing in to my rescue, but they do not.

After five minutes, I *totally* expect that they'll come for me—hoofing around the corners and up out of the musty places—but they do not.

I scan the rooflines and the doorways and the mouths of all the different alleys that lead into and out of this place and I see nothing that looks even a little bit like the Captain and a fully equipped bomb disposal unit. I see faces peeking out at me from darkened windows and see rats scuttling along between the trash piles. I see roughs and toughs and street creatures come slithering out of their myriad little holes and begin edging close because it is a hot summer afternoon and I am a man sitting on a box in the middle of a parking lot who is obviously in some kind of distress and, really, there just isn't that much on TV anymore.

"It's a bomb, you idiots," I say. "You should run."

I don't say it loud because I can't really say it loud without risking annoying the Cyclot in my hand. But I say it loud enough, and words like "bomb" and "run" have a tendency to carry further than their duller cousins, don't they? Everyone hears me. Most of them run. But not all of them.

There's nothing more I can say, of course. If a man tells you he has a bomb and you *don't* run, there's just nothing more that logic can do to convince you.

Zen. The Zen of incalculable experiences. Of moments that can't nothing be done with them but to live through them or die of them. I close my eyes. I feel the sun on my face and the faint breeze on my skin. I inhale slowly but deeply and try to appreciate all the unusual smells that have collected in this little corner of the world—balmy trash and hot tar and dirty pavement and piss and old oil and, faintly, food cooking somewhere and, even more faintly, flowers. Honeysuckle. There is something about it that reminds me of the warm exhaust from a clothes dryer running. Something from my childhood. A memory cut loose from its moorings and drifting. A smile fits itself onto my face despite my nearness to exploding because I am in the moment, wholly and completely, and it is not a bad moment. Mostly because I still have it. As last moments go, it would be a pretty shitty one, but I'm not done in just yet.

When I open my eyes, the remaining fools have drawn close. There are perhaps a half-dozen of them and they shuffle forward crouched over and staring, breathing through their mouths. They are like Neanderthals seeing fire for the first time, unsure of whether or not they should try to eat it, fuck it or pray to it.

"Let me say this to you," I say to none of them in particular. "If I could run away right now, don't you think that I would?"

This stops them. There is, among the assembled company, some bare evidence of cogitation.

"That I am *not* running away could mean one of two things. First, it is possible that I am such an ace-high badass motherfucker that I have no fear of even the whole lot of ya'll together. That I am just waiting to open all your pipes and leave you choking on your own jam while I walk away, cool as cats. Please let me assure you that this is not the case.

"Second, it is possible that I am not *able* to run away. That something more fearsome than even just the smell of you all together is keeping me rooted to this here box. I would present to you as evidence of this conjecture, my right hand." I cut my eyes in the direction of my bandaged hand and the terribleness it contained. "This one's my right hand in case any of you were confused. If I move, this will explode. If it explodes, I will die. You will die. Probably some of the people in the houses and shacks yonder will die. There won't be no time to run or get away. It'll just be over, get me? None of us will ever feel a thing."

Wearing my easiest, warmest smile, I look around at the assembled crowd and shine my teeth at them. I was enjoying myself. Really, I was.

"So tell me," I continue. "In which of these instances do you fellas come out ahead?"

My briefcase is sitting on the ground next to the box. I am, of course, somewhat concerned that one of them might make a grab for it and scamper off, but that concern is a distant thing. All the more so when the first of the crowd breaks and runs. Where logic and the invocation of self-preservational reflex had failed, simple economics had prevailed. There was no profit to be made here. Nothing worth the possible risk to life, no mater how squalid that life may be, and, shortly, the rest follow him in running off, quickly or slow. And then I am alone again—just me and the rats and the giant mantises, which, likely, had once been someone's pets—and this makes me sad because it means I don't have no one to talk to. I close my eyes and begin counting to ten thousand.

Counting to ten thousand takes roughly two and a half hours. I started because I had nothing else to do, and I make it only to to nine hundred and four before hearing the scuff of footsteps approaching, this time from behind me.

"Do not turn around, Duncan," says the Captain.

"Tell me you brought the bomb squad."

"I brought a pair of scissors and a pair of barbecue tongs."

"Oh, well that's just as good then."

The Captain came alone, but he assured me that he was not *really* alone.

"We had to leave you sitting for a while," he tells me.

"Why?"

"So Carmen could feel safe getting away. This is how he does things, and since we like Carmen, we play along. We also had to be sure no one was following either you or him. But mostly because it was funny."

"Seriously?"

"Yup. We've all been watching you Duncan. Could've sold tickets. I mean, you were a spy. You know how fucking dull it is most of the time. But watching a guy that might explode if he moves? Let me tell you, that is *riveting*."

"You're less amusing than you think you are," I says to him. "Can you get this out of my hand now?"

"Yeah, I can. Stay very, *very* still."

He did not hesitate, nor was he timid. Not in anything he did, and not when nose-close to powerful explosives neither, which, honestly, was a disconcerting thing to see. True fearlessness that wasn't in any way a put-on or the grim acceptance of one's own dumb fate. He clipped through the layers of bandage one at a time and let the rags of them fall across my knee, humming some little snatch of some little ditty to himself while he worked. When I listened close, it came to me that he was humming the "Flower Duet" like from my dream and I felt a chill and closed my eyes back up again, wondering if this was it. The end, and the world all come a'tumbling down around me.

I mean, it wasn't. Obviously. Because I'm here talking to you about it. But I'm just saying that that was weird. Weirder than your everyday weird, and weird enough to raise an apple in my throat that I had a hard time swallowing.

"You okay there, Duncan?" the Captain asked me.

"Sure," I said. "But can I ask you something?"

"This would be a fine moment for it."

Really, I just wanted to stop him humming, and he couldn't hum while he talked, so I asked, "What are you thinking getting your explosives from the guy with the melty-face and the lobster hand? Were you looking for a bargain or something?"

He chuckled. Snipped through another layer of bandage and, suddenly, I could feel the cool blade of the scissors against the hot flesh of the back of my hand. "The thing about bomb makers is, not many of them grow old, you know? So you know how you tell which ones are good at it?"

"How?"

Another snip. And then air on my skin.

"The ones who are good at it are still alive. The ones who are bad at it are not. Stay real still now, okay?"

The Captain stood up. He dropped the scissors and took the barbecue tongs from where he'd tucked them into his belt and carefully grabbed the top of the glass tube with them.

"Okay. Let go."

I opened my hand. Nothing exploded.

The Captain took a step back.

"Now get up and open the case for me. Watch where I put this. Remember which one it is. This is not something you can forget, understand?"

I did as I was told and watched as the Captain slid the tube of Cyclot-8 into the one open slot in the box. Upper right corner on the hinge side.

He let it go, tossed aside the tongs and carefully closed the box, fastened the latches, laid both hands on top of it, took a breath. "Well. That was fun, wasn't it?"

"You do know how to show a fella a good time, Captain. We done here? Or maybe you want me to, what? Juggle a few hand grenades?"

"Can you?"

"Never tried, but I am clever."

The Captain sat down on the box that I had recently vacated. From out of his jacket he took a plastic baggie filled with tight, lovely handrolls. Took one for himself. Offered the bag to me. He lit his with a battered silver Zippo. While sitting on a box full of explosives. I took his lighter and lit my own. While standing next to a man sitting on a box full of explosives. Somehow, it felt fine. As though, after what we'd just done, nothing so simple or obvious as plain stupidity was going to kill us.

The Captain took a long drag and exhaled through his nose. He picked a bit of tobacco off his tongue, examined it, then looked back at me.

"What about pulling a Last Man Standing? You ever try that?"

I laughed. "What, like in real life? No."

"I've been reading your paper, Duncan," he said, his voice easy and conversational. "You pulled a lot of jobs in your time. You were a solid operator. Good head. Good eye for the small things. You did a lot of stupid things and made them look smart."

Yes, my legend was good. It'd been carefully scrubbed and re-assembled by the best possible man to do so. Too bad so much of it was just a pleasing fiction.

"There's no way to make a Last Man Standing look smart," I said. "It only works in the movies."

"Yeah, that's true." The Captain tapped his cigarette and looked up sharpish toward the mouth of one of the alleys a split-second before I saw the nose of a white hydrogen-conversion van poking through it, scraping its side mirrors on the walls to either side. "But from what I understand, you spent some time with a bunch of actors, didn't you?"

That was true. I'd hidden out for a time with a troupe of travel-ing thespians of some small repute. Almost a year, actually. We did the popular hits: *Hamlet, Star Wars, Death of a Salesman, Troilus and Cressida*, the first couple seasons of *Friends*. I played a passing fair Obi-Wan, a genius Patroclus, and as good a Monica as any man before me. When required, we could play as a passable band. Even did a little bit of stage magic and circus stunts when the rube quotient of the small towns along the Missouri border was fright-fully high. Almost every man among us was the sort that was run-ning from a bad name left behind somewhere. And while the pay was no great shakes, no one hardly ever noticed that we all made our real eating-money in dragged-up border crossers, fugitives in bolshie gowns and low heels, and the sorts of things as was easy to smuggle inside wigs, falsies, and Thersites's comically oversized pantaloons.

"For criminals, they weren't bad actors," I said. "But as actors, we was much better criminals. At our best, I still don't think even we could've made it work."

The van rolled up close and I grinned to see Miss Holly Bright behind the wheel, one of her eyes black, a cut beside it closed with a pink band-aid. Like a fool I even waved at her.

"That's funny," the Captain said. "Because they seem to have a bit more confidence in their abilities than you do."

Like more of a fool, I stood there with my hand up and turned to look at him. "What?" I asked.

"Your friends. They seem to think they could pull it off. Provided they had the right roper that can take it through the send. Of course, I did offer them a very good payday if they pulled it off. That might've influenced their opinion of themselves some."

"You're fucking kidding me."

The Captain pursed his lips and shook his head. "Nope. Didn't I tell you I had the perfect job for you?"

"But how did you—"

The Captain crossed his arms. "Really, Duncan? They live in a giant bus with clown heads painted on it. How tough do you think it was to find them?"

"Thalia and Melpomene," I said. "Comedy and Tragedy."

"Clown heads."

"Says you."

"Honestly, there's not much I can't do once I put my mind to it, you know? It took me about a week to bring them in. And if you hadn't pulled your little stunt with Holly up there in Great Times, I wouldn't have had them cooling their heels in the bunkhouse for the past two days on top of that. But now, there's a man I need to have a few words with, and he's not the sort I can just call up at the corner bar. We need him popped clean from the world and vanished, so we're pulling a Last Man Standing."

"Wait," says me. "This is bosh. If I'm the roper and my old crew is standing as spielers, you and yours'll work as our come-alongs, right?"

"You'll have some help, yeah. Whatever you need."

"Then why do you need me? If you've got the bodies to make a snatch, why not just drop him on the street?"

His Captainness took a thoughtful drag and squinted up into the sun like there was answers to all life's mysteries writ in the sky. "Because sometimes I take orders same as you do, Duncan. When it is to my advantage, anyhow. So we're working a proper OSS hierarchy on this. Right from the top. And the orders move from God to his angels to me to you."

"So then who's the Last Man Standing?"

"We'll get to that. But for right now, worry about your end. You're the roper. You have your team. And you've got two days to put it all together. Now help me get this stuff in the van without blowing it up, okay? We're on the clock."

It was my first time in a dog's age seeing these men that I had lived with and worked with and cut capers with for near on a year, but there was no time for catching up and telling tales over beers and the like. There was six of them. I knew four as well as I knew any man alive, save perhaps Gordon. We shook hands, them and me, commented on the loss of hair or the gain of weight, expressed a certain, brief amount of shock each that the others was still above snakes, and then got on about our business.

It was my first time inside the bunkhouse—the Captain's office and keeping-place, home to himself and the permanent members of his crew—but I didn't have the time to appreciate it and saw little of it save what they called the staging room, which was just a garage, or old warehouse space maybe, where we practiced and re-practiced and re-re-practiced our blocking. We all rumbled around there like marbles in a box, worked on our patter, ate MRE beef stroganoff and peach cobbler that tasted like the plastic in which it'd been bagged. When I slept, I did so wrapped in a blanket that smelled of diesel fuel and mold, in an inexplicable clawfooted bathtub shoved off in a corner.

After a day and a night of rehearsing, the Captain asked what I thought and I told him I thought that maybe some of us would make it out alive. Not all of us, but maybe half.

"That's not good enough," he said. "This has to go smooth."

So we got back to work, called in the OSS entry team and shooters that'd been lent to the Captain by their local commanders, drilled with them and guns full of blanks that filled the whole room with smoke and the sharp smell of spent powder. I'd been told that we would be facing between ten and twenty men, likely, and that two of them would be the Captain's—agents-in-place that'd been among the enemy for a long time and were aching for a way out. So them, us, and the principal all needed to survive. No one else could. Full down, those were the orders. The shoot team needed to make a clean sweep of it. We experimented with blinders and concussion grenades. Tear, vomit, and nerve gas (of the non-lethal variety), tagged mites, booby traps, trained wolverines in tiny parachutes—anything that might improve our odds. In the end, I decided that simpler was better. Lots of bangs. Lots of blood. Fast, fast, fast. Once I brought in the Captain's bag team as well, we had the whole operation down to fifty seconds and I was feeling good.

"If there's seven of us inside," I said to the Captain, "and your people don't kill any of my people, I figure we can get out losing one or two."

"You okay being one of those two?"

"Hell no. I'm gonna be hiding under a damn table."

"Then it isn't good enough yet."

I shrugged. "We're on a deadline, hoss. There might be a moment when good enough is the best we get."

It was the two inside men that were proving to be the most trouble. And when it wasn't them, it was the unknowns—the fact that I knew nothing of the arrangement, the room, the array of forces. After a while, all we were doing was losing sleep practicing for something that we wouldn't understand the lay of until the moment we had to perform. And though it was nice to be able to get the patter down, work out the crossfire, let everyone know where they had to be standing and when, in the end we were just making a pretty show leading up to the big event, and weren't none of us could tell how that was going to play for a paying crowd.

Still, rehearsing death scenes is always fun. There was some goofing, flubbed lines, missed marks and the casual, japing cruelty of seasoned professionals trying to keep their energy up even after the thirtieth or fiftieth iteration of the vital second. Flobbert, one of the new men, could not die in any way that even vaguely resembled the way any living thing ever had until Jaime, one of my old acting friends, told him that he ought to pretend he was faking the rigors of orgasm, and after that he got it right off. At one point, Del Harper, another friend, a man I'd shared a room with, a bed and every meal, fat or lean, for a year, refused to die, took up two guns and, in a hurricane of lead, called out to me to leave all this grim make-believe behind, imploring me with weeping soap opera histrionics to ride with him for Uruguay where all the banks stand unguarded and none of the women wear underpants. We laughed until we cried, all of us, then dried our eyes, reloaded our guns, and got right back to practicing. It was good to see my old friends again, even if I was just preparing them all for dying.

Later on that second night, when sleep resolutely refused to come to me, I went roaming. No one had told me outright that I was confined to the staging area. At no point did I run across a sign that said DUNCAN, GO NO FURTHER. So, to me, that was as good as permission to get about snooping.

Sadly, it was a disappointment. And if there is anything like a theme to these stories I'm telling you—something that unites them sweetly in a smooth commonality—it would be the notion that everything you was expecting to be wondrous turns out, in the end, to disappoint.

I mean, think on that a spell. The Captain expected me to be some trig linguist who could be his babel fish among the Techny and pull his bacon out of the fire if things went sour. As it turned out, I knew just enough to keep us all from being murdered in the remains of an old 7-11. Jack, Asa, Julie and me expected Great Times to be this plum gathering place for men of vile intentions, but it ended up a small, mean dump, more tumble-down than hellzapoppin'. Rufe, I'm guessing, did not expect his life to end in that place. Jack had held high notions of being a horse baron and had gotten his brains blown out in the dirt over the rescue of a girl who didn't need rescuing in the first place. All of us, I suspect, get a different and poorer future than the one we expect.

It was little different with the bunkhouse of Captain James Barrow. Where I expected to throw open doors and find rooms full of kung fu ninjas dodging fire and practicing with throwing stars or laboratories where fussy Englishmen designed submarine cars, wristwatch lasers and razorblade hats, instead I found a closet full of stockpiled toilet paper. Another that was empty save for a dry mop without a bucket and one small girl's rain boot with ladybugs on it. A kitchen where no one had done the washing up for quite some time. A long, low, gray room, waterstained and dark, filled with mismatched desks and chairs patched with duct tape which was twice as grim as the room I'd labored in at the Castle. A rec room of sorts which, to its credit, was somewhat comfortably appointed in the way of maybe a college dorm or the green room of a small-town playhouse, with a dark and wobble-legged Dungeons & Dragons pinball machine in one corner and far too many lamps.

"If you're looking for the secret volcano fortress, that's in the basement."

I turned at the sound of Jemma's voice and tried not to look like I'd been caught with my hand in the cookie jar. She was standing, back down the way I'd come, leaning against the wall with a cup of something in her hands. She was barefoot, wearing shorts and a plain tee shirt, her hair pulled back in a loose ponytail fixed with a twist of wire.

"Snooping?" she asked, smiling in a sly way that made her look both childish and fierce.

"Course not," said me. "Just got lost looking for the bathroom. Hope I didn't wake you."

She shook her head. "Not at all. I'm in the night room tonight and the Captain is keeping me company. Sorta." She toyed with the handle on her cup. "You, uh, want to join us maybe?"

And I said, "Sure," and, "Why not," because I was trying to sound cool and disinterested even as something hopped in my chest like a frog. "I mean, if y'all don't mind a third hand in the ring."

She smiled at me, ducked her head and said to come on along if'n I was coming, then turned and went back the way I'd come from.

It is ridiculous how little of good spying is like a James Bond movie, you know? And how much of it is like asking a girl out of a first date. Some men (like Gordon, for example) could never reconcile that in their muddled heads. But me, it suited just fine.

The Captain waited in what was colloquially referred to as the night room—a communications center of sorts, with two wooden desks hunched in a corner, a curling map of the Western states pegged to the wall, and a well in the center formed of scavenged couches and chairs and two tables pushed together. There were a couple TVs of Archie Bunker vintage, a flatscreen that appeared to have been on the losing end of a knife fight, and an archeological strata of trash and gadgets and dirty plates and doodads and old magazines turning slowly to compost that, if excavated, might've spoke volumes about the Captain and his crew. It was nice if your tastes ran toward shag carpeting and bachelor peculiarity.

"Ah, Duncan Archer," said himself, his boots up on the lower of the two tables before him, a scattering of opened beer bottles surrounding them. "The inimitable Duncan Archer. The profoundly perplexing Duncan Archer."

Jemma leaned over and bumped her shoulder into my shoulder. "He's a little drunk," she said.

"I am *not* a little drunk," said the Captain. "And I'd prove it to you if that harpy hadn't hidden my guns."

I looked at Jemma and she raised her eyebrows at me and grinned.

"So, Duncan Archer. Tell me something," said the Captain, but then gave no particulars. Not *tell me something about yourself* or *tell me about the man who's tasked you to spy on me.* I was, briefly, at a loss.

"It's a game he plays," said Jemma, sliding around me and going to sit in a straight-backed wood chair with its back turned to a desk covered in old-fashioned wired telephones, ancient cassette-tape answering machines, and bunches of phone cables bound in clumps with colored zip-ties. "Especially when he's a little drunk."

The Captain turned and stuck his tongue out at Jemma, who responded with a one-finger salute.

"He means tell him something he doesn't know," she continued. "About yourself or something. Come and sit."

"Okay," I said. "I'm game." I sat across from the Captain in a gut-sprung armchair made of cat hair and rusty leaf springs, put my elbows on my knees, and thought for a minute. "Okay. Those actors down there? My old friends? Two of them are OSS deserters like me."

And the Captain, he makes this honking sound like a gameshow buzzer and he says, "Nope, already knew that. Del Harper, interpreter, Cleveland office, and Duane Harris, data analyst, straight from the nest, Washington D.C." He sniffed and rolled his eyes. "They're deserters, Duncan, but not like you. You gotta drink."

He rattled around among the bottles until he came up with one that sloshed when shook and handed it to me. "Go on, now. Take your medicine."

The best thing that could be said of the beer that the Captain and his crew drank was that it was technically a liquid and, in a world shy on good refrigeration, was generally cold. Beyond that, it was thick and it was dark. As a delivery method for alcohol into the bloodstream, it lacked near every pleasant quality and tasted like it'd been brewed from poison stump water, day-old coffee, mercury, uranium mine tailings, moldy lemon peels, heroin tar, and sour barley taken from the field behind a witch's shack. The Captain euphemistically referred to it as a stout and claimed on many occasions to actually like it, though it was truly and indisputably awful, so I suspect that had more to do with politeness and expediency. In near any instance, I would've sooner drank mouthwash or wine coolers had there been any around. But to be neighborly, I chewed through a couple swallows, caught my breath, and said simply, "That's a powerful brew."

"Logue makes it," the Captain said. "Down in the motor pool."

"He use leaded or unleaded?"

His Captainness chuckled wetly. "Yeah, its got a bite to it. Your turn again. Tell me something."

I cleared my throat. "Well, under normal circumstances, I'd play this kind of game to lose, but considering the forfeit, let me consider a moment."

I told him that Julio Reconquista de la Teja was a transsexual and that, had Jack August not been killed at Great Times, we had this scam working where we were going to become rich horse barons so that he could get his plumbing properly reconfigured, and the Captain said he knew that. That he'd spoken with the both of them and that the both of them had mentioned the horses in a wistful sort of way—in the way of men who wished, all of a sudden, that their lives had followed a slightly different trajectory—and that made me feel bad all over again for the blood and wreckage I'd brought unto them.

"Drink," the Captain said.

I told him that, before the world ended, I'd been on track to become a lawyer, and he told me my summer job when I was 17 years old had been running files for a law office at 1818 Market Street in Philadelphia—a position secured for me by my mother, a litigator for a different firm four blocks away.

"Drink," he said.

"The Captain doesn't lose this game very often," said Jemma from her chair. And I asked how personal I was allowed to get. Like was I allowed to tell him what I dreamed about last night?

And no, said Jemma. It had to be a fact. A thing that had happened.

"So a thing that could conceivably be known?" I asked.

"That depends highly on how much you want your head fucked with," said the Captain. "I'm not sure you want to walk away from this little—" the Captain burped, "—this little party wondering how it was I know the name of your beloved childhood pet or the last time you jerked off."

I told him that the last thing I done on the day that Philadelphia burned was ask my phone where I could get some frozen yogurt. That on a perfect summer day I'd come down off the 36th floor where the law firm was, walked out into the courtyard at Market and 19th, asked my phone where I might find some froyo, gotten my answer and only then looked up to see the hullabaloo in the streets. The running and the squealing brakes of cars and a city bus turned sideways. I was turning away when I saw the enormous

Type 1 come crawling over the stock exchange building, crumbling masonry turning to powder in its metal hands, the sun shining through raised dust onto the banded dome of its metal head.

And the Captain said, "Wow. Frozen yogurt?"

"Yup."

"And you were there? I mean, *right* there?"

"Yeah."

"Frozen yogurt." He shook his head. "That has to be one of the worst end-of-the-world stories I've ever heard."

I grinned with one half of my face, as the other half seemed to have gone numb or briefly to sleep. "That's how you know it's true. It's them as say they were Rambo-ing it out on the streets or whatever that you know was actually fifty miles away and looking in the other direction when it all happened."

"Cheers to that," said the Captain.

"Drink," said me.

"Roger that," said him, and took a bottle and upended it into his person.

"So, if I understand this game correctly," I said, "now it's my turn. So, your Captainness, tell me something."

He laughed. He choked a little on the dregs of his stout. He wiped his mouth on the sleeve of his jacket and looked at me with bright eyes only slightly swimming, and said, "The trick here is not beating you because I know so much that you don't know. It's deciding what among the million things I *could* tell you that would actually be . . ."

"Not a violation of mission security?" Jemma suggested.

". . . funny," finished the Captain. Unprompted, he took a second swallow from the bottle in his hand. "Okay, you see all those telephones going currently unmanned by the lovely Jemma Watts?"

"Lovely *and* intelligent," said Jemma.

"The lovely, intelligent, and dutiful Jemma Watts? Those are our mayday phones. Every one of them is a number known by one or more of my people in the field. They're all cold drops. Unwired. Not even voice mail, but actual answering machines for those who need to pass messages to us in a hurry. We've got . . . what? How many now, Jemma?"

"Twenty-eight active currently. Fifty total."

"And they're all fake businesses. Like dry cleaners and insurance adjusters and, like, cobblers or whatever . . ." He was fading slightly, the Captain. Unbidden, he drank again.

He had the same set-up as Gordon and the boss did, with me calling into Pork Chop Express Carting and Haulage. Which was not surprising to me at all, since I knew where he'd learned it.

"Some of them, though, are actual businesses that we run," the Captain continued. And my favorite is Tuttle's Heating and Cooling, run by Harry Tuttle. Who is me, under one of my many hats. I have gone to people's houses and actually fixed their furnaces. And the funny part is, no one has ever gotten the joke."

I knew that. It was in the Regulator's file, under known aliases: James Barrow, a.k.a. Harry Tuttle. I opened my mouth to say so, then closed it again. I looked at the bottles of beer in front of us and could taste the evilness of the brew still lingering like a fur coat on my tongue. It killed me a little to lose at a game I could win. I had to force my mouth to work.

"Huh," I said. "I didn't know that."

The Captain laughed. "Well of course you didn't, Duncan! Like I said, the things you don't know . . . *Whew.*"

I chose a bottle and I drank from it, eyeing the Captain as he and Jemma launched into a discussion of some of the other numbers they had set up and the jokes of them. "*Brazil*," he said. "You remember that movie, Duncan?"

"I do," I said.

"That was my favorite movie of all time. Well, maybe my second or third favorite. But it was up there, you know? Top five for sure." Then wistfully. "*Brazil* . . ." Then sadly. "Fuck." Then in a voice that was uncharacteristically small and almost boyish, a thing that almost got lost in the dim and closeness of the crowded night room. "How long has it been since I saw a movie?"

I got my brief the next day, thirty minutes before we were due to go in for the first time. The Captain did it leaning on the hood of an old pickup truck with a covered bed and blooms of rust coming up from the wheel wells. He was eating chicharones shook up with hot sauce from a greasy paper bag and licking his fingers at the end of every sentence. He seemed none the worse for wear after last night's exertions.

"You are Harry Plum," he said. "Dealer in booms and bangs. You have for sale twenty tubes of Cyclot-8 liberated from the Hiawatha, Kansas armory during the unpleasantness. The going price is $100,000 in gold by weight. They have it, so don't let them tell you they don't."

"And who are 'they?'" I asked.

"Legion of Terror," said the Captain. "Or what remains of them, anyway." He held out the bag to me but I demurred. "Your loss."

The Legion of Terror were the former henchmen of Dinosaur Joe, he explained. Dinosaur Joe was currently in the territorial supermax at Florence, but when he'd been loose, he'd had it all— stupid nickname, secret lair, crazy schemes, and a private army of low-rent psychopaths and mama's boys who dressed up in ridiculous costumes and ran around causing trouble for the boss.

"Also, he had dinosaurs," said the Captain, licking his fingers. "You know, hence the name."

Real, honest-to-Jesus dinosaurs. He grew them in his Honeycomb Hideout or whatever—cooked up from a mish-mash of genes and goop and spare parts. Or at least that was the story. No one had ever actually, you know . . . seen one.

Anyway, the Legion of Terror very badly wanted their leader back. But in order to bust him out of the supermax, they needed explosives.

"Enter Harry Plum," said the Captain, and smiled, his cheeks stuffed with chicharones. "This is just a first pass. Take your two best men. You know Maria's?"

"The Mexican restaurant on Federal?" I asked. Because that was another thing that'd survived our own peculiar version of the apocalypse: taquerias. And thank the good lord for it.

"Yeah. You're meeting them there. Jemma will give you a ride."

We did the first pass, ate tortilla chips and salsa made from melons, g-mod tomatoes, and hot sauce straight from the bottle, drank margaritas, and I watched one of the Legion of Terror throwing up in the street after we were done.

At the first actual meeting a day later, we discussed terms: twenty tubes of Cyclot-8 for $100,000 in gold. They brought a sample—a slug about the size of a cigar tube. Just looking at it, I knew it was the worst fake gold I had ever seen, so smiled and told them how pleased I was at its loveliness and weight. The L.O.T. were ridiculous and dim, wearing pieces of uniforms that made them look like Confederate extras in a Civil War costume drama and constantly spouting off bits of nonsense about dinosaurs or how the Western Confederacy was going to operate when their glorious leader rose to the throne.

Harry Plum, for his part, was aloof and distant—a man who was happy to make a deal, but didn't *need* this deal to make rent. He didn't care about politics or sides or feuds. He had no interest in the L.O.T.'s plans for world domination or the suspect genius of Dinosaur Joe. This was just business. I carried my case with me everywhere I went and wore my automatic under my arm. The Captain had procured for me a nice suit, black with a subtle taper. I wore it exceedingly well.

Back at the bunkhouse after the first meeting, I saw Dogboy and the Captain sitting together by the big roll-up doors eating tacos.

The Captain was kicked back in a folding chair, his back against the wall. Dogboy was squatting beside him, half an al pastor hard shell held between his strange front paws.

"That's him if you want to say something," the Captain said to Dogboy, bobbing his chin in my direction.

Dogboy looked up at the Captain, then at me—his head tilted in that peculiarly doggish way, tongue lolling slightly, taco crumbs all over his muzzle. He rose onto two legs (which was never the most comfortable way for him to walk, not after being shot, but did make him feel more human) and loped over to me with long strides. I had to stop myself from jerking back at his approach— from upping sticks and just plain bolting at the reflexive fear of feeling his attention turned, suddenly, to me.

"You're Duncan," he said, his voice thick-tongued and slobbery, but understandable. "You were there that night. On the road."

I said that I was.

"You saved my life," said Dogboy. "Wouldn't no one else have done that." And then he stuck out a paw that wasn't quite a paw, but wasn't really a hand neither, and I felt the ridiculous urge to *say* shake rather than just do it, but then I did.

"Thank you," Dogboy said.

His hand was hot. His claws scribbled against the inside of my wrist. And then the moment was over and Dogboy turned and hobbled back to sit beside the Captain, pick his taco up off the ground, and get back to his lunch.

When I looked down, I saw that my hand was still extended. I quickly shoved it in a pocket and walked off to not think about what I'd just done.

There was a second meeting with the L.O.T., in a parking lot on the edge of the contraction zone fronting a block of long-abandoned nail salons, car insurance offices, and the smashed remains of a

Baskin Robbins ice cream shop. They brought more men this time and so did I—my entire troupe, decked out in the drag of cheap gangsters, all tracksuits and snap-brims or slouchy suits of the sort that could be gotten off the rack at the relief office, in colors from garish to horrible.

This time, my job was to act the waffle, being pushed around by my own men, and to ultimately convince the L.O.T. that, because of the highly unstable nature of the product I was selling (coupled with the highly unstable nature of my men), the only place we could possibly do the hand-over of gold for boom jelly was in a garage which the Captain and his people had chosen as ideal for the theatrics we had to stage. Doing that by making them embarrassed for me was the easiest way my troupe and me could figure, and it worked a treat. The actors and I had our crossfire down cold. They hollered and they stormed at the suggestion that we meet for the hand-off at one of the L.O.T.'s facilities, then hollered louder when I tried to push for a neutral territory like a parking garage or a men's room. We chawed at each other there in the parking lot for a solid five minutes—snipping and biting and dropping, here and there, into deep cant or bits of Ruska. The freeze-out was perfect. The L.O.T. just stood there, blinking at each other, not knowing what to make of us. And then one of my men set in to screaming and hit me with his hat, which was the thing that finally pushed the L.O.T. over the edge. They threw their hands up like to shush us or to cool us out, and quickly agreed that the meeting place didn't much matter to them after all, so they'd be happy to do it at our garage the next day if only we would all shut up and stop acting like such children.

"Thank you, gentlemen," said Harry Plum, looking down and wearing a face of fearsome but contained embarrassment. "Three o'clock then. And I apologize for all this unpleasantness."

We did two fast, final dress rehearsals with the entire team in the actual garage immediately after the meeting, then bugged out for the bunkhouse—wanting to leave the space cold in case the Legion of Terror suddenly became smarter than was their reputation and put a watch on it. The Captain dismissed his loaner teams from the OSS with orders to meet back at the bunkhouse at noon for gear-up and final mission prep. Once they were gone, he spat on the floor and went upstairs without a word.

"He seems cheerful," I said to Logue, who was standing near me, watching the doors roll down behind the last of the OSS shooters.

"Shut up," said Logue.

"I'm just saying," I said. "He seems rather more prickly than usual."

And Logue turned to me. "This the place where I'm supposed to tell you all the secret thoughts of the Captain and why he doesn't play well with others? Fuck you."

And then he turned and walked away.

That night we drank water and everyone went to bed early. I stayed up a while with the Captain, Barnum and Strange, Joker Haws and Logue, running through the entire dance on paper time and again, explaining every move we were going to make and showing them all the places where things could go wrong. When I was done, the Captain looked around the table, nodded, then gave me a final brief.

"This is the man we want," the Captain said, shoving a tablet across the table at me. On it were several pictures of the same small, odd-looking man with a doughy face, glasses, and hair parted straight down the middle of his head. "That's the Chemist. Ignatz Walton. He's your Last Man Standing. The idiots are going to try to surprise you with him tomorrow. He'll come along with the money, after the send, and he'll ask to test the Cyclot before the money is handed over."

"No," I said.

"Yes," said the Captain. "These are the orders from on high."

I put my head in my hands. "This changes everything," I muttered. "This fucks up every move in the final act."

The Captain's voice was calm and level when he spoke. "Explain to me how."

I looked up and told him I could count the ways. "First, there's no way to test Cyclot without a whole lab setup," I said. "Not without blowing it up."

"He knows that," said Barnum.

"He's a smart man, the Chemist," said Strange.

"But the Legion of Terror are not sharp sticks," said Barnum. "They don't know shit."

"Which is just one of the reasons why I'm a big fan of this guy," said the Captain. Then, to Barnum and Strange: "Also, stop talking like that. It weirds people out."

The two of them smiled.

"He's just pretending, my man Ignatz, and taking a nice paycheck for doing it," said the Captain, pulling the tablet back to his side of the table and swiping through the photos. "I love this guy. I really do. He used to work with Dinosaur Joe before Joe went inside. Worked with lots of other people, too. He's really gotten around. But he's the only chemist that the L.O.T. have available to them, so according to our people inside, they're planning on springing him on you at the last minute. They figure that, if the Cyclot is fake, you'll panic and run."

"But it is fake," I reminded him.

"All but the one tube," he said. "Upstairs, they're worried that Ignatz *might* be able to tell the difference between the real stuff and the fake stuff just from pretending to test it, so you have to make sure that he goes for the one real tube."

"That's the second problem. There is no reasonable way to guarantee that. It's a one-in-twenty chance he grabs the right one. It's not something we've rehearsed for. We have no script for it. Him being there puts another body in the room at the critical moment.

Worse, it puts another body in the room in close proximity to live explosives. We can't do it."

"No choice," said the Captain. "Those are the orders I have been given. The OSS bosses want this guy badly and they have a whole act planned out for him." He paused them, looked me in the eye. "So I want you to understand this, Duncan. You listening?"

"Yeah," I sighed. "I'm listening."

"No, are you *really* listening?"

"Captain, I am *really* listening."

"Okay. The OSS bosses want this guy badly. They want him taken with the Cyclot—the *live* Cyclot—in his hand so there'll be no way he can run. Their shooters will take down all the L.O.T. targets and then snatch him up while he's standing there like an idiot with a tube of powerful explosives in his hand. That something you can understand a little bit?"

I said yes. That was something I could surely understand.

"They gave me my orders. I have now given those orders to you. But if something were to happen during the execution of the mission which required someone to call in the shoot team early? If the Chemist maybe had a chance to run and a clever fellow had maybe put a bag team in place to snatch him away in the confusion . . ."

"The entire mission would be ruined," I said. "A complete failure."

"That's what it would look like, yeah. And all because one man made the call too early. Just by a few seconds. Because maybe something went wrong with the setup at the last second or someone was out of place? That could totally happen, you know, what with this whole mission being so rushed and everything?"

"Hmm," I said.

"Something to think about," he said.

"It surely is. I think maybe I'd better wake my team and have a bit more practice. Just to make sure nothing like that happens."

The Captain smiled. "No, let them sleep. You can drill it in the morning. In the meantime, why not show me here on these papers how things *might* go wrong tomorrow."

It was well after midnight by the time we were done. I waited until 3 AM and stepped outside for a cigarette. I took a little walk around the building. Then I took a walk around the block.

Nerves, I told myself. *Tomorrow is a big day and you're very nervous.*

I walked around the block again. On my third turn, when I was sure no one was following me, I took from my pocket the new burner that Gordon had given me three days ago, which I'd taken from my briefcase before leaving, and let it speed dial the only number it knew.

It went to the same cold-drop—Porkchop Express. I waited for the beep.

"He's pulling a Last Man Standing," I said, gave the address of the garage and the time. "Primary is Ignatz Walton, also known as the Chemist, and he's planning a drop-out and snatch of his own. I'll be on-site for confirmation tomorrow. And I'm gonna need a new phone."

Without breaking stride, I twisted the phone until it snapped and dropped one piece into a dumpster as I walked past, the other into a rent in the earth which, in the dark, seemed to go down a mile.

I was living in the moment. All Zen all the time.

In the end, what it all came down to was trading fake boom jelly for gold that was so impure it might just as well have been slugs of lead painted yellow and tossed in a canvas sack with a dollar sign drawn on it in crayon.

The meeting was scheduled for 3 o'clock. The Captain brought in a couple of ex-OSS dressers to help my actors and me gear up, then we loaded the box full of Cyclot-8 into the back of the pickup truck and all climbed gingerly aboard. We were on-site by 2 and all in our first positions. The Legion of Terror were, of course, late.

When they arrived, they were loud and pushy and tumbling over each other like puppies. There were fourteen of them—two of whom were the Captain's inside men and twelve who was already being fitted for knotty pine tuxedos and didn't even know it. They saw the box of Cyclot set on a table with its lid propped open, and half of them made a dash for it like it was filled with candy.

Like professionals, my actors broke position as natural as actual humans in order to restrain the exuberance of the L.O.T., and after some shoving, loud words and exhortations to stay the fuck back so's all of us might walk out of this garage un-blown-the-fuck-up when our business was concluded, they faded back to their marks like it was nothing. Not one of them had drawn their guns. Which was good because not one of them had anything but blanks in them.

Everything from there on out was a dance. Harry Plum was all business, and I played him once again as a man in control, a man who just wanted to get the botheration of his day's business out of the way so he could get back to playing handball or strangling cats or whatever it was amused him when he wasn't selling explodables to damn fools.

"I, uh, don't see a nice, tidy pile of gold here, gentlemen," I said to the assembled, not bothering to address anyone in particular because I hadn't bothered to learn a one of their names. "A hundred thousand dollars in gold is heavy. I don't figure you all are carrying that in your pockets."

There were chuckles from the L.O.T., and one of them—a chunky thing with a shining face so greasy that he appeared to be sweating lard in the tin-roof heat of the garage—stepped forward.

"Had to make positive that you were true first. True blue. That you had what you said you had and weren't having any second thoughts about dealing with the Legion of Terror."

At which point every idiot in the room pumped their fist and chanted *El Oh Tee! El Oh Tee! El Oh Tee!* because, apparently, not a one of them had the good sense God gave a goat.

"Oh fuck me," I said, lowering my head and pinching the bridge of my nose.

I waited for the cheers to die down, and when I looked up again, I was wearing a face of sour exasperation. "Please tell me you guys aren't going to try to make this like a movie now, where you tell me you have the gold, but you don't have it *here*, and then we have to go *get* the gold and you don't have *enough* gold and then I have to kill all of you and feed you to the pigs on my farm in Ordway. Because I am a motherfucking professional, guys, and I just don't have time for that."

We had these code words, both as a fallback in case the drone mites and pickup microphones and the fiberoptic cameras and all the other electronic surveillance equipment that Jemma had laid into the garage all failed at the same moment, and as a way to keep me and my guys on our timing. They were like act breaks—first this happens, then this, you understand? A way for us to recover the script when things grew messy.

Farm was the first. It meant that the preliminaries was done and now was time to start the send. The minute I said it, my guys started moving.

"Fuck this, Harry. Close 'er down, huh?"

"Seriously, bru. We gone. Gots plenty more buyers for this what isn't feckin' childrens."

Two of my guys started walking toward the box of boom jelly, meaning to pack it up and take it all away. Another threw his hands in the air and made as if headed for the door.

"Tol' you this was just the apex of futility, didn't I?" said the one of mine closest to me, and I whipped to him on my toes and gave him a smart smack in the mouth, backhand, but with a sound that really carried. He spun down to one knee, hand over his mouth, fake blood drooling from between his fingers.

The greasy little fat man said nothing. Nor did any of his paj-animals in their silly costumes. I pointed a finger at him and said, "You. Tell me now. You have the gold?"

He looked at me, eyes wide, trace of a smile playing around the squishy bits of his cheeks. "We got the gold," he said.

"Show me. Now. We count. We trade. We leave. That's the way *business* gets done."

The man's face folded in on itself and I saw his hands coming up in a placating gesture and I knew, right then, that we had them roped.

"Okay, look," he said, then chewed at his own cheeks as if he couldn't stand the taste of the next words that had to come out of his mouth. "We have the gold, but it's not here."

"Oh, you cocksuckers!" I yelled.

At which point two of the L.O.T. touched leather and started hollering about *what did you call us* and *no one talks to the Legion of Terror that way*, and my guys all unlimbered their iron and then so did most of the rest of the L.O.T., and suddenly it was all beer and skittles with shouting and pistol-waving and damn fools in their gray-belly costumes shaking their guns at my guys like that was the way you made the bullets come out. And all was right with the world as I stepped to the center of the room with my hands raised and bellowed at the top of my lungs, "*Everyone shut the fuck up!*" because now I and mine knew for certain who the Captain's two undercovers were, and so did everyone watching the fun on TV at home.

306

Cocksucker was the second code word, of course. We were two-thirds of the way home.

"Look," I said. "Look! Everyone shut up and put your guns away. Do it now and maybe we can all still get what we want today. I'm bored already and I want this done with."

Slowly, my fellas holstered their weapons and moved to third positions. Two of them closed the box of Cyclot and fixed the latches. Lifted it with exaggerated care off the table on which it'd been sitting and set it down on the cement floor of the garage. I cut a third off the room and positioned myself near the back wall, then turned to the L.O.T.'s spokesman and asked him, "You really have the gold?"

"Course we do," he said. "The Legion of Terror doesn't—"

"Yeah, yeah, yeah. Whatever. You have *all* of it? And somewhere close by?"

"Yeah."

"Well then take the Superfriends here and go fucking get it then. We'll wait, what . . .?" I turned to my guys, and they argued a moment before we all came down on twenty minutes, and not one more.

"You get back with the gold in twenty minutes, we do business. You don't, we're gone. Understand? I don't like any of you. My guys *really* don't like you. But I hate wasting time more than I hate you right now, so you've got this one chance to make it right." I looked around the garage. None of them seemed to be moving.

"The fuck are you all staring at? The clock is running. All of you, get out of my garage. Come back with the money or don't. I seriously do not give a fuck right now."

And with that, I pulled out a conveniently placed chair, sat down in it, leaned back against the wall and waved my fingers at them like shooing away flies. In a disorganized and confuzzled mob, they turned and slunk out the front doors, toward their woolly mammoths or Terrormobiles or whatever it was they'd arrived by.

And that, my friends, is how you do the send.

Once they were gone and we'd gotten the all-clear from our spotters outside, we all breathed out and flexed our smiles at each other. The show wasn't over yet, but it was coming close now.

It took the Legion of Terror eighteen minutes to make it back. In that time, we'd had a final meeting, adjusted a few details of the final act, tested our personal electrics, moved the Cyclot box nearer the back wall and its conveniently placed exit, propped open that door with a chunk of cinderblock, and by the time they were hustling through the big roll-doors at the front of the garage, we'd all moved into our final positions. Mine was outside the back door having a cigarette with one of my guys. We wanted to make sure everyone saw the back door. *Knew* it was open. We particularly needed the Chemist to see the back door, know it was open, smell the fresh breezes and freedom just on the other side of it, because, despite what the OSS might've required, this was the door we needed the Chemist to go out when everything fell apart. We needed him to run like a mother and not even think about it. My guys and I had practiced it this morning. We thought there was a 50/50 chance of it going the right way, which wasn't bad.

The Legion of Terror entered, all full once more of brash and swagger. The sweaty fat one was dragging a carry-on bag with wheels. And behind him walked the Chemist, just goggling around at everything, a look on his face like everything in the world was new to him and being seen for the first time.

It was time to bring the house down.

"I'll go in first," I whispered to Flobbert, the man I was outside the door with. "Give it a ten-count, then you follow. Make a show of adjusting the cinderblock. Leave the door as wide as you can make it."

And then Harry Plum took the stage for one last time. He yelled, he blusterated, he snatched the wheelie-bag away from the Legion of Terror's headman, yanked down the zippers and made cooing noises over the mound of the world's most impure slug gold contained within—even going so far as to call a couple of his hard boys over to feel the weight of it and briefly skylark about the boats and hookers it was going to buy for them.

When Harry seemed to first catch a sight of the Chemist poking around through a pile of scrap metal by the side wall, he exploded in apoplectic fury over the Legion of Terror bringing someone new in to the negotiations at this late a date, but then cooled immediately when the L.O.T. explained that they weren't stupid and that they were damn-sure going to have someone test the boom jelly before they paid good money for it.

"Well," I said. "That's reasonable, I guess." Then, distractedly. "Luka, Jerry, get a tube for the nerd to sniff at, will ya? And be fucking *careful*. I swear to god, you blow us all up, my spirit will come back and ghost-fuck your wife every goddamn night."

Luke and Jerry (being played by Del and Flobbert) broke from their places and moved to the box.

I hawked and spit onto the floor, checked the front door and the back door, watched the Chemist walk slowly toward Luka and Jerry and the box. Watched Luka and Jerry open the box. Watched the Chemist reach into the short jacket he was wearing and pull out a test tube and dropper—the fake accoutrements of his fake business today.

"Hey," I called. "Wait a minute."

I started walking over toward them. I put myself in a direct line between the front doors and the Chemist's body. We were all in the air now. Running on changes to the final act that'd been made just hours ago, with no one but us knowing about them.

"Let me get the tube out, butterfingers. I just don't trust you not to drop it."

Butterfingers was the last word. It meant the finale had arrived.

Somewhere, there was a rush of booted feet. A clacking of rounds going into chambers. The OSS shooters were in no position to question the timing. All they could do was go when I said the word.

I counted my own steps. One, two, three, four, five. That was my mark. And all I could do now was wait for the bangs.

I died two seconds after the shoot team came through the door. I knew it was my time when I felt the pinprick heat against my skin of the tiny magnesium charges going off inside the blood squibs surgical taped to my tee shirt. Then it was my death scene, which was the most *important* death scene because I was the star and the director of this massacre, both. I had to stagger. I had to whuff out a big breath as my shirt and parts of my jacket were blown to ribbons and streamers of fake blood spattered out ahead of me. I had to reach, at the last, falling second, for the Chemist who stood just a pace away from me, and break my fall against him to smear him all down the body with blood and save myself doing terrible things to my knees—which, hate to admit it, were getting as old as the rest of me and would not have enjoyed the shattering impact with the concrete floor of the garage.

I could not look around to see what was happening elsewhere. I was dead and there was no time. I could smell it, though— the acrid sting of gunsmoke—and I could hear it—screams and cries of surprise and the stiff, sharp *brrraaap* of controlled bursts from modern assault rifles firing low-velocity, low-caliber rounds at wicked rates into meat which just seemed to attract them like honey does flies.

I was busy. There was nothing I could do but my part, and I wanted to play it well. I let myself slide down the Chemist's body, painting him in my own fake blood. I looked straight into his eyes and let him see the life go out of mine.

The weird thing? His were as dead as mine already. They were, if anything, faintly amused.

I hit the ground. Threw out an arm. Squirmed just a little. No one who dies by the gun ever goes quietly 'cept them that's head-shot, and we didn't have the skill or equipment to simulate that among our dead men. Eventually, I went quiet.

I watched, through my dead eyes, the Chemist's ankles. If all had gone right, the shoot team would have put down every member of the Legion of Terror. The Captain's two undercovers would be trading fake shots with them right now, both of them firing into the roof, moving, firing, rotating their positions until the undercovers could run out the front doors and the shoot team could follow them, which should have been the signal for the OSS handlers to come in and collect their prize. Ten seconds, it would take. Ten long seconds, during which the Chemist had to go out the back door lest the OSS handlers have time to come for him. I listened to the cacophony. Ratatat small arms. The rip of automatics. Shouting for effect. Running feet. My men would all be pretend-dead. The L.O.T.'s would be for-real-dead. And then there would be the Chemist. The Last Man Standing.

Covered in blood and surrounded by dead men, but the last man standing. His only choice would be to run out the back door, which was propped open and waiting for him. *Calling* to him, really. Freedom. Escape. He wouldn't know that the Captain's bag team was out there waiting on him. He wouldn't know that he was running into a dog-leg alley at the end of which waited Barnum and Strange, Joker Haws, Lud Margate, and Laszlo Gazsi with a shock-rod, a bottle of ether, a rag, and a van, its windows blacked-out with tin foil.

I watched his ankles, our Chemist. I counted seconds. The racket was tapering off. Then it was stopped as the action moved outside.

He was alone now in the ringing quiet and haze of gun smoke. Every sane man in the world would, at this point, run like hell.

But the Chemist, the crazy motherfucker, he *walked*. He bent down, looked at me in my pretend-dead eyes (which, because no one can fake being actually dead in the eyes to a man who has seen real dead men before, I had to make just-a-little-bit-alive-yet eyes), smiled a strange and distant smile, and then walked out the back door.

Well, I thought. *That's that then.*

My order had been for all the make-believe dead to stay that way for sixty seconds or until I called clear. When we rose from the places of our dying, there was much shouting and carrying on and questions of what had happened to the Chemist and what had happened to the plan.

Still, my men cheered and slapped backs, as they'd been instructed to do. They'd done their parts. Played their roles. They couldn't care less about the greater concerns of them as were paying them for their time. So despite all the real and truly dead leaking their vitals onto the stained cement of the garage, there was a festive, post-curtain feeling in the air because we had, in fact, done the nearly impossible. We'd pulled a Last Man Standing for a paying crowd and run the gank like pros.

The OSS shoot team came back in. The OSS handlers yelled at anyone who would listen to them. Medical units and an OSS cleaning crew descended in white panel vans marked like various down-on-their-heels fish merchants and furniture repairers. These men were not of the Captain's coterie neither, but support teams of the greater realms of the OSS infrastructure, and I'd been told by the Captain to expect them because he had one more small trick for me to play. Harry Plum was not quite finished with his work yet, and though the show was all done, I could not linger. I had one more job to do.

Of my men, one—Duane Harris—had been lightly injured about the face by concrete shrapnel kicked up by a bullet that'd barely missed him, and another, Ozzie Lawton, had sprained his wrist, so flamboyantly had he hurled himself at the ground in his death throes. Of the Captain's two undercovers, one had taken a pistol round in the chest (which was stopped by his spidersilk long-johns) and another sting to the arm which was a clean in-and-out but was bleeding like he'd flat-out burst. The other was unharmed in any way. None of ours had been killed, which was just remarkable and something which I take the pride of, even today.

I was dripping fake gore that smelled sweet and stuck the tatters of my clothes to me. My face was sticky with it. My hands like a butcher's. I relaxed near the front doors, smoking a cigarette, watching the cleaners in their gloves and coveralls bagging bodies and fitting them into 55-gallon drums marked with biohazard trefoils while the handlers and shoot teams tried to ask a hundred different questions to anyone who crossed their gaze, trying to get a handle on what had gone wrong and a search organized and moving on the fly for a man who'd just simply up and disappeared.

I waited on the technicians that came to fetch up the slug gold, the fake boom jelly, and the one tube of the real stuff, which had been marked now and fitted in with its mates. It took some time, but eventually both boxes were loaded into the back of a truck that'd once belonged to Oliver's Meat & Seafood and I promptly sidled up and stole that truck, driving it off without no man even giving me a sideways look. All was a commotion in and around the garage. Everyone was busy fussing at something.

My men had their own evac and rally orders. As did the Captain's bag team, who were under special instructions to be as sneaky as ever they could be since the Chemist was a high-value snatch and the greater portion of the OSS would certainly be anxious to find him now that he was, ostensibly, in the wind.

The Captain, in case you haven't noticed yet, was not a man who cottoned much to sharing.

As for me, I'm sneaky just on general principles. My instructions had been clear: to watch the technicians load the truck, to steal the truck, and then to bring the truck full of ill-gotten goods back home to the bunkhouse by most direct route.

But in all the uproar, that had seemed un-smart to me and so, like I'd ignored that earlier bit about letting the Chemist get close enough to test the Cyclot, I ignored that order as well, made a field expedient decision, and drove the truck straight to the Nob, enlisted Hippo and the least shaky of his drunks into helping me unload its valuables into the bar's wheezing, mostly functional beer cooler, and then made it rain enough half-eagles that everyone save Hippolite himself would drink themselves into forgetfulness by the time happy hour was done.

For my man Hippo, I offered him a nice delivery van in exchange for five undisturbed minutes in his men's room and his recalcitrance and stoicism on the subject of trucks, mysterious bags, and my bloodied and ragged appearance in general.

"I was never here, Hippo. You understand?" I said. Which was awesome because, really, how often in life does a man get to say that without being laughed at?

I cleaned up as best I could, ditched the top half of my savaged suit into a bag, and bought an only somewhat disgusting denim jacket off one of Hippo's regulars that fit me well enough that I could hail down a cab without anyone immediately calling the beeps on me or shooting me for being a zombie.

The cab got me to within walking distance of the bunkhouse and I did the rest of the distance on foot. When I came into the staging area, I found the Captain in a temper—pacing the floor in his shirtsleeves, hollering at the walls and at Jemma and at Logue, and, when the spirit moved him, kicking whatever fell within his range.

I thought it was me he was furious at and strolled in with hands up and apologies already in my mouth.

"Captain," I said. "I'm sorry, but it took me as wise that I didn't—"

"Duncan!" he shouted, whirling in my direction and pointing at me with both hands. "Boom. That's one. We're halfway home."

I said, "Huh?" because I am just clever that way.

"Of course he appears to be missing one truck," the Captain continued, cocking one curious eyebrow at me. "One truck full of gold and explosives. Which is somewhat . . . discouraging. But I'm sure he has a reasonable explanation. Please, Duncan, favor us with your reasonable explanation."

I said, "Uh . . ."

"Quickly, Duncan."

"The Cyclot and the gold are safe. It seemed wise to stash them in case there was any heat coming. The truck I kinda gave away, but that's not important. I know where it is if we need to borrow it back. But is there something going on here that I'm missing?"

The Captain spun away from me and slapped a hand down on the roof of the pickup truck that'd been our briefing table once. In a far corner of the room, Dogboy slunk in through a door and crouched, panting, in a shadowed corner.

Jemma looked at Logue and Logue looked at the Captain and then Jemma looked at me.

"The bag team are missing," she said. "We know they grabbed the Chemist. We had contact from them en route as they were leaving the site. But they should've been back almost an hour ago now and we haven't heard a word."

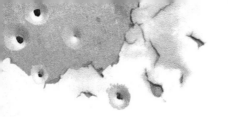

EPISODE

6

Lawyers, Guns, and Money

IT WOULD TAKE DAYS TO FIGURE OUT WHAT HAPPENED TO THE Chemist. Most of it—say 90% of it—we had in the first hour or two, and that's almost always the way of these things. Getting that last 10%, though, is inevitably and unquestionably a bitch, because that last 10%? That's the truth of a thing, and truth doesn't never come easy nor cheap.

Which, come to think of it, is something you must understand better than most. I mean, you're the ones been sitting here listening to me for all this time. So give us a drink, huh? And a smoke, as well. How long have I been talking now? Hours? Days? I believe I've earned a bit of kindness.

That's right. Pour it tall. Give me a light, too. Okay.

Now listen. Because this is where things get strange.

316

The Captain is pissed. He is in a twist and does not handle it gracefully. He is not a man accustomed to things going in ways that he does not understand, in ways that he has not seen coming along the bright curve of the horizon. An ace planner, him. Learned it at a tough school and never forgot a trick. But as you well know, there's much more to it than that.

So in the staging area, in the moments just before things go from bad to seemingly-less-bad-but-actually-much-*much*-worse, the Captain shows his petulance and, maybe, the true face of himself when forced to live, temporarily, among us mere mortals for whom time is only what they see on their watch. He beats his fists. He kicks things, rages, hollers, curses God, the devil, and the OSS. He throws, for lack of a more elegant word, a tantrum.

Off and out of the range of his conflusteration, Jemma explains to me that the bag team—Barnum, Strange, Lud Margate, Joker Haws, and Laszlo Gazsi—has gone missing, along with, of course, the Chemist. No word, none forthcoming. There is, from all of them, just a silence which the mind fills with ten thousand worst possibilities as the absence of the Captain's men becomes a bucket into which we might all pour our most terrible fears.

"Can't even get eyes," says Jemma quietly, meaning cameras, mites, drone video, anything. "The whole area has just gone dark."

Logue looks at the Captain and then looks away. He looks back, sidewise, as though attempting to witness an eclipse without going blind from it. And though he doesn't actually peek from behind his hands, I imagine him a boy—an enormous boy—watching a scary movie on the couch from behind the cage of his own knotted fingers. The Captain's temper is spooking Logue. Is shaking his roots-deep belief in the man's unique infallibility.

The faith that Logue had in the Captain was always scarifyingly complete. And you'd think it was simplicity or a lack of nuance in the big man's thick head, but that wasn't it at all. For most people, I think, it's falling in love that's enough to convince them that all life's inequities and terrible failures of promise are, on balance, worth suffering for the moments of grace which come of seeing one's best self reflected in another person's eyes. The reason we don't all die of first love—and the almost inevitable, inexplicable ways in which first love goes wrong—is because that first taste is enough to convince us, even through the pain of its walking away, that a life spent chasing the next would not be a life ill-spent.

But there are a few people for whom loyalty eats the heart right out of love. Who live in the fire of a zealot's faith in a cause, an ideal, a man. And Logue was indisputably of the second sort. He was an atheist, as far as I knew. An ascetic in innumerable ways. Occasionally a humorless stone of a man with the moral give of a brimstone tent preacher. But he saw his best self only as it was reflected back to him by the Captain and lived for his belief in the man's rightness and goodness which, in a way, was like love. A different kind of love, maybe. More pure and uncomplicated. And coming from where he did—having been Logue Ranstead before falling into the Captain's company and seeing what that Logue Ranstead had seen—none of this was surprising.

But I'm getting distracted. None of that matters just now.

Logue looks and then he looks away. He looks and looks away again. And then he sees Dogboy slinking around on all fours in the shadows at the back of the staging area, locks onto him like a missile, and calls out to him, loud. Logue heaves himself to his feet and goes pounding down the length of the room toward him, which Dogboy don't like even a little bit. His hackles go up and he skins his lips back from his vicious teeth.

Dogboy barks at Logue in the way of a man yelling *Bark!* and Logue shouts right back at him, yelling "Report! Report, goddammit!" because Logue knows—or hopes he knows—that Dogboy, who'd been set out on the trail of the bag team the minute they'd gone silent, has information. Something to jerk the Captain out from the deeps of whatever blue-deviled place he's found himself in.

And I am watching all this unfold. Beside me, Jemma is shouting at Logue. And the Captain, in his huff, pauses to see what his lieutenants are carrying on about, and when he catches sight of Dogboy looking ready to do terrible things to Logue and Logue walking purposeful into the scythe, he steps quickly between them before one or the other commences to biting.

"Logue," he says. "Logue." And Logue, still rolling forward like a meat tank, puts a finger out to point and the Captain snakes a hand up quick, catches that finger and the hand where it lived, gives them a twist and, somehow, Logue suddenly finds himself spun right round, pointing at a rack of spare tires, with the Captain behind him, giving him a desultory shove in the back.

"Play nice, Logue," he snaps. "Get a hold of yourself."

And the heartbroke pain on Logue's face for being manhandled that way—for being shoved about and spoken sharp to, especially by the Captain—is awful, even if it only lasts for the space of a breath. Logue drops his hand. He screws his face into a hollering, red-bloomed knot and looks over his shoulder.

But the Captain has, just as quickly, forgotten about Logue completely. "Dogboy," he says, reaching out a becalming hand. "Please give me some good news."

And Dogboy growls. He twists his head around and cuts his yellowy-blue eyes at Logue, then settles. In his slurpy, husking voice says, "News is I found 'em. But it ain't good."

Things happen fast. Things happen without us really thinking. When we're not looking, the whole world can change, just like *that*. That's something you need to remember.

Dogboy told the Captain that he'd found the van, crashed into a retaining wall on 56th Avenue, right at the interstate overpass, a bare mile or so from the garage where we'd run the gank on the Legion of Terror's best and brightest. Said he'd found the bag team, too—all laid out on the street in a row. The Chemist, of course, was gone.

Dogboy could move quick when he needed to. Could go 'cross rooftops and through the hedges and hides, bounding like a jackrabbit, moving like bad news, running like the devil knew he did it.

But what he couldn't do was carry five men on his back at the same time. And since no one had thought to give him a radio when he'd been put on the scent, he'd had no choice but to leave the Captain's men where he'd found them. He couldn't even move the bodies (which, in the moment, he'd assumed were all dead) because he was rightly afeared of the possibility of being seen abroad on the streets and being recognized for what he was. A nightmare walking.

So he'd come back home again, running with a mouthful of here's-where-it-gets-worse, but it'd taken him near on an hour to get there, find the van, count the perished, and get back again, and the mission was almost ninety minutes cold now. Those men had been lying there a long time. By this point, all the gold and the boom jelly that I'd liberated from the OSS technicians was no doubt being missed dearly. And no matter who it was that'd thieved the Chemist away from the Captain's men, pretty soon someone was going to come knocking with questions that needed answering. Tribulations had we—and in number fastly multiplying.

"First things first," said the Captain. "We bring our people home."

"And if they's actually dead?" asked Logue.

"Then we bury them with honors," said the Captain. "Wake them loudly, mourn them properly, and then find out who needs to pay the goddamn butcher's bill."

And that was when Doc Holcomb, who'd been manning the phones at the night desk (which, even in the day, was still called the night desk), came into the staging area and hollered out that he'd just taken a call.

"What line?" asked the Captain.

"CosaNostra Pizza Delivery," says Holcomb.

"That's Barnum and Strange," said Jemma. "The extraction line."

Relief, palpable, though short-lived.

"So they're alive," said the Captain, turning to Logue, reaching out and shoving him lightly. "You see, you big baby? The day is improving."

Logue grumbled like a mountain with the itis. Jemma rattled around behind me, pawing through a shelving unit cluttered with tools and machine parts and leaking cases of oil. Dogboy licked his own nose.

"They left an address," said Doc.

"Of course they did," Jemma shouted, and stood up with a tool belt hung over one shoulder, a sloshing red gas can in one hand. "What are you all standing around for? Grab your bag, Doc. We're rolling."

The Captain grinned. "I remember the days when I used to give the orders around here," he said. "You heard the lady. Rescue mission. Let's go."

Logue and Doc Holcomb jumped into the rusting heap of a pickup that the Captain had lately been kicking at in his temper. Himself, Jemma, and me piled into Marlene.

It took three tries and threats of terrible violence before Logue could get the pickup started, but the world had been falling to pieces for so long that any man who wasn't amazed daily by the amount of stuff that still actually worked at all was a man possessed with either too much optimism or too little imagination for catastrophe.

Marlene, on the other hand, started at Jemma's first kiss with the key, but that was because Marlene was a soulful machine and deeply loved. There's magic in that. Ask any machine.

We pulled out and into the afternoon's heat, to streets curiously devoid of traffic. Jemma had the marconi tuned to Radio Free Georgetown and the news was all bad and strange and worse.

The mountain strongholds were closing their walls against reavers, trolls, armed survivalists, and Jayhawkers. Pirates were plying the skies. Roads were snaking off in the night. Going gooey and melting away to nothing. Maps were untrustworthy now, and there was late word of a whiplash tornado on the Kansas border that'd wiped a refugee encampment completely off the map—just lifted it up and hurled it across the horizon. The Free Republic had gone quiet, its domes and arcologies polarized to midnight blackness, and there was said to be riots on the streets of the Queen City, though the closest thing to that I'd seen was the farmers marching on the Castle a few days ago, and that'd hardly been riotous. A little tear gas never hurt anyone.

The DJ was Nico Fury and she had a voice like honey on a razor blade. "Things are coming asunder, my babies," she said. "Watch the skies. Keep an eye to them you love. Now let's have some music."

She played R.E.M., "It's The End Of The World As We Know It," but all the words seemed to be wrong. I knew that song pretty well, and twisty as the world had become, I could say with a reasonable amount of sober certainty that there were no lyrics in it about plagues of snakes and dinosaurs and temporal redaction. I mean, how do you even rhyme that? Autumnal traction? Vestigial hobgoblin? It was a mess. But who knew? Maybe it was a cover.

Even still, it seemed a bit on the nose, and I was going to say something to Jemma, but then I saw her looking at the Captain and I saw the Captain looking at her and she looked like she was going to be sick right there in her lap and he looked like he'd just seen his own ghost go strolling by whistling.

"Revision?" she asked.

"I think so," he said. "Start making calls. Anyone you can think of. You have a phone?"

Jemma nodded and told me to hold the wheel while she dug in her pockets and came up with an old-fashioned flip-phone that looked a lot like my burner. She took the wheel back. The roads were still quiet—not entirely desolated, but more than a mite emptier than they ought to have been, considering the hour and the day and the general rumbustiousness of the city at large. There was something unsettling about it. That took you right in the belly like the pounding of a bass drum or eating a bad piece of fish. It was spookifying, like all the animals of the forest had suddenly caught wind of something big and bad and mean come stomping and had gone to ground in fear and tremblement.

Jemma dialed a number. It rang and rang. Finally, she hung up.

"Who was that?"

"Watchmaker."

"Try someone else."

She thumbed in a second number, fought with the wheel to jink around a dog that came dashing out onto the blacktop like it was spoiling for a fight, then held the phone cradled against her shoulder. I could hear it ringing in the stillness of Marlene's cab. With each unanswered tone, Jemma looked more and more like she was going to cry. Eventually, she disconnected.

"Who was that?"

"Anthony."

"Who?"

"Anthony Macklin. One of our spotters. Bald guy? Looks kind of like a ferret?"

"Tony the Ferret," said the Captain. "Yeah."

"Well, he's not answering either, Cap."

"Yeah, but he was always flighty."

"It's a revision," Jemma said. "A redaction."

"It's the Chemist," said the Captain. "He's fucking with things."

"What makes you think—"

"Reasons," interrupted the Captain. "I've got reasons. You ever known me to not have reasons?"

"Yes."

"When it's important?"

Jemma considered for a moment, then said, "Somewhat less yes."

"Well there you go then. This is important. And I have reasons. And I'm not completely sure this is—"

"It is," Jemma said. "I can feel it." She hauled Marlene around a corner, squealing the tires, and came up on a dead man lying in the street, a laughing knot of battle police looming over the body. She roared past them, not slowing, Logue and Doc Holcomb trailing her in the second truck. Another corner and there was a wall, partly decorated in an Old States battle flag done in dripping spray-bomb that made the red stripes look like they were bleeding.

"Fourteen stars," said Jemma.

"Wishful thinking," said the Captain.

"They're not stars," I said. Because they weren't. They were tiny mushroom clouds.

"Cap . . ." said Jemma.

"Oh, now that's just creepy," said the Captain.

Jemma made eleven calls. Many went unanswered, and each of those she took like an invisible punch. Those that were answered, she would smile, bite her lip, say, "Check," and then wait for the person on the other end to say "Check" and then she would hang up. Say "Thank you," and hang up. Say "Oh, thank god," and hang up. She drove one-handed better than most people would with three, but eventually, the roads got dicey and she folded the phone up against her chin and dropped it in her lap.

"Five checks," she said. "Two of the numbers were just plain dead."

The Captain nodded and stared out the windshield. "Five," he said, "is five more than none. Which isn't really proof of anything, but *is* better than having no proof at all. We need to get our people and get home."

I asked him, Captain, you're in such a rush, why not just fly down in that lovely Osprey you have? Plenty of room, that. Nice and fast. Man could make a properly dramatic entrance and exit when flying.

And the Captain, he gives me the cold eye like a man who'd told a joke that now had to be explained to the slowest rube in the group.

"Duncan," he said. "We *stole* that."

"Okay," says me. "So where do you keep it stashed then?"

Jemma answered for him. "They had to return it before anyone noticed it was gone."

The Captain nodded. "We are the good guys after all."

"Most of the time," Jemma said.

"Are we almost there?" he asked.

"Couple more blocks."

The bag team, in various states of distress and discombobulation, were holed up in a burned-out office park, abandoned by all but the Queen City's least savory elements—rats and roaches, brainless monsters fried on the warp and weft of the weird, and a Dianetics testing center that'd colonized the one standing corner unit.

The five of them had crawled into the rubble of a former telemarketing firm like raccoons, and when we pulled up, Barnum and Strange, in their matching black suits and mirthless airs, were crouching close over the other three with their pistols in their hands, looking like they meant to use them on the very next thing they saw moving.

"Somebody here order a pizza?" the Captain yelled out the window as Marlene crunched to a rocking halt in the lot.

Barnum pointed to Strange. Strange pointed to Barnum. The Captain pulled his head back inside and said, "I'd fire those two if I wasn't worried they'd show up in my bedroom some night with long knives."

We loaded up the survivors into the beds of the trucks and were on our way in minutes. The Captain instructed Logue to stay close to Jemma on the drive.

"Dangerously close, understood? Things are getting gooey and I can't have you wandering off because we've just done one rescue and I don't want to have to make another."

"Won't need rescuing," Logue said. "You might, but not me."

"Your confidence is what makes you so cute, Logue."

The roads were different on the way back. Too many strange turns and dead-ends. Everyone noticed but no one said anything about it. I saw something huge and winged cross the blaze of the setting sun, and when the radio crackled with news of border ruffians and street fights between the King's men and groups of armed insurgents with Jayhawker sensibilities, the Captain shouted "Music!" and stabbed at the buttons until he got it to play Led Zeppelin, coming in from somewhere on the plains all dirty and scratchy with static. We rolled through the streets of Denver in the pinking of the dusk while Robert Plant sang "When the Levee Breaks."

"Things are falling apart fast," Jemma said.

"We're not going to let that happen," said the Captain. "I have a plan."

"Care to share it?"

"No."

Jemma drove in silence for a moment, then, "Do you *really* have a plan?"

"No," said the Captain. "Not yet. But I have a feeling that one will come to me."

"Really."

"I'm clever, Jemma. All the girls say so. Plans are what clever men have. So yes, one will come to me. And if one doesn't, maybe Duncan will come up with a plan, won't you, Duncan?"

"Me?"

"Why not?" the Captain asked. "I'm tired. Maybe it's your turn to save the world now."

And I didn't have the heart to tell him that I might've been the one who'd wrecked it all up in the first place.

The bunkhouse was right where we'd left it. The Captain seemed to find this more surprising than I was comfortable with.

We turned the staging area into a surgery, dragging tables into the center of the floor, sweeping them clean of junk, and moving lights to shine on the wounded.

"This is a gentleman's game and it's played by gentleman's rules," said the Captain. He'd stripped down to a white tee shirt, now bloodied, and wore long gloves, taped to his arms just below the elbow. The gloves were pale yellow, like a chick's down, except where they were slicked with claret. "We forget that at our peril."

All hands were taking part. I, for example, was tasked with the vital duty of holding a cigarette to the Captain's lips every time he bellowed for a smoke, and of rolling fresh ones whenever he'd sucked them down to the roach.

"Oh, fucking hell I'm going to be sick. Smoke!"

And I raised my hand to him and felt the heat of the burning ember glowing against the skin of my fingers as he inhaled and sucked the smoke deep into his lungs and held it there like a balm against airing his guts right there on the floor. The Captain could cut, you see, and the Captain could sew in a pinch, but the Captain, he hated blood and the sight of the insides of men open to the world.

When he exhaled, he did it through gritted teeth, used a towel to sponge away the blood welling up in a hole in Laszlo Gazsi's ribs—the towel growing more plush as it drank and reprocessed all that delicious fluid—and then groaned and looked away as he reached down and felt around the margins of the hole.

"Doc!" he bellowed. "Non-penetrating, upper chest. I think I can feel the piece of shrapnel just under the skin."

Doc Holcomb was handling the most serious injury suffered by the Captain's bag team—a neck wound on Joker Haws that'd opened him up like a pig on a hook and spilled the best part of him all over 56th Avenue. It'd been a piece of plastic that got him—a little arrowhead of it, sharp as a shaving razor. Blown out of the van's dashboard display was the guess, or maybe the steering wheel collar. Doc had IVs running into both of Joker's arms, clone platelets and packed cells. He'd clamped off the big external carotid and was trying to graft in a patch that he'd had typed and printed whole while Joker was on the table, but it was tricky.

"Cut him," Doc yelled back to the Captain. "It's safer than trying to pull it out. Cut him, remove the foreign object, irrigate with little doctors, then use the meat glue to stick him back together. Same goes for the big face lac and the one on his belly. Irrigate and glue. I'll look at his foot when I'm done here, but if the toes start going gray, just cut 'em off. We can grow him new ones."

"The hell you will," said Laszlo, who lay peaceably under the Captain's knife, numbed and paralyzed from the neck down with an electric spinal. "Keeping my own toes, me. You take them, I wait 'til you sleeping, Cap, and snip-snap. You wake up minus something ver' precious, hear?"

"Smoke!" gurgled the Captain. And I obliged. Then Laszlo asked me to roll one for him and I did, planting it in his mouth like a stake.

Lud Margate was on another table, being attended to by Logue who was stitching closed tears in the envelope of Lud's flesh like he was darning socks, humming a little tune to himself and biting off the thread after every knot and spitting Lud's blood onto the floor. Jemma was assisting by threading silk onto the hooked needles Logue used and occasionally stopping to gently smooth back Lud's hair from his forehead and make jokes with him. When slivers of glass or plastic or, in one case, a metal screw had to be pulled from Lud, Logue would lay a massive forearm across Lud's neck and shoulders to hold him down and say, "Hush, now. You ain't dying."

Laszlo's foot was a hamburgered mess. Lud's arm had been broke in addition to him being holed variously by all manner of interesting bits of this and that. Holcomb had thought that Joker'd cracked his rib bones and was maybe dying when he'd been brought in, but it'd turned out just to be a wicked bruise from hitting the steering wheel and so Doc had ignored it save for injecting a tube full of constructors and modified clotting factors straight into the un-ruined side of Joker's neck to find and repair any internal damage where what little blood he had left in him might still be leaking into his dark and crevicey places. After the most vital repairs had been affected, he'd uncapped a Sharpie marker with his teeth and quickly drawn a swollen head and two dangling balls on Joker's up-angled and lividly purple bruise to turn it into a giant penis.

"He's gonna find that super funny when he wakes up," Doc insisted, and even Logue had laughed, which was something of passing wonderment owing to its dodo-bird rarity.

Barnum and Strange were unharmed—or mostly, anyhow. Strange had a scratch on one cheek that he petted like it was a cat, and Barnum claimed to be suffering from a powerful ennui. Plus, both had been fuzzed by a spark grenade—as had Lud, Laszlo, Joker Haws, and, presumably, the Chemist—and that will straight up fuck with a man. Light him up from the inside like a turkey in the microwave and make it hard for him to remember simple things like his name or favorite brand of breakfast cereal.

But whoever'd done it could have killed them and didn't. Had pulled them all out and away from the van (which had gone nose-first into a retaining wall and support pillar at the 56th Avenue interstate overpass) and lined them up on the pavement neat as you please, according to Dogboy, and had even slapped a pressure bandage on poor Joker's leaking neck, which had undoubtedly saved his life. But then they'd also pilfered the Chemist right out of the wreckage, which was absolutely unsporting of them, considering the great pains we'd gone to in stealing him ourselves.

"A gentleman's game," the Captain repeated as he pitched a dart of bright and blood-slicked aluminum into an old coffee can being used as a basin. "And we are just the fucking gentlemen to play it." He slapped Laszlo on one bare and electrificatedly benumbed shoulder. "I'm going to go outside and throw up now, Laz. But when I come back, I'm going to fix up your face so it leaves a big, mean pirate scar. Ladies love scars."

The Captain turned sharply then on his heel and made for the normal-sized door set in between the two tractor trailer–sized roll-up doors that let in on the staging area from the wobbly world outside. Watching him go, I could see the gray-suit men still standing there—the lawyers, hungry-eyed and top-hatted, mostly, clustered up and waiting with billable-hours patience in the V made by the noses of two parked cars and having themselves a picnic supper of little cakes, brought sandwiches and coffee from a thermos. I could hear the Captain yell, "Percy, you wanna talk? Come watch me barf. And bring me a cup of that coffee, too."

I rolled a cigarette for myself and, when I was finished, saw that it had an almost perfect bloody thumbprint on the paper. Shrugging, I lit it anyway, with the Captain's steel Zippo, and went to see if Logue and Jemma needed any help.

Percival Blythe and his associates had been at the bunkhouse door when we'd returned with the injured—lurking under the porch lights like process servers or vacuum cleaner salesmen—and they'd been waiting politely while we worked on plugging up the holes in our people because Logue had threatened to twist the head off any one of them who came too near.

Not in so many words, of course. Big man like him, all it took was him snapping the hood ornament off Percy Blythe's black town-car with one hand and sticking it in his pocket. After that, the threat was just generally implied.

The Captain had to have known from the start that the OSS were going to come with questions. Even if the Last Man Standing had gone perfect and he'd slipped away into the Weird with the Chemist in his possession leaving none the wiser, the OSS were going to come. And I'd known going in that the blame would fall on me as the man who'd altered the plan and called in the OSS shoot team early.

Which I was fine with, and fearless of any consequence, for I had made my peace with its necessity. We had a story all worked out, the Captain and me, and were steeled against any questions that might get asked. I was just a freelancer, after all. An actor. A nobody. Had things gone right, it would've been just another mistake in a long line of them because if there was one thing the OSS should have been accustomed to, it was things going absolutely spot-on wonderful right up until the moment that everything fell to pieces.

This, though, was something different. The Captain's men had been caught in possession of the Chemist, stolen right out from under the nose of the OSS regulars. Squatting in the dust and the ruin of the office park while Doc Holcomb did triage and field assessments on the wounded, Barnum and Strange had given their best accounting of what had happened. They'd taken the Chemist walking, they said—just strolling down the alley behind the garage, hands in his pockets like he was out for a stroll, all covered in fake blood and nastiness. He hadn't put up any fight. He'd extended his own hands for the zip-cuffs and bowed his head for the bag even though the Captain's bag team hadn't thought to bring an actual bag with them.

"Showed him the ether bottle and the zapper," said Barnum.

"Like we were giving him a choice," added Strange.

"And he just stood there and gave his head a little shake."

"Like he was saying there was no need."

The Captain had asked if he'd said anything at all, and Barnum and Strange had said no. Not for the whole drive. They'd loaded him into the van. Lud, Laszlo, and Joker rode up front on the bench. Barnum and Strange had been in the back with the Chemist. No rough stuff. No words passed between them. They'd driven for a minute, maybe two. Lots of turns. Their escape route had been planned to get them clear of the site as fast as possible and into the cover of the workaday world. But then, at 56th Avenue, they'd rolled over a crippler mine—a wide-pulse electromagnetic charge that'd killed the engine and all the van's electronics in an instant, with the additional benefit of giving strokes and seizures to any other electrificated gizmos in the area (hence Jemma's blindness in the area). They'd gone straight into the retaining wall at about thirty miles an hour. And OSS security had been waiting.

One spark grenade into the cab. Another into the back. Goodnight, Irene. After that, everything was clear as pudding.

"How do you know it was the OSS?" the Captain had asked.

"Anyone else would've killed us," said Barnum, shrugging. And Strange had nodded his assent, stroking the scratch on the side of his face gently.

The Captain hadn't been able to argue with that logic. And when we'd all seen the OSS gray-suits waiting outside the bunkhouse as we pulled in, we'd known for a fact it was true. The whole thing was just too neat to be otherwise.

"They came quick," I said. "In my experience, the Office's investigators are somewhat more inept."

"Those aren't investigators," the Captain had said. "Those are lawyers."

"Oh," said me. "Well that's much worse then."

We'd pulled the trucks up to the big doors. Logue had climbed out to open one. Doc Holcomb was hollering for haste and to ferry everyone inside and to get tables laid and lights brought in. All was a hullabaloo of shouts and scrambles and furious action. But as the Captain was striding up, the lawyer-iest of all them gathered gray men—the one with the baldingest head and most impressive paunch, with the finest gray suit, mirror-polished shoes, most glossy black tie and a pocket square, red as fresh blood and perfectly folded—stepped up and said to him, "Why Mr. Barrow. I'd heard you'd died."

"Rumors of my demise et cetera et cetera, Percival. I'd heard you'd grown back your hair, but that obviously wasn't true either."

And that was it. The Captain had brushed right by them then without so much as a sidewise glance. His tactic seemed to be that of a small child or an irresponsible adult: a dogged belief that if he ignored Percy Blythe, his lawyers, and the complications that they represented, maybe they would all just go away.

Unsurprisingly, that didn't work.

From outside the staging area, I heard the Captain calling my name.

Or, rather, I heard him calling *a* name, not my name, but when I looked up, his eyes were boring into me like drills, as though he could transmit to me, telepathically, all the mysteries living in his shouting out some other fella's name and hoping I responded.

I turned to Logue and Jemma. "You think he's calling me, right?"

"Seems to be," said Logue, who was fighting a losing battle with a band-aid, trying to get it unstuck from itself.

"Just stay loose," said Jemma. "He's obviously up to something."

"I should be worried, shouldn't I?"

"You ever known a bunch of lawyers at the door to mean good news?" asked Lud from the table. He was pulling now from a bottle of white lightning, his body covered with rough stitches and dried blood and pink Hello Kitty band-aids.

"And Percy is not a friend to us," added Jemma.

"Who is he?"

"Management," said Jemma. "Percival Blythe, the Office's chief of legal affairs."

"Hates the Captain," said Logue.

"*Seriously* hates the Captain," added Jemma. "You should go."

So I did. With my hands dug in my pockets and trying to look like a man unweighted by the cares of the world. It was pressing on toward night now, the light from the staging area spilling out into the growing dark like the white heat of civilization. The Captain and Percival Blythe were standing apart from the rest of the lawyers and their cars and their picnic supper, around by the corner of the big door, just on the edge of the light. Percy had dug a finger under his tie and loosened it just enough to give his wattles room to breathe. The Captain had stripped off his gloves and dropped them onto the cracked pavement of the small lot outside the staging area. His spring-loaded little Jesus gun was still strapped onto his right forearm, and his thumbs were hooked into the belt he still wore, with his pistol and his sword. For him, that was casual Friday through and through.

"Evening, Captain," I said. "You need me?"

"So this was your operation?" asked Percival Blythe, stepping between the Captain and me with a finger cocked and pointed and a look on his face like the Captain had been feeding him lemons at gunpoint. I stopped short and gave him a slow, up-and-down kind of look.

"Classified," I said, and was thrilled to see the tiny explosion of mirth that lit behind the Captain's eyes at my impertinence. "And who are you when you're not wearing that fancy suit?"

"My fault," said the Captain. "Dorian, this is Percy Blythe, ambulance chaser for the OSS. Percy, this is Dorian Bloom. An old friend. He ran the Last Man Standing operation."

I raised my nose a couple inches like I didn't like Percy's smell. "I'd shake your hand, but I have blood all over mine. Or maybe, as a lawyer, you're accustomed to that?"

Percy wrinkled his nose and reached inside his jacket for a small notebook and a pen. "Bloom?"

"Bloom," repeated the Captain. "Dorian Bloom. He's an actor. Dorian, show him."

I turned to the Captain. "What?"

"Show him. Act something."

"Um, okay . . . I, uh . . ."

The Captain laughed with a snapping coldness. "I'm kidding, Dorian. Percy and me, that's what we do. We kid. Right, Percy?"

The OSS's chief legal mind looked up from his notebook briefly and said, "No."

"You sure about that?" asked the Captain. "I'm pretty sure you'd prefer me kidding with you rather than . . . something else."

A thin smile creased Percy's face—just a line, upturned at either end like a child's drawing of a bird in flight. "Are you threatening me, Mr. Barrow?"

And the Captain cocked an eyebrow. "Yes. Did you not get that? Dorian, wasn't I clearly threatening Percy?"

"That was the impression I got," I said.

"I mean, if you missed the nuance, I could be clearer."

"Please do," said Percy. "And remember that this is all being recorded for posterity."

"Good. Then have this for your record. I'm kidding with you because all my men look like they're going to live, so I'm feeling good. But if it were otherwise, they would've never found your body, Percy." He tapped a thumb against the butt of the big Colby on his hip. "Yours or any of your associates."

And the conversation really kinda went downhill from there.

Percy accused the Captain of having orchestrated the escape of the Chemist, which had only been foiled by the fortuitous intervention of an OSS sweeper team that saw a van speeding wildly from the scene. The Captain countered by claiming that the Chemist had escaped out a door left unguarded by the OSS team leaders, and had only been caught when his backup team spotted him running and secured him for transport back to a safe location.

"Meaning here," said Percy.

"No, they were going to take him out for pancakes first," said the Captain. "Seemed only neighborly."

The Captain accused the OSS of then attempting to blow up his people in an ambush which nearly killed one of them. Percy said that the OSS sweepers were attempting to prevent the kidnapping of a valuable asset by rogue operators who should really know their place by now and accept that the grownups in the room know better when it comes to the needs of the United States government.

"Rogue operator?" asked the Captain. "Is that what they're calling me around the office now?"

"Traitor has a nicer ring to it, I think, but I've always been a poetical sort," said Percy. "The boss has made it known that no one is to use that word, though. Traitor."

"Made it known . . ." mused the Captain. "Were there memos? A meeting? Was lunch served?" Then to me. "I hope there was cake. I like cake."

"I'll keep that in mind for your birthday," I said.

Percy said, "The last person who called you a traitor got his fingers caught in a paper shredder. All ten of them. The message was pretty clear."

The Captain smiled. "Nice to have friends in high places."

"You think Nimrod will protect you forever." Percy sniffed. "You're wrong."

"I think you would be scared to say his name out loud if he was within twenty miles of here," said the Captain.

"He's not the man you remember, James. I'm not sure if he ever was."

The two of them stared at each other. In their eyes was the weight of a shared history that I would never completely understand. They'd been young together, the Captain and the Lawyer. Had traveled vastly different paths that, were you to plot them, would curl around and around each other like two snakes humping. Like one of them walked with his pockets full of lead and the other with shoes made of magnets. They were men who could have entire conversations without ever saying a word, but eventually Percy broke. He looked at me.

"You ever wonder exactly who it is you've hitched your wagon to here, Mr. Bloom?" he asked.

"Not once," I said. "And anyway, I'm afraid of horseys."

Percy continued his questioning after that. "Had the operation been carried out as ordered, the principal would not have been in a position to run in the first place. He would've had a handful of unstable explosives and no opportunity to leave the scene. Can Mr. Bloom explain why he called in the shoot team before the principal was immobilized as ordered?"

"Ignatz pulled a gun," said the Captain.

"A gun?" said Percy incredulously. "The Chemist pulled a gun."

"Or a knife? Which was it, Dorian?"

"Gun," I said.

"Or a ferret," said the Captain.

"It was totally a ferret," I agreed.

"A really mean ferret. Weaponized. He was getting ready to throw a ferret at Dorian."

"So the principal assaulted you with a ferret," said Percy. "You want that on the record?"

"Well, *attempted* assault," I said. "He never got a chance to throw it, so . . . I guess that would be attempted assault with a deadly rodent, wouldn't you say, Captain?"

"Is a ferret a rodent?"

"I think so."

"Okay, then yes. I concur. 'Principal attempted to assault Dorian Bloom with a very angry ferret and Mr. Bloom responded in a self-preservationy way by triggering capture phase before principal was fully secured.' Put that in your little notebook, Percy."

When Percy asked if he could have a room at the bunkhouse to perform interviews in a more civilized fashion, the Captain refused, claiming that his cleaning lady hadn't been in yet this week and that the place was just a mess. When Percy asked if his associates could interview the members of the Captain's backup team, the Captain refused.

"They've had a rough day, being blown up and all. They're all getting hot cocoa and being put straight to bed."

"Then what about your crew, Mr. Bloom?" Percy asked, turning to me. "The other actors?"

If they'd followed orders, my team, in all their blooded costumery, would have left the scene in the garage by whatever best expedient was available to them and would've been hiding out just then at a safe house the Captain had chosen—which, really, was just a bar with a kitchen that made very good tacos and a couple of rooms upstairs with very good locks on the doors. They'd been told to hold there for three days and, if no further word was forthcoming, to simply filter out one at a time and get back on about their lives, with the thanks of a grateful kingdom in their back pockets, expressed in the form of Old States dollars. Many, many Old States dollars. Enough to eat and drink on for a good, long time. Which, I thought, was nice—considering I hadn't yet been paid a dime for all my hard work.

"They're on their way to Las Vegas," I said. "We're all booked for three weeks at the Sands. I might be able to get you tickets if you ask nicely."

"Anything else, Percy?" asked the Captain.

At which point, one of Percival's associates approached us slowly. A young one, his hair cut in a junior G-Man brush, wearing a suit that looked like it was stuffed with two hundred pounds of rocks. "Excuse me, Mr. Blythe?" he said. "Sorry to interrupt, but I'd like to speak with Mr. Bloom for a minute."

Percy looked at the man. The Captain and I looked at the man. Then the Captain looked at Percy and asked, "Who the fuck is this?"

And Percy actually shrugged. He said, "Tom Lakey. One of my investigators. Tom, what is this about?"

"I just have a couple questions for Mr. Bloom, sir. Relating to another investigation. I believe he'll know what I'm talking about. It'll just take a minute."

Percy gave a flummoxed look to the Captain and the Captain looked sharpish at me, but neither of them said no and young Tom just kept walking until he was close enough to touch me on the shoulder and say, "This will just take a minute, Mr. Bloom. If you could come with me."

He was smooth. I took three steps without even thinking about it. Percy asked the Captain if he still wanted that cup of coffee or anything. I felt the weight of Tom Lakey's hand on my shoulder, steering me, and I took two more steps before it occurred to me that this man was leading me off toward the far corner of the bunkhouse, out of the square of light falling from the open roll-up door and into the dark, and that, maybe, that wasn't somewhere I wanted to go with a strange boy I'd just met. But the minute I dug my feet in and made to stop moving, he hit me.

It was just one shot, but it was a good one—catching me right in the side, below the ribs, and folding me up like an envelope as it felt like every breath I'd ever took was suddenly forced out of me.

My legs went, but Tom Lakey caught me and held me up, his fists knotted in the stinking denim of the jacket I'd taken off the rummy at the Nob. I felt one of his hands snaking quickly inside the jacket. His mouth was close to my ear, and he was whispering. Talking fast.

"Sorry about this, man. There wasn't any other way to get to you. That's a new phone in your jacket. The boss wants you to call in as soon as possible. He has a message: Train 1066 to Goodland. Got that?"

I groaned in as affirmative a way as I could manage.

"Train 1066 to Goodland," he repeated. "Okay. I'm gonna hit you again now. Sorry."

And he did—lifting me out of my sag, standing me up and firing a pulled punch into my guts that was still enough to drop me onto my hands and knees, retching and sucking for air.

"And if you *ever* come near her again, I will kill you!" Tom Lakey shouted at the top of my head. "You understand me? I will fucking kill you!"

I saw his foot coming back for a kick, but then he was tackled and went down hard beneath the Captain. Logue wasn't far behind. Neither were the other law-dogs, Percy, Jemma. It was a party. I wrapped one arm around my belly and threw the other one up to try to get them to pay attention to me, but no one seemed to notice.

"Wait," I gagged. "Stop!"

I coughed, fell forward with my forehead on the pavement, then dragged myself back up. "Stop," I said again. "Let him up, Cap. Please. I deserved that, okay? This . . ." I wheezed, sucked in a thimbleful of air. "This is nothing to do with nothing, please. I . . ."

"He fucked my sister," shouted Tom Lakey from the ground, and I thought, *Okay, let's go with that then,* so said, "Sure," and "Yes, I did," and reiterated around gasps how I'd apparently defiled this man's sister and so absolutely deserved the punching I'd gotten and that brother Tom was only defending the honor of his kin and really ought to be let up and not stomped to death, please.

So the Captain regretfully climbed off Tom. Jemma knelt down and helped me to my feet. Percy's associates picked their man up off the ground and brushed ineffectually at his suit while Percy himself stared at Tom with a disbelieving eye and said, "Mr. Lakey, that was rather out of line, don't you think?"

Tom Lakey spat onto the pavement, strung a few more threatening words together for my benefit, then yanked himself free from the clutches of his mates and went stomping off in the direction of the cars.

Percy turned to the Captain and said, "Maybe that's enough questions for tonight, you think, Mr. Barrow?"

The Captain didn't argue. We watched from the doorway as the rest of the lawyers loaded up into their cars and as Percy had some harsh, whispered words with Tom Lakey, who now hung his head and looked appropriately chagrined. He never met my eyes. Never even glanced back in our direction.

Once the picnic fixings had been cleared and the cars had gotten themselves straightened out, Percy's rolled slowly past and the passenger window came down. He leaned his head out.

"I'm glad all your people are okay, Mr. Barrow," he said. "Truly. We should remember that we're all on the same side here. The *winning* side. You understand?"

The Captain said nothing. The window went up. The cars crunched off through the darkness of the small parking area, but he made no move to leave. I felt the weight of the phone in my jacket like a rock, hot with potential and possibility, and the aching in my guts like a reminder of age. I sucked breath through my teeth and felt the place where the younger man's first punch had taken me.

"So was she worth it, Duncan?" the Captain finally asked.

"Who?"

"The girl. Tom Lakey's sister."

I smiled a bitter smile and tried to straighten up without wincing. "The sad thing, Captain, is I don't honestly recall."

He turned to me in the dark. "How did he know who you were?"

"I don't know. I've never seen him before."

"But he knew you. Obviously. Even though I was calling you by a different name, he knew you."

I looked at him, willing my eyes to blankness, my heart to lightness. "Captain, if I knew, I'd tell you. I don't recall a girl named Lakey, but there's apparently one out there who remembers me. And not nicely. Sad to say, she's probably not the only one."

The Captain watched me for a long minute. There were wheels turning in his head. Plans hatching. In the unscared boyishness of his eyes, the faintest traces of old worries like the massive body of an iceberg hidden mostly beneath the icy blue-green sea. He knew that the OSS had been tipped to his intentions with the Chemist.

He *had* to know. And in that moment, I had the reward of one of those rare times when I knew something that the Captain did not. I knew *exactly* who'd tipped the OSS.

Because it'd been me.

I hadn't meant to, but when I'd called in to the Pork Chop Express dead drop on the night before the operation to update the boss, I'd told him precisely what was going to happen. Had said something to the effect of *The Captain means to steal this man and run off with him into the sunset.* And the boss would've had just enough time to arrange a contingency op, were he so inclined. If he hurried. And got a little lucky.

It had to have been him. Him and Gordon Navarro and all their Tom Lakeys and other magical little elves, working in the dark, which was their preferred medium. They'd gone to a great deal of trouble to steal the Chemist back from the Captain, and then risked more just to pass me a message that would, presumably, help the Captain get him back. *Train 1066 to Goodland.* The boss would've known that I would understand the reference. That I would've known *exactly* what it meant.

There are only two things of note in Goodland, Kansas. Or *were* only two things of note. One was the burnt remains of a giant easel that had once held a giant reproduction of Van Gogh's "3 Sunflowers In A Vase."

No, I don't know why.

The other was an OSS secure facility called Sunflower Field, meant for the keeping and long-term interrogation of high-value targets. A prison, put bluntly. The kind don't no one ever come out of, mostly.

And Train 1066 was the once-monthly train that ran there— from Golden, through the Free Republic of Boulder and Denver, then the Flatlands and Goodland and on to points east, carrying produce, timber, uranium, gold and consumer goods to market, and, every now and again, prisoners to Sunflower Field. I knew that because it was the train that'd taken me there, once upon a time, and that's not the kind of thing one quickly or easily forgets.

I watched the Captain. I watched him stand there in the square of cast light, staring off into the darkness beyond for a time that, at first, felt only long, then uncomfortable, then painful. The phone inside my jacket had become heavy as lead and I bit down hard on the urge to say something. When interrogating a suspect, the most potent weapon at your disposal is silence. Not threats. Not drugs. Not electrodes or car batteries or claw hammers or sacks full of oranges or boxes of starving wolverines. Just silence.

The guilty talk. They can't help themselves.

I watched the Captain's eyes. I watched his face. And he knew. I was *sure* of it. But then he broke, a smile blooming on him like a false dawn.

"Jesus, man. You look *gray*." He laughed and slapped me on the shoulder. "They're just lawyers, Duncan. We deal with mad scientists and rebel warlords and kings. What kind of a 'rogue operator' would I be if I didn't know how to handle some lawyers? Now just relax, okay? I have a job for you. Quite suited to your talents."

He turned his head and shouted over his shoulder for Holcomb. I heard the doc's voice from inside saying that no one else had volunteered to clean up and that he'd be out in a minute, and the Captain pulled a face.

"Never fast enough," he muttered. "Nothing around here ever happens fast enough for me."

He looked out across the parking lot again and scratched at his arm where the straps for his Jesus gun were rubbing him red. I tried to take a deep breath and regretted it. Jemma bent down to pick up a stone from the broken pavement and then chucked it off into the dark, listening to it rattle.

"We have to get the Chemist back," the Captain said. His voice was quiet, like he was talking to himself, but then he turned to me and repeated himself, louder. "We have to get him back. There's no option there."

"Abjuration," said Jemma. Logue grunted and crossed his arms over his chest.

"No," said the Captain. "We've come too far to let it unravel like this."

"We can stop it?"

"I don't know. But we can try."

Jemma bit her lip. The Captain kept talking—mostly, I think, for my benefit. Or maybe just to hear himself. To try and fill the dark with his voice so that it did not fill up all on its own with monsters. "You know how people say, 'Oh, it's not the end of the world,' when they're trying to give someone a little, uh . . . *perspective* on their problems? Like, 'Oh, I broke a nail' or "Oh, the kids are all on heroin again,' and then someone says, 'Well, Nancy, it's not the end of the world.'"

No one else answered, so I did. "Sure, Captain. I've heard people say . . . something like that."

"Yeah, well if we don't recover the Chemist, it will be the end of the fucking world, I promise you that. The end of this one, anyway. The end of us. He knows so much, that man. The Chemist. Ignatz . . ." The Captain let that name hang, his voice running out into an *Sssss* . . . and a sigh of thoughtfulness "He's seen so much. And I need him." Another pause. A breath. "I'm gonna get him."

"This something you seen?" asked Logue. "Something you know?"

And the Captain whipped around on one heel to face Logue. "What haven't I seen, sweetheart? What don't I know? I'm Captain James Barrow. The Western States boogeyman. I know *everything*. When people say my name they say it with awe. They speak in terrified whispers."

"You know they don't really do that, right?" asked Jemma.

But the Captain blazed now. He threw his arms out wide. "Bad men run when they see me coming. Ladies swoon. They lift up their children to me so that later, a hundred years from now, those children can tell their own great-great-grandchildren that they once touched the hand of Captain James Barrow."

"Oh, Jesus . . ." said Logue, rolling his eyes.

"Want me to tell you how you'll die, Logue?"

"No, I do not."

"Or when?"

"No."

"But maybe it's tomorrow. Maybe it's in five minutes. Do you want to know?"

"Is it in five minutes?"

"No."

"Then no."

The Captain reached out and patted Logue on the cheek, spun, leapt and landed facing us all. "World as it is today, we're always twenty minutes from the apocalypse. Losing the Chemist, that makes it more like five. That man, he moves the clock. I think that's why I'm so sweet on him. But we're not too late. We can get him back. We *need* to get him back. So we will. Because we're all there is standing between glory and the end of all things, you understand? Just us."

From the open door, Doc Holcomb came strolling out. "Did I miss the pep talk?" he asked. "Which one was it?"

"Ladies swooning. Bad men running," said Jemma.

"The one where he tries to tell me how I die," said Logue.

"Ooh, I like that one. Did you go for it, Logue?"

"No."

"Good choice."

The Captain darted forward, all spastic enervation and lightning in his hair. "My good horse doctor," he said. "Are the patients all secured for the night?"

"Yup," said Holcomb. "They'll all live. Just hosing everything down."

"Do you have a table left for one more case?"

"What?" asked the doc. "Who else is hurt?"

And the Captain whipped a hand out, popped his wrist, and I saw the spring-loaded pistol leap into his hand.

"Duncan is."

And that was when he shot me.

It was not the best day I've ever had.

Intermission: Abjuration, Revision, Redaction, Loop Recursion

Have you, since our last contact, done anything that you feel might jeopardize your cover, your legend or your mission?

No, but I'm about to.

Do you feel like, at this time, you are under any threat of physical harm?

Ask the man who just shot me. I'll bet he has some pretty strong feelings as to my physical safety and well-being right now.

Is there any further information you wish to disclose regarding your mission or its principal which we have not already discussed?

Yes.

Six days before the world ended, I saw the man with no arms on the streets of Philadelphia.

Four days before the world ended, a new building appeared on a street that I'd been walking down every day, twice a day, for weeks and years. It wasn't there, and then it was there. I saw a building grow out of nothing and become real.

Six days before the world began to end, I was at work. Summer job. Center City, Philadelphia, like I told to the Captain when we were playing our game of Tell Me. It wasn't nothing, the job. Just running files in a law office that handled a lot of small claims.

Personal injury. Slip-and-fall. I got in every morning at a few minutes before eight. Left every evening at a few minutes after five. I spent a lot of the time in between hiding out in the stairwell smoking bowls, taking long lunches, walking files all over the city for attorneys who were too cheap to pay a courier service. My mother knew one of the partners pretty well, and she'd gotten me the job. I wasn't there to impress anyone.

This was before everything went sideways. Or from the early days of the slide, maybe. Depending on how you look at such things. From a time before you could watch things coming apart on every corner. The days when we thought everything was fine as cream gravy.

We took the train in every morning, my mom and me. She usually slept, her hair wet, occasionally in mismatched shoes. She was the kind of person who was always late for things. Always rushing. But she was a partner, so who was going to complain?

At the station, I went one way, she the other. Her office was at Broad and Walnut, a few blocks away. It made more sense for her to get off one station earlier, at Market East, but she always stayed on the extra stop with me. She never said why.

Six days before the worst day, I walked to my stupid, pointless summer job. I went up the elevator. I made sure a couple of the stuffed suits saw me. I ducked out to smoke a bowl. When I came back, there were no files waiting for me, so I went to my desk, lit up my screen, checked my mail, checked for any messages from my friends about the night before, then tapped my feet on the ugly industrial carpeting of my cubicle and tried not to think about how little time that had all eaten out of my day.

At ten, a file came in. It was marked personal and confidential, which meant it would have to go to an actual person, not just some secretary. A drag, true, but one which would reasonably take a certain amount of time and therefore facilitate my dawdling. I zipped downstairs, went through the lobby, out the doors, and took a left on Market Street.

That was when I saw him. The armless man.

It wasn't just that he had no arms, but that he appeared to be of a place where arms had never been thought of.

He was shirtless and barefoot, standing on the sidewalk at 19th and Market Street in a dirty pair of pajama bottoms looking around as though he'd just been dropped there from another planet. His feet were filthy, his belly sunken enough that I could count his lower ribs, but he was shaved. His hair, though longish, had recently seen a comb. And where he should have had arms, there was only smooth, pink and undisturbed skin.

I stared. He hadn't seen me yet. I walked a few paces to get clear of the door, then a few more to get a better look at him.

He was not crazy. I'd spent enough time in the city that I knew from regular old street-side crazies, and did not see in this man the glaze in the eyes of one who spent an inordinate amount of time talking to parking meters. He was mad, that was certain. Scared, maybe, too. His eyes were clear and wide and his mouth a little bit open, and he was turning in a slow circle. Looking around at all the buildings and the people and busses passing and pieces of trash blowing in the street.

I was maybe fifty feet away. Then forty. And there was something about the scene that disturbed me beyond the armless man at the center of it. Something which I couldn't quite name—like a flavor on the back of the tongue that you know but can't attach to a solid, knowable taste like *apple* or *mustard* or *cinnamon*. The wind blew and men grabbed for their hats and women pinned down their skirts. The sun dimmed as a cloud passed in front of the sun and then, suddenly, I had it.

No one else was looking at the armless man.

And I don't mean that they were studiously avoiding looking at him. You can tell when someone is choosing not to look at the elephant sitting on the coffee table. This, though, was different. They simply didn't see him. Almost no one saw him. There was a pretty girl in a black dress with orange polish on her toes and an iced coffee in her hand who stared right at him. There was a businessman in a cream-colored summer suit furiously stabbing at his phone and trying hard *not* to look. There were two kids smoking cigarettes at the corner, sitting up on the decorative planters, slack-jawed and gawping, and a round, thick-necked working man in paint-stained carpenter's Dickies and a faded Phillies tee shirt who had his head tilted like a dog's, like he'd just heard his name misspoken from far away.

But that was it. No one else saw him. And even when he started talking, no one saw him. And even when he started screaming.

This was the Abjuration. It wasn't called that then. It wasn't called anything yet. But it was an example of what would *later* come to be called the Abjuration—the willful repudiation of incongruous reality; the unwillingness of the brain to process that which it could not, or *would* not, rationalize as existing. Those who did not see the armless man on the street that day were not ignoring the armless man. They actually could not see him. They were selectively blind. We all were at times. We saw what our brains chose to allow us to see and were spared the rest as reality and dimensionality and the orderly structure of the universe unraveled like a cheap rag rug beneath us.

Two days later, a building appeared around 21st and Market. It happened on the other side of the street from where I usually walked when I was delivering files or getting lunch, but it happened. One day, there were two identical blue-black skyscrapers set right next to each other, mounted to the earth in granite facades like twin knives bedded in sheaths of stone, nothing between them but an alley I'd never been down, a small stone arch, a whiff of hot garbage. The next day, there was a third building between them, set back in its lot with a lovely little open plaza before it, a fountain, a TV screen the size of a billboard. The space that had once been nothing but an alley had stretched impossibly to accommodate. The building itself was thirty stories, give or take. Made of pale stone slashed with red, hung with ivy and buntings. The windows were all black glass that seemed to shimmer as though made of falling water that never went anywhere.

I thought, *this is just one of those things . . .*

A hiccup in the brain. Of *course* the building had always been there. Somehow, I'd just never noticed. It happened all the time.

Right?

Everyone just walked on by. No one even looked up. Except for a handful of people standing, huddled, on the opposite sidewalk. Two ladies in business attire, another in running shoes and tight shorts, a homeless man, a transit cop, a bicycle courier. They stood in a close knot, their shoulders and elbows and hips all touching, all of them staring at this building that wasn't, but then was.

I stopped close to them. The bicycle courier was shaking his head. The transit cop was crying. One of the women was cursing hard under her breath, over and over and over again.

"Did you see the video, too?" the girl in the running shorts asked.

"No," I said. "What video?"

So she took out her phone and she showed me the video. The accidental video, shot by some tourist, somebody in town for a party, something. There are three friends standing on the sidewalk, roughly where we were all standing just then. They're smiling, laughing, sticking out their tongues. Behind them, there are just two buildings. The person holding the camera says something. The three friends all shout "Happy Birthday, Laura!" And somewhere between "Birthday" and "Laura" the whole world changes. A building is born from nothing, perfectly placed, perfectly whole.

The person holding the camera says, quite clearly, "Holy shit. Did you just see that?"

The video had been shot at 2:18 AM. I saw it at 10:44 AM of the same day. It already had 11 million views and the very first comment—the only one I could read on the girl's phone—was, "I don't get it. What is it? I didn't see anything happen."

Abjuration. Revision. Redaction. Loop Recursion.

Ignorance, followed by corrective action, followed by the elimination of incongruity, followed by the repeating of time and events in their new, consistent parameters. A temporospatial version of the See No Evil/Hear No Evil/Speak No Evil monkeys.

That was the way of the world when it all came apart. That is the way of the world now. Anyone who lived through it knows that it can happen again at any moment because it really is just one of those things. Witness the impossible once and all you can do, for the rest of your born days, is wait, cringing, for it to happen again.

Four days after I saw the building that wasn't, then was, I saw a giant robot smash through Center City Philadelphia. I saw it climb over the rubble of the Stock Exchange building and reach for me, its dumb eyes and idiot mouth a terror beyond my capacity to describe. I ran, following the directions on my phone for the frozen yogurt place that I'd been asking about just a moment before because, in my panic, I couldn't think of anything else to do. In the dark and the dust and the smoke and the dying, I followed my phone to safety. And frozen yogurt. This was the beginning of the end of the world.

This was 2011. It was a Wednesday. I was 17 years old.

EPISODE

7

A Multi-Dimensional Man

I WAS NOT SHOT BAD, AND I'D BEEN SHOT BEFORE, SO I DID NOT wail and I did not weep but, instead, like a gentleman, I simply passed out in a heap on the cracked pavement. Someone carried me inside. Someone lay me down gently upon a bed still warm from the trials of other wounded, recently vacated. Doc Holcomb, I presume, stopped up the hole the Captain had put in me, topped me up to the brim with vital fluids, cured me of all my vital ailments save, of course, confusion over why his Captainness had seen fit to shoot me in the first place and a hollowing fear that I knew precisely why.

And then I slept and slept.

I'd been shot in New Jersey as a young man and nearly died of it. I'd been shot in a trailer park outside of Jacksonville, Florida. I'd been shot in Magnolia (not by Joe Castillo, but by someone else whose story is of no consequence here), though that'd been nothing. Just clipped my ear and gave me a tiny bit more character than the volumes of it I already possessed.

I was stabbed in Amarillo during a bar fight I was attempting to flee and leaked crimson all over my favorite shirt. I still miss that shirt. Got beaten down in Emporia, Kansas. Again in Sidney, Nebraska, by a bunch of drunken militia in tall boots with steel toes who would've killed me if they hadn't gotten bored halfway through, tossed me into the street, and just gone back to looting the Git 'n Split. I was shot again in Joplin, Missouri, by a dwarf named Lamar, but that had been an accident, so I'm not sure if it counts. Then I was beaten *and* shot in Raton, New Mexico, and coughed blood into the snow while the party of OSS hunting centaurs that'd run me down pawed at the wet earth, spat on me, and blew gouts of steam into the frozen air. That last adventure led more or less directly to my visiting Goodland, Kansas, where the hurts visited upon both my person and my everlasting soul were rather so frequent and harrowing that they don't bear mentioning.

There is a piece of me that believes these injuries unremarkable—that would argue there is not a breathing man of consequent age who does not carry upon him the scars of existing in a world of such exquisite fuckery as ours. But then there is another piece which knows beyond argument that I have brought this all upon myself. For loving cards and girls and barstools. For hating the last word, the final moment, and closing time. For being like a magnet to the lead in bad men and, worse, to the iron in good ones.

But no matter. Now I'd been shot in Denver, too. I was filling the map. And though I thought I knew the reason (because the Captain had gotten trig to the fact that I was informing on him to powers that might've effected the vanishment of the Chemist, Ignatz Walton, whom he'd been so keen to steal), when I came around a few hours later, the first thing I noticed was that I was alive. The second was the weight of the phone still inside my jacket where Tom Lakey had put it. And the third was the Captain, sitting in a chair by my bedside and watching me with an amused air.

"You shot me," I said, my voice croaking for want of water or, preferably, powerful spirits.

The Captain nodded. "Yup. I did."

"So I didn't dream that?"

The Captain shook his head. "No, you did not."

I mused upon this a moment, glancing cautiously down to where my formerly fashionable trousers had been scissored into one half of a pair of fiercely ugly shorts and where the stark whiteness of a fat bandage around my thigh marked the place where the Captain's bullet had gone in and, presumably, come back out again.

"You want to tell me *why* you saw fit to put a bullet in me, Captain?" I asked.

He pursed his lips and crossed one leg over the other. He tented his fingers below his chin in a way that he thought made him look professorial or wise but really only made him appear as some boob doing a poor impression of Sigmund Freud. "It's important you understand that *I* didn't shoot you, Duncan, but that Harry Plum was shot by the OSS during the raid on the garage. That's where we need to start this conversation."

I told him that I didn't understand. He said that was because I was not so bright. I told him that I was surely bright enough to secretly pee in his Frosted Flakes every morning until I felt he'd drunk enough of my urine to square us for the shooting. He said that most mornings he just preferred toast.

"Oh, you surely do not want to know what I could do to that butter, hoss," I said, and he laughed and I let him and he apologized for shooting me but didn't really mean it because, in his recollection of the moment, he'd had a good reason. He'd been struck, he said, by inspiration.

"So to celebrate, you shot me."

"I did indeed."

"You're an asshole."

"I've been told as much, but I don't really believe it. Honestly, I think I'm just misunderstood."

He informed me then that I was going back. Back to the Legion of Terror. That Harry Plum—wounded in glorious service to the cause—was going back, offering fire and bloody vengeance upon them that had just so callously made a dozen and more of his and theirs dance the machine gun ballet.

"But wait," said me, in a moment of uncharacteristic restraint. "Weren't *we* the ones who just perished all theirs?"

And the Captain said, "Well, strictly speaking, it was you. But I certainly wouldn't mention that when you meet them."

He had a plan, did the Captain. His brilliant inspiration. And while it'd started with holing me, it rolled on with Dogboy put back out a'hunting, his nose full of the stink of Ignatz Walton, and Logue pulling up false pieces of flooring from the staging area in the bunkhouse and unhiding boxes of RFID locators, scissor grenades, poison gas, de-assembled disintegrator rays, and worse. Jemma was missing—*out gathering* was all the Captain would say of her—and Barnum and Strange had been roused reluctantly from their sick beds (where they'd been sulking over warm tea and toast) and sent to fetch back the two undercover men who'd been the Captain's eyes inside the L.O.T. He wanted them back *toot sweet.* Faster than fast. He expressed his sense of urgency to his two odd ducks by threatening to kick them if they dawdled and promising them hearty handshakes, medals and steak dinners if they rushed.

"You planning a war, Captain?" I asked.

"Trying hard to stop one," he said, distracted, and then fast-walked off to harangue Logue and sit before a bank of mostly decrepit computers which he laid into with language that would've given a blush to a donkey-show barker.

Doc Holcomb came to check on me.

"You bleed a lot," he said.

"Happens every time someone puts a fresh hole in me."

He sniffed and told me I was as cured as the Captain wanted me. "You probably feel pretty good right now. You could walk if you wanted to. Hell, amount of endorphin analog in ya, you could jog on two bloody stumps and not notice. But it's still bad, the wound. You're plugged, stitched and disinfected. Kind of thing you could've gotten done on the street. I threw a couple million knitters in there so you'll heal a bit faster, but Cap wanted you limping and in pain. Said so quite specifically. So once the happy juice wears outta you, you will be. Guaranteed. But it won't kill you. Leg won't fall off. None of that. How are you with pain?"

"I prefer it in other people," I said.

Hours passed, or maybe days. Maybe minutes. Time was twisting itself in knots, and I was largely ignored, biting down on the urge to lay hands to the phone in my pocket but wanting badly to touch it, as though it were a talisman now, fat with luck and knowledge. I needed to get clear of the Captain and his people. That was job one. I needed to call in to the boss. The need to report was strong. My aching desire to have some questions answered stronger.

Holcomb had gone to bed. At one point Laszlo Gazsi came thumping out into the staging area on a pair of crutches with the handles wrapped in graying surgical tape, and when he saw me, he asked what'd happened. I told him I'd trade a story for a drink of anything but the house beer and he produced an old sports bottle half-full of potato vodka that tasted like sucking fire and made my eyeballs hot in their sockets.

"Fell on a bullet," I said. "It was the damndest thing . . ."

We talked for a time, Laszlo and me. Not about anything of consequence, but just words, light as candy floss and about as substantial. We were talking when Jemma came back, and she smiled weakly at me as she came through the door. Waved, too, but seemed to forget how halfway through. She had Miss Holly Bright with her, and two other men I did not know—some other thralls of the Captain's, I guessed. Two of the dozens and dozens of competent men and experts in felony, thuggery, and larceny, both petty and grand, who waited at his beck and call.

"More of the Captain's commandos?" I asked Laszlo, the words leaving, perhaps, a bit more bile on my teeth than I'd intended.

"Survivors," said Laszlo, shaking his head. "We're reasonable safe here, all'n together, but Captain's trying to rescue as many of him friends as possible 'fore the big Scorekeeper takes 'em all off home."

I looked again and regretted my bitterness. One of the men trailing the two ladies was elderly, shuffling along in one house slipper with his hair mussed from sleeping, and the other was plainly out of his gourd.

"Scorekeeper?" I asked.

And Laszlo rolled his eyes skyward, showed his palms to the ceiling. "Scorekeeper," he said. "Ain't no God or Jesus to me, see? But they's a scorekeeper up there an' he a *cruel* muthafucka." He drank a pull from the bottle and handed it to me. "Scorekeeper keep track of this world and t'other. Add 'em up. Make ever'ting copacetic. And the Captain, he have reg'lar and true conversations with the Scorekeeper. That's *fact*. See that old man there?"

He pointed to the be-slippered gentleman currently shuffling his way across the floor of the staging area.

"Him's the Watchmaker. Run him a clockworks shop down in the Red Lights and sell bangs out the back door. Major big bangs, mostly to the Captain. Off the books like. And the other, that's Malcolm the Spider. Him a full-time listener. Run a cell net up top of the Hickenlooper Building that the Captain use most frequent." Laszlo paused long enough to take the bottle back from me, have a pull, cough, and shake his head. We watched as Holly Bright helped Malcolm the Spider make his scrabbling way across the open middle of the floor, eyes the size of radar dishes, tuned skyward in search of freak transmissions, his hands slapping at the floor.

"Never in his right mind, that Spider," Laszlo said. "But he seem somewhat more disturbed tonight than is customary."

Jemma asked for the Captain to turn on the radios.

"Which one?" himself asked.

"All of them," said Jemma. And the Captain started flipping switches, making a dozen-some boom boxes and transistor radios and hacked Walkmen and rack systems all come to life until the room echoed with Ry Cooder and static and Buck Owens and the Buckaroos singing "Act Naturally" over the husky tones of Nico Fury talking of devastation and loss, of sky-opening storms, fields of red roses sprouting, towns appearing, stillborn and cold, from the dead earth, and DJ A-10 from Flatlands 90.5 relaying lists of the missing in a series of border assaults by reformed Kansan militia. Music and voices boomed around the high ceiling. Discordant tunes and the fuzz of weak signals and reports of fire and death and the end of all things rattled on our ears like fistfuls of gravel thrown on a tin roof.

In the riot of sound, the Captain asked Jemma how many she'd tucked away and how many she'd lost completely and she said she didn't know. That counting was not something she felt she could do rightly any more. Holly stumbled over to look at me once she'd gotten Malcolm the Spider comfortably folded away beneath a table covered in staling snacks and medical supplies and she had blood all over her hands. I couldn't tell if it was hers or someone else's.

"Bad night out there in the Weird, see?" said Laszlo, mostly to me. "Bad, bad, bad. Revision and redaction taking more than OSS long knives *ever* could."

"We miss you out there, Laz," said Holly, and smiled a vicious smile. "It's your kind of night."

"Sister, I keepin' myself to myself tonight."

Holly looked at me, an unmuted and inexplicable fury dancing like match flames in her eyes. "Don't think you're blameless," she said.

"I'm just studying up for the part of man shot by bad men," said me. "The world was unhinged long before I gave a shit."

She spat on the floor and went to stand by Jemma, the fingers of one of her hands tangled all up in Jemma's pale blonde hair while she squatted near the big doors and wept quietly at the hurricane of sound and voices that swept the room like rain.

The night was the worst and, come the day, the world was a different world. Holly and Jemma went out into the wrack, returned, went out again. Dogboy came slinking back in and asked after the Captain, then lay near the stairs, panting. He'd found nothing, he said, which both was and wasn't the truth. In actuality, he'd found a hundred thousand things, but none of them the Chemist. The streets were crazy. He'd ducked battle police and patrols of soldiers with eyes like acid-eaters. He'd fought a robot and won. He'd seen monsters rooting through dumpsters and long trains of refugees snaking in from the contraction zone, their paths lit like neon rivers by fogs of bioluminescent mites.

Logue prowled, lion-like, through the dark places around the bunkhouse. He sounded the alarm when, briefly, 200 Colorado National Guardsmen in full MOP gear—plastic-and-charcoal suits and baggy head-sacks with monster-face NBC re-breathers—materialized in the parking lot. They flickered into existence as silently as the approach of bad news until 200 pairs of terrified eyes, like children's eyes waking from a dream into a worse dream, stared at us over the iron sights of 200 automatic rifles. The Captain had scrambled us paltry few into the breach at Logue's alarm. I'd hopped, a grenade in each hand. And then, in what by all rights ought to have been the moment of our dying, the soldiers all just as quietly de-materialized as Barnum, Strange, and the Captain's two wayward undercover men came strolling through the heart of them, walking through the vapor of bodies, blind completely to what we were seeing.

"They looked worse scared than we do," muttered Laszlo, sitting with his back against the door frame, his crutches tossed aside and a pistol in his lap, sweat coursing down his face.

"Somewhere out there," said the Captain, "other versions of us are having a much worse night than we are."

Barnum, Strange and the undercovers had stopped when they saw the guns and hard looks of them as were pointing them. Barnum said, "Something is happening here that we don't understand."

Strange nodded, wide-eyed, his hands held well out from his body, but said nothing.

The Captain holstered his pistols and ran a hand through his hair until it stood up straight off his head. I wondered how long it'd been since he'd slept or had a shower. His face was puffy from exhaustion.

"This is too much," he said to himself, his voice small in the long reach of the broken night beyond the doors. "Too much, too fast." Then he shook himself, squared his shoulders, and told Barnum, Strange and the undercovers to get inside. "I think you two might've just saved our bacon somehow, but I'll be damned if I thank you just for showing up." He turned sharpish on one heel and strode into the deepness of the bunkhouse.

"We're heroes," said Barnum, to Strange.

"Wonder if we should ask for rasises," said Strange, to Barnum.

When the sun came up, it turned the day the color of rotting fruit. Inside, the two undercover men drifted through the room with the languid wonderment of astronauts just returned to the embrace of gravity. They looked like men whose organs were still trying to find their proper places. I hopped to the comfort of a chair that had seen better days, touched fingers gingerly, worriedly to my leg, and watched the two of them moving in slow orbits about each other. When the Captain called out to them, neither responded until he used their cover identities, Lee Staples and Arthur Finch.

"Finch," he said. "Lee. I believe you both know Harry Plum?"

"We've met," said Lee.

"Who shot you?" asked the one called Finch.

"He did," I said, pointing to the Captain.

"What'd you do to piss him off?"

"He wasn't quite Harry Plum enough," the Captain answered for me. "Now he is."

Both Finch and Lee had been inside the L.O.T. for a long time. Finch for a little more than a year. Lee for nine months. And they'd both been phenomenal betrayers in their time.

"Was these two that helped put away Dinosaur Joe before the Kansas troubles," said the Captain, reaching out and grabbing Lee by the back of the neck and shaking him. "Was these two handed him to me on a plate. They've done their time. Seen all there is to see. Earned the glorious retirement that you bought for them, Harry, with your Last Man Standing routine."

"And we're thankful," said Lee, who was a younger man, his black hair pushed straight back off his forehead, his muscles like smooth river stones beneath his skin. "We never thought we were going to be able to walk away."

"Yeah . . ." said the Captain. "And that's the thing, Lee. Finch. I need the both of you to go back. And I need you to take Harry here back inside with you."

Lee Staples and Arthur Finch were far from happy, but happy was not what the Captain was concerned about. There was some amount of yelling and intemperate language. After months and years spent pretending to be members of the Legion of Terror—of going to meetings and swearing allegiance and shouting *El! Oh! Tee!* at the tops of their lungs like fools every time the situation demanded it, of drinking the Kool-Aid and reciting epic poems to the greatness of Dinosaur Joe and planning missions of sabotage and mayhem that always seemed to fail at the vitalest moment through idiocy, bad luck, or an overabundance of psychotic enthusiasm—they had been out for just a bit more than twelve hours.

"You have no idea what it's like," said Finch. "Inside, I mean. With them."

The Captain shrugged. "I have *some* idea. I took your reports. I listened to you talk and talk."

"They're crazy," said Lee. "All of them. Every one."

"We're all crazy."

"Not their kind of crazy," said Lee.

"If I never see one of those uniforms again in my life, I'll die a happy man," said Finch.

"I burned mine," said Lee. "First thing, Captain."

The Captain said that didn't matter. That nothing mattered now but getting back in. "A couple days," he said. "Week tops. You're only going in for one thing."

And he didn't say what the thing was. He shut his mouth. Looked from one man to the other.

"What's the one thing?" asked Finch.

And the Captain smiled because he knew he had them. He knew they'd go.

"I have a plan," he said. "Worry about making contact first."

The Captain needed the Chemist. He just couldn't get at him. To start, he had no idea where the man was. He had notions, of course. Suspicions. He figured maybe the OSS were keeping him in a run of offices they kept downtown, in the spastic and strokey husk of a dying skyscraper. Or maybe a containment facility in the contraction zone called The Pit which was used by the interrogators as a workshop for countless of their little projects. He thought perhaps they'd have him in Percy Blythe's favorite hidey-hole, which was a tumble-down blackout of a house on a dead block just off 6th Avenue. He made calls, did the Captain. They went unanswered. He called in markers and found all doors shut to him. He sent Dogboy to snuffle around and made Barnum and Strange knock on doors, pretending to collect for widows and war orphans. Every hole he poked into was a dry one.

"They'll want him close," The Captain mused. "He's a shiny, shiny prize and they'll want to play with him as much as they can."

And even if he'd found the Chemist, he couldn't touch the man with his own hands. He couldn't steal him a second time. Not without crossing the OSS in a way that he couldn't come back from. So he needed cats-paws, which was going to be the Legion of Terror. And Lee and Finch. And me.

I had my own notions. I couldn't just walk up and tell him what I knew, you understand? I had no way of telling him about the train, about Goodland, without explaining how I came by the information, and I could not explain how I'd come by the information without explaining about the boss and my true nature. Without blowing my cover. And as I'd already been shot by him once, I was not keen on seeing the bangy end of his pistols a second time.

But I had an idea, too. All I needed was some time.

For a day and another night, survivors of the abjuration and revision drifted in or were brought. From one of her trips out into the Weird, Jemma hauled back a scrofulous gump in sprung braces with skin the color of road dust, and a broken angel with shredded wings twitching from holes torn in a leather vest and eyes like infrared cameras. She also carried dinner in both hands. Green chile in a milk jug. Tortillas steaming in a paper sack. What she didn't have was Holly Bright.

"Family dinner," she sing-songed, and tables were pushed together, plates and mismatched eating irons rustled up from drawers and odd places and laid out for many and more. Bathtub wine and house beer were offered in quantities comforting to all. A bottle of cactus juice of unknown terroir. The wounded, the halt, the mad and the lame all gathered together to pass plates, mutter to the ghosts in their heads and eat as much as they could manage.

The Captain sat at the head of the table, talking big and telling jokes. The rest of the seats filled in. I took a place in the middle of one long side and Jemma slid in beside me. I asked her how she was, how she was holding together, and she said that she wasn't. "I'm faking it pretty good, though, aren't I?" she said, smiling at me. "I mean, can you tell that I'm having a breakdown right now?" She had a tortilla in one hand and green chile was leaking down into the sleeve of her jacket. She looked about twelve years old, her hair ratted and her eyes red-rimmed.

"Not a bit," I said. "You look as perfect as you did the day I saw you walking into the Nob to ruin my life."

She laughed, too loudly, and drank tequila too fast. I asked after her charges—the Captain's dregs—and she just shook her head. I asked her about Asa August and Julie, and she said she'd had no orders to go looking for them. I asked after the Watchmaker, pretending like I knew who he was—that I knew more than I did—and she said he was fine. Had been sleeping when she and Holly had come kicking through the doors and hadn't known the slightest thing had gone wrong.

"Abjuration," I said.

"Abjuration," she repeated, nodding.

I sipped at my tequila. "What about Reggie?"

She shrugged, running the tip of one finger around the rim of her cup. "We looked. No sign of him."

I asked if she'd checked Miss Kitty's and she had. No one had seen him. "His house?" I asked.

"Nothing. Empty."

"Has he called in? All those phones you watch over?"

"Not since last time I checked."

I shook my head. "I liked Reggie," I said. "What number was his?"

"Guess," she said, smiling weakly, and when I said I had no idea, she told me. "Persephone Horse Farms."

I laughed. "Appropriate."

"Yeah, the Captain has a strange sense of humor."

"Doesn't he though . . ." I said, massaging my leg gently above the bandage, feeling a hot edge of pain creeping in, and in my head, the voice of the planner in me. The old field agent. *That's one thing done.*

When I asked after Miss Holly Bright, Jemma knocked the plastic cup she was drinking from against the cut-glass tumbler beside my plate. "She's out there in it," Jemma said. "Doing what she does." And then she drank. And I drank so as not to be rude or outpaced. And then she continued, talking into her cup. "Lost track of her a few hours ago, but I'm not worried. Child of the whirlwind, that one. Heart full of chaos." She looked up. "You like her?"

"I'm worried about her," I said. Which, in truth, meant I thought I might need her.

"You tried to rescue her."

"I did. I felt . . . responsible."

"You felt *something*, that's for sure." She looked away, off and out into the emptiness of the staging area.

"Why Jemma Watts," I said. "Are you insinuating that I have feelings for a coworker?"

She chuckled. "That's cute, champ. Eat your dinner before it gets cold."

I bumped a shoulder against her shoulder and stuffed my mouth with green chile and tortilla before I said anything stupid. When

I looked up, the Captain was watching me with eyes like a dog hunting.

Lee Staples and Arthur Finch explained that contacting the L.O.T. was no simple thing. There were cells, each independent but linked through captains and commissars and a hundred different overlapping and tangled systems of codes and ciphers and secret methods of communicating.

"It's like every one of them read a different spy novel and try to use every trick, all at the same time," said Lee.

"Bad spy novels," added Finch. "The system is ridiculously complicated and stupid."

"Do what you have to," the Captain said. "Remember: You two and Harry here were the only survivors of the OSS massacre at the garage in which all of your friends and all of Harry's men were killed and the Chemist taken into custody. And Harry is pissed now, aren't you Harry?"

"I'm certainly pissed about certain things," I said, rubbing again at my leg, the ache of it like a bad tooth, pulsing now with every beat of my traitorous heart.

"Right. He's angry, in possession of high explosives and looking for revenge and you two have convinced him that the best way to *get* revenge is to help the L.O.T. get their chemist back."

"They'll understand the revenge part," said Finch. "The rest of it they won't honestly care about."

"All the better. How long is it going to take?"

"Lee has already made the first contact." Finch said.

And Lee said, "Phone tree—that was the start. Code words. Cold drop to a cell phone sitting in someone's mother's basement." He shook his head. "I had to sing a fucking song, you believe that?"

"Which song?" Finch asked him.

"'Glorious Rise Of The Dinosaurs.'"

Lee whistled quietly. "That's a long song."

"I know. Can't believe I remembered the whole thing."

"Anyway," Finch continued. "It'll take them some time now while they all argue over whether or not we're traitors or spies sent by the King to infiltrate their terrifying ranks or whatever. They do that a lot. Argue over who's loyal enough. Who's peddling them. Who's in and who's out, you know? It never comes to nothing."

"Except for when it does," added Lee.

Finch shrugged. "Except for when it does. Then a whole lot of people get killed. But that doesn't happen all that often, really."

Doc Holcomb watched the night desk while Jemma slept. I waited until I knew he was there alone and then hauled myself up the stairs and told him I was hurting.

"Supposed to be," he said. "You been shot, remember?"

I dropped myself heavily into a chair and hissed through gritted teeth. "I been shot before, Doc. Enough to know from how much it ought to pain me. This is something else, though. You got anything that could take the edge off?"

He hemmed and he hawed, but my whining can be incredibly persuasive, and, eventually, he gave in. "I got something," he said. "But I have to go downstairs and get it out of my supplies. Can you stay here and watch the phones for me?"

I massaged my leg and made terrible faces. "Should I be expecting them to do anything sneaky?"

"No, just, if one of 'em rings, listen in on the message, take it down word for word, and tell me when I come back, okay?"

"Will I have to get up?"

"No. Just listen. That's all."

"Then I am your man, Doc," I said, waving a shooing hand at him. "You can count on me, et cetera, et cetera. Just hurry, okay?"

I listened to the scrape of his shoes in the hallway, and as soon as he was far enough away that I was reasonably certain he wouldn't turn around and come back, I bounced up and limped quickly over to the desks covered in phones.

There were fifty, according to what Jemma had said on the night that me and the Captain had played Tell Me. Twenty-eight of them currently active. I needed just one: Persephone Horse Farms. Colonel Arthur Reginald Molesworth's panic line. I needed to know which it was. And I needed its number.

The phones were various but unlabeled, sitting in their nests of wires. There were old-fashioned-y rotary phones and wired cradle phones and touch-tone phones and brass-fitted Princess phones and a phone shaped like a football and another one shaped like the head of Darth Vader. Each sat beside its answering machine—neatly, spaced more or less equally from its neighbor—which told me that, at one point, there'd been a plan. An organizing principle to the system which, likely, had been Jemma's.

Fifty phones. Twenty-eight active. Likely fewer after the recent Abjuration, but still. I stood, staring at the desks, wondering how long it was going to take for Doc Holcomb to get back from his mission of mercy. I opened the top drawer on the first desk and it was empty. I opened the others and found messes of papers, scribbled notes, cigarette ends, a stapler with no staples, disposable chopsticks, the nubs of pencils with Chinese characters stamped on them, crushed beer cans, rubber bands, a bullet, a Rubik's Cube. I wondered how much time had passed. Stopped. Breathed slowly. Listened.

It was a lot of phones. A lot of names and numbers to keep track of. Anyone who did it a lot would have a key somewhere. There was logbook where each call was recorded—it's time, number, content, duration, character, principal, more. None of that helped me. I lay the book aside, closed my eyes and forced myself to think.

Think, I told myself. *If it was your job—every night, sitting in here, in the dark, waiting for phones to ring. Waiting on disaster.*

Every night, night after night. And then, the call. What would you do? Scramble for the logbook, a pencil. Look for the light on the answering machine, listen to the voice coming through the line.

I eased myself down into the chair that Holcomb had been sitting in. The chair Jemma had been sitting in the last time I was here.

You would have to be quick. You would have to know immediately who was calling, from where, to what number. You would have to know what fake message applied to each agent in the field. Some you would know right off, but others you wouldn't. Some phones would ring more frequently than others. But you would always have to know just how to react. Who to take seriously. Who to ignore. Twenty-eight phones is a lot. Twenty-eight operators in the field. You'd have to know who was who and who was important and who was not, because even though the Captain might claim that everyone was important here, in his little rebel kingdom, that simply isn't true. There was more important and less important. You would have to know, immediately . . .

I opened my eyes and looked at the wall behind the desk. It was covered three-deep in notes and maps and dirty pictures and jokes and lunch orders, all tacked right to the wall, all stacked on top of each other. There was nothing that looked like a list. Nothing that would help.

Call comes in, anyone sitting the desk would have to know how to behave. To what level of panic they should rise. They would have to know, even before the message was done running, who was calling. Would have to start writing fast . . .

I pulled open the top drawer of the first desk again. The empty one. Pulled it all the way out, laid it on my knees and flipped it over. I smiled. There, on the bottom, were two five-by-five grids, carefully drawn in thick black marker. Each block represented one phone. Twenty-eight of them were labeled with initials, descriptions and numbers. The night desk cheat sheet. I ran my finger down the columns and found *P. Horse Farm, A.R.M.* and looked at the number. I heard footsteps ringing at the top of the stairs, took a breath and read the number three times. Said it out loud, under my breath.

Said *remember this number*, which would be enough for me. I was good at remembering.

Quietly, I fitted the drawer back into place and pushed it closed. I stood, hobbled back to the chair I'd been sitting in and fell back into it—head back, eyes closed. I heard Holcomb come through the door.

Think pained thoughts, I said to myself.

That was two things done.

Doc brought me ibuprofen and acted as though he was shitting gold into my hands. He added a strip of six analgesic patches that I could thumb onto my skin for additional relief.

"Ain't much," he said, "but it's what I have that won't make you feel healed or just not care. Cap wants you limping, so you'll have to be limping."

I thanked him just the same, dry-swallowed the pills and asked him if there was somewhere I might find some clothes that weren't either covered in sticky fake blood and half-missing (as my trousers were) or ripe with alcoholic bum stink (as my jacket was). He pointed me in the direction of a room on the second floor where racks upon racks of clothes hung, most fuzzy with dust or hideous or both, but from bits and pieces I was able to assemble a passable summer suit. It was wine-colored, cut narrow, with a shirt that had maybe once been white but was now the color of old bone. I still had my hat and my hat still had the goggles Logue had given me sitting on the brim. And I still had my boots, into the pipes of which I'd dropped Tom Lakey's burner and the pain patches that the doc had given me.

The leg hurt like the devil. That wasn't entirely a lie. But I was medicating with liquor and cigarettes and needle-thin joints cadged off of Laszlo Gazsi who was as bored as I was with all the sitting and waiting. I limped when I walked, which was just as it was supposed to be. When no one was looking, I'd sit, rub my leg, and scream away the hurting without opening my mouth.

You know how, in movies, it used to be that a fella could take a bullet or two to his non-vitals and keep right on fighting the aliens or the commies or whatever? He could shrug it off like a hole the size of an index finger punched through flesh and bone and sinew by a piece of metal traveling 900 miles per hour was a mosquito bite.

I hate those movies.

Putting on the suit, I felt sharp again. Nearly whole. I'd taken a whore's bath in a sink on the second floor because I hadn't yet figured out where the showers were. In a fogged mirror over the basin, I'd examined the livid, purply-black bruises along the sticks of my ribs from the punches I'd taken, then re-wrapped the dressing onto my leg. The ibuprofen had done nothing. Thumbing one of the patches onto the hot skin above the hole in me was like spitting onto a bonfire. I'd put my pistol back on, groaning as I snaked my arms through the straps of the shoulder rig, then sat down in a quiet stretch of hallway, popped the snaps on my briefcase, took out a copy of the *Westward* and scanned the masthead until I found Gordon Navarro's name, listed as gardening editor.

I told you he was a journalist, right? And I told you there has never been a better cover story for a spy.

There was a number listed for him, but I didn't call it directly. I flipped through the pages instead, found what I wanted, then sorted through my own phones until I found one that had a signal and called the main number for the paper.

A receptionist picked up on the 9th ring. Her name was Pretty, which I thought a bit presumptuous, but she had a nice voice and told me that La Rata wasn't at his desk today and wasn't expected (typical). I explained that I needed to have a correction made (a request that puts the fear in all journalists everywhere) and asked for his voicemail. Pretty said she would inform Mr. Navarro personally that I'd called, and then connected me.

You've reached the desk of Gordon Navarro, gardening editor at the Westward. *I'm not at my desk right now, but if you leave a message, I'll get back to you just as soon as I'm done pruning my snapdragons or whatever.*

Beep.

"Mr. Navarro," I said. "This is Jimmy Fields and I have an urgent correction I need made. In your July 15 issue, page 26, third column, fourteenth line, it should read 'Tomorrow, 3pm, 5pm, 7pm, and 9pm.' Again, that's page 26, third column, fourteenth line, three, five, seven, and nine. Thank you for your time."

Click.

That was three things done. The day, I told myself, was improving.

Then I went looking for the Captain.

Come to find, the Captain was looking for me, too. We crossed paths near the stairs, which I'd been standing at the top of, considering the descent with some dread.

"Choose that outfit yourself, or did you lose a bet?" he asked.

I straightened up and showed him the underside of my nose. "And I'm going to take sartorial remonstrance from a man's been wearing the same get-up since the day we met?"

"Big talk for a man who looks like he just skinned a pimp," he said, "Come have a word with me, Duncan. There's business to attend to."

And then he pushed past me and took off walking at speed, the way he always done. He was headed for his office, and I hobbled after as best I could. But when he saw how much he was outpacing me, he stopped, turned back, flashed his teeth and, without a word about it, dashed back and inserted himself under one of my arms. He half-carried me all the way along to his office because, on the one hand, he didn't like to be kept waiting but, on the other, was just a man who couldn't never leave a friend behind.

He could *shoot* one, sure. If it suited his purposes. But I haven't a doubt he would've also carried me on his back all the way to the distant ocean if the ocean was where we needed to be.

Logue was waiting by the door to the Captain's office to report that the Ragamuffin Army had arrived to defend the shop and were, at that very moment, downstairs touching stuff, fighting with each other, and stealing everything that wasn't nailed down.

"They's awful," said Logue. "And sticky."

"There anything vital down there that you want *not* liberated as spoils of war?" the Captain asked.

"Sure. Plenty."

"Well nail it down, then," he said, pushing open the door and ushering me inside. "Deal with it, Logue. In two hours, this place is going to be their clubhouse, so you might as well get accustomed to it."

I eased myself down into a chair. "Two hours?" I asked.

"We're upping stakes," said the Captain. "Pulling out."

"Why?"

"Have to," said the Captain, who scooted behind the monumental clutter of his desk and began spinning around in his chair, without no plain notion of explaining things any further.

"Okay," I said. "Why do we have to?"

The Captain caught his heels on the legs of his chair, looked at the empty doorway, and hollered for Logue to come back. The big man poked his head back in the door. "What?"

"Finch ought to be knocking around downstairs somewhere. I think I saw him. Can you send him up?"

Logue nodded, turned, and went clumping off back down the hallway.

The Captain closed his eyes and bobbed his head back and forth for a few seconds, then yelled, "Logue!"

We both heard him sigh. Heard his steps. He poked his head back around the doorframe again. "What?"

"You know you're my best friend, right?"

"I've heard you say so."

"You know we couldn't do any of this without you."

"That's what I always tell you."

Logue stood. The Captain stared at him.

"What, you waiting around for more compliments?" the Captain asked. "Go see to the kids. Get Finch up here. We've got a goddamn world to save and you're standing around sponging up niceties? Lord have mercy, Logue Ranstead . . ."

"I'm gonna smother you in your sleep one of these days," Logue promised, then turned and left. Again.

"Fuck you for thinking that I ever sleep!" the Captain shouted after him, then looked at me. "That was fun," he said, and smiled broadly. Then he went back to spinning in his chair.

"Captain?" I asked.

"Duncan Archer," he said, but did not stop spinning.

"Why do we have to leave?"

"Because we do," he said. "Because it's time."

"So because you say so," I said.

He slapped his hands down on his desk, causing a minor land-slide in papers stacked on one corner and overturning an empty cup of noodles with a pair of chopsticks sticking up out of it. "You know why everyone calls me Captain, Duncan?"

I shook my head.

"Because I'm the fucking Captain, that's why. Because I'm in charge. I give the orders. People follow the orders. That's just how this shit works."

"Not saying I disagree, Captain. Just curious is all."

"I can see the future," he said.

"No you can't."

"Yes I can. No one's told you? I'm magic."

I shook my head. "Shit . . ."

"I'm *remarkable*."

"You're something, all right."

"Duncan!" he snapped, the lash of his voice taking me right in the neck. "Look at me. Look in my eyes." And I did. "You're right. I can't really see the future. But I *know* the future. One version of it. Because I've seen it happen. Because I spent a long time in a small room studying it. Every possible permutation. Because I'm not from here. You understand that, right?"

I said nothing.

"Tell me you're smart enough to have figured that out," he said. "That you asked someone. That someone here told you how . . ." He voice trailed off. And again, I said nothing.

He started again. "Abjuration," he said, and then he counted on his fingers. "Revision. Redaction. Loop Recursion. There is this world and then there is the other world. The world that those soldiers came from last night. The giant robots. All this war and fuss and consternation. The world that is trying very hard to eat this world."

I did not give him the benefit of looking shocked. Of looking confused. Of looking anything but slightly disbelieving, marginally suspect and a little bit bored.

The Captain raised an eyebrow at me as though momentarily perplexed. A single line appeared between his eyes, which was, in him, a sign of depthless exasperation. He picked a piece of paper up from one of the stacks on his desk and held it flat in his palm.

"This world," he said. Then he picked up a second sheet, held it just above the first. "The other world," he said. "And all these other papers? *Other* other worlds. Minor variations in the quantum observables. Chaotic inflation, symmetry breakage, disparate modal realities. Bubbles in an infinitely ergodic universe. But fuck them.

They don't matter much to us here and now. What does matter? Our world and the other world, which, tragically, have moved too close. Or been brought too close. We have our timeline—" he fluttered the bottom sheet, "—which I should really say is *your* timeline. And then we have the other." He shook the top sheet. "Which is where I came from. Then this happened."

He closed his fist, crumpling the two sheets together.

"It's a mess. A tangle. Mathematically speaking, the two timelines are trying to resolve themselves. Which we experience as a process of changes in our understanding of the universe that we call abjuration, revision, redaction, and loop recursion. As intrusions of physical objects, modes of thought, spatial infrastructure, and what-not, moving from the other world into this one. Followed by a revision in our memories of what this world was like before the change. Followed by the removal of aberrational structures, latent physical manifestation of the former, pre-revision world, disappearances, fugue states. Followed by loop redaction—a pinching off of all paradox-inducing Calabi-Yau manifolds. They're moving toward a massive wavefunction collapse, these two worlds. Only one world can win out. We're all just particles in this. Pieces of an equation as big as the entire universe. The math doesn't give a damn how it all resolves itself, but I do. And the OSS does. We have a difference of opinion over how it should turn out, them and me, but I intend on winning because I know what will happen if I don't win. Because I've *seen* it. When all is said and done, there will be one world again. One observable reality. All will grow quiet in the universe once more."

The Captain dropped the balled up paper on his desk. "You understand this, right?"

I blinked, kept my face neutral. The one line between the Captain's eyebrows became two.

"Look, the reason for all this mess over the past couple days is the Chemist being taken by the OSS. He was supposed to end up with me because if I get him, the world goes one way. The

OSS gets him, the world goes another way, understand? He is a causal structure. A hinge element. The problem is that the two timelines? They operate under slightly different physical laws. Minor derivations in constants. Too small to matter to anyone but the scientists, but the result is that my world, since the first recorded interaction between the two, has stretched about thirty years further down the curve than this one. So I've seen thirty more years of history than you have. Studied it. Plotted a course through it. I have worked very hard to make myself important to the math. I have made sure that I matter. That what I do has *consequence*."

He tilted his head and looked at me.

"So what you're saying is that you're from another dimension?" I asked.

"From a parallel universe, if you're more comfortable thinking about it that way."

I leaned forward just a little and lowered my voice. "Are you Jesus?"

The Captain opened his mouth. He made a noise like he was choking. He closed his mouth again and closed his eyes and dropped his head into his hands.

And then I laughed. Couldn't help it.

The Captain looked up. "You're fucking with me?" he asked. He rolled his eyes and breathed out sharply, slapping his palms down on the desk. "Duncan, you're *fucking* with me. Oh, that is not cool." And then he started laughing, too.

"No," I said, trying to get my teeth into my laughter and failing completely, squeezing them down only into manic giggles. "No . . . It was a good speech. Really, Captain. I mean, you were so *serious*." I leaned back in my chair and did my best impression of him— which, if I do say, was spot on and brilliant. "Paradox-inducing Calabi-Yau manifolds and modal realities and blah blah blah."

"Those are totally a thing," he said, around gasping breaths. "It's science, man."

Which just set me right off again on a storm of snorting hysterics that went on until I covered my face with my hands and held my breath. *Science,* I thought. *It's science.* "I particularly liked the part where you said you were a time traveler."

"Yeah? That one always gets them," he said, laughter still bubbling up out of him. "No one ever buys that. Not the first time." He sighed and flicked tears out of his eyes with his fingers. "I mean, not until I tell them how they die."

And then, of course, the whole thing was a lot less funny. I felt that contrarianism was what was needed here, in healthy, large doses, and so I said to him, "Bullshit, Captain," and, thinking *please don't shoot me again* "You're fucking mad."

He looked at me. He tilted his head one way, then the other. He grinned.

"Sure," he said. "Who isn't? But then you've got to ask yourself, Duncan. Whose office are you sitting in?"

When Finch stepped in, he found us staring at each other, red-faced, eyes gleaming, breathing deep. He looked, saw the crumpled paper on the desk and, likely, the look on my face.

Finch said, "Aw, he gave you the ball of paper speech, didn't he?"

Finch said, "Duncan?"

Finch said, "I know what you're thinking right now, man. Don't ask."

Finch said, "I can come back later if you guys want . . ."

The Captain was crazy. I know that. But *everyone* was crazy then. It was the end of the world.

But the Captain was crazy in a different kind of way. He was crazy from knowing too much. He was crazy from having seen too much and from holding too much in his head. He was crazy from being a man who was absolutely convinced of his rightness and specialness. Of his importance, even when that importance was only in his mind. Who felt, in a very real way, that if he didn't get his way, the world would end. Not figuratively, but literally. The *universe* would end. In his head, he was responsible for the fate of every person, every cat, every tree, every worm, every stone, every particle, every star, every planet, every alien sun. He was a fanatic because he had to be. Because to be anything less was either to admit that he was wrong, that he mattered as little as the rest of us ultimately did, or that he was willing to give less than all of himself to the only cause that had ever truly mattered.

The Captain was crazy. But later—years, days, I don't know—he would tell me about myself. The myself of his world. He would tell me how there were a million little things about this world—my world—that bothered him for their pointless differences. Songs and TV shows and brands of soda and the names of things. In so much, there was an internal consistency. A huge and smothering quilt of sameness. But then something would catch him—a song with the wrong lyrics, a street that ended in a different place—and it would be like a barb in his eye. He couldn't *not* notice the differences and they ate at him. People, he said, were the worst. All of us were ghosts to him. Most of us, anyway. When he told us he knew how we would die, what he meant was he knew how we died in *his* world. In what he considered the real world—a place so wicked and so broken that he had chosen to anoint himself the agent of its destruction in favor of one he thought he could shape the better himself.

So he would tell me that, in his world, he'd thought for the longest time that I was dead. That I had never made it out of Philadelphia on that worst of worst days. That I'd never gone underground and waited out the wracking contractions of abjuration, crawled through the flooded, mad, and squirming tunnels, emerged into the light of a gone world, made my way to New Jersey (a story for another day, I promise). Never saw Manhattan melt under the heat of a brief and furious second sun being born, never fought with a boy on the roof in the dawn light and killed him over nothing (over air, over breath) as I pumped rosy, young claret out into the dying world. Never saw Buffalo or Rochester or Wheeling, West Virginia, or Magnolia, Arkansas, never became an operator for the OSS, never had Gordon Navarro handed to me, never betrayed, never ran, never hid, never saw the inside of Sunflower Field, never left it, never came here, to Denver—the Queen City—or to the Free Republic, never found myself in the employ of King Steve on a Tuesday afternoon when one James Barrow came stepping in to ask for a translator.

"But you see how that's impossible, right?" he would ask. "Because you *were* there. Because you are here. Because I knew you would be. It bothered me for a long time, Duncan. It still bothers me."

But he did find me, he said. It was his proudest moment. The moment he figured it out. Or thought he figured it out. All that time, all that study, under the harshest of task-masters. Being quizzed. Being tested time and again as he was made to memorize a million-million things about a world that, to him, was make believe. Was an impossibility but would, in his future, be real. Flash cards. Mnemonics. Spreadsheets. Memorization games that made him like an idiot-savant, able to spit out whole histories of people when triggered. A thousand names and dates and places. The OSS's most perfect agent, the Captain was. The most secret. The most valuable to them that made him, shaped him, aimed him, and loosed him on this world. And when he'd found me, he said, it'd all clicked. It'd all made sense.

"Of course I knew you," he would tell me. "And someday you'll understand it, too. But not today."

He didn't tell me. Wouldn't. It was one of those things, he said. I just had to figure out for myself.

Sitting in the office, the Captain talked to Finch. Finch talked to me. Lee, he said, had made contact through a phone tree operated by one of the other L.O.T. cells. From a phone tree to a cold pass to a handshake meeting to a debrief by whatever leadership could be rousted out of their nests and dark apartments and mother's basements. That was where Lee was now—being debriefed in one of the L.O.T.'s pillow forts somewhere. There was panic in the ranks, Finch said. Wild accusations. There were so many dead, so quickly, and no one knew who to blame.

Finch cracked his knuckles. "That's one of the great things about dealing with idiots," he said. "They're so accustomed to being the ones who fuck things up that they assume all of this was somehow their own fault."

Lee had a cover story, and it was simple: OSS had come in shooting and we'd run. That was all. No heroics. No big, complicating details that might have to be corroborated later. When the shooting started, there'd been a rout. Everyone had tried to run. Lee would act appropriately surprised if anyone told him that we were the only three who'd tried to make contact.

"So why aren't you with him now?" asked the Captain.

"Wounded," said Finch, pointing at his arm. "Harry and me, both. We're recuperating somewhere off the streets and waiting. Harry has the explosives or some of the explosives or one of the explosives. Lee doesn't know exactly because Harry is being cagey, aren't you, Harry?"

"Apparently, I am," I said.

"Honestly, none of the Legion is really bright enough to ask too many questions," Finch said. "Really, they just don't care."

"You're sure?" asked the Captain.

"I'm sure enough. You took out Leo Purvis and Cal Miller in the raid. Those were two of their big thinkers and even they couldn't probably get through a *People* magazine without moving their lips. You any more sure yet about where the Chemist is being held?"

The Captain shook his head. "Things are hot right now. I can't get anything from any of our usual sources. Everything is just . . . quiet. But we'll find him."

"And if you don't?" Finch asked.

"It has to be one of those three locations—the offices, the Pit, or Percy's clubhouse. I just can't see them bringing him anywhere else."

"Why?" I asked.

Finch and the Captain both looked at me.

"You keep asking that question," the Captain said. "It's getting annoying."

"Okay," I said to him. "So it's annoying. But tell me why. If it was you, would you keep him close?"

The Captain shook his head and looked at Finch as though to continue on with the conversation, ignoring me and my pestering interjections, but then he stopped. He narrowed his eyes and looked back at me.

"What do you mean?" he asked.

"I mean, if it was you. If you'd kept hold of the Chemist like you'd intended. Would you have brought him here? Some place those lawyers and the rest of the OSS all know about?"

I was taking a chance—dancing a little bit close to the fire—but it was necessary. I had to put the doubt in him. Get him off his track of thinking we were just going to pop over next door with the Legion of Terror and borrow his man away again. The Captain had to be primed and ready to believe the train to Goodland story when it came to him. When I, carefully, handed it right to him.

"I might've," said the Captain.

"No you wouldn't," I said. "Because I wouldn't if it was me, and I'm really hoping you're smarter than I am."

Finch raised an eyebrow. "Man's got a point, Captain."

"Shut up," he said to Finch without even looking at him. "Duncan, if you know something . . ."

"I don't *know* anything," I said. "It just seems that you're focused on these locations you know about, and I'd think those would be the least likely places for them to keep the man because they're places you know. That Percy *knows* you know."

The Captain watched me. He didn't speak.

"Those Regulators," I said. "The ones that lived. They were put on you by the OSS, right? To harry you and yours. That's what you said. And you took them, nice and clean, at Great Times. But I notice that they're not here at the bunkhouse, are they? Because you put them somewhere *else*, didn't you? Somewhere not so easily accessible to them as might want to take them back."

Snatching his gaze away from me suddenly, the Captain swore under his breath.

"All I'm saying is that, if it was me keeping hold of the Chemist, I'd want him far and away from you. I'd want him buried in a hole somewhere that you've never looked in before."

"Kansas," said the Captain. "They'd take him to Kansas."

Which, honestly, was more of a leap than I expected him to make, but he was getting there by different means.

"The OSS," he continued. "The *other* OSS. Percy's OSS and Injun Joe's OSS. They're hot for the Kansans. Have been for a long time. The Western Confederacy has grown too strong for their tastes, and they feel that the best way to knock it down a peg is to tangle it up in battles with the Kansans, who are rather more friendly to ideas of America and reunification than King Steve is." He looked back at me. "Personally, I prefer the chaos. The rugged individualism of the West. An ascendant Confederacy. It's one of the many tactical points on which the OSS and I disagree."

"Which is why you're getting called a traitor around their offices," I said.

And the Captain smiled. "Oh, there are many reasons for that."

Finch just shrugged. "Okay, well one way or the other, we're going to need to know. And soon. I think Lee can probably get the Legion riled up. He was always better at speaking their language than I was. And Harry will have to sell them on making the attack, wherever it is. But the trick is to do it fast, before they get bored or forget how pissed off they are."

The Captain asked how much longer Lee was going to need and Finch said he didn't know. Finch asked how long before they were abandoning the bunkhouse and the Captain said hours, and not many of them.

"We need to make some jack moves," said the Captain. "Something to mix up the history a little. Dilute the immediate importance of the Chemist being in the wrong place and try to cool out the revisions. Plus, this place stinks of lawyers now. Honestly, I'm surprised that Percy hasn't been back with his troops."

"He was just here to twist the knife, Captain," Finch said. "You gotta know that. He thinks he pulled a trick on you and wanted you to be sure you knew who did it."

The Captain leaned back in his chair and rubbed at his eyes with the heels of his hands. "I do honestly hope that's all it was," he said. "There's still a chance they don't know who the Chemist really is, but they're not stupid. Even if he doesn't talk, they're going to figure it out eventually. The longer they have him, the better the chances of them being able to tell their asses from a hole in the ground."

Finch and Lee had a lovely doss arranged for themselves in a sushi bar in Cherry Creek that'd been partially collapsed during the Kansan withdrawal and now functioned as a perfect little clubhouse for two boys with big secrets. The Captain and most of his crew were falling back to a warren of gutted offices in the Chase Bank building, which most of the natives gave a wide berth because of the rumors of it being haunted—rumors that had been started and lovingly tended by the Captain himself. The only problem was, they were a little bit true, those rumors. There was part of a damaged machine brain still functioning somewhere down in the guts of the building, controlling the flow of nana and ensmartenment, causing the building to occasionally try to clean itself, perform routine maintenance on a million backed-up urgent repair requests or eat itself from the inside out.

"It's totally safe," the Captain insisted. "Totally, one-hundred-percent mostly safe." And then he laughed. "What's life without a little risk?"

The wounded were being evac'd by Doc Holcomb to a safe house close by where he'd tend to their hurts and be linkman between the Captain and his ragamuffins, who, even as we were all preparing to abandon ship, were pawing at everyone's things, drinking all the coffee, and rolling on the floor fighting over who was sleeping where,and who was in charge of what square foot of floor. They'd been instructed to keep to the first level. To not mount the stairs except under the most extraordinary of circumstances, and not to leave the premises until relieved or ordered into the streets. The Captain had called them all together into formation and given them the what-for, stalking up and down before them like Patton with Tuesday dogging his heels with her ice axe in hand.

"This is your fort," he told them. "And who comes into your fort?"

"No one, sir!" they answered in unison.

"If you are challenged, who are you?"

"Bunch of useless kids, sir!"

"But who are you really?"

"Your army, sir!"

"Goddamn right you are," said the Captain, looking them all over with beaming affection. "Medals for everybody that lives. Ice cream for anyone who does something heroic, like blooding any lawyer that steps foot on the grounds. Try not to break anything. Don't steal too much. If you see something that looks dangerous . . . I don't know. Wear a helmet or something. Army dismissed."

Engines were started. Trucks and vans and cars, all loaded to the axle-stops and burning fuel that was as dear as blood. The Ragamuffin Army melted into the place, poking into every corner and hole, and the Captain squatted down and reminded Tuesday to report four times a day to the doc, who would pass along any orders or messages that needed passing. Tuesday saluted by tapping the blade of her axe to her forehead.

"How many of yours are missing so far?" he asked her.

"Four," she said. "But one of 'em was dim, so say three. Redaction's a bitch, in'it?"

"They may come back."

"Don't never count on good luck, sir."

"Then we'll take four of theirs in trade. Fair?"

"Make it double. Three of em's was good and shiny and worth two of any O-man."

"Come here." The Captain said and hugged the girl fiercely. She dissolved into it like, for a second, she'd remembered beneath the dirt and bruises what it felt like to be a child. And then it was done. The Captain stood.

"Roll out!" he yelled.

I caught him as he was making for Marlene, Dogboy loping at his heel. "Oh, Captain," said me.

"You can ride with us, Duncan. Get in the back."

"Actually, I'm going to head for Miss Kitty's if it's all the same. Need a shower, some personal bits and pieces. A drink might go down nice, too."

He shook his head. "Not secure," he said. "Things are too loose right now. I can't have you out of sight."

I stepped a pace closer. There was never going to be a better opportunity than this to get myself popped clear for a little bit, so I took a risk and pushed it. "I also have to pick up the boom jelly from where I stashed it, don't I?" I said. "Someone has to. Plus the gold, if you want it back. Harry Plum has much and more he needs to get done before he's ready to turn freedom fighter for the L.O.T., and I have errands of my own need doing, too."

The Captain bit his lip, slapped the tailgate of one of the trucks as it passed and headed out the door, then looked back at Marlene idling away precious ounces of fuel. Jemma leaned her head out of the window and hollered for him to come on. I opened my mouth to say more, but snapped it closed again. The trick was not to look too anxious. To make him give the order to me.

"You want to take Dogboy with you?" he asked?

"Nah. He'll scare the hookers."

He looked back at Jemma, who gave him a come-along face, squinted his eyes in thought, then asked, "You need anything? Money? A gun?"

"I'm covered, Captain."

"Go then," he finally said. "Stay in touch. You know where we'll be?"

"I do," I said.

"Finch and Lee? You know where they're holing up?"

"I do."

"Okay. Don't be far. I'll send someone for you when we're ready to send you back in. If you run into any trouble, you come running, understand? I need you, Duncan. You die or disappear, I'm going to be very put out."

I saluted, turned sharply on my good leg, and limped off as quick as I could manage before his Captainness had a chance to change his mind. Outside, the day was hot and bright and seemed scoured clean of all darkness. I could see the mountains rising in the distance, the blue of the sky and the white of the clouds. The broken pavement of the lot was drifted with dust, the bones of small animals, Styrofoam packing peanuts and hundreds of hand-bills for Banjo Oblangata and the Critical Malfunctions playing a free show in Prospect Park. In the distance, fingers of black smoke rose straight into the still air like cracks in the beauty of the natural world and I aimed myself in their direction, using them, the conversations of birds and the far-off chatter of auto-matic weapons like compass points to guide me, limping, back into another life.

It was time to make a phone call.

I never was all that good at being just one man. Being two was exhausting.

I knew this fellow once called Dink Leslie. Knew him in jail, at Sunflower Fields. He was ex-OSS, like me. A runaway. He'd spent the bulk of his career as a deep-cover asset, worming his way into the houses of petty kings and border lords on the western frontier. Gathering, like me. Working out of a suitcase, like me.

I spent most of my time in solitary. Restrictive confinement. Just me and my bruises. But not all the time. I spotted Dink on the first time I found myself in the yard—forty-four minutes of walking in a circle on a path worn down to dirt by the resigned tread of a million footsteps, a hundred dead men walking, all blinking into the pure Kansas sunlight.

Most of the mudsills confined in Goodland were humps. Gray-faced, silent, once-dangerous men broken now into shambling husks with all the bite of kicked dogs. But Dink was different. Dink was, for lack of a more flowery description, happy.

He looked up into the sun like it was a revelation. He looked down at the ground like it was growing rolled joints and hundred dollar bills. Where other men trudged, he strolled—hands in his pockets, a bounce in his step.

We weren't supposed to talk in the yard, but we did. Everyone who still had his teeth had the knack of speaking without looking, of mumbling through lips barely moving, of talking from behind hands or into shoulders or whatever. We were watched remotely. There were no guards. No one knew when the eyes were on them and when they were off.

Anyway, Dink Leslie had been undercover for years, and he told me that when he'd run, he'd done it because he couldn't take being two men any more. Being three men. Four. Being the sum total of all the men he'd pretended to be and going to sleep at night with the memories of what they'd all done and waking with their tics and their histories and their various awfulnesses all tangled up inside him like ropes knotted in a musty locker.

"Come a day," he said to me, "when being one man was all that mattered. Lord give us each twenty-four hours in a day, and that's hardly enough to be one whole man. Being two just means that both is shorted. Both is fighting, always, inside of you. And it isn't ever the goodest one that wins."

The happiest day of Dink Leslie's life was the day he got bagged by the OSS. "Because they was coming for *me*," he explained. "They said, 'Dink Leslie, you coming with us,' and I said, okay then. That's who I am now. I'm just one man." His head, he said, went quiet. His heart, he said, beat for only one. He was Jonathan Robert "Dink" Leslie, and that was fine. It'd been so long since he'd been himself that he had the first peaceful sleep he'd known in years while his head was bagged in the back of an OSS osprey.

I was thinking about Dink as I limped away from the bunkhouse. As I found a road somewhat traveled and flagged a rickshaw being run by a kid that couldn't have been more than thirteen, wearing mad aviator goggles and a pair of canvas sneakers held together with silver tape. As I rode back to Miss Kitty's, massaging my leg, trying hard to not never look back over my shoulder. Trying to behave only like a tired man heading finally for home, such as it was, because I assumed I was being followed. Being watched. Being tracked, somehow, by the Captain. By the boss. By Percy Blythe or Clarence Doolittle. By enemies, known and unknown.

I felt that I wasn't. But maybe I was. I couldn't be sure. There is a special third ear that modern men grow, made for hearing the cloying, distant buzz of drones circling lazily. For hearing the gnat song of mite clusters taking an inordinate interest, suddenly, in the tap of one's footsteps. I'd been unconscious for a good while at the bunkhouse. Could the Captain have tagged me? Probably. Of course he had. Maybe.

I closed my eyes and turned my face skyward as though just enjoying the warmth of the sun. Then I cracked an eye and scanned quickly for the moving dot. The aberrant smudge against the blueness of the sky. I imagined my skin a finely tuned dish for receiving the gentle caress of radar pulses sweeping, the pin-point pressure of an optical tracking laser as, somewhere high above me, a finger-sized, fire-and-forget missile rolled out of its magazine and into the firing cradle. Once upon a time, men feared demons and monsters of inestimable evil. Now our paranoia is of the drone, the camera mite, the buzzing autofocus of the surveillance eye. *And* demons. *And* monsters. *And* waking up one morning knowing somehow, in some deep but untouchable place, that abjuration and revision have taken from us some vital detail about the world-that-was. That while we slept, magical elves have snuck in and rearranged all our psychic lawn furniture. Sometimes I feel that we've been offered the shit end of the stick.

My leg itched fiercely. Scratching it set off fireworks of pain. My room at Miss Kitty's, I thought, would likely be compromised. Too many ears in the main rooms. I shook the burner Tom Lakey had given me out of my boot and had the rickshaw driver drop me a block away from the whorehouse and hobbled the rest of the distance on bootleather. Inside, I was greeted like an unexpected relation arriving in the middle of dinner. Madam turned her nose up at me, even as I made my apologies. I gritted my teeth at the turns of the stairs, but climbed to my room in the attic, collected some things, then hopped back downstairs, ate two pain killers out of my private supply, and washed them down with a shot of Devil Eyes from a bartender I didn't recognize and who demanded cash payment. After that, I paid for a bath and a girl to give it to me.

"I gotta pay extra for you to help me up the stairs?" I asked of the little dove who'd taken my eagle.

"Gotta pay extra for everything, cowboy," she said, smiling.

"Some things never change."

Inside the room, she ran the bath, stripped out of the yoga pants and University of Colorado sweatshirt she'd been wearing (day hookers rarely have to try very hard), and eased herself into the steaming water.

"You coming, baby?" she asked.

"At just seeing a girl take her clothes off? Not since I was a young man."

She laughed and held out a hand to me. I shook my head. "Soap up. Splash around. Make a play of it, okay? And I'll give you an off-the-books double if you forget anything you hear, deal?"

The girl shrugged, closed her eyes, her whole demeanor changing in the turning of a second. "Your dime, man. I'll never turn down a hot bath."

I took out the burner, let it dial its number, and waited. It rang and rang. It clicked through. I listened to the encryption tones climb, listened to the click.

"Secure," I said.

"Secure," said the boss. "You alone, Duncan?"

"Alone-ish," I said.

"Where are you?"

"Safe in the arms of the Lord."

"Funny."

"Start talking, boss. I don't have a lot of time and I'm paying for every minute."

"Did you get my message?"

"I did."

"Train 1066 to Goodland."

"That was the gist of it. How long do I have?"

"Five days until they move him."

"Where is he now?"

There was a pause. "Can't say," the boss said.

I told him to hang on a second, then turned to the girl. "You know how to sing, darlin'?" I asked.

"Got a voice like a lark," she said.

"Then sing me something, will you? I'd dearly like to hear it. And can you . . ." I mimed putting hands over ears. "Earmuffs, sweetheart. If you please."

She shrugged, cupped her ears, and began to sing "Mercedez Benz" like Janis did, but in a voice that was like a mother singing to her child—so sweet and breathy that it broke a tiny little piece off my heart.

I put the phone back to my ear. "The fuck you mean you can't say?"

"I mean I can't say. He'll be on the train. You're going to have to take him on the train."

"We *had* him at the garage," I said. "Was it you that took him off the Captain's team?"

"Not personally, no, Duncan."

"You and fucking Gordo? You set that up?"

"Yes."

"Why?" I asked, a rasping edge in my voice that I smoothed with a deep breath. With thoughts of free whiskey, sunshine, cigarette trees and fluffy kittens. "Why would you take him and then expect me to get him back?"

And the boss, he said nothing. I could hear him breathing. I could hear him lick his lips.

"Train 1066," he finally said. "You've got five days to prepare."

"He shot me, you know. The Captain? Shot me in the leg."

"I know."

"You know?"

"I know."

I chewed on that a minute. Dink Leslie was executed not long after I had the pleasure of speaking with him. Two in the head in a basement room tiled from floor to ceiling. He'd died staring at a floor drain, knowing in his final instant exactly what was coming. I like to imagine that he was cool with it. That he was happy enough because he was dying as Jonathan Robert "Dink" Leslie and no one else.

The OSS is not kind to its wayward sons. The company's retirement plan almost always pays out in lead. Everyone knows that. Stay in long enough, it's just one of those things you learn.

"I need a meeting," I said.

"I'm on a plane right now," the boss said. "Bad timing."

"Yeah, it's always bad timing, isn't it?" I took a deep breath, smiled at the girl. "What if I can't get to him? The Chemist?"

"You have to. You have to take him on the train between Denver and Goodland. You're clever, Duncan. You'll come up with something."

"I'm gonna need some things from Gordon next time I see him."

"He got your message. He'll be there and he's been instructed to give all possible aid. Make this happen, Duncan. It's important."

It's important. *Everything* was important. There wasn't never a day that wasn't important.

"The Captain is insane, you know."

"James Barrow," the boss said. "Call him James Barrow. And yes, he's an odd duck."

"He thinks he's from another dimension."

"No, Duncan. He *is* from another dimension."

"Funny."

There was a quiet moment. The phone rustled and popped like the boss had put his hand over it. I could hear muted voices, but not what they were saying. Then the boss was back.

"I'm not joking. James Barrow is a lot of things, but he's not a liar. James Alexander Barrow was born, raised and trained one world over. He was an OSS forger and paper-hanger. A small-time asset for a case officer called Joe Tanner who, not coincidentally, was also called The Captain because he was, in fact, an actual Captain, unlike Mr. Barrow, who was never anything of the sort. But there was a . . ."

And then the boss said some stuff I can't recall. Some stuff about the Captain and about . . . something. It's strange. I'm a good rememberer. Always have been. I know 899 stories about the Captain and every one of them is true. I could tell you about the time he sent me into the Seven Hills to make war with monsters and rescue an actual princess. I could tell you the name of his sister, his shoe size, or what he said the time we were happened upon by the territorial police while trying to break into one of the Free Republic domes.

"Why, gentlemen, you're just who I was hoping to find," said him, taking me by the back of the neck like a rug-pissing dog. "Look what I found trying to weasel his way into your fancy little Eden."

I spent eight days in jail before he got around to springing me. Not a long stretch, but still.

The boss once told me that I am a man defined not by what I done or what I seen, but by them things that I can't remember. Them things that I am *incapable* of knowing, for reasons which I am also incapable of knowing. It was my own private Abjuration, I think. A redaction so careful and so precise that it just couldn't be shook. The universe—this one, the other one—they don't fuck around when it comes to balancing their equations. Ain't none of us anything more than quanta to them. Just grist for the mill of reality, ground terrible fine.

I could lie to you. I could spin you such a wonder as to make your heads spin. As I've already told you, I am not a man over-burdened with veracity or guilt for making a tale sing true, if not factually. But I find even that . . . difficult. To speak in the vicinity of them things I am predisposed to not know makes me uncomfortable. It *hurts* me in a way that's like a fist inside my head, squeezing.

I'm sorry. I truly am. I know what you want to know and I know what you need to know. I know what's on the line. But believe me when I tell you that there are ways at this information. Just not ways that involve an easy walk or a straight line.

"I don't understand."

That's the next thing I can comfortably recall myself saying to the boss.

And "You never understand," said the boss to me. "You know how many times I've told you this?"

I said nothing.

"This is the 19th time I've told you this, Duncan. You never understand and you never remember. I'm not sure you *can* remember. But you have to accept. I'm going to play you the song now. I'm sorry."

I recall saying *no*, saying *please* and then nothing. I don't know what song he meant. Or why it was played. I mean, I *know* probably. Somewhere. But I can't recollect it for you.

Sorry.

I do remember yelling. Scaring the girl in the bath, I reckon. The smell of ancient dust and warm steam and flowers. And then it was just me standing there, phone in my hand.

"You're all insane," I said. "Fucking hell, you're all insane."

The boss chuckled. "You should think about that, Duncan. If everyone around you is saying one thing and you're the only one saying different, who's the crazy one?"

"Another dimension. Really."

"The world is full of strange things. Trust me, James Barrow isn't even the strangest. Get the Chemist back, Duncan. Gordon knows what to do."

"See? And that's how I know you're crazy. Letting the fate of the world hang on La Rata."

"Anything else?"

"Can I have a raise?"

"No. Get to work. You've got five days."

And the phone in my hand went quiet. The boss had hung up.

I dropped the burner back into my boot and motioned for the girl to take her hands down.

"You hear any of that?" I asked.

"Let me see your coin and then I'll tell you."

I rooted in my pocket and gave her my last two eagles. She nodded her approval. "Didn't hear a damn thing," she said, closing her eyes and settling back into the bath. I leaned my back against the wall and slowly let myself slide down to the floor. The boss had been right. I was clever. I had the beginnings of a plan, but it wasn't a good one. It was ridiculous and stupid and risky, involved explosives, betrayal, guns, and lies upon lies. Also dinosaurs.

"That was a real pretty song," I said to the girl. "You've got a beautiful voice. You ever think about singing for a living rather than getting on your back for strangers?"

"Trust me, cowboy. Fucking strangers is a better living than singing to 'em. More dependable, too."

I sighed. "You may be right about that."

"Speaking of which," she said. "You paid your dime. You want that bath now?"

"I'd love to, darlin'," I said, patting at my gimpy leg. "But I got this hole in me right now that I shouldn't get wet."

"Got a wet hole of my own," she said. "Wanna see?"

I wish I could tell you that I demurred in a healthful and gentlemanly fashion and got right on about the business of saving the world, but what can I say? I'd paid, after all. All I got was what was coming to me.

E P I S O D E

8

Last Train to Goodland, Part 1

I LIT A FIRE. I PUNCHED A COP. I KILLED A FRIEND. I RODE A DINOSAUR across the plains of Eastern Colorado.

Why am I telling you this? You *know* all of this. You know exactly where it's going.

I betrayed the Legion of Terror a second time because some men are just so dim that they deserve betraying. I betrayed the boss because some men are just so weak and so stupid that they can't help but betray those who are trying to help them. Or *claim* to be trying to help them, anyhow.

The Captain would tell me that I saved millions. That was his defense for everything—for every good and bad thing he ever did and was ever done by those who gathered under his flag. He would say that I did terrible things but that, really, I had no choice. That the things I done were the things I had to do. That I had *already* done, depending on how one conceives of the clockworks of the universe and everything in it. The Captain would tell me that this made me no less deserving of punishment, and then would deliver it. Even the punishment was part of the plan. And one fucked with the orderly progression of time and time's doings only at one's great and fearsome peril, as we had all so lately learned.

So I burned and I betrayed and I killed and I rode a charging triceratops across the flatness and shaved fields of the No-Man's Land of the Colorado/Kansas border. I rescued the Chemist. I don't know even today that it was worth it. It might have been, but I'm not sure. I ended up with vomit on my pants and brains on my sleeve and, according to the Captain, bought back a few more minutes from Doomsday and the end of all things. But the Captain was probably insane, so what did he know?

Only everything. Or so he claimed.

You know all this. That's what bothers me. I love to talk, it's true. Love the sound of my own voice, me. Love making myself out the hero. Or at least not the most villainous among the coterie of villains with whom I ganged.

So I'll talk. I'll talk because so long as I'm talking, I'm still precious to you, right? I still have some small worth?

You listening? Here's what happened. Most of it, anyway, and mostly true.

It was a busy few days.

I played that night at Miss Kitty's simply because there was no reason not to. After getting kicked free of the Captain, having my call with the boss and my bath, I had some time to kill. My leg ached fearsomely, but every time I felt that hot snake of pain start moving through me, I just drowned the sonofabitch with another beer.

The room jumped. The crowds were there waiting when I came downstairs and they just kept coming, refreshing themselves as the front door banged open and closed and open and closed. I played "Jack Straw" and they threw pennies at me, trying to sink them into the mug of beer I had setting on top of that Regent and cheering for themselves when they did. I played "Rocket Man" and "Backstreets" and "Werewolves of London" and a kind of drunken Irish lullaby that I'd first heard done by Arthur Guinness Talking back when I was still a traveling man and a ripper for the cause. Tore it up one side and down the other, they had, in a dim and divey public house in the North Country where the bass player claimed to own 10,000 acres of uncut timberland and a parrot he'd taught to play poker and curse in Yiddish.

I played as good a version as I could without any accompaniment, then cooled it out with a choppy version of "Take Five" that rolled right into one of Banjo Oblangata's originals—a footstomper called "Twenty Minutes into the Future"—that wanted badly for East Coast Dave's fast hands and Czerw Mulligan's electrificated fiddle, but I did alright. Least I think I did. By the last chorus, I was whipping my sweat-lank hair back off my forehead with my free hand, and when it was all over, I chugged down the lager in my mug until the coppers rattled against my teeth.

Triumphant, I strode to the long oak. As I always did, I imagined hoots and cheers of surpassing joy from the crowd I'd labored to entertain and, this time, might not even have been imagining them. I ate pickled eggs and cubes of tofu in a slick of sweet soy sauce and rice, white and plain, then I charged back to the Regent and played a second set that was as dark and hot and ugly as a bruise.

The crowd swelled. It was a pleasure-eating monster with hundreds of legs and half as many heads, starving for all the good times in the world. Everyone alive, it seemed, wanted some bought company that night, or maybe just the warmth of a loud room full of strangers. The working girls and boys bobbed their heads to the music when they weren't bobbing for something else. The bartenders dashed the length of the bar like they was being whipped to a lather.

Reggie never came, but that meant nothing. Any one of the lushes and lonelyhearts who mobbed Miss Kitty's that night could've been an informer for the Captain or the boss or Percy Blythe or the grim and loveless half of the OSS. I played "Lawyers, Guns and Money" and sang like I didn't care who was listening. I played "Roadhouse Blues" like the 88's was on fire. At one point, I played "Secret Agent Man" and looked all around to see if the irony of it was enough to spark any guilty smiles, but I saw none that weren't directly related to liquor, graft or pussy, so sang the whole goddamn thing in Spanish like the Plugz once done, hit a sour last chord, then pushed back on the bench, hunched over, did "Innocent When You Dream" by Tom Waits and, with the whirlwind roar of the mob still echoing in my ears, retired to my bachelor's quarters alone.

I proved Tom wrong, dreamt of betrayal and being pulled apart by hounds, but woke at ten minutes 'til one in the afternoon with a smile regardless and a sharp eye besides.

"Busy day," said me to myself. "Busy, busy day."

I had to meet with Gordon and had arranged, through the call I'd made to him at the Westward, to do it at a flower shop he'd mentioned in his column. We were scheduled to meet at 3pm, with fallbacks at five, seven and nine. I had every intention of being there at three. But first, I had to pack.

There was, in dealing with the abject calamitousness of living in that falling-to-pieces world, two ways in which one might cope, stuff-wise.

The first was to over-prepare for every possible disaster and strangeness—to go out into the Weird like some overcompensating Boy Scout, weighted down with bug spray, antibiotics, snacks, anti-radiation meds, extra ammo, cab fare, rope, pure water, band-aids, a can opener, change of socks, goggles, harpoon gun, body armor, compass, gas mask, burn ointment, sunglasses, flashlight, snow-shoes, shovel, the name of a good lawyer, and a hand grenade, just in case. That was the Captain to a T. On any given day, his pockets were like an old lady's purse—full of tissues and hard candies, squirreled away in case of need.

The other way was to accept the fact that the world was a mess and to know stepping out into it that one can never truly be prepared. To trust in your native wit and divine providence to see you through when things got sticky.

That, in a word, was me. It was an agreement I made with the world and myself a long time ago—the understanding that the surest way to prevent your being eaten by a sea monster was to always carry a loaded harpoon gun with you, but that, in such prevention, the harpoon gun just became more weight to carry.

So I left the harpoons at home; wore my gun, my fancy suit and my good boots; shoveled the burner, Julie's knife, three additional cell phones and the regulator's paperwork all into my briefcase; salted my pockets with whatever cash I could lay hands to; then tossed a plastic baggie full of handrolls into my hat, jammed it down onto my head, and went more or less barehanded into the warp of the world. I trusted that, if I should happen upon a kraken while walking down a country lane, I would have the presence of mind to simply hide. Or run the fuck away. I was feeling good.

Outside on the street, I spotted the first tail almost immediately— a bloody-eyed and nerve-ish little man I recognized from his late keeping in Miss Kitty's parlor the previous night. He could not have been easier to spot if he'd been wearing a sign—a man alone, still in last night's beer-stinking drag, ghosting the streets with nowhere to be and suddenly taking an interest in a road sign the minute I came out the door. Staring up at it like it was imparting to him God's own secrets of the universe.

I kinda wanted to kiss that man right on the mouth because he was just so *expected*. His presence confirming my every dark thought and paranoia. Had he been shouting "I'm acting casual!"

at the top of his lungs, he wouldn't have been more obvious, and I guessed straight off that he was the radioman for a street team—relaying my particulars of dress, carriage and comportment, the time of my departure and direction of travel to one or more two-man pavement units who'd pick me up moving and do the actual footstepping work of following me about my business. There was no way he was alone. He didn't look bright enough to find his own hat. And if he'd been even a little bit good, I never would've seen him at all.

Still, the mood I was in, I took it as a challenge. A bit of sport to keep me sharp for the rest of the day's fun. Had no idea who'd put him on me, but it didn't much matter at the moment, so I just hailed down a pedicab and had it take me to the market yard in front of the Castle where a half-eagle bought me a child's backpack with one broken shoulder strap and a once-white tee-shirt with a New York Jets logo on it, number 19 on the back. I dawdled about the market, poking at this and haggling over that, making myself as fat a target as possible for whoever might be watching, then paid six more eagles for two plastic liter bottles filled with gasoline (which went into the backpack, wrapped in the tee-shirt) and another half for a coffee, white and sweet, from Katarina, the shark-mouth coffee-seller who'd rated a hug from Jemma once upon a time.

"Pleasant to see you again, Katarina," I said as she poured my coffee without really looking away from the book open in front of her.

"You, too, cowboy," she said, but I knew in my heart she didn't mean it.

"You still studying hard?" I asked. "Pretty and smart. That's a dangerous combination."

She glanced at me. "I'm sorry, do I know you?" she asked.

"Duncan," I said. "Duncan Archer. We met a couple of months ago. I was here with Jemma Watts, getting coffee for the Captain?"

She sighed, a touch more deeply than was necessary, added the milk, carefully marked her place on the page (it was a different textbook this time: *Nucleic Acids and Mycology*, 4th edition), and then looked up at me.

"Duncan Archer?" she asked.

I smiled. "That's me."

"Do you have any idea how many cups of coffee I pour in a day, Duncan Archer?"

I allowed that I did not. She said it was a lot. I told her it must be nice to be so popular. She said, "Point is, I cannot remember every person who buys a coffee from me and I'm sorry that I don't remember you."

I nodded sagely. "Maybe it's the hat," I said, pointing at it, as though maybe she hadn't noticed it sitting on my head. "I wasn't wearing it last time."

"It's not the hat."

"No?"

"No."

And "Oh," said me, hinting at a deep well of disappointment. "Well, next time I'll endeavor to make a more lasting impression. Thanks for the coffee."

She shrugged and looked back at her book. "Whatever you say, cowboy."

"Duncan," I said, and tapped my hat to her. "Duncan Archer."

And then I turned my back and walked off into the crowd in the vague direction of the Nob, doubled-back out of her sight and, from around the billowing corner of a blousy tent offering a hundred different magic potions, each of them swirling with heavy metals and a billion inert constructors, I watched her through the swirl of bodies out for a day at the market. She was on the phone—dialing, waiting, rolling her lovely purplish eyes. And then she was talking. It looked to me like she was leaving a message, and I wondered which one of the phones back at the bunkhouse was hers. What number she called when she had a tidbit for Jemma Watts.

I waited until she was through, until she sighed and cupped her face in both hands and looked back down at her book. Then I dumped the coffee out on the ground, flattened the cup and stuck it in my back pocket. I didn't like coffee. I liked chicory. And I knew just where to get some.

I made another slow, meandering circle around the fringes of the market yard, just to make sure the pavement artists had me well in their sights, and then it was up to the Castle and straight in through the front doors amid the clutter and bump of the daily traffic. My tails, I knew, would be flustered. Tougher to follow a man indoors than out—particularly into what was an effective dead-end for those who didn't have appointments for important business within.

So they would pull back, form up around the obvious exits. They'd wait for me to come out again because, to a rational person, once I was inside, where else could I go? I'd run a hundred pavement teams myself. I knew all the protocols and best practices. And it pleased me no small amount to be able to use all that wicked and hard-earned knowledge to my own foul ends.

I had no appointments, but I was sneaky. I knew tricks. I took the door off the lobby that I used to pass through each day at work—back when I was pilfering from the King and pretending to know something about roads. It was nondescript, that door. Overlookable, propped full open, and watched over by a tubby thing called Leon who I knew was bored with watching said door by about 9:15 every morning and catatonic by noon. I strode up powerful, like I was walking on lightning, raised my briefcase at him, knocked on it with the knuckles of my other hand, and said, "Road works, Leon," which was enough. He snuffled at me groggily and I just never stopped moving.

Hallway, hallway, the offices of petty bureaucrats and plutocrats and pencil-pushing, dead-eyed disaster-crats who, like me, had seen a dollar to be made from the attempted ruination of the Queen City and had jumped at it. Loved them. Crooks to a man. The Royalty's finest swindlers.

I passed through the dank bullpen of the waterways committee, the slightly more chic digs of the communications and data engineering subunit, hooked a clean-ish mug from someone's unwatched desk and made right for the canteen where I poured myself a full measure of hot, woody chicory and luxuriated over it for ten whole, peaceful minutes while sitting at a sticky table and thinking quite deliberately of nothing much at all. Of girls and the atomic glow of irradiated sunrises and the clink of pennies against my teeth. Fuck them as were dogging me, I thought. There wasn't a man in the world who meant me well—who wasn't using me for some perfidious end or actively trying to kill me right dead—so let 'em sweat, whoever they were. There were, I reckoned, fewer and fewer moments of bliss offered to a man as the land fell daily into deeper and deeper enstrangement. And whosoever didn't take what rare opportunities for joy or fun that the wrecksious world presented ought to just eat a bullet now or pray mightily for the return of khaki pants, cubicle walls and television shows where idiots sang and danced for money.

When I was done, I got up, poured another cup, drank it down fast, made for my old environs among the roadways working group, found my old desk and my old window with its view out over the giant robot head which, still, had not been removed, stole all the pens, fine paper, binding clips, gnawed pencils and a stapler without hardly stopping to think about it, then passed on through the nearest doorway, down a short hall, and out through a fire exit whose alarm had been handsomely disabled long ago—a thing I knew because I was the handsome man who'd done the disabling.

That door let out onto a small yard, the yard to a beaten path between the body of the Castle and its palisade wall, the path to a gate rarely used because by "gate" I really mean a loose bit of wall-piece useful to them as wanted to sneak out midday for a cold beer or a bit of a walk without having to explain one's self to the likes of Leon or one's bosses.

I slipped out, clean of all tails, and ducked into the first cab that presented itself.

"14th and Wazee," I said. "Don't spare the whip."

I leaned back then, pulled my hat down low, massaged my aching leg, and let the *clopclopclop* of cab's automatic horse tick away the fastly running minutes of my day.

When Gordon Navarro had found me at Sunflower Field, I was a wreck. Two years, twenty-nine days inside, and all of those spent in a solitary, nine-by-twelve box excepting those precious moments spent outside and above ground in the yard for exercise and those hours and hours and hours spent in the hands of the OSS interrogators who asked me again and again what it was that made me turn traitor and again and again what it was I'd hoped to gain by the downfall of mom, apple pie and the U.S. of A.

For a month, I laughed at them. I was younger then and could afford it. I laughed at the notion of there being anything left of the U.S. of A. to fall down. They would shake their heads and march me back to my cell, hoping for better results the next day.

For three months, I tried to reason with them—asking, *Hey, have you seen it out there?* and *Best case, gents, how many stars do you still count on Old Glory?*

Fifty, they would say.

Nothing has changed, they would say.

Now tell us, why do you hate America?

There was something sick at the heart of the OSS. Something broken or black or cancerous. I'd known this before walking away. Hadn't known precisely what it was that was wrong—couldn't lay a finger to a specific thing and say *this is what is ailing us and here is how it might be cut out*—but I'd known that there was something wrong and growing wronger and that was why I'd gone left on a day when I'd been ordered to go right and then just ran and ran until I couldn't run any more. Until Raton, New Mexico, where they'd taken me in a sting that, five years earlier, I would've seen coming a hundred miles off. Honest, I was shocked they was still hunting after me. I was harmless as a mouse to them then. My own man with my own concerns. But the OSS would eat itself hollow at the least hint of infidelity. The OSS don't never forget.

It took being caught to show me plain what had soured in those boys. The institutional insanity that caused those most loyal to get up every morning, pull their pants on, salute a flag that represented only a dream of past days, and then go off to work hurting and murdering them as claimed to see the world in a different light.

You gotta understand this. In the good old days, the Office of Special Services had a mandate to protect and preserve the remains of this torn-apart world. To govern the chaos, police the weird, to see and to report and report and report on the divergences wrought by changes that no one claimed to understand and to shepherd the scattered flocks through the storm. The OSS had been born of the dissolution of the United States. A grunting, blood-soaked, squalling idiot-child come heaving into the twilight of civility—the last functioning arm of a splintered and reliquary system. Tasked with the maintenance of a wracked memory of America, working among the hodge-podge remainders of kingdoms and fiefdoms and secessionists and kings, we hunted mad scientists, toppled petty, stupid despots, ended wars, guarded the light, bandaged the wounds and, most important, maintained an endless vigil so that, someday, someone might be able to track a course back through bedlam and know how the world now received unto us had come of the world-gone-by. They—*we*—were the good guys. The guards in the madhouse of the Abjuration. Not there to cure, but to maintain, to protect and to understand so that, someday, wiser heads might come along and put the whole mess of everything back together again right.

But that had changed somewhen. At a certain point, the OSS had begun to think of itself as the doctor, attempting to impose a reality of its own devising. To shape a truth that suited them in ignorance of the truth that was. Madness, you understand, is not a rejection of reality in favor of fantasy; it is the imposition of a *different* veracity on the bones of the true.

Now tell us, they'd say, who convinced you to turn your back on America?

Who are you reporting to?

Who did you betray us to?

My interrogators showed remarkable patience with me, but this, like all things, had a limit. One of them hit me for the first time on day 99. And after that it was like a dam done broke. All bets were off.

In his newspaper column, Gordon had called Gerstmann's Flowers at 15th and Wazee "a place to get away from it all," which was exactly what I was looking for. I had the cab drop me a block away and did the last stretch on foot, limping a little, but doing my best to bury it under the guise of a cheerful fellow out for a slow-loping afternoon stroll.

I passed Gerstmann's at 2:30 from the opposite sidewalk and kept on shuffling by. I didn't have the feeling—the learned, tingling tightness between my shoulders—that I was being actively followed, but sometimes it was tough to tell. If my tails hadn't picked up the cab (and I didn't think they had), I figured I was in the wind. But that was no reason not to be careful.

Across the street from the shop was a run of mixed-use red-brick buildings—shops on the ground floor, apartments above. Most of them had been shot-holed during the troubles, some parts leveled, the rest abandoned save for the scavengers and scroungers who inhabited every corner of things. I ducked down an alley like a man ambling after a misplaced cat, found a back door loose on its hinges, leaned against it until I felt the remains of the lock snap, and slipped spiritously inside. A ghost, me. There but not there and taking great care to leave no footprints.

I had to keep moving, but the perch I wanted was a second-floor window spiderwebbed with cracks that I'd seen from outside and which looked directly across at Gerstmann's front door. Lacking wings, a second-floor window involved stairs, and I stood there at the base of them, looking at the broken railings and missing risers, breathing deeply, trying with all my wit to convince myself that I didn't really need to go up them. That staying rooted comfortably at ground level was plenty good enough and that doing the proper thing and the wise thing in going up the stairs to a good hide was just the acme of foolishness since it would surely do further harm to my gimp leg, which I might need later since hopping everywhere was both awkward and impractical.

I went up anyway. Slowly. Part of it, I crawled.

Upstairs, another door, and now I was limping again for real. Could feel something loose and hot in the place where the Captain's bullet had been. I leaned on the frame, took a breath and knocked loud. A warrant knock, like the booming hand of God.

"King's business," I bellowed, in a voice lower and rougher than my own. "Open the door or we're coming in."

I listened, heard nothing, tried the knob, found it mercifully unlocked, so twisted it and shoved the door open while standing well clear, which was fortuitous as the scattergun blast that followed mortally wounded only the wall opposite the door and not me.

It was a one-shot booby-trap, the gun just a milled pipe with a single buckshot shell stuck in one end, the whole thing crudely fixed to the floor and angled upward, an improvised hammer and firing pin wired to a tension line. I kicked it loose with my good leg, shut the door behind me, and hobbled to the window, passing carefully around the trash on the floor, the half-dozen bare mattresses, the books swollen with dampness. On the wall around the window frame were a child's crayon drawings of flowers and suns and stick-figure people. The flowers all had faces and most of them had teeth. The sun was red and furious. And though they held hands or the strings of balloons and stood on scribbled grass done in cerulean blue, didn't none of the crayon people look particularly happy with the world they'd been drawn into.

I sat, stretched out my leg, touched a finger to the drawings and could feel the waxiness of the marks on the wall. I tried to imagine the mind of the child who'd made them. Who'd never known a world of normalcy and steadiness and sanity. One of full refrigerators and quiet nights and crickets and flowers without teeth. Where the sun brought the day and the moon chased the night and things didn't just appear and disappear like dreams. Where armies didn't march in the streets and giant robots didn't shudder the ground and the rain was not poison and the earth did not split and crack and grown train tracks and televisions. One where clocks told time with the regular *tickticktick* of provable truth.

I took out a cigarette and lit it. Scratched at the foot of a stick-figure Daddy with a look on his round face like he knew something terrible was creeping up on him from behind. Through the window, I could see Gerstmann's. At 2:45, Gordon Navarro ghosted the front door. I saw no one following him. No suspicious vehicles. Not even the odd twinkle given by conglomerations of mites sparkling in the sun.

At five minutes to 3pm, I watched him approach again. He had a bag over his shoulder and was wearing a rumpled suit the color of stormclouds. He went in through the front door, and as he was going, I saw him glance back over his shoulder, eyes quickly scanning the line of windows opposite.

He didn't see me. The glare, the cracks—I was more or less invisible. But at least I knew he was being careful.

By the time I got back down the stairs again, my leg was throbbing. Putting any weight on it at all drove a hot nail of pain into me. I lit another cigarette in the shelter of the downstairs door and saw that my hands were trembling Not a good sign. And like the man said, I still had miles to go yet before I could sleep.

"Fuck it," I muttered and went hop-stepping out into the alley. From the alley to the street, grunting at every step. From the street to Gerstmann's, through the front door, quick as a cripple ever could. I was pouring sweat by the time I touched the door handle, and stepping into the cool air and scent of growing things was like slipping into cool water. Like stepping into another, sweeter world. It made me want to lie down and sleep for a year.

But I didn't. I relished the touch of refrigerated air on my skin, the dryness and the softness of it. I eyed the swirling colors of the cased G-Mod flowers, the bursting impossibility of them in a city that, in large part, had difficulty feeding itself and keeping the Kansans out. I'd seen grown men rolling in the dirt like dogs down in the red lights, fighting over unequal portions of grilled field mouse, but here, there were flowers.

But what the hell, right? Someone had to do it.

Gordon stood in the middle of the shop talking to a small, stooped elf of a man with tufts of white hair sprouting from behind his ears and the delicate hands of a concert pianist or professional bomb defuser. The man wore an apron, the pockets of it festooned with syringes, phials, hook-bladed scissors, scalpels, and a hand-held monocular partiscope. Gordon smiled and patted him on the shoulder. When he saw me, he gently turned the little man in my direction and pointed me out to him.

"Herr Gerstmann," he said, "this is my friend, Jimmy."

Gerstmann shuffled forward and extended a hand. I shook it. "Pleased to meet you," I said.

Gerstmann looked me up and down without releasing my hand. "Your friend, he seems sick," he said to Gordon. "He here for a little milk, too?"

Gordon smiled. "No, doctor. We just need to use your cooler for a little bit. No one in until we're through, okay? I owe you." Then, turning to me and smiling his junkie smile: "Herr Gerstmann has a nice side business mixing up cocktails. Got some prize poppies growing in the back. Beautiful strains of sativa. Grows some of his own biological reagents, too, cooked in with the plant DNA. Extracts the funner compounds and mixes them with milk. Just like the old Cordova, right?"

"Milk ist gutt for growing bones," said Gerstmann.

"Opium is good for secret agents," said Gordon. "But not right now. Busy busy, like little bees. That's what we are. Come on, Jimmy. Can you walk? It's just here in the back."

I walked. Not happily, but I walked. Gordon guided me to a big silver door with an impressively large handle—a walk-in cooler, and one of three.

"Right here," he said. "Quick now."

"Quick ain't an option, Gordon," I said.

The door opened with a squeal and a hiss, and icy fog rolled out around our ankles. I peeked in and saw a rich man's fantasy of electronics and lab equipment, a table, chairs, a surgical table.

"Need to get you clean," Gordon said. "That's first. Then I'll see about your leg."

"You a doctor now, Rata?" I asked. "Expanding your skill set?"

"Best one you're gonna find in the next ten minutes," he said. "Gotta keep you in one piece for a few more days. Boss's orders. So get in and lay down on the table. Leave your bag and briefcase outside."

"The hell I will," I said.

He frowned at me. "I promise no one will touch it," he said. "But I'm going to fry any mites you might have on you, and the EMP will scramble your phones if they're inside. The cooler is shielded. We're totally secure." Gordon mimed a hurt face, a pouting lower lip. "What, you don't trust me, Jimmy?"

I laughed.

"Come on, bud," he said. "I'm your friend, remember? I'm the good guy."

"Then Lord help the wicked."

"Fuckin'-A right."

Gordon shut the door behind us and the cold was so delicious I wanted to suck it inside myself and hold it like an ice cube against my heart.

At Sunflower Field, I thought Gordon was there to kill me. It seemed appropriate. I always knew he was going to rise. We'd worked together for a time after Magnolia, then went our separate ways, stepped out together occasionally, when circumstances threw us back into each other's orbits. He'd always been a bright boy. Crooked as a bent nail. Had all the loyalty of a rented snake. A perfect OSS man. And though I hadn't kept a careful track of him in the years that passed between our dealings with the Castillo brothers in Magnolia and my eventual, final fall in Raton, I'd heard things. He'd become a field agent in his own right. Then a handler. A case officer. There'd always been the odor on him of manipulation from on high—of a special friend somewhere in management acting as the angel on his shoulder, but I'd never given that much thought. Knowing Gordon, I thought it more likely that he'd turned his every borrowed skill against his own people. Extorting and blackmailing his way into promotion after promotion by holding photos of his bosses in bed with schoolgirls, Dalmations, Hoover vacuum cleaners, or all three at once. He'd always kept to his legend as an investigative reporter. It was his true calling. Gordon always had been a man who loved nothing like he loved finding the truth of a thing—the uglier and more sordid the better. That love had served him so, so well.

I was in my cell and then, suddenly, he was there in my cell with me. The interrogators had broken me ages ago, but wouldn't let me go. Like dogs, they just *worried* me. Gnawed me to the bone. The questions never stopped, and though I wasn't holding out anything, they seemed to believe that I still had something to give. Some name. Some detail. I was a good rememberer. Always had been. Could hold entire conversations in my head forever, parrot 'em back unmussed. Knew languages, cants, was a helluva actor, as has been amply established. And so they didn't trust me. They'd turned me inside-out, but still thought I was hiding something. They combed my guts daily for it.

I was in my cell, swallowing blood, curled on the floor, resetting dislocated fingers with my teeth. I was probably crying. I did that a lot. If they'd been using the electrics on me especially. Or the memory drugs. All of it fucked me up. I thought Gordo was a hallucination. I thought he was an angel dressed in a devil's drag. I thought, briefly, that I'd finally died. That something inside me had finally let go and that he was my penance. My albatross. My Virgil.

I was in my cell and then Gordon was in my cell. Missing the one eye that the OSS doctors had pulled from his head to get at the recording gear he'd worn inside his skull when he was only an *actual* reporter. His eye patch was black as an empty socket. He was squatting over me. I could hear his fancy shoes squeak. He laid a hand on my shoulder and I screamed and tried to scramble away, but he held me there. He leaned down close. He put his lips right to my ear, close as a lover.

"We're going to kill them all, Jimmy," he said. "Everyone that done this to you. We're gonna fuck 'em right the hell up. You and me. I promise."

The table in Gerstmann's cooler was like lying on a slab of ice, and the EMP flash, when it hit me, tasted like chewing nickels and felt like I'd sloughed off a single layer of invisible skin.

Gordon was behind a console. "Shit," he said. "You're still broadcasting. What the fuck."

I squirmed out of my pants. My leg was bleeding, but the bandage had drunk up most of it. Gordon came at me dragging a tray of instruments behind him.

"Look," he said. "I can't give you anything for the pain. Can't afford to have your head messed up just now. I'm going to put a block on the area though while I work. When it comes off, you're either going to feel a little better or a whole lot worse."

"Wonderful," said me, then gritted my teeth and waited for the worst.

Gordon scissored off the bandage, exposed the area, clucked his tongue over the mess of me, then put my leg on an electric nerve block which, for the few minutes it was operating, was like a reprieve from the consequence of bad actions. I felt nothing as Gordo took the knife to me, working fast and with reasonable cleanliness, razoring through the stitches and dissolving the meat glue that Doc Holcomb had stuck me back together with, opening the wound back up and then digging into it with a probe, the tweezers, then pliers.

"Look at this," he said, and held up a little nugget of something he'd pulled out of me. He smudged off the blood and the goop with his thumb and then the sleeve of his jacket and showed me something about the size of an antibiotic capsule, densely packed with electronics when he cracked it open, shielded in lead foil.

"It's an RFID locator. They jammed it in your fucking leg, bru! Lojacked you." He shook his head. "That's hardcore."

I reached out and took it from him. Stared at it like there was mysteries in it, written upside down. So worried about the Captain's tails, and here, he hadn't needed to put a man on me at all. Had me broadcasting like a radio all the time. Which made them as *had* been following me the other side's heartbreakers for certain, which, I suppose, did answer one nagging question, at least. I thought about where I'd been. What I'd done. As far as I could think, my movements hadn't given anything away. I'd done nothing out of the ordinary. Except for coming here.

"Location only?" I asked.

"Yup. But pretty accurate. To within five feet or so, especially if the reader is close."

"Constant or pulsed?"

"Depends on the tracking program, but the signal is constant."

"How's the fail rate?"

Gordon shrugged. "It's not a long-term solution."

"So they break is what you're saying?"

"Everything breaks, Jimmy."

"Good enough," I said, laid the tracker down on the edge of the table and smashed it with a metal basin from the tray of instruments Gordon'd dragged over. Then I lay back down and closed my eyes. "Now close me back up and make it pretty. We have work to do."

For a junkie and a spy, Gordon made a pretty good nurse. His hands were steady. He was sober. Only caught him picking his nose once. All in all, I felt I had a reasonable chance of surviving his care. And the mercy of the nerve block was sweet—so much so that I had in me a biting fear of him switching it off and the pain rooting in home again.

"I had a tail on me when I left Miss Kitty's this morning," I said. "Probably had one when I left the bunkhouse yesterday, too. I shook 'em at the Castle, put my face in front of one of the Captain's watchers so he'd hear where I was and not worry over me, but I need them all gone for good. I'd thought the Captain might've had someone on me, but—"

Gordon shook his head. "No. You've got a lot of fans right now, Jimmy. A lot of people wondering about where you go when you're not at home. But the Captain is overextended. The recent . . . unpleasantness has stretched him badly."

"Jesus Christ, Gordon. Which unpleasantness do you mean? It's not like we're experiencing any shortage."

"The unstuckness of everything," he said. "The falling apart-ness."

"The Abjuration, you mean?"

He nodded, stuck a threaded needle in his mouth while he held sponges on my leg with one hand and rummaged for something with the other. It reminded me that there were words that Gordon didn't like saying—his fear being that speaking them aloud would draw them close. Make them real. It was a childish superstition, of which he had many, each more colorful and ridiculous than the last. "A lot of Barrow's people are walking around right now with their brains leaking out of their ears. He just doesn't have the bodies to keep a team on you. Hence the electronics, which was a dick move, for sure, but maybe the only option he had."

"So then who's following me?"

Gordon said nothing. He bent to his darning and his hand moved quickly.

"Gordon, seriously. Who is it?"

"Clarence Doolittle," he said. "Your friend. Or his people, anyway. Which are nominally Percy Blythe's people, but really, they're his people. All of them. Young, vicious, loyal. Main-body OSS from the boots up. Hate 'em all. Least fun crowd you've ever seen."

"Well what do you have for assets then?"

"Me?" Gordon asked, glancing up. "You're kidding, right?"

I pushed myself up on one elbow. "The boss said you'd be able to give me what I needed, Gordon. What I need right now is some peace and distance from them that appear to want me in the dirt."

"That list," he said, "seems to be growing longer every day."

"Perils of a life so full of whiskey and deviltry."

"I mean, Barrow? He's supposed to be your best friend right now and even he shot you for being annoying."

I rolled my head on my shoulders and tried not to look down at what Gordon was doing. "The Captain shot me for not being shot enough to pass for a survivor of a massacre. Again, perils of also being very fucking good at what I do." I stared at the side of Gordon's face, the blade of his nose, the faint pinkening of scar tissue extending beyond the edges of his patch. "So do you have a counter-surveillance unit?" I asked. "Someone we can use to scrape the watchers off me for a couple days?"

Gordon chuckled. "Bud, I've got eighty-seven dollars in my pocket, my service automatic, and a few weird friends. You want CoIntel support? How 'bout I buy you one of those fake-nose-and-glasses things."

I sighed, lay back again and closed my eyes. "What about a ride?"

"Now that I can help with," Gordon said. "Got me a Cadillac, because I'm *fancy*. Where are we going?"

"You volunteering to ride shotgun, Rata?"

"I'm your man, Jimmy. Always have been. What do we have to do?"

I explained my plan to him while he finished putting me back together and thumbed sticky painkilling and antibiotic patches onto my skin, all in a row down my thigh. He warned me before switching off the nerve block. I bit down on the inside of my cheek and told him I'd try to be brave.

"I won't tell if you cry," he said.

"Bullshit," I muttered.

"Yeah, you're right. I'd put that shit on my blog. Sucks to be you."

I held my breath. He flipped the switch. It wasn't as bad as I thought it would be, but Gordon still had to help me put my pants back on, which was humiliating enough. He had a car parked behind Gerstmann's—a gas-burning Cadillac Seville, as promised, of boxy lineage, cream over brown, with a blue velour interior decorated in brass thumbtacks and images of Mexican saints. He helped me hobble the distance, laid me down in the backseat, staring up at the ripped headliner, and, ten minutes later, we were pulling up in front of the kudzu field and tumble-down shack that Arthur Reginald Molesworth had once called home.

"This the place?" he asked.

I told him that it was. He said that it spoke poorly of the paychecks collected by the Captain's irregulars and I told him I was walking proof of the man's parsimony.

"Well, *limping*," Gordon added.

"Shut up."

"Stitched my initials into your leg, Jimmy. Just so you never forget me."

"Park somewhere inconspicuous," I said. "Let's get this done."

I carried my briefcase and the backpack I'd picked up at the market. Gordon offered to carry me, but I just took his arm instead, walking like his bride. We hurried across the yard to the porch, to the rattly stairs, to the door, locked but only in theory.

"Check," said Gordon.

I gave the street a quick scan and saw no one paying undue attention. No king's men. No beeps, though they'd been crawling everywhere during the drive. "Clear," I said.

Gordon laid his weight into the door and had to hold it up to keep it from collapsing inward. We both ducked inside and he propped the door back into the frame.

"That's not going to fool anyone," he said.

"Not going to matter. Come on."

Inside, the room was the same as when I'd last left it. Empty. Dirty. Smelling of abandonment and shit. I scuffed along the floor until I found the edge of Reggie's trapdoor—the entire square of it laying flush to the floor.

"There's probably a trick to this," I said.

Gordon walked a fast circle around it, looked to the four corners of the room. Then he raised a leg and slammed his heel down along one edge. The opposite side popped up, fell and landed crooked.

"Trick found," he said.

"And if it'd been booby-trapped?" I asked, thinking about the last door I'd gone through.

He bent down and lifted the cover free. "I was hoping it would only kill you. Then I could take the rest of the day off and get high."

There was a hole. A ladder, which would've been murder on my leg, but it was short and I was able to go down it hopping with one foot. Then darkness.

"You have a flashlight?" I asked.

"In the car," said Gordon.

I swore, dug in my pockets, found a box of matches and lit one. "Holy shit," I said.

Gordon's eyes bulged. "Look, man. I have seen some weird shit in my time, but this . . ."

The match burned out. I lit another. Gordon found a light switch and turned it on, flooding the single room with antiseptic white light and the humming, from somewhere, of batteries quietly draining.

The room was square, bunkered in cement, about the size of a cheap motel room. It was decorated in a homey fashion—a bed mounded with covers, a writing desk all snowdrifted in papers and hard-bound books splayed open, an old-fashioned, boxy rotary phone sitting in an open drawer. There was a kitchen area with scrubbed pans hung from hooks, a sunny yellow teapot, and folded tea towels on a sideboard.

But every inch of the walls were covered in pictures of horses. Pictures carefully razored from books, torn from magazines, done in paint and mounted in frames. There were amateurish sketches in pencil and black charcoal on onionskin paper that'd obviously been traced from other pictures. Old photos of men on horses, of soldiers gathered with their horses, of automatic horses and meat horses and, repeated over and over again, a younger, heartier Arthur Reginald Molesworth astride his dear Persephone or standing beside his dear Persephone or rubbing down his dear Persephone. There was a fully kitted-out military saddle on a sawhorse, Remington repeater in its scabbard, saber in its own, the stirrups dragging on the ground. Leaning imperiously against one wall was a lance—white, ringed in red—still tipped with its directional explosive charge. And on the wall opposite the bed, a horse's taxidermied head, mounted and wreathed in black flowers, glass eyes staring crookedly out into the great beyond. Below it, a brass plaque that read simply: Persephone.

"Fuck me, Jimmy. This is a murder house. We're totally going to be murdered here and turned into skin suits. I'm telling you, this is a bad, weird place." Gordon was turning in fast, spastic circles, his voice squeaky with panic. With goofy, pointless, ridiculous fear, considering some of the places he'd been and the things he'd seen. I told him to shut up, but I felt it, too—the sudden, irrational feeling that the damn horse was watching us. That *all* the horses were watching us and judging us. That they knew what was coming. That Reggie was going to come stepping out of some hidden panel in the wall wearing only a moldering horse head and carrying a honed axe.

"Quick's the action, motherfucker," I said to him, tore my eyes from the walls and from Persephone's dead eyes, and walked to the desk. I took a deep breath. Behind me, I heard Gordon continuing to scuff around in circles, muttering under his breath. I laid a hand to the phone's receiver in its cradle and dug up the number I'd memorized from the night desk cheat sheet I'd found. *P. Horse Farm, A.R.M.* I picked up the receiver, took the flattened coffee cup from my back pocket, fluffed it out and fitted it over the mouthpiece, making a bell out of it that would distort and echo my voice just enough to cover any roughness in tone or accent. I thought about the time I'd spent with Reggie—of the nights he'd spent at his table near my piano at Miss Kitty's, the trip to Great Times, our conversations in the dark. I needed the tone and tempo of his voice, the taste of it in my mouth. The way he chose his words. The ruff of his mustache. I cleared my throat. With my free hand I drew my automatic. I closed my eyes. I said, "Persephone."

I said, "Per*se*phone . . ."

I said, "Per-SE-phon-ee."

I dialed the number. It rang. And rang. Then there was a voice that I recognized immediately as Jemma's.

Thank you for calling Persephone Horse Farms. We're not able to come to the phone right now, but if you'd like to schedule an appointment, please leave your name, contact information, and preferred times after the beep. And have a horse-tastic day!

"Right," I said. "Ahem. Your Chemist, gents? I've found him. Or rather, found where he will be. A worthy prize, I hope, because he's not going to be in the easiest of locations for a proper assault. Not without cavalry, you know. Horses, that's what you need. My Persephone, for one. But he's being moved, and soon. Out to Kansas with the dregs and criminal elements, on train 1066, headed for Goodland and points beyond. Thought you might like to know. Or that our Piano Man might want to know, as I've heard he's planning something in a rescuing sort of fashion. Again, that's train 1066, headed for Goodland, Kansas. Set to depart sometime in the next four days. And now I've—"

With my gun aimed skywardly, I pulled the trigger once, dropped the receiver, yanked the cord from the body of the phone. Sighed, and said under my breath, "Sorry, Reggie."

I turned and Gordon was frozen, crouched, one hand on his own gun, eyes big as plates.

"Warn a man!" he snapped.

"Snap the banger off the end of that lance," I said, pointing with my pistol at the knight's arms leaning against the wall. "And grab that backpack for me."

He did. I took out the two bottles of gas, uncapped them, soaked the tee-shirt with a measure from one, laid it over the papers and books on the desk, put the explosive head from the lance in the middle of it, then dumped the rest of that bottle over the desk and the floor.

"Mind your shoes," I said to Gordon. "Get up the ladder. We're done here."

He went. I handed my briefcase up to him, then the other bottle and the backpack, then dragged myself back up the rungs one-legged. Caught my breath at the top. Wiped my hands on the lapels of my jacket.

"Other bottle up here," I said to Gordon, then dug in my pockets, took out my matches and handed them over. "Burn it. Whole thing."

"Why me?"

"You can probably run faster than I can. Give me a head start, okay?"

And I went out the door without looking back, hobbling in the direction of Gordon's Cadillac with my briefcase in my hand. When La Rata went sprinting past me, I knew it was done. He had the car running when I got there and fell into the back seat. We both heard the boom of the explosive detonating.

"We have another stop to make now," I said.

"Something else to light on fire?"

As he pulled out into the slow progress of traffic, I opened my briefcase, took out the regulator's paperwork, and flipped to the smudgy page dealing with Arthur Reginald Molesworth.

"Not quite," I said. There was a second address listed on the page. A street address a couple miles away. "Now we just have to make sure that Reggie doesn't come back to life."

The address led us to a partially reclaimed stretch of 6th Street where the Royalty construction crews were re-growing houses as fast as the demolition teams could dissolve the old, dead and crippled ones. It was still a little Wild West-ish, with a lot of old bungalos and ranches with scavenged plywood over the windows and doors, the blacktop chuckholed with blast scars and yards full of piled bricks, scorched timber or the damp insides of smart houses piled like mounds of rotten meat. There was a fuzz in the air of rogue nanites clouding together in their techny-sexual attempts to trade information. I could still read the cryptic spray-painted sigils of search teams who'd combed the wreckage when it was still fresh and smoking—faded now from the acid rain and scouring elements, but legible. Knots of scabby run-around kids in pulpy, homebrew body armor and rebreather masks ranged up and down the shattered sidewalks scraping the heads of aluminum bats on the broken cement like match heads.

The battle police had a hardpoint at the corner, about ten houses down from Reggie's neat, boxy ranch, which was good because it meant the cell reception was probably good and there might even be the fizzing remains of a wifi network. Double-good because it also appeared unmanned—a playground for the local toughs who'd climbed it to plant flags and spray-bomb the mini-dishes with smiley faces, anarchy signs and the logos of long-gone sneaker companies.

I pointed out Reggie's house to Gordon as we passed and told him to circle around again, park at the corner and get out.

"Check the house," I said. "Quietly."

"Because you can't walk?"

"Yup."

"Not because you expect me to be walking into a trap?"

"Nope."

Gordon stared at me a long moment. "I liked you more un-shot. Allowed me to indulge my essentially lazy nature."

"I liked me more un-shot, too," I said. "Make it quick."

He did. While he was about it, I rummaged through his glove compartment, checked under the seats and inside the headliner, tapped the door panels from the inside. When I didn't find anything illegal, incriminating or untoward, I assumed the car must've been so recently stolen that Gordo hadn't yet had the time to leave his criminal effluent all over it. There was no way he'd become clean and professional enough to have a car that wasn't a rolling indictment of every bad habit and foul impulse that drove him.

When I saw him coming back down the street with his hands in his pockets and his lips pursed for whistling, I was reminded that he was never the greatest spy that had lived neither.

"Someone's been in the house recently," he said as he climbed back in behind the wheel. "Dishes in the sink. Bed's mussed. Doors and windows are all locked."

"Any notion of *how* recent?"

Gordon shrugged. "Didn't exactly leave his day planner out for me to find, Jimmy. No way to tell. Within the week for sure. Probably the last couple days."

I swore under my breath, doffed my hat, and took a handroll from the bag.

"He might have been revised," Gordon said. "Lot of that going around lately."

"Might could be," I said, "but on this particular point, I require a bit more in the way of certainty. The Captain spent two days trying to collect as many of his people as he could after the Abjuration started. Trying to preserve as much of his continuity as he could. Reggie was never found. The Captain's people looked plenty hard, far as I know. But in order for my cover to remain intact and for me to stay above snakes, I have to be sure that Arthur Reginald Molesworth stays gone."

As things would turn out, I probably should have phrased that differently.

I asked for my matches back from Gordo, lit my smoke and rested my head against the dash.

"Now that your tracker has gone dead, Barrow is going to be looking for you. And your pal Doolittle is still abroad, too."

The complicating truths of both of those things I knew, full and well, and said so. "The trick is to get found now by one and not the other. If Percy orders Clarence to lift me, all of this has been for nothing."

"Clarence is really good, bud. He's a corker, and he's got assets to burn. He wants you bad enough . . ."

"I know."

I took a drag, blew it out, handed the cigarette to Gordon, who smoked silently for a minute then handed it back to me.

"I have an idea," he said.

"I'd love to hear it."

"It's not elegant."

"When have you ever been?"

Gordon laughed, drummed his hands on the wheel. "Super spy shit, man," he said. "I got this. You got a phone?"

"I have a selection of them."

"Then give me one and get to limping. I'll stake the house here. You find a lift back to wherever you have to go, do your thing, get back into the Captain's vision, whatever. And by the time you get there, I promise that I'll have caused enough trouble that the OSS will have bigger things to think about than your dumb, gimpy ass."

I asked him what he was going to do, and he just smiled at me, plucked the cigarette from between my lips and stuck it in his own mouth. "Watch me work, Jimmy. Watch me fucking work."

I gave Gordon one of my phones. We traded numbers and promised to keep in touch. I eased my way out of the car, hobbled a block and then leaned against a canted street sign until an independent hack with a buckboard full of choreboys, hooly dregs, and rusticated remnants come up out of the gray places heaved into view, all pulled along by a patched warhorse and two street-cleaning robots. He was driving a route, the hack, from the outskirts to the kingdom's heart and back again, twice daily, but it would take me close to Colfax Avenue and the Castle, so that was good enough. I paid my nickel, hopped onto the board, hauled myself through the huffery and stink of broken-down men, and found enough room to sit with my bum leg out straight and my hat down over my eyes, trusting in the natural camouflage of penury and uglification to keep me unnoticed until the ride came to a complete stop.

☢

Getting me out of Sunflower Field had been a trick—requiring a certain imperiousness and sense of entitlement which Gordon was perfect at affecting when it suited his purposes.

"Do you know who this is?" he'd bellowed at anyone who'd listen. "Do you know who you have here? This is Jimmy Fields, you idiots. Jimmy motherfucking *Fields*. And I have orders to take him from you, but I swear to fucking god, you dimwit, thumb-sucking, masochistic little twerps had better clean him the fuck up and have him looking pretty as his goddamn graduation day picture before I walk him out that front door, or there are certain men in management—men who *remember* Jimmy Fields and what he did for the cause—who will make it their goal to memorize every single one of your names and bring down such an ocean of shit upon your heads that you will never, *ever* see the beach. You understand me? You hearing what I am saying to you right now? Get me medics, get me housekeeping, get me the graduating class of the nearest goddamn beautician's college—whatever you have to do. You will make this man feel like a *princess* for the next thirty minutes and hand him to me so shining and pretty that I'll want to kiss him right on the mouth."

The trick is to not rush. The trick is to demand impossible things. To act like every other person in the world is a stupid, worming, minimum-wage button-pusher as un-acquainted with the machinations of the wise and intelligent men who direct their daily toil as a slug is with the higher realms of quantum mechanics. Gordon had no papers giving him permission to take me out of one of the OSS's most favorite oubliettes. No recognizable mandate to remove me from the care of my torturers. He had nothing but one name—one *big* name—and that he saved like the last bullet in a gun.

In the meantime, all Gordon had was Gordon's rage, Gordon's towering sense of superiority, Gordon's deep and passionate love for pushing around the craven and the dumb.

"Thirty minutes. That's what you have. Twenty-nine minutes now."

He spoke as he held me up—one arm wrapped around me, holding me under the arms while I rolled my head against him and smeared blood onto his suit. He walked me straight out the door of my cell and down a hallway, hollering and blusterating to any and all, and when he reached the security station where transfers were made in and out of the Secure Housing Unit where I was kept, all the management of Sunflower Field was waiting on him, arrayed in a phalanx and ready for war.

The trick is to do the unexpected.

"Here," he'd said, and heaved me into the arms of the most senior-looking officer. "Clean him up. Make it look like you haven't spent the past two years beating the ever-loving shit out of one of the best undercover men this company has ever had."

"I'm sorry," said the officer. "Mister . . .?"

And Gordon had stepped back, folded his arms, fixed his one eye on the man who had deigned speak to him. "Whatever this man has told you," he'd said. "Whatever words have come out of his mouth. Every syllable, every burp, every grunt. You need to forget it right now." He passed a hand slowly in front of his eyes. "Wipe it away, just like that. You don't know him. You never saw him. You never saw me. The two years you spent torturing and confining Jimmy Fields? They are *gone* from your books five minutes after we walk out the front door. Every man who touched him, every man who talked to him, every man who was ever in a *room* with him has the choice between voluntary retirement, effective yesterday, or staying at their desks and explaining to Nimrod Kane precisely why they have been complicit in holding one of his level 1 case officers in this dirty fucking hole in the ground for the past two years. There'll be a team from the Falls Directorate visiting tomorrow, 9am sharp. Director Kane will be with them. So will you be here to meet him, mister . . .?"

The officer had crumpled like he was made of paper. Like Gordon had come to him with a basket of kittens and a can of gasoline and offered him two choices: compliance or the match.

One name was all Gordon'd had and one name was all he'd needed to send the small and the meat-cow ignorant scurrying before him.

I don't know how he spent the next half-hour, but I was taken away, bathed, mended, studded with a year's wages in analgesic and antibiotic patches, shot up with vitamins. My teeth were brushed, my hair cut and combed. I was put in a fresh suit of clothes (short at the wrists and ankles, but clean) and, at the end of it— twenty-eight minutes later—the manager of the Sunflower Field facility stepped into the room, shooed everyone else away, and said to me, "We'd like to apologize, Mr. Fields. The courage and forti- tude you've shown while in our care has been an inspiration to all of us who've pledged our loyalty to the OSS, and we will use your example to further refine our techniques for information gathering in the future."

And then he'd leaned close, his eyes darting around a room that he must've known was bugged. "Please," he whispered. "I've got eighteen years with the company, Mr. Fields. I have a family. A son. If you could mention to Director Kane that I never had any idea who you were—"

Two years, twenty-nine days inside, nothing more than an hour's exercise each day, walking in a circle, 'round-and-'round, and it still took three housekeepers to pull me off the manager. When Gordon Navarro came striding in, saw me being held back, blood in my teeth and on my knuckles, and the manager on the floor, choking on his own teeth, he clucked his tongue like a mother hen.

"Oh, Jimmy," he said. "That was somewhat less than gracious. You ready to go now?"

I spat a gob of the man's ear onto the floor and nodded my head.

We walked straight out the front door of the place, Gordon with one arm around me to steady me. It was a cold day—the sky hard and blue and the ground crusted with frost. My breath steamed. My chest ached.

"Just keep walking, Jimmy," Gordon hissed. "We're almost clear. Just keep walking, okay? Don't fall now."

I did not fall.

Ten minutes after I'd climbed out of Gordon's Cadillac, a bomb threat had been phoned into the City and County building. It came through a desk chief in the OSS records office: biological agent thought to be in the ventilation system, information from a solid source. The desk officer had hit the panic button and the whole place was evacuated out into the sunshine and greenery of Civic Center Park like someone'd opened a tap on a keg full of government leeches and royalty men.

Which might've been nice, for them. Cause for a picnic lunch or maybe nipping off down the block for a cold pint. Certainly what I would've done. But them as labor honestly for the King and crown and the OSS besides are a humorless, wet-blanket bunch, and they were punished for their selfless loyalty when, five minutes after that, purple gas was spotted rising from a sewer grate on Bannock Street, which crossed the foot of the park. The panic it caused in those put on the street was remarkable. It took an hour for the King's men to restore order with sticks and barricade foam. Kansan jayhawker elements were immediately blamed for the dog-dirty assault on the pillars of civic governance, but that became a tougher story to sell when, fifteen minutes after the first call, the 6th Avenue home of a private legal office led by one Percival Blythe was hit by a second gas attack—canisters thrown by hand through first floor windows, no suspects apprehended.

As it turned out, the gas used in both events was nothing more than marking smoke. Mildly irritating when inhaled, but basically harmless. No one knew that, though, until after Percy's entire office had been decon'd and all occupants (including Percy himself) thrown into the back of an OSS emergency NBC response truck, stripped naked, hosed down, shot up with atropine and adrenaline, and filled full of nanite hunter-killers through full-face ventilators.

That was Gordon's picayune notion of a distraction. Of sowing panic in the ranks of the enemy. It'd taken him two phone calls—one to that desk chief who was already on the dime of the boss, another to a small-time tribe of Russian gangsters who owed him favors for inglorious deeds done in the past. They'd dropped the purple smoke bomb into the sewer on Bannock Street, made their way to 6th and filled Percy's office with the same. To them, it was a lark. Good for a laugh and a way to while away a plummy afternoon. For me, hopping off the board and stepping out into the riotous agitation, it was the space I needed to make it cleanly to the Nob in time for happy hour.

Hippo was behind the bar. I recognized every regular sitting there and was sure that none of them were informants for Clarence Doolittle, Percy Blythe or the OSS, which had at least *some* standards for physical and mental fitness that no frequenter of the Nob Hill Inn would ever meet.

I knew that the Captain's people would be looking for me. With their tracker dead, they would have to do it the hard way, but, knowing my tastes and proclivities, the Nob would be one of the first places they'd check. I didn't know how long it would take them to get the message from Reggie. Or from me pretending to be Reggie. I didn't know how long it would take them to pass that information to Lee and Finch, for Lee and Finch to pass it to the Legion of Terror, for the L.O.T. to be convinced that wisdom dictated an assault on a moving and guarded train in order to recover their man. But according to the boss's phone call, I'd had a lean five days to get the Chemist off that train and back into the Captain's hands, and I'd already burned through the best part of two of them. The clock was ticking.

Still, sometimes a man has to follow his gut. And what made sense to me then was a drink and a smoke and a breather from the action of the day, so I asked for the one, lit up the other, fell onto a stool around the horseshoe curve of the bar, and asked Hippo how he'd been keeping since last we'd been in each other's company.

He said he'd been well. I asked him if anyone had been around asking after me, and he said I was suffering from inflated notions of my own importance, which made me laugh. It was easy there, you know? With Hippo, the smashed and the fuddled with which he surrounded himself, the sour smell of last night's beer and the soft haze of smoke pooling around the lights. I felt as if I were teetering on the edge of a hole, its bottom stuffed with pillows and teddy bears. It was a hole, sure. But hitting the bottom of it didn't look so bad from where I was standing and I wondered who, really, would be harmed by my just throwing myself in? Eventually, another abjuration would come along—and another and another—'til a revision would finally catch up with me, inevitable as hangovers and damnation, and I'd forget who I was, where I'd been, where I was going. I'd be just another casualty then. Another old soldier broken beyond anyone's reasonable use and peaceful in my own mind for not recalling a lick of the days when, once, I'd been tasked with the saving of the world.

I sipped my whiskey and smelled gasoline on my hands, closed my eyes and tried not to think about how it'd gotten there. On the radio behind the bar, Bob Dylan was singing "Not Dark Yet," which was one of Hippo's favorite songs. We'd spent a night once talking about nothing but that. Not favorite songs in general, but just that one. Just one song. I'd left lit like a roman candle—I recall that. Smiling so wide that I caught the moon in my teeth. That'd been about a week before I threw my lot in with the Captain.

"Fuck it," I said to my drink. "I ain't done just yet."

I waved Hippo back over, slid an eagle across the bar and told him to use it to dent my tab, then asked him about the packages I'd left with him—the suitcase full of dirty gold and the box full of boom jelly that he'd been sitting on for me since the events at the garage—and he said they were right where I'd left them, untouched and unbotherated, because he was a good man and wise and, further, wouldn't for a hundred dollars lay hands to anything that I'd touched first.

"Never know what's gonna be full of snakes, do I?" he said. "Or what's going to blow up in my face."

"Smart," said me, tapping a finger on my temple. "The world is a strange and a perilous place these days, Hippolite, my brother, and I do appreciate your discretion and generous nature. Speaking of all that, do you still have that truck I gave you?"

He did, and I told him I needed to borrow it back—promising that I'd return it unharmed just as soon as I could and knowing that every word of that was a lie.

I was poking around his cooler, trying to figure the easiest way to get the gold and the case full of Cyclot-8 back into the truck with one leg and no help when help suddenly presented itself.

"Bunch of little people here to see you," Hippo said, sticking his head through the door.

"Little people? You mean midgets?"

"Kids. Of a sort. One of 'em's calling herself Tuesday and has an axe."

"Reinforcements," said me, under my steaming breath, the smoke of my living twining up through my smiling teeth like proof of my devilish heart.

Hippo blinked at me. "The world you see when you wake up in the morning is a lot different than the one I see, isn't it."

I smiled. "Not so much. It's just more . . . flavorsome."

"That's kinda just another word for different, isn't it?"

"Guess so."

"I always thought you were just a drunk and a card cheat."

I stood straight, slapped my hands together and squared my shoulders. "I am both of those things, Hippo," I said. "I'm just some *other* things, too."

Out in the bar, a deputation from the Ragamuffin Army was waiting on me. There were three of them, chattering away to each other in something that only barely passed as English and hungrily eyeing the liquor and the pockets of the gathered rummies who, for the most part, were recoiling from them, as though unfettered youth was anathema to whatever little numb places they'd carved out for themselves at the Nob. Or maybe it was just the goatish smell of the starveling little monsters.

Tuesday twirled her axe when she saw me. "You's not dead yet, topper," she said. "That's me losing a fair wager then."

"Who was it betting on me still being aloft and breathing?"

"Him that sent me to fetch you."

"Well," said me. "That's a vote of confidence in me then, isn't it?"

"Yeah, you'd think that, but he only bet me a nickel. Anyway, he's arching for you. Sent usn's to find you, gather you up and bring you home." She tapped her axe against her leg. "Willing or no."

One of the other two monsters standing with her—one with a strawberry mark on the evil half of his face and a leather jacket two sizes too big—piped up then. "Said to give us each five dollars, too."

"For our troubles," agreed the third.

"Shut it, Shortcake," Tuesday said without looking at him. "We's working and will comport ourselves like perfessionals."

"Perfessionals need cash, Toos," said the one called Shortcake.

"To get paid, like," said the other. "Fat stacks."

She spun then and, like a flash, had the pink blade of her axe laid gentle and precise right along the unmarked cheek of Shortcake. "You'll get my dick in your eye, you speak again that ain't saying 'yessir' or 'nosir' to me, read?"

"Army," said me. "I may have a solution to your cash flow problems. How you feel about helping me load a truck?"

Shortcake had eyes only for the blade tickling his eyelashes, but the other had presence enough to spit at my shoes. "Manual labor is beneath them as is smart enough to steal and rob, geezer. Go fuck you an' your truck."

I shrugged. "What you'll be loading was stolen by me, so that counts, right? Or is that too abstract to meet the tenets of your manifesto?"

The little monster looked at me like I had squirrels in my hair.

"An eagle apiece to them as pitches in," I said. "Cargo is this way. Truck is around the back. And no one gets axed who doesn't deserve it."

The Captain, as it turned out, was on the move again—spreading himself thinner and thinner as a ward against the troubles of eggs and baskets. So rather than the bunkhouse, the haunted offices or his fallback safehouse (two of the three of which I had not, at that point, even seen), Tuesday directed me out into Commerce City where the feed pumps, black labs and grow houses made a maze of a place that, even before it had been eaten by history, had already been a maze.

I drove slow. The truck, with the Cyclot in the back, was a moving bomb just waiting for an excuse to go off. But no matter how many times I explained this to the children, they pounded the dashboard, called me grandma and asked if I wanted them to get out and push. I'd ordered all three of them to ride up front with me in the cab because having them rattling around in the back with the gold and explosives had seemed like a gloriously poor idea for more reasons than I had fingers to count them, but after long enough in their company, the notion of having them all blown to a fine pink mist seemed not altogether a bad thing.

Finally, we came to a crumbling red-brick lump of a place that'd once been a voting machine warehouse for the city (back when the city was a city and voting was a thing that people did), but was now the headquarters and secret lair of the Human Liberation Front.

Well, not *secret* exactly. They had a giant H+ flag that flapped from the roof. At street level, the walls were tagged with biohumanist graffiti and animatic propaganda posters advocating the joys of transhumanism. And on the front door was a giant biohazard trefoil wearing a pair of bunny ears and the warning, in six-inch hazard-yellow caps: YOU WILL BE CONVERTED.

The HLF were pranksters, mostly. Rhizome cowboys and aberrant geneticists into extreme genome tinkering and preaching a deliberately muddled gospel of mutantism, miscegenation, and biological impurity. They'd once made the Wells Fargo building grow an enormous and pendulous pair of tits. They'd once released a thousand miniature shuggoths into the wind, all stuffed with candy like piñatas, and handed out sticks to the people. They'd once thrown a parade out front of the Castle where everyone had to come dressed as their favorite engineered nuclease series and more than 500 people had shown up, his Stevenness included, in the drag of a 33-34 amino acid TAL effector.

Anyway, they were more than a trifle odd. But they were also quite trig and talented makers, and effective psychological terrorists besides, and the Captain, as was his way, liked collecting freaks and so had made a temporary home there among them.

We went in the front door, the Ragamuffins and me, through a false-front that appeared for all the world like the hard-scrabble offices of a local benevolent society, complete with precarious stacks of leaflets, dirty coffee mugs, scavenged desks covered in animatic stickers for local bands and transhumanist organizations, a corkboard with offers of housecleaning services, notices about candle-light vigils and lost dogs, and a poster on one wall with a kitten hanging from a tree branch that said *Hang in there, baby*.

There was a closet door at the back, and Tuesday went through it without hesitating. It led into a closet full of office supplies which was only a closet until she did something clever with her hands and the back wall of it snicked and hissed and drew back with a slight pop like an air lock equalizing pressures.

Beyond it was a real office—a bare room with one desk in the middle of the floor and one man behind it wearing an ear-piece and holding an automatic rifle across his knees. Tuesday saluted him with her axe, but did not slow, kept right on moving past him, to the single door behind him.

"Watch the mines," he said, looking at me, and I looked down and saw the floor dotted with pressure triggers over which Tuesday and her boys skipped without the least bit of concern. I went careful, my breathing thick, and hit the far door with a gasp of relief, nearly falling through it onto a factory floor of sorts—high-ceilinged and glaringly lit.

I limped along, following the trail cut by the Ragamuffins as they wound through the busyness and loudness, cutting around a pod of chugging 3D printers here and a sling-lift gantry crane there hoisting something that looked like an enormous blower motor but was doubtless something far more sinister. We ducked under tarps and went around safety gates that'd been pegged down around gaping places in the floor and, following jumpily around a showering waterfall of sparks from a high-mounted industrial cut-em-upper somewhere, I nearly walked straight into Logue Ranstead, who stood amid a knot of tee-shirted, work-booted, tail-having, furry-bodied, occasionally scaled, occasionally slug-headed, occasionally winged or polydactylated young men and women staring intently at computer screens, glowing tablets, or old-fashioned-y scroll-printed papers. Logue himself was jumpsuited, his arm strapped into a tele-sense waldo, wearing some sort of magical, complicated, and steely multiocular octopus on his head—staring into the invisible ether and, like as not, doing terrible things to whatever lived there.

I must've stared, gape-mouthed. I might've said something like "Erp," or "Hurnff" because one of the women standing near to Logue laid a careful hand on his shoulder, interrupting him in the middle of saying things so un-Logue-Ranstead-ian that, had I been blind and far, far stupider than I am, I would've thought coming from a different man entirely.

"The isometries are all fucked, is the problem here. You have a 12-bar motion chain and not enough ternary links. If the topologies overlap, you'll have a . . . What?"

He looked up, pushed the octopus clear of his face, and turned enough to spy me gawping like a rube at his fanciness. His face went through several rapid, stunning contortions of expression before finally settling on its default air of vaguely annoyed in general and specifically disgusted with me.

"There is so much in this world that you will never understand, Duncan," he said. "I'd explain it to you if I had a thousand years to spare. Now fuck off and let the grownups work."

I walked on, afeared first of being lost and left behind but also finding myself, for one of the very few times in my life, completely at a loss for words.

The Captain had encamped himself deeper within the building, free of the clatter of the shop floor and in among, one presumed, the management. When I finally caught up with the Ragamuffins and came staggering in, I found him sitting behind a desk laid with a nest of cell phones and paper maps, legal pads, snacks, file folders, a hand grenade, and a laptop computer that looked heavy as six bricks with wired-in cabling that hung down from a hole cut in the ceiling. He was wearing a tee-shirt—black with FUCK A MUTANT written on it in the same shouty yellow caps as was emblazoned on the front door—plus boots and braces. His gun belts hung from the back of the chair in which he sat.

He shouted my name when first I stumbled across his threshold, but didn't look up from stabbing spastically at the keyboard with two fingers. Shouted, "Tuesday, my girl!" Shouted, "And you other two!"

Then he said nothing. Went back to typing. If that was what you could call it.

I waited politely. Tuesday stood at a ferocious attention. Shortcake scratched at his face.

"Captain?" I ventured finally, and he held up a finger for silence, which cut his typing speed in half. A man squeezed into the office past us and held out a loose sheaf of papers to the Captain.

"Signal intercepts," the man said. "Latest from Three Wide and the border runners."

The Captain extended a hand, snapped his fingers, snatched the papers away when they were presented to him. "You're a prince," he said. "A prince among men."

The man nodded. He had gray-furred rabbit ears growing out of either side of his head, almond eyes black as pools of oil, and too many fingers. When he withdrew, I smelled pressurized oxygen and zinc solution on him like a hot day at the beach.

"Army," said the Captain all of a sudden. "You found my man."

"Second place we looked," said Tuesday.

"Where was the first?" I asked, aside to Tuesday.

"Hook shop."

"Yeah, that makes sense."

The Captain cleared his throat. "Complications?" he asked. "Troubles?"

"Legation," said Tuesday. "Streets are getting hairy. Beeps are rolling heavy-armed. Gas attack on the C-and-C had everyone in a fright."

"Someone hit Percy's office, too," said the Captain. "I would've paid an honest dollar to be there to see that."

I kept my face neutral. Not even a twinkle in my prettiest eye.

"Your topper here has a lot of people snooping on him, too," Tuesday added. "Walkers and watchers on all the cobbles." She sniffed. "It's almost like he's important or something."

"Scored me a nosey," said the one that wasn't Shortcake.

"Did you now?" asked the Captain.

Tuesday scowled at her man, then looked back. "O-man prowl team. Closing on the boozer where this'n was getting his tongue wet and wasting our precious time. We in'ercepted them in the alley, demanded a toll, iced 'em when they reached."

"How many?"

"Just two. Shock sticks only. Just like you ordered, sir."

"That's a good girl. What's our rule?"

"Only perish them that deserves it."

"That's right."

"We got off clean after that. Fetched him. No tails. Your topper is off their grid for the now."

The Captain nodded, dismissed the urchins, told them not to steal anything on their way out, and bid me sit. He asked me how the leg was feeling and I told him it felt like I'd been shot in it, and he said that was good.

"We got him, Duncan," he said. "The Chemist."

"You already grabbed him?" I asked, feigning wonder tinged with relief.

"No, we *found* him," the Captain said, tossing aside the signal intercepts and planting his elbows amid the wreckage of the desk in front of him. "Know where he is and where he'll be going. So you're on. The last ride of Harry Plum."

"I don't exactly like the way you say that."

He waved a hand at me. "Don't act like you're afraid of dying," he said. "Hell, man, you died just a few days ago, remember? Didn't seem to slow you down too much."

"So where is he?" I asked.

"That's the better news," said the Captain, beaming now like he'd swallowed a searchlight. "I kinda don't even want to tell you. Let it be a surprise."

I affected patience, but poorly. Folded my arms. Made my mouth into a line of surpassing severity.

"He's on a *train*, Duncan. Train 1066 to Goodland, Kansas. You're going to get to rob a fucking train!"

Then, finally, I grinned. "That is some serious cowboy shit, Captain."

"I know. I'm actually a little jealous. But then, I guess I'm going to get to rob a train, too, because that's how we're going to do this now. You're going to go in with the L.O.T., get things all crazy, blow some stuff up, make a nuisance of yourself. And then, before the Legion all get themselves killed, I'm going to jump in with a small team, grab the Chemist, you, Lee and Finch and exfil the hell out of there before anyone gets wise."

He was excited, the Captain was. Joyous. He slapped his hands on the desk and gestured broad as he spoke, running down plans and lists of who was doing what—glad, I think, for someone else to talk to, even if he was really only talking to himself.

"We've got the Maclusky twins on transport," he said, counting on his fingers. "The Watchmaker is providing hardware. Dogboy is coming. Barnum and Strange. It's gonna be a *party*. I'm gonna get Logue out of the house again, which'll make him happy as ducks. And when we get out of there with the Chemist in hand, we win, you know? We get back to where we're supposed to be. Get the wind on Percy and his idiots. We get the Chemist and the Chemist gives us answers. We squeeze him and miracles will come out. Enough to buy a little breathing room for King Steve and the Western Confederacy. "

He stopped short, seemed to remember that I was there. "You haven't seen Reggie, have you?"

"No," I said. "I played at Miss Kitty's last night and he wasn't there. Jemma said she and Holly hadn't been able to raise him after the revision."

He pursed his lips and scowled. "Yeah, that's bothersome. Reggie is a good man. He's survived a lot in his time."

"He saved my life at Great Times," I said, which was the truth. Didn't do the same for Jack August, but not for lack of trying. "Plus, he liked my piano playing, which speaks to his good taste and merciful nature."

The Captain grinned. "He liked you," he said. "Said you were a good man. Vouched for you early when I wasn't so sure about you."

"Again, the man is obviously a fine judge of character," I said.

"Okay, well just keep an eye open, okay? He's a lost dog right now, and I'd very much like him back someday. And in the meantime, you're on, okay? Lee has got the Legion primed. Finch is waiting on you. That train rolls in something like three days now, and you have to have them lathered up, in place and ready to fight. You can do it?"

"I can do it," I said.

"You're sure?"

"Absolutely not. But I'm sure gonna try."

"Good man."

There was some discussion of logistics after that. Exchanges of numbers and communications protocols and fallbacks. Spy stuff which, from long and painful experience, was mostly about what to do when everything went tits-up and precisely wrong. Because most of the time, that's exactly what everything did. At one point, I asked him if that was really Logue Ranstead I'd seen out on the floor, dressed up like a smarty and saying words longer than the Logue I knew had any business chewing on.

"We are none of us who we appear to be," the Captain said, seemingly distracted by a bit of something smudging the mess of his desk. Then he looked up at me, showed me a mouth full of daggers and eyes as cold and blue as a bombardier's. "Shouldn't you know that better than anyone?"

I swallowed the billiard ball that suddenly rose in my throat. I did not blink. Did not look away. Screamed at my own brain to continue breathing and pumping blood. "Why whatever do you mean, Captain?" I said, trying to sound as airy and indifferent as I surely was not.

He said nothing. I watched the rise and fall of his shoulders as he breathed. Felt the titanic weight of his eyes on me. "How many men have you been while in my employ?" he asked, then suddenly shifted his gaze to the ceiling and began counting on his fingers. "Chester Thewlip. Dorian Bloom. Harry Plum. Who were you to that road crew outside Boulder?"

"Dexter McThorphan," I said, trying not to gasp.

"Right. That was a good one."

"I was inspired."

"I mean, who haven't you been to me, Duncan? And in such a short time. We are all liars now. We are what we are when we need to be. None of us are who we pretend to be any more."

As we talked, HLF men and mostly-men came and went, dropping off papers, pointing at maps of the Colorado/Kansas border, asking cryptic questions and receiving equally cryptic answers. I could've sworn I saw Nils Sorenson from the Green Willow clave passing by in the hall, but I wasn't sure. The Captain obviously had something working beyond the immediate job of cross and double-cross, but I didn't see fit to broach on it. I had worries of my own, and they were legion, but I let none of it show in my face. Let none of it cloud me.

After Gordon Navarro took me out of Sunflower Fields, he jumped the border into Colorado, crossing in the middle of the night at a place where the imaginary line was watched by two sleepy soldiers who stank of the brake fluid they were cooking into moonshine. He scuttled me to a motel in Burlington where I slept on and off for two days and every time I woke, I saw him sitting in the dark next to the door with a shotgun across his knees.

We left the motel on the third day, moved to a different motel and Gordon fed me peanut butter sandwiches on bread that tasted like sprouted grass. The TV in the room showed nothing but snow, but there was a radio that worked. We listened to classical music and didn't talk and stared at the walls until they seemed to be falling inward upon us.

We moved to Cheyenne Wells after that, stayed a night in a bare room with two mattresses on the floor and cased LAW rockets stacked up high along the walls. In the morning, Gordon left, returned with a doctor who searched me, inside and out, for tracking devices, recorders, the dust of unfriendly mites still clinging to my skin. When he pronounced me clean of all possible ears, he saw to the mementos that my interrogators had left me with. He re-set my broken fingers, treated my infected burns, installed four new teeth to replace those of mine that had been swallowed or gone missing. Both of my eyes were bad, but he couldn't do anything to fix that. Didn't have the proper equipment. He told me I should probably get new ones grown and, maybe, try not get hit in the head so much in the future.

When he was done with me, he handed Gordon a paper folder with six morphine styrettes and two cell phones—both identical burners, not at all unlike the one that I would later carry, hidden in my briefcase. He also told him about a decent place to get Mexican food, and that night we ate tacos and yellow rice with meat that might've been vat-grown buffalo but was probably dog.

"Was that true, what you said to them at the Field?" I asked him. "Nimrod Kane?"

"Of course not," Gordon told me, shoving half a taco in his mouth and chewing thoughtfully. "Well, kinda."

From Cheyenne Wells, we moved to Lamar, then La Junta. We stayed in the cheapest motels when there was cheap motels to be had, or in rooms that were obviously on some kind of OSS list for places to stay when you were having the worst night of your life. At the motels, Gordon paid in cash, gave fake names, called me his wife. If anyone looked strangely at my bruises, my scars, the hollow and haunted look I wore twenty-four hours a day, he'd grin and say, "Guess he should've listened the first time, huh?" And then he'd laugh, because spousal abuse humor always kills in the sticks.

We didn't talk. When we did talk, we talked about old times. Our good days together—which were really only good now that they were over. Or about the weather. Or about the car. Or we'd make fun of the locals, which was what we did the most of.

Through the most of it, though, we said nothing. If I ever tried to ask any questions of him, he deflected them. When one of his phones rang, he would look at the number, take it or not, but hardly ever say anything. I assumed he talked more when he was out of my hearing. Or when I was sleeping. I slept more than I had ever slept in my life. Gordon hardly slept at all.

In a town called Kleinburg that was little more than a truckstop, six fast-food restaurants that looked like they'd been recently mortared, a cheeseburger place called Griff's, a hot-sheet motel called the Lucky 7, and two bars situated directly across the town's one street from each other, we went out for drinks one night and Gordon told me that he hadn't been lying at the prison. Not completely.

"Nimrod Kane," he said, "sent me looking for you."

Nimrod Kane was the director of the OSS. Control. The boss. An iconoclastic man who was rarely heard and almost never seen by the rank-and-file and seemed, if the rumors were to be believed, to hate everyone who worked at the agency he directed. So of course La Rata knew him. Had spoken with him. Was taking his orders directly from him.

"Bullshit," I said. "You're just planning on selling my organs, aren't you?"

"Only if you die on me. And at this point, it looks like you're going to survive."

Then we got blind-drunk and I danced with a pretty girl in tooled cowboy boots—which was remarkable because, prior to getting so lit, I hadn't known how to dance at all.

In the morning, Gordon told me that the drinking hadn't really helped. I couldn't really dance when roostered either. We sipped black coffee, he bought a bag of cheeseburgers from Griff's, and we moved again.

Driving south of Pueblo, he left the remains of the highway suddenly and drove off into the poisoned land beyond. There was a washboarded ranch road, but not much of one. The minute the snow started falling, we lost it. Eventually, Gordon stopped the car, waited, saw a plane flying over, and followed its path to a private airstrip.

At the airstrip, there was a small house—cozy and tidy like a lighthouse keeper's cottage in a fairy tale destined to end badly.

In the house, there was a man who'd laid out a lunch, made coffee, made coffee, opened a bottle of mezcal. He had one leg. The other was just a spring-steel blade. One of his eyes had an optic like a spotter's scope. There were plug-holes running in an arc behind his right ear, all limned in gold. The man never gave his name or offered his hand to shake. As soon as he had us situated, he vanished as completely as a ghost in daylight.

The plane was a Lear whisperjet—old fashioned to the point of ostentation. Gordon's phone rang. He picked it up and said, "Yeah, I've got him."

He said, "He's alive. Let's leave it at that."

He said, "Yeah, there's lunch."

He said, "Well come on in then, boss."

Nimrod Kane walked with a limp. He had a nest of scars on his face and the hair-fine wires of an audio implant in his right ear. He wore sunglasses and carried a battered, brown briefcase and talked in a warm voice that felt immediately comforting even when he was saying terrible things.

And he said a lot of terrible things that afternoon. He told me that he needed me. That he'd had Gordon take me out of Sunflower Field for one reason, and that if I fucked it up, Gordon had orders to take me right back again, break both my legs and dump me in their dooryard. I'd never see daylight, he said. I probably wouldn't live out a week.

"You're a deserter," he said. "A liar, a thief. That's the only reason I'm talking to you. Anyone who'd risk what you did to get away from the OSS right now is a man I think I can trust. A man I have something in common with."

"I'm also a helluva dancer," I said, but he didn't get the joke.

There was, he said, a schism at the core of the Office of Special Services. There were those who wanted to see it go one way, and those who wanted to see it go the other. The problem was, those who wanted it to go the other? They were mostly dead. Or missing. Vanished so completely that, like black holes, they could be detected only by the darkness of their lack. The problem was, Nimrod Kane was one of those who wanted it to go the other.

"As the boss, you'd think that kind of thing would be up to me," he said. "But you'd be very, very wrong."

He told me all about the Captain—though, as it turned out, he didn't tell me nearly enough. He said that I was going to be put in the path of one James Barrow. That I was to be recruited. That I was to make my way into his organization and report from the inside. And that if it didn't take the first time, we'd just have to try again. He explained how James Barrow was special. Was a man under his personal protection, acting on orders and for reasons that even he barely understood. James Barrow, the Captain, was Nimrod Kane's favorite weapon in the battle between the two halves of the OSS. Was his sword, and, in turn, Nimrod was the Captain's shield.

"Listen," he said. "You're there to watch him. To get close and be his man and to tell me every little thing he does and says and thinks and plans. He's a good man, Mr. Barrow, but he's wild. I need to know what he's doing before he does it. So I can protect him."

"Control him," I said.

"That, too. Being the good guys in this isn't easy. And it's never clean."

"Tell him about the Chemist," Gordon said.

I looked at Nimrod Kane. "Yeah, boss. Tell me about the Chemist," I said.

So the boss told me about the Chemist. How this one stupid, ridiculous little man was, for a brief and shining moment, going to be one of the most important people in the world and the focus of much dying and consternation. Because he wasn't really a chemist. Or rather, he'd *become* a chemist, but only after being a physicist for a very long time. Dr. Ignatz Walton was one of the men who'd discovered that this world was not the only world, and one of the men who'd opened the door between. As far as anyone knew, Nimrod said, of the seven people on the experimental team in 2011 that had discovered Superpositional Heisenberg Anomaly A, Ignatz Walton was the last survivor. The man who'd created the Abjuration.

"So I find this man," I said. "I help your Captain find this man, and that's it? I'm done?"

"Done?" asked the boss.

"Done," I said. "As in free to walk away and never think about the OSS again."

And Nimrod just laughed. "Oh, no," he said. "That's just what we're doing tomorrow." He leaned back slightly in his chair, raised a finger and pointed it at me, then at himself, then at me. "You and me? We're together in this for *life*."

The boss left after that. Stood, coughed, limped back out the door. He hadn't eaten a bite. Gordon and I sat, listened to the plane power up, scream down the runway, and lift off into the frozen sky. In the silence that came after, I turned to him and asked him what he'd done. Why he'd bothered springing me from Sunflower Field. Why he'd gotten me involved in this after I'd tried so hard to get out.

Gordon looked at me closely, like he was searching for something in my face—some humor, some forgiveness, some understanding. Then he shook his head and looked away, out a window and up into the hard blueness of the winter sky into which Nimrod Kane's plane had flown.

"Trust me when I say this, Jimmy," he said. "I really had no choice."

The Captain asked me what I knew about trains and I told him that I'd watched a lot of Thomas the Tank Engine when I was a boy.

He asked me if I thought my leg was going to hold up, and I asked him if I was going to have to run any marathons.

"You have a phone," he said. "You have a gun. You have your legend in place. I'm just trying to figure where this might go wrong."

"You're giving me three days to convince a gang of psychopathic dinosaur nuts to attack a moving train full of OSS agents as a cover for you to swoop in and steal your favorite chemistry teacher or whatever. I can't see any way in which that could go wrong."

"Are you happy?" the Captain asked, out of nowhere.

"I am," I said without missing a beat. "I cannot for the life of me understand half of what you're about with all this, but I'm about to rob a train, Captain. And who gets to do that? You know what this is?"

"What?" he asked.

I paused to take a cigarette out of my hat and light it, grinning like a death's head as the smoke laddered up and out of my mouth. "This is way better than rebuilding roads."

E P I S O D E

9

Last Train to Goodland, Part 2

THE CAPTAIN SENT ME ON MY WAY WITH A WINK AND A GRIN AND orders to meet Finch down in Cherry Creek just as quickly as ever I could.

I left the HLF's clubhouse the way I'd come in—which is to say limping, but also backtracking my way through hallways that seemed to curve and sway as though they'd been laid by drunks, and through the open, vaulted cathedral of a shop floor where it rained sparks and stank of ozone and 3-in-1 oil. Somewhere in that mess of screaming hydraulic presses and terribly complicated what-not was Logue Ranstead, worrying over his isometries and other un-Logue-Ranstead-ish things. I did not see him again on my way out.

The truck was right where I'd left it—spray-bombed now with transhumanist graffiti, but left otherwise alone. Tuesday and her royal guard were lounging around on top of it, exuding a sense of feral youth and aggressive boredom.

"When I was a kid, I had friends who used to surf the top of trucks like that," I said to them. "Cars, too. Heard about kids who did it with trains, but I never knew any."

"Seems like a pointlessly stupid way to die," said Tuesday. "Glad I didn't never know none of your idiot friends."

I folded my arms, but immediately felt a bit too fatherly, so unfolded them and let them hang instead. Then stuffed my hands in my pockets. "Mind telling me what you're doing up there then? I'm a busy man. Got places to be. And this here is my loyal steed."

"Relieving you of your gold," said Tuesday.

"Robbery," said Shortcake, leering.

"Not really," said the one who wasn't Shortcake.

"Orrrderrrs . . ." drawled Tuesday, stretching in the fading afternoon sun like a cat. "Captain has need of pesos, so we's lightening you of yours."

"The Captain mentioned no such thing to me," said me.

And "Didn't have to, did he," said Tuesday, rolling to her feet and staring imperiously down upon me. "Cuz he mentioned it to me."

Not particularly caring what happened to the rolling suitcase full of dirty gold I'd taken off the L.O.T. then liberated from the OSS—and trusting, actually, in Tuesday's loyalty to the Captain above all lesser things—I waved a hand at the back of the truck and bid them make haste with the unloading all by their lonesomes. I'd already stolen the stuff twice. I certainly wasn't going to be involved in carrying it away a third time.

In the Creek, there'd been a bombing which turned out to be just one of the former Kansan prisoners of war running off from his work crew and exploding all over a building that'd already been made terribly unstable by the violent enthusiasms of other Kansans come before him. He blew up, the building came down, nuns and puppy dogs were crushed beneath the rubble. Whatever. All rebuilding work had been suspended and King Steve had put his men into the streets—marching squad-by-squad, parade formation, to comfort the swells with their guns and shiny buttons. Liberal as the man might've been, there are some humors that can only be quelled by a show of precisely what's waiting for them as mean to misbehave.

I stuck to the clearest paths but still crawled, laying on the truck's horn, inching forward through the press of a crowd that was a pickpocket's wet dream. The streets were choked with the city's flotsam—veterans and objectors rubbing shoulders, froth-mouthed evangelists leafleting the heathens, street-walkers and burly-boys, dealers and healers, schizophrenics having passionate arguments with gutted parking meters, the halt, the lame, vicious packs of feral children with teeth like ivory thumbtacks, all driven down into the Creek by the weight of the weird in the city's core and, as ever, the dandies strolling the cobbles with their walking sticks and haze of nanites, looking around as though they woke up every morning seeing a different world than the one that was laid out for the rest of us.

At every major intersection, exo's stood, ten feet tall and fierce as drawn knives, their gun-arms hot, battle ribbons snapping from whip-poles that rose from the cooling units on their backs. And not to be outdone, the battle police—decked out shiny in their black dress uniforms and mirror-face helmets—scuffled with every jaywalker, jack-roller and malingerer within reach of their shock rods. Dust from the collapse choked the streets. Mixed with tear gas. Mixed with smoke. Everyone who was anyone was out in it, trying hard to turn nothing into a proper Red Lights riot. It was a mess, but one that was attracting the finest quality of people.

It was getting on toward dark by the time I reached the vicinity of the ex-sushi-bar where Finch and Lee lived, and Finch was there waiting for me. We reversed course, drove through smoke and searchlights. Something somewhere was on fire and burning enthusiastically. With the windows open, we could hear the flat pops of small arms fire and the fierce trumpeting of a war elephant, so naturally we closed the windows and pretended we'd heard nothing at all.

"Things are shaking themselves to pieces," Finch said. He was driving because he was the one who knew where he was going. Also, so I could rest my leg.

And I wanted to tell him, *good*. I wanted to say, *fuck 'em all* because, really, the more trouble, the more madness, the more cover there was for me. The easier it was for me to move. And, God's honest, what did I care about more right then than me? The OSS was looking for me. Percy Blythe and Clarence "Injun Joe" Doolittle were abroad, actively sniffing after my trail. Good odds that they were also after Jemma and Logue and Barnum and Strange and the Captain and everyone else, too, but I was, in so many ways, the prize.

I mean, wasn't I? I was the only linking factor between the Legion of Terror, the Chemist, and the Captain. Percy thought I was a freelancer and an actor called Dorian Bloom. The L.O.T. thought I was a Kansan arms dealer called Harry Plum. The Captain thought I was an ex-OSS linguist and field man called Duncan Archer. All of them were right and none of them were right, all at the same time. I was what I was—the man in the middle, holding everyone's hands. If I got bagged, everything would come a-tumbling down.

Which was why it was vitally important that I not get pinched. Which was why I rode with my head down and my hat low. Which was why I said to Finch that until the sun was fully down, I'd have felt a lot better about things if someone would kindly set a few more fires.

"There's people live here, man. You've got to remember that. People who got nothing to do with what we're about. Who are just trying to get on about their lives and not die from someone else's politics."

I flinched as a shower of rocks spanged off the side of the truck. "I'm trying hard not to die from someone else's politics, too, Finch."

"You chose your side," he said, hooked a hard left a block short of where the beeps were laying down ballistic foam barricades across the road, and straightened out. For a moment, the setting sun glittered through the standing remains of one giant Kansan robot leg. It was beautiful in a way that made me miss things like cameras and gentle moments of self-reflection. "Most of these people just want to wake up breathing tomorrow morning."

I sniffed. "Anyone ever tell you that you have a way of making the end of the world seem a lot less fun?"

"Just wait," he said. "The Legion, they're all very excited to see you again. They haven't killed Lee yet, so I'd say you have a fair chance of convincing them to take on that train. And when you do, things are going to get very weird very fast."

The Legion of Terror were, in their full and fanatical flowering, just as maroony as Lee and Finch had claimed. Their secret lair was an underground bunker in the contraction zone, accessed through a Starbucks on the surface that still hummed with enough live nana to be able to affect minor repairs and cleaning. As such, it *gleamed*, that place. All green and cream and scrubbed brick, lustrously glowing in the dark amid a Golgotha of lesser enterprises—a smashed tax preparer's office, a dry cleaner's that wore its shattered windows like black-eyes in a stunned face, a bar that looked like it'd been kicked by a giant boot.

Seeing something like that in the day would only be strange. Coming upon it in the fraught darkness of an evening—to turn a corner amid the rubble fields and bones of long-gone taquerias and to see it radiating there with its softly glowing lights and warm, buttery shades—tripped some ancient fear of traps and predation. It was like when, in the middle of the hard rock desert, the

Roadrunner would chance upon a plate and a sign: FREE BIRD-SEED. Or when Bugs Bunny would spot a voluptuous girl bunny out in the forest, all rabbit tits and red, red lips. You know that it's a set-up. You know that there's a grand piano twisting in the blue sky above the free birdseed with the Coyote on the other end of the rope. You know the girl bunny is made of fizzing dynamite.

"We're going in there?" I asked Finch.

He nodded, threw the truck into park. "Okay," he said. "You ready, Mr. Plum?"

"No."

"Trust me. Staring at it doesn't make it any better."

"You ever watch any Bugs Bunny cartoons?" I asked.

He grinned at me. "The girl rabbit made of dynamite? Yeah, it's just like that. Come on."

We left the truck, walked in through the front door of the Starbucks (every table polished, the brushed aluminum accents spotless), around one end of the counter, and into the back.

"Game face," Finch whispered out of the side of his mouth. "We're on."

I followed him close. I would've ridden on his back if I hadn't thought it would appear undignified. He stopped in front of an unmarked door—smooth and battleship gray. There was no knob or handle, so Finch just stood, watching the door as though waiting for it to do something clever.

And then it did—splitting down the middle like a parting curtain and flowing aside like water. Beyond it was an elevator platform.

"Nice trick," I said.

Finch bobbed his head. "You first, Mr. Plum," he said, his voice suddenly deeper, his spine the more straight. "The Council is waiting on you."

Down and down. The elevator was slow and grinding but it'd been so long since I'd known an elevator that actually *worked*—that was safe to ride in a building taller than three floors that hadn't gone insane from viruses, rot, or loneliness—that I was charmed regardless. To have such a thing as an elevator in a world of giant robots and fire-breathing dragons was, in its own, dull, pedestrian way, remarkable.

"The truck . . ." I said, aside to Finch.

"No one around here is stupid enough to come within a hundred feet of it. The Starbucks has already eaten all the foolish or overly curious neighbors."

That did not make me feel better at all.

The Council of the Legion of Terror was seven middle-aged men who should've known better than to be playing outlaw in a hole in the ground. They were seated on a raised platform at the far end of a long, low room stuffed with their fellows, in chairs of varying ostentation, dressed like drum majors from the University of Bad Taste—all epaulets and gold braids, cutaway coats the color of electric limes and jangling with microchip medals, green vinyl capes with silhouette collars that looked like they'd been made from seven different shower curtains took from the guest bathrooms of seven different grandmothers. Some wore gloves with clawed fingers. Some wore scaled pimp boots with stacked heels. All of them wore rubber dinosaur masks, partially enlivened and pasted to their faces in ways that made them look more horrible than real—two Tyrannosaurs, three things with flared nostrils and beaked mouths, two spiky things that looked like angry horn toads.

The rest of the Legion looked only worse. If there was a costume contest being held, the Councilmen would've won places two through eight, for sure, but any bed-sheet ghost would've taken top prize in a walk. To stop from laughing I bit my tongue 'til I tasted blood and, in my head, promised to hit Finch very hard when this was all over and done with for not telling me what was going to be waiting for me in the basement of the most scarifying Starbucks in the zone.

Should I describe for you the ridiculosity of the next interminable hours of my life? The songs that needed singing, the epic poems that needed reciting? There was raucous debate and fistfights among the rank-and-file, tests of strength, one formal duel, a snack break where cupcakes and jugged 'shine were passed around, and I had my hand shook by a double-dozen fools in green-dyed union suits with their hair spiked up like lizard frills, all of them wanting to know how I'd been shot and where I'd been shot and how I'd been keeping since the terrible events of that terrible day and such-forth and so-on. Sweat poured down the necks of the Councilmen and soaked their shirts, but not a one of them moved to pull off their masks. I was threatened with kidnapping, face-punching, and execution, all in the first five minutes, but I had Harry Plum's bluster, Harry Plum's impatience, and Harry Plum's towering rage at them that'd done him sour, disrupted his business, and put a bullet in him—all of which played well in that echoing room with its audience of willing psychopaths.

The Councilmen hollered and stomped. The hoi polloi on the floor hollered back and stomped their own feet. I was told that I was unworthy. That I was an outsider and therefore dirt-like in my insignificance before the great and awesome will of Dinosaur Joe. I argued that I'd bled right alongside the best and luckiest of theirs and that mine own men had died under the same guns, sucking the same last breaths.

"The OSS cravenly bushwhacked us both in the midst of our business," I said. "And all I'm offering is a chance to get blood for blood and your man back."

They howled that this attack I proposed was not in keeping with the 79 precepts laid down by Dinosaur Joe. And then all 79 were recited. From memory. Followed by a song.

Divisions grew on the floor. There was them that said that the Chemist wasn't a member of the Legion and, therefore, not subject to their protections. Others insisted that the Chemist had been a favorite of Dinosaur Joe before the glorious leader had gone inside to do his time, and that triggered another song (which, judging by the content, was called something like "Fuck Everyone Who Ain't Dinosaur Joe"), and some more scuffles amongst the volunteers until a compromise position was reached which stated that while the Chemist was not a *member* of the Legion, per se, he had been a proven friend and confidant of Dinosaur Joe and therefore was subject to the honors, benefits and protections of full membership—but that I was certainly neither and ought to be killed right fastly for knowing now where their secret headquarters was and for having witnessed many of their sacred observances.

There was, briefly, round agreement that this should be the way to proceed until a small but vocal dissenting sect began shouting that mine or the Chemist's membership in the Legion was not really the goddamn point here because what this was all *really* about was taking vengeance on the OSS for the true members that had been killed by them in the garage, and that if Harry Plum was offering his services than that made him, too, a friend of the Legion.

It was Lee who made that careful, needle-threading argument, and it got him some cheers and slaps on the back by them as was nearest to him. And then someone demanded a somber reading of the names of the dead, attended by the striking of a gong that looked like it'd been lifted from the lobby of a second-rate Chinese restaurant. This went on until the gong-striker botched the gonging somehow, which got *him* dogpiled by furious Legionnaires who claimed the man was a traitor for deliberately befouling their venerated rituals with his clumsy gong-hitting, and for the most part, this was the way that things went for what seemed hours and hours and hours—just arguing and fuming debate, followed by hitting, followed by songs, followed by more arguing, with occasional pauses for small-group discussions, trust exercises, liquor, the re-aligning of loyalties on the floor and bathroom breaks.

After one particularly long shouting match between one group of the rank-and-file who argued that, in volunteering my services to the Legion, I had effectively made myself their property, and another, larger group who insisted that volunteering to help the Legion was the same as volunteering *for* the Legion and that, perforce, I ought to be treated like any other new recruit and ignored completely until I'd proven myself in honorable combat with another member, I stopped saying anything at all. I just stood by, arms folded, eyes hopping from one Councilman to another.

In time, the ruckus died down enough that I could be heard, and I asked, "What does a man have to do to become a member of the Legion of Terror?"

"You have to be recommended for membership by another member in good standing," said one of the spiky-heads.

"Okay, so that's done, isn't it? Finch brought me here. I think that counts as a recommendation."

"The recommendation has to be seconded by—"

"Seconded," said Lee from the back of the room. And, to my credit, this second was echoed by several other voices.

"Good," I said. "Next?"

"You have to be educated about the history of the Legion and the validity of our claim to the throne of the West."

"Don't care," I said. "You want the throne? Good for you. Stupid thing to want, but whatever. Next?"

"You have to memorize the 79 Precepts and the Song of—"

"No, that's stupid. Next?"

"It's not stupid!" insisted one of the Councilmen. "It's a part of our venerable—"

"No," I said. "Trust me. It's stupid. And anyway, there's no time. What's next?"

"Swearing allegiance to Dinosaur Joe and your brothers in the Legion of—"

"Done," said me. "I swear to the Great and Powerful Whatever that Dinosaur Joe is awesome, that I love you all like brothers and that, for the next few days, I am your man in all things. Now is that it?"

"No," said a different dinosaur head. "There's also the trial by combat, which has to be witnessed by—"

I spun to my left, ignored the hot spike of pain that went shooting through my leg, and hit the man nearest me with everything I had, burying a fist in his stomach, just below his ribs. I gave him half a second to gasp and fold double, then hit him again in the side of the face—dropping the punch on him like a hammer, hitting hard enough that my hand and arm went numb nearly to my elbow. The man fell to the ground in a heap and didn't move. I turned back to the Councilmen in their fancy chairs.

"Done," I said, shaking my hand and flexing my fingers. "What else?"

In the stunned quiet, one of the dinosaur heads—the bigger of the two Tyrannosaurs—leaned forward and said, "Tell us about this train our Chemist is going to be on."

I smiled and said, "That's where things get tricky."

Train 1066 to Goodland was a bullet. A maglev sling train with a nose like a .45 caliber slug and 64 cars gliding along behind it in perfect, frictionless comfort. The track for it had been grown from seeds sown by a machine built for nothing else—spidering along the landscape from the outskirts of the Republic of Boulder, south through Golden and the foothills to Denver, and then all the way to Kansas City on 14 legs, stopping every 171 feet to blast a hole, excrete a magnesium-and-niobium-charged growing medium and plunk down a seed full of root assemblers, constructors, and link maintenance mites. Then it would move on. The machine had been built on the orders of King Steven, who'd submitted his plans and designs on a series of cocktail napkins covered in a surprisingly deft draughtsman's hand, and had required a reinforced armored platoon to protect it on its travels—King Steve's hand-picked bestest, keeping the spider safe from outlaws, idiots and them as saw all flailings in the direction of civilization as counter to the anarchic delights of living in a post-rational world. The King's armor buried 74 of their own along the way, but the track itself, once it'd grown up proper, was self-maintaining. And on the flats, the train traveled at upwards of 200 mph.

"You can't catch it," I said. "You can't hardly even *see* it as it goes past. The track is unbreakable, more or less. And the stations it pulls into along its route are fortresses."

Again, there was yelling. An insistence that the Legion of Terror was certainly up to the challenge of breaking the everloving shit out of this miracle of modern engineering even if none others were. They had, they'd insisted, broken all sorts of stuff in their time. It was one of the things at which they excelled.

"The beasts . . ." I heard someone deep in the room say. "Bring out the beasts." Which, of course, made me look for who'd said that because . . . Well, because that's strange, right? Because that's not the kind of thing that anyone would find comforting hearing in a big room full of strangers who were all quite obviously bananas and dressed like thrift-store dinosaurs.

"There is one place where the train's speed . . . its really rather *phenomenal* speed, you understand . . . is not an issue," I explained. East of one of the last flatlands settlements it passed—a place called Waltz, which wasn't nothing more than a few tin shacks, a hundred silos and an enormous repair yard for the machines that brought in the harvests in the south—was a place where the track ran in a long, snaking "S" in order to get itself aligned with the border towns of Kansas, of which Goodland was one. The train always stopped in Waltz to take on cargo, offload machine parts coming from those places in Colorado where people actually lived and did things like build complicated machine parts, and allow them as were aboard to get off, stretch their legs, have a piss, smoke a little, and be able to say that they'd seen something of the countryside on their journey, even if what they saw was nothing but flatness and brownness and old-fashionedy farmers with their toolbelts, level B hazmats tape-wrapped at the wrists and ankles, and packs of heeled biogen hounds with eyes like radar dishes. American Gothic, circa the end of the world.

I knew all this because Waltz was where I'd took the last breath of clean air I'd had before passing into Goodland myself. Where I'd last seen sky that was all my own. A horizon uncut by chainlink and razorwire.

They told me to run in Waltz—the four guards that were riding with me, who'd taken me out of the secure car where we'd been playing cards to pass the time. They'd put a cigarette in my mouth, lit it for me (because, with my wrists shackled, I couldn't do it myself), and told me to have a good look 'round. To remember what the sky looked like and the air tasted like.

"We'll give you ten steps," they'd said, grinning and running their thumbs over the butts of the service automatics they wore in palm-reader ID-lock holsters. "Kindest offer you're liable to get in the next hundred years."

As things turned out, they were wrong about that. But there were many times over the following *two* years where I'd thought hard about it. Dreamed about it, really. Wondered how bad it could've hurt—dying and all, their bullets taking me in the back where I couldn't see them coming, pulling the life out of me in crimson streamers as they flew. I wondered if it could've possibly hurt worse than what was being done to me by them as had once been my side, you know? The OS-fucking-S.

"Waltz," I said to the Councilmen. "That's the only chance you have."

And again, I heard from deep in the room, "The beasts. . ." Only this time, it was more than one voice.

"Only chance *we* have," said the biggest of the dinosaur heads.

I sniffed, affected Harry's haughtiest and most high-hat sneer. "You look like you oughtta be in a parade. Don't get all fucking semantical with me now."

We could, I reckoned, try to blow the track. I explained that the Cyclot-8 might make a hole large enough that couldn't be healed in time for the train to pass over it. But if we did it in enough time for the train to stop, it would just backtrack to Waltz at the first sign of trouble. And if we waited until the train was right on top of it, all we'd do is derail the thing, and run the risk of killing the Chemist in the wreck.

Again: "Bring out the beasts . . ." I glanced quickly over my shoulder, then turned back.

"The other option," I said, "is the crazy one. That we take the train moving."

"Beasts."

"It'll accelerate slow through the curves—35, maybe 40 mph, tops. They won't bother cranking the speed up, because now they have to stop at the border, too. At the checkpoints."

". . . beasts . . ."

"Bring the beasts . . ."

I continued, but the whispered glossolalia was spreading. I looked again over my shoulder, then back at the Councilmen. "The best point," I explained, "would be at the top of the first curve. Twenty miles from Waltz, about thirty from the border. They're beyond all rapid aid there, and moving as slow as ever the train does. That's where we'd take it. Make a rush on it, if you have the wheels—"

"Get the beasts!"

"Bring out the beasts!"

"—to be able to run up on 'em then."

I'd thought, in my last moments of freedom aboard train 1066, that if there was going to be a rescue for poor Duncan Archer, that would be where it would happen. My guards had tucked the cards away. They'd done with the taunting. I recall resting my head against the wall of the train car as it sailed slowly along. Closing my eyes. *If the cavalry is going to come*, I'd thought, *this is the place.* I'd had some friends at the time. It wasn't beyond the bounds of reason that some of them might attempt a rescue.

Except that it was, of course. No one was coming for me. Not until Gordon Navarro did.

"Beasts!" came a multitude of voices from the floor, now attended by the stomping of feet and the susurration of bodies rocking and surging together. "Beasts!"

I spread my hands and appealed to the Councilmen. "I'm not the only one hearing this, right?"

From somewhere, someone began chanting "El! Oh! Tee! El! Oh! Tee!" and that was picked up even faster. They were calling for blood now, these fools. Howling for it. And the Grand Poobahs up in their fancy chairs damn well knew what side *their* bread was buttered on and were glancing left and right at each other's rubber dinosaur faces, knowing that there was no backing down now. That their lots was thrown.

"Battle," one of them said.

And "battle" said another and "battle" said the one after that until, finally, it came to the last of the Tyrannosaur heads, who stood up and spread his arms and shouted, "Battle!" At which point the room just erupted into all manner of bedlam and foolishness and bouncing and head-butting and chanting and I closed my eyes thinking, not for the first time, that the world was just a whole lot stupider now than it had been when I was a young man. That talking them of low brain-wattage into nonsense had become altogether too easy and that maybe if everyone appreciated good whiskey, pretty girls and breathing a little bit more, there'd be fewer suckers out there willing to fight and die in the petty wars begun by the sharp, the mendacious and the wicked.

At the head of the room, the main Tyrannosaur gave a speech full of big words and fire. When his breath gave out, one of the other dinosaur heads stepped into the breach. On the floor, there was dancing and carrying-on and things continued on apace for quite some time with each of the head men making sure that he took his fair piece of the speechifying and got covered in the glow of this new, inevitable victory a'borning. I listened as long as I could, but I was tired. My leg was a blossom of pain unfolding and my hand hurt and there wasn't really no piece of me that wasn't sore for one reason or another. What I wanted was a nice drink and maybe a nap, but instead, I saw the biggest of the Tyrannosaur heads trying to sneak off down one side of the platform upon which the Councilmen's chairs were set, and I limped over to him.

Three days, I told him. That was basically what we had remaining to us before train 1066 rolled. And I asked him if he really believed he could get all his honorable and respectable brothers-in-arms or whatever into place in time.

"These dummies?" he said to me. "If I opened the front doors right now, they'd *run* there."

The man reached up and started wrestling his mask off, grunting and cursing as he tried to get a hold on the sweat-slick rubber where it'd glommed alive-ishly onto the wattles of his neck and struggling to get the whole thing up and over his head. When he finally succeeded in extricating himself, he was flushed, blotchy, his cheeks mottled, his breath coming in gasps. His graying hair was plastered to his scalp, his rheumy eyes set deep into a face with more wrinkles than a gas station map.

"*Hate* this damn thing," he said, staring into the eyeholes of the mask. "It's hot and it smells like a rotten foot in there."

"Then why do you wear it?" I asked him.

He shrugged. "Better to be a boss than not to be. And the men expect some traditions to be held to. Especially in Joe's absence. If we didn't wear the masks, they'd freak out. Maybe decide that they had some notions of their own about how things ought to be run. And then where would we be?" He pulled off his green gloves and fanned himself with the soaking mask. It was soupy-hot in the main room of the Legion of Terror. Loud like the inside of a can of dry

466

beans, vigorously shook. "Hope you're right about all this business, Mr. Plum. Wouldn't want to be you if we got there and there's no train. Or worse, no Chemist."

"I'm right," I said. "No doubt. And we'll get him, too. See some of these OSS types in the dirt, I promise you." I paused, looked about at the fool's bacchanal frolicking up all around us. "Gotta ask, though. What the hell's all this carrying on about beasts? *Get* the beasts, *release* the beasts. What is that?"

"Dinosaurs," said Tyranosaur head. "We don't use 'em for every fight because they're big and temperamental and they stink like you wouldn't believe. And it's a schlep to get to where they are, too. Way out on the plains, the ranch is. But in this case, it seems the men have spoken." He blew out an exhausted breath. "They want the big show."

"Wait," I said. "You mean *dinosaurs* dinosaurs? Like, you have actual dinosaurs out on a ranch on the plains?"

And the chief Tyrannosaur looks at me, tilts his head, mops his face tiredly with the palm of one hand. "Of course we have dinosaurs," says him. "Our leader's name is Dinosaur Joe. And that would be a pretty fucking stupid name if he didn't have actual dinosaurs, wouldn't it?"

I was not trusted to go to the ranch. Good as my swears and my beating down of that one, poor man had been, it wasn't enough to buy me full membership in their little club, so it was decided by dinosaur-head fiat that myself, Lee and Finch would remain behind, guarded by what I assumed to be the dimmest and least likeable of the Legion's soldiery—two scrappy and scrofulous creatures called Squirrel and Fat Randy.

Me, they knew as suspect. And Lee and Finch had also been painted with the stink of possible traitorousness simply by their having survived something that all others had not. The only sure way to prove your loyalty to the Legion? Die in its livery, gloriously or not so. All dead members were heroes by default. All them living was just one wrong step or word away from being named a betrayer.

We were told that we'd be sent for once things was rolling and mostly prepared. Two days, most. Lee and Finch were to watch me. Squirrel and Fat Randy were to watch Lee and Finch. And alls I needed was to arrive with my booms in hand, no more.

And then I was told that if anything went cross—if there was even the leastish smell that I was playing the Legion of Terror anything less than completely square—I would be executed on the spot. Fat Randy was solemnly handed an enormous revolver with a barrel almost as long as his forearm, and he drooled over the thing like it was made of pussy.

I didn't feel it my place to remind anyone that I still had my automatic under my own arm. That I had Julie's knife. That I was, presumably, in possession of twenty vials of the angriest conventional explosive made by man. It was all for show, these threats and such. If they'd been intending on putting Harry Plum in the dirt, they'd already had ample opportunity.

Not that I underestimated the potential for a sudden, psychotic reversal of opinion, mind you. Just that I was feeling somewhat more confident with three-on-two odds as opposed to one-versus-a-multitude.

The Legion of Terror drifted out into the night, passing through doors that led deeper into their underground lair or up the lift and out through the Creepiest Starbucks in the World. I kept my lips clamped tight and my mind on my business, but I did get the chance to pass a quick look and a terse nod with Lee and Finch while Fat Randy dancingly held the big revolver up above his head and slapped at Squirrel with his other hand as Squirrel hollered about getting his turn holding the gun and trying to jump for it.

We passed the remains of the night in the quiet of the lair, eating off the remains of the snacks that'd been laid in for the meeting, reddening our noses with lashings of jugged party liquor, and pacing careful circles around each other like five strange dogs curious about each other but too polite or domesticated to just come out and sniff each other's butts.

Squirrel, I learned, had come across the northern border from Cheyenne four years ago during the winter famine. He'd weighed 87 pounds when he'd staggered into the refugee camp at Campion, which had been a rich recruiting ground in its day for the war chiefs, militia commanders, and mad scientists looking for henchmen. The White Rose Guard, the Thunder Brothers, Laddie Cullen and his Columbine Riffs, the Redlegs, La Raza, the Mollys, Juanito Dada and the Maelstrom Riders—they'd all been there. But Squirrel had fallen hard for Dinosaur Joe and the Legion of Terror because, in his words, "They'd been the leastwise ridikerlous."

Also, they claimed to have dinosaurs. And, as I can truthfully attest, among boys of a certain twig and toggery mentality, one can not discount the enervating spark lit by the promise of dinosaurs.

Fat Randy, on the other hand, had been a local recruit. He had a girlfriend, currently in Canada, who Squirrel insisted did not exist. And a job at a fish farm in the zone—tinkering with the feed composition and chemical mix in the growing vats and keeping the rats and cats and feral dogs out of the tanks.

"You, uh . . . You ever need you some fish, I got the hook-up," Fat Randy said, winking at me. "Back door deal, you know? Fifty-pound block of frozen carp protein just off the feeder bring a pretty profit for a man knows how to move it and don't mind the smell."

I told him I would certainly think about it, but that my business—which was to say, Harry Plum's business—was primarily in guns and bullets and things that went boom. If Harry Plum were to suddenly go to market with a truckload of frozen fish, people would wonder what had happened to him. Whether he'd suddenly discovered heretofore unknown pacifistic tendencies. Which would likely result in him being shot in the face quicker than a man could say "fish popsicle."

"Nothing wrong with the fish business," Fat Randy said sniffily. "The genetics are clean, the money is good. So you think about it, Mr. Plum. You know where I'll be."

Eventually, we slept. Woke. Puttered around. Squirrel disappeared for a while and came back with coffee in a samovar and china cups. When I made a move toward one of the doors that led deeper (presumably) into the Legion's hideout, Fat Randy waved the big pistol lazily in my direction.

"Come on now, Mr. Plum," he said, slurping in a loud and pleasuresome way at his coffee. "If'n I shoot you, I won't never be able to talk you into getting into the fish business with me." He spoke without ever looking at me. Without ever raising his voice. "Plus I know Squirrel don't want to clean up the mess of you."

"Why me?" asked Squirrel.

"Him holding the gun gives the orders, Squirrel. And I orders you to do the scrubbing up if I has to spread Mr. Plum out over yonder wall."

Squirrel thought about that a moment.

"Well okay then," he said. "So long as I got something to do."

They were insane, them two. Less or moreso than their contemporaries was hard to call, but they were amusing, and watching them together made the time go, right up until it didn't anymore, and then Fat Randy started whining about wanting to go out catting.

"What," he asked, "are we waiting for, really? I mean, other than our orders, right? And thems can't possibly come a'fore tonightish."

"True," said Squirrel, who sat on the floor hugging his knees to his chest and chewing distractedly on his own pants.

"Was we told specifically—and I mean orders-wise—that we was to stay down here?"

Yes, I thought. Lee, who was sitting near me sipping coffee, said nothing. Finch was laid out on the floor against the far wall, sleeping or pretending to sleep.

"No we was not," said Squirrel.

"No we was not," agreed Fat Randy. "So what we should do is go out and get us a bit of sunshine, I think. Maybe find a place with drinks . . ."

"And girls," Squirrel added.

". . . and girls, which I was just about to say, Squirrel. A place where we might all unwind a bit. Relax. Stay loose and limber and ready for action."

"And meet girls," added Squirrel.

"And perhaps meet girls, yes. Although I've no need of girls as Darlene, my girlfriend, does me just fine."

"Imaginary girlfriend," said Squirrel, and giggled and rocked, but Fat Randy was on a roll now.

"A place where a man might stretch out and find a moment of repose," he said, spreading his arms as if to embrace the notion of normalcy and proper relaxation. "That's what we need. Place where a man might find himself among like-minded company. Because—and I swear to you this is true—a man expecting action will always go the faster and better into it if he approaches with a relaxed and uncomplicated mind."

"Ninja mind," said Squirrel, hopping up and striking a Kung Fu pose.

"A ninja mind, yes," said Fat Randy. "That's just wiseness, is all. That's simple knowing of smartness." And as he said that, he was scratching beneath his chin with the sight blade of the big revolver so, you know . . . he was a man who knew from wiseness.

"Maybe we should just sit tight," I offered, as tenderly as one might. In the way that one might approach a baby chewing on a hand grenade. Or how one might talk a bear into putting down a chainsaw. But all my gentleness and prudence was for naught because, immediately, Fat Randy's eyes narrowed to piggish slits and I knew I'd made a mistake.

The pistol barrel lay against the pillowed line of his jaw. It moved as he seemed to chew over my suggestion. "Why do you say that?" he asked.

"Because there's only going to be one shot at this train," I explained, bulwarking what had only been sagacity on my part. Emblematic of a deep and passionate desire to not go anywhere where girls, loud music, and corn liquor, indelicately imbibed, might be further rattle whatever was already loose in Fat Randy's brains. "And if something were to happen—if we weren't here when the time came for—"

"*Why* do you say *that?*" Fat Randy asked again, lowering the gun now, his eyes locking onto me. "Because you're expecting something? Because someone is coming here?"

"What?" I said. "No." And then "What?" again.

Squirrel dropped his ninja pose and muttered under his breath, "I'll go find a bucket . . ."

Fat Randy stalked forward. The gun found me. Summoning all the coolness that lived in Harry Plum's icebox heart, I looked into the barrel and saw only blackness. The difference between life and death that was measured in the weight of the trigger pull. "Who's coming here, Mr. Plum?" he asked. "Is someone coming for us?"

"Randy . . ." I said.

He stopped short, snapped the gun up at the ceiling, arm bent at the elbow. "A member of the Legion of Terror must always be on guard against betrayal and double-dealing," he said, reciting rather loosely from the 79 Precepts of Dinosaur Joe. "A member of the Legion of Terror should not ever put his . . . Uh . . ."

Trying to help, Squirrel piped up from the other side of the room. "Put his trust in someone who ain't . . ."

"No, that's not it. Shouldn't never *have* trust in someone who ain't also . . ." Fat Randy trailed off, thinking, the pink tip of his tongue poking out of one corner of his soft mouth, the gun now wavering.

"No member of the Legion of Terror shall lay his faith in matters of importance upon any man who is not one of his brothers in the Legion," said Finch, rolling over from where he'd been laying and rising slowly to his feet. Fat Randy lowered the gun to him and Finch said, "Don't point that at me, fat boy. I'll feed it to you." He turned and asked Lee what he thought. "Sounds right to me," said Lee.

"You're outvoted then, Mr. Plum. Four members to none. Let's go get a drink."

We took the truck. I lifted the case of Cyclot out of the back and, with Lee's help, took it back down into the bunker.

"You can't argue with them, man," he said, once we were out of ear shot. "Nice as that performance was before the Council, you're still a nothing to them. If you're not a member of the Legion, you're an enemy of the Legion. That's just the way it works."

"Just like the Girl Scouts," I said.

We stashed the case off in a corner, beneath a tarp, then stacked dirty dishes and jugs of 'shine on top and got back into the elevator.

"For disagreeing with him publicly, Fat Randy was obliged to kill you."

"Just like the Girl Scouts," I said.

I drove. Finch rode up front with me because he said he didn't trust me now. That I'd made myself suspect with my refusal to drink with the Legion. Lee, Squirrel and Fat Randy loaded into the back.

"All in all, you're doing very well," he said to me once the motor was going and the radio was cranked, blowing static like a storm. "How you feeling?"

"Alive. So far."

"Oh, we'll keep you alive long enough to get to the train, that's for sure."

"Appreciate that," I said. "This gonna work?"

Finch thought about that a minute. "Honestly, I didn't think you'd get this far. I gave the Captain fifty-fifty odds that the Council would have you killed on the spot."

I drummed fingers on my knee, drove one-handed. Out the side window I caught a flash of movement. Something loping along the ground, running a course roughly parallel to the one I followed. There and then gone. "He never told me that," I said.

"Yeah, well why would he have? Wouldn't have done nothing but make you fearful. And Harry Plum, from what I've seen of him, isn't a fearful man."

I was quiet for a time. The truck jounced and rattled over the rough paths and through the gray daylight. I saw the darting leap of something pacing us again, out of the corner of my eye and thought it must be Dogboy because Dogboy was, at that moment, the least bad thing I could think of and I was laboring at remaining cheerful.

"What was the fallback plan?" I finally asked.

"What do you mean?"

"If they'd killed me. What was the fallback plan for getting the Chemist?"

"There wasn't one," Finch said. "Lee and me would've exfil'd at the first opportunity and gone to ground. Cap said the King has a doomsday plan in place, but I don't know what it is."

"The King?"

"King Steve," Finch said. "Didn't you know they were pals?"

Well of course they were. Why wouldn't they be? I shook my head and drove on while, somewhere in the corner of my eye Dogboy or something worse than Dogboy loped on, pacing us and skittering along through the odd quiet of the day.

Finch chose the bar—a place on the edge of the zone called Hellmouth's that was accustomed to a certain uniqueness among their clientele. It was a blister dome, gray as a raincloud. There were teeth painted on the front entrance and the door opened vertically so, walking in, you felt like you was being swallowed up, body and soul.

There were, as promised, girls there. Some even of their own free will. There was also gun hands and gangsters, deserters, loons, fierce knots of costumed hard boys giving off a goatish stink of trouble looking for a place to settle, lab crews still in their white coats and looking like a convention of pharmacists all drinking shots of snake wine that smelled of un-cut kerosene, doomy bikers in ratty feathers and lacrosse pads playing out some kind of freaked-up Mad Max fantasy, and, of course, just plain drunks. Hellmouth's catered well to them of the henching persuasion—with one whole stretch of wall behind the bar plastered with pictures of the honored dead draped in loops of black g-mod carnations. Men in dinosaur green and HLF tails and bunny ears, uniformed Redlegs, other men in ridiculous hats and plasmid blouses that made them look like giant, fat bumblebees. The house shot was overproof cherry brandy, sriracha, and a sprinkling of gunpowder. It was called, unsurprisingly, "the Hellmouth," and it didn't taste as bad as it sounds, but only because it tasted much, much worse.

We drank. For a time, things were peaceful. Squirrel and Fat Randy sat with their elbows down and their heads together, daring each other to go talk to a variety of girls but never actually, you know, going. I drank. I saw Lee and Finch touching liquor to their lips and then emptying glasses into their boot-tops or onto the floor. That seemed the soul of wisdom, but also a terrible waste of perfectly serviceable hooch, so I did not participate in any such profligate sleight-of-hand. Even among the mad, a man must maintain certain standards of decorum. Must live by whatever rules govern him. And one of mine was to drink what was laid afore me in as amiable and gentlemanly a fashion as possible until such time as amity and anodyne goodwill was no longer profitable or prudent. The peaceable sharing of drinks is what elevates man above the monsters of this world. It's what makes us better than the night-mares we have created.

We'd been at table better than an hour when I saw Miss Holly Bright come strolling in through the door-mouth. She looked nine feet tall in shitkicker boots, Daisy Dukes, a leather fringe purse the same shade as an old bruise, and an HLF t-shirt with a flying giraffe on it holding a laser cannon. It read simply NATURAL SELEC-TION IS FOR PUSSIES.

She went to the bar and ordered a beer with a beer chaser. She paid in hard coin, which was unusual for these environs and got her noticed by all the wrong people. She grinned at the room like she was chewing bullets and then locked onto Fat Randy with eyes as cold and passionless as bombsights, stood, downed one beer, hoisted the other, and came sauntering over like she owned the place complete.

"Legion of Terror," she said. "Yo, dinosaurs are wicked sexy."

And that, as they say, was that.

The great thing about idiots is that they're idiots.

And I don't mean that to sound as flippant as it does, because it's not. What I'm saying is, a true idiot—an honest and thoroughgoing representative of the species—tends to be an idiot in all things. Sure, there are idiots out there who are in some ways *not* idiots—who are maybe idiots when it comes to trigonometry but not in understand-ing fine points of ballroom dancing. But real, true, purebred idiots are not like that. They're idiots in every which way. They can be defined as such because their reactions to any situation, to any new stimu-lus, come out of their essential idiocy. Given a universe of possible options, an idiot will always choose the one which hews most closely to their native state. In this way they are absolutely dependable.

Idiots are a case officer's bread and beer. To a field man, they are vital. Idiots can be talked into anything. They are trustworthy.

They are unwavering. You know what you're getting with your idiot. Accept the limitations of their essential idiotness and there are, ultimately, no surprises.

Holly Bright sat for 45 minutes, bellied up to the table with us. She drank shots and laughed loudly. She kept touching Squirrel and Fat Randy, paid a fair amount of pleasant attention to Lee and Finch. Me, she called "Suit" and mostly ignored me unless she couldn't reasonably do so. When forced to interact, she did so with a stilted politeness that screamed an absolute, asexual indifference. Squirrel, she treated like a very cute puppy. She acted like Fat Randy was an Adonis of a man. A bubbling cauldron of sensuality and manly vigors. She licked her lips. Hung on his every stuttering word. Stopped short of climbing into his lap, but just barely.

And to Fat Randy and Squirrel, this all made total sense. As though of *course* a strange, beautiful young woman would approach them, be enthralled by their every utterance, laugh at every muttering attempt at humor, swoon at pick-up lines that were old when Jesus used them. None of this struck them as at all strange. Because they were idiots. And idiots can never see it when the fix is in.

At 46 minutes, Holly wobbled drunkenly to her feet, hooked her purse off the back of her chair, giggled, said she had to pee, and then immediately toppled over and caught herself against me.

"Whew . . ." she said, smiling and biting her lip. "Those shots went right to my head. You boys certainly do know how to drink." Then to me, "You mind escorting me to the ladies room, Suit? Just need an arm to lean on is all."

Fat Randy began to push himself blearily to his feet and offer his assistance, but Holly laid a hand on his arm. "Save your strength, baby," she said. "You get us another round. Let the square here walk with me. I promise I won't run off with him. And when I get back, you can tell me all about your karate lessons."

Because that was the story Fat Randy had been telling her. About the karate lessons he took when he wasn't dressing up like a chunky, sweating dinosaur groupie and how deadly he'd become with his hands.

I got up and walked Holly to the bathrooms at the back of the bar. She leaned heavily against me, giggled wetly, told me how cute she thought Squirrel was. "Like one of those cats," she said. "The ones without any hair that are always shivering and shitting on the floor? So cute . . ."

I got her to the door and felt her hands suddenly go vise-tight on my arm. She never stopped moving, dragging me along with her, still laughing. She hit the door heavily and we staggered inside. There was one other girl in the bathroom, but she left quickly when she saw Holly whooping and stumbling. I smiled an apology as she squeezed past me. The instant the door closed, Holly stood up straight.

"Lock it," she said, then stalked purposefully over to the sink, jammed a finger down her throat and skillfully reversed the drinking process—evacuating all the shots she'd put down in one coughing spasm. She cursed. Ran some water into one hand. Rinsed her mouth out and spat. Cursed again.

"First thing," she said, wiping her chin with the back of her hand. "Captain needs to know if we're a go on the train. If the L.O.T. are going to attack."

I told her that things seemed to be leaning in that direction. She said she needed more assurance than that. I told her that the big men and the troops had all lit out last night to collect their dinosaurs and that the plan was for us and the moron twins to meet up with them out on the plains when everything was in place.

"Then what the fuck are you doing out here drinking?"

"That's a complicated story," I said. "It was this or get shot by Fat Randy."

She shook her head. "Give me a number," she said. "A percentage."

"A hundred percent that they're going to try. Maybe seventy-five percent that they actually get their shit together enough to find the train and make a go of it."

"Okay," she said. "That's good enough for the Captain to gear up the team then. Second thing: You're blown."

"What?"

"Half-blown, anyway. Someone knows Dorian Bloom is here. Not sure if they know Dorian Bloom is Harry Plum or that Harry Plum is Duncan Archer, but there's an OSS blackout team on the way with battle police in support. It's not your fault. It was one of my coat-tailers. She got lazy and didn't notice the tail on her, then got pinched just as you and Finch were rolling in last night. Cap put Dogboy in the field as soon as he heard. We've been hunting them all night, without a lot of success. Then you all decided to go out for drinks and things got messy. Best guess is that we've got about . . ."—she reached into her back pocket and pulled out an old pocket watch without a chain—". . . twenty minutes until they hit this place. Maybe less. But don't worry, there's a plan to cover your getaway."

"Well that makes me feel much better then."

"Don't get smart," she said, sliding the watch back into its place. "Third thing: Would I get anything additional, anything at all useful out of fucking either of those two dipshits you're running with?"

"No. They're idiots."

"Well thank god for that," she muttered, then turned back to the sink, ran some fresh water into her hands and splashed her face, looked into the mirror, scowled, looked back to me. "Number four: Take off your jacket."

I did. She told me to hang it on the back of the door. I turned to the door, saw no hook, and was turning around to tell her so when

I found her nearly on top of me, taking my wrist, getting me in an arm lock and jamming a needle into my wrist. It was over before I had time to protest. She pushed back away from me, held up the syringe and smiled. "That's five cc's of dedicated tracker nanites, bud. Pheromone trigger. To a calibrated sensor, like maybe the one in Dogboy's nose, you're now gonna stink like a fart in church. Cap had a lojack on you, but it failed for some reason. So now, if you live long enough, we'll have a way to find you on that train and pull you out before the worst happens. Keep Finch and Lee close to you so we can scoop them up, too. Those are orders. Got it?"

I rubbed my wrist, smearing a spot of blood onto the cuff of my shirt. "Got it. Anything else?"

"This," she said, reached into her purse, put away the syringe, and came back out with a military-grade tear gas grenade, which she tossed to me. "You and me are going to cause a ruckus now. You ready?"

I smiled. "This is my kind of date."

"Shut up and listen, okay?"

"For what?"

She walked to the door and leaned an ear against it. "You'll know when you hear it. I have some friends out there. They're about to have a problem with your friends. When they do—"

There was a scream, high and piercing. A babble of raised voices. The crash of shattering glass.

Miss Holly Bright nodded at me. "Baby, they're playing our song," she said. "Give me thirty seconds, then come out, pop that smoke, start yelling cop, get your people, and get the fuck out by anything but the front door."

She opened the door. The sounds of bad things happening close by flooded in and she darted right into the middle of it, which always seemed to be her most rightwise place. I stepped clear of the bathroom, snaked my way quietly around the curving wall, counted to thirty, and pulled the pin on the grenade. I knew that things were going to get nasty fast. I took a deep breath. Then one more. Then I underhanded the grenade down along the wall, saw the magnesium igniter pop, and started yelling at the top of my lungs, "Cops! Cops! Everybody run! The beeps are coming in!"

Fat Randy had a hostage—a topless cocktail waitress who, near as I could recall, had not been topless before becoming making Randy's acquaintance.

Squirrel was dancing with a fat man in biker leathers, throwing wild punches with his head down and his eyes closed. The fat man had Squirrel by the front of his pale green Legion of Terror outfit and seemed to be trying very hard not to hurt him. There was a crowd of gawkers all shouting and throwing things and generally elevating the commotion. Pressing in close, Lee and Finch had their hands out and were trying to cool down an advancing knot of angry, spitting leather boys, beefed up by what passed for security at Hellmouth's—two sharp-looking bouncers in identical suits with eight arms, two tasers, and a cricket bat between them.

Half the crowd startled the minute I said "Cop" and, at the first whiff of CS, everyone tried to run in every single direction at once. I kept yelling and kept moving—fighting the scatter patterns of the rapidly panicking crowd to get to Randy, at whom I bellowed, "Beeps, Randy! Let the girl go. We gotta run!"

Randy said something bombastic about fighting cops, but he unwrapped the boiled ham of his arm from around her head and she bolted like a spooked fawn. The fat man dropped Squirrel. I caught Lee's eye and twirled a finger at him. *Wrap it up.* Then I pointed to the back wall of Hellmouth's. *Time to duck out the back way.*

Lee grabbed Finch. Finch collected Squirrel. I saw Fat Randy turning in slow circles in the center of the room near what had been our table and hollering about how he'd take on any cop that wanted a piece of him, so I circled, came in low on his blind side, hit him with two hard shots in the kidney that dropped him like a cow hit with a bat and he immediately began to cry.

Someone tripped over him and went sprawling. Someone else stepped on his hand and he curled into a ball. I circled back to his other side like a crab, found my briefcase on the floor, grabbed it, then bent down and got my face in Randy's face.

"Randy," I said. "You okay? Someone hit you!"

"Ow," said Randy. "Owowowowow . . ."

I heaved him onto the fat meatloaves of his feet. The gas was filling the room. I coughed and spit and we ran for the back wall, found Lee and Finch and Squirrel, and there discovered that Hellmouth's had no back door. It was a dome. There was only one way in and out.

Or, rather, one *traditional* way.

Randy had the big revolver shoved in his pants like a dumb gangster. I reached for it. He slapped at my hands and I restrained myself from hitting him again, even though I really wanted to. I yanked the gun free, aimed it low at the wall and pulled the trigger three times.

Three huge booms in such a confined space. Three ragged holes in the skin of the dome. I handed the revolver to Lee, bent down—my eyes watering now, my breath burning in my throat as the dome's air recirculators sucked at the tear gas and whipped it like a hurricane all around the room—popped the catches on my briefcase, and took out Julie's knife.

It was sharp, thank the good Lord, and with it I sawed us an exit. I pushed Lee through first, then Squirrel. Finch and me together dragged Randy out into the heat and the chaos of the day. I hadn't been the only smart boy in Hellmouth's. It was leaking gas and people from a half-dozen fluttering gashes in its skin. We tumbled onto pavement, rolled, gasping, in broken glass and gravel, laughing at our own good fortune. I shoved the knife into my belt, rolled onto my belly and got to my feet. There was a twinge in my leg—buried beneath the numbness of cheap liquor and the adrenaline of the moment—but I stood. And that was when I saw the actual cops descending. Battle police in their business blacks, clubs and shields in hand, mirrored face shields gleaming in the sun. They were early, which was gauche. And feeling bangy, which was just vulgar.

We ran. Into the ruin of a strip mall behind Hellmouth's, out through a blast hole in the wall of a barbershop, into a narrow alley, ducking and scrambling as blind-fired bullets slapped the cinder-blocks near us—puffing dust and spraying needles of stone in our faces—then backtracking, going another way, crawling through a window that let out into a sheltered courtyard full of ripe dumpsters and a carpet of cockroaches, through a squeezeway so narrow we had to shimmy along it single-file, then popping out into the open and the sun for long enough to see the truck—my truck—burning like a torch in the lot where we'd parked it; two OSS gray-suits standing close by, stubby little machine pistols in their hands. One of them was smoking. The other casually raised his weapon and stitched a man in a lab coat who ran past, grinning as the man's legs went out from underneath him and he sprawled in the dust and rubble of the ruined world.

"Go," I hissed, and pushed Fat Randy away from the truck and the O-men at an angle. "Quick, you pudgy fuck. Move it."

Fat Randy sniffled and groaned, but ran and made such a loud-ness of it that the O-men turned in our direction, raised their guns, fired like they were watering a garden. Bullets went everywhere except into us. I'd say it was miraculous except that it wasn't. We were probably fifty feet away and guns like theirs were barely accu-rate with the barrels pressed firm against the target.

We went back into the wreckage, popped out, went back in. It was hide-and-seek, played for lethal stakes. When we ran smack into two beeps coming sharpish around a corner less than a block clear of Hellmouth's front door, I pushed Fat Randy into the first one and punched the second square in his face shield, which I figured was enough to break his nose, at least. Lee was right on my back, press-ing the barrel of the revolver into the chest of the one I'd hit and pulling the trigger. The gunk of his body armor absorbed the report but didn't stop the bullet. Blood spattered the wall behind him, and I could hear him choking in the shock of his perishment. Fat Randy squirmed like an octopus on top of the other beep, pinning him to ground beneath his own shield. To save the cop's life, I kicked him in the side of the head as hard as I could. Then I kicked him again. And again. When he went limp, I stopped.

"Keep moving," I said, dragging Randy once more to his feet. "We don't find a ride out of here, we're all dead."

As though to punctuate the seriousness of my point, we all heard the hiss-shriek-boom of an air-to-ground missile lasering in on its target. The drone snapped past right above our heads. In a second, Hellmouth's had become just another crater in a place that seemed to grow them like wildflowers. A fireball bloomed then collapsed. Black smoke smeared the blue sky. Debris rattled down like the sky had split and begun raining stones. Briefly wonder-struck, we stared up into it like children, slack-jawed in the face of thunder and lightning and all other manifestations of God's unearthly wrath.

It took us another hour to squirm and sneak and slither our way through the cordon. Eventually, Squirrel proved his usefulness by stealing us a car. It had no rubber on the wheels and only a thimble-full of gas, but we rolled on bare, sparking rims and chugged it to within six blocks of the Starbucks before it sputtered, gave a final resigned gasp, and died. We rode with our guns in our hands. No one said a word. And when we all piled out again, Fat Randy took us not to the main entrance, but to a falling-down garage that he said concealed a back door.

This was good because I knew that, having missed me at Hellmouth's, the OSS surveillance would be regrouping at the last place they'd had a positive ID on Dorian Bloom—the World's Creepiest Starbucks—in the hope that he would return there to give them a second shot at bedding him down for good. And honestly, I'd had no idea how I was going to deal with that problem if that was where Fat Randy and Squirrel had taken us.

The wreck of a garage sat like a shell around a perfectly functional second garage within. And from this inner garage, there was a ramp that led down into the bunker we'd so recently left. In as few words as possible, we all agreed that, if we made it back inside undetected, none of us would breathe a word about what we'd done to the Legion's dinosaur heads.

"It's best that they don't know the kind of trouble we made," Fat Randy said, nodding sagely as he waddled down at the head of our merry little band. "I don't know that they'd appreciate right now the kind of efforts the cops was making to take down Squirrel and me. Ain't that right, Squirrel?"

Squirrel nodded and said nothing. He had a grin on him like a knife wound in a pumpkin. We all got below, rinsed out our eyes, scrubbed our faces, rubbed the gravel from out of our hair. Lee gave Fat Randy the revolver back, but Fat Randy raised his hands before him and said to give it to Squirrel.

"It's his turn now," he said. "Only fair."

Squirrel took it and sniffed at the barrel, pointed it at his own face, tried spinning it on his finger. As a group, we decided it might be best to just lay the gun aside for the time being. Finch went looking for coffee. I sat and rubbed my leg.

It was less than a half-hour before the Legion came back for us. There was just one man, stepping silently into the room from one of the many doors, dressed in slick ceramic hardplate and tall riding boots with wicked looking spurs jangling at his heels. His armor was tinted green and had a ridge of chromium spikes running down the spine. He walked with a rigid sort of purpose and, upon discovering us all laying about down there in the basement, looked us over like something unpleasant he'd found floating in his breakfast cereal.

"Let's go," was all he said, then turned sharply on his heel and went back out the door again. Finch and I took the case of explosives and I balanced my briefcase on top. Lee took the revolver.

"Ninja mind," said Squirrel to Fat Randy, nodding as we followed the man through an up-slanting hallway and into a different garage where a six-wheel electric cargo truck sat idling silently.

"Most assuredly ninja mind," said Fat Randy. "That is a man ready to do some serious wrecking."

It took us eight hours to drive to the middle of nowhere—out into the largeness and the flatness of the plains. We slept the night in the truck's bed, parked in what had once been Burlington, Colorado but was now only an ashy wreck of house bones and the crumbled memories of things that'd once been things. Homes where families had been raised. Shops where the business of the day had once gone on. In the night and the dark, I wandered a bit. No one moved to stop me because, really, where was I going to go? I hobbled in circles and kicked at the ground with my one goodish leg. In the lee of a broken wall, I found a Coke can, smashed flat, and tried to remember when was the last time I'd drunk a cold Coke.

It was longer than I could honestly recall.

I sat with the wall between the truck and me and opened my briefcase on my knees. I sorted my things, tucked away my knife, checked the load and action of my automatic, unloaded and reloaded the clip, then checked my phones. On one, there were four missed calls, all from the phone I'd given to Gordon, and one wavering bar.

I bounced the phone in the palm of my hand, eased myself up enough to look back at the truck, then settled back down. I closed my eyes and opened my mouth a little to hear better. And in that way I sat, for an hour or more. I heard a hundred small things but none of them were the sounds of a man moving to get the drop on me. None of them were the rustlings of anyone feeling awakeish and lighting out for a stroll.

I enlivened the phone with my thumb and stared at the screen. I touched the missed call and the phone reached out over incalculable distances to find Gordon Navarro in whatever place Gordon Navarro kept himself on nights laden with freights of worry. Strip clubs. Whorehouses. Bars of villainous aspect. A man who liked to roll deep in the dirty, was Gordo. To surround himself with characters who, he presumed, had done worse than him to earn their eagles on any given day.

Gordon picked up on the first ring and said my name. It sounded so loud that I closed my eyes and waited for the cool touch of a pistol barrel on the back of my neck.

"Insecure," I whispered. "Observed."

"Copy," he said. "I settled your problem."

"Which one?"

"The horseman. He was still alive."

"Was?"

"Was. Sorry, Jimmy. Makes you feel any better, he never saw me coming."

I hissed into the phone like a snake. Just "Ssssssss . . ." because I wanted to say so much, but couldn't. Didn't have the words. Lost the command of them in the moment that Gordon Navarro told me he'd killed Arthur Reginald Molesworth. For me.

"You're welcome, you ungrateful f—"

I hung up. Switched off the phone. Laid it carefully back in my briefcase, closed my eyes, and hung my head. The night was dark and long and filled with terrible things. I was only one among many, and likely not even the terriblest. But thinking that gave me no peace at all.

At dawn, we rolled out. Fat Randy complained of the hour. Squirrel rubbed at his eyes like a child. The day was cloudy and, in the distance, feed irrigation systems turned and bot harvesters crawled the perfect rows of g-mod corn and wheat and soy and bamboo and microchip bushes and opium poppies.

I rode in silence and no one bothered me. Harry Plum had a temper, that was known. Was whipped by bitter humors. No one wanted to rile him when he was looking blue.

Two more hours of slow jouncing across washboarded ranch roads and I saw the maglev rails for the first time. Seeing them hit me with a spike of old fear that I swallowed like a dry second tongue. Another fifteen minutes and we were crawling behind a low rise—a gully cut by some ancient river, long gone to dryness. There was red stone. Granite sparkling with mica flakes. Brown dirt and a tangle of scrubby, low bushes with leaves that looked like they were made of wax, at which stood a triceratops, placidly chewing.

It was 9am or near to it when we pulled into the temporary bivouac of the Legion of Terror. There were fifty of them, plus a handful. A monstrous conglomeration of a tank. Three triceratops, all told. A herd of raptors—six feet tall standing and looking young and ripe and vicious in a way that only truly wild things do. The raptors were collared and chained and staked out inside a pen made of electrificated wire. As we pulled in, they were eating a cow that appeared to have been brought along for just that purpose. It'd been a live cow fairly recently, which was a rare thing. But maybe not so rare to men who can make their own dinosaurs. The triceratops, for their part, were just ambling around eating anything green and staring up at the sky as though waiting for something to alight upon them.

When they opened their mouths, they made a sound like a giant blowing his nose.

For a moment, a childlike awe subsumed every other awfulness in me. "Holy shit," I said.

"I know," said Finch, standing beside me with his arms crossed. "No one ever believes it until they see it. Not for nothing, but Dinosaur Joe was a goddamn genius."

Train 1066 to Goodland was due to pass in about five hours.

After all it'd cost, I really hoped that the Captain would be there.

EPISODE

10

Last Train to Goodland, Part 3

IN THE HIGH NOON SUN, I SQUATTED ON THE CURLING LIP OF A BURL in the land and watched two children warily approach the bullet-holed body of a Kansan war robot.

It was a small one, the robot. Maybe twelve feet tall and standing lurched over on the apron of a fallow field, just a few paces off a frontage road that'd returned mostly to dust. It'd been splashed hastily with the separatist colors, as though buckets of paint had been dumped over the welded-on armor at its shoulders, but still showed the flaking safety orange of its previous life on some assembly line before it'd been drafted, de-pacified and turned out to fight.

The children were a boy and a girl—her 4 or 5, him just a couple years older. Somewhere between hay and grass. *Brother and sister*, I thought. Or maybe neighbor kids, forced together into friendship and adventures simply by a lack of other options. Both wore heavy

490

boots with lug soles, probably printed for them down at the community feed, and patched, hand-me-down field pants, rubbery and yellow, with bibs and straps like overalls that made them both look like they'd just stepped off the world's most adorable crab boat.

The boy wore goggles, but had his rebreather hung around his neck, okay, apparently, with breathing in whatever DNA chaff he kicked up in his passing, unafraid of the recursion going on in his lungs, the blastomas of free assemblers and broken helices that would grow there. The girl had strawberry-blonde curls and a cheap surgical mask over her face. Through the binoculars, I could see the pock marks on her cheeks from where virulent colonies of wild carrier phages or spore bacteria had been clumsily removed. Probably by her father, with a pocketknife honed on cement. When she coughed, she sounded like a two-pack-a-day smoker with seventy years already behind her. Obviously, her family was poor.

The two of them approached the robot, moving slow. I could see the plasticky summer grasses growing up through the skeletal hydraulics of the machine's feet, the cracked shell of one of its fairing panels sprouting tufts of bird's nest, and the blackened rims of the holes where a surfeit of violence had finally forced it into shutdown. It had an arm that'd once been a plasma welder with a licking tongue of blue-white flame hot enough to melt steel. The other was a re-mount chain gun. She'd been a tank killer, that 'bot; her heuristic intelligence filled completely up with an aching want to detonate the Chobham slabs of Western Confederacy battle tanks, peel back the smoking steel, and smash all the soft, squishy people inside. If you could believe the kill marks etched into her armor, she'd been very good at it. Problem was, you could never believe the kill marks.

I watched as the boy took something out of his overalls—a package swaddled in cloth. He carefully unwrapped it and it was a gun. A small, flat pistol which he loaded and cocked with a flourish and held out to the little girl.

She did not take it immediately, but he convinced her. Showed her how to hold it with two hands, to keep her little arms out straight. I watched as he coaxed her tiny finger inside the trigger guard, watched her turn her face away and jerk the trigger—the shot going wild and the sound of it nothing more than a distant hand clap.

Beyond them, far and away, I could see the plume of dust that signaled train 1066 slowing for the first curve. It was maybe ten miles away on a straight shot. More like fifteen following the track. For what it was worth, the Legion of Terror had chosen their ambush position well.

Again, the boy showed the girl how to hold the pistol. He held her hands. Helped her aim at the hulking wreck of the dead war robot. Another hand clap. Another miss, even from just fifteen feet away. The girl tried to hand the pistol back to the boy, but he refused. Held up his hands and backed away a step.

The Legion had their tank backed up down the frontage road. I could hear its engine, hot and growling, from where I squatted, but it would be invisible to the train until it was too late. It would shoot once, then move, but if its first shot missed the mark, things would become inestimably more complicated. I'd been assured that the tank gunner was good. That he would not miss.

I assumed he would miss.

One more try. The girl aimed carefully. Through the binoculars, I saw the pink nub of her tongue poking out the corner of her mouth. The boy stood just behind her, a smile on his face like he knew something secret.

She squeezed the trigger. The gun fired. The bullet struck the robot square, instantly sparking off some ancient threat response protocol, sucking juice from reserve batteries, grinding the almost-but-not-quite dead machine into a sudden, spastic life. Its chain gun arm twitched up like it was weightless, as though it didn't weigh five hundred pounds. Ballistics programs back-traced the path of the bullet in a fraction of a second and locked onto the threat—not understanding that it was a five-year-old girl with someone's daddy's plinking gun. The barrels were already whining up to speed, spinning with an awful grinding sound and the girl was standing there, screaming, not moving, the gun still in her hand and her hands over her ears as the robot quaked and rattled in place and the targeting system found her.

The barrels spun but there was no murderous hail of bullets. Just a clacking sound like a storm door banging in the wind. The thing was out of ammunition.

Behind her, the boy was laughing. He'd obviously played this game before. But the girl wouldn't stop screaming. Even after the 'bot had settled back into inaction. Even after the barrels had ground to a scouring halt, she was crying. And when the boy approached—slowly, carefully, to take the pistol from her hands—she hit him with it. A wild, flailing haymaker that caught him over the eye and sent him to his knees with both hands pressed to the spot where she'd blooded him.

"Good, you little shit," I said to the wind. "You deserved that." Then I checked the train's position one more time, turned, and slid down off the hump of earth behind which the Legion had hidden their test-tube beasts. Their dinosaurs.

"Train's coming," I said to the chief monster wrangler in his fancy hardplate armor and high boots. "Saddle 'em up."

There are two ways that the universe works. In all its glorious clock-work splendor, there are two possible ways that it keeps from shaking itself to pieces every time a butterfly farts.

The first option is a theory which says that everything is real. That the world as we know it is the world as we know it. That every action builds a chain of consequent reactions and that these, too, are hard and real and unforgiving. It says that everything that happens, from the depths of the mundane to the apex of the fantastical, is both the logical result of things that have happened before and the catalysts of things *yet* to occur. The world and your experience of it, says this first theory, is real *because* it is the world you experience. Quanta shift states. Electrons hop valences. Atoms couple and decouple. Water flows. Mountains tremble. Stars burn. The robot in the field shudders and goes quiet, its ammunition long ago spent.

The second theory, on the other hand, is actually true.

Dinosaurs up close smell terrible. Like heavy moss and a fat man's sweat and a deep and animal funk like old tee shirts left too long in a gym locker. They smell of the grass the way I can vaguely recall a greenhouse smelling—like too much life packed into too small a space. But mostly, they smell of shit.

I sat, smoking a cigarette, with my back to the exposed and sun-warmed red rocks. I watched the dinosaur experts from the L.O.T.'s secret ranch tightening girth straps and flank cinches, running the saddle rigging under and around the massive bodies of their triceratopses while they stood, laconically chewing at whatever greenery they could find and, occasionally, hissing, blowing, or making noises like an old man standing up. There wasn't never a moment that I didn't comprehend the anachronistic strangeness of what I was doing. The wild improbability of it. In a world of dragons and dogboys, of high-hat weirdoes with rabbit ears and girls with wings and children walking around with tails and eyes of etched Vogel crystal, there remained something primally effecting about being so close to a living, breathing, blood-pumping monster that hadn't walked the earth in millions of years. Something lost, but now found again. A miracle of abjuration and crossover and whatever strange genius lived in the head of Dinosaur Joe. The world was richer and stranger for having honest-to-Jesus dinosaurs in it again, I felt. For as twisted and broken as it might've been, it was still a world replete with wonderments fit to boggle even the most jaded of eyes.

As I sat smoking, Squirrel sidled up beside me. He wore a door gunner's vest, dyed a sickly shade of green, that looked like it'd last seen duty over Khe Sahn. He had a bit of rope tied around the middle of it like a belt and had stuck what was either a short sword or a long knife through it. A cutlass, I guess it would've been. A pirate's sword. And he carried a long-barreled shotgun over one shoulder, beautifully scrolled. A collector's piece back in the day's before it'd become valuable solely for its ability to spit lead. The uses of all things now reduced to their most elemental or most clever.

"I just seen one of them pointy-heads shit something the size of a toddler," he said, grinning. "Never seen nothing like that before in my life."

I looked up at him, squinting at the lovely, bright sun burning on his shoulders like a fiery grace, and reminded myself that different things impress different people. That some men see dinosaurs cropping the bluestem and are reminded of the odd magic that lives now in a land governed by no rightwise compacts, and that others could still be awestruck by a really big turd.

"You keep your head down out there, okay, Squirrel?" I said.

He patted the stock of his shotgun like it was baby in need of burping. "Gonna get me some O-men today, Mr. Plum. Fucking A."

I'd like to say that I lamented all them that I was riding off to their deaths—Fat Randy and Squirrel and all their friends. I'd like to say that I had a moment of regret, knowing what was coming and the lies that I'd told them, but I did not. It was a question of loyalties. Of knowing who I was fighting for and who I wanted to see ultimate victory. But it was a hard nut, that. I'd been an O-man once. Was, arguably, one again now—whether in the employ of the Captain or the boss. And yet I was unleashing this rabble upon *other* O-men, and whomever they had on the train with them. Turning on them that had once been brothers to me and dragging behind me them as I'd promised a temporary brotherhood to. They was all men who thought they was doing right. All of them enflated with grandiose notions of duty and vengeful propriety. Really, all I was concerned with was my own skin and getting through the coming conflagration with all or most of my blood still inside me. And sitting there as Harry Plum, obsessed with his notions of comeuppance, was easier than sitting there as Duncan Archer, for sure. So the truest question was really only in deciding who was the bad guy. Who deserved what they was about to get.

I shaded my eyes and looked around for Finch and Lee. It was going to be time to go soon.

As previously stated, there are two ways that the universe works. The first way is that everything is true and real and consequent. There is one world and we make our way in it as best we can.

The other option is similar, and yet vitally different. The second theory allows that, yes, things are real. You still have to pay your bills and feed the cat and if you throw a rock at a window, the window will shatter.

Except . . .

Sometimes the rock will shatter. And that's real, too.

Sometimes the rock will vanish in transit, leaving the window unharmed. And that's real, too.

Sometimes the window will shatter, but rather than breaking into a thousand glittering, sharp shards, it will shatter into a thousand tiny penguins. Sometimes the penguins will fly away. Sometimes the penguins will approach, thank you for freeing them from their glassy prison, and make you King of Tiny Penguin Land. And that—all of it—is also real.

The thing that's amusing to consider but terrible to know for certain is that the second theory is the true one. It's the difference between everything being real and EVERYTHING being real. All of you, somewhere, are King of Tiny Penguin Land.

The triceratopses, rigged as they were, could each carry five men, and that was where I was riding—alongside Lee and Finch, the three of us waving from one of the Cadillacs of this strange parade. First-class seats all the way.

The raptors were leashed with lengths of chain, three to a lead, and collied by handlers on armor-plated three-wheel ATV's with balloon tires and roll cages.

The bulk of the L.O.T.'s boarding forces were loaded into the cargo trucks that'd brought the beasts and their supplies and upon which defenses had been hastily erected overnight—iron grate and corrugated steel and uprooted road signs bolted and welded onto the low-rise beds to provide some cover for them as would be riding into the thick. There was a psychotic DIY flavor to it all that I found not entirely uninspiring in its rattletrap and scrappy optimism. Seeing the drunk, whooping, ridiculously attired men piling into the trucks with their mish-mash array of small arms, pig-stickers, spiked hair, green tatters of uniform, and useless bits of re-re-recycled armor was like watching a procession of ghosts. Their fates had been decided long ago by men they never knew, by forces they didn't imagine as being arrayed against them. The unnamed chorus of this tragedy in the offing, alive here only so they might die conveniently to my cause somewhere close by. Wanna know why I joined up with the OSS in the first place so long ago? Because it sucks to be a Red Shirt. To be one of the little people manipulated into dying by the big-and-distant.

The saddlery the Legion's dinosaur handlers had devised was clever, and allowed for two men to ride like saddlebags on each side of a triceratops—standing in stirrups thrown over its flanks and holding tight to bullropes, hidden mostly behind the bony shield of its massive head. A fifth, then, lay himself belly-down aback the flaring crest, on a seat made special for it, threw his legs around the monster's massive torso, and more or less drove the thing with nasty, gleaming rib hooks on his heels and reins that were like jumper cables clamped to an iron bit in the dinosaur's mouth. Like chewing on a live power line, it was. The only way one might get twelve tons of angried-up monster to turn on a dime.

I'd scavenged up a bit of stretch-rope and had tied my briefcase slant-wise across my back. The case of Cyclot-8 was secured to my ride's hindquarters on a padded seat of its own that I'd devised with an eye toward making it appear protective of the ostensibly unstable boom-jelly. I'd been worried over the one actual tube of the stuff I was in possession of—the one that I would need to prove my worth and actually bring this dumbshow to its proper, fiery conclusion— but had come up with an inspired last-minute solution. I'd stuck it right to the thick skin of my dinosaur with a glob of polymer resin that I'd later need to stick it to the train itself, then smoothed a profusion of silver duct tape right onto the rough flesh of the beast, avoiding the odd tufts of spiny hair-ish whiskers that sprouted hap-hazardly from its up-close ugliness, and left the tube stuck there, perilously close to my head once I'd actually mounted up. If it blew either out of plain, cussed annoyance or a million-to-one hit from a bullet, I would never know. A fine pink mist with no regrets I would be. But in the meantime, it was the smoothest ride I could offer and I said a quiet little prayer to it and the temperamental gods of explosives that my boom-jelly remain unjostled enough that I might employ it as this ridiculous plan demanded and live long enough to see it done.

Lee and Finch took the pegs across from me. The dinosaur driver took his place in the saddle. I asked him if his beast had a name and he scoffed at me, glowering down from his seat with a ferocious disdain.

"Ain't got no name," he said. "Gots a brain the size of a walnut and don't know from nothing but eating, shitting, and stomping shit to death." He raised himself up slightly then, looking out over the crest of the triceratops's frill as though sighting something on the horizon, then sank back and patted the thing with surpassing gentleness upon its massive shoulder. He looked at me again, tilted his head just so, and smiled a soft little smile. "But when I gots to call her something, I calls her Daisy," he said. "She's a good girl, and just as brave as stupid can make her."

He glanced around again and then leaned down close to me. "I'd really appreciate it if me and her both lived through this day, Mr. Plum. So you do what you gotta do then get right the fuck away from us, clear?"

"Crystal," said me. And then I patted Daisy on her heaving side, my own heart hammering, my own voice a little tight with anxiousness. "Just get me close, Daisy. I'll do the rest."

The final set of pegs—those directly in front of me—were ascended to by a humorless L.O.T. commissar, giving Finch, Lee, me, and the driver all the stink eye in one all-encompassing and practiced glance.

"To death," he growled, drawing a gleaming revolver from his belt with the hand that wasn't gripping his bullrope, "and the greater glory of the Legion. Any of you quail in the face of the enemy, I will hole you where you stand."

"You have got to be fucking kidding me," I said.

The man looked back at me. "I assure you that I am not. I'll be watching you, Mr. Plum. Fail us, and you'll taste lead."

I shook my head. Between Lee, Finch, and my own self, we outgunned this growling, Saturday matinee dimwit three-to-one. I did not envy that man's odds on seeing the next sunrise, which I reckoned as a fair sight poorer even than that of all the others pledged to Dinosaur Joe's doomed cause.

The two theories on the governance of the universe and everything in it have to do with waveforms and the care and keeping of them. They have to do with Schroedigerian arguments about ambiguously dead cats and boxes, discussions of the consistent histories of quantum propositions, Hugh Everett's relative state, the Copenhagen Interpretation of reality, both gross and fine, and an understanding of the Heisenberg Uncertainty Principle which, to science-y types, says a lot of things, but to you and me, here and now, says just one: When you look at a thing, you change it. When you look at a thing, you make it real.

The signal for us to move out and begin the assault was to be the tank firing. An impossible thing to miss. Or so you'd think.

The signal for the tank to fire was to be the boom of the train's shockwave projector detonating—a necessary bit of equipment on a train which, in its best moments, traveled at 200 miles per hour through land which was occasionally abounding with cows, feral hounds, monsters of varying size and mental capacity, tumbleweeds, Kansans and highjack enthusiasts of all stripes. It was a tuned sonic cannon, mounted on the bulletish nose of the machine, which, when triggered, would blast the holy whatsis out of anything within its cone of effect.

From what I dimly understood of the workings of such fancies, it was a thing that could only be used infrequently—requiring charging or reloading or something of the sort after every use. And the Legion of Terror had made fully sure that the train's engineer would blow the thing by erecting across the train's path a barricade of scrap metal, beer bottles, wood scrap, a ladder, and the rusted carcass of a junked Ford Fairlane convertible that they'd found dead in a pole barn not far away. In their surpassing cleverness, the strategic minds of the Legion had also thought to adorn their fortification with a couple of less-wise brothers-in-arms who'd been ordered to plink away at the train with long rifles at a distance the minute it came out of the curves and into the straight approach—just to get the attention of the driver, you understand. To make it look as though the barricade meant business and wasn't there as just a pointy distraction to keep folk from noticing all the dinosaurs.

The firing of the shockwave projector would also be an impossible thing to miss. Or so you'd think.

All of this was, as I'd said, a far better plan than I'd thought the Legion could come up with when left to their own think. There was a rational organization to it—a sense of making the best of a bad situation and an employment of their limited resources in the wisest ways possible. When it'd all been described to me—one of the chief dinosaur heads scribbling diagrams in the dirt with a stick— I'd felt a thin, tepid confidence. A weak tea of conviction, as it were. A sensation of less than complete and abject incredulity regarding the possibility of any of us surviving long enough to actually touch the train itself. It was what had kept me from scratching Duncan Archer's Last Will and Testament onto the rocks of our final hide— though even then, just barely.

But what I hadn't taken into account—what I had, howsoever briefly, forgotten in the rising excitement of the moment— was that the L.O.T. was peopled almost exclusively by idiots and psychopaths for whom dying in the name of Dinosaur Joe was the best possible future they could hope for. They were men who feared nothing because they were men who believed with their whole peppercorn hearts that a photo on the wall at Hellmouth's and being remembered by their friends for being the first one shot, blown up, trampled by dinosaurs or just generally killed to death by any lethal expedient available was a fine thing to hope for and a good way to spend an otherwise lovely morning out upon the Eastern Plains.

And so thusly did the commissar riding before me rap on the hip of Daisy's driver with his shiny pistol and order him to move forward and out of the lee of our cover early just so, like a small and un-bright Patton, he could get a look at the lay of things for himself.

And so thusly did the other triceratopses and the other triceratops riders *also* begin shuffling forward—fearing, perhaps, that Daisy was looking to get an unfair jump on them when it came to all the coming fire and the rapidly aborning proof of their mortality.

And so thusly did them minding the raptors (which had all taken to screeching and slashing at each other with their vicious claws) clamber aboard their ATV's, snap fast their chains, and gun the engines. So, too, them driving the cargo trucks full of the terminally foolish—each of them inching forward, spitting dirt from beneath studded off-road tires, jockeying for position and angling for a head start.

And so thusly did someone inside the L.O.T.'s grumbling duct-tape-and-Bondo wreck of a tank see all this confusticated hubbub amid the rocks and, apparently, think that they'd missed their cue to action. So without having given the gunner his chance at glory, its driver began clanking and grinding the thing forward into a more advantageous firing position—meaning one from which they could actually see the train which was, as yet, still sailing easily through the backside of its last curve before entering our ambush zone and, as yet, well outside the effective range of the tank's main gun.

And so thusly did the geniuses manning the barricade, seeing the tank on the move, convince themselves that they, too, had waited overlong and so began firing wildly at the flank of the train as it rolled broadside to them and suddenly began cranking up its own speed as someone inside it with a bit more in the way of brains than was possessed by them outside it no doubt thought to themselves that something untoward was likely in the offing and that the best way to deal with it would be to go really, *really* fast until any and all troubles was left far behind in the dust.

Once the tank moved, the likelihood of its gunner hitting anything other than air fell to nothing-plus-one.

Once the dinosaurs broke cover, the likelihood of us having anything remotely resembling surprise on our side went right out the parlor door.

And, really, once the carefully conceived plan had been as thoroughly banjaxed as it had been in just a handful of seconds by the meddling brainlessness of fools, there was really only one thing left to do.

We charged.

In bed together one day, Jemma Watts talked to me about the ways of the universe. She tried to educate me, such as she could, but I was, as you can imagine, powerfully distracted.

Oh, should I have said "Spoiler Alert?"

But you wouldn't get that joke, would you?

If this story goes on long enough—if you keep me alive long enough to get there—then you'll understand. Then maybe I can tell you a love story rather than this one, all full of bad men and dinosaurs and betrayal. But I digress . . .

She says to me, "Duncan, darling, sweetness, love of my ever-lasting life. What you have to understand is that Iggy's mistake was in looking, but it wasn't really a mistake because looking is what we do."

And then she rises, naked as the daylight, from the warm and tangled island of bedclothes we'd made for ourselves. She walks through shafts of buttery yellow sunlight to an oak dresser where-upon sat a tin pitcher sweating beads of condensation. In her passage through the brightness of our room, it seemed that she'd become suffused with light—her cornsilk hair awash with micro-scopic lightnings, her skin glowing as though radiating photons I was uniquely calibrated to see—and I loved her.

"We can't help but look," she says to me, pouring water from the pitcher into a cup, then turning, smiling at me and walking back barefoot across a floor of polished hardwood, leaving behind perfect footprints on the wood that vanish like a fog of breath on a mirror. "Looking is what makes us human."

What happened next was madness.

Because, as the Captain had said, the Chemist was important—because, as the boss, Nimrod Kane, had explained to me on that frozen day in the sitting room of an airport keeper's house, the Chemist would, for one brief and shining moment, be the *most* important man in the world—so did the universes twist and buck all about the moving point of the Chemist's singular existence. We had thrown the dice the moment we'd moved on the train, and as we whooped and hollered down upon it, they were still tumbling. All was a wild slew of probability. A storm of superpositional waveforms and decoupled quantum histories, functions split off from broken equations flying 'round like bullets—the shrapnel of shattered classical mechanics. It was an abjuration to end all abjurations.

The world vibrated like watching the reflection of all and everything seen in moving water. The land rippled. Tornadoes snaked down fat fingers that danced across the muddled earth. I and everyone about me unfolded into an infinity of ourselves, then accordioned down into mere multiples then died and didn't die and exploded and didn't explode. Rain lashed and wind blew and blisters swole the ground and burst until rock and stone and dirt and grass hung in the air like the movie of the world had gotten stuck in its projector and begun to burn.

The raptors grew huge. Became a dozen Godzillas stomping across creation, and then shrank to the size of terrier dogs—yapping and exceedingly mean. A vanguard of Kansan war robots grew up out of the dirt, rising like zombified machinery from the sour earth that held them. Their guns chattered. Their torches flared. But they were ghostly and insubstantial. Daisy passed clean through one and I closed my eyes, cupped my palm ridiculously over the tube of Cyclot-8, and pressed my head to the hot, stinking body of my dinosaur like a child praying to an unnamed god that closing his eyes might make him invisible to the monsters even then descending on him in the smothering dark.

It did not work. There was no lord of the quanta to hear my entreaties. No benign intelligence who might vouchsafe my continued existence simply because I was the one telling this damnfool story.

I died. And then died again. And then again and again and again. I exploded, was shot, fell, was trampled into jelly by the pounding feet of triceratopses charging across the Eastern Plains. I swallowed fire and ate bullets and screamed and laughed and, like a wild and unsolvable variable threading an impossible course through a complex equation, some of me also lived and stood high on my stirrups and roared out the fury of my immortal triumph from the back of a dinosaur bearing inexorably down upon a train.

The L.O.T. commissar looked back at me and I bit off his head. Exultant, I turned my eyes to the swirling bruise-purple sky and swallowed a twister whole.

The L.O.T. commissar looked back at me and I cowered.

The L.O.T. commissar looked back at me and I roared all the louder.

The L.O.T. commissar looked back at me and I didn't even notice. My eyes were still closed. I only opened them when I felt the tickle of his pistol in my hair and felt the warm spray as Lee, ever the most efficient of murderers, put one round cleanly through his head.

"Hold it together, Mr. Plum!" he shouted across Daisy's back. "We're almost there."

Lightning forked the land behind him. Fighter jets smoked the sky. We rode with a war party of Comanches, the warriors painted with their death faces, carrying their buffalo hide shields and war hawk clubs, rattling in their bone armor as their ponies kept pace. Arthur Reginald Molesworth galloped at their head, mounted astride his beloved Persephone, his lance couched, his eyes black, exit wounds torn through his cheek and the shattered plane of his forehead. Gordo, it seemed, had double-tapped him in the back of the skull. Kissed twice, just to make sure. As I watched, Reggie turned in his saddle to look at me, showed me his rictus grin with his torn cheek flapping and broken teeth, then spurred Persephone on, outpacing us all, the explosive tip of his candy-cane war lance lowered for action.

And out above and beyond it all, Train 1066 squiggled like a silverfish speared with a pin, squirming along maglev tracks that wavered in a fluttering film-loop progression between iron rails spitting sparks, smooth super-cooled maglev rails, and bizarre rococo froths of swooping chrome and pulsing Gernsback radiator coils. I leaned out beyond Daisy's crest and tried to fix my eyes on the engine—to pin it in place in my eye and my mind and thereby resolve the uncertainty of its fluttering probability density. When you see a thing, you make it real. A man with no arms, an impossible building, a dead friend, a train. I watched it and I whispered *train, train, train . . .*

"Make it there," I said to myself, "or ain't none of us gonna be King of Tiny Penguin Land."

You know that last story was a lie, right? About Jemma and me? I mean, not all of it, but most of it. Here's another version. Maybe truer, maybe not.

In bed together one night, Jemma Watts talked to me about the ways of the universe. She was *smart*, was Jemma. So smart. And so sad for knowing what she knew.

She says to me, "Duncan, there's something you need to know."

And I says, "Jemma, darling, sweetness, love of my everlasting life, there's nothing I need to know that I don't know right now."

She smiles sweetly and distantly. I can feel the twitch of it against my chest where she lies. "What you have to understand," says she, "is that Iggy's mistake was in looking, but it wasn't really a mistake because looking is what we do. It's what we all did. Superpositional Heisenberg Anomaly A was just out there waiting for someone to look in the right place, in just the right way. I know you hate him, but if he hadn't found it, someone else would have. It's what came after that . . ."

And her voice, small already, dissolves into nothing and she clings to me as the bombs fall and the crumbling walls rattle and plaster falls down on us like snow. When she kicks free of the scratchy blanket we'd found and steps onto the rotting carpet, she is naked as anything but hard to see in the darkness, shot through here and there with scratches of guttering light.

Not that I didn't try to see her, of course. I would've burned the eyes out of my head from staring, watching her pick her way carefully through the mess and ruination of our room, our dark island, and making for the gun cases and wooden crates stacked carefully against the far wall. Upon them sat a dented tin bucket, filled with melted ice and the last of our beers. Even in that place, her body seemed to reject the darkness and glow with a weak flame. Her considerable brightness and goodness and joy at a low ebb, but not extinguished. I see the livid bruises on her pale skin. The tangles of her hair. Her fingernails blacked with blood. And I love her.

She talks to me about the project Ignatz Walton had led while she fishes in the bucket for unopened bottles, her voice and the rattling of the tin pail the only sounds in a sudden, delicate quiet. The 2011 experimental team—seven men and women working on a tiny piece of a larger program investigating quantum field theory, working out some small fillip of Born's Law or Born's Theorem, collecting experimental data on negative-energy particle movements in observer-biased space. The so-called quantum tunneling effect. None of what she says makes any sense to me. None of it matters, and I am barely listening anyhow.

"The funny thing," she says, "is that the work was expected to fail. It's why the team didn't even really have a name. Just the 2011 experimental team. It was due diligence, that's all. Academic cover for the larger, more prestigious work being done on the West Coast. But Iggy was young. His career was staling already, and he was wild.

Obsessive. And the anomaly was just sitting there in the math, waiting to be discovered."

She has two bottles by their necks in one hand. With the other, she takes some cold water from the bucket and splashes it on her face. From outside, there is a shriek and a crash—the room briefly lit with a cold, white radiance that turns everything photo-negative. Jemma is a black, girl-shaped hole against white space, her hands and fingers skeletal.

"That was close," I says to her. "You should come back to bed."

But she walks instead to the windows, tears back the black plastic sheeting we'd stapled in place two days ago, and lets all the horror of a world torn up by warring come spilling in. Proof, maybe, of the Captain's failure. Of Ignatz's. Of ours.

"We can't help but look," she says, standing there, staring out into the fire and all the nightmares abroad and walking. "Looking is what makes us human."

The train reaches the makeshift barricade and triggers its shockwave projector, reducing what the L.O.T. had built there to so much shattered chaff. A billion toothpicks, all following probabilistic arcs of their own as they blow and flutter, and one Ford Fairlane tumbling through the air like a toy.

"Follow the man on the horse," I shout to the man driving Daisy, pounding on his shin with one balled fist to get his attention.

"What man?" he shouts back, and I wonder, briefly, what reality he is experiencing. What he can see and what he can't.

The tank rocks to a quaking halt and fires. In a thousand worlds, the shot goes wild. In a hundred, the shell misfires. In ten, it strikes home somewhere on the body of the train. In one, which happens to be *my* one, it spirals in like it's riding a laser, misses the point of aim (which had been the driver's compartment of the engine), but slams into one of the magnetic suspensors three cars back.

The train sags. There is a gout of sublimating liquid helium like a sudden stormcloud, a flare of melting niobium alloy as the current running through the suspensor magnets heats them in an instant to about ten thousand degrees, and then just the sparks of metal grinding on metal.

A hundred Comanche warriors are redacted from the universe. The train loses its impossibly airstream design flourishes. For a moment, the wavering of the world cools and settles and we are chasing only a bullet train across the ruin of Eastern Colorado on dinosaur-back. This is how I know that, for a moment, we are winning out against probability. Charging ahead of the Gaussian curve. It is our moment.

"The engine!" I yell. "Get me to the engine!"

The driver looks down across his shoulder at me. "You're supposed to open the car the Chemist is in."

"Change of plans!"

Aboard the train, the defenses are becoming more organized. Bullets fly. Shoulder-fired rockets sizzle through the air. Wisdom: A triceratops doesn't really feel small calibers. They're too big, too tough, and, frankly, too dumb to notice anything so trivial as gunfire. Daisy shrugs off the chugging impacts of assault rifle rounds fired from gun slits in the leading cars of Train 1066, and I, being small, weak and well acquainted with being shot, cower behind her crest, one hand knotted in the bullrope, the other still ridiculously shielding the tube of Cyclot-8 taped onto her hide.

I can hear the booming of the tank's main gun firing somewhere off to our right. The sky is blue again, but a steaming rain lashes us, and a wind that blows flower petals, plastic bags, cigarette butts, sheet music, bone meal, and leaflets for free massages and Pentecostal church services—the flotsam of time's ejecta. We are angling in toward the train—a closing course, doomed to collision. I watch across Daisy's back as a different triceratops takes a rocket in the shoulder and flops down into the grass, trumpeting and rolling madly. All them as had been riding her are thrown and mostly crushed beneath her, their juicy demises masked by a haze of kicked dust. Further off, one of the trucks has jounced close enough to the train to attach itself to one of the cars with a spiderweb of magnetic grapples and gobs of carbon polyurethane. The Legion of Terror swarm across like pirates boarding a crippled merchantman—knives in their teeth and pistols in their belts. There are drones aloft, having launched from security cars near the rear of the train, but they die in the air like poisoned birds, hitting patches of air so thick with hunter-killer nanites that they appear like snaking tendrils of fog, alive with malicious intent.

Daisy's driver hauls her head around, trying hard to keep her thick, bony skull between us and all the fire coming from the train that now sails in a veil of sparks. Finch dies and comes back—a stunned look on his face as though he'd briefly seen the sweet hereafter and found it not entirely to his liking. Then he dies again—bullets taking him in the hip and ribs and neck—and doesn't come back. His feet slip from the pegs. He hangs for a long second from the rope, but then falls away. Lee does not reach for him. He doesn't even look back. That kind of shit only happens in the movies.

The tank booms again. A glancing hit from a 120-millimeter high-explosive shell sending a curling wave of fire rippling down the length of the train. It is lovely but ineffectual.

And then, suddenly, I can see the tank as it crosses in front of us. Black smoke belches from every ventilating hatch—its engine screaming and overstressed as it races on a course less steeply angled than ours. The main gun fires on the move, aiming low, damaging another suspensor, but it isn't enough. Machine guns chatter. Rockets slam into its sloped armor. There's fire on the rear deck.

And clear of the curves now, the train's engineer is dumping power into the coils. Angling suspensors to lay on speed. The bullet-nosed engine seems almost to crouch for a moment, just waiting to leap forward with renewed vigor as the driver sees flat-open track ahead of him, running all the way to the safety of the Kansas border.

He will run away from us if given the least chance to do so. Outpace us in an instant.

But then the tank plows into the berm of the maglev rail as the train's engine blows past. It bounces high as its tracks bite and claw at the dirt and then it buries itself in the body of the train—shearing itself to pieces like driving straight into a massive meat-grinder. The crash is loud. The impact stunning. Pieces of tank and pieces of train fly everywhere. I feel the tickle of something razoring open my scalp, a jerking impact on my back that nearly knocks me loose from Daisy. Like something horribly, suddenly alive, the train screams. It grows wings of flame as emergency brakes lock onto the rail. It is moving, but slow. Limping. Dragging the twisted innards of the tank along beside it like an anchor.

And ten seconds later we are galloping alongside the engine. We are close enough to touch it, and I tear free the tube of Cyclot, lean out, arching my back, and jam it onto the smooth skin of the train.

The resin sticks. Streamers of tape flap in the wind. The detonator is in the cap of the tube. A friction igniter like a road flare. Pop the cap and you have five seconds to run before a tiny bead of white phosphorus pops into a brief and flaring brightness.

"Go!" I yell at Daisy's driver. "Get clear!"

He hauls on the reins. The massive beast seems to turn away with an old lady's doddering slowness. To amble off slowly, thinking, perhaps, about her knitting or coupons or many cats. I can feel Daisy's feet pounding the ground, but we seem to be going nowhere. I count five seconds and nothing happens because, likely, I'd counted five in the time it took to blink, to gasp half a choking, panicked breath.

So I count five again and still nothing happens. I look back and see a raptor scampering along the top of the train—running along the roofs of the cars with its head scything back and forth, dragging twenty feet of chain behind. I see the wreck of the tank gouging a trench in the dirt, uprooting bushes and small trees. I see, far in the distance, something rocketing into the curves of the maglev rail—reinforcements, I guess. Dispatched from Waltz. Or maybe some automated repair vehicle coming to the site of a massive, dinosaur-related breakdown. In the moment, it does not occur to me that this is probably the Captain coming. The final act of all this trouble and bother. I had expected . . . I don't know. Something somehow *more* fantastical than dinosaurs, though I'll be fucked if I can tell you what that might've been.

I look at Lee who is looking at me.

I open my mouth, say, "I don't know what—"

And then the Cyclot goes off.

In both theories on the inner workings of the universe there is a central conceit: That reality is scalable. That the essential indeterminacy of very small things translates to an elemental indeterminacy in larger things.

This is rational because all large things are, at their core, made of very small and dithering things. We know the small things vacillate wildly. Appear and disappear. Move when they oughtn't. Do things with a kind of gleeful recklessness that break all the laws that man has tried to impose on the structures of the universe. And so, naturally, we assume that large things—like atoms and rocks and penguins and people—must do the same. That if we are made of inconstant matter then we, by nature, are as unstable as that which makes us.

Only that's not true. Not *completely*. The discovery of Superpositional Heisenberg Anomaly A by Ignatz Walton and the 2011 experimental team proved, with gutting ramifications, that to look at a thing makes it real. Gives it a weight of realness in conjoined relation to its probability and observational bias. But the Abjuration proved that there are limits. That the universe and everything in it is only one of many, maybe infinite, universes-and-everythings, and that each of them are self-correcting independent of observational bias. Reality is what you see. But it is also what you are *allowed* to see. Man occupies an as-yet entirely privileged and unique niche in that we are the arbiters of the real. We see. We experience. We cement into being all that exists by accepting it as existing.

That's what Jemma was trying to explain to me. As humans, we can't help but look. We are made—if we have been made for anything—for that most primal and important of purposes. We *see*, and thus does the world exist.

But that begs an important question. One which you, particularly, ought to be powerfully concerned by. If seeing makes a thing real, then does telling serve the same function? If I told you only one story of me and Jemma lying in bed together, would it have been true and real simply because I said so?

Of course not. Because I am a liar and have told you so.

But if you believe me, does *that* make it true?

Think before you answer that. Think hard about everything you think you know. Is it the seeing? Or is it the believing?

The Cyclot did its job. It peeled the engine of the train open like a tin can, opening a rent in the skin of it that Lee and I could climb through like a door.

There were red lights flashing. Fire suppressant foam dripped everywhere. Alarm bells put forth a great and caterwauling clamor as though they'd been waiting all the quiet years of their existence for just this one moment to shine.

The engineer was gone, but Lee found one of his shoes. The driver was still in his compartment and alive, but it didn't take a lot for Lee and I to convince him to wind the generators down and bring Train 1066 to a shuddering, final halt.

He asked why we were doing this. He shouted because both of his eardrums were ruptured.

"I hate this goddamn train," I told him. "But I got no particular quarrel with you. If you climb off and run like hell, I'll bet you live long enough to tell this story for free beers somewhere far away."

It was good advice and he took it deeply to heart. I thought for sure that Lee was going to try to shoot him down as he ran, but he never raised his pistol. Instead, he turned to me. "Okay," he said. "What's next?"

"I'm sorry about Finch," I said to him.

"Who?" he asked.

"Never mind."

We moved backward through the train because there was really nothing else to do and nowhere else to go. Forward into battle out of no great sense of duty, but simply from a dearth of better options. The next car was the generator car, and we squeezed through a narrow passageway between crackling, cooling walls of great groaning and panicked machinery so recently tortured that we could smell the sharp ozone smell of its dying. Beyond that was the coolant recirculator—all cracked and twisted and leaking a hundred poisons. We pulled our shirts up over our noses and held our breath, hoping it would be enough. We lived, so I figure it was.

With the train stopped, the L.O.T. swarmed aboard. They blew and burned open doors, released their raptors against the OSS agents riding as security (their numbers bulked up by hired Regulators who could be spotted plainly by the way they ran as soon as the train came to rest), and killed relentlessly anything their monsters left behind.

To the OSS's damnable credit, they didn't just roll over and die. They rallied their defenses quickly, established control of a few cars, and dug in hard. They knew what the L.O.T. were there for and had no intention of giving the Chemist up easy.

Later, I would wonder how far off they thought help was when they sealed the doors of the cars immediately surrounding the secure transport unit in which the Chemist was being kept. They knew there was no surrendering. No chance of quarter. And yet they held their ground. I wondered what it was they'd seen when the world had tied itself in knots. And if they'd thought they were winning.

Six cars in, Lee shot a Regulator who'd unwisely stayed to fight. He barely broke stride, fired six times, stopped to reload, and then moved on.

"Gonna get worse the farther we go," he said.

"I'm just hoping to find the bar car," I told him and smiled, sitting down to rest on the arm of a passenger seat. "That was a joke."

"I know," he said. "Just didn't think it was very funny. The Captain is coming, right?"

"He gave every impression that he was."

"Because I want to go home now."

Another car back, we picked up three L.O.T. gunmen who were enthusiastically charging in the wrong direction. Getting them turned around was as simple as pointing the way toward violence and letting them have their head. The next car was ripped open like an envelope and festooned like an abattoir. My head ached and I was limping again. I could feel blood leaking down my leg and more of it matting my hair. My case felt loose and rattly where I'd strapped it to my back, but there was no time to stop and check it.

"Keep moving," I said and leaned my weight on the backs of empty seats at every opportunity.

We found a dead raptor. We crunched through carpets of shell casings. Ahead of us, we could hear the pops of small arms and then the thudding of a heavy machine gun that punched rounds through the bulkhead in front of us and put us all on the floor.

We waited. There was screaming, the screech of a dinosaur, and then a tumult of voices. One of the L.O.T.s advancing with us crawled forward on his belly and pushed open the door between cars and we saw two raptors scrambling over seat backs and hurling themselves at a makeshift OSS hard-point to tear apart the two gray-suits manning a single heavy gun on a bipod. As soon as the big shooter went quiet, three L.O.T. dinosaur handlers stood up holding pistols and shock rods and pushed forward into the next car, driving the beasts ahead of them. Lee and the three L.O.T.s followed. I did not.

Lee glanced back at me. "You okay?" he asked.

I nodded.

"You're still on the floor."

"That's only because I'm not sure I can get up."

He came back to me, leaned down, and got an arm under me, but when I looked down at my leg, I saw my pants soaked with claret and so looked away.

"Only way the Captain finds you is if you're with me," I said. "That's just the way of things. So we might want to hole up here," I said, then sniffed. "You smell something?"

"I don't want to answer that question," Lee said.

"Get down," I told him. "Low."

And he did, easing down across the aisle from me, in the space between the seats where feet and briefcases normally go. The three gunmen we were traveling with had stopped short of the far door, hesitating. Then they started backing away.

"What is it?" Lee asked.

"Gas, I think."

A raptor crashed into the door, lost its footing, clawed its way clumsily back up, and then came charging back down the aisle in our direction, its mincing little hands held limply in front of its chest.

The L.O.T.s dove for the passenger seats, scrambling to get out of its way, but the monster was unconcerned, suddenly, with snacking and passed by without slowing, it's long, hooked claws skittering on the blood-slicked floor.

The gas, when it came, drifted through in wisps at first—grayish-white and smelling of sulfur. I heard a howling that wasn't from a dinosaur. A growling and a baying like from a hound.

"This is it," I said to Lee.

"You sure?"

I looked at the spreading pool of blood under my leg and felt the sick, dull pounding in my head. "I'm sure that it'd better be."

He nodded, popped up to his feet, and shot down the three L.O.T.s in front of us, quick as you please. Two he shot in the back as they tried to get themselves untangled from where they'd hidden from the raptor. The third he got as the man tried to crawl away.

Then he dropped back down beside me. "We're clear," he said. "What now?"

"Now we sit still and wait."

The cloud grew thicker and I watched it roll slowly down the length of the car toward us—expecting to see the Captain striding through it in our direction. But I did not. And then certainly expecting it *now*. And then not seeing him again.

I heard coughing and choking. Gunshots. Screeches and howling. The smoke looked wet. Sticky. Like a lethal fog thick with droplets of poison. And still no Captain.

I swore, pushed Lee aside with one hand, sat up and raised my pistol and emptied the clip into the two windows opposite us.

"Help me up," I said. "Quick. Then get your head out the window if you can. That's not tear gas."

He dragged me to my feet and more or less threw me across the aisle into the opposite row of seats. I dragged myself forward as the first coughing fit took me, got my best leg underneath me and lunged for the window.

The safety glass crunched. I knocked out as much as I could with the butt of my pistol and one bare hand then tried to drag myself up over the lip of the casement, but couldn't quite make it. I took a breath, but it was mostly poison. It tasted of tin and rotten eggs and I felt my stomach knot. In a panic, I folded my bad leg under me, got a foot-hold on one of the seats, and pushed.

Pain exploded through me. I know that I screamed. I know that I managed to squirm my head and shoulders out the window before the top edge caught on the briefcase strapped to my back, and so I just hung there for a second or two, breathing raggedly and looking out over a green and sunlit field in which a single triceratops stood, pleasantly cropping the grass.

When I felt something grab at my legs, I tried to kick it away. I tried to struggle, but there wasn't much of me left. My breath was rasping. Black ink was bleeding in around the edges of my eyes. I flapped my arms as best I could. I thrashed my hips. Train 1066 had nearly brought me to my death once, and I could not believe that now it was going to do it again.

I was pulled back inside the train. The air was heavy and gluey with gas. I caught my chin on the edge of the casement then fell on my face, sucked in a reflexive breath and curled double from gagging and coughing.

Strong hands grabbed my shoulders and I fumbled for my pistol.

Strong arms rolled me onto my back.

I looked up into a twisted face in a rubbery, clear mask—a snubbed snout, delicate fur, a lolling tongue.

"I got 'im," Dogboy said. "They's in hand. Everyone pull out."

I stared and I choked. When Dogboy asked, "Finch?" I shook my head.

"We're even now then, you and me," he said wetly, voice muffled by the mask. "Glad I could make us square."

And I wanted to say something pithy. I wanted to tell him that I wasn't keeping score, that I wasn't that kind of man, or at least that I appreciated the gentlemanly way in which he chose to pay what he owed. But he was already receding from me down a dark hallway. He was already falling away into darkness. So in the end, I said nothing. For once, I just didn't have the strength to get the last word.

Intermission: An Orthogonal Solution to a Problem of Nested Quantum Indeterminacies

I woke to the sound of bells and, contrary to all literary convention, I had no notion, however brief, that I'd died and gone to heaven. Hurt too bad for that, me. Felt altogether too badly in all conceivable ways for to be anything but alive and suffering for my latest crop of sins and foolishness.

I was on a cart, laid flat on the hard boards like a corpse but altogether too animated with pains to be one. There was a makeshift shade erected over me, made of a bedsheet covered in tiny pink flowers, faded by a thousand washings and strung between four poles. There was a fresh-ish pressure bandage knotted thickly about my thigh and the pipe of that trouser leg was crackling stiff with dried blood. Lee lay beside me, his skin sallow, his breathing wheezy. I tried to sit up, but the moving caused some sort of landslide in my lungs. I coughed until I vomited, hanging my head off the back of the cart, pushed up on one elbow. Looking down, I saw blood speckling my jacket, my hand. There was a blobby chunk of something stuck to my sleeve that I figured was probably a bit of the commissar's brain. And then I threw up again.

"It's awake," said a voice from the front of the cart.

"One of them is," said another.

"But they're both alive, and the other one is in much better shape. He'll live without any tending," said the first.

"Fine," said the second. "I owe you a Coke."

Barnum and Strange. They rode side by side, severe as Baptist ministers in identical black suits furred with road dust. One held the reins of a yoked ox with loops of tiny bells hung around its neck. The other carried an assault shotgun across his lap, the fat drum of ammunition knocking against his knee every time the cart swayed.

We were nowhere, a vast and dusty flatness where not even scrub grew, following a path that might've once been a water route or a highway for snakes. Behind the cart in which I rode was another—a gypsy wagon like a giant's steamer trunk on four spindly wheels, towed by two street-sweeping robots with their optics smashed in and driven by an old woman in homespun and a flopping sunhat. I rolled onto my back and shaded my eyes with one hand. The smell of me was nauseating. The sky above was the color of bleached denim. I had the terrible thought that we had failed somehow—that the mission had been unsuccessful and that the Chemist remained unrescued, rendering all recent hurts taken and blood spilled for naught.

I tried my voice and spoke in the language of sandpaper. I swallowed, took a deep breath, and tried again.

"Did it work?" I asked.

Strange looked back over his shoulder at me, then over at Barnum. "It's speaking," he said.

"We have orders not to talk to it," Barnum replied.

"Really?"

"Not to engage in any way. It's confused, the poor thing. Probably going to die anyway."

Strange looked at me again, then raised his eyes to something behind us and made the slightest come-over-here motion with his chin, then looked back at Barnum again.

"I don't like these orders," he said.

"It's not a matter of liking. Orders are orders."

"But it won't understand."

"Orders. Are. Orders," Barnum repeated, tugged gently at the reins, and clucked his tongue. And that was that.

The woman on the gypsy cart had whipped up her team of street-sweepers and drawn even with the back of the cart in which I rode. I noticed her boots first—heavy, steel-shank tankers—and the trench knife sheathed there. Then the gray-green cuffs of a field jacket poking from the sleeves of her dress. The large and scarred hands. When she looked up, I saw myself briefly reflected, doubled, in the mirrored lenses of her aviator sunglasses.

"Saw you lost your lunch back there, Duncan," she said, smiling wide enough to show white teeth.

"Nice hat, Captain," I said. "So did it work?"

I could not tell if he was nodding, bobbing his head to some soundtrack playing in his head alone, or if it was just the swaying of the cart. "You did brilliantly, boy. Everything I could've hoped for and more. And lived to reap the rewards of a job well done, besides."

"The Chemist?" I asked.

"Yup," he said, reached back and rapped knuckles on the box of his wagon. "Sleeping peacefully, I should think. He's had a rough couple of days."

And I laughed until I coughed and I coughed until I thought I was going to cry and then curled myself into a ball and closed my eyes.

"Oh, no," I heard the Captain say. "No rest for the wicked, Duncan. There's something I need to show you."

"Later," I said.

"There is no later, Mr. Archer. But we're almost there. Just hang on a couple more minutes."

We jounced along, hooked around a thin scrim of trees, and climbed a bump in the land that fancied itself a hill. The Captain talked about nothing. About dinosaurs and Dogboy and the weather. His voice was just a pleasant hum in my ears. Summer cicadas of my youth. The cart rocked. The day's warmth was numbing. The bells on the ox jingled.

"Duncan?" he asked.

"Yes, Captain," I said.

"Duncan, you have to open your eyes now. We're there. You have to see this."

I had fluttered out of the world, but he drew me back. The cart had stopped and we sat on the crest of a pimple on the land's flatness. The Captain stood, my hat in his hand, taking one of my cigarettes from out of its crown. He offered me a hand and pulled me forward until I was sitting on the edge of my cart, feet dangling, looking off toward Kansas and to where the silvery snake of the maglev rails crossed the border. We were perhaps five miles away. Train 1066 was a crawling smudge on the land.

"Took us a couple hours to get the train running again. Logue wanted me to thank you for not just wrecking the thing. Made his job a lot easier, though cutting that tank loose was no picnic."

I looked at the Captain. He popped a match alight and touched it to the tip of the handroll in his mouth.

"I'd offer you one," he said, "but I don't want to think what it would do to your lungs right now."

The train inched along. I watched it because there was nothing else to watch. I asked what I was seeing and the Captain winked, stretched his back, and said, "An orthogonal solution to a problem of nested quantum indeterminacies."

He raised his hands like a conductor, touching his fingertips to his thumbs, then suddenly spread them.

"Boom," he said.

And sitting there, I watched eleven mushroom clouds growing in a line down what I imagined to be the Colorado/Kansas border, blossoming into towering umbrellas of furious light—the train, the crossing, the low-slung little border towns all lost behind a curtain of debris and dirt lifted from its rightful earthbound place, tossed skyward and vaporized.

We watched in silence—me, the Captain, Barnum and Strange. A minute, maybe two. There was wind and then there wasn't. A rumble and then none. Finally, the Captain turned to me.

"Seen enough?" he asked.

"I didn't want to see this in the first place," I muttered.

"Yeah you did. You had to."

"Says who?" I asked. "Who told you I had to see this?"

"You did," said the Captain, then held up a finger. "There'll be time for questions," he said. "Lots and lots of questions." He turned then, stepped quickly to his cart and took something from the seat.

"And many of those questions," he said, "are going to be mine."

When he turned back to me again, he was holding my briefcase—one whole side of it torn open by whatever had hit me when the tank exploded.

"It's always seemed so important to you, this case," he said. "Dogboy figured you wouldn't have wanted it left behind."

I stared at him. Over his shoulders, the mushroom clouds swelled and darkened, towering above him like wrath. The whole day was going gray. Barnum and Strange stepped up on either side of me. They did not touch me, but then, they didn't have to.

The Captain stepped forward, looked deeply into my face and smiled. He reached up and patted me on one cheek. "We should probably have a talk, you and me."

EPISODE

11

Bleeding Kansas

I TOLD YOU ONCE, VERY EARLY ON, THAT I KNEW THE TASTE OF THE Captain's pistol in my mouth and how it felt to have the thick barrel of it knocking against my teeth from upon a day when he damn near executed me. This, then, is that moment I was recalling. This, then, is the proper place for it—a point in the telling that is not an ending, but which finds me finally (or somewhat finally) on a bump of land fringed with a curtain of shade trees, overlooking the livid hell of the Colorado/Kansas border whereupon, lately, eleven small but ferocious surplus nuclear warheads borrowed from the black armories of King Steve had done the one thing for which they'd been designed.

I was, I recall, stunned beyond reaction. And hurt beyond caring. And exhausted beyond all but the most token, smart-mouth resistance when the Captain had begun asking me his questions.

He'd patted me on the cheek, the Captain had, and I'd felt the heat of his fingers pale before the radiant malice in his smile as he'd held the remains of my case between us. Seeing that, I'd known immediately that I was skunked. That there was no way out for me but the gun.

It's all done now but the dancing, I thought. And so, when the Captain had queried, I'd answered him with half-truths and outright lies and curses upon him, his kin and kind. When he'd ripped from the guts of my split-open briefcase the Regulator's paperwork that I'd bought for five dollars from the car parking man at the Brown Palace, I'd claimed I was writing a historical novel with deep, romantic undertones and that they were my notes. The Captain had thrown the whole sheaf of them at me and I'd laughed as the pages all fluttered about. As Barnum and Strange went scampering off after the windblown paper, leaping and slapping pages from the air like children. And when the Captain had taken out my phones, I'd said they were phones and that, if he was confused, I'd be happy to show him how they worked.

"Delighted to help you out, Captain," I said. "As ever I have been." And then I'd smiled back at him with blood in my teeth and vomit on my breath and that was when he'd gotten angry and took out his gun and bid me cease my prattle by shoving the barrel in my mouth.

That he had me on my knees was more my choice than his. My leg was done in by then. It would never, in fact, work rightly again and I would always have a limp. Sometimes I would try to pass it off as dashing—evidence, wasn't it, of a life dramatically lived?—but most times it was only a hobbling bother.

Oddly, I had very few regrets as I tongued the barrel, tasting gun oil, leather and the smoky pepper of spent powder. I snorted breaths through my nose and looked down at a clump of pages that'd blown up against my knee. The one that I could read was the first page of the profile on Jemma Watts—her name, her known aliases, known addresses, known associates and, in one corner, a smeary black and white photo that described her the way a man with no tongue might an orange and did her loveliness no justice whatsoever.

I thought, in that moment, that if even this bad picture of her was the last thing I saw before the Captain blew the brains out of me, that would be okay. Not *wonderful*, of course. But okay. I had, after all, seen so much already. To ask more might've been mistaken for hubris by whatever god oversaw the wrack and ruin of the Weird. Or maybe that's only how I recall it now. I know for certain that I hardly fought it at all.

"Any more jokes?" the Captain asked.

And I said nothing.

"More lies?" he asked.

And I said nothing still.

He shouted for Barnum or for Strange to hold my case for him and there was a rustling and a ripping. A grunt as something was torn free. With just the slightest of upward pressure on the gun in my mouth, the Captain made me lift my eyes to him. Made me watch as he held in one hand the no-longer-hidden dumb phone that was my lifeline to the boss, Nimrod Kane.

"And this, Duncan?" he asked. "Have anything clever to say about this?"

"Fuck you," I said into the gun. "I'm tired."

"What?"

"Foxtrot uniform charlie kilo uniform," I said, making an equally unintelligible mash of it, speaking only in vowels as my mouth was full of iron.

A line appeared between the Captain's blue eyes. The slightest wrinkling of perturbation. "This always works better in the movies," he muttered. And when, momentarily frustrated, he yanked the pistol out of my mouth, the sight blade chipped my front tooth and the barrel trailed a long thread of drool, which, for a lingering movement, hung in the harsh light rather prettily.

I coughed, spat in the dirt, and said, "I don't know about you, but this is really more homosexual subtext than I'm comfortable with, Captain."

I'd honestly thought he was going to laugh.

But he didn't laugh. His face was a crumbling mask—the hardness in him warring against confusion and rage and the pain of betrayal. He raised the pistol to me again and then his hand fell away. He opened his mouth and closed it again. He looked at the phone in his other hand and stepped a pace closer to me and put the gun to the top of my head.

"Who does it call, Duncan?" he asked. "Just tell me."

There was a pleading edge to his voice and, for an instant, I believed everything I'd already learned about the Captain. That he was an alien here. That he did not belong.

"Tell me!" he roared.

That he was a man who knew with a cold fixity everything that was going to happen save for the myriad ways that the evils of small men might ultimately fuck with his big designs. That he was a man who knew the future, but was consistently enraged by unexpected alterations to the script he'd memorized. That, in knowing the future, he was a creature who could not comprehend betrayal, and yet was now feeling it for the first time.

"You didn't see this coming, did you?" I asked him.

He pressed the gun tighter against the crown of my head and the words fell like stones from his lips. "Who does it call?"

I looked up at him from my knees. The day was growing grayer with the clouds he'd made blotting out the sun. There was a smell of scorched earth, like cinnamon burned to ash. Far in the distance, I could hear a grumbling like summer thunder rolling in from miles off. A disturbance in the sudden quiet of the shattered day. And suddenly I thought I knew something that I hadn't before. That if I could accept the absurdity of the Captain himself—this man from another world, farming mushroom clouds here in order that he might make this place better than the one he'd come from—and swallow his whole story, then I could understand something else as well.

"There's only one number in it, Captain," I said. "Dial it and see for yourself."

Ages and ages ago, while still a schoolboy spy going through OSS battle school and learning the ropes of my trade, there'd been a lecture on resisting interrogation. In a freezing barn south of Ashtabula, a round and waddling former police detective had droned on about defensive posturing, behavioral resistance and going to our happy places while nine of us sat on our hands on bound-up bales of rotting hay and tried not to doze off while he blathered.

Ohio then was a DMZ. Half-melted. Ripe with impossible monorails and mystical greenwoods and an ogre king living in the ruins of a crumbling hotel atop Little Mountain. It was a place made for the OSS—twisted by the Weird and as unstable as a one-legged chair. Ruinatious things grew in the fields there and crawled loose in the dark. Mad scientists ruled the low places with their jeroboams, DNA plasmids, thermal cyclers, BamH restriction enzymes and 3D printers. The chawed-up borders of what had once been the Buckeye State stood like a ribbon of madness separating the crumbling, tenacious, industrial civility of the East from the full-throttle crazy of the Plains Nations. We spent our mornings practicing tactical fast-insertions and running teams of coup-counters through the abandoned suburbs collecting forks and buttons and pretending they were the enemy's choicest treasures. Afternoons we slogged in the mud and climbed cargo nets, beat each other with sticks and punched nickel-groupings in paper targets from ten yards out. And evenings we were talked at by whatever learned men the Masters could coax out of their holes with the promise of a warm meal and branded whiskey.

Because we were young and dumb and made of iron, there was nothing the ex-detective said that night that meant a thing to any of us. We were field agents in training. Future case officers. Cold and practiced killers. Interrogation? First, they'd have to catch us.

And this man, he must've known that he was speaking to deaf ears. That he was instructing barn owls and cold mice more than us front rank of the rational world. Right at the end, he came clean and admitted that all he'd told us was so much bunk and hoakum.

"Someone wants information out of you, they're gonna get it," he said, sighing and stuffing his meatloafish hands into straining pockets he'd already stuffed with wrapped sandwiches and plastic airline bottles of scotch. "Doesn't matter how hard you are. How much of a badass you think you are. Resistance is fucking pointless because you just ain't as hard as a hammer is, you wanna know the truth."

The ex-detective chewed his lip. Looked around at us, all bleary-eyed and snot-nosed. "But I don't know. When they catch you—and they *will* catch you—lie through your goddamn teeth, that's my advice. Tell a hundred different stories just to confuse the fuckers. Swear every one of them is true. And I'll tell you this, when you're out of every other option? Just pass out. Just . . . drop. Just give up. Worst thing that happens is you buy yourself a minute of breathing room. Another minute of life. And sometimes a minute is all you need for a miracle to happen."

The Captain flipped open the phone and he dialed the only number it knew. Kneeling there with my eyes closed and a final "fuck you" to the Lord almighty whispering upon my lips, I expected any number of things to happen.

I expected it to ring and for Nimrod Kane to answer.

I expected it to ring and for someone else to answer.

I expected it to ring and ring and for no one to answer.

I expected it to blow up in his hand. To electrocute him. To turn into a small and glossy-black turtle and bite him on the ear.

I expected there to be no bars. That the disturbance of a tactical nuclear strike and the consequent agitation of all the atoms or the ions or whatever it was that made voices travel through the air like magic would render the thing just a dumb piece of plastic, incapable of doing anything more than looking like a phone.

What I did not in a million alternate universes expect was to kneel there, expecting the bullet, and then to hear, quite clearly, the trilling song of a phone ringing somewhere behind us.

I looked up. The Captain jerked his head up and craned his neck around. A pistol had materialized in the hands of Barnum. Strange had the assault shotgun pressed to his shoulder. Both of them were looking out and down toward the thin backdrop of trees where, somewhere, a cell phone was caterwauling an annoying, factory-default ring.

I said, "Well this is peculiar." Which, apparently, was the sign for the world to grow only stranger.

The ashen air seemed to waver, like heat rising from summer blacktop. Bits of the landscape began to move in ways that landscape oughtn't, rose up and became men in fluttering, reactive optical camouflage cloaks—all armed with rifles that they kept decorously pointed at the ground. There were two, then four, then six and, at the center of their line, the bobbing, bodiless Cheshire Cat head of Nimrod Kane from whose vicinity the ringing phone did bleat.

"Really?" he said. "You're not going to hang up? Hold on a second . . ."

Nimrod's head became Nimrod's head and a sharp V of a dark suit as he held up one finger and unfastened something of his camouflage so that he could reach inside his invisibility cloak and come out with a phone which he unfolded, put to his ear and answered.

"Hi, James," he said brightly. "It's me, Nim. We both know you're not going to pull that trigger, so how about you just put the gun away now, huh? It's gauche and makes you look even crazier than you are."

Above me, I heard the Captain say, "Nim?" His voice was that of a child caught not stealing candy from a drawer, but planning an elaborate heist at a candy factory. Amused and frightened and confused and dauntless, all in equal measure.

"The gun, James. Put it down."

I felt the barrel of the Captain's pistol scrape through my hair and fall away.

"Now tell Tweedle Dee and Tweedle Dum to holster their iron, too, okay? My guards get a bit froggy when I go out in the world and they prefer to be the only ones with guns in their hands."

The Captain asked, "How did you—"

And Nimrod interrupted, pinning the phone between his ear and his shoulder briefly while he patted around himself for something that I figured had to be a cigarette. "I honestly didn't know which would freak you out more," he said. "Materializing like this or staying hid and just making you dance. I'm glad I chose this option, though. I think it was the right choice, dramatically speaking. Something about the . . . I don't know. The *mystique* of it appeals to the showman in me. I mean, it's been a dog's age, hasn't it, James? I just wanted to make an impression, me." He took the phone away from his ear suddenly, held one hand over it and shouted, "Strange! Barnum! Mr. Barrow told me to tell you to holster them pistols before something messy happens. Do it now." And then he put the phone back to his ear. "James? I'm going to hang up now because this game is getting silly."

And then he did—snapping the phone closed and tucking it back inside his jacket and dramatically throwing both wings of his cloak back over his shoulders and straightening out the hood so, for the first time, he became the front half of a whole man in a sharp, dark suit, wearing a copse of late summer trees about his neck and on his back. From out of his suit he took a flat, white box and, from it, extracted a single, machine-rolled cigarette, all white and perfect, which he sniffed at like it was the finest Havana cigar. He looked at me. "Duncan? How you doing over there?"

"Poorly, boss," I said.

A smile fluttered across Nimrod Kane's face, passing quickly as a bird's shadow. "Yeah," he said. "You surely have had yourself a day . . ."

He hung the coffin nail from his lip and looked around himself. From another pocket, he took a battered silver lighter, coaxed from it a flame, and touched it to the end of his cigarette. The smoke wreathed him and stirred in the fitful breeze, twisting itself into dragons and spaceships and other once-fanciful things. "This is fun, don't you think?" he asked no one in particular. "It has been so long since I've been out amid the madness."

"Nim," said the Captain. "I mean, how . . ."

Nimrod grinned and gave the Captain a wink, then turned to the men who flanked him. "Okay, gentlemen," he said. "Up we come now. The grownups are going to talk, so make yourselves scarce." Limping, he began making his way up to the crown on the hill as his honor guard of invisible killers wavered away into nothingness once more—a man attended to by ghosts, walking with violent spirits at his right and left hands.

And though it wasn't the best timing in the world, that was when I finally chose to take the advice of that long-gone police detective I'd known once in a frozen Ohio barn and simply passed out.

While I slept, the armies of the Western Confederacy passed me by. That rumbling we'd heard earlier? That was the early-arriving armored divisions rushing to take their places along the border. They were followed by rank upon rank of exos flying brilliant battle flags, engineer units in donut-wheeled trucks loaded with blacked-out cargo containers and heavy excavators rushing to the fore. The infantry marched in proud lock-step. Drones swarmed the air. More containers came slung beneath the swollen bellies of heavy-lift airships, and the pulsing *thwopthwopthwop* of their fan engines infiltrated my dreams like the sound of a massive and beating heart.

It was full and unnaturally dark by the time I woke and found myself lying in the shadows outside the light and heat of a small fire kindled atop the same wood-fringed hill on which we'd earlier perched. Someone had been kind enough to throw a sheet over me—the sere and sun-faded flowery bed linen that had previous been the roof over the cart that'd kept the sun out of my eyes when there'd been a fair chance of my dying.

The carts themselves were gone. Barnum and Strange and Lee all appeared to have absquatulated while I napped, though I couldn't swear to that. There was, near to hand, a plastic bottle of water laid down for me, but though afflicted with a powerful thirst, I felt it too neat a trap. Conscious but with my eyes re-closed, I lay and measured my breathing—listening to the conversation taking place around the fire between the Captain and Nimrod Kane.

How convenient would it have been had they, as in the old movies that the Captain is so fond of, laid out in their ignorance of my wakefulness, the whole broad reach and roundness of their plans and deepest, most intimate feelings on the many worlds and our places in them? How sweet, though middling, a grace note it would have made.

But instead, they appeared to be talking about a dog they'd once known. Because that, truly is the way of the world. If I have learned anything throughout the sweep of all my adventures, past and yet unfolding, it is that the confounding of convenience and neatness is the universe's most primal order.

"You remember the way he would sit with the thing?" Nimrod asked, his voice seeming younger somehow, curlicued with old mirth dredged up from some deep place. "In his lap, with it getting its hair all over his suit?"

And the Captain laughed. "God," he said, "that thing was ancient as bones. It smelled like cheese all the time, too. I watched it one day, in the office, and it slept for 14 straight hours. I would've sworn it was dead except for all the farting. What the fuck was its name, though?"

"It was something stupid," Nimrod said. "He'd named it something long and stupid after some TV show or something."

"What did he call it again?"

"Ollie."

"Ollie. That's right. . ."

"Ollie, Jesus. Short for Oliver?"

"Maybe."

"It was something British, I think. He said the dog was British, so it deserved a—"

"Lord something?"

"No. That doesn't sound right."

The Captain groaned. I smelled cigarettes and the charry smell of drifting woodsmoke. The ground beneath me was hard and, in the distance, I heard the sharp and clanging sounds of hard work being done by other hands, the rumble of machinery, an occasional guttural bellow like an elephant arguing against the inequities of the world.

"Oliver . . ." Nimrod said. "Percy loved that stupid dog back when he still had something like a heart."

"Careful, Nim," said the Captain. "Keep talking that way and you're going to delude yourself into believing he was human once."

"But he was, wasn't he? And not just human, but a good man. A friend."

"That was before he went over to the dark side."

"Before he tried to kill you, you mean."

"The first time."

There was a pause, then Nimrod, saying quietly, "I don't know why, but it bothers me that I can't remember the name of Percy's dog. Makes me wonder if I'm slipping, you know? I've always been such a good rememberer."

"It's the world that's slipping, not you," said the Captain. "Things change so much. It might be that he never had a dog now. Or that he didn't have one there, but did here. I mean, think about it, Nim. Way things are, one of us shouldn't remember the dog at all."

"But I do."

"And so do I. But it's impossible, isn't it? There's no mathematical way that both of us were ever together in a place where we could've both known Percy when he had Oliver."

"That's true," said Nimrod. "So then which one of us knows this?"

"Maybe we should wake the boy and ask him if *he* remembers."

Another pause. I felt the metaphysical weight of two sets of eyes on me. And then Nimrod's voice again. "No, let him sleep. Things are going to go hard for him soon enough. Let him have a little peace."

"You're too protective of him, you know."

"Wouldn't you be?"

The Captain chuckled, but it was a dark thing. A mordant piece of him, generally buried, bubbling briefly to the surface. "I am not the man you want to answer that question, Nim. Not tonight."

The fire flickered. I cracked an eye and saw a piece of the darkness detach itself and go fluttering toward the fire—one of Nimrod's men.

"Word from Ranstead, sir," he said. "They're almost ready below."

Nimrod looked at the Captain and the Captain shrugged. "Your call, chief. There a reason to wait?"

"My penchant for laziness and liking for another drink and a few more stories," he said. "The fire is warm and the night is long and tomorrow is—"

I missed the rest of what Nimrod said because, suddenly, another voice interrupted. A whispering voice from directly behind and above me—like someone crouching in the dark, close enough to touch me. Or sitting. Lurking, in any case, and powerfully creepy for it besides.

"He knows you're awake, you know," said the voice, and I was prevented from just flat-out killing its owner by the deadening effect of repeated shocks and the fact that sleeping rough had numbed most vital parts of my overtaxed anatomy. So short of flying into a hellacious fury of bloody murderousness, instead I began to roll lumpily in the direction of the voice, rather in the way an enormous walrus might. But a hand stayed me.

"No. Don't. I'm not going to hurt you. I owe you my life, apparently. Or my freedom, at least."

"Ignatz?" I whispered.

"Who else would it be? They left me here to watch you. Which is ridiculous because, as I said, Nimrod must know that you're awake. He has to. And yet he's pretending he doesn't know. You find that strange? There must be something he wants you to hear, you think?"

"Ignatz?" I said again. Because I am, as I have repeatedly said, quite clever.

The Chemist sighed in the blind dark. "This is a big moment. Not something he'd forget. So he must've known that you'd wake when you did and hear what you've heard. Did it mean anything to you?"

"They were talking about a dog," I whispered. "Meant nothing."

"Hmm . . ."

"What do you mean, *hmm*."

Ignatz ignored me. I felt his hand fall from my shoulder and then, as if second-guessing the wisdom of leaving me to my own sea-cow devices, he put it back again.

"I wasn't sure it was you, you know? I saw you in the garage that day for the first time, but I wasn't sure. You remember the garage?"

"Of course I remember the garage," I hissed. "None of this botheration would've been necessary if you'd just—"

"If I'd just what?" he interrupted. "No. Don't say that, please. It makes me think you're stupid and I don't want to think of you like that." A pause. A beat in the stuttering heart of the universe. "It all would've happened just the way it did because it had to. I mean, it happened other ways, too. It happened in all ways, in infinite variety, which is the glory of the multiverse, I guess. But it happened the way it happened here because that was the way it happened, you understand?"

"You're all maroony," I said. "The whole crazy fucking lot of you, every one."

And "Shh . . ." the Chemist said, patting my shoulder like he might a fussing animal, and, "Quiet now," and then, continuing, his voice like sour honey in my ear, his words wisping and thin and stilted like a man new to language and still finding his way with it. "I couldn't believe it, really. That day? Seeing you there? The . . . improbability of it was astounding. I've done the math. I have. It's what I did while I was being kept. In my head, I did it. You are so . . . *odd*. Such an unlikely histogram, uh . . . What name are you using now?"

And here's a thing that's funny to me now, but only because I know what's coming next. In the moment, it wasn't funny. It won't seem funny to you. But it's funny. Trust me.

I opened my mouth to answer Ignatz. To say *Duncan Archer, at your service*, or something equally all-overish. But then I stopped because I didn't know who, in that moment, I ought to claim to be. Was I Duncan Archer to this so-called important man? Was I Harry Plum? Was I the actor, Dorian Bloom? I closed my mouth and said nothing.

"It doesn't matter," the Chemist said. "I could call you Larry. Or Carl. I could call you Mildred. That would be funny, I think. I imagine I'm going to have a different name soon, too. Because Ignatz Walton died on that train, I imagine. Spectacularly. *Definitively*, as they say. An orthogonal solution to a problem of nested quantum indeterminacies—that's how I explained it to Mr. Kane before he gave me over to those OSS men."

I perked up. "What was that?" I asked.

"What?"

"What you just said."

"That I died? Well, I mean not *really* obviously, but—"

"No. After that. That phrase you used. An orthogonal . . ."

"An orthogonal solution to a problem of nested quantum indeterminacies? Yes. What I mean to say is—"

I sat up. I took the bottle of water from beside me and drained away half of it in a single pull.

"Hey," said the Chemist. "That was mine."

"The boy appears to be awake," said the Captain, looking at me over the low flickers of the fire.

"He would be, yeah," said Nimrod, then turned back to his man again. "Give the order," he said. "Let's get it started so we can get it finished."

I tried to stand up but couldn't. My bad leg was numb and senseless and my good leg was asleep.

"You going to come join us, Duncan?" asked Nimrod without looking at me. His man was already flickering back into invisibility—wrapping his camouflage cloak around himself and pulling up the hood. It would've been a frightening effect had I not seen a hundred worse things since breakfast.

"That depends," I said, stalling while I tried to lift my own legs into some kind of useful posture. It was like hoisting deadfall timber while sitting down. "Captain, you still planning on shooting me?"

"At the moment, no," said the Captain. "Be brave, Duncan."

"I'm being prudent. I mean, you've already shot me once."

"That was necessary."

"So you say."

"That was necessary," said Nimrod.

"So you both say. Wasn't neither of your legs getting shot in."

Nimrod said, "He's got us there," and laughed.

The Captain told him to shut up and to stop taking my side. "Don't be a baby," said the Captain, to me. "Everyone gets shot sometimes."

"And you almost shot me again today, too."

"That," he said, "was a misunderstanding. I thought you were a spy."

"I *am* a spy," I said.

"I mean the bad kind."

"So do I."

Nimrod snorted, seeming over-all charmed by every damn word that fell out of me. "His honesty is a refreshing change, don't you think? Reassure him, James."

"Stop calling me that," the Captain said.

"Well I'm certainly not going to call you Captain."

"Fuck you," he said to Nimrod. Then, to me, "Duncan, I promise not to shoot you again tonight, okay? Now as your Captain, I order you to come over here and drink with us."

From behind me, I heard Ignatz Walton stand. He said, "He took my water so I'm coming, too," and then stepped over me.

In the end, I crawled.

Below us and away, lights bobbed in the darkness. Great machines chugged and strained at mysterious tasks. There were tanks and trucks and many bodies. The sounds of beasts put to the whip. There was a fog—a high and swirling wall of it—demarcating what I imagined to be the border between Colorado and Kansas, and the sense of many, many men going ferociously about some important task, which only made me think that I was very glad not to be a part of it. My job, I thought, was finished. Let some others shoulder the burden of the afterclaps now. For better or for worse, I'd done what I was meant to do, brought the Chemist back alive, and thought that maybe now I'd simply be allowed to slip off into some quieter existence. To find a bottle and a card game, men to cheat, girls to lie to and maybe a piano to play. To pick up with my solitary-ish and juvenile life where I'd left it off, more or less. To walk away.

But I was a man made for remembering and I remembered what Nimrod Kane had said to me the first time we'd met. The *last* thing he'd said to me. I'd asked him if, once I'd met the Captain and informed on the Captain and helped the Captain find this Chemist he was hunting after—if, after all that, I'd be free to fuck off and go on my merry way.

And Nimrod, he'd said *No.* He'd said, *That's just what we're doing tomorrow. You and me? We're together in this for life.*

Of all the lies he told me then and after, it figured that that would be the one time he was telling the truth.

In the meantime, I'd dragged myself to the fire and hadn't protested when a drink was pressed into my hand, nor when Nimrod shook loose a rolled cigarette for me and lit it. I hadn't said a word when the Chemist set in to pestering the Captain over what his new name might be—whether he'd get to choose it or have a hand in the choosing of it and whether he'd have only one or if there would be options.

"Ignatz," he said, "was never a nice name to have. I'll be glad to be rid of it. I wonder, though. Does changing the name change the man?"

And I just sat. I drank my drink slow and relished every tiny sip of smoke I allowed myself off the cigarette I'd been given, even when it tore up my sore lungs to do so. I stared off into the dark and tried to make sense of the firefly dance of lights in the distance. To catalog the sounds and make some whole picture of everything that had been done and appeared, still, to be in the offing.

Twice, invisible men materialized near to Nimrod and said things to him that I either could not hear or did not understand. Briefly, him and the Captain talked of Logue Ranstead and the Chemist, too, asked after him in a brotherly way that implied he somehow knew the big man, which I found unlikely in the extreme. But in this world, who knew? It was easier, sometimes, to just believe everything on its face and let the lies eventually disappoint you. To live a life of grinning acceptance as anathema to the exhaustion of patently cynical disbelief.

For my part, I said nothing. In my mind, I was adding two and two. The four, though, was eluding me. I felt as though, if I were only a man possessed of slightly more brains, it would all snap to right nicely. If only I'd cogitated upon something in the years between the beginning of the end of the world and the end of the beginning of it that wasn't the false pass, the throw, tickling the 88's, how to shoot and run and lie, and the long con.

"You're quiet, Duncan," said the Captain.

"I am," I replied, nodding.

"That's unnatural."

My cigarette had burned down and my hand missed it already. I scratched at the side of my face and felt dried blood flaking away under my nails. "Perhaps it's my natural state," I said. "Maybe everything else has been an act."

"If that's the case, then I would prefer you go back to acting. I found you more pleasant company as a spy and a liar."

I shrugged. "I do have a question," I said.

"I imagine you have more than one."

"One that's vexing me, for certain. Before you tried to shoot me—"

"First time or the second time?" the Captain asked.

"Second time."

"Go on."

"Before you tried to shoot me the second time, you told me that I'd told you to bring me here. To this hill. That I'd told you there was something I'd need to see."

And the Captain allowed that, yes. He'd said something to that effect. And I asked him *when* I'd told him this thing that I had most assuredly not told him at all, and he said that it'd been in the morning, before the assault on the train. He intimated that, perhaps, I simply did not remember.

"No," I said. "I'm a good rememberer. But doesn't that strike you as strange?" I asked.

"Strange is something of a relative term, Duncan. I mean, strange compared to what?"

I waved a hand at him. I said that if we were to take as given that I had called—that, presumably, I'd had a reason to want to be right here at just the right moment and time to step off for a chat with my handler while surrounded by certifiable loons and all their dinosaurs—then what was it I'd been expecting to see?

"I asked you that same question," said the Captain.

"So what did I say?"

"You said 'an orthogonal solution—'"

"—to a problem of nested—" I chimed in, speaking over him.

"—nested quantum indeterminacies," finished Nimrod.

The three of us looked at each other.

"That's weird," said Ignatz Walton, whose words they'd been in the first place. "How did you guys do that?"

"It was me called you, James," Nimrod said. And then to me. "I've always been good with voices, you know? With languages." He reached up and touched one ear. "Aunt Nells like my Aunt Nell, me."

I nodded again.

I smiled.

And "Fuck you," I says to Mr. Nimrod Kane, Director of the OSS. "Who are you?"

The Captain said something unsweetened about me not being the sharpest nail in the box or the brightest piano player at the whorehouse, and I ignored him. I watched Nimrod who watched me and then tipped his head to one side and told me he was my father.

I reeled, of course, because, you know, my poppa was a rolling stone or somesuch. A poor choice my mother had made a long time ago, who'd chickened and ran about the time that I learned to walk. A man made only of random phone calls, court documents, age-inappropriate Christmas gifts from back in the days before all Christmases was cancelled forever, and birthday cards that always arrived two or three days late. He was nothing to me but an absence, and me my mother's son complete.

Across the fire, the Captain breathed into his hand and droned, "Luke, I am your faaatherrr," and laughed. "*Revenge of the Empire.* Great goddamn movie."

"*Empire Strikes Back*," said Nimrod.

"What?"

"*Empire Strikes Back*. That's what it was called here."

"That's a stupid title."

Nimrod shook his head. He looked at me and said my name. Snapped his fingers. He said, "Duncan? Okay, so that's not really true. I was kidding. I'm not your father." He said that he'd figured if he said that first, I wouldn't go out of my head when he told me the actual truth. That he thought it would be funny. "Of course I'm not your father. That's ridiculous. It makes no sense."

And I asked him again: "So who are you?"

"I'm you," he said.

"All grown up," said the Captain.

"Thirty-two years, two months, three days, six hours, forty-four minutes of difference," said Ignatz. "Between this universe and the anomalous parallel. I've done the math, but the seconds get a little slippery."

"You're me," I said.

"I am," he said.

"From the other . . ."

"Dimension, yeah."

"You gonna freak out?" asked the Captain, leaning forward, his eyes glittering in the firelight. "I have a fairly large bet out on it and I wouldn't mind making some money off you."

I did not freak out. Partly to screw the Captain out of his wager and partly because Nimrod Kane being an older version of me actually made the world make *more* sense, not less. The truth of it chimed with a certain resonance, like a bell in my head. It answered questions, not the least of which being why anyone would trust me to do a job like the one I'd already been entrusted to do. Why he would've come for me in my duress at Sunflower Field, sending my old friend Gordon Navarro to fetch me. I mean, who would I trust more than me? I loved me. Most of the time, anyway.

"If you're not going to cry, I'm bored with this conversation," the Captain said.

And I turned on him snappish. "I rode a fucking triceratops today," I said. "I feel as though my capacity for wonderment while in your company is a thing grown boundless."

The Captain chuckled, then asked Nimrod, "Did you always talk like this?"

"I've always had a love for language," he said.

"You must've gotten beaten up a lot as a kid."

"Come on," said Nimrod, heaving himself crookedly to his feet. "The fun's all about to start. Let's go watch the show."

They stood near to the round top of the hill, the three of them in a line and me sitting, wearing the flowered sheet I'd been covered in like a cape around my shoulders, my fingers knotting in the grass, and together we looked out over the darkness and all we could survey. The night was cool. The land below us was an imaginary char world of ash and churned earth and devastation. I imagined I could see the glowing hearts of atomic cores—eleven of them that would live for ten thousand years in the graves they'd dug for themselves in the fury of their awakening.

I mean, I couldn't see any of that, really. I couldn't see anything at all. But in the stuffed and thickly darkness of that nuclear midnight, I imagined all manner of riotous things. Despite all claims made to his Captainness, my mind was more than a little bit blown, I can tell you. There wasn't a minute that went by that I didn't find my eyes drifting to the face, the hands, the body of the man who claimed to be me, aged and wise, and wondering what had happened to me to turn me into him. Every wrinkle on him was a destiny if he was telling me the truth. Every scar a promise. It was disconcerting, but I tried not to let it get to me.

Eventually, Nimrod caught me looking. "It's only going to get stranger the more you think about it," he said.

"Not rightly sure it could get stranger than it is," I replied.

"That's only because you don't know Nim very well yet," said the Captain, and then Nimrod looked at him and said, "You understand how ridiculous that is, right?"

The Captain made a face. "Is it or isn't it? I mean, you know *him*, Nim. But he can't know you at all. Not half of you, anyway." He shrugged. "The most interesting half."

"Ontology is a sucker's game," said Nim, then, to me: "You want me to play you the song?"

Instantly, my head began to hurt and I flinched away.

"Nim, don't do that to him," said the Captain. "It's not nice."

"Shut up, James. Duncan? Do you want me to play you the song?" From inside his jacket, he took out a minirecorder with a small speaker and held it up.

"Put it away," I said. "Please."

"It'll make everything easier," he said.

I shied like a horse but couldn't take my eyes off the recorder in his hands—something in me knowing the magic that dwelt inside. "Because it'll make me remember?"

"No. It's never made you remember. It makes you . . . accept."

"Fuck you, then."

Then he leans in closer to me and shakes the recorder in his hand a little. "It's funny," says him, "but I've never understood what it was with you—with me. With *us* and this song. With the flowers."

"'Flower Duet,'" I says. "But not just the song."

"It's just the song. The song is what . . . I don't know. *Roots* you, I guess."

And "It's not just the song," I says to him again, emboldened of a sudden. Brave, briefly, or wreckless in the face of irrationality and fears and the knowing of things that I didn't know.

Nimrod's head goes shake, sadly or resignedly. "Whatever it is. I've never understood what it is about it."

"Yes you do," I says. "If you really are me, you understand exactly what it is."

"So tell me then."

"Why should I tell you? You said you're me, right? And if you are me then you understand exactly what it is."

"I know," Nimrod said, then crouched down beside me. "But this is the part where you tell me. Because as weird as this is, you as the younger me remember this thing that me as the older you does not. I don't know if I've forgotten it or if, for some reason, I just can't know. But I do know that this is the part where you tell me because I *remember* you telling it to me now. Right here, in this place."

I stared at the recorder in his hand. "So what if I don't?"

"You will."

"Why?"

"Because you already have. Because I remember it happening, just like this."

I thought about that for a minute and licked my lips and felt sweat prickling in my hairline as anxiety clawed at me, the fear of a song that I suddenly knew the origin of and the meaning of in the way that, suddenly, you might remember the name of a high school girlfriend decades later. And not just her name, but the smell of her skin and the feel of her hair running through your hands and the precise pitch of her voice and a single, perfect moment of her, all round and whole, like it'd just happened five minutes ago.

"On the day," I said, my eyes fixed on the recorder, my throat feeling sandy and my voice ancient and creaking. "The first day of the end of everything. When I was standing there in the plaza out front of 1818 Market Street in Philly and I saw the giant robot come smashing through the Stock Exchange building across the street . . ."

Nimrod shrank a little back from me and winced like he'd eaten a bad plate of shrimp or something.

". . . All was a riot," I said. "A panic. There was fire and smoke. And blood. Bodies fell from the red hands of the Type 1, or were crushed beneath the relentless smashing of its feet. And there was all these little machines, too. 'Bout the size of dogs or maybe a little bigger. Had these red eyes. Mouths full of chrome teeth. Whip tails like rats. And I ran before them. Was drove, really—in a crowd. A stampede."

"Frozen yogurt," said Nimrod, his voice ghostly.

"Yup. That's right. Frozen yogurt. I'd been asking my phone for a place to get me some frozen yogurt when it'd all happened and the directions was still on it. Couldn't see nothing in the smoke and the press of bodies, but I could see my phone, so I followed it—"

"—down into Suburban Station, right. The train station."

I nodded. "Down into the train station. And there was always these kids from the local schools down there, underground, by the entrance to the dead tracks."

"And they would always be playing music."

"Busking for change, yeah."

"It was violins, mostly. Cellos. They were from some music school."

"And on that day, I threw myself down the stairs on JFK Boulevard, went underground, and there was two kids, a boy and a girl, one playing the violin and one singing, and they was doing the 'Flower Duet.'"

"Standing by the flower sellers," said Nimrod.

"Where the buckets had all been kicked over and the flowers all trampled."

"The whole place, it smelled like flowers and smoke."

"And right in the middle of it, right across from the frozen yogurt place, they played and sang the 'Flower Duet' while the crowds fell down the stairs and smashed down the doors. The last thing I heard before going into the tunnels."

Nimrod whistled, low and soft. "I've always remembered that day," he said, "but never that piece of it. Those two kids playing that song. It was so strange."

"It was the end of the world," I said.

"And then the tunnels. The dark. Jesus . . . Going to New Jersey. To the Shore. And that summer. I stayed in the—"

"—in the Sunflower Motel—"

"—with that girl—"

"Yeah."

"Resonance," said the Chemist, breaking the drifty, back-and-forth Nimrod and me had going. This remembering of memories that we both shared but had lost, forgotten, suppressed.

"What?" we both said at the same time.

"Resonance," the Chemist repeated. "Resonant improbabilities, really. It's the name for the perceptual skewing of random, discreet objects in an individual cosmology. Like, do you remember how, back before, you would buy a car and, suddenly, you see that same car everywhere on the road? Or you would hear a song for the first time, one that you'd never heard before, and suddenly you hear it everywhere. It's the ontological weight of importance given to a unique object biasing its frequency of appearance in a closed perceptual space."

"Coincidence," I said.

"There's no such thing," said the Chemist. "Coincidence is the colloquial term given to an aberration in the statistical Gaussian distribution. Resonant improbability is what you're talking about. You hear the 'Flower Duet' being sung in a place that smells of crushed flowers. You stay in a place called the Sunflower Motel . . ."

"Sunflower Field," Nimrod said, quietly.

I closed my eyes. I hung my head. I thought of my first solo job for the OSS, of the dream I'd had while on the road to Good Times, of Gordon Navarro's cover job in Denver and the place where we'd met and a million other things. When I opened my eyes again, I saw my fingers knotted, holding closed the sheet under which I'd napped, and the tiny, wash-faded flowers printed on the fabric.

"Sorry," said the Chemist. "Was that too much? I sometimes forget how—"

"Shut up, Ignatz," said the Captain. "Give 'em a minute."

"Not me," said Nimrod. "I knew this was coming."

"Then give Duncan a minute. It looks like his brains are coming out his ears."

They weren't, but I appreciated the concern. I looked up at Nimrod, who stared out over the field below us, and saw myself in him. All the broken pieces put together into a whole, and I wondered how I'd gotten there and if him standing beside me made me more or less unkillable for the next—

"No, it doesn't, Duncan," he said, answering my thought. "The future can always change. It doesn't like to, but it can. Everything is breakable to a clever man." Then he turned to the Captain. "You have the gadget?" he asked.

From out of his jacket, Captain James Barrow took a thick and stubby pistol, all plasticky and orange. A flare gun. He reversed it quickly in his hand and offered the butt of it to Nimrod. "The honors, Nim?"

And Nimrod shook his head. "It's your op, James. Bring it home."

In the dark and the flickering fire, it was now the Captain's smile that was white and huge as a Cheshire's. "I was hoping you'd say that," he said and pointed the gun at the sky like he meant to mug it all. "Here we go."

He pulled the trigger and a single point of light went whistling skyward, almost immediately met by a hundred more. Mortar flares and artillery illumination rounds and air-drop parachute flares that all burned with a hot and blinding whiteness. It was as if a star field had erupted all afresh over this one patch of blasted borderland—every sun new and burning with the fury of youth.

And below was a battlefield, laid as neat as something on a table. A game of war, all set and waiting, just west of the hot, wet scars of the nukes the Captain had lashed across the border. There were a hundred tanks and a thousand robots and men as teeming as ants who all took the raising of this curtain of stars as a signal to fire their guns and run about and clash with dozens upon dozens of dinosaurs of varying shape and description.

Cannons roared. Artillery erupted. Machine guns chattered in rippling, sparking lines all up and down a series of excavated lines in dragon-tooth arrangement. I saw a saddled allosaurus fall under the pounding of shoulder-fired anti-tank weapons—the cork-screwing paths of their rockets sketched in hissing smoke, the brief flare of their impacts like more flowers blooming in fast-forward. Bodies cascaded off its back in strange, doll-like lifelessness, to fall among the pounding feet of three tyranosaurs who charged into a group of Western Confederacy war robots that held their ground and lit the night with chattering chain guns and gushing flamethrowers.

Beside me, Nimrod gave a low whistle. "Wow, James," he said. "How'd you get the King to go for all this?"

"Steve owes me big," the Captain said, his hands shoved deep in the pockets of his trousers as he rocked back and forth on his heels. "I introduced him to his girlfriend."

"Among other things."

The Captain nodded. "Among other things. Quiet now. Watch this part coming up. They're gonna see this shit in K.C."

From behind us, there came a whistle that grew into a shriek and then a series of shattering sonic booms as a wing of supersonic fighter jets streaked overhead and dropped a line of napalm along the scar line left by the nukes. A curtain of fire erupted, towering fifty feet high.

The Captain cheered. Nimrod Ooh'd and Aah'd like he was watching a fireworks show, all recent metaphysical conundrums forgotten in the wash of booms and flames and the simple pleasures of watching things blow up.

"That was all Jemma there," said the Captain, shouting over the sudden, sucking rush of wind. "Her and Holly and Holly's team lifted six tankers of Cheyenne kerosene. Carmen Schuler cooked it down for us. Even Steve doesn't know that we got to one of his air defense men for the delivery."

"Holly do that bit for you, too?"

"No," said the Captain. "Barnum and Strange, believe it or not. Not their usual M.O., but the man was crooked and I needed a hard ask."

The dinosaurs went mad at the sight and the heat of the flames and died under the guns of the Western Confederacy. I watched one of the tyranosaurs take a war robot in its teeth and throw it into the air like a toy. I saw triceratopses running mad into lines of exos that clubbed them down with their massive fists and lines of infantry breaking and reforming under panic charges by hunting packs of raptors. Long-distance artillery boomed from somewhere far behind us and seemed to bracket the battlefield with smoke and fire. Lines of tanks leveled their guns at berms, fresh-cut into the tortured land, from which sparked a perfection of small arms and sheaf rockets.

But there was something wrong about the entire scene. The fire, the artillery targeting, the dinosaurs.

"This is fake," I said, then turned to look up at the Captain and repeated myself. "This is fake, isn't it? It's a set-up."

"Says who?"

"Says me."

"Good thing no one listens to you then, huh?" he asked, then gestured broadly to the game playing out before him. "What you're seeing here are the valiant armies of King Steven and the Western Confederacy coming to the aid and defense of their uppity and ungrateful Kansan brothers, defending them bravely from a dastardly midnight incursion by the Legion of Terror."

"The hell it is."

"But can't you see the dinosaurs? They're right there, all big and bitey with their teeth and whatever. And all the stuff exploding? It's all very exciting, Duncan."

"It's fake," I said, smiling.

"Now why would I go to all the trouble of faking a giant battle on the Kansas border with tanks and airplanes and dinosaurs and all this *stuff* in full view of the Kansan Home Guard currently cowering on the other side of that completely irradiated patch of land down there? You'd think I was trying to stop a war or something. To make the Kansans owe King Steve a debt for defending them against a horde of rampaging dinosaurs and crazy people. I mean, that's ridiculous, isn't it Nim?"

"Completely ridiculous," agreed Nimrod. "It's like you think Percy Blythe and the OSS was secretly backing the Kansans with guns and money and federal troops in mufti. Like maybe the OSS *wanted* the Kansans to scrap against the Western Confederacy in order to weaken both sides in advance of a war with the Old States being orchestrated by certain highly placed officers within the Office of Special Services."

"But that would be crazy," added the Captain. "Because we *are* the OSS, Nimrod and me. And we certainly don't want that to happen."

"No, we do not," said Nimrod. "The Director of the OSS secretly aligning himself with a rogue operator—"

"Thank you," said the Captain.

"—in order to subvert the wishes of the larger intelligence community and the remains of the United States government? That would be treason, Duncan."

"Man would have to be insane to attempt something like that."

"Completely off his goddamn rocker."

I looked back down to the field at the play war being waged there and grinned and grinned like maybe the Captain had been right and my brains really had gone to liquid. "Which is why you two did none of it. It was the Legion of Terror all along."

The Captain beamed down upon me. "You're getting smarter, Duncan."

"Gonna make a proper traitor out of you yet," said Nimrod.

"Now how about we all shut up and watch the movie, huh?" said the Captain, folding his arms across his chest. "It's not like there's anything good on TV these days. Let me have what entertainment I can make for myself."

Down below us, the guns blazed and the fires burned and robots fought dinosaurs in the churned-up mess of a radioactive wasteland. And the Captain was right. It was all a pretty good show.

Coda: Old Scars

It took about 45 minutes for the big show to wrap up, but we were gone before it burned itself down to embers—the four of us loading into two nondescript trucks sitting at the wooded base of the hill, each with two of Nimrod's ghosts riding shotgun and a third acting as driver.

The Chemist rode with Nimrod, as they claimed to have things to talk about. I rode with the Captain, which was fine, as I had things I wanted to ask him. As I've said before, he was an impatient man, but not one who'd ever abandon a friend. When it became plain that I could not make it down the hill under my own power in any way other than rolling, he lifted me onto his back and carried me.

We rode showing no lights, the drivers wearing night-vision goggles and not sparing the lash as we lit out over ranch roads and cattle trails that were washboarded and chuck-holed and awful. I was surprised when we turned for Kansas rather than aiming ourselves back for the comforts of the Queen City, and was moved to gently inquire as to what the Captain had in mind for his next frolic.

"If I told you that, there would be no surprises," he said. "And wouldn't that be a dull life."

"Dull or no, I'm a little skittish about traveling so close up on the place that you just Hiroshima'd, Captain."

He waved a dismissive hand at me and explained that he hadn't actually used atomics on the border, but rather a few thousand pounds of Cyclot-8 that'd been cooked up by Schuler, his crab-handed explosives man. Eight ounces of the final order had gone to me. The rest of it had gone into the ground along the border.

"Certainly looked convincing, didn't it? It's the mushroom clouds that scare people, but that same effect can be gotten by using large-scale conventional explosives. Any vacuum bomb will do it. Thermobarics. In this case, zero-oxidizer gel explosives buried in place two nights ago. We even had the border crossing and the closest settlements evacuated. Said we thought someone in the area had a nuclear bomb and everyone just scattered. Remarkable how motivating such a thing can be."

"And it turned out to be true, too."

He shrugged. "Well, true-ish. The Kansans will figure out soon enough that it wasn't real nukes, but we only needed to keep them on their own side for the night. By morning, there's gonna be nothing but dead dinosaurs, the bodies of fifty-odd L.O.T. henchmen, a big mess, and King Steve waiting to shake hands and have his ass kissed by every Kansan born with lips."

We drove through the night and made Colby, Kansas by dawn, where there was breakfast, hot coffee (which I spurned), and a horse doctor to see to my leg and all the other bits of me lately weathered by the recent unpleasantness.

"If you were a meat horse, I'd like as tell your owner to fetch in his pistol and put you down," said the doctor, probing gently at the thrice-opened and twice closed wreck of one of my two favorite legs.

I told him that the Captain had already tried that yesterday, but that it hadn't took. "I might not look like much right now," I said, "but I'm scrappy."

The doc put me under with dental gas because he said it was all he had. I expected to wake again adrift—the Captain, the Chemist, my older self and all his drivers and ghosts gone off on whatever adventures the two-legged have when they leave the cripples behind.

In space for two hours, I floated, warm and brainless, tuned to the broadcast frequency of rocks and lead. When it was done and I came swimmingly back to the surface, the Captain was beside me waiting.

"You done resting now, Princess?" he asked.

Nauseated and lying on a mat of crinkling old newspaper on a padded table in the veterinarian's office, I turned my face to the wall and said, "I have some complaints about the company health insurance policy."

Twenty minutes later we were back in the trucks and moving again.

Kansas was a mess. Though no recent battles had been fought on its soil, and though King Steve had ordered the Western Confederacy troops halted at the border back when they'd been chasing down the routed Jayhawkers, abjuration and a yen toward weird science had shredded what little fabric of consistent reality Kansas had ever had.

Ever a vexatious place, ever a scurrilous and unpoised place, ever a place where the rubbing up of modernity against its manifest time-warp backwardness made strange music in the cornrows and long flatnesses, Kansas now was just a junk drawer for the multiverse. The place where bad ideas went to be believed in by fools.

The skies were the color of piss and mercury. The corn moved even when there was no breeze. Heading south, we saw rats eating the eyes out of a scorpion big enough to wear a saddle, and we was passed on the road by wedge-nosed hovercraft blazened with Bible verse on their armored skirts and flying Christian Scientist battle flags.

The Captain would not allow the radio to be turned on. The future, he said, was still too fragile to be set in place by the knowing of it by the likes of us.

"That like an actual rule? Or are you just making that up?"

"Doesn't really matter, does it?" he said. "Call it a safety precaution. Until this new version we've set in motion has some time to set itself, our knowing anything could still alter its path."

"You're saying it won't be real until we know about it?"

He shrugged. "I'm saying nothing is. But that's the way things have always been."

Outside of Garden City, we saw the dome head and gun-black eyes of a giant, doddering robot breaking the line of the horizon like the topsails of a corn-going schooner spotted from around the curve of the earth. It walked like a drunk and we switched direction to give it a wide berth.

When we needed fuel, we followed the distant glow of pole-mounted floodlights to an old highway rest stop, but pulled right back out again when we saw the inviting, neon-coiled diner there shiver in place and yawn—showing a dozen rows of chromium teeth and a gleaming Formica tongue.

"It swallowed a dog!" one of the bodyguards yelled. "It swallowed a dog! It swallowed a dog!" And after that, Nimrod's men simply mined the road with cripplers, waited for the next segmented tractorpede to come booming down the blacktop, then detonated the EMP charges, blew open the sealed compartment where its intelligence lived, burned out the dogbrain expert system that drove it, and siphoned all the switchgrass ethanol out of its massive tanks.

Their work attracted scavengers—small-time road gangs dressed in stained Highway Patrol uniforms or nightfighter camos or cloaks made of stitched-together teddy bear heads. When the brigands drew too close, Nim's Praetorians all activated their invisibility cloaks and wavered away to nothing.

The gathered mobs scattered, knowing what had to come next if they stayed put, but when they were all gone and the bodyguards swirled back into being, not a one of them had even moved.

"The things that people want to believe are so much more powerful and affecting than the things that are true," Nimrod said.

He was standing by the open back door of one of the trucks where I lay across the back seat smoking one of his cigarettes and keeping my leg elevated. "My boys could've torn that rabble to bright ribbons. Laid 'em out, cut off their heads and paraded them around on sticks. But no one would've cared because men like that have seen it all before. But turning invisible? That looks like magic. And magic still scares the pudding out of the dim."

If there was a point to all our footstepping around the wrack-and-ruin of Kansas, it was not one that was immediately apparent to me. I suppose it should've occurred to me that we were on the run, but it never did.

One night, in a tumbledown motel room outside of a pop-up town called Blessed made entirely of collapsible geodesics and safety-yellow bubble domes surrounded by the shiny petals of solar collectors, I found a radio on the nightstand and dared turn it on, so soft that I had to hold my ear to its dusty speaker just to hear.

The Captain, the Chemist and Nim were all outside, seeing to the midnight loading of the trucks with supplies taken on in Blessed. I crouched down and listened, but got only static and more static until, finally, I caught the wisp of a voice—a girl, her voice choked with panic.

". . . in Kansas City. They're flowing out now. The city is on fire. I don't even know how many dead. If anyone can hear me, please help. Please . . ."

I turned it off, my supper sinking like a weight in my belly, feeling as though, by knowing, I'd made those flames and the terror in that girl's voice true. That I'd been complicit in whatever terrible thing was happening in Kansas City.

When I turned around, the Chemist was standing in my doorway, watching me as I crouched by the nightstand, fingers trailing down the cracked plastic body of the old radio. "We're ready to go," he said. "You need a hand?"

We drove through the night, headed east across open land. I rode again with the Captain, and he seemed edgy. Excited.

"Something happening, Captain?" I asked.

"Always something happening," he said. "Just a matter of getting to where the action is."

We talked as Nimrod's men drove and kept a watch on the road ahead of us. We had fuel and food and clean water, wooden cases full of mysterious things stacked high in the backs of the trucks and lashed to the roof. The Captain was in the front seat. I was in the back, my bum leg outstretched.

I asked him about the Chemist and about Nimrod Kane, and he seemed to talk just to fill the long dark. He explained how there'd always been a plan in place to put the Chemist in the wind—to use him to bait the wrong-headed parts of the OSS—but that he and Nimrod had disagreed on how it ought to be done.

"Nim knows the past," he explained to me. "But the past he knows is only the parts of it that *you* know. Or that you will know. And right now—at this point in time—you don't know all that much. But me, I know the future, which means that he should just give up and let me win every argument."

The Captain did his best to explain, but the language for what he was trying to tell me never has really existed. Not in any whole or reasonable way. Their disagreement regarding tactics and the proper ways that one might fuck with the future history of the world, he said, led to the snatching of the Chemist by the Captain, then the re-snatching of him by the OSS, under gentle guidance from Nimrod, then the re-re-snatching of him from Nimrod by Percy Blythe, who squirreled the Chemist away and forced Nimrod to set up the great dinosaur-back train robbery and final re-re-re-snatching of the Chemist by me for the Captain and all the tumult that attended it—including but not limited to the shooting of me, the abjurations that followed, and all that came after.

"It was a wreck of a thing," the Captain explained. "Nim and I both knew where things had to go, but we disagreed about the way to get there. In the end, what needed to happen, happened. It all came together. It always does."

He sighed and checked his left wrist, on which he had strapped a profusion of watches. Three or four at least. He squinted out the windshield at the position of the moon and the stars and reached out a hand and brushed his fingers across the face of the radio. "Almost time," he said to himself.

He explained how there'd always been a plan in place. He had his men inside the L.O.T. and an intention to use the Legion as his cat's paws for the final disappearance of the Chemist—who was, as far as anyone knew, the last surviving member of the team that'd wrecked up the world and caused the Abjuration. All he needed was an excuse to use them. And lots and lots of dinosaurs.

"Finding the Chemist on that train," he said. "That was the excuse."

And as for the dinosaurs?

"That was easy," he told me. "I mean, Dinosaur Joe helped, of course. He was happy to. Gave him something to do that wasn't staring at the walls out in Florence. He gave us the basics, but we still needed to sequence all that DNA and get the things grown. And do it in a hurry. That kind of thing takes a lot of processing power. We needed something like—"

"A machine brain," I said.

The Captain turned around in his seat and pointed at me, his fingers in the shape of a cocked pistol. "Bingo," he said. "Good thing I'd recently found one, huh? And had passed it along to the kinds of guys who could grow 10,000 shuggoths for a prank or make a building grow a pair of tits for fun."

The Captain checked his watches again, and I recalled (with an odd sort of wistful yearning, like for better and simpler times) my first day with the Captain. His rescue of me from the drudgery of the King's roadworks. Riding in Marlene. Calling on the Green Willow Clave. Nearly dying. I remembered driving off with our stolen machine brain and how the Captain had traded it to a furry man in a clapped-out pickup truck for a bunch of sacks of what might've been magic beans or candy for all I knew. I remembered clocking that one fella with the rabbit ears that I'd thought was a peculiar hat but wasn't. The HLF had gotten a long head start on building the Captain his dinosaurs.

"Hey," he said. "You just never know when you might need something like that. If I hadn't used them here, I would've found some other thing to do with them. That's the thing about knowing the future, Duncan. I know the way it's *supposed* to go pretty well. But getting there is always a fucking adventure."

He sighed and looked one more time at his watches. "Shut up now, okay? I like you less and less the more you talk."

I watched him as he reached for the radio, switched it on and twirled the dial down fast to Flatlands 90.5. A voice came through, pure and strong and round and full, offering up the news of the day.

. . . the arrival of King Steven in Goodland, Kansas, to meet with Lord Phillip and his ministers following the battle of Tulip Draw. The entire area is on lockdown, cats and kittens, so stay well clear of the border today. Ain't nothing much left to see anyhow but bones and soldiers as the last of the Legion of Terror appear to have been eliminated from . . .

"That safe?" I asked. "I thought the radio was off-limits."

"Shh . . ." he said.

. . . a quiet day in the Flatlands, which is something none of us have seen in too long a time. So with no more news to report, how about I play a request? Haven't gotten one of these in ages, but from Captain James Barrow to Oliver St. John-Mollusc and all the boys in the Office

of Special Services, here's Faith No More doing "We Care A Lot," right here on Flatlands 90.5, the Voice Of The Future . . .

I laughed and said, "Oliver? The dog?"

The Captain nodded. "The dog. Percy's dog. I knew I'd eventually remember the name of the damn thing."

The song came crashing on, all slappy bass and pounding drums. In the front seat, the Captain closed his eyes and nodded his head along with the music.

I asked, "So what—"

"No more talking," he interrupted. "I need some rest before morning."

He laid his head against the glass of the passenger side window. From the back seat, I stared at him.

"Seriously," he said, smiling. "I'm going to sleep."

He was quiet for a moment, then cracked one eye and looked back at me.

"It's been fun, though, hasn't it?" he asked.

"It has," I said. "Not all of it, but enough of it."

"Yeah, well just wait 'til you see what comes next."

Then he closed his eyes again and, in time, he really did fall asleep. Which I knew because he snored all the way through the dawn and on into daylight. I listened to the radio and smoked my cigarettes until they were gone. I watched the fresh day get born through the smoked glass of the windows and wondered if it was a better one or a worse one than the day before. I wondered how much of that was owing to me—either the current me or the Nimrod Kane version of me with his limp and his scars and his head full of stories. I wondered if, wherever we were going, Jemma and Logue and Dogboy and all the rest would be there to meet us.

And eventually, I slept, too.

ACKNOWLEDGEMENTS

Books are weird things and weird books doubly so. The number of people I would need to thank for helping me put this one together would be prohibitively long and bizarre (for example, how would I thank the *real* armless man I saw on the streets of Center City who gave me the inspiration for a pivotal moment in the story?), so let me just leave it at this:

Thanks to all the freaks, the night creatures, the broken and the botched who populated my actual world during the writing of this and, inevitably, bled over onto the page. "Like likes like," as Duncan once said. None of this would have been possible without you.

Thanks to Fleetwood Robbins for consistently questioning my understanding of the criminal world and the motivations of those who populate it, and for keeping a close eye on all the airships and dragons and giant robots and mad scientists. I like a guy who doesn't flinch when there are sea monsters, but can't abide it when the guys stealing the horse semen don't appear to be fairly cutting in all their henchmen. See ya at Hellmouth's, bud.

Thanks to Richard Camp for understanding Duncan Archer's voice even better than I do. I swear to anyone reading this part that this book would have been a damn sight less flavorsome, word-wise, had it not been for his perfect ear for the dialect of the powerfully strange. Also, there would've been a lot more commas if he'd had his way, but ain't none of us perfect men . . .

Thanks to the real East Coast Dave, the real guys in Arthur Guinness Talking (Andrew Samrick most notably), the real Banjo Oblangata, Benny the piano player, my man Sparky for not asking what the favor was, everyone at the real Nob Hill Inn and the very real city of Denver, Colorado, for being the perfect place to watch the world fall to pieces.

Finally, an extra-special thanks to Parker Finn, the real Tuesday and General-For-Life of the Ragamuffin Army, and to my boy Mad who loves trains and loves dinosaurs and who, one awesome after-noon, decided that the coolest thing in the world was to have his dinosaurs attack his trains.

I could not have agreed more.

ABOUT THE AUTHOR

Jason Sheehan is a former dishwasher, fry cook, saucier, chef, restaurant critic, food editor, reporter, and porn store employee. He was born and raised in Rochester, New York and though he has since fled the rust belt repeatedly, he still harbors an intense fondness for brutal winters, Friday fish fries, Irish bars and urban decay. As a young nerd, he fell hard for Star Wars, Doctor Who, William Gibson, Roger Zelazny and the spaceships-and-rayguns novels his father would leave on his bedside table. He dreamed of someday befriending a robot, stealing a spaceship and wandering off across the stars in search of alien ladies and high adventure. Since that hasn't happened (yet . . .), he now writes about it instead—which is almost as good. And yet despite all this, his mother still kinda thinks he should've been an orthodontist.

Kindle Serials

This book was originally released in Episodes as a Kindle Serial. Kindle Serials launched in 2012 as a new way to experience serialized books. Kindle Serials allow readers to enjoy the story as the author creates it, purchasing once and receiving all existing Episodes immediately, followed by future Episodes as they are published. To find out more about Kindle Serials and to see the current selection of Serials titles, visit *www.amazon.com/kindleserials*.